NEW TOEIC
新多益閱讀題庫大全

緒論 Preface

　　一言以蔽之，「NEW TOEIC 新多益閱讀題庫大全」的目的是透過對多益的學習，讓廣大讀者「掌握正確的英文學習方法」。

　　對於現代人來說，多益英語能力測驗是評價一個人的英語實力的標準，而且成了聘雇職員時的參考指標，因此很多大學生和準備就業的年輕人都投資大量的時間努力準備多益考試。基於這樣的現實情況，作者想為廣大讀者提供「多益學習和影響我們的人生工具——英語學習」的方法，因此編寫了本書。

　　這本新多益閱讀題庫大全徹底分析了跟多益相關的龐大內容。本書的誕生是將多益實戰問題的龐大單字、文法、閱讀理解資料，經由長時間的從不同角度和研究基準分析而萃取出的精華。並且在本書中詳細地介紹了多益測驗的基本框架和有關學習方法。用最簡潔的方法，正確地列舉了征服多益閱讀測驗的必考試題。因此，只要完全掌握本書的內容，不僅能順利地通過多益測驗，而且有助於提高職場英文文件閱讀的能力。

　　除了嚴格選定最多的實戰問題的這項優點外，有別於其他將題目與答案混為一冊的編法，本書特別將解答本獨立出來，以方便讀者能對照查詢。本書將多益的最新題型徹底分析整理，並採用學習者最有效率的吸收方式編輯而成。這種將龐大的資料壓縮，並讓考生有實戰感覺的模擬測驗，一定能成為考生的最好助手。

　　最後，Hackers多益網站（www.Hackers.co.kr）會讓多益學習更加有趣，而且該網站在韓國已成為點擊率最高的英語學習網站，因此充分地體現了「結交朋友，跨越年齡，共同發展」的Hackers哲學。（編註：本服務為韓國原書提供之服務，與本出版社無關）。

　　學習並不是一個人的練習，透過學習形成互相幫助的團體，透過互助的練習，建設更美好的社會，最終建設健康的競爭和協助共存的社會，這就是我們出版的精神。從這種意義上看，充滿熱情和精神的「NEW TOEIC 新多益閱讀題庫大全」並不僅僅是為了取得較高的英語成績，而是透過向每一位讀者傳播健康的哲學來共同建設美好的社會。

David Cho

CONTENTS

本書特點

01 最大數量收錄最新實戰試題

本書針對文法、單字類題型、閱讀理解的最新動向，收錄了豐富的題目，讀者在做完這本書裡的題目之後，能夠充分體會實戰感，同時也能夠提高成績。

02 NEW TOEIC 最新動向完全分析

本教材詳細分析了 NEW TOEIC 新變更的不同類型題目，並將有關文法、單字、閱讀理解問題的變化趨勢反映在基本原理的分析和實戰問題上，使讀者能夠充分應對 NEW TOEIC。

03 融合了基礎知識和實戰問題的書

本書不僅是一本徹底分析整理最新動向的多益試題書，而且是一本能夠讓讀者練習大量最新類型考題的試題集。這樣的構成，對於無論是想打好基礎的考生還是想體會實戰感、提高分數的考生，都會有幫助。

04 新多益核心問題的系統整理

以原理為中心，系統地整理了新多益的文法，使讀者能夠在不看基本文法書的情況下，直接使用本書精心準備的新多益文法。在每一頁都會簡單易懂地解釋一項核心問題，並可利用每頁配備的最新類型問題加強所學內容。

05 收錄了新多益考試頻繁出現的單字

書中收錄了最近兩年已出的試題，並網羅過去五年間的重要考古題，迎合了最新的多益考試動向。解題的同時學習單字，增加讀者的字彙量。旁邊的解釋幫助讀者在短時間內提高學習效率。

06 集中攻破閱讀理解中頻繁出現的文章結構

集中學習多益中頻繁出現的文章結構，提高讀者的閱讀及解題速度。這是一種新的階段式學習法，是經過釋義和分單元類型的練習來厚實基礎，最後達成解答實戰試題的目的。

07 能夠鞏固各單元學習內容的充足練習題

在解實戰題目前，為了充分鞏固各單元所學的內容，本書準備了比實戰題目簡單的試題。在解練習題的時候能夠復習前面所學的內容，也可以和實戰題目做對比。

08 收錄了最新的已出試題和模擬實戰測驗題目

在各單元結束之前有最新的已出試題和模擬實戰測試題目。其中不僅包含了相關單元的題目，還包含一部分以前所學單元的題目，使讀者重溫以前所學的內容，強化記憶。

09 包含30日內必考單字表

將最近五年間的文法測驗部分及單字測驗部分出現的所有單字按日分配，使讀者在30日內完成記憶。不僅對已出單字進行了分類和變形的整理，更收錄了易混淆單字，還新加了同義字，使讀者能夠與 NEW TOEIC 中找同義字的題目作對比。

10 收錄了詳細的解釋和分析

透過詳細的解釋和分析，讀者能夠掌握各單元所學的解題方法。解答和分析在另一本書中，方便讀者同時閱讀題目和解析，旁邊另外整理了每篇文章的單字和片語，使讀者擁有更高的學習效率。

本書構成

01 診斷考察

在練習本書的學習法之前，讀者透過練習與實戰非常接近的「診斷測驗」，就可以在檢測自身實力之後制定對應的學習計畫。特別是在診斷測驗中，針對答錯的題目對自身弱點進行專門學習，這對系統學習會提供很大的幫助。

02 GRAMMAR 愉快地打基礎

在 Grammar 的相關收錄中，本書整理了最基礎必要的文法項目，成為讀者提高實力的堅強後盾。對進行基礎學習的讀者來說，這是再好不過的學習平臺。

03 POINT 文法說明

本書整理了在新多益中出現的所有文法項目，使讀者能夠循序漸進地學習。連文法說明的範文都採用了新多益考試的 Part5 形式，以便培養讀者發現問題的能力。

04 新多益實戰試題——新多益試題是這麼出的！

為了使讀者能夠應用在頁面上端所學的文法要點，在頁面下端提供了三道實戰題目。用這三道題目練習所學知識，使讀者在即時理解文法要點的同時，熟悉實戰模式。

05 VOCABULARY、READING 洞悉出題類型及戰略

徹底分析 Vocabulary 和 Reading 的出題類型，收錄了一定要掌握的核心事項和解題戰略。透過熟悉各種類型試題的解題方式，幫助你有效地積累實力。

06 HACKERS PRACTICE

透過對多益中出現的文章進行分析，可以牢固地練習和復習每次學習的內容。在掌握英文文章結構方面對讀者有巨大的幫助。

07 HACKERS TEST

在完成各部分的學習內容後，將相關的所有實戰題目類型進行綜合的練習，使學習內容和實戰得到聯繫。

08 實戰模擬測驗

最後透過實戰試題與學習成效作對比，檢測自己的真正實力。與初期的診斷考察做比較，可以感受到實力的提高。

09 30日必考單字表

將最近五年的已出單字分成30日份的單字表，使應試者經由每天學習一日份的多益單字來積累實力。

10 另一本解答本

可視為書中之書的解答本，集中了詳細的正確解答、分析、翻譯，使讀者能夠確切地完成學習。

關於 TOEIC

什麼是多益？

TOEIC 是 Test Of English for International Communication 的縮寫，是非英語母語人士，針對語言能力中原本的「議事溝通」能力為重點，評測日常生活或國際業務等方面需要的實用英語能力的考試。開發目的在於，透過綜合考察應試者的英語綜合實力，測試應試者在需要使用英語的環境中應用英語的能力。出現在多益考試的內容，比較學術性，更以以下的實用性內容為主。

- 協助開發：研究，產品開發
- 財務會計：借貸，投資，稅金，會計，銀行業務
- 日常業務：預約，協商，行銷，販賣
- 技術領域：電器，工業技術，電腦，實驗室
- 事務領域：會議，秘書業務
- 物品採購：購物，產品諮詢，貸款支付

- 飲食：飯店，會餐，晚餐
- 文化：劇場，體育，郊遊
- 健康：醫療，保險，醫院診療，牙科
- 製造：生產線，工廠經營
- 職員：錄用，隱退，薪資發放，晉升，雇用機會
- 住宅：不動產，搬家，企業用地

多益考試的構成

多益考試由 100 道 Listening Comprehension 試題和 100 道 Reading Comprehension 試題構成。共 120 分的考試時間，其中 Listening 45 分鐘，Reading 75 分鐘。Listening 由 4 個部分（照片敘述、應答、短對話、短獨白）構成，Reading 由三個部分（完成句子、短文式克漏字，閱讀測驗）組成。題型是從 3~4 個選項中選擇一個答案的客觀題形式，答案要標記在另外提供的 OMR 答題卡上。

多益應試引導

1 多益考試申請

〔通訊報名〕

· 全台含離島共 19 處報名表領取點，並可網路下載報名表。

· 請前往郵局購買郵政匯票，受款人請註明：忠欣股份有限公司。請將報名表填妥後連同郵政匯票。以掛號寄至 (106) 臺北郵政第 26 之 585 號信箱「TOEIC 註冊組」收。

〔網上報名〕

由 TOEIC 首頁連結至網路報名平臺後依畫面指示進行線上報名作業，使用上若有任何疑問請洽 (02)2701-8008 轉分機 318 或 319。

2 應試

· 測驗前 15 分鐘入場，遲到者不得入場應試，請考生注意。

· 必須準備有效證件（國民身份證正本或有效期限內之護照正本），文具（鉛筆和橡皮擦），准考證（注意：准考證須先自行黏貼好照片）。

3 成績單及證書

· 每次測驗成績單預計寄送日及網路成績預計查詢日請參考官網公佈資料。

· 測驗成績兩年內可重複申請。

· 測驗日起六個月內，可申請成績復查或補發。處理費 NT$200 元，且經完成申請手續不得要求退費。

· 測驗日起兩年內，可申請多益英語測驗證書，每份 NT$600 元，且經完成申請手續不得要求退費。

與多益相關的 TIPs

1 在多益考試日之前提前確認考試地點。

2 考試當天若沒有國民身份證正本或有效期限內之護照正本，則不能考試。要注意駕照、居留證、健保卡、學生證、信用卡等皆不能作為身份證件。

3 一旦開始考試，一切都需要使用英語表述，不要由於受到環境影響而緊張。

4 選錯答案並不扣分，所以即使有不會的問題也要在答案紙上選上答案。

5 多益考試後面並沒有預留填答案的時間，請聽到答案後立即在答案紙上作答，並注意作答的順序。

→ 請搜尋臺灣多益官方網站（www.toeic.com.tw）可以得到更詳細的資訊。

關於 NEW TOEIC

台灣從2008年3月的定期考試起施行NEW TOEIC。NEW TOEIC把重點放在測試實際商業情況中可能使用的單字運用能力，長篇文章的聽力與閱讀能力，隨即整體對話與文章變長，強化了單字問題。

NEW TOEIC 的特點

· 增加了對話和問題的長度。
· 增加各個國家（英國、加拿大、澳洲、紐西蘭）的英語發音與語調。
· 增設了短文填空的題型取代挑錯的題型。
· 在閱讀部分增加了帶有兩篇文章的雙篇閱讀。

舊多益 與 NEW TOEIC 結構比較

結構	舊多益		新多益		時間	分數
	內容	考題數	內容	考題數		
聽力測驗	Part 1 照片描述	20	Part 1 照片描述	10	45分鐘	495分
	Part 2 應答問題	30	Part 2 應答問題	30		
	Part 3 簡短對話	30	Part 3 簡短對話	30		
	Part 4 簡短獨白	20	Part 4 簡短獨白	30		
閱讀測驗	Part 5 單句填空 (文法/單字)	40	Part 5 單句填空 (語法/單字)	40	75分鐘	495分
	Part 6 挑錯	20	Part 6 短文填空 (新增)	12		
	Part 7 文章理解	40	Part 7 單篇文章理解 雙篇文章理解 （新增）	28 20		
TOTAL	7 Parts	200題	7 Parts	200題	120分鐘	990分

舊多益與新多益的區別

1. 聽力測驗

- PART 1 　由原來的20道題變成10道題，但是題型沒有變化。
- PART 2 　保持原來的30道題，題型沒有變化。
- PART 3 　對話變長。

　　在舊多益中，一段對話有一個問題，但是在新多益中，一段對話有3個問題。另外，原來的A-B-A形式的短對話變成A-B-A-B形式的長對話。總之，對話的長度增加了1.5倍～2倍，因此需要記憶的內容增多了，難度也提高了。

- PART 4 　增加了考題數量，文章也變長了。

　　由原來的20道題增加到30道題，而且文章也變長，問題數量增多。比以前更需要提高聽和理解長篇文章的能力。

- 發音變化　使用了幾個國家的英語發音和語調。

　　除了美式發音外，還增加了英國、加拿大、澳洲的發音和語調。熟悉美式發音的考生會對英式、澳洲式發音有些陌生，因此平時需要熟悉各種發音。

2. 閱讀測驗

- PART 5 　保持原來的題型和考題數。
- PART 6 　廢除了挑錯的題型，新增了短文填空的題型。

　　取消了尋找錯誤文法的題型，新增了在一篇文章中的3個空格內填寫相應單字的短文填空的題型，因此單字測驗的比重比以前高了些。其中有些題目只看有空格的句子，就能填寫出正確的答案，但有些題目只能在上下文中尋找答案。

- PART 7 　增加了考題數，而且增加了帶有兩篇文章的雙篇文章理解（double passage）。由原來的40道題增加為48道題。在考題方面，縮減了原來根據單篇文章回答的閱讀題，新增了根據兩篇文章回答的閱讀題。總之，閱讀負擔比以前來得重。

各單元的考題類型

Part V 單句填空（40道題）

Part V是把一個句子中的空白處，從4個選項中選擇正確的答案填入的題型。大概會出現25道文法問題和15道單字問題。這40道題需要在20分鐘內完成，這樣在閱讀理解部分的時間才不會太少。每個問題需要在25-30秒內完成。

1 文法

這是測試看英語文章的能力和文法知識的類型題。比起死記硬背膚淺的文法知識，還不如提高迅速理解文章構造的能力來得更有效。有深度地學習文法知識才是得到高分的辦法。

The ------- step of this project will be to present our proposal to the board of trustees and the acting CEO.

(A) final
(B) finally
(C) finality
(D) finalize

解說　需要的是修飾名詞（step）的形容詞，所以選（A）final。

2 單字

這類題目是測試在實際生活或商業情形中運用單字的能力。不要停留在光背單字的常見涵義，而是需要透過例句來理解各個單字在各種情形下的用法（usage）。

The company, known for its air-tight food -------, began manufacturing non-stick pans in an attempt to hold a broader part of the kitchenware market.

(A) dishes
(B) bowls
(C) containers
(D) plates

解說　選項中裝食品時不漏氣的容器是（C）containers（容器）。

Part VI 短文填空（共12題）

在一篇文章中的3個空格選擇恰當的單字或詞類的類型。共有4篇文章和12道題，為了要騰出時間給後面的閱讀理解，需要在5分鐘內完成，所以每道題要在20～25秒內完成。有些填空只需看空格所在的句子就能解答，但有些填空需要讀完全文並理解文章的來龍去脈才能解答。

In an urgent announcement yesterday, TNA Electronics issued a ------- for a total

1. (A) regard
   (B) request
   (C) resignation
   (D) retirement

recall on all Chop-O-Matic blenders. After an unusually large number of complaints received by their customer service hotline from consumers, the company stated they had no choice but to officially acknowledge a malfunction with a part used in the Chop-O-Matic. A company spokesman said the component used to hold the blades in place was not properly aligned during assembly. Because of this -------, the cutting

2. (A) risk
   (B) defect
   (C) characteristic
   (D) alteration

device can easily become dislodged, injuring users. The company wished to offer customers their sincerest apologies by providing full medical compensation for those harmed and ------- all returned products with a newer, safer version of their Chop-O-

3. (A) replacement
   (B) replace
   (C) replacing
   (D) replaced

Matic blender.

解說

1. 透過對「以所有Chop-O-Matic攪拌器為主發表回收的___」這一句子的理解，在空格處應填的詞是（B）request（要求）。（A）regard是「關係」、「考慮」，（C）resignation是「辭職」，（D）retirement是「退休」的意思。

2. 此題需要觀察分析前文。在前文中提到了「零件沒有正確排列在位置上」，所以與之對應地，應選擇（B）defect「缺陷」。

3. 透過對「提供醫療賠償並對半成品提供換貨來道歉」這一句的分析可知，空格之前的and聯繫著providing和空格，並由此可知，空格處應填與providing時態一致的Ving形式，即（C）replacing。

Part VII 閱讀理解（共48題）

閱讀理解由「一篇文章」和「兩篇文章」類型構成。

1 一篇文章 （Single Passage）(28題)

讀完一篇文章後在2-4個問題中選擇適當答案的類型。出題文章的類型爲書信、廣告、新聞等常在日常生活中見到的實用文章。一共九篇文章，需要時間爲25分鐘，所以每篇文章要在2分30秒～3分內完成解答。

This is an important memo informing all employees of a new policy regarding the usage of computers in the office. Due to an increase in personal use of computers during working hours, disciplinary measures have been initiated. To begin with, all staff members will have their computers monitored daily. Eventually, only approved websites will be accessible on work computers. Additionally, to turn on the computer you will have to enter a log-in name and password. That way we know who is using the computers for personal reasons. This policy will take effect as of June 10th. Mrs. Anderson will be taking your password requests this week in room 354. You will be able to register anytime after June 2nd.

Q: When will the new monitoring system begin?
(A) After the first of the year
(B) Next week
(C) June 2
(D) June 10

解釋　問題的核心是 " new system begin"，我們可以發現在本文中第7行用 " This policy will take effect" 來代替表現。新規定在 " as of June 10th" 實施，所以正確答案是（D）June 10。

2 兩篇文章 (Double Passage) (共20題)

讀完兩篇相關的文章後在5個問題中選擇恰當答案的類型。一共出4組「兩篇文章」的題目,需要時間為25分鐘,所以每組題要在5~6分鐘內完成。因為是兩篇文章,所以文章長、問題多,但問題的類型和解題方式跟「一篇文章」相似。「兩篇文章」中有些問題要結合兩篇文章的內容解題,所以建議對這一類問題要加以練習。

TO: All Staff
FROM: Nathan Perch, HR Manager, Superior Advertising Agency

Once again the festive season draws near, and planning is underway for our annual Christmas party. This year's promises to be an extra-special affair, as we've been lucky enough to have the menu designed by Albertus Fabiola of the High Street Bistro and Grill. The tentative plan for the menu is as follows:

1. Pasta Salad with avocado, red onion, and sesame dressing
2. Hawaiian barbecued salmon with a coconut cream sauce
3. Chicken breast stuffed with goat cheese and olives

Please inspect the choices carefully and get back to me within the next week with your feedback or suggestions, and we will endeavor to take them into account when making the final selections.

TO: Nathan Perch
FROM: John Dory, Marketing Division Chief

Nathan:

We were very excited to hear of the plans for the Christmas gathering and thrilled that you managed to secure such an eminent chef as Mr. Fabiola. Overall, we were very satisfied with the menu, though a few of us thought that the second suggestion might be spiced up with the addition of roasted vegetables. The coconut cream sauce would match well too. If you are able to take our request into account, I am sure it would be much appreciated by all the staff here in Marketing.

Kind Regards,
John

Q: What item does Mr. Dory suggest changing?
(A) Vegetable and noodle salad
(B) Coconut cream sauce
(C) Grilled seafood
(D) Spiced potatoes

解釋　問題是問 Dory 先生建議要換的食品是什麼?在第二篇文章第3行的 "the second suggestion might be spiced up with~" 中可以看出提議要換第二種菜單。至於什麼是第二種菜單,可以在第一篇文章的第6行 "2. Hawaiian barbecued salmon~" 中找到。所以與 barbecued salmon 同義的(C) Grilled seafood 是正確答案。

自我診斷和學習方法

*回答第24頁的診斷測驗題，然後根據測驗的成績，選擇適合自己程度的學習方法。

level 1
我已經不是初學者！
走出基礎課程！

（診斷考核 15~22分）

這是為剛踏入多益學習或英語基礎課程不扎實的人所準備的學習法。這個等級的學習者應同時抓好教材中的 Grammar 和 Vocabulary 部分。紮實的學好文法和多背單字是走出基礎課程的捷徑。即努力學習並消化 Grammar 和 Vocabulary 部分後再學習 Reading 的方法。在 Grammar 部分要熟悉每頁中的重點並練習下面的3道多益實戰考題，不要因為沒有基礎知識而放棄和氣餒，要嘗試利用上面的內容去解題。在解題的快樂中增加對多益題型的熟悉，你會自然而然的走出基礎課程。在本書中的 Vocabulary 單元可以使你在簡單快樂的解題和背單字中，不知不覺地提高紮實的單字實力。

level 2
一個階段 Up! Up!
攻進中間分數段！

（診斷考核 23~35分）

這是為需要通過多益考試，但始終提不高成績而苦惱的人所準備的學習法。這個階段的學習者也應同時抓好教材中的 Grammar 和 Vocabulary 部分。紮實的文法和單字量對提高解題能力有很大的幫助。即多背 Vocabulary，在做 Grammar 學習時不要光解題，要分析每一道題，會有很好的效果。建議這一類的學習者在解題時多做深入分析會對提高成績有很大的幫助。不惜多利用一些時間來分析所有的題目並記住所有的單字，這會讓你驚訝的發現多益成績在不知不覺中提高。

level **3**

哎！多益成績為什麼
這麼不盡人意？
我要成為多益高手！

（診斷考試 36~45 分）

「多益成績上升一點，只要是一點點…」、「這次考試要是多答對5題…」、「要是達到這個成績不僅就業，其他方面也會很順心…」，如果你就是這樣想的人或為就業而焦慮的人，這個單元就是為你們設立短期目標並快速提高成績為目的而制定的。不要為過去的失敗而懷疑接下來的一個月。只要下定決心並依照本書提供的四週（或八週）學習計畫來試試看。完成後去參加考試的話，你也應該可以成為多益高手。

level **4**

RC 450分就是我！
以滿分畢業多益！

（診斷考試 46~50 分）

這是為已經取得了別人羨慕的成績，但還是希望得到滿分的人所制定的學習法。本多益書中多角度的收錄一切可能在多益考試中出現的題目，讓你提前練習所有的題目。解題時應另外整理好模糊或生疏的題目。不略過這些題目是非常重要的。因為若做錯的題目是由於你「不知」的文法或單字造成的，那麼你還是會犯同樣的錯誤。必須找出錯誤的文法、單字和閱讀技巧才能得到滿分。只要以「非找出不懂的地方不可」的意志去學習本書，就一定能得到滿分。

學習計畫

01 單獨學習	1. 熟讀本文中的文法重點、單字目錄、閱讀攻略。 2. 以學習內容為基礎解下面的實踐題或 Practice。但不要馬虎的去做題目，要努力在每一道題中仔細套用學習的內容。 3. 以考試的態度解 Hackers Test。這時應該縮短時間限制並有意識的對題型做出分析。 4. 解完後對照正確答案，對做錯的題目再次確認。
02 小組學習	1. 彼此相互激勵可以營造良好的讀書氣氛，增加學習慾望，故可與同要要考多益的同學組成學習小組。 2. 跟著進度在家讀本文中的文法重點、單字目錄、閱讀攻略後參加學習小組。 3. 在學習小組組員之間用預習的內容來做小測試或口頭測試。文法中的重點用口頭方式問答的方法，單字和閱讀用單字考試的方法。 4. 學習時以考試的態度去做 Hackers Test。若縮短時間會更有效率，且互相公開錯誤的題數以良好的刺激學習。 5. 對照正確答案後一起確認錯誤的題目。一起討論不懂的題目直到徹底了解為止。
03 錄影學習	1. 由於錄影學習不受時間的限制，很多補習班都會把上課的情況錄影下來，以便學生做錄影學習，但也因此很多考生無法控制時間，有一課沒一課的上。進行錄影學習時，應該制定好學習時間，然後按時參加錄影學習。 2. 在錄影學習之前，必須預習和複習。首先熟悉本文內容，並回答問題。如果有不清楚的部分，就應該在課堂上認真聽講。另外，要經常翻看印象模糊或容易出錯的考題。
04 課堂學習	1. 在課堂上必須全神貫注地聽老師講課，如果有不理解的部分，應該及時發問。如果在課堂上沒有機會問，就應該利用下課休息時間問問題。 2. 下課後應該複習當天所學的內容，而且要記錄經常出錯的問題和很難理解的考題。

Study Plan A.　Grammar+Vocab → Reading 混合學習型

	Day	1st Day	2nd Day	3rd Day	4th Day	5th Day	6th Day	7th Day
1st week	Grammar	診斷(Part 5/6) (p.24~27)	Ch.1-2 (p.44~61)	Ch.3 (p.62~67)	Ch.4 (p.70~77)	Ch.5 (p.78~85)	Ch.6 (p.86~93)	Ch.7-8 (p.94~107)
	Vocabulary	Ch.1 (p.246~251)	Ch.2 (p.252~257)	Ch.3 (p.258~263)	Ch.4 (p.264~269)	Ch.5 (p.270~275)	Ch.6 (p.276~281)	Ch.7 (p.284~288)
2nd week	Grammar	Ch.9 (p.110~117)	Ch.10 (p.118~125)	Ch.11 (p.126~133)	Ch.12 (p.136~145)	Ch.13 (p.146~155)	Ch.14 (p.156~163)	Ch.15 (p.164~175)
	Vocabulary	Ch.7 (p.289~293)	Ch.8 (p.294~298)	Ch.8 (p.299~303)	Ch.9 (p.304~308)	Ch.9 (p.309~313)	Ch.10 (p.314~317)	Ch.10 (p.318~321)
3rd week	Grammar	Ch.16 (p.176~187)	Ch.17 (p.190~195)	Ch.18 (p.196~205)	Ch.19 (p.206~213)	Ch.20 (p.214~223)	Ch.21-22 (p.226~239)	實戰 1.2(Part 5/6) (p.445~451) (p.469~475)
	Vocabulary	Ch.11 (p.324~327)	Ch.11 (p.328~331)	Ch.12 (p.332~335)	Ch.12 (p.336~339)	Ch.13 (p.340~343)	Ch.13 (p.344~347)	
4th week	Reading	診斷(Part 7) Ch.1-2 (p.28~37) (p.354~365)	Ch.3-4 (p.366~377)	Ch.5-6 (p.378~393)	Ch.7-8 (p.394~405)	Ch.9-11 (p.406~423)	Ch.12-13 (p.424~443)	實戰 1.2(Part 7) (p.452~468) (p.476~492)

*「診斷」是「診斷測驗」，「實戰」是「實戰模擬測驗」的縮寫。

→ 「四週完成型」依照上面表格，「八週完成型」就把上面表格中一天的分量利用兩天完成。

→ 想要在兩週內短期完成本書，就要把兩天的分量在一天內完成。

Study Plan B.　Grammar → Vocab → Reading 順序學習型

1st week
Grammar

Day	1st Day	2nd Day	3rd Day	4th Day	5th Day	6th Day	7th Day
	診斷 Ch.1 (p.24~37) (p.44~53)	Ch.2-3 (p.54~67)	Ch.4-5 (p.70~85)	Ch.6-7 (p.86~101)	Ch.8-9 (p.102~117)	Ch.10-11 (p.118~133)	Ch.12 (p.136~145)

2nd week
Grammar

Day	1st Day	2nd Day	3rd Day	4th Day	5th Day	6th Day	7th Day
	Ch.13-14 (p.146~163)	Ch.15 (p.164~175)	Ch.16 (p.176~187)	Ch.17-18 (p.190~205)	Ch.19 (p.206~213)	Ch.20 (p.214~223)	Ch.21-22 (p.226~239)

3rd week
Vocabulary

Day	1st Day	2nd Day	3rd Day	4th Day	5th Day	6th Day	7th Day
	Ch.1-2 (p.246~257)	Ch.3-4 (p.258~269)	Ch.5-6 (p.270~281)	Ch.7-8 (p.284~303)	Ch.9-10 (p.304~321)	Ch.11-12 (p.324~339)	Ch.13 (p.344~347)

4th week
Reading

Day	1st Day	2nd Day	3rd Day	4th Day	5th Day	6th Day	7th Day
	Ch.1-2 (p.354~365)	Ch.3-4 (p.366~377)	Ch.5-6 (p.378~393)	Ch.7-8 (p.394~405)	Ch.9-11 (p.406~423)	Ch.12-13 (p.424~443)	實戰 1.2 (p.445~492)

* 「診斷」是「診斷測驗」，「實戰」是「實戰模擬測驗」的縮寫。

→ 「四週完成型」依照上面表格，「八週完成型」就把上面表格中一天的分量利用兩天完成。

→ 想要在兩週內短期完成本書，就要把兩天的分量在一天內完成。

多益診斷測驗
Diagnostic Test

READING TEST

In this section, you must demonstrate your ability to read and comprehend English. You will be given a variety of texts and asked to answer questions about these texts. This section is divided into three parts and will take 75 minutes to complete.

Do not mark the answers in your test book. Use the answer sheet that is separately provided.

PART V

Directions: In each question, you will be asked to review a statement that is missing a word or phrase. Four answer choices will be provided for each question. Select the best answer and mark the corresponding letter (A), (B), (C), or (D) on the answer sheet.

01 In spite of the decreasing amount of silver, the value of the metal has fallen ------- in the past years.

(A) sharp
(B) sharply
(C) sharpness
(D) sharpen

02 Unlike ------- writers who prefer specializing in a specific genre, freelancers usually work with many literary types.

(A) much
(B) more
(C) the most
(D) many

03 Donors are assured that 90 percent of the money they contribute goes ------- to the implementation of the organization's social programs.

(A) uniquely
(B) directly
(C) easily
(D) exactly

04 It is important for ------- interested in doing an investigative piece to check their sources and ensure their stories are accurate.

(A) journalists
(B) journal
(C) journalism
(D) journalistic

05 The entire staff would like to congratulate Mr. Richards ------- his winning the "Employee of the Year" Award.

(A) to
(B) in
(C) with
(D) on

06 Dealing with angry customers everyday became too ------- to handle, so she quit the receiver position.

(A) frustrate
(B) frustrated
(C) frustrating
(D) frustration

07 Part of Mary Tyler's role as public relations manager is to attend several private and business ------- each week.

(A) functions
(B) practices
(C) values
(D) aspirations

08 Hank ------- from depression, having lost his job in January from budget cutbacks in the service department.

(A) will suffer
(B) was suffering
(C) will have suffered
(D) suffer

09 The company decided to give her a chance, ------- doubts regarding her ability to perform such high-level tasks.

(A) but   (B) yet
(C) nevertheless   (D) despite

10 The convention is an excellent ------- of bringing commodities buyers and suppliers together in one place.

(A) approach   (B) means
(C) technique   (D) instrument

11 Please be reminded that we are not responsible for any damage to the product due to careless use, intentional misuse or ------- customer negligence.

(A) other   (B) the other
(C) another   (D) others

12 Sales of small cars have been so high in Asia that the German auto maker is ------- into entering the Asian market.

(A) watching   (B) looking
(C) searching   (D) viewing

13 ------- the remodeling is finished, the office cubicles can be put back in place and regular work hours can begin again.

(A) As soon as   (B) However
(C) While   (D) In time for

14 Before taking your car out of the parking garage, be sure that nothing ------- your view.

(A) concedes   (B) notices
(C) obstructs   (D) intensifies

15 A thorough ------- of the journal article is needed before it can be published next month.

(A) revising   (B) revision
(C) revise   (D) revised

16 The proposal should be ready next week, ------- how long it takes the architects to finish the floor plan.

(A) resulting from   (B) partly because
(C) depending on   (D) certain

17 The speakers will be on the radio talk show ------- their views on energy issues in North America.

(A) introductory   (B) introduce
(C) introduction   (D) introducing

18 ------- renting a vehicle, verify the exact amount to be paid for licenses and maintenance costs.

(A) Rather than   (B) When
(C) Because   (D) As though

19 The ------- profitability of the X-27 is about ten percent higher than previous models of this machine.

(A) overall   (B) overcast
(C) overdue   (D) overwhelmed

20 Please let me know if there are office spaces still available ------- lease in the new complex.

(A) into   (B) as
(C) for   (D) with

Directions: In this part, you will be asked to read an English text. Some sentences are incomplete. Select the word or phrase that correctly completes each sentence and mark the corresponding letter (A), (B), (C), or (D) on the answer sheet.

Questions 21-23 refer to the following advertisement.

Happy Pharmacy Valued Customer Day

We are pleased to announce that Happy Pharmacy will be celebrating its tenth anniversary next week. We recognize that our success is in no small part due to the support we receive from customers like you. In -------, we would like to invite you to participate in our Valued Customer

      21 (A) apprehension
          (B) appreciation
          (C) appeasement
          (D) applause

Day on April 26. Visit any of our convenient locations and you will be treated to sandwiches and refreshments, as well as a 15% discount on all purchases over $20.00. In addition, you will get the chance to meet local health practitioners, try out new products, and enter your name to win a complete set of vitamins courtesy of Happy Pharmacy. So, we hope that you will take advantage of this great opportunity to save money and get to know the health services in your area. We hope to ------- offer more events like this

    22 (A) recently
       (B) conclusively
       (C) continually
       (D) timelessly

in the future. A flyer with our store addresses ------- for your information.

      23 (A) enclosed
         (B) is enclosed
         (C) has enclosed
         (D) was enclosed

Questions 24-26 refer to the following e-mail.

From : Breakgen Productions
To : Darcey Kerr
Subject : DVD Order

Dear Ms. Kerr,

Thank you for your recent order for a copy of our DVD box set of Werewolf Killer. Unfortunately, we have discontinued this box set version and will be unable to fulfill your order as -------. We apologize for

24 (A) request
(B) requesting
(C) requests
(D) requested

any inconvenience this may cause. We do offer an alternative version of this DVD that contains the original broadcasts as well as other additional features. Bonuses include ------- unreleased footage,

25 (A) presently
(B) previously
(C) purposefully
(D) generally

a documentary about the making of the program, and an interview with the director. Because of this ------- material, the DVD has become one of our bestsellers.

26 (A) essential
(B) supplemental
(C) excessive
(D) promotional

The only other difference between the box set and this version is the external packaging. Of course, should you decide to purchase a copy of Werewolf Killer and find that it is not suitable, you may return it for a full refund.

Sincerely,
Elmo J. Pudd
Customer Service Department, Breakgen Productions

PART VII

Directions: In this part, you will be asked to read several texts, such as advertisements, articles or examples of business correspondence. Each text is followed by several questions. Select the best answer and mark the corresponding letter (A), (B), (C), or (D) on your answer sheet.

Questions 27-28 refer to the following invitation.

The Embassy of Spain
requests the pleasure of your company
at a reception and dinner
to welcome
the new Ambassador of Spain Antonio Martinez
on Friday, the twenty-second of August
at 7:00 p.m.
The Town Hotel
Manhattan, New York City
Black tie
RSVP
Regina Davis
Vanderbilt Offices
Manhattan, NY
461-2007

27 What is the reason for the dinner?

    (A) To award an outstanding manager
    (B) To receive a dignitary
    (C) To introduce a new executive
    (D) To welcome a visiting delegation

28 What is the recipient asked to do?

    (A) Bring a companion
    (B) Be on time
    (C) Prepare food
    (D) Reply to the invitation

Questions 29-30 refer to the following information.

5ᵗʰ Annual Bazaar

The community center is pleased to announce that it will be hosting the Midwestern Women's Association's 5th annual bazaar next weekend. Items to be sold at the event include home-made quilts, freshly baked pies, jam, and hand-made crafts. All participating community members are asked to bring at least one item, whether material or food, to sell or add to the potluck dinner. Of course, donations are welcomed and will be used to improve the community center facilities. We are considering the installation of a media center for the education and convenience of the community youth who aren't fortunate enough to have access to such technology. With your contributions, it will also be possible to organize and hold more meaningful events for the community. As always, please spread the word to your neighbors about the event next Saturday. A sign-up sheet is located on the bulletin board in the main hall. It is sure to be a time of warmth, friendship, and community!

29 What are people coming to the event asked to do?

(A) Bring the entrance fee
(B) Provide food for their family
(C) Participate in remodeling the center
(D) Ask other local residents to attend

30 What is suggested in this text?

(A) Financial assistance will be appreciated.
(B) Donations are mandatory.
(C) All community members are required to come.
(D) The community center is newly built.

Questions 31-33 refer to the following job advertisement.

Wanted

Executive Housekeeper
We are looking for an individual with an energetic personality. The qualified candidate will be responsible for managing, and overseeing all public areas of the compound. A minimum of 3 years experience in a similar position is required.

Convention Services Representative
Assists the manager in ensuring maximum sales, profit and guest satisfaction of Catering Services through proactive selling, maximization of incremental revenue of confirmed bookings and securing repeat bookings. Must have a minimum of 2 years experience.

Front Desk Agent
The Front Desk Agent is responsible for the professional and efficient operation of the reception desk. Previous experience necessary. Must be outgoing and 'people-oriented' and have excellent oral and written communication skills. Possesses the ability to deal with pressure in a graceful and courteous manner. Position must be filled today.

Guest Service Agent
Guest services for arriving guests. Responsibilities include door person and valet. Driver's license is necessary. Must be able to lift up to 80 lbs and work standing for long periods of time. Full-time position. May require extended work hours on weekdays and weekends.

E-mail resume and all pertinent information to hrd@fairfield.com. Those applying for supervisory positions must include two letters of reference.

31 Who might have put up this ad?

(A) A housekeeping agency
(B) A convention hall
(C) A large hotel
(D) A recruiting firm

32 What is a requirement of the Front Desk Agent job?

(A) A minimum of 3 years experience
(B) Good interpersonal skills
(C) A degree in hotel management
(D) Proficient typing skills

33 What should be submitted for the executive housekeeper position?

(A) Letters of recommendation
(B) A copy of college transcripts
(C) A copy of a driver's license
(D) A certificate of training

Questions 34-37 refer to the following article.

"A Firm to Start Work on Public Underwater Tube Project"

The city has announced that Christenson & Dawson has won the annual engineering contract out of twenty major engineering companies that competed for the bid. The agreement awards the company permission to design and build San Francisco's proposed underwater tube, the addition of which is forecasted to greatly improve transportation in the city. Citizens are hoping it will resolve the existing traffic problems. In particular businessmen want the commuting convenience. Simultaneously, government officials expect the media attention to the project to give a boost to the sluggish tourist industry. All in all, there is great pressure from all of these sections of the population on the winning company.

In light of its importance, the project manager, Josh Pratt, has acknowledged that this deal must be supervised by a highly experienced and reliable company. The selection committee adhered to the strict rating standards it had developed a year prior to the competition. Ten of the potential contractors were dropped within the first week of review and only one applicant, who eventually won the contract prize, scored high on all of the criteria set forth by the critics. The committee asserts that because of its impeccable track record with similar projects and phenomenal reputation, Christenson & Dawson is the company best equipped for the job.

In response, a representative from Christenson & Dawson has said that the job will receive the same attention and care as their other projects. He has assured the public that the creation of the line is of the utmost importance, but that also no other projects will be ignored, while also expressing the company's eagerness and excitement regarding the upcoming challenge.

34 What is this article about?

(A) Completion of a design project
(B) The excellent reputation of Christenson & Dawson
(C) The presentation of an award
(D) Granting of a major engineering contract

35 What is NOT one of the potential community benefits of the project?

(A) Incoming money from visitors
(B) Better traffic conditions
(C) Federal funding for the project
(D) Appeal to travelers

36 What is correct about Christenson & Dawson?

(A) It met the standards determined by the committee.
(B) It had a strong competitor until the final stage of the review.
(C) It won the bid despite a lack of experience.
(D) It will give its entire attention to this project.

37 The word "dropped" in paragraph 2, line 4, is closest in meaning to

(A) discarded
(B) consulted
(C) eliminated
(D) recruited

Questions 38-40 refer to the following letter.

October 21, 2004

Carrie Wynand
Wadley Mortgage Firm
Woodland Hills, CA

Robert Hartshire
1219 North Street
Helmsley Park, CA

Dear Mr. Hartshire,

This is in response to your inquiry regarding the mortgage trainee position we advertised in The California Herald. We would like to congratulate you on your interest in becoming a mortgage banker. There has been an overwhelmingly favorable response by mortgage brokers to the possibilities afforded by an online system that has resulted in record double-digit growth.

The mortgage banking team consists of professionals who are setting industry standards for innovation and service. Wadley Mortgage emphasizes the need to expand its system into the technological world. Therefore, we support the professional development and training of our employees. We firmly believe that the key to success rests in the quality of our bankers. Therefore, we are proud to offer people the opportunity to take part in our training program.

To participate in our program, you will need to submit the following: an application using the application form available on Wadley Mortgage's website, a letter of reference, your resume (including a cover letter). After you submit the required documents, the selection committee will post their decision on the website, which you may access with the code sent to your e-mail account after the entire application has been received.

.Once again, thank you for your interest.

Best regards,

Carrie Wynand

Carrie Wynand
HRD

38 What is the purpose of this letter?

(A) To inform the applicant that he was rejected
(B) To remind the applicant his documents are incomplete
(C) To respond to a potential participant
(D) To tell the applicant when he can get the results

39 What should the candidate do next?

(A) Indicate interest by calling Ms. Wynand
(B) Visit the office for an interview
(C) Send a reply via e-mail
(D) Provide the necessary paperwork

40 What is correct about the letter recipient?

(A) He works at Wadley Mortgage.
(B) He has previously contacted the firm.
(C) He has already applied to the program.
(D) He has experience in the banking industry.

Questions 41-45 refer to the following e-mail and schedule.

From: Sylvia Broadleig
To: Frank Tawker

I had committed to demonstrating the new Smart Microwave at the Hometech section of *the Future in Electronics* exhibition tomorrow in my role as Head of Product Development. However, due to a complication with our new blender, I have to work on finding a solution and thus won't be able to make it. Harvey Hampton in Promotions was wondering if you could take my place. Information about the event is as follows:

"Mark your calendars because *the Future in Electronics* is coming to you! The exhibition features such themes as Hometech, Fast Lane, Tomorrow's Toys, and Innovative Workplace, being brought to you by Time Savers Inc, Brute Automotives, CompuGames, and Gold Computers respectively. It will be held at the Michigan Exhibition Center from Friday, the 15th to Sunday, the 17th of September."

Future in Electronics

Hometech
See what the future holds in store for your everyday home life. Hometech will demonstrate the latest in technology in home appliances. Join us in the Great Lakes Exhibition Hall for the opening ceremony and get your picture taken with Penny Heartthrob, the official face of Time Savers Inc.

Fast Lane
Get a glance at the latest developments in automotives being presented in the East Parking Lot. Meet the Brute Racing Team, learn how engines are manufactured and even test drive a 500 Series Convertible. While you're there, don't forget to enter the draw for a brand new Coupe Hybrid Truck and really start living life in the fast lane.

Tomorrow's Toys
Bring the kids to check out Tomorrow's Toys in the Main Concourse, where they can try all the newest and coolest in computer games, video games, and electronic toys. Take home some of the many free trial games offered to any child under 12!

Innovative Workplace
Move your office or work environment into the 21st century with Innovative Workplace in the Foster Exhibition Hall. Make sure to stop by on Saturday to hear Ingrid Goldstein, CEO of Gold Computers, talk about all the exciting advances in the world of Electronics and the Workplace.

41 Who is Sylvia Broadleig?

(A) A promoter at Brute Automotives
(B) A researcher at Time Savers Inc.
(C) A model at CompuGames
(D) A designer at Gold Computers

42 What does Sylvia want Frank to do?

(A) Make an appearance at a company event
(B) Meet a deadline for a blender
(C) Change his position to promotions
(D) Exhibit the newest car model

43 Where will you most likely find a gas stove?

(A) At Hometech
(B) At Fast Lane
(C) At Tomorrow's Toys
(D) At Innovative Workplace

44 What is the prize for the draw?

(A) A computer game
(B) A test drive
(C) A new microwave
(D) A vehicle

45 Where will Innovative Workplace be held?

(A) The Great Lakes Exhibition Hall
(B) The East Parking Lot
(C) The Main Concourse
(D) The Foster Exhibition Hall

Questions 46-50 refer to the following article and email.

Dialatron Corp. has confirmed speculations that they are making huge changes in the company with the introduction of Mrs. Barbara Starduster, as the new President of Overseas Marketing. Having finalized an employment contract with Mrs. Starduster, Dialatron stated they are now fully capable of moving forward with their goal of becoming the leading cellular phone manufacturer world wide. They have also introduced Ila Singh, formerly with Ring Telecommunications, to become the head of Marketing for Asia, and Bob McCloud, to lead the European division. Singh and McCloud will both report directly to Mrs. Starduster. Dialatron also declared they have secured Ms. Fiona Toledo, who left her position as main accountant to Handheld Electronics Inc., as their head figure cruncher and expect to see a rise in the profit margin. Ms. Toledo vowed to make miracles happen and will keep Mr. Abraham Goldberg, company Treasurer, and Ms. Annabella Binoche, Financial Analysts, on her staff. Dialatron Corp., already dominating the domestic cellular phone market, currently holds 25% of worldwide sales. With continued restructuring and an influx of fresh ideas, they are predicting that figure will double in the next year.

From: Barbara Starduster
To: Ila Singh, Bob McCloud

Greetings you two,
It's been a hectic two weeks and I'm impressed with what we've accomplished so far. But we have been confined to the office and have not had enough opportunity to converse in a more natural atmosphere. Therefore, I'd like to suggest an informal gathering where we can get a chance to know each other over dinner. I've made reservations at Gibbons', for 8:oop.m. this coming Friday. It was suggested to me by a good friend who has impeccable taste in establishments. I hope to see you both there so we can sit down and have a nice chat over a scrumptious dinner. Please let me know if this is convenient for you.
Barbara

46 What does Dialatron want to do?

(A) They want to settle a financial dispute.
(B) They want to downsize their accounting staff.
(C) They want to support a local restaurant.
(D) They want to sell more cellular phones overseas.

47 Where was Fiona Toledo formerly employed?

(A) At a telecommunications company
(B) At an accounting company
(C) At an electrical appliance company
(D) At a marketing firm

48 Who is Bob McCloud's immediate supervisor?

(A) Ila Singh
(B) Barbara Starduster
(C) Fiona Toledo
(D) Abraham Goldberg

49 What is Gibbons'?

(A) A residence
(B) A company
(C) A restaurant
(D) An office

50 Why did Barbara choose Gibbons'?

(A) It has good food.
(B) It's not expensive.
(C) It has a good atmosphere.
(D) It was recommended.

正確答案請查看解答本 P.2

* 檢查完後到 p.18 查看適合自己的學習方法

NEW TOEIC 新多益必考文法

☑ 從詞性分類，詳細解析新多益必考之文法

☑ 例句中英對照，邊學文法也能邊學會話

☑ 中英翻譯、解答同步呈現，讓學習更有力

☑ 收錄考古題和新題型解題之必備文法觀念

☑ 擴充單字量並加強文法觀念，輕鬆拿高分

GRAMMAR

GRAMMAR

1 多益文法的特點

● 多益中的文法都來自與實際商務交流相關的文章。

多益中的文法主要考察日常生活或公司業務中的英語活用能力，因此，多益會選擇實務商業對話中的一篇文章，以其中用到的文法來出題。所以，即使是已經掌握了文法，如果不能真正理解商業文章的內容，也可能選錯答案。因此，對沒有職場生活經驗的人來說，不能只侷限於學校裡和日常生活中所學的簡單會話，還要熟悉一些與商業有關的主題和單字。

● 多益試題裡有特定的文法題目類型。

多益考試旨在考察考試者對日常生活中基本文法掌握的準確度和靈活度。因此，多益中會反覆出現一定類型的題目，它們考察的只是相當基本和實用的文法。所以，與其系統整理和記憶所有的文法，還不如針對多益的核心文法類型反覆練習達到熟練的地步。

2 多益文法問題類型

● 單句填空（Part V）

這部分的考試是要考生在題目中的四個選項中選擇一個正確答案來填空。選擇的同時也要注意正確的詞性、連接詞、時態，使文章符合基本的文法規則。

[例題]

Kathleen O'Connor ------- decided to accept the position of assistant to the executive that was offered to her by Mr. Warren.

(A) finalize   (B) finally   (C) finalized   (D) final

翻譯：Kathleen O'conner 終於決定接受 Warren 先生任命的祕書一職。
解說：在四個選項中選擇了詞性正確的（B）finally，使文章文法正確且完整。

● 短文填空（Part VI）

這部分的考試是在一篇短文中設置三個空格，在四個選項中選擇一個適合這個空格的答案。要選擇恰當的詞性、介系詞、連接詞使文章的文法通順並且意義明確。

[例題]

Growth Focus, a leading business journal, announced the release of a 52-page special publication entitled "Inside the Booming Chinese Internet Sector." Praised by experts for its in-depth scrutiny, the report contains ------- information concerning the Chinese investment climate, and is being
      (A) valuable   (C) value
      (B) valuably   (D) valued
made available free of charge to customers who sign up for a one year subscription to the magazine.

翻譯：一流商業雜誌《Growth Focus》宣稱將發行52頁的《透視方興未艾的中國興網路業》特刊。這篇因深入調查而獲得專家好評的報告，記載了有關中國投資環境的寶貴資訊。訂閱本雜誌滿一年的訂戶可免費獲得這本特刊。
解說：透過「以形容詞修飾名詞」的規則，選擇可以修飾名詞information的形容詞（A）valuable做答案。

3 出題比率

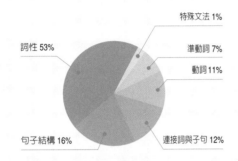

特殊文法 1%

準動詞 7%

動詞 11%

連接詞與子句 12%

句子結構 16%

詞性 53%

〔各種文法範圍的出題比率〕

4 NEW TOEIC 的趨勢及戰略

- 掌握好句子的結構才能做對更多的題目。

從前只要掌握較多的多益文法和單字就能在考試中順利過關。但最近,增加了需要瞭解句子構造才能解決的題目。因此,區分句子的必要成分和附加成分(修飾語),以及掌握句子結構的能力就倍顯重要,對於這一點要進行重點練習。

- 每次考試必然出現1～2道難解題目。

從前只要掌握好多益中經常出現的基本文法項目,就可以獲取高分。但是,最近每次考試都會出現1～2道難解題目。這種題目,解題重點不在文法和單字知識,而在於單字的用法,所以必需充分熟悉單字的多樣用法(usage)。

- 增加了短文填空

取消了找出文法錯誤的題型後,在NEW TOEIC Part 6中新增加了短文填空。這雖然增加了閱讀文章的負擔,但這類題目只需閱讀包含空格的句子便可充分解決,所以不會太難。另外,即使在相關的文章裡找不出答案,也可以從上下文中的提示中輕鬆解答。因此,實際上會感到比從前考試中的Part 6更簡單。

Section 1 句子結構

Chapter 1

主詞、動詞

啊哈!! 愉快地打基礎

1

動詞指的是句子中描述動作或狀態的部分，主詞指的是那個動作或狀態的主體（誰 / 什麼）。

Kathy ate an apple. Kathy 吃了蘋果。

這個句子中描述的動作 "ate"（吃）就是句子的動詞。還有 "ate" 的主體即「誰」吃的，所以 Kathy 就是句子的主詞。

2

所有的句子都要有主詞和動詞。

Kathy an apple.（X）Kathy 蘋果
ate an apple.（X）吃蘋果

以上句子都是錯誤的。第一個句子中沒有描述動作（動詞），所以是錯誤的。第二個句子中的動作 "ate" 沒有主詞，所以也是錯誤的。所有的句子都必須同時有主詞和動詞才能成立。

3

句子〔主詞 + 動詞〕與句子〔主詞 + 動詞〕之間必須要有連接詞。

Kathy exercises she goes to work.（X）Kathy 運動 她上班。
　句子1〔主詞1 動詞1〕　　句子2〔主詞2 動詞2〕

句子1〔主詞 1 動詞1〕與句子2〔主詞 2 動詞 2〕之間在沒有任何連接詞的情況下連接在一起，意思不明確。句子〔主詞 + 動語〕與句子〔主詞 + 動詞〕之間必須要有連接詞。

Kathy exercises before she goes to work.（○）Kathy 上班前做運動。
　句子1〔主詞1 動詞1〕連接詞　　句子2〔主詞2 動詞2〕

01 可放在主詞位置的單字或字組，即具有名詞性質

❶ 能夠成為主詞的單字或字組即具有名詞性質。

名詞片語	The top <u>executives</u> agreed to negotiate with the union. 最高董事會同意與勞動組織協商。
代名詞	<u>They</u> are having a team meeting today. 他們今天有一個小組會議。
動名詞	<u>Operating</u> the machinery is difficult. 操作那台機器很困難。
不定詞	<u>To meet</u> the president was a privilege. 與那位長官見面是一種殊榮。
名詞子句	<u>What</u> Jane needs for her office is unclear. Jane的辦公室需要些什麼還不太清楚。

→ 畫線的部分是主詞，多益考試中往往會從這部分設置問題。

注意！ 不定詞充當主詞的情況並不多。不定詞經常用於表示虛主詞的真主詞。此內容會在 Chapter 2 中的 02「虛主詞 it 結構」中詳細介紹。

❷ 動詞、形容詞等不能成為主詞。

A rushed ~~decide~~ should be avoided under any circumstances. 在任何情況下都要避免倉促做決定。
　　　　 decision

→ 主詞的位置應該是名詞（decision）而不是動詞（decide）。

The financial ~~healthy~~ of the company is in doubt. 那家公司的財務健全度令人質疑。
　　　　　 health

→ 主詞的位置應該是名詞（health）而不是形容詞（healthy）。

注意！ 1. 要注意貌似形容詞的名詞。

applicant 名申請者	delivery 名運送	denial 名拒絕	proposal 名提案
complaint 名不滿	strategy 名戰略	disposal 名處理，處分	withdrawal 名提款

2. 要注意常用於動詞或形容詞但也可以用於名詞的單字。

prospect 名前景 動調查	respect 名尊敬 動尊敬	request 名邀請 動邀請	review 名動再檢查
help 名幫助 動幫助	charge 名費用 動索價	raise 名抬高 動舉起	check 名支票，停止 動檢查，阻止
deal 名交易 動處理	leave 名休假 動離開	effect 名影響，效果 動導致	increase 名增加 動增加
offer 名提供 動提供	pay 名傭金 動支付	control 名控制 動控制	interest 名利息，興趣 動使發生興趣
objective 名目的 形客觀的	respondent 名應答者 形應答的	alternative 名選擇 形替代的	representative 名代表者 形代表的
normal 名常態 形普通的	individual 名個人 形個人的	potential 形潛在的 名潛力	original 形原來的，獨創性的 名原物

❸ 主詞的單、複數要與動詞的變化一致

The ~~prospects~~ of increased revenue <u>awaits</u> us next year. 明年收入增加的前景在等著我們。
　　 prospect

→ 為了與單數形式的動詞（awaits）對應，應使用單數（prospect）做主詞，而不是複數（prospects）。

多益實戰考題　　　多益會出這樣的問題

⊙ 填主詞
　這種題型填入名詞片語的答案出現的最多。

1. Please remember that the ------- of electronic devices is prohibited during takeoffs and landings.

(A) operation　　　(B) operate
(C) operated　　　(D) operator

2. Personal ------- left behind on seats in the theater are brought to the lost and found department, but most are never claimed.

(A) belonging　　　(B) belongs
(C) belongings　　　(D) belong

3. The new ------- that is going up at Williams and 3rd will accommodate hundreds of commercial enterprises.

(A) structural　　　(B) structurally
(C) structured　　　(D) structure

02 虛主詞 it

❶ it 用來代替動詞不定詞片語或 that 子句中的長主詞。這時稱 it 為「虛主詞」，而原來的長主詞稱為「主詞」。

It is important <u>to open negotiations with the Brazilian firm</u>. 與這家巴西公司進行洽談是很重要的。
　虛主詞　　　　　　　　　　　　實際主詞（to 不定詞）

It is understood <u>that Mr. Gann will resign fairly soon</u>. 看來 Gann 先生很快就會辭職。
　虛主詞　　　　　　　　　　　實際主詞（that 子句）

❷ it 強調名詞或介系詞片語時與 that 搭配，並組成「it ~ that 強調句」。

It was <u>Jane</u> that gave a speech. 演講的人就是 Jane。
　　　被強調的物件

It is <u>in the conference room</u> that the most important meetings take place.
　　　　被強調的物件

最重要的會議就是在這個會議室中舉行。

注意！ 被強調的物件是人時，也可以用 who(m)；是表示事物的名詞時，也可以用 which。
　　　It was Patrick <u>who</u> won the game. 在遊戲中獲勝的人就是 Patrick。
　　　It was the song <u>which</u> captured my attention. 吸引我注意力的就是那首歌。

❸ 虛主詞 it 的位置不能被別的單字替代。

~~That~~ was a cat that was stuck in the tree last night. 昨晚卡在樹上的是一隻貓。
　It
→ that 不能替代虛主詞 it 的位置。

~~There~~ is possible that nobody will attend the meeting. 有可能誰都不會參加會議。
　It
→ There 不能替代虛主詞 it 的位置。

多益實戰考題　　　　　　　多　益　會　出　這　樣　的　問　題

⊙ 填虛主詞、實際主詞。

1. When deciding what food to serve guests at a party, ------- is always best to choose dishes that can be prepared ahead of time.

  (A) there　　　　　(B) what
  (C) that　　　　　 (D) it

2. It is mandatory to ------- a work identification card when you first enter the company.

  (A) obtain　　　　　(B) obtaining
  (C) obtainment　　　(D) obtained

3. Although the two copywriters in the office are often at odds with one another, ------- is clear that they have respect for each other's work.

  (A) there　　　　　(B) it
  (C) what　　　　　 (D) that

正確答案 P10

03 虛主詞 there

❶ there用於表示「有…」，構成「there +動詞（be, remain, exist..）+實際主詞（名詞句）」的形式。

There are <u>eleven offices</u> on this floor. 這層樓有11個辦公室。
虛主詞　　　　主詞（名詞片語）

There remains <u>some doubt</u> over her level of dedication. 對她的奉獻程度存疑。
虛主詞　　　　　主詞（名詞片語）

There exists <u>a possibility</u> that the company will be bought out this year. 這家公司今年有被收購的可能。
虛主詞　　　　主詞（名詞片語）

❷ 在如同「there+動詞+主詞」的句子結構中，主詞不能是動詞。

We will contact you if <u>there</u> are ~~cancelled~~. 如果有人取消預約，我們將與您聯繫。
　　　　　　　　　　　 cancellations
→ there are後面的主詞位置上，應該是名詞（cancellations）而不是動詞（cancelled）。

多益實戰考題　　　　　　　　　　　多 益 會 出 這 樣 的 問 題

⊙填虛主詞、實際主詞

1. ------- remain significant challenges for the fledgling company as it tries to gain a foothold in a highly competitive market.

(A) It　　　　　　　(B) There
(C) He　　　　　　　(D) They

2. The publisher prints an apology on the second page of the magazine when there are ------- of fact in previous issues.

(A) errs　　　　　　(B) erroneous
(C) errors　　　　　(D) erred

3. I'm hopeful that somewhere in the city ------- exists a position with the hours and benefits I seek.

(A) there　　　　　(B) it
(C) he　　　　　　(D) what

正確答案　P10

Hackers Skill　　要區分虛主詞it和there的差別。

· 若動詞意思為「是… / 做…」則用it，若意為「有…」則用there。
When you want to travel, it(there) is a good idea to plan ahead. 如果你想去旅行，提前擬定計劃是正確的做法。
There(It) is a guidebook in each language. 有包含各種語言的說明書。

· 當it做主詞時，動詞後面可跟名詞、形容詞、介系詞子句等，但there做主詞時，動詞後面只能跟名詞。
It (There) is <u>fair</u> to give him a chance. 給他機會對他來說是公平的。

04 謂語的位置可以有「(助動詞+)動詞」

❶ 可成為文章謂語的是「(助動詞+)動詞」。

The supervisor oversees an entire office. 這位主管管理整個辦公室。
The supervisor can oversee an entire office. 這位主管可以管理整個辦公室。

❷ 「動詞原形+ing」或「to+動詞原形」的形式不能成為謂語。

The supervisor overseeing an entire office. (×)
The supervisor to oversee an entire office. (×)
→ 雖然overseeing和to oversee形如謂語,但並非謂語overseeing(動名詞、分詞),to oversee(不定詞)這樣的成分稱為「非謂語動詞」。

❸ 名詞或形容詞不能成為句子中的謂語。

Jake ~~arrival~~ a few minutes late for the meeting. Jake在會議中遲到了幾分鐘。
　　　arrived
→ 謂語應是動詞(arrived)而不是名詞(arrival)。

This company ~~compliant~~ with government regulations. 這家公司遵守政府的規定。
　　　　　　　complies
→ 謂語應是動詞(complies)而不是形容詞(compliant)。

注意! 有一些詞既可用做形容詞、名詞也可用做動詞,要避免混淆。

function 名功能 動運作	question 名問題 動質問	name 名名字 動命名,任命	document 名文件 動用文件證明
finance 名財政 動融資	cost 名費用 動花費	experience名經驗 動經歷	access 名接近 動接近
process 名過程,程序 動處理	purchase 名購買 動購買	claim 名要求,主張 動要求,主張	place名場所 動放置
influence名影響 動影響	transfer 名移動 動移動,挪動	contact 名接觸 動接觸	demand 名要求,需求 動要求
feature 名特色 動以…為特色	schedule 名日程安排表 動預定	deposit 名保證金 動寄存	service 名服務 動修理,提供
complete 形完整的 動完成	separate 形個別的 動分離	secure 形安全的 動看守	correct 形正確的 動校正

多益實戰考題　　　　　　　　　　　　多 益 會 出 這 樣 的 問 題

⊙填謂語

2. The new regulation from the Department of Transportation ------- a change in the manner in which rest time is calculated for commercial vehicle drivers.

(A) requires　　　　　(B) requiring
(C) to require　　　　(D) requirement

1. The value of the dollar ------- yesterday against the Japanese yen after skirmishes in the Middle East died down.

(A) rising　　　　　(B) to rise
(C) risen　　　　　(D) rose

3. Salaried employees ------- a ten percent increase in wages last year as an incentive to increase production.

(A) receipt　　　　　(B) to receive
(C) received　　　　(D) receiving

正確答案 P10

Hackers Skill　　謂語不能是非謂語動詞或其他詞性的詞(名詞、形容詞)。

05 謂語要有恰當的單複數形式、時態和語態

❶ 謂語要與主詞的單複數形式一致。

The <u>results</u> of the inquiry ~~was~~ made public today. 那次調查的結果在今天發表。
were

→ 主詞是複數形式（results），因此謂語也應為複數形式（were）。

❷ 謂語要與句子的時態相一致。

Randy ~~joins~~ the firm <u>seven years ago</u>. Randy 在 7 年前加入了那家公司。
joined

→ 因為有表示過去的 seven years ago，因此謂語也應該為過去形式 joined。

❸ 謂語要有正確的主動 / 被動語態。

The accounting reports ~~checked~~ by a team of auditors. 結算報告由審查團檢查。
were checked

→ 根據主詞（The accounting reports 與 a team）以及動詞（check）之間的語意關係，可知謂語應用被動語態 were checked。

They ~~were used~~ their savings for a charitable cause. 他們將存款用於慈善事業。
used

→ 根據句意可知，是主詞「他們」使用了「存款」，是主動語態，因此謂語應用主動語態的 used。

注意！ 有關謂語的單複數形式、時態、語態，將在 Section 2 動詞片語中的 Ch5，Ch6，Ch7 裡詳細介紹。

注意！ 所謂的「謂語」（Predicate）的定義即為「在句子內包含動詞且用來描述主語的部分」。所以一般句子的基本構成為「主語＋謂語＋賓語」，若主語、謂語、賓語的部分皆以一個單字為代表，就會變成一般我們耳熟能詳的「主詞＋動詞＋受詞」（即 SVO: subject + Verb + Object）的說法。很多文法在講解時會儘量減少使用過多文法專有名詞，所以常會有直接以「動詞」來代替「謂語」的說法，例如 "Subject-Verb Agreement" 通常會講成「主詞動詞一致性」而非「主語謂語一致性」。

多益實戰考題　　　　多 益 會 出 這 樣 的 問 題

⊙ 填謂語

對於這裡主要出現的題目，可以首先排除答案中不能用做謂語的詞，再挑選有正確的單複數形式、時態、語態的詞做為答案。

1. A notice about the vacancy ------- on the company message board.

(A) were posted　　　(B) have posted
(C) to post　　　　　(D) will be posted

2. Mr. Franzen ------- Joyce Marcus head inspector of the company's several factories located in the southern region of the country.

(A) name　　　　　(B) named
(C) is naming　　　(D) namely

3. When CSI Peripherals ------- its sales division, one middle manager and three assistant administrators were dismissed.

(A) was restructuring (B) was restructured
(C) to restructure　　(D) restructures

正確答案　P11

❶ 祈使句沒有主詞，以動詞原形開始。

Place the report on my desk. 把那份報告放在我的桌子上。
Please complete this form and sign at the bottom. 請填寫這張表格並在最下面簽字。

注意！ 祈使句中省略了 you，為表示禮貌語氣，在動詞前經常加 please。

❷ When 子句 / If 子句＋祈使句：做⋯的時候 / 若做⋯、做⋯

When investigating an insurance claim, follow all company procedures.

在調查保險金索賠請求時，一切都需依照公司的程序進行。

If you would like to request a transfer, submit this form.

如果你想要請求調動，要提交這份申請表格。

→ 在多益考試中，與以簡單的祈使句開始的文章相比，更多文章中的祈使句含有 if 子句或 when 子句，並在其中考謂語用法。少數祈使句中也會出現 whatever 等子句。

❸ 不是原形的動詞、名詞等不能成為祈使句中的謂語。

Please ~~has~~ a seat. 請坐。
　　　　have
→ 除了動詞原形，第三人稱單數形式、過去式等動詞都不能成為祈使句的謂語。

Whatever your destination, ~~relying~~ on J Net for quality service.
　　　　　　　　　　　　rely

無論目的地是哪，若想得到高品質的服務請使用 J Net。
→「動詞原形＋ing」（動名詞、分詞）不能成為祈使句的謂語。

When negotiating a partnership, ~~trial~~ to be open-minded. 當洽談合作時，盡量試著敞開心防。
　　　　　　　　　　　　　　try
→ 名詞和形容詞不能成為祈使句的謂語。

多益實戰考題　　　　　　　多 益 會 出 這 樣 的 問 題

⊙ 填祈使句中的謂語

1. When making a presentation, ------- discussing matters already known to the audience.

(A) to avoid　　　　(B) avoids
(C) avoiding　　　　(D) avoid

2. Whatever your investment needs, ------- on Farallon Services to provide the information and advice you need to make a wise investment.

(A) counts　　　　(B) count
(C) counted　　　　(D) counting

3. If the strategy fails to meet the team's objectives, ------- the plan in order to determine where its weaknesses are.

(A) evaluating　　　　(B) to evaluate
(C) evaluate　　　　(D) evaluation

正確答案 P11

HACKERS PRACTICE ● ● ● ● ● ● ● ● ● ● ● ● ● ● ● ●

Practice 1 在兩個選項中選擇一個正確答案。

01 The technician (working / worked) night and day to get the security system running.

02 The (complete / completion) of the new office will enhance our operations in Europe.

03 The freshness of the vegetables at the market (vary / varies) depending on the time of year.

04 (Reduce / Reducing) the amount of paper wasted in the office is one of the manager's priorities.

05 Investment activities for the agreement (comprise / comprisal) cash payments as well as stock transfer.

06 (It / That) was important to finish discussing the recent deal before moving on to other business.

07 All assignments should (send / be sent) to the director's mailbox by the Saturday deadline.

Practice 2 改正錯誤。

08 Efficient is the most important consideration in the company's decision about whether to relocate.

09 When Joseph completes the audit, he concluded that it needed to be revised.

10 When uncertain about what to do in a work-related situation, asks your supervisor.

11 The information Robert provided is several months out of date.

12 There is known that high salaries contribute to staff retention and loyalty.

13 The engineer estimation that the building will need three thousand tons of concrete.

14 Its downtown locate means that the office is in a prestigious business district.

Part V

01 Management ------- on resource allocation for the coming quarter will have to be set aside until the director arrives from his business trip.

(A) decides   (B) decide
(C) decisions   (D) decisive

02 The price of a sketch or an oil painting ------- the frame and the cost of delivering the artwork to the buyer's address.

(A) include   (B) including
(C) includes   (D) inclusion

03 Commuters arriving at the Logan Square station had no choice but to use the stairway because the ------- was being repaired.

(A) escalate   (B) escalator
(C) escalation   (D) escalating

04 The lipstick samples ------- back to the manufacturer when it was discovered that a number of the lipstick cases were defective.

(A) were sent   (B) were sending
(C) sent   (D) being sent

05 Director Patterson's ------- was that the institute should move its headquarters to Austin, Texas.

(A) conclusion   (B) conclusive
(C) conclude   (D) conclusively

06 Sales revenue ------- significantly since the launch of the company's new ad campaign.

(A) increase   (B) will increase
(C) has increased   (D) increasing

07 If you plan on renovating your apartment, be sure that the changes you make ------- with the stipulations in your rental contract.

(A) compliant   (B) complying
(C) compliance   (D) comply

08 The training department requires even seasoned employees to attend safety courses because ------- of accidents is paramount in the workplace.

(A) prevent   (B) prevention
(C) to prevent   (D) preventable

09 Katherine Bryant ------- Purcell Firm forty years ago, making her one of our longest-serving employees since the firm was first established.

(A) joining   (B) join
(C) joined   (D) joins

10 The Japanese ------- backed out of the World Peace Conference when more than half its members came down with the flu the day before their flight.

(A) delegate   (B) delegated
(C) delegation   (D) delegating

11 The chef ------- a cooking clinic for housewives to teach them how to make consommé and other French soups.

(A) to organize   (B) organized
(C) organization   (D) organizing

12 The sudden ------- of Harvey Wyman as executive director has left the corporation in a state of uncertainty.

(A) resign   (B) resignation
(C) resignedly   (D) resigned

13 Approximately half of the employees at Sabian & Randolf, Ltd. ------- to work by subway.

(A) commute   (B) commutes
(C) is commuting   (D) has commuted

14 By the end of the first quarter, the company ------- estimated profit by over ten percent.

(A) exceeding   (B) had exceeded
(C) was exceeded   (D) to exceed

15 The ------- of the agreement forced the lessee to comply with the legal requirements necessary to obtain a new contract.

(A) cancel   (B) cancellation
(C) canceling   (D) cancelled

16 The project development director ------- evaluations for all projects administered in the last quarter to be on her desk by tomorrow morning.

(A) have expected   (B) expects
(C) to expect   (D) expecting

17 The Board overwhelmingly ------- the proposal made by the marketing division, considering it too complex at the present stage of expansion.

(A) rejected   (B) rejecting
(C) reject   (D) was rejected

18 ------- has been so little information on some health concerns that it is difficult for the individual to decide whether or not he should see a doctor.

(A) He   (B) It
(C) That   (D) There

19 The new main office was housed in a bright and modern building, but its ------- was inconvenient for employees who didn't have a car.

(A) locate   (B) to locate
(C) located   (D) location

20 When having an important document delivered, ------- the receiver that the package is on its way.

(A) notification   (B) notify
(C) notifies   (D) notifying

Part VI

An Impeccable Approach to Textiles

In the world of textile manufacturing, with types of companies as endlessly varied as the fabrics that they produce, one company ------- like a crimson dress in a sea of black. Thread

21 (A) stand   (B) stands
(C) standing   (D) to stand

Manufacturing is a small family enterprise that has secured a dedicated list of clientele from young hobby seamstresses to big name designers like Claude La Tour. Their dedication to pushing the limits of textile capabilities gains ------- with every new product released, and

22 (A) tension   (B) momentum
(C) progress   (D) probability

shows no sign of abating. Furthermore, no other ------- has yet been able to create a product

23 (A) compete   (B) competing
(C) competitor   (D) competitive

superior to theirs. Thread states that the reason for this lies in their ability to produce silk that is known worldwide as being softer than a spider's web, yet more durable than steel. Thread plans to broaden their range of fabrics by commencing the production of ultra-fine cotton. The company ------- great demand when the first rolls of cloth come off the

24 (A) hopes   (B) anticipates
(C) believes   (D) deems

assembly line next summer.

正確答案 P12

Chapter 2

受詞、補語

啊哈!! 愉快地打基礎

1

受詞是動詞的陳述對象，是及物動詞後面必須要附加的句子成分。

I like pizza. 我喜歡比薩。

這裡動詞 like 作用的對象 pizza 就是受詞。若沒有受詞 pizza，則會因「不知道喜歡什麼」而使句子意思不完整，成為一個錯誤的句子。

I like.（✗）我喜歡。

2

有些動詞需要兩個受詞。

My girlfriend gave <u>me</u> <u>chocolate</u>. 我的女朋友送我巧克力。
　　　　　　　　受詞1　　受詞2

這裡動詞 give 有兩個受詞，因而句子變成了四部分。（主語＋動詞＋受詞1＋受詞2）此時，受詞1為表示「對…」的間接受詞，受詞2為表示「具體事物」的直接受詞。用於這種形式的動詞有：grant, teach, instruct, send, buy, bring, tell, offer 等。

3

補語補充主詞或受詞。有些句子中，動詞後面必須要有補語才能使句子完整。

He is a magician. 他是魔術師。
I find magic exciting. 我認為魔術很有趣。

這裡的 a magician 是補充主詞（He）的一個主詞補語，exciting 是受詞（magic）的補語。若沒有補語，則會不知 He 是誰，也不知 magic 如何，因而導致語意不完整，成為錯誤的句子。

He is.（✗）他是…。
I find magic.（✗）我認為魔術…。

01 可在受詞位置的詞：有名詞性質的詞

❶ 能成為受詞的詞是有名詞性質的詞。

名詞片語　Jake has enough business <u>sense</u> to run his own company. Jake 有足夠商場上的判斷力來經營自己的公司。

代名詞　I can't find <u>them</u> anywhere in the office. 我找遍了辦公室都找不到它們。

動名詞片語　Fred hates <u>working</u> overtime. Fred 討厭加班。

動詞不定詞　Helen wants <u>to get</u> a new job. Helen 想找新的工作。

名詞子句　I agree <u>that</u> we need new filing cabinets. 我同意我們需要一個新的檔案櫃。

→ 畫線部分的受詞是核心部分，多益考試常在這部分出題。

❷ 動詞、形容詞等不能當受詞。

The company guarantees ~~deliver~~ in five to seven days.
　　　　　　　　　　delivery

公司保證在 5～7 日內送貨。
→ 受詞應是名詞（delivery）而不是動詞（deliver）。

Planners designed the ~~productive~~ with the teenage consumer in mind.
　　　　　　　　　　　product

設計者針對年輕消費者的心理設計了產品。
→ 受詞應為名詞（product）而不是形容詞（productive）

多益實戰考題　　　　多　益　會　出　這　樣　的　問　題

⊙填受詞

2. Working in the field helped the trainees to formulate a better business ------- that would address the problems raised by Mr. White.

　(A) strategic　　　(B) strategical
　(C) strategy　　　(D) strategize

1. Reliance Property Developers takes great ------- in announcing that we have purchased eleven square kilometers of land in the Hartford area.

　(A) please　　　(B) pleasure
　(C) pleasant　　　(D) pleasurable

3. The manager posted a note stating that the staff should know the revised ------- for company tours.

　(A) proceed　　　(B) proceeds
　(C) procedural　　　(D) procedures

正確答案　P14

02 虛受詞 it 結構

❶ 在含有受詞補語的句子中，將動詞不定詞和that引導的子句放在後面，用it代替它們原先的位置。

I found ~~to use the software easy~~. 我發現這個軟體很容易使用。
　　　　it easy to use the software
→ 將句子中的實際受詞為動詞不定詞片語（to use the software），在它的位置放上虛受詞it並把整個實際受詞放在後面。

The entire staff thought ~~that the CEO didn't attend the seminar peculiar~~.
　　　　　　　　　　　　it peculiar that the CEO didn't attend the seminar

全體職員都對CEO沒有出席研討會感到奇怪。
→ 實際受詞為that引導的子句（that the CEO didn't attend the seminar），它被放在句子後面，原本的位置則由虛受詞it代替。

> **注意！** 當受詞不是動詞不定詞片語或that引導的名詞子句，而是名詞或者名詞片語時，不用虛受詞it。
> Mrs. Tyne's leadership made ~~it~~ possible the expansion of the company.

❷ 用虛受詞it的例句 "make it possible"

The machinery will make it possible to increase productivity. 這個機器將使生產力提高變為可能。
→ 在make it possibale句型中，實際受詞的動詞不定詞片語（to increase productivity）和虛受詞it必須一起出現。

Revisions to the contract will make it possible ~~negotiate~~ interest rates. 合約的修改將使利率的協商變為可能。
　　　　　　　　　　　　　　　　　　　　to negotiate
→ make it possible句型中，實際受詞不能為動詞（negotiate），而應該是動詞不定詞片語（to negotiate）。

> **注意！** make it possible句型中，也可用easy、difficult、necessary這樣的形容詞代替possible的位置，它們的句意分別為「使主語成為…變得簡單 / 困難 / 必要」。
> The teacher made it easy to skip class. 那位老師使蹺課變得容易。
> He made it difficult to talk by constantly interrupting. 他使講話被經常打斷變得困難。

多益實戰考題　　　　　　　　多 益 會 出 這 樣 的 問 題

⊙填實際受詞

2. The whole community found it unreasonable ------- the city proposed building a landfill site within a 20 mile radius of the city limits.

(A) which 　　　　(B) about
(C) that 　　　　(D) when

1. The proposed budget increases would make it possible ------- added support to each sector of the firm.

(A) give 　　　　(B) gave
(C) to give 　　　(D) in giving

3. To develop a spirit of creativity in the office, supervisors should make it a point ------- the initiative of each employee.

(A) recognize 　　　(B) to recognize
(C) of recognizing 　(D) recognized

03 可以當補語的成分：名詞或形容詞

❶ 可以成為補語的成分是有名詞或形容詞性質的詞。

- 有名詞性質的詞

  名詞片語 Previous work experience will be an <u>advantage</u> for applicants. 有工作經歷的申請者將具有優勢。

  動名詞 His specialty is <u>designing</u> databases. 他的專長是設計資料庫。

  動詞不定詞 The important thing is <u>to include</u> your phone number. 重要的是要包括您的電話號碼。

  名詞子句 The problem is <u>that</u> we do not have sufficient capital. 問題是我們沒有充分的資本。

- 有形容詞性質的詞

  形容詞 The new investments are <u>profitable</u>. 新的投資有利可圖。

  分詞 We found the art exhibit <u>fascinating</u>. 我們發現這次藝術展非常有趣。

  →畫線部分是補語的核心部分，多益考試常在這部分出題。

❷ 補語不能為動詞、副詞。

All employees are ~~cooperate~~ with the new policy. 所有職員都要配合新的政策。
　　　　　　　　　cooperative

　→補語應為形容詞（cooperative）而不是動詞（cooperate）

Excellent acting made the performance ~~excitingly~~. 出色的演出使表演非常精彩。
　　　　　　　　　　　　　　　　　　exciting

　→補語應為有形容詞作用的分詞（exciting）而不是副詞（excitingly）。

❸ 可以接主詞補語的動詞、可以接受詞補語的動詞

可以接主詞補語的動詞	be 是…	become 成為…	get 成為…	seem 像是…	remain 仍然是…
（連接動詞）	turn 成為…	taste 有…味道	feel 感覺…	look 看起來是…	sound 聽起來像…
可以接受詞補語的動詞	make 把…做成	keep 保持…	find 發現…	consider 認為…	call 叫成…

She <u>became</u> a professional musician. 她成了一位專業音樂家。
Mr. Shaw had always <u>considered</u> himself a self-motivated individual. Shaw 先生一直自認是個主動的人。

注意！　1.一般動詞不定詞做 remain 的補語。形容詞 / 分詞做 keep 和 find 的補語。

　　　　The reports remain <u>to be filed</u>. 報告還沒有整理好。
　　　　The heater will keep the room <u>warm</u>. 暖氣會使房間保持溫暖。
　　　　2.make sure 是習慣用法，注意不要把 sure 寫成 surely。
　　　　Make ~~surely~~ that you lock the supply closet. 確認你有把物品保管室鎖上。
　　　　　　　sure

多益實戰考題　　　　　　　多 益 會 出 這 樣 的 問 題

⊙填補語

　解題時首先排除動詞和副詞。其次，名詞和形容詞做
　補語的情況最多。

1. The salesmen have been very ------- in their attempts to get us to purchase a beachfront property.

(A) persuade　　　　(B) persuasive
(C) persuading　　　(D) persuaded

2. It was a great ------- that Brian Mann did not receive the Employee of the Year award because he had worked so hard.

(A) disappoints　　　(B) disappointed
(C) disappointing　　(D) disappointment

3. Although I'm ------- about your situation, I have to consider the best interests of this company.

(A) empathetic　　　(B) empathize
(C) empathizing　　　(D) empathically

正確答案　P15

04 名詞補語 VS. 形容詞補語

❶ 如果補語與主詞或受詞是對等關係，則補語是名詞。

Alice is a ballet dancer. Alice是芭蕾舞者。（即「Alice = 芭蕾舞者」的意思）
After two months, Jack became a general manager. 兩個月後，Jack成了總經理。（即「Jack = 總經理」的意思）
→ 主詞（Alice / Jack）與主詞補語（a ballet dancer / a general manager）是對等關係，所以補語為名詞。

People called him a liar. 人們稱他為騙子。（即「他 = 騙子」的意思）
We all considered his speech a masterpiece. 大家都認為他的演講是傑作。（即「他的演講 = 傑作」的意思）
→ 受詞（him / his speech）與受詞補語（a liar / a masterpiece）是對等關係，所以補語為名詞。

❷ 如果是說明主詞或受詞的補語，則補語是形容詞。

The paintings are impressive. 那些畫讓人印象深刻。
She seemed bothered at work today. 今天工作時她看起來有些憂慮。
→ 主詞補語（impressive / bothered）是在說明主詞（the painting / she），所以補語為形容詞。

The manager made the workers nervous. 那位經理使工人們緊張了起來。
The bank keeps its depositors satisfied with insurance guarantees. 銀行使存戶在保險的保障上感到滿意。
→ 受詞補語（nervous / satisfied）在說明受詞（the workers / its depositors），所以補語為形容詞。

注意！ 虛主詞（it）—主詞（動詞不定詞或that引導的子句）做補語的情況
It is my recommendation for you to move into a higher level class. 我給你的建議是轉到更高級的課。
It is recommendable for you to move into a higher level class. 讓你去更高級的課的建議是可行的。
⇨ 這種情況無論補語是名詞（recommendation）還是形容詞（recommendable）都正確。但必需注意的是，這種情況下如果名詞（recommendation）沒用所有格形式（my）而單獨出現則是錯誤的。

It is a pity that you can't continue working with us. 你不能繼續和我們一起工作真是一件讓人遺憾的事情。
It is pitiful that you can't continue working with us. 你不能繼續和我們一起繼續工作，真是太遺憾了。
⇨ 補語無論是名詞（pity）還是形容詞（pitiful）都正確。但這種情況如果名詞（pity）沒有冠詞（a）而單獨出現則是錯誤的。

多益實戰考題　　　　　　　　　　　　　多 益 會 出 這 樣 的 問 題

⊙填補語
經常會出現要求在補語位置填形容詞的題目。

1. Mrs. Heinz is ------- that the company will be more successful next year.

(A) optimistic　　　(B) optimism
(C) optimist　　　　(D) optimistically

2. Because prices at department store sales were quite -------, shoppers did not think it necessary to compare prices.

(A) competition　　(B) competitive
(C) competitor　　　(D) compete

3. It is ------- for investors to check a company's performance before purchasing any shares.

(A) advice　　　　(B) advisable
(C) advise　　　　(D) advisor

正確答案 P15

Hackers Skill　　若補語是用來說明主詞或受詞時，一定要為形容詞。

The bank keeps its depositors satisfaction(→ satisfied) with insurance guarantees.
銀行使存戶在保險的保障上感到滿意。

HACKERS PRACTICE ● ● ● ● ● ● ● ● ● ● ● ● ● ● ● ●

Practice 1 在兩個選項之間選擇一個正確答案。

01 Your reservation for the workshop will not be (complete / completion) until we receive full payment.

02 Sandra lacked the (mature / maturity) needed for someone in a position of such responsibility.

03 The company made the associate (proud / proudly) by electing him as vice president.

04 Investors in the company expressed (amazing / amazement) at the rate of return they received.

05 James asked his broker to keep him (inform / informed) about developments in the market.

06 Unless you send us a written (confirmation / confirmed), we are not able to ship the order.

07 The new database becomes (operational / operationally) as soon as Mr. Mills gives authorization.

Practice 2 改正錯誤。

08 When applying for a business loan, you need provide your bank account information.

09 Many people consider credit cards convenience and safe to carry.

10 Sudden budget cuts made it necessary lay off two hundred employees.

11 I found professional workshops incredibly help and productive.

12 Mrs. Fields prefers sharing office tasks to working alone.

13 It is always wisdom to review a contract before signing an agreement to all of its terms.

14 The insurance company offers its customers numerous coverage options.

正確答案　P15

Part V

01 Speedy Carrier cannot guarantee ------- of packages in cases where natural and unavoidable calamities occur.

(A) deliver   (B) delivery
(C) delivered   (D) deliverable

02 An outstanding tenor and a captivating plot made last night's opera at the Carnegie Hall very -------.

(A) exciting   (B) excitable
(C) excitedly   (D) excitement

03 Starting up the consulting firm is a ------- that Mr. Richards is eager to take up.

(A) venture   (B) venturesome
(C) ventured   (D) venturing

04 New factory workers must have their superintendent's ------- for requisition of any supplies needed for the assembly line.

(A) approve   (B) approval
(C) approves   (D) approvingly

05 Customer complaints have become much more ------- since we installed the automatic messaging system that filters calls.

(A) managing   (B) manage
(C) manageable   (D) management

06 The ------- of the company's financial officer has left a vacancy that the CEO is trying to quickly fill.

(A) resigned   (B) resignedly
(C) resignation   (D) resign

07 Accounting graduates are required to obtain ------- to establish their credentials as licensed public accountants.

(A) certify   (B) certified
(C) certifiable   (D) certification

08 Points earned on the purchase of any of the products are not ------- to other customers.

(A) transfers   (B) transfer
(C) transferable   (D) transference

09 The company normally requires each applicant to be interviewed, but they made an ------- for Mr. Payne because of his outstanding résumé.

(A) exceptional   (B) exception
(C) except   (D) excepting

10 The health club management keeps customers ------- by providing quality service and discounted memberships on a monthly basis.

(A) satisfaction   (B) satisfy
(C) satisfyingly   (D) satisfied

11 I don't consider it helpful ------- the manager for advice, as he seems to know less than anyone else.

(A) ask   (B) to ask
(C) by asking   (D) asked

12 Meat packing plants must be given a week's ------- before an inspector from the Department of Agriculture visits the plant.

(A) notice   (B) notices
(C) noticed   (D) noticeable

13 Please be ------- and refrain from speaking loudly or causing a disruption during the speaker's presentation.

(A) considered   (B) consider
(C) consideration   (D) considerate

14 Each year, the reclusive writer ------- 25 percent of his yearly earnings to an orphanage located just outside of the city.

(A) donates   (B) donating
(C) are donated   (D) to donate

15 Computer game manufacturers are often ------- even in times of economic slowdown because the games they produce are usually addictive.

(A) profitable   (B) profitably
(C) profit   (D) profiteers

16 Jeff Myers prefers a job that offers the ------- he enjoyed while completing his internship at Rytech International.

(A) flexible   (B) flexed
(C) flex   (D) flexibility

17 It is ------- that with the glut of digital products coming into the market the electronics industry is entering a challenging phase.

(A) cleared   (B) clearly
(C) clearest   (D) clear

18 The firm was granted an ------- to file its corporate tax with no penalty as long as it makes the necessary tax prepayments.

(A) extend   (B) to extend
(C) extension   (D) extensive

19 The artist, whose paintings are currently on exhibit at the Parkinson Art Center, gets his ------- from the works of Monet and Degas.

(A) inspire   (B) inspiring
(C) inspired   (D) inspiration

20 Most recruiters admit that it is an ------- for candidates to have a strong background in at least one foreign language.

(A) advantage   (B) advantaged
(C) advantageous   (D) advantageously

Part VI

P.O. Box Information

For those with frequent changes of address, or who wish to maintain privacy in terms of their mail, acquiring a post office box guarantees ------- and convenience. Once you have selected the size

     21 (A) secure   (B) secured
             (C) security   (D) securely

deemed the most suitable for your requirements, you will be asked to submit a completed registration form. Due to high -------, applicants should be advised that a wait of up to 3 months

     22 (A) demand   (B) technology
             (C) elevation   (D) election

may be requisite. After approval for ownership of a box is granted, further complications in receiving your mail remain ------- as the P.O. box section of the post office is open from 7:00

     23 (A) minimal   (B) minimize
             (C) minimizing   (D) minimally

a.m. to 10:00 p.m. daily, including weekends and holidays.

Note: Our ------- states that we are not responsible for theft due to lost or stolen keys. Should

     24 (A) customs   (B) symbol
             (C) preparation   (D) policy

such incidents occur, please notify the staff immediately.

正確答案 P15

Chapter 3

修飾語

啊哈!! 愉快地打基礎

1 修飾語增加句子中的必需成分（主詞、動詞、受詞、補語）的作用。

<u>She is lying</u> under the tree. 她躺在樹下。
　必需成分　　　 修飾語

主詞 She 和動詞 is lying 是文章不可少缺的成分。在必需成分（她躺著）之後增加了「場所」under the tree（在樹下）這個資訊。

2 修飾語是可有可無的附加成分。

He is running with his dog. 他和他的狗一起跑步。
He is running. 他在跑。

即使沒有修飾語 "with his dog"，句子也成立，因此稱為「受詞補語」。

3 一個句子中可以存在多個修飾語。

Of all the people I know, <u>Jackie was the best saleswoman</u> that I had ever worked with.
在我認識的所有人當中，Jackie 是我所共事過最好的銷售員。

句子中必需成分（Jackie ~ saleswoman）雖然只有一個，但修飾語可以有多個（Of all the people，I know，that I had ever worked with）。

01 修飾語的成分

❶ 可以成為修飾語成分的詞

介系詞片語　<u>In</u> the park, I saw Janice. 我在公園看到 Janice。

to不定詞片語　I came here <u>to see</u> you. 我來到這裡是為了看你。

分詞（片語）　The people <u>invited</u> to the party were my friends. 受邀參加聚會的人都是我的朋友。

關係子句　I respect my colleague <u>who</u> works extremely hard. 我敬佩非常認真工作的同事。

副詞子句　<u>When</u> we arrived, we sat down for a cup of tea. 我們到達後，坐下來喝了茶。

→ 畫底線的部分是修飾成分的核心，多益中常在這些部分出題。

❷ 修飾語的位置

● + 主詞 + 動詞

[<u>Despite</u> an extensive audit], <u>the error</u> <u>was not discovered</u>.
　　　　　修飾語（介系詞片語）　　　　　　主詞　　　　　動詞

儘管是大規模的審核，但是沒有發現錯誤。

主詞 + ● + 動詞

<u>These desks</u> [<u>remaining</u> in the hall] <u>must be removed</u> soon.
　主詞　　　　　修飾語（分詞）　　　　　　動詞

這些留在大廳的桌子要儘快的移走。

+ 動詞 + ●

<u>Darren</u> <u>decided</u> <u>to take the new job</u> [<u>although</u> it would be challenging.]
　主詞　　動詞　　　　受詞　　　　　　　　修飾語（副詞子句）

雖然新的業務很有挑戰性，但 Darren 還是決定接受。

❸ 尋找修飾語的步驟

● 尋找句子的動詞 → 尋找句子的主詞 → 用〔 〕標記修飾成分。

<u>Candidates</u> [applying for the job] <u>must pass</u> a background check. 求職應徵者需要通過背景審查。
　 2）主詞　　　　 3）修飾成分　　　　　 1）動詞

→ 先找到句子的動詞（must pass）之後再找主詞（candidates），最後找出修飾語的部分。

多益實戰考題　　　　　　　多 益 會 出 這 樣 的 問 題

⊙ 填修飾語。

會出現去掉不能成為修飾成分的名詞、動詞後，填入修飾語的問題。

1. ------- the new supervisor is mild-mannered and soft-spoken, she is very firm about getting work done on time.

(A) Even　　　　　(B) Then

(C) If　　　　　　(D) While

2. The membership packages ------- are offered by the book club are based on the reading needs and tastes of the members.

(A) they　　　　　(B) that

(C) those　　　　(D) these

3. The newspaper publisher submitted to an investigation, ------- that charges of plagiarism against his star reporter would be dealt with quickly.

(A) ensuring　　　(B) be ensured

(C) ensure　　　　(D) ensures

正確答案　P18

02 以「片語」引導修飾的部分和以「子句」引導修飾的部分

❶ 以片語引導修飾的部分是沒有主詞、動詞的「片語」形態，屬於介系詞片語、to 不定片語、分詞（片語）。

介系詞片語 <u>Because of</u> a decrease in orders, the company ordered fewer supplies.
因為訂單減少，所以公司訂購了更少的物品。

to不定詞片語 The consultant suggested several strategies <u>to reduce</u> overhead costs.
顧問提出了幾個可以減少總經費的方法。

分詞（片語） Employees <u>going</u> on the trip will be issued plane tickets tomorrow.
出差的職員明天會拿到飛機票。
→ 畫線部分的介系詞（because of），to 不定詞（to reduce），分詞（going）以片語引導修飾的部分，這是多益常考的。

❷ 以子句引導修飾的部分是有主詞、動詞的「子句」形態，屬於關係子句、副詞子句。

關係子句 The arena is a place <u>which</u> hosts sporting and musical events.
圓形舞臺是舉行運動比賽和音樂活動的場所。

副詞子句 The request cannot be approved <u>until</u> Mrs. Charles signs this form.
那個要求直到 Charles 夫人簽名才能被批准。
→ 畫線部分是關係詞（which），副詞子句連接詞（until）引導修飾成分子句，多益常考這些部分。

❸ 區分引導出片語修飾語或子句修飾語的詞

• 修飾語中沒有動詞時 ⇨ 引導修飾語的是介系詞、to 不定詞、分詞。

• 修飾語中有動詞時 ⇨ 引導修飾語的是關係詞、副詞子句連接詞。

She left <u>without</u> a word to anyone. 她沒有對任何人留下隻字片語就離開了。

→ 修飾語（without a word to anyone）中沒有動詞，所以是以介系詞（without）來引導。

<u>Unless</u> conditions improve, I'm going to have to change companies soon.

假如情況沒有好轉，我會立即換公司。

→ 修飾語（Unless conditions improve）中有動詞（improve），所以是以副詞子句連接詞（Unless）來引導。

多益實戰考題　　　　　多 益 會 出 這 樣 的 問 題

⊙ 填引導修飾語的詞。

2. The breakdown of a major piece of machinery ------- production forced the owner to announce a temporary plant shutdown.

(A) since　　　　　(B) during
(C) while　　　　　(D) except

1. ------- this is only Ms. Planter's third week, she has quickly become a standout in company presentations.

(A) Although　　　　(B) In spite of
(C) Nevertheless　　(D) However

3. ------- the problems Team B is experiencing, the manager decided that it would be best to give the team a little more time to write its project assessment report.

(A) Even if　　　　　(B) Since
(C) Nevertheless　　(D) Because of

正確答案 **P18**

HACKERS PRACTICE ● ● ● ● ● ● ● ● ● ● ● ● ● ● ● ●

Practice 1 找出修飾語後用（ ）標記。

01 In spite of a scheduling conflict, Jacob attended the annual meeting.

02 Shoppers purchasing less than ten items can use the express checkout lane.

03 The man read an article whose topic dealt with working relationships.

04 A valuable employee is one who is diligent, trustworthy, and self-motivated.

05 Industrial automation has laid off numerous trade union members from the assembly line.

06 Rob was disciplined for using funds without proper permission.

07 While Dan waited in the office lobby, he read a magazine article.

Practice 2 在兩個選項中選擇正確的答案。

08 Craig's version (unless / of) the events contradicted statements made by other witnesses.

09 A meeting was called (to resolve / resolve) the conflict between the coworkers.

10 Mrs. Bishop worked (even though / despite) she was suffering from the flu.

11 Miners (working / work) in the coal industry face significant health risks.

12 (Because of / Because) Andy delivered excellent results, his boss granted him a raise.

13 A market analyst is a position (and / which) is highly valued on Wall Street.

14 Our division will work on the sales project (during / while) the next month.

Part V

01 The meeting was still a success ------- the guidance of the vice president and others in senior management.

(A) though   (B) without
(C) unless   (D) even

02 All products in the catalog are available in our online store, ------- customers to shop from the convenience of their homes.

(A) allows   (B) allow
(C) will allow   (D) allowing

03 ------- Mr. Zimmerman prefers sitting at a desk and facing a computer, Mr. McNally would rather meet people and talk to them.

(A) Regarding   (B) While
(C) However   (D) As soon as

04 ------- the wide range of services offered by the agency, it is surprising they have a fairly narrow clientele base.

(A) Meanwhile   (B) Then
(C) Considering   (D) Again

05 Please give us your mobile phone number ------- Mr. Saunders has other questions to ask you.

(A) in case   (B) even if
(C) despite   (D) therefore

06 The women ------- our organization are either full-time housewives or college students who want to make a difference in our community.

(A) join   (B) joining
(C) will join   (D) will be joining

07 ------- the number of people using public transportation has increased, traffic along the main thoroughfares is still heavy.

(A) For   (B) In spite of
(C) Also   (D) Although

08 A reminder was sent to the staff that wise ------- of company supplies would decrease monthly expenditures.

(A) utilization   (B) utility
(C) utilize   (D) utilizer

09 In the business world today, there is a growing optimism ------- the rising value of the dollar.

(A) view   (B) with respect
(C) over   (D) refer to

10 The Miracle Skin Company has received hundreds of inquiries ------- it ran its first advertisement in all the major dailies.

(A) before   (B) by
(C) since   (D) past

11 The company's standing in the telecommunications industry was forged ------- years of putting the customer's needs first.

(A) regarding   (B) but
(C) when   (D) through

12 Visitors ------- in the library after nine p.m. are asked to use the exit doors in the east wing when leaving.

(A) have remained   (B) will remain
(C) remaining   (D) remain

13 ------- any changes, the proposal will be presented at a special meeting of sustainable development organizations next week.

(A) Except   (B) Barring
(C) Unless   (D) Because

14 Delegates from the ITO have gathered ------- the practicality of current import/export laws.

(A) to analyze   (B) analyze
(C) analyst   (D) analysis

15 ------- worries that the government will be unable to control the budget deficit, it is expected that national spending will reach an all time high.

(A) Nevertheless   (B) Despite
(C) After   (D) However

16 ------- new competitors have flooded the market, management does not view them as a serious threat to business.

(A) In spite   (B) For
(C) Regardless of   (D) Even though

17 On behalf of the entire staff, I ------- to announce the opening of our new head office in Cedar Rapids.

(A) with pride   (B) am proud
(C) proudly   (D) have pride

18 The studio is expected to release five more films before the end of the year ------- their summer movie makes a good showing at the box office.

(A) there   (B) so
(C) if   (D) then

19 The company is strict about having progress reports submitted ------- the end of each week.

(A) early   (B) when
(C) by   (D) promptly

20 Companies are decreasing the amount of fuel they use ------- higher prices for energy sources have begun to cut into their profits.

(A) except   (B) as
(C) until   (D) at

21 The company will redesign a vacuum cleaner it put out in the market two months ago ------- the many complaints it has received.

(A) given   (B) were given
(C) have given   (D) gave

22 The investigation team questioned all of the associates ------- in the alleged plot to embezzle company funds.

(A) involves   (B) involve
(C) involved   (D) involvement

23 The best sales companies teach their sales representatives how to sell a product ------- seeming too aggressive.

(A) except   (B) otherwise
(C) without   (D) whereas

24 The work took much less time to accomplish ------- the manager organized the staff into task groups.

(A) following   (B) after
(C) soon   (D) by

25 Consumer confidence in the company ------- over the months, due in part to a strategic merchandising campaign.

(A) increase   (B) increasing
(C) to increase   (D) has increased

26 All members ------- the project team should report to the conference room at 2 P.M. for a special meeting on project proposal writing.

(A) once   (B) unless
(C) of   (D) when

27 An effective manager should not only be able to delegate responsibilities but also give ------- to the staff.

(A) encouragement   (B) encourage
(C) encouraging   (D) encouraged

28 ------- the overwhelming response to the musical, the performance will be extended for another two weeks.

(A) Although   (B) Because of
(C) Despite   (D) Since

Section 2 動詞

Chapter 4

動詞的形態與種類

啊哈!! 愉快地打基礎。

1

動詞有五種形態

① 原形（動詞原形）
I work for an advertising company. 我在廣告公司上班。

② 第二人稱單數現在式（動詞原形 + s）
She likes to go camping. 她喜歡露營。

③ 過去式（動詞原形 + ed / 不規則變化）
I visited my parents last week. 我上週探望了我的父母。
Brian told me a funny story. Brian 告訴我一個很有趣的故事。

④ 現在分詞（動詞原形 + ing）
I am playing a trumpet. 我在吹小號。

⑤ 過去分詞（動詞原形 + ed / 不規則變化）
The cat was saved by a stranger. 那隻小貓被一個陌生人救了。
I had brought some cookies to school. 我帶了一些餅乾到學校。
⇨ 過去分詞 (past participle) 用縮寫 p.p.來表示。

2

動詞分為不需要接受詞的不及物動詞和需要接受詞的及物動詞。
不及物動詞如 1、2 形式裡的動詞，及物動詞如 3、4、5 形式裡的動詞。

① 形式（主詞 + 不及物動詞）
She smiled. 她笑了。

② 形式（主詞 + 不及物動詞 + 補語）
Mark is smart. Mark 是聰明的。

③ 形式（主詞 + 及物動詞 + 受詞）
Dogs like swimming. 狗喜歡游泳。

④ 形式（主詞 + 及物動詞 + 間接受詞 + 直接受詞）
She sent me a flower. 她送了一朵花給我。

⑤ 形式（主詞 + 及物動詞 + 受詞 + 受詞補語）
I found Mark wise. 我發現 Mark 很有智慧。

01 助動詞 + 動詞原形

❶ 助動詞 (will / would, may / might, can / could, must, should) 後面必須接動詞原形。

I will ~~to call~~ you. 我會打電話給你。
      call
→ 助動詞（will）後面不能接 to 不定詞片語（to call），只能接動詞原形（call）。

We could ~~going~~ to the park today if you would like to. 如果你願意，我們今天可以去公園。
        go
→ 助動詞（could）後面不能接動詞的 Ving 形式（going），只能接動詞原形（go）。

All campers should ~~remembrance~~ to bring the following items. 所有的露營者都要記得帶以下所列的物品。
             remember
→ 助動詞（should）後面不能接名詞（remembrance），只能接動詞原形（remember）。

She will ~~forgives~~ you. 她會原諒你的。
       forgive
→ 助動詞（will）後面不能接第三人稱動詞單數（forgives），只能接動詞原形（forgive）。

注意！ 1. 助動詞和動詞原形之間可以有 not 或副詞，所以注意不要混淆。
      Employers should <u>not automatically</u> dismiss complaints by employees.
      雇主不能不自覺地無視職員們的不滿。

      2. 以下的助動詞後面也接動詞原形。

| ought to 應該… | had better 最好… | would like to 喜歡… | used to 曾經… |
| have to 必需… | is able to 可以… | is going to 將會… | |

      Shelly used to <u>work</u> at Greenspan. Shelly 曾經在 Greenspan 工作過。
      He is able to <u>run</u> every morning before work. 他可以在每天上班之前去跑步。

❷ 否定句或倒裝句中的助動詞後面也要接動詞原形。

They did not ~~arrived~~ until 2 p.m. 他們直到下午 2 點才抵達。
          arrive
→ 否定句中的助動詞（did）後面不能接動詞過去式（arrived），只能接動詞原形（arrive）。

Never did I ~~thought~~ about switching careers. 我從沒想過要更換職業。
        think
→ 倒裝句中的助動詞後面不能接動詞過去式（thought），只能接動詞原形（think）。

多益實戰考題   多 益 會 出 這 樣 的 問 題

⊙ 填助動詞後的動詞原形。

2. To achieve success in today's competitive environment, companies must ------- a solid business plan.

(A) to establish   (B) establishing
(C) establish   (D) establishes

1. The corporation's plan to overhaul the employee benefits program will ------- because it has the full support of the staff.

(A) success   (B) succeed
(C) succeeds   (D) to succeed

3. The book was delivered by an international courier, but it did not ------- until three weeks after the expected delivery date.

(A) arrival   (B) arrive
(C) arriving   (D) arrived

正確答案 P22

進行式（be + Ving）／被動式（be + p.p.）／完成式（have + p.p.）

❶ be Ving 和 p.p.與 be 動詞、have 動詞結合並組成進行式（be + Ving），被動式（be + p.p.），完成式（have + p.p.）等。

進行式　　She is looking out the window. 她正望著窗外。

被動式　　Rental cars were brought back here. 租的車被送回這裡了。

完成式　　I have seen Lion King. 我觀賞過《獅子王》。

注意！助動詞（may, must, can...）後面的 be 動詞用原形 be ，而不是 am, is, are, was, were。

Susan may be finishing her project tonight. Susan 今晚可能會完成她的企畫。

Rental cars must be brought back here. 必須把租的車送回這裡。

❷ be 動詞和 have 動詞後面不能接動詞原形。

Edward is ~~watch~~ a film this evening. Edward 今晚會看電影。
　　　　 watching

→ be 動詞後面不能接動詞原形（watch），所以換成 V ing 形式（watching）的進行式。

The form must be ~~submit~~ by Tuesday. 那個表格必須在星期二之前提交。
　　　　　　 submitted

→ be 動詞後面不能接動詞原形（submit），所以換成 p.p. 形式（submitted）的被動式。

I have ~~see~~ the new advertisement. 我看過那個新廣告。
　　　 seen

→ 助動詞 have 後面不能接動詞原形（see），所以換成 p.p. 形式（seen）的完成式。

注意！當 have 表示「擁有，吃」的意義時是一般動詞，而不是助動詞。

The company has critical financial problems. 那個公司有重大的財務問題。

多益實戰考題　　　　　　　　　　多　益　會　出　這　樣　的　問　題

⊙ 填「be 動詞 +Ving / p.p.」或「have 動詞 + p.p.」

2. Environmental groups have severely ------- the auto industry's lackluster efforts to reduce harmful emissions.

(A) critical　　　　　　(B) criticized
(C) criticism　　　　　(D) criticize

1. The astute manager discerns unspoken employee gripes even before they are -------.

(A) express　　　　　　(B) expression
(C) expressive　　　　(D) expressed

3. Real estate values have been ------- from year to year in most parts of the United States.

(A) rise　　　　　　　(B) rose
(C) risen　　　　　　(D) rising

正確答案　P22

03 容易混淆的不及物動詞和及物動詞，形式 3 和形式 4 動詞

❶ 不及物動詞需要有介系詞才能與受詞搭配，及物動詞則是直接與受詞搭配。

意義	不及物動詞＋介系詞＋受詞	及物動詞＋受詞
說	speak to a group 對團體說 talk to your customer 跟你的顧客說 talk about the problem 談論問題 account for your absence 為你的缺席解釋	mention his absence 提到他的缺席 discuss the issue 討論提案 instruct me to hire programmers 吩咐我雇用程式設計師 explain the contract 說明合約
回答	reply to letters 回信 react to the updated version 對新版本做出回應 respond to a question 回答問題	answer the question 回答問題
同意／反對	agree with (to, on) their sales policy 同意銷售策略 object to the plan 反對那個計畫	approve the request 接受邀請 oppose the new system 反對新系統

The supervisors were asked to ~~explain~~ for the high absentee rate at work.
　　　　　　　　　　　　　　　account

負責人被要求解釋工作的缺席率過高的問題。

→ 受詞（the high absentee rate）前有介系詞（for），所以只能用不及物動詞（account），不能用直接可以跟受詞搭配的及物動詞（explain）。

❷ 要區分只有一個受詞（that 子句）的形式 3 動詞和有 2 個受詞的形式 4 動詞。

形式 3 動詞＋受詞（that 子句）	形式 4 動詞＋受詞 1（對象）＋受詞 2
say / mention / announce (to me) that 說 suggest / propose / recommend (to me) that 提議 explain / describe (to me) that 說明	tell / inform / notify me that 告訴 advise me that 建議 assure / convince me that 使確信

The supplier ~~said~~ the purchaser that they had new stock.
　　　　　　told

供應商告訴購買者他們有新的貨品。

→ 因為有兩個受詞（the purchaser 和 that they had new stock），所以要用形式 4 動詞（told），而不是形式 3 動詞（said）。

多益實戰考題　　　　多益會出這樣的問題

⊙ 用正確形式的動詞填空。

1. The Chief of Security ------ to us that we should take the highest precautions to ensure no information was leaked to the press.

(A) informed　　　(B) convinced
(C) notified　　　(D) mentioned

2. The council ------ the director that continued support of the Baker project might result in financial loss.

(A) advised　　　(B) explained
(C) recommended　　(D) announced

3. My stock broker ------- me about a safe investment plan that would secure my financial future.

(A) gave　　　(B) told
(C) suggested　　(D) recommended

正確答案　P22

04 有建議、要求的主句後的 that 子句要用動詞原形

❶ 主句中出現關於建議、要求的動詞 / 形容詞 / 名詞時子句要用「動詞原形」。

動詞	request 邀請	ask 請求	suggest 提議	propose 提議	recommend 建議
	insist 主張	command 命令	order 命令	require 要求	demand 要求
形容詞	imperative 強制的	essential 必需的	necessary 必要的	important 重要的	
名詞	advice 忠告				

The hotel manager <u>requests</u> that any meetings ~~are held~~ in the conference room.
be held

飯店經理要求無論什麼會議都要在會議室舉行。

→ 主句中有表示要求的動詞（requests），所以子句中的 be 動詞要用原形（be held）。

It is <u>essential</u> that the process ~~is completed~~ in a timely fashion.
be completed

在適當的時機完成這個過程是必需的。

→ 主句中表達需求的動詞（essential），所以子句中的 be 動詞要用原形（be completed）。

My <u>advice</u> is that she ~~takes~~ more classes in business communications.
take

我的建議是她還要多選修一些商業溝通課程。

→ 主句中表達建議的名詞（advice），所以子句中的動詞要用動詞原形（take）。

注意！ 上面那些動詞、形容詞、名詞雖然在主句中出現，但不表達提議或義務等涵義時，that 子句不能用動詞原形。

A recent cancer study <u>suggests</u> that exposure to sun <u>make</u>(→ makes) our skin prone to cancer.
最新的癌症研究表示使皮膚在紫外線曝曬會導致皮膚癌。

⇨ 這個文章中的 suggests 是「表示」或「揭示」的意思，而不是「提議」的意思，所以在 that 子句中不能用動詞原形。

多益實戰考題　　　　　　　　　　　多 益 會 出 這 樣 的 問 題

⊙ 在關於建議、要求的主句後的 that 子句中填入動詞原形。

2. The manufacturer insists that the defective air bags ------- replaced in spite of the high cost of recalling thousands of affected cars.

(A) are   (B) be
(C) have   (D) has

1. The Trattoria Restaurant requests that patrons ------- reservations for a table at least two weeks ahead of time.

(A) makes   (B) making
(C) made   (D) make

3. Due to the urgency of this matter, it is imperative that Mr. Lambert ------- one of our customer representatives by 5 p.m.

(A) is contacting   (B) will contact
(C) contact   (D) contacted

正確答案　P22

HACKERS PRACTICE ● ● ● ● ● ● ● ● ● ● ● ● ● ● ● ●

Practice 1 選擇正確的答案。

01 Crystal will gladly (accept / acceptance) her boss' offer of a promotion and a raise.

02 It is important that the city (receive / receives) state funds for its budget.

03 The famous author was asked to (speak / mention) to Harvard's graduating finance majors about the meaning of success.

04 Should you (be / are) unable to attend, have my secretary send you the minutes from the meeting.

05 Jessie (would like / was liked) the opportunity to serve on the committee for international diplomacy.

06 Despite the financial benefits, most people in the community (oppose / object) the construction of a chemical plant.

07 The commentator failed to (mention / notify) to us that the source for the story was unreliable.

Practice 2 改正錯誤的地方。

08 You had better turned in those evaluations before you put in a request for time off.

09 Kate has apply for some vacation time for this coming August.

10 It is imperative that you will submit all reports in a timely fashion.

11 A ceremony will held in honor of Mrs. Stansfield's many accomplishments.

12 Only on Saturday afternoons does the clinic accepts walk-in patients.

13 She is compile the documents and should have them ready for you shortly.

14 It is essential that we to remain aware of our competitors' activities.

Part V

01 The fee must ------- within two days if you do not wish to forfeit your reservation.

(A) be paying   (B) be paid
(C) to pay   (D) have paid

02 While Harman's used to ------- imported furniture, it is now sticking to local products to avoid the hassles of customs.

(A) have sold   (B) sold
(C) sell   (D) selling

03 It is essential that no unauthorized persons ------- into the building once it has been locked by the security personnel.

(A) admitted   (B) admit
(C) be admitted   (D) admittance

04 Until recently, the Family Entertainment Arcade located in the mall ------- not generating the revenue its owners expected.

(A) is   (B) was
(C) has   (D) being

05 Financial advisers suggest that setting aside cash for emergencies ------- it easier for the first-time investor to recover from losses.

(A) makes   (B) be made
(C) make   (D) made

06 Because the positions need to be filled immediately, applications for the positions indicated below ------- be received or postmarked no later than March 21.

(A) might   (B) ought
(C) need   (D) must

07 The notice on the community bulletin board requested that the purse ------- to its owner and stated that a small reward would be given.

(A) returns   (B) returning
(C) be returned   (D) to return

08 The two leading construction firms have indicated their ------- in bidding for the Swanson Tenement Project.

(A) interested   (B) interesting
(C) interest   (D) interests

09 At the meeting we will ------- about the problem concerning the misuse of company telephones and fax machines.

(A) object   (B) oppose
(C) talk   (D) discuss

10 More supplies may ------- if the participants run out during the week-long conference.

(A) requisite   (B) be requisitioned
(C) to be requisitioned (D) be requisitioning

11 Your team will need to meet and prepare a timetable when you ------- ready to begin work on the new project.

(A) be   (B) are
(C) have   (D) will be

12 The canned chicken soup manufacturer insists that all the cans -------, regardless of losses to the company.

(A) recall   (B) recalling
(C) be recalled   (D) are recalled

13 The director ------- not agree with the company president, as he believes that the word processing software market is already glutted.

(A) is   (B) was
(C) did   (D) has

14 A 60-item test was given to the applicants to eliminate those who did not ------- the basic knowledge requirements for the job.

(A) meet   (B) meeting
(C) be met   (D) to meet

15 The final report should ------- on the more recent findings rather than on the data collected a few months ago.

(A) base (B) based
(C) be based (D) to be based

16 ------- the sudden collapse of the firm, hundreds of people found themselves without a job.

(A) As (B) Although
(C) However (D) Because of

17 Faced with a huge decrease in sales, the company ------- half of its employees and closed down two factories.

(A) dismiss (B) dismissal
(C) dismissed (D) was dismissed

18 The stock room manager ------- the window display designer that the fall display would have to wait because of a delay with the shipment.

(A) explained (B) informed
(C) announced (D) proposed

19 Only after one of the employees expressed concern did they ------- investigating harassment claims against the supervisor.

(A) started (B) starting
(C) starts (D) start

20 As there are so many calls for computer system repairs, the company technician has ------- his supervisor to hire additional workers.

(A) ask (B) asking
(C) asked (D) been asked

Part VI

New Drug Said to Knock Out Stress

With PharmaNext currently holding a ------- on work-related stress relieving drugs, MediComp

21 (A) monologue (B) monotone
(C) monogram (D) monopoly

has unveiled their new product in a coup attempt on the market. According to a company spokesperson, Stress-Out TM ought to ------- in not only treating stress induced illnesses and

22 (A) aid (B) to aid
(C) aiding (D) aided

pains, but also provide the worker with a balanced mix of multi-vitamins to improve one's immune system. Having received certification from the federal drug administration, MediComp has ------- a few companies with free trial versions of the drug. Studies showed that

23 (A) supply (B) supplier
(C) supplying (D) supplied

employee ------- improved after only two weeks and employees stated they felt healthier and

24 (A) creation (B) productivity
(C) execution (D) abundance

more energetic. The drug is said to be made of 100% organic herbal material and will not cause any side-effects. It will be readily available at all major pharmacies by next month.

正確答案 P23

Chapter 5

主詞動詞一致

啊哈!! 愉快地打基礎

1 動詞的單複數形式要與主詞一致。

A dog barks. 一隻狗在叫。
主詞（單）動詞（單）

Dogs bark.（幾隻）狗在叫。
主詞（複）動詞（複）

第一個句子的主詞 a dog 是單數，第二個句子的主詞 dogs 是複數。
所以第一個句子要用動詞單數形式 barks，第二個句子要用動詞的複數形式 bark。
像這樣動詞和主詞的單複數形式一定要一致。

2 動詞的單數形式是動詞原形加 -(e)s，動詞的複數形式就是動詞原形。

原形	單數形式	複數形式
visit	visits	visit
watch	watches	watch
do	does	do
have	has	have

The girl has lots of ideas about what to write.
那個女孩對於要寫什麼有很多想法。

The children have lots of ideas about what to write.
那些孩子們對於寫什麼有很多想法。

動詞的單數形式和複數形式只用於一般式，在過去式中動詞的單複數形式是一樣的。

The teacher encouraged the students to speak freely.
The teachers encouraged the students to speak freely.
老師（們）鼓勵學生自由討論。

但 be 動詞在過去式時的單數形式和複數形式是有區別的。

原形		單數形式	複數形式
be	（現在）	am / is	are
	（過去）	was	were

01 主詞的單數形式對應動詞的單數形式，主詞的複數形式對應動詞的複數形式

❶ 主詞的單數形式對應動詞的單數形式，主詞的複數形式對應動詞的複數形式。

The lunch menu changes daily 午餐菜單每天更換。
→ 主詞（The lunch menu）是單數，所以動詞用單數形式（changes）。

The ferries have restaurants that are open for all three meals. 那些渡輪上有供應三餐的餐廳。
→ 主詞（The ferries）是複數，所以動詞用原形（have）。

注意！ 1. 主詞的單數形式有可數名詞單數和不可數名詞，主詞的複數形式也有可數名詞複數。以下是在多益中常出現的名詞。

可數名詞單數	a client, a manager, an employee ...
不可數名詞	information, equipment, furniture ...
可數名詞複數	representatives, plans, people, goods, funds, savings ...

2. 要注意以下雖以 - s 結尾，但不是名詞的複數形式的詞。

學科名	economics 經濟學, statistics 統計學, mathematics 數學
專有名詞	World Satellite Atlas, Times ...
其他名詞	news, the United States ...

❷ 動名詞 / 子句充當主語時用動詞的單數形式。

Reading a book makes me want to fall asleep. 讀書使我想睡覺。
→ 動名詞（Reading a book）是單數，所以動詞用第三人稱單數形式（makes）。

What I remember about her is a willingness to negotiate. 我對她的印象是她擅長協商。
→ 子句（What I remember about her）是單數，所以動詞用原形（is）。

❸ 主詞和動詞之間的修飾語與動詞的單複數形式無關。

Services [at this hotel] ~~includes~~ airport pick-up. 這個飯店的服務包括機場到飯店的接送。
                            include
→ 注意不要把動詞（include）前的修飾語（at this hotel）中的 hotel 看作主詞，以免錯用動詞的單數形式。

The statement [drawn up by Werner Accountants] ~~provide~~ a benchmark for evaluation.
                                                  provides
Werner Accountants 制定的報告書提供了評價的標準。
→ 注意不要把動詞（provides）前的修飾語中的 Werner Accountants 看作主詞，以免誤用動詞的複數形式。

多益實戰考題　　　　　多 益 會 出 這 樣 的 問 題

⊙ 填入與主詞（動詞）一致的動詞（主詞）單複數形式。

2. As the members of management have come to realize, the ------- of implementing the new business proposition has to be studied further.

(A) prospect　　　　(B) prospective
(C) prospects　　　　(D) prosperous

1. The recent meeting between the two companies ------- that a deal is near.

(A) imply　　　　(B) implies
(C) was implied　　　　(D) implied

3. A decrease in the supply of clean water sources ------- sales in water purification products.

(A) aid　　　　(B) aids
(C) aiding　　　　(D) was aided

正確答案　P25

Hackers Skill　　先去掉修飾語，再統一主詞和動詞的單複數形式。

02 與表示數量、表示部分 / 全部的主詞之單複數形式保持一致

❶ 表示數量的詞為單數時用單數的動詞,複數時用複數的動詞。

表示單數數量的詞	表示複數數量的詞
one (+ 名詞) each (+ 名詞), every + 名詞 the number of + 複數名詞 somebody, someone, something anybody, anyone, anything everybody, everyone, everything nobody, no one, nothing	many / several / few / both + (of the) + 複數名詞 a number of + 複數名詞 a couple/range/variety of + 複數名詞

<u>One of the trainees</u> has scored perfect on the company procedures test. 其中一位受訓者在公司常規考核中得了滿分。
<u>Every person</u> at this meeting looks exhausted. 每個參加會議的人看起來都很疲倦。
<u>Many schools</u> have football teams. 很多學校都有足球隊。
<u>Many of the employees</u> take vacation time in the summer. 有很多職員在夏季休假。
<u>A variety of methods</u> are used to obtain information. 為了獲得資訊而使用了很多方法。

注意! many, several, both 等單字獨自做主詞時也視為複數。
Many <u>predict</u> rates will be rising soon. 有很多人預測稅款會增加。

❷ 表示部分或全部的詞做主詞時,of 後面的名詞決定動詞的單複數形式。

all, most, any, some, half, a lot (lots) part, the rest, the bulk, percent, 分數(幾分之幾)	+ of +	名詞單數 + 動詞單數 名詞複數 + 動詞複數

Half of <u>the annual profit</u> goes to paying taxes and insurance fees. 支付在稅款和保險費上的費用是年度收入的一半。
→ half of 後面的名詞(the annual profit)為單數,所以動詞用第三人稱單數形式(goes)。

Roughly half of <u>the employees</u> at K Company commute to work by bus. K 公司有大約一半左右的職員搭公車上班。
→ half of 後面的名詞(the employees)為複數,所以動詞用複數形式(commute)。

多益實戰考題　　　　　多 益 會 出 這 樣 的 問 題

⊙ 填入與主詞(表示數量、表示部分 / 全部)一致的動詞單複數形式。

2. Every employee ------- to consider what his or her prospects are for career advancement and personal growth, and HRD will provide counseling services to assist them.

(A) have needed　　　(B) needs
(C) needing　　　　　(D) to need

1. A wide range of colors ------- to have been used in the painting, but we will not know this for sure until after the artwork has been cleaned.

(A) appear　　　　　(B) appears
(C) is appeared　　　(D) are appeared

3. All of the consultants' suggestions about the company's position regarding the upcoming merger ------- into consideration by the CEO.

(A) is taking　　　　(B) was taken
(C) will take　　　　(D) have been taken

正確答案　P26

03 有連接詞連接的主詞動詞一致

❶ 主詞與連接詞 and 連接時用動詞的複數形式。

The president <u>and</u> the director are working on the plan. 董事長和總經理正在執行這個計畫。

→ 單數名詞 The president 和 the director 用連接詞 and 連接，所以動詞用複數形式。

注意！ "Both A and B" 的情況下動詞也用複數形式。

Both the flower bed and the garden <u>need</u> to be watered. 花床和花園兩者都需要澆水。

❷ 主詞與連接詞 or 連接成（A or B）形式時由 B 來決定動詞的單複數形式。

Two vans <u>or</u> a bus is needed to take those children somewhere.

需要兩輛貨車或一輛巴士才能把那些孩子們送到其他地方。

→ 複數名詞（Two vans）和單數名詞（a bus）與連接詞 or 相連接，所以依照 or 後面名詞決定動詞用單數形式（is）。

注意！ 由 B 來決定動詞的單複數形式的其他例子

Either A or B	A 或 B 中一個
Neither A nor B	A 和 B 都不是
Not A but B	不是 A，而是 B
Not only A but (also) B	不僅 A，且 B 也
B as well as A	不僅 A，且 B 也

❸ in addition to~, along with~, together with~ 等修飾語不影響動詞單複數。

<u>Mr. Clarion</u>, [along with his partners], ~~think~~ the new venture will work.
　　　　　　　　　　　　　　　　thinks

不僅他的同伴，連 Clarion 先生也相信新的冒險會行得通。

→ 修飾語（along with his partners）對動詞的單複數沒有影響，所以依照單數主詞（Mr. Clarion），動詞要用單數形式（thinks）。

多益實戰考題　　　　　多 益 會 出 這 樣 的 問 題

⊙ 填入與連接詞連接的主詞一致的動詞單複數形式。
主要會出現與 and 或 or 連接的主詞問題。

1. Mr. Burns and the secretary of our Arlington branch ------- to the weekend gathering.

(A) is coming　　　　(B) are coming
(C) comes　　　　　(D) has come

2. The chef's assistant and I ------- a special menu for this evening's wine tasting event, which will be attended by some top sommeliers.

(A) am preparing　　(B) prepares
(C) are preparing　　(D) has prepared

3. The federal government, along with the cooperation of leading industrial companies, ------- to create more jobs for skilled workers.

(A) is pushing　　　(B) are pushing
(C) pushing　　　　(D) have been pushed

正確答案　P26

04 形容詞子句中主詞先行詞和動詞的單複數形式保持一致

❶ 形容詞子句中主詞先行詞和動詞的單複數形式保持一致

單數先行詞 複數先行詞	+ 主格關係代名詞 (who, which, that) +	動詞的單數形式 動詞的複數形式

We have hired <u>an associate</u> who has experience in international sales. 我們雇用了有海外銷售經驗的人。

→ 先行詞（an associate）為單數，且為形容詞子句的主詞時，在子句中用動詞的單數形式（has）。

<u>Receptionists</u> who don't have database experience are useless in today's job market.
沒有資料庫經驗的接待員在職業市場上沒有價值。

→ 先行詞（Receptionists）為複數，且為形容詞子句的主詞時，在子句中用動詞的複數形式（don't have）。

❷ 不要混淆先行詞和先行詞後面的修飾語中的名詞。

<u>Offices</u> [in <u>this building</u>] that ~~is~~ currently leased on a monthly basis will be subject to additional charges.
are

這個大樓裡依月租繳費的辦公室要承擔附加費。

→ 先行詞（Offices）為複數，所以在子句中用動詞的複數形式（are）。注意不要把關係代名詞（that）前的修飾語（in this building）中的單數名詞（building）看作先行詞，這會導致子句中的動詞用複數形式（were）的錯誤。

<u>The virus</u> [in <u>the computers</u>], which ~~were~~ passed on by e-mail, was removed by a computer technician.
was

電腦中透過電子郵件傳播的病毒被技術人員清除掉了。

→ 先行詞（The virus）為單數，所以在子句中用動詞的單數形式（was）。注意不要把關係代名詞（which）前的修飾語（in the computers）中的單數名詞（computers）看作先行詞，這會導致子句中的動詞用複數形式（were）的錯誤。

多益實戰考題　　　　　　多 益 會 出 這 樣 的 問 題

⊙ 填入與主詞（先行詞）一致的動詞（子句中的動詞）單複數形式。

2. Each year, we send representatives from our firm to job fairs that ------- at college campuses throughout the country.

(A) held　　　　　　(B) are held
(C) are holding　　　(D) was held

1. Files that ------- in the main facility are being removed in an effort to computerize all records and data.

(A) were stored　　　(B) have stored
(C) was stored　　　 (D) stores

3. The number of users who ------- support has increased since the company released the latest version of its software.

(A) require　　　　　(B) requires
(C) is required　　　 (D) are required

正確答案 P26

HACKERS PRACTICE ● ● ● ● ● ● ● ● ● ● ● ● ● ● ●

Practice 1 選擇正確的答案。

01 Plans to open an office in Asia (was / were) delayed for several months.

02 Employees at this firm that (is / are) currently salaried will be asked to pull overtime this week.

03 (Many / Much) fear that small business taxes will rise next year.

04 All computers in the office (was / were) damaged in the fire.

05 The guests brought to the convention (is / are) from the international branch in Germany.

06 Savings (bank / banks) in the western region have begun to increase loan activity.

07 The supervisor, together with investigators, (is / are) going to confront the accountant about fraud accusations.

Practice 2 改正錯誤的地方。

08 A car and a truck is on sale during the year-end clearance program.

09 Half of the stocks listed on the exchange pays annual dividends.

10 Several guests request that the hotel swimming pool be opened early.

11 The news warn that the airline industry is on the verge of collapse.

12 Uniform with company emblems are required by airlines for both security reasons and customer convenience purposes.

13 Accurate information is needed to make business and economic decisions.

14 Reducing waste through increased recycling are both practical and necessary.

正確答案　P27

Part V

01 All ------- for long distance phone calls made from the office are the employee's responsibility.

(A) charge   (B) charging
(C) to charge   (D) charges

02 Members of the labor union unanimously ------- the introduction of a six-day work week.

(A) were rejected   (B) rejecting
(C) rejects   (D) rejected

03 The price of the vacation package to London ------- airfare, hotel accommodations, meals, and the services of a professional tour guide.

(A) include   (B) including
(C) inclusion   (D) includes

04 Target and Macy's chain stores are popular with the public, and ------- offer quality goods at affordable prices.

(A) one   (B) them
(C) both   (D) either

05 The quality of beef served at the hotel ------- depending on where it was purchased.

(A) to vary   (B) varies
(C) varying   (D) vary

06 North America's Atlas, featuring articles on individualism and capitalism, ------- in August by Russell Palmer.

(A) publish   (B) to publish
(C) will be published (D) have been published

07 Questions ------- the recent changes in employee benefits and eligibility should be addressed to Mr. Henderson in personnel.

(A) concerning   (B) concern
(C) concerned   (D) concerns

08 A medication is known to be dose-dependent when its effects ------- as its dosage varies.

(A) change   (B) changing
(C) to change   (D) changes

09 Flight attendants who do international trips report that the most common ------- they receive is for an extra blanket or pillow.

(A) requested   (B) to request
(C) request   (D) requests

10 A customer has called to complain that the product he ordered last month ------- not yet arrived.

(A) is   (B) are
(C) has   (D) have

11 Salespeople who ------- their interactions with customers on a case-to-case basis are more effective than those who stick to the same approach with everyone.

(A) handle   (B) handles
(C) are handled   (D) handling

12 The flu epidemic will probably ------- an increased demand for over-the-counter remedies.

(A) stimulates   (B) stimulated
(C) to stimulate   (D) stimulate

13 The cheap cost of labor in developing countries ------- as a motive for companies to move production overseas.

(A) is seen   (B) has seen
(C) see   (D) seeing

14 During the annual company evaluation, employees should point out the various aspects of the company's system and organization that ------- improving.

(A) need   (B) is needed
(C) needs   (D) needing

15 Work on such infrastructure facilities as power and water supply, as well as roads and telecommunications, ------- shape in the small town of Loleta.

(A) to take   (B) taking
(C) has taken   (D) take

16 We would like to assure the staff that the benefits of having an annual physical exam far ------- the inconveniences associated with such tests.

(A) to outweigh   (B) outweigh
(C) outweighing   (D) outweighs

17 Disallowing the use of inappropriate language at the workplace ------- a longstanding rule that has been enforced since the company's establishment.

(A) have   (B) has
(C) is   (D) being

18 The reason ------- were so many people in the office yesterday was because the CEO held interviews for a new assistant.

(A) it   (B) they
(C) that   (D) there

19 We would like to inform the participants that the fees for the two-day educational event ------- reference materials, lodging, and meals.

(A) cover   (B) to cover
(C) is covered   (D) has covered

20 With corporate ownership increasing in the Eastern hemisphere, many ------- that labor jobs will triple over the next five years.

(A) predicting   (B) to predict
(C) predict   (D) has predicted

21 The selection committee ------- to review the resumes, portfolios, and reference letters of each potential candidate.

(A) want   (B) wants
(C) wanting   (D) have wanted

22 The pharmaceutical firm that makes these sleeping pills has emphasized that it cannot be held responsible for any injury or death that ------- from improper use of the pills.

(A) result   (B) results
(C) resulting   (D) have been resulted

23 The aforementioned increase in pay is offered only to ------- who have completed the required two year full-time employment contract.

(A) employ   (B) employer
(C) employees   (D) employment

24 Over the last decade, the level of interest in the federal retirement plan shown by small scale investors ------- due to a rise in personal investments.

(A) has declined   (B) decline
(C) were declined   (D) declining

25 The tips listed on the first page of every issue ------- buyers determine what computer accessories they really need and where to buy them.

(A) help   (B) helping
(C) is helping   (D) to be helped

26 After completing his doctorate in anthropology, Jeff Damon began working for a research organization that ------- in Biblical studies.

(A) to specialize   (B) specializes
(C) was specialized   (D) have specialized

27 The number of individuals being recruited by the company this summer for temporary jobs ------- to exceed fifty.

(A) is expected   (B) are expecting
(C) expects   (D) expecting

28 We have ------- that the market will continue to allow for small business opportunities, and the unemployment rate will decrease accordingly.

(A) confide   (B) confided
(C) confident   (D) confidence

GRAMMAR | 動詞

正確答案 P27

Chapter 6

時態

啊哈!! 愉快地打基礎

1 表現動作或狀態的動詞在不同的時間裡有不同的形態,這叫動詞的時態。

She worked on the paper last week. 她上週寫了那份報告。
She works on the paper a little bit every day. 她每天寫一點報告。
She will work on a paper tomorrow. 她明天會寫報告。

就像上面例題表示動作的 work 有 worked, works, will work 等變化來表現時間。這種表示時間的動詞形態的變化叫時態。

2 動詞時態有簡單式、進行式、完成式,並以不同的形態來表示時間。

· 簡單式:表現特定時間內動作的狀態,並有「動詞 (+ s)」,「動詞 + ed」,「will + 動詞」等形態。

現在 Club members meet every Wednesday at 7 p.m.
俱樂部會員們在每週三晚上 7 點見面。

過去 Club members met in various locations in Grand Folks.
俱樂部會員們在 Grand Folks 的很多地方聚會過。

未來 Club members will meet today after school.
俱樂部會員們會在今天下課後見面。

· 進行式:表現在一個時間點上動作一直進行著,且用 "be + Ving" 形態。

現在進行 Jane is walking. Jane 正在走路。

過去進行 Jane was walking. Jane 當時正在走路。

未來進行 Jane will be walking to work. 那時 Jane 將的在走路去工作的途中。

· 完成式:表現在特定時間點之前發生的事件或從過去一直進行到那個時間點的動作或狀態,並用 "have + p.p." 的形態。

現在完成 Denise has left. Denise 離開了。

過去完成 Denise had left already. Denise 在那之前已經離開了。

未來完成 Denise will have left by that time. Denise 那時將已經離開了。

01 現在式 / 過去式 / 未來式

❶ 現在式表現出反覆動作或一般事實。

She usually charges high fees for her consulting service. 她的諮詢服務一向索價很高。
→ 為表現索價的反覆動作,所以用現在式（charges）。

A good supervisor creates a nice environment. 一個優秀的管理者會製造良好的環境。
→ 為表現優秀管理者的一般特徵,所以用現在式（creates）。

❷ 過去式表現出已經結束的過去動作或狀態。

Miguel instituted the Art Appreciation Program two years ago. Miguel 在兩年前設立了這個藝術鑑賞節目。
→ 設立藝術鑑賞節目已經是在兩年前結束的事,所以用過去式（instituted）。

❸ 未來式表現對未來狀況的猜測或意向。

We will go to the beach tomorrow. 我們明天會去海邊。
→ 為表現明天去海邊的意向,所以用未來式（will go）。

注意！ 現在進行式（be 動詞 + Ving）和「be going to + 動詞原形」的形態也是表現未來預定的事或將要發生的事。
I am seeing Cathy on Tuesday night. 我將在星期二跟 Cathy 見面。
I am going to get married next Sunday. 我將在下禮拜日結婚。

❹ 表示時間的子句中用現在式來代替未來式。

When you will finish the course, a certificate will be sent to you. 完成那項課程後,將會把結業證書寄給你。
              finish
→ 以 when 開頭的時間子句中不能用未來式（will finish）表現未來。應用現在式（finish）。

If you will want, there is left-over food in the fridge. 如果你想吃,冰箱裡有剩下的食物。
        want
→ 以 if 開頭的條件子句中不能用未來式（will want）表現未來。應用現在式（want）。

注意！ 1. 引導條件、時間子句的連接詞有 when, before, after, as, once, if, unless, by the time 等。
       2. 引導條件、時間的連接詞的子句之外的主要句子中,不能用現在式來代替未來式,而直接用未來式。
       When you finish the course, a certificate is sent(→ will be sent) to you.
       ⇨ 表示時間的 when 子句中用現在式（finish）來代替未來式（will finish）,但在主句中應用未來式（will be sent）,不能用現在式（is sent）。

多益實戰考題   多 益 會 出 這 樣 的 問 題

⊙填入動詞的正確時態。

2. Mr. Sanders ------- out of the country until next Friday, but you can contact him by e-mail if there are matters of urgency.

(A) is being　　　　(B) will be
(C) will have been　(D) has been

1. Mr. and Mrs. Robertson, who ------- the Save the Children Organization, will be giving speeches at our company dinner tonight.

(A) founding　　　(B) foundation
(C) found　　　　(D) founded

3. If management ------- Ms. Fernandez to rewrite the project analysis over the weekend, they will have to pay her for overtime.

(A) will ask　　　　(B) asks
(C) will have asked　(D) would ask

正確答案　P29

02 現在進行式 / 過去進行式 / 未來進行式

❶ 現在進行式（am / is / are + Ving）表現出現在時間點上正在進行的事件。

She is living in Canada at the moment. 她現在在加拿大生活。

→ 為了表現在現在時間點（at the moment）上生活在加拿大，所以用現在進行式。

注意！ 1. 表現反覆的動作時用一般現在式，而不是現在進行式。

Mr. Clark is usually giving(→ usually gives) us snacks in the afternoon. Clark 先生通常在下午給我們零食吃。
為表現反覆給零食的動作，所以應用一般現在式（usually gives），而不是現在進行式（is usually giving）。

2. 表現現在正在發生的事件時應用現在進行式，而不是一般現在式。

The dog barks(→ is barking) at the cat. 狗正在對貓吠叫著。
⇨ 因表現了正在發生的動作，所以用現在進行式（is barking），而不是一般現在式（barks）。

❷ 過去進行式（was / were + Ving）表現出在特定的過去時間點上正在進行的事件。

I was watching TV at eight o'clock yesterday. 昨天八點的時候，我正在看電視。

→ 為了表現在過去特定時間點（at eight o'clock yesterday）在看電視的過程中，所以用過去進行式。

❸ 未來進行式（will be + Ving）表現出在未來的特定時間點上正在進行的事件。

At this time tomorrow I will be lying on the beach. 明天這個時間我正躺在海灘上。

→ 為了表現在未來特定時間點（At this time tomorrow）時會正躺在海灘上，所以用未來進行式。

❹ 不能用在進行式的動詞

情感動詞	surprise 驚訝	shock 使震驚	hate 恨	prefer 寧願	want 希望	believe 相信
狀態動詞	include 包括	need 需要	be 是	know 知道	exist 存在	

I ~~am preferring~~ the sound of the sea. 我更喜歡海的聲音。
　　prefer

→ 情感動詞不能用進行式（am preferring），所以只能用一般現在式（prefer）。

The president ~~is being~~ out of the office. 董事長現在不在辦公室。
　　　　　　　is

→ 狀態動詞不能用進行式（is being），所以只能用一般現在式（is）。

多益實戰考題　　　　　　　　多 益 會 出 這 樣 的 問 題

⊙ 填入動詞的正確時態。

1. The majority of home designers believe that more people in the United States ------- in townhouses or gated communities by the year 2020.

(A) had been lived　　(B) lived
(C) will be living　　(D) is living

2. Facilities at the university recreational center ------- an Olympic-sized swimming pool, five racquetball courts, and an indoor track.

(A) are including　　(B) include
(C) includes　　(D) has included

3. No one was more ------- than the company president to discover that a few of his most trusted employees had resigned and joined the competition.

(A) shocking　　(B) shock
(C) shocked　　(D) being shocked

正確答案　P30

03 現在完成式／過去完成式／未來完成式

❶ 過去完成式（has / have p.p.）表現的是：從過去發生到現在或剛剛結束的事件；過去的經驗；過去發生並影響到現在的事件。

He has served **for 5 years on the board of Brown University.** 他在 Brown 大學委員會裡工作了五年。
→ 從過去五年工作到了現在，所以用現在完成式（has served）。

I have **already** finished **my project.** 我已經完成了我的企劃。
→ 剛剛完成了這個項目，所以用現在完成式（have finished）。

I have **never** visited **Mexico.** 我沒去過墨西哥。
→ 去墨西哥是一種經驗，所以用現在完成式（have visited）。

I have lost **my watch.** 我遺失了我的手錶。
→ 在過去遺失了手錶說明現在沒有手錶，所以用現在完成式（have lost）。

注意！ 1. 在完成式句子中表示持續的涵義時用 for 或 since，表示已經結束時的涵義時用 already 或 just，表示經驗時用 ever、never、yet 等。

2. 現在完成式和現在完成進行式都可以表示一個事件從過去一直發生到現在，但現在完成進行式更強調表示這個事件正在進行的意圖。
In the last few months, it <u>has rained</u> heavily. 前幾個月下了很多雨。
It <u>has been raining</u> a lot lately. 這幾天一直在下雨，已經下了很多了。

❷ 過去完成式（had p.p.）表現過去特定時間點之前發生過的事件。

When the party finished, my sister had **already** departed. 派對結束時，我的妹妹已經離開了。
→表達了過去特定時間點（結束派對時）之前妹妹已經離開的事實，所以用過去完成式。

❸ 未來完成式（will have p.p.）表示未來特定時間點之前發生的事件在那個時間點上結束。

I will have studied **for 5 years by next December.** 到明年 12 月時我就已經研究五年了。
→表達了從過去開始的研究到未來特定時間點（next December）時將達到五年的時間，所以用未來完成式。

多益實戰考題 　　　　　　　　　　　多 益 會 出 這 樣 的 問 題

⊙填入動詞的正確時態。

1. This year the car industry ------- many investors because automotive products now make up 15 percent of the country's exports.

(A) attract 　　　　　(B) has attracted
(C) attracting 　　　　(D) had attracted

2. By exercising at the gym during lunchtime, she could relieve work-related stress that ------- built up from the morning.

(A) are 　　　　　(B) would
(C) has been 　　　(D) had been

3. Next fall, Irene ------- employed with this corporation for over a decade as an advisor to the president.

(A) has been 　　　(B) is
(C) had 　　　　　(D) will have been

正確答案　P30

❶ 常與過去式，現在式，未來式，現在完成式一起使用的表現。

過去式	現在式	未來、未來完成式	現在完成式
yesterday 時間表現 + ago last + 時間表現 in + 過去式 * 但 until 不能與未來完成式一起使用。	usually often each month (year) generally	tomorrow next + 時間表現 by / until + 未來式 as of + 未來式 by the time + 主詞 + 現在式動詞 when + 主詞 + 現在式動詞	since + 過去式 in the last (past) ~ over the year

She ~~has started~~ to work for this firm last year. 她去年就開始在這家公司工作了。
　　　started

→ 有過去時間表現（last year），所以用過去式（started），而不是現在完成式（has started）。

She ~~taught~~ English since she moved here. 她自從搬到這裡以後就在教英文了。
　　has taught

→ 句中有表示從過去時間點到現在的「since + 表示過去時間點的片語」，所以主句中的動詞不能用過去式 (taught)，而是用現在完成式（has taught）。

She ~~has served~~ for 14 years by the time she retires. 到她退休時她將已經服務滿 14 年了。
　　will have served

→ 句中有表示未來時間點的「by the time + 主詞 + 動詞現在式」，所以用未來完成式（will have served），而不是現在完成式（has served）。

❷ 主句為過去式時，子句就用過去式或過去完成式。

Mr. MacKenzie explained that the fiscal report ~~is completed~~ the preceding week.
　　　　　　　　　　　　　　　　　　　　　　was completed

MacKenzie 先生解釋他上週就完成了財務報告書。

→ 主句時態（explained）為過去式，而且子句中也提到了過去的事件，所以子句中用過去完成式（was completed），而不是現在式（is completed）。

注意! 主句為過去式，但子句中的動作或狀態一直延續到現在時間點時可以用現在（完成）式。還有句子中提到現在時間點以後預定的事件時可以用未來式。

The financial analyst thought that market conditions have improved. 財務分析師認為市場環境已有改善。

⇨ 雖然主句是以過去式（thought）寫成，但整個句子表示景氣好轉的狀況到現在一直都持續著，所以子句使用現在完成式（have improved）。

The company spokesperson reported that the press conference will be held on Thursday.
公司發言人宣佈新聞記者會將在星期四舉行。

⇨ 雖然主句是以過去式（reported）寫成，但以現在的時間點看來，記者會是在未來的時間舉行，所以子句使用未來式（will be held）。

多益實戰考題　　　　　多 益 會 出 這 樣 的 問 題

⊙填入與時間表現一致的動詞時態。

2. Last week, a newspaper columnist ------- an article that triggered an investigation into the university's admissions practices.

(A) writes　　　　　(B) has written
(C) wrote　　　　　(D) have written

1. Television viewership ------- slightly since the advent of the Information Age and the invention of the personal computer.

(A) drop　　　　　(B) will drop
(C) has dropped　　(D) dropping

3. Management was informed that the shipment from the branch office in Paris ------- the following Thursday.

(A) arriving　　　　(B) would arrive
(C) have arrived　　(D) has arrived

HACKERS PRACTICE ● ● ● ● ● ● ● ● ● ● ● ● ● ● ● ●

Practice 1 選擇正確的時態。

01 When Martin (reads / read) the contract, he discovered that he had been deceived.

02 William reluctantly (attends / attended) the seminar, but he surprisingly found it very helpful.

03 After returning from vacation, we learned that a storm (had damaged / damages) our house.

04 James (retire / retired) years ago, but he still has stock in his old employer.

05 The reports estimate that earnings (will double / has doubled) by the end of next year.

06 If you (believe / had believed) that there may be financial wrongdoing, please notify your supervisor.

07 What the new IT specialist knows about data systems (was / will be) useful when the office updates its computer programs.

08 As soon as the board (makes / will make) its decision, the managers will implement the plan.

09 The Pioneer Fund (has been / is) the company's biggest earner in the past four years.

10 The manufacturing company (needs / is needing) to increase production capacity in order to keep pace with its competitors.

Practice 2 選擇正確的答案。

11 Mr. Hyland will have served as CEO of the company for ten years (since / by the time) he retires.

12 Jeffery has analyzed stock market figures (in / since) 1991 when he joined a firm on Wall Street.

13 Steven, who previously worked in the sales department, is a manager in the head office (two years ago / at the moment).

14 The company (once / usually) requires three years of experience for all job applicants.

Part V

01 The employees in the accounting division were stunned to learn that three of their co-workers ------- that very morning.

(A) had fired
(B) will have been fired
(C) had been fired
(D) fired

02 Mr. Keating ------- Rick Chang as officer-in-charge for the duration of his European business trip last Wednesday.

(A) designate
(B) is designating
(C) has designated
(D) designated

03 When Mr. Arellano and his team ------- the write-up, please have them send it to my desk immediately.

(A) will finish
(B) would finish
(C) finish
(D) will have finished

04 Since last Thursday, window cleaners on a scaffold ------- the windows on the south side of the building.

(A) have been washing
(B) are washing
(C) have been washed
(D) were washed

05 By next fall it ------- time to integrate the recently developed data system.

(A) is
(B) will be
(C) was
(D) had been

06 A competent manager ------- opportunities for his employees to improve themselves professionally.

(A) created
(B) create
(C) creates
(D) creating

07 An environmental group recently released information indicating that pesticide companies ------- testing procedures to determine the levels at which toxic substances were harmful to humans.

(A) develop
(B) developing
(C) had developed
(D) had been developed

08 Until the beginning of this year, the amusement park ------- not attracting many visitors.

(A) has
(B) was
(C) is
(D) being

09 A new printer for the faculty room ------- purchased as soon as the requisition slip is signed.

(A) will be
(B) would be
(C) had been
(D) has been

10 In the past ten years, the number of Americans using 90 percent of their disposable income to pay off credit card debts ------- by 30 percent.

(A) has been rising
(B) will have risen
(C) was rising
(D) has risen

11 Participants were asked to complete an ------- at the conclusion of the photography workshop.

(A) evaluated
(B) evaluation
(C) evaluator
(D) evaluative

12 Because of the weakening economy this year, any purchases in new assets and properties ------- carefully studied over the next several months.

(A) have
(B) have been
(C) will have to be
(D) will have been

13 Once you ------- filling out the form, please proceed to the main hall to the left of the lobby.

(A) have completed
(B) will complete
(C) having completed
(D) are completing

14 The stylish new mobile phones are the best-selling products the company has designed in the ------- year.

(A) next
(B) past
(C) following
(D) future

15 Analysts predict that agricultural biotechnology ------- little interest for investors because of the opposition to genetically modified products.

(A) hold   (B) held
(C) will hold   (D) have held

16 If you ------- any problems with your new word processing software, check the handbook first before consulting online technical support.

(A) had experienced   (B) experience
(C) were experienced (D) experiencing

17 As of this coming Tuesday, Anne Porter ------- the head of Research and Development for five years.

(A) to be   (B) was
(C) had been   (D) will have been

18 Although online brokers usually ------- the least in commissions, they require you to do your own research instead of giving you advice.

(A) charging   (B) charges
(C) charge   (D) are charging

19 Ever since Mr. Smith ------- head of the town's community center, he has been holding at least two meetings per week.

(A) was elected   (B) will elect
(C) is electing   (D) had elected

20 The supervisor thinks that the factory's production capacity ------- by the end of the year, provided a new group of full-time workers is hired.

(A) will double   (B) has doubled
(C) had doubled   (D) been doubled

21 Recently, those in managerial positions ------- in more seminars and lectures on positive leadership and motivation for employees.

(A) were participated
(B) are to be participating
(C) have been participating
(D) will have been participating

22 The two law firms ------- more clients now that they have joined forces on their goal to provide affordable legal advice.

(A) receives   (B) receiving
(C) are receiving (D) were received

23 By the time the two new large printers are installed, demand for the popular publication ------- twofold.

(A) has increased   (B) had increased
(C) been increased   (D) will have increased

24 ------- there has been a concerted effort by the company to increase its market share, the results have been disappointing.

(A) Although   (B) Even
(C) In spite of   (D) Nevertheless

25 Please make sure that the client understands that payments must be made before the product -------.

(A) will deliver   (B) will be delivered
(C) deliver   (D) is delivered

26 Mr. Benson said that the maid never ------- to clean his quarters the whole time he stayed at the hotel.

(A) comes   (B) came
(C) come   (D) coming

27 Effective next month, employees ------- asked to participate in our new recycling program by carefully disposing of waste in the appropriate containers.

(A) was   (B) to be
(C) will be   (D) had been

28 As a temporary worker, we will notify you if a job that fits your experience and interests ------- available.

(A) become   (B) becomes
(C) became   (D) will become

Chapter 7

主動語態、被動語態

啊哈!!愉快地打基礎

1 主動語態是主詞「做…」的意思，即主詞是行為的主體，被動語態是主詞「被…，遭受」的意思，即主詞是行為的對象。被動語態的基本形式是 "be + p.p."。

主動語態　　I designed this building.

被動語態　　This building was designed by me.

第一個句子「我設計了這個建築物」表示主動意思，所以用主動語態。
第二個句子是「被…設計」的被動意思，所以用被動語態。

主動語態的形式　動詞的現在／過去／未來式	be + Ving（進行式）	have + p.p.（完成式）
被動語態的形式　be + p.p.	be being + p.p.（進行式）	have been + p.p.（完成式）

2 把主動句中的受詞放到主詞的位置時，句子就會變為被動句。

主動語態　　<u>Carol</u> <u>cooked</u> <u>dinner</u>. Carol 做了晚飯。
　　　　　　主詞　動詞的主動語態　受詞

被動語態　　<u>Dinner</u> <u>was cooked</u> <u>by Carol</u>. 晚飯是 Carol 做的。
　　　　　　主詞　　動詞的被動語態　by + 行為主體

3 主動語態的受詞變被動語態的主詞，所以只有能接受詞的及物動詞才有被動語態，而不及物動詞不能有被動語態。

We were arrived in Prague.（×）

We arrived in Prague.（○）我們到達布拉格了。

不及物動詞（arrive）不能接受詞，所以不能改為被動語態。

多益中常出現 take place（舉行，發生），rise（升起），occur（發生），consist（構成）等不及物動詞以被動語態出現的改錯題。

01 主動語態與被動語態的區別

❶ 主動語態中及物動詞後須接受詞，在被動語態中則不接受詞。

The assistant is used the computer. 助理使用那台電腦。
　　　　　　uses

→ 不能接受詞的不及物動詞（is used）後面有受詞（the computer），所以應改為主動語態（uses）。

A new machine will install. 新的機器將被安裝。
　　　　　　　　be installed

→ 在主動語態裡一定要接受詞的及物動詞（install）後面沒有受詞，所以應改為被動語態（be installed）。

❷ to 不定詞的動詞和關係動詞的語態區分也跟有沒有受詞有關。

The tenant is supposed to be paid the rent on July 1. 房客被要求於 7 月 1 日繳房租。
　　　　　　　　　　to pay

→ 不接受詞的被動語態 to 不定詞（to be paid）後面有受詞（the rent），所以把 to 不定詞改為主動語態（to pay）。

The draft was supposed to discuss in the workshop. 這個草案應該拿到研討會上討論。
　　　　　　　　　　to be discussed

→ 在主動語態必接受詞的及物動詞（to discuss）後面沒有受詞，所以用 to 不定詞的被動語態（to be discussed）。

A famous author who is written children's fairy tales is signing autographs today.
　　　　　　　　　　writes

一位著名童話作家將在今天舉辦簽名會。

→ 不接受詞的動詞的被動語態（is written）後面有受詞（children's fairy tales），所以改為主動語態（writes）。

We have received all of the items that list in the files. 我們接受了列入那個檔案中的所有物品。
　　　　　　　　　　　　　are listed

→ 在主動語態必接受詞的及物動詞（list）後面沒有受詞，所以改為被動語態（are listed）。

多益實戰考題　　　　　　多 益 會 出 這 樣 的 問 題

⊙ 用謂語的恰當語態填空。

2. ------- the mailing of the package, you will need to add five dollars more to the shipping fee.

(A) To expedite　　　　(B) Expedited
(C) To be expedited　　(D) Will expedite

1. The e-mail addresses and telephone numbers should be ------- carefully in the blanks provided.

(A) written　　　　(B) write
(C) wrote　　　　　(D) writing

3. You must fill out the tax form, a copy of which is ------- to the contractual agreement you received on the first day.

(A) attach　　　　　(B) attachment
(C) attaching　　　(D) attached

正確答案　P33

Hackers Skill　　及物動詞後面有受詞時用主動語態，沒有受詞時用被動語態。

02 形式 4、形式 5 動詞的被動語態

❶ 有兩個受詞的形式 4 動詞為被動語態時，其中一個受詞留在動詞的被動語態後面。

主動語態   She gave her sister the car. 她把那輛車送給了她的妹妹。

間接受詞變為主詞時的被動語態   <u>Her sister</u> was given the car. 她的妹妹得到了車。

直接受詞變為主詞時的被動語態   <u>The car</u> was given to her sister. 車被送給了她的妹妹。

→ 間接受詞（her sister）變為主詞並成為被動語句時，直接受詞（the car）會留在動詞的被動語態（was given）後面，看起來像是為動詞的被動語態接了受詞。其實不是這樣的，所以做題時要注意這一點。直接受詞（the car）變為主詞並成為被動語句時，動詞的被動語態後面接「介系詞 + 間接受詞」（to her sister）。

注意！ 一般的形式 4 動詞（give, send, grant）等的直接受詞變為主詞並成為被動語句時，動詞的被動語態後面接「介系詞 to + 間接受詞」。但有 buy, make, get, find 等形式 4 動詞時，就要把介系詞 to 替換為 for。
The house was built <u>to</u>(→ for) homeless people
那個房子是爲無家可歸的人所建造的。

❷ 接受詞和受詞補語的形式 5 動詞成為被動語態時，受詞補語留在動詞的被動語態後面。

· 受詞補語為「名詞句」的形式 5 動詞的被動語態

主動語態 Victoria considered him a genius. Victoria 把他視爲天才了。

被動語態 He was considered a genius. 他被視爲天才。

→ 受詞（him）變為主詞成被動語句時，名詞句受詞補語（genius）直接留在動詞的被動語態（was considered）後面。要注意不要把這個看作是動詞的被動語態接了受詞的錯誤句。

· 受詞補語為「to 不定詞片語」的形式 5 動詞的被動語態

主動語態 He asked me to send a stamped envelope. 他拜託我寄一個附上了回郵的信封。

被動語態 I was asked to send a stamped envelope. 我被委託寄一個附上了回郵的信封。

→ 受詞（me）變為主詞成為被動語態時，to 不定詞的補語（to send~）直接留在動詞的被動語態（was asked）後面。

注意！ 1. 名詞句做受詞補語的形式 5 動詞有 consider（認為，把…視為），call（稱呼），elect（選舉）等，to 不定詞句受詞補語的形式 5 動詞有 advise（忠告），ask（邀請），expect（期待），invite（請求），remind（提醒），require（要求）等。

2. 請注意不要混淆了 consider 的形式 3 動詞和形式 5 動詞的用法。
The committee <u>is considered</u>(→ is considering) promoting her. 委員會考慮要將她升職。
⇨ 本句中 consider 是「考慮」的意思，也就是形式 3 動詞，當後面接受詞（promoting her）時，只能使用主動語態（is considering）。

多益實戰考題   多 益 會 出 這 樣 的 問 題

⊙ 用謂語的恰當語態填空。

2. Though somewhat new at making presentations, Paul Blakely is ------- the best public speaker of the team.

(A) consider   (B) to consider
(C) considering   (D) considered

1. Ray Murphy submitted a requisition form yesterday to make certain he ------- given a projector for today's presentation.

(A) has   (B) have
(C) is   (D) are

3. The research team ------- to make back-up files of all their work to prevent loss of valuable data.

(A) reminded   (B) was reminded
(C) will remind   (D) was reminding

03 情感動詞的主動語態 / 被動語態區別

❶ 及物動詞表示感情動作時，主詞是感情主因時用主動語態，主詞是受感情的對象時用被動語態。

趣味 滿足	interest 使發生興趣 fascinate 迷住	excite 使興奮 encourage 鼓勵	amuse 使歡樂 satisfy 滿意	please 使高興
失望 不滿足	disappoint 使失望 tire 使疲倦	discourage 使沮喪 trouble 使煩惱	dissatisfy 不滿意	depress 使消沉
荒唐 衝擊	bewilder 使迷惑	frustrate 挫敗	shock 衝擊	surprise 驚嚇

The results of the negotiations ~~were pleased~~ both of the attending parties. 協商的結果令所有參與的人都很高興。
               pleased

→ 主詞（The results）是使人高興的原因，所以用動詞的主動語態（pleased），而不用動詞的被動語態（were pleased）。

I ~~am pleasing~~ to hear that you are feeling better. 聽說你的身體有好轉，我很高興。
  am pleased

→ 主詞（I）是感到高興的物件，所以用動詞的被動語態 （am pleased），而不是動詞的主動語態（am pleasing）。

The regional director ~~was dissatisfied~~ the workers by refusing to give salary raises.
                  dissatisfied

區經理拒絕了調薪的請求，使員工感到不滿意。

→ 主詞（The regional director）是使人不滿意的原因，所以用動詞的主動語態（dissatisfied），而不用動詞的被動語態（was dissatisfied）。

The workers ~~dissatisfy~~ with management's handling of the situation. 員工們對管理階層的處理情況感到不滿。
          are dissatisfied

→ 主詞（The workers）感到了不滿，所以用動詞的被動語態（are dissatisfied），而不是動詞的主動語態（dissatisfy）。

The news ~~was surprised~~ the man. 新聞使那個人感到驚訝。
         surprised

→ 主詞（The news）是使人驚訝的原因，所以用動詞的主動語態（surprised），而不是動詞的被動語態（be surprised）。

The man ~~surprised~~ by the news. 那個人被新聞嚇到了。
    was surprised

→ 主詞（The man）是受驚嚇的對象，所以用動詞的被動語態（was surprised），而不是動詞的主動語態（surprised）。

多益實戰考題　　　　　　　多益會出這樣的問題

⊙ 用謂語的恰當語態填空。
常出現只要求填入 be 動詞後面的現在分詞或過去分詞的題目，而不是要求單字的原形。

1. Young businessmen who set up venture companies should guard against being ------- during the first year of operations.

(A) disappoint   (B) disappointed
(C) disappointing   (D) disappointment

2. When he took up cooking, Jerry Porter was ------- to learn how easy it was to make inexpensive, great-tasting meals.

(A) fascinate   (B) fascinating
(C) being fascinated   (D) fascinated

3. The manager ------- her staff with news of an upcoming bonus if sales figures reached company goals by the end of the quarter.

(A) encourage   (B) was encouraged
(C) encouraging   (D) encouraged

正確答案　P34

❶ 形式 3 動詞的被動語態 + 介系詞

be amused at ~ 對…感到高興	be surprised at ~ 對…感到驚訝	be worried about ~ 擔心…
be pleased with ~ 對…感到高興	be alarmed at ~ 對…感到驚慌	be concerned about / with ~ 擔心…
be delighted with ~ 對…感到高興	be astonished at ~ 對…感到驚訝	be bored with ~ 厭倦…
be satisfied with ~ 對…感到滿足	be frightened at ~ 對…感到驚恐	be tired of ~ 疲倦…
be gratified with ~ 對…感到滿足	be shocked at ~ 對…感到震驚	be ashamed of ~ 對…感到羞愧
be disappointed at ~ 對…感到失望		be convinced of ~ 確信…
be interested in ~ 對…有興趣	be absorbed in ~ 熱衷於…	be equipped with ~ 配備…
be involved in ~ 關於…	be indulged in ~ 沉迷於…	be covered with ~ 被…覆蓋
be engaged in ~ 從事…	be devoted to ~ 獻身於…	be crowded with ~ 被…擠
be associated with ~ 關聯於…	be dedicated to ~ 獻身於…	be based on ~ 以…為基礎
be related to ~ 關係於…	be skilled in ~ 努力，熟練於…	be exposed to ~ 暴露在…

This hotel room is equipped with luxurious baths and tiles.
這間客房具備豪華浴缸和磁磚。

The strength of the alloy is closely related to the quality of the ore.
合金的強度與礦石的質量有密切的關係。

❷ 形式 5 動詞的被動語態 + to 不定詞片語

be asked to 被邀請做…	be required to 被要求做…	be expected to 期待做…
be told to 被告知做…	be urged to 被命令做…	be allowed to 允許做…
be reminded to 被提醒做…	be advised to 被建議做…	be intended to 為了做…
be encouraged to 被勸告做…	be invited to 被邀請做…	be scheduled to 打算做…

The project managers are required to fill in forms and get them signed.
專案經理被要求填好表格後簽字。

Employees are reminded to use office e-mail only for business purposes.
職員們被提醒只能因公使用辦公室的電子郵件

多益實戰考題	多 益 會 出 這 樣 的 問 題

⊙ 用謂語的恰當語態填空。
除了填入正確動詞語態的問題外，最近還出在形式 5 動詞的被動語態後面加 to 不定詞片語的問題。

1. The accounting team is ------- to providing accurate billing statements and resolving all customer enquiries within twenty-four hours.

(A) dedicating (B) dedicated
(C) dedicate (D) dedication

2. As a member of our office you are invited ------- the annual charity auction.

(A) attending (B) to attend
(C) attends (D) attend

3. We are truly ------- with the positive consumer response to our new marketing strategy.

(A) delight (B) delighting
(C) delighted (D) delightedly

正確答案 P34

HACKERS PRACTICE ● ● ● ● ● ● ● ● ● ● ● ● ● ●

Practice 1 選擇正確的時態。

01 Judy (implies / is implied) that she was treated unfairly by management recently.

02 Sales (expect / are expected) to decrease as a result of the recession.

03 The budget director (rejected / was rejected) the plan to cut back on spending.

04 The business owner was (frustrating / frustrated) by the lack of adequate capital to make investments.

05 Artists (have painted / have been painted) a large mural on a wall in the conference hall.

06 The plans for the merger (will take / will be taken) at least a month to evaluate.

07 Jason was (exciting / excited) to learn that he was being considered for a promotion.

Practice 2 改正錯誤的地方。

08 Employee motivation is closely relating to the success of a company.

09 The building will be undergoing renovation for the next three weeks.

10 A proposal for a partnership offered to an Italian firm last week.

11 This product made for busy working moms who need help in the kitchen.

12 All assembly line workers are advised wearing protective eyewear and gloves while working.

13 A lifelong honorary membership in the firm has granted to the retired CEO.

14 The company is dedicated to its goal of introducing products that are modern, functional, and affordable.

正確答案 P34

Part V

01 After consulting with a systems analyst, they were able to pinpoint what office procedures should be -------.

(A) streamlining   (B) streamlined
(C) streamline   (D) to streamline

02 A number of clients have been ------- with the firm since it was reorganized in an attempt to decrease expenditures.

(A) dissatisfying   (B) dissatisfy
(C) dissatisfies   (D) dissatisfied

03 A replacement for the outgoing advertising manager has not yet been -------, but the possibilities have been narrowed down to five applicants.

(A) chose   (B) choice
(C) chosen   (D) choose

04 Each year, Gibbins Foods, a local food manufacturer ------- five thousand cans of vegetables to the city's homeless shelters.

(A) donates   (B) to donate
(C) donating   (D) are donated

05 The contract stipulates that an employee is ------- to do overtime during weeks that presentations or special reports are being prepared.

(A) requirement   (B) requires
(C) required   (D) requisition

06 Dr. Juan Taveras, who ------- the first neuroradiology training program in the United States, will speak at the 10th International Neurological Conference.

(A) developed   (B) developing
(C) development   (D) develops

07 A power distribution system would need to be ------- should the owner ever consider expanding the plant.

(A) installation   (B) installed
(C) install   (D) installing

08 The campaigns that ------- assigned to the broadcasting division have been scrapped due to lack of support.

(A) having   (B) were
(C) be   (D) had

09 The announcement in the newsletter is meant to ------- Mr. Meyer's remarks on the merger between the two communications firms.

(A) clarified   (B) be clarified
(C) clarification   (D) clarify

10 No matter what the brand, computers purchased at this shop will be ------- free of charge for a full year from the date of purchase.

(A) service   (B) servicing
(C) to service   (D) serviced

11 First class seats are ------- with Internet hook-ups, global telephones and faxing capabilities for all of your airborne professional needs.

(A) equip   (B) equipment
(C) equipped   (D) equipping

12 The manager is ------- to announce that Morgan & Co. will be giving stock options to all interested employees.

(A) please   (B) pleased
(C) pleasant   (D) pleasing

13 After today's planning session is completed, the members of each group will be ------- a report of their team's objectives for the next three years.

(A) generation   (B) generate
(C) generated   (D) generating

14 We would like you to be escorted ------- our assistant manager who will give you a tour of the company's offices and facilities.

(A) with   (B) from
(C) by   (D) into

15 The East Valley Mall will be ------- later during the holiday season to allow shoppers to meet their last minute gift preparation needs.

(A) close   (B) closes
(C) to close   (D) closing

16 To meet the special needs of our branches in Asia, a total of twenty-four trained staff will ------- to Japan, Hong Kong, and Thailand.

(A) send   (B) be sent
(C) be sending   (D) have sent

17 The problem between the management and some of the staff ------- at the emergency meeting to the satisfaction of those involved.

(A) resolves   (B) is resolving
(C) has resolved   (D) has been resolved

18 Membership at the exclusive sports club ------- benefits ranging from the use of all sports equipment to discounted rates at the club's restaurant and bar.

(A) includes   (B) to include
(C) have included   (D) including

19 The new CEO will ------- at a dinner to be held at the residence of a member of the Board of Directors.

(A) be honoring   (B) be honored
(C) honor   (D) have honored

20 The introduction of the specially trained conflict resolution advisors ------- to reduce tension between management and frustrated employees.

(A) expected
(B) is expected
(C) has been expecting
(D) will have been expecting

21 If the director ------- that the top candidate was still a consultant for Master Lines, Inc., he could have given others greater priority.

(A) tell   (B) telling
(C) had told   (D) had been told

22 ------- the machine's continued operation, a thorough check by maintenance personnel should take place bimonthly.

(A) To be ensure   (B) To ensure
(C) Will ensure   (D) Ensured

23 The winners of the logo contest are ------- to be at the dinner this evening, which will begin at 8:00 P.M. at the International Plaza Hotel's Blue Room.

(A) plan   (B) plans
(C) planning   (D) planned

24 In order to reduce the number of customer complaints, all telephone representatives are asked ------- the new guidelines.

(A) following   (B) being followed
(C) to follow   (D) to be followed

25 To test the efficacy of the product, the bottles ------- in water mixed with the recommended amount of the sterilizing liquid.

(A) were washing   (B) were washed
(C) have washed   (D) being washed

26 Participants in the seminar were ------- to make hotel reservations by the date indicated on the list of hotels.

(A) advisable   (B) advisory
(C) advising   (D) advised

27 Before structural renovations take place, all businesses must ------- the building as indicated in the official notice issued last month.

(A) vacant   (B) vacancy
(C) vacate   (D) be vacated

28 Access to the computer terminals ------- during evening hours, so it is necessary for us to finish the work during the day.

(A) restrict   (B) to restrict
(C) is restricted   (D) has restricted

正確答案　P34

Chapter 8

假設語氣

啊哈!! 愉快地打基礎

1 假設語氣文章用於假設與現在或過去事實相反的情況。

If I were rich, I would travel the world. 如果我很有錢，我會去環遊世界。

If I had been rich, I would have led a very different life.
如果我曾經有錢，在過去我就會走向一個完全不一樣的人生。

第一句話中用「如果我很有錢」來假設了與現在事實相反的情況。（現在不是有錢的人假設了如果自己是很有錢，那他將會去環遊世界。）
第二句話中用「如果我曾經有錢」來假設了與過去事實相反的情況。（過去不是有錢的人假設了如果當時自己是有錢人，那他在那個過去的時間點就會走向一個完全不一樣的人生。）

2 假設語氣的句子一般以 if 開頭，並用特殊時態。

If I won a million dollars, I would faint.
如果我贏了一百萬美元，我會昏倒的。

假設語氣句子中為了假設與「現在事實」相反的情況，在 if 子句中用「過去式」（won），在主句中用「助動詞的過去形式 + 動詞原形」（would faint）。

If I had won the lottery, I would have sent many poor teenagers to college.
我要是中了樂透彩，我早就讓那些貧困的青少年上大學了。

假設語氣句中為了假設與「過去事實」相反的情況，在 if 子句中用「過去完成式」（had won），在主句中用「助動詞的過去形式 + have p.p.」（would have sent）。

3 要區分假設語氣句和以 if 開頭的條件子句。

If you experience any difficulties, please contact one of our customer service staff.
如果遇到困難，請與我們的客服人員聯繫。

If I have a midday break tomorrow, we will meet up for a lunch meeting.
如果明天中午我有休息時間，我們就可以見個面一起吃午餐。

就像這兩個句子一樣把某件事看作事實的用法叫直敘法，這樣的 if 子句叫條件子句。條件子句並不是用特殊時態，而是用一般的時態（表示現在式用現在時態，表示過去式用過去時態）。

01 假設語氣未來式 / 過去式 / 過去完成式

❶ 在假設語氣未來式 / 過去式 / 過去完成式文章中，if 子句與主句的時態一致。

未來式	If + 主詞 + should + 動詞原形, 主詞 + will (can, may, should) + 動詞原形	不可能實現的未來假設
過去式	If + 主詞 + 動詞過去式 (be 動詞用 were), 主詞 + would (could, might, should) + 動詞原形	與現在事實相反的假設
過去完成式	If + 主詞 + had p.p., 主詞 + would (could, might, should) have p.p.	與過去事實相反的假設

If rain should come **today, we** will move **the party indoors.**
倘若今天下雨，我們將會把派對改在室內。 ⇨ 今天下雨的可能性很小。

If computers were **cheap, I** would buy **ten of them for my home.**
假如電腦便宜，那我就會買十台電腦放在家。 ⇨ 事實上電腦不便宜，所以不可能買十台。

If Nancy had come, **Jeff** might have turned **down the invitation.**
假如 Nancy 來過，那 Jeff 會拒絕邀請的。 ⇨ 因為 Nancy 沒有來，所以 Jeff 接受了邀請。

注意! 「if + 主詞 + should~，命令句」表示鄭重地建議，當發生問題或需要幫助時，他們會提供服務。這種句型常出現在多益考試中。
If you should **experience any problems with your telephone service,** <u>please report them to the front desk.</u>
當電話服務出現問題時，請與櫃枱聯繫。

❷ 混合假設語氣中 if 子句和主句的時態不一致。

If 主詞 **had p.p.,**	主詞 **would** 動詞原形	「如果…（現在）就…」
假設語氣過去完成式	假設語氣過去式	

→ if 子句裡用了表示與過去事實相反的「假設語氣過去完成式」，主句中用了表示與現在事實相反的「假設語氣過去式」。

If I had asked **for time off last month, I** would be **on vacation now.**
要是上個月申請了休假，那我現在應該在休假中。 ⇨ 上個月沒有申請休假，所以現在不在休假中。
→ if 子句中用了表示與過去事實相反的假設語氣過去完成式 (had asked)，但在主句中用了表示與現在事實相反的假設語氣過去式 (would be)。

注意! 混合假設語氣的主句中常出現表示現在時態的單字 (now, today)。
If I <u>had talked</u> **with my boss last week, the problem** <u>would be solved</u> **by** <u>now</u>.
要是上週跟上司提到這件事的話，那現在應該解決了。
⇨ if 子句中用了假設語氣過去完成式，但主句裡以 now 表示是現在假設語氣，所以用假設語氣過去式。

多益實戰考題　　　　　多 益 會 出 這 樣 的 問 題

⊙ 填假設語氣動詞。
出現最多的是填入假設語氣過去完成式的題目。

2. If personal income taxes had been lowered, the national economy ------- much more quickly.

  (A) recovered
  (B) has recovered
  (C) would have recovered
  (D) has been recovered

1. If measures had not been taken to reduce company expenses, the added costs would ------- by the customers.

  (A) assume　　　　(B) have been assumed
  (C) had been assumed　(D) be assuming

3. If the client had come on time, these negotiations ------- completed by now.

  (A) would be　　　　(B) would have been
  (C) wouldn't have been　(D) would not be

正確答案　P37

02 沒有 if 的假設語氣：假設語氣倒裝和區分 without

❶ 假設語氣中可省略 if，這時可以調換主詞和助動詞的位置寫成倒裝句。

未來	If + 主詞 should + 動詞原形，主詞 + will (can, may, should) + 動詞原形 Í Should + 主詞 + 動詞原形，主詞 + will (can, may, should) + 動詞原形
過去	If + 主詞 + 動詞過去式 (be 動詞用 were), 主詞 + would (could, might, should) + 動詞原形 Í Were + 主詞 + 名詞，形容詞等，主詞 + would (could, might, should) + 動詞原形
過去完成	If + 主詞 + had p.p., 主詞 + would (could, might, should) have p.p. Í Had + 主詞 + p.p., 主詞 + would (could, might, should) have p.p.

If Arnold should <u>call</u>, he can come at any time. 如果 Arnold 打電話來，他隨時都可以來。
⇨ Should Arnold <u>call</u>, he can come at any time.

If Brad and I were not <u>friends</u>, I would be interested in dating him. 假如 Brad 和我不是朋友，那我就會有興趣跟他約會的。
⇨ Were Brad and I not <u>friends</u>, I would be interested in dating him.

If he had worked harder, he would have gotten the promotion. 他如果當時再多努力一點，很可能早就會升職了。
⇨ Had he <u>worked</u> harder, he would have gotten the promotion.

❷ If 子句可以被「without + 名詞」代替成為假設語氣。

假設語氣過去式	主詞 would 動詞原形 +「without + 名詞」(= if it were not for + 名詞)　　假如沒有…將會…
假設語氣過去完成式	主詞 would have p.p. +「without + 名詞」(= if it had not been for +名詞) 假如沒有…（過），就…

I couldn't do it <u>without you</u>. 假如沒有你，我就做不到。

I could never have done it <u>without you</u>. 假如沒有你，我當時不可能做到。

注意！ 也可以用 otherwise 代替 if 子句。

He took a taxi; otherwise (=if he had not taken a taxi), he would not have made the meeting on time.
他當時叫了輛計程車，否則的話，他就不能準時到達會議了。

多益實戰考題　　　　　　　多 益 會 出 這 樣 的 問 題

⊙ 填假設語氣動詞。
會出現填 should 或 p.p.等假設語氣中的動詞等題目。

2. Had the team submitted the report on schedule, the manager ------- to postpone the meeting of the Board of Directors.

(A) did not have　　　　(B) would not be had
(C) would not had　　　(D) would not have had

1. Had the contract ------- earlier, we might have been able to discuss the conditions and make a decision before the week's end.

(A) deliver　　　　　　(B) delivered
(C) been delivered　　　(D) were delivered

3. ------- you need any assistance while staying at our hotel, please don't hesitate to contact any of our staff.

(A) Perhaps　　　　　　(B) Whether
(C) May　　　　　　　 (D) Should

正確答案　P37

HACKERS PRACTICE ● ● ● ● ● ● ● ● ● ● ● ● ● ● ●

Practice 1 選擇正確的答案。

01 If it had not been for inflation, Jamie would (save / have saved) more money.

02 The team (can / could) never have done such a good job without Steve's input.

03 If I had filled out the application on time, I would (be / have been) working there now.

04 Kelly would not (take / have taken) the job if she had known about the other offer.

05 But for the dedicated efforts of our staff, the business (will / would) have crumbled under the competition.

06 If people (used / have used) public transportation more, the air would be less polluted.

07 Had the flight been cancelled, we would (miss / have missed) the meeting.

Practice 2 改正畫線部分。

08 If Joseph <u>applied</u> for the job, he would have been hired.

09 If it were not for its loyal employees, the company <u>is not</u> where it is today.

10 If Jack <u>asked</u> the workers politely to work overtime, they would have at least considered it.

11 Had the client called about the problem, it <u>will be</u> solved immediately by the representative.

12 If Erin <u>bought</u> that house, she would have put herself into deep debt.

13 If she <u>has finished</u> her work this week, she would have gone shopping with us.

14 Our public relations department <u>shall have been</u> more prepared to handle the press' questions.

Part V

01 If customers were unhappy with the quality of a product, the store ------- it or provide a refund.

(A) would exchange   (B) exchange
(C) have exchanged   (D) will exchange

02 Had we ------- that Mr. Robbins had a case pending in criminal court, we would never have hired him for the job.

(A) been known   (B) knew
(C) know   (D) known

03 The company ------- never have won the account without the support of the very talented copywriters in the advertising division.

(A) would   (B) need
(C) must   (D) can

04 If all members of our staff were consistently productive, it is likely that our output ------- greater.

(A) have been   (B) would be
(C) been   (D) be

05 The reductions in the budget will have serious ------- on what projects will be executed in the next quarter.

(A) implicating   (B) implicates
(C) implications (D) implicated

06 If insolvency laws do not change and continue to favor creditors, many small-scale companies ------- bankrupt.

(A) have gone   (B) will go
(C) went   (D) goes

07 The supervisor commented that the manual could ------- better had the company hired an editor to go over the material before it was printed.

(A) organize   (B) be organized
(C) have organized   (D) have been organized

08 The health clubs in the city ------- amenities such as weight machines and separate saunas for men and women.

(A) is providing   (B) provide
(C) provides   (D) providing

09 The recurring problem of unheated rooms would ------- if the owner had responded to the tenants' initial complaints.

(A) have been elimination
(B) had been eliminated
(C) have been eliminated
(D) have been eliminating

10 Had the president ------- that an important client was waiting, he would have asked him to wait in his office.

(A) been informed   (B) be informed
(C) informed   (D) inform

11 The director ------- out of the country until next month, during which time his assistant will take charge of ongoing projects.

(A) has been   (B) will be
(C) is being   (D) will have been

12 If plans ------- made sooner, Gilbert & Sons would be conducting the feasibility study for the Safeway Water Project by now.

(A) were being   (B) was being
(C) had been   (D) have been

13 If the error had not been reported immediately, the customer ------- his order until after the Christmas season had ended.

(A) would not have received
(B) would not receive
(C) did not receive
(D) would not be received

14 The internet service provider requests that subscribers ------- certain that their systems are protected with a reliable anti-virus program.

(A) made   (B) making
(C) make   (D) to make

15 If it had not been for a tip from my broker, I ------- thousands of dollars in doomed stocks.

(A) was lost   (B) have lost
(C) would lose   (D) would have lost

16 ------- the machine parts arrived promptly, we would have been able to finish assembling the machine in time for its first run.

(A) Have   (B) Had
(C) Should   (D) Were

17 A world-renowned economist ------- that except for the euro, currencies around the world will continue to devalue.

(A) is predicted   (B) predict
(C) predicts   (D) predicting

18 If preparations had been made for the presentation, it ------- much easier to sell the proposal.

(A) would be   (B) has been
(C) had been   (D) would have been

19 The original documents would not have materialized ------- continued efforts from our ever dedicated and thorough research team.

(A) so as   (B) as to
(C) in that   (D) if not for

20 Had estimated figures been more accurate, strategists would ------- a better financial plan to tackle the budget deficit.

(A) create   (B) be creating
(C) have created   (D) had been created

正確答案 P38

Section 3 非謂語動詞

to 不定詞

啊哈!! 愉快地打基礎

1 to 不定詞（to + 動詞原形）出於動詞。但 to 不定詞在句子中不能當做謂語，而是當名詞，形容詞，副詞等來使用。

I to like apples. （×）
I like to travel abroad. （○）　　　　我喜歡海外旅行。
I want something to eat. （○）　　　　我想要吃的。
I work to make money. （○）　　　　我為了賺錢而工作。

從上文中可以看出 to like 不能做動詞角色，to travel 在動詞 like 後面以名詞角色做受詞，to eat 在名詞 something 後面做修飾它的形容。還有 to make 以副詞的角色做動詞 work 的目的。像這樣動詞原形加上 to 形成的 to 不定詞片語的詞性不確定，因而可以在句子中充當多種身分，所以我們把它叫做「不定詞」。

2 to 不定詞在句中不能當做動詞，但保持動詞的性質，所以可以接受詞和補語，也可以被副詞修飾。

I want to learn magic.　　　　我想學魔術。
I want to be a magician.　　　　我想成為魔術師。
I need to exercise regularly.　　　　我需要規律地運動。

從上文中可以看出 to learn 接了受詞 magic，to be 接了補語 a magician。
還有 to exercise 被副詞 regularly 修飾。像這樣的「to 不定詞 + 受詞 / 補語 / 副詞」形式稱為「to 不定詞句」。

01 to不定詞的作用

❶ to不定詞作名詞、形容詞、副詞等作用。

- 像名詞一樣做主詞、受詞、補語。

  主詞　　To observe is one way of learning new things. 觀察是學習新事物的方法之一。

  受詞　　You need to call a service technician. 你應該打電話給技術服務人員。

  主詞補語　The goal of the meeting is to reach a decision. 會議的目的是做出決定。

  受詞補語　Janice helped Craig to write the report. Janice 幫助 Craig 寫報告書。

- 像形容詞一樣在名詞後面修飾它。

  修飾名詞　He has a letter to type. 他有一封信需要打（字）。

- 像副詞一樣表示目的，原因和結果等。

  目的　　I am writing to inquire whether more funds are available. 我寫信的目的是想詢問能否籌集更多的資金。

  原因　　I am pleased to grant Betty a promotion to vice president. 我很高興把 Betty 升到副董事的職位。

  結果　　He called the center only to find out the tickets had sold out. 他打電話到售票中心發現票已賣光。

→ 底下畫線的部分是 to 不定詞的核心部分，多益考試中常考這部分。

注意！　1. to 不定詞可以做實際主詞和實際受詞。

It is important to ensure the money is safe. 確保錢財的安全是很重要的。

Lewis will make it a point to reward employees based on performance. Lewis 會視表現來獎勵職員。

2. to 不定詞表示「目的」時，可以用 in order to，so as to 代替 to。

He applied for a bank loan in order to finance a small business. 他為他的小規模事業向銀行申請了貸款。

3. 表示人的行為和目的（為做…）時，不能用「介系詞 for + Ving」，只能用 to 不定詞。

For passing the test(→To pass the test) he had to work hard. 為了通過考試，他必須努力學習。

表示了人要通過考試的目的，所以要用 to 不定詞，不能用 for Ving。

❷ 動詞不能到 to 不定詞的位置。

You promised ~~look over~~ my report! 你答應過要檢查我的報告！
　　　　　　　to look over

→ 為成為動詞（promised）的受詞，不能用動詞（look over），只能用做名詞角色的 to 不定詞（to look over）

The memo indicated a need for the factory ~~enhance~~ its efficiency. 備忘錄指出這家工廠需要提高效率。
　　　　　　　　　　　　　　　　　to enhance

→ 為修飾名詞（a need），不能用動詞（enhance），只能用當做形容詞角色的 to 不定詞（to enhance）。

多益實戰考題　　　多 益 會 出 這 樣 的 問 題

⊙ 填 to 不定詞。
　最常出現的是表示目的的 to 不定詞作副詞的題目。

2. The purpose of the program is ------- museum staff with the know-how and feedback to set priorities and identify areas for change.

(A) provide　　　　　(B) provided
(C) provision　　　　(D) to provide

1. The firm temporarily closed one of its branch offices ------- operating expenses.

(A) will reduce　　　(B) reduces
(C) reduced　　　　(D) to reduce

3. The Dogwood Company is pleased ------- that you can now purchase seeds and all your gardening needs directly from their website.

(A) to announce　　　(B) announcement
(C) announced　　　(D) be announcing

正確答案　P40

❶ to不定詞有「to + 動詞原形」的形態。

Use this telephone line ~~to communication~~ with the main office. 請用這支電話與本部聯繫。
~~for communicate~~
to communicate

→ to不定詞後面不能接名詞性單字，只能接動詞原形。而且不能用for代替to。

❷ to不定詞（to + 動詞原形）的被動語態是 to be p.p.，進行式是 to be Ving，完成式是 to have p.p.。

I really didn't like to be told what to do. 我真的不喜歡別人對我下命令。
→ 為了表示不是我下命令，而是我被下命令，用to不定詞的被動語態（to be told）。

I observed that the students appeared to be cheating during long exams.
在長期考試中，我似乎看到學生作弊。
→ 為了表示作弊的動作在進行中，用to不定詞的進行式（to be cheating）。

It is nice to have finished the work. 完成工作太好啦。
→ 為表示完成工作的時間點（finish）在感到高興的時間點（is nice）之前，用了to 不定詞的完成式（to have finished）。

注意！ need，deserve，require 後的to不定詞的被動語態可以用 Ving 替換。
Your hair needs to be cut. = Your hair needs cutting. 你該剪頭髮了。

❸ to 不定詞需要主詞時的連接方式：to的前面接「for + 名詞」或「for + 受格代名詞」。

His parents' goal was for Rob to become a doctor. 他父母的願望是讓Rob成為醫生。
→ to 不定詞前接「for + 名詞」（for Rob），表示要成為醫生的是Rob，而不是他父母。

In order for us to do a good job, we must have more time. 為了讓我們能把工作做好，我們需要有更多的時間。
→ to 不定詞前接 「for + 受格代名詞」（for us），表示是我們要把工作做好。

多益實戰考題　　　　　　　　　　多 益 會 出 這 樣 的 問 題

⊙ 填入to不定詞中的to或動詞原形或in order to。

2. Now that the new branch has opened, the company can use this opportunity to ------- business in Latin America.

(A) expand
(B) expanding
(C) expanded
(D) have expanded

1. Mr. Cummings, who is leading the new project, would like all the team members to come together ------- brainstorm ideas about marketing strategies.

(A) for
(B) to
(C) as
(D) with

3. The landlord will shut off the heating system in the entire building ------- determine why some floors are not being properly heated.

(A) as if
(B) such that
(C) in order to
(D) in spite of

正確答案 P40

Hackers Skill ｜ 不能用「to + 名詞」或「for + 動詞原形」來代替「to + 動詞原形」。

03 可以接 to 不定詞的動詞、名詞、形容詞

❶ 可接 to 不定詞的動詞

動詞 + 受詞（to 不定詞）					
願意	want to	need to	wish to	hope to	desire to	expect to
計畫	plan to	aim to	decide to			
提議 / 約定 / 拒絕	propose to	offer to	ask to	promise to	agree to	refuse to
假裝 / 設法	fail to	serve to	pretend to	afford to	manage to	

動詞 + 受詞 + 補語（to 不定詞）					
願意	want to	need to	expect to	invite to	ask to
鼓勵	encourage to	persuade to	convince to	cause to	
強調	force to	compel to	get to	tell to	require to
允許	allow to	permit to	enable to	forbid to（禁止）	
告訴	remind to	warn to	advise to		

動詞 + 補語（to 不定詞）		
	remain to 尚待　　seem to 好像　　appear to 看似	

Management <u>wants</u> to reorganize the marketing division. 管理階層希望重組行銷部。

Their commitment to quality <u>enabled the company</u> to win the contract. 對品質的精益求精使那家公司成功贏得合約。

How well this plan will work <u>remains</u> to be seen. 這個計畫會進行的如何還得拭目以待。

❷ 可接 to 不定詞的名詞

ability to 能力	authority to 許可權	capacity to 能力	chance to 機會	claim to 主張
decision to 決定	effort to 努力	need to 必要	opportunity to 機會	plan to 計畫
readiness to 願意	right to 權利	time to 時間	way to 方法	wish to 希望

Chefs should have the <u>ability</u> to create different dishes. 廚師要有做出多種料理的能力。

❸ 可接 to 不定詞的形容詞

可能	be able to 有能力做…	be ready to 準備做…	be willing to 願意做…	be likely to 很有可能做…
熱情	be eager to 非常渴望做…	be anxious to 非常希望做…		
感情	be pleased to 對…感到高興	be delighted to 很高興…		
判斷	be easy to 容易做…	be difficult to 難於做…	be good to 有利 / 適合於…	be dangerous to 做…有危險

Jody should be <u>able</u> to work well with the new employee. Jody 應該有跟新職員和睦相處的能力。

多益實戰考題　　　　多 益 會 出 這 樣 的 問 題

⊙ 填 to 不定詞。

1. Having failed ------- a consensus, the manager asked that the decision be postponed.

   (A) creating　　　　(B) created
   (C) to creating　　　(D) to create

2. Please take time ------- the names on this invitation list and feel free to add anyone whom we might have missed.

   (A) review　　　　(B) be reviewed
   (C) to review　　　(D) reviewing

3. The CEO believes that the staff will be able ------- on the Albers Project once the staff evaluations are completed.

   (A) concentrate　　　(B) concentrating
   (C) to concentration　(D) to concentrate

正確答案　P40

04 有些動詞不能接 to 不定詞，而是接原形不定詞來做受詞或補語

❶ 使役動詞（make，let，have）+ 受詞 + 原形不定詞

Mrs. Banks <u>let</u> us ~~to~~ take the day off. Banks夫人讓我們休息一天。
→ 使役動詞let的受詞補語不能用to不定詞，而是要用原形不定詞，所以要省略to。

注意！ 1. 以「受詞補語」這種形式表示被動意義時，受詞補語不能用原形不定詞，而是要用p.p.。
He will have his car repair(→repaired). 他會讓他的車得到修理（他會把車送去修理的）。
⇨「他的車被修理」表示了被動語態，所以用p.p.（repaired）來代替原形不定詞（repair）。

2. get有「使…」的意思，但這時的受詞補語用to不定詞，而不是原形不定詞。
I got Ted <u>host</u>(→to host) the reception. 我讓Ted主持那個宴會。
I got the project (to be) <u>authorized</u> by management. 我使企劃得到了管理階層的認可。
⇨以「受詞補語」這種形式表示被動意義時，get也能接p.p.的受詞補語。這時的p.p.是省略了to be p.p.的to be而形成的。

❷ 準使役動詞help（+ 受詞）+ 原形不定詞 / to不定詞

Vince <u>helped</u> Carol (to) complete the assignment. Vince幫忙Carol完成了任務。
Company retreats <u>help</u> (to) strengthen employee relationships. 公司的休養計畫加強了職員之間的關係。
→ 準使役動詞help的受詞補語都可以用原形不定詞和to不定詞。

❸ 感官動詞（hear，see，watch，notice）+ 受詞 + 原形不定詞 / 現在分詞

I <u>saw</u> her cross the road. 我看到她過馬路。
I <u>saw</u> her crossing the road. 我看到她正在過馬路。
→ 感官動詞saw的受詞補語都可以用原形不定詞和現在分詞。現在分詞強調動作的進行狀態。

注意！ 以「受詞補語」這種形式表示被動意義時，受詞補語要用p.p.，而不是原形不定詞或現在分詞。
I heard my name <u>repeat</u>(→repeated). 我聽到我的名字反覆地被叫。

多益實戰考題　　　　　　　　多 益 會 出 這 樣 的 問 題

⊙ 填原形不定詞。

1. The training program offered by the company can help ------- your future work options.

(A) broad　　　　　(B) broaden
(C) broader　　　　(D) broadly

2. The general manager will have his assistant ------- the proceedings of the meeting and prepare a report for senior management.

(A) transcribe　　　(B) to be transcribed
(C) be transcribing　(D) transcribed

3. Employees who want to do volunteer work sponsored by the company are to let their supervisors ------- before the end of the week.

(A) know　　　　　(B) to know
(C) known　　　　　(D) knowing

正確答案　**P41**

HACKERS PRACTICE ● ● ● ● ● ● ● ● ● ● ● ● ● ● ● ● ● ●

Practice 1 選擇正確的答案。

01 The CEO will be happy (win / to win) a vote of confidence from the board.

02 It is possible to (custom / customize) this program if it does not suit you.

03 The ability (type / to type) quickly and accurately is a valuable skill.

04 Darren let problems in his personal life (to influence / influence) his performance at work.

05 Your presence at the administrative office is required for the wage claim (proceed/to proceed).

06 Sonia arranged to have the package (deliver / delivered) to the office overnight.

07 Your suggestion will enable us (improving / to improve) the quality of our products.

Practice 2 改正錯誤的地方。

08 The employee had no right signing for the shipment brought to the office Saturday.

09 The accountants want to be warned when the IRS is coming to visit.

10 The head office must send the approval slip for Mr. Reynolds start working with us.

11 The manager will have a study do by the research department.

12 If you want to keep your job, you'd better be willing put in more effort.

13 If you don't have time today, get the assistant to bring the files over to management.

14 There are different ways attract business to areas where unemployment is high.

正確答案 P41

Part V

01 Mr. Coulter designated a room for archive storage in order ------- the loss or damage of important documents.

(A) to curtail   (B) to be curtailed
(C) curtailed   (D) curtailment

02 Customers who need ------- lengthy documents over the Internet should have their network connection configured to optimize large data transfers.

(A) receive   (B) to receive
(C) receiving   (D) reception

03 It was important ------- the presentation before giving it to the over 200 business school graduates in the audience.

(A) rehearse   (B) rehearsal
(C) to rehearse   (D) rehearsed

04 If you ------- to order a copy of this report, please fill out the attached form and mail it to the following address.

(A) have liked   (B) were liked
(C) had liked   (D) would like

05 The company can either deliver the customer's purchase or arrange ------- the customer to pick up his order at a convenient time.

(A) of   (B) from
(C) for   (D) to

06 Employers should make it routine ------- the strengths of each employee in order to use their talents to full advantage.

(A) to assess   (B) for assessing
(C) assess   (D) assessed

07 The problem is that nobody in the office has the authority ------- make a decision regarding her employment status.

(A) for   (B) with
(C) to   (D) as

08 Mr. Rosenberg had his secretary ------- out copies of the agenda to each of the members of the Board of Directors.

(A) is mailing   (B) mail
(C) mailed   (D) to mail

09 The supervisor has taken a more active interest in the way the elite sales force -------.

(A) managing   (B) manager
(C) is managed   (D) manages

10 Some customers prefer ------- a minimum balance in their checking accounts rather than pay monthly fees.

(A) to maintain   (B) is maintaining
(C) maintained   (D) maintain

11 How the public will react to the soft drink's new formula remains ------- seen.

(A) to be   (B) being
(C) have been   (D) been

12 Customer complaints show that there may be a need for Net Manage ------- the present quality assurance and monitoring systems.

(A) enhance   (B) to enhance
(C) enhancing   (D) to enhancing

13 Please ------- park your cars in the commercial lot next to our building, as it is for client use only.

(A) no   (B) not
(C) not to   (D) do not

14 The building owner has a policy of letting lessees ------- to unoccupied units if they are dissatisfied with their present unit.

(A) to move   (B) be moving
(C) move   (D) to be moved

15 As a still-life photographer, Mr. Bryant aims to ------- a particular mood when he snaps the shutter.

(A) capture   (B) captured
(C) capturing   (D) have captured

16 Lack of sleep is a major ------- in the unbelievably fast service of Small World 24-hour international delivery corporation.

(A) to factor   (B) factored
(C) factor   (D) factorable

17 The candidate promised to ------- prescription drug prices by as much as 30 percent if voted into office.

(A) low   (B) lower
(C) lowering   (D) having lowered

18 A notice about our annual system upgrade ------- on the company bulletin board, detailing what steps should be performed by next week.

(A) posts   (B) posted
(C) to be posted   (D) was posted

19 Having been unable ------- the performance evaluations, the manager put several projects on hold until the evaluations were finished.

(A) complete   (B) to complete
(C) completing   (D) completion

20 If a client is not utterly satisfied ------- an ad campaign, we will return to the drawing board to start again.

(A) by   (B) to
(C) with   (D) for

21 Three people from the research department have been asked to investigate ways ------- non-taxable imported goods into the country.

(A) bring   (B) of bring
(C) to bring   (D) bringing

22 With the prices of natural gas and other energy sources increasing, utility companies are now encouraging people ------- energy.

(A) conserve   (B) conserved
(C) to conserve   (D) for conserving

23 I am calling ------- whether the factory will accept visitors on either Friday afternoon or Saturday morning.

(A) inquire   (B) to inquire
(C) inquired   (D) inquiring

24 I have enclosed two reference letters, and hope that this will serve ------- my credentials.

(A) to verify   (B) to verifying
(C) to be verifying   (D) to verification

25 Until a complete inquiry -------, no action will be taken by the president on the harassment case filed by a clerk.

(A) conducts   (B) is conducted
(C) is conducting   (D) will be conducted

26 For further help ------- the program, please refer to the instructions on our website or e-mail us with your specific question.

(A) install   (B) to install
(C) installed   (D) be installed

27 The projects committee advised the proposal writer ------- to the project beneficiaries in order to determine their real needs.

(A) talk   (B) talking
(C) talked   (D) to talk

28 Several new waiters and salespeople were hired ------- the influx of customers during the long holiday season.

(A) to handle   (B) handling
(C) to be handling   (D) to be handled

正確答案 P41

Chapter 10

動名詞

啊哈!! 愉快地打基礎

1　動名詞（動詞 + ing）雖然是基於動詞形成的，但動名詞在句子中的是當做名詞，而不是動詞。

She cleaning the house everyday.（×）
I hate cleaning.（○）我討厭打掃。

上文中的 cleaning 在句中當做名詞並作 hate 的受詞，而不是當做動詞。

2　動名詞仍然有動詞的性質，所以可以接受詞或補語，還可以被副詞修飾。

I like playing baseball.　　　　我喜歡打棒球。
Becoming a doctor is not easy.　當醫生不容易。
Eating slowly is a good habit.　細嚼慢嚥是個好習慣。

根據上文可知，playing 可以接受詞 baseball，Becoming 可以接補語 a doctor，Eating 可以被副詞 slowly 修飾。像這樣「動名詞 + 受詞 / 補語 / 副詞」的形態叫「動名詞句」。。

01 動名詞的作用、形態、及該動作所應對的主詞

❶ 動名詞可以在句中當做名詞並作主詞、受詞或補語。

主詞位置　　　<u>Providing</u> a loan **will allow the bank to collect interest.** 貸款可以讓銀行徵收利息。

受詞位置　　　**Stan enjoys** <u>playing</u> **golf**. Stan喜歡打高爾夫球。

介系詞受詞位置　**The director aims at** <u>reducing</u> **corporate debt**. 部長希望減少企業負債。

補語位置　　　**John's hobby is** <u>listening</u> **to music**. John的愛好是聽音樂。

→ 底下畫線的部分是動名詞的核心部分，多益考試中會常考這部分。

❷ 動詞不能取代動名詞的位置

Sarah is thinking about ~~buy~~ **a car**. Sarah正考慮買一輛車。
　　　　　　　　　　　　buying
→ 介系詞（about）的受詞不可以是動詞（buy），應該用做當名詞的動名詞（buying）。

❸ 動名詞（動詞 + ing）的被動語態是 being p.p.，完成式是 having p.p.。

Karen loves being looked **at in her new dress.** Karen喜歡自己穿著新衣服時的樣子被（別人）看到。
→ 不是Karen在看，而是被別人看。所以用動名詞的被動語態（being looked）。

He denied having lied. 他否認他撒過謊。
→ 撒謊的時間點（lie）是否認（deny）之前，所以用動名詞的完成式（having lied）。

❹ 動名詞需要指示做此動作的主詞時，動名詞前的名詞（代名詞）用所有格。

I don't mind John's going **with us.** 我不介意John跟我們一起去。
→ 動名詞的主詞是動名詞前名詞的所有格（John's）。即表示做 "going" 這個動作的主體是 "John"。

His going **with us is out of the question.** 他跟我們一起去是不可能的了。
→ 動名詞的主詞是動名詞前名詞的所有格（His）。即表示做 "going" 這個動作的主體是 "He"。

多益實戰考題　　　　　　　　　　　　多 益 會 出 這 樣 的 問 題

⊙ 填動名詞。
　出現最多的是動名詞作動詞的受詞或介系詞的受詞的題型。

2. Department heads distributed a memo reminding employees to refrain from ------- their cell phones during company meetings.

(A) to use　　　　　　(B) using
(C) uses　　　　　　(D) use

1. ------- regular donations to local charities from business profits is not only personally rewarding, but is good for developing a reputation.

(A) Give　　　　　　(B) Gives
(C) Giving　　　　　(D) Given

3. The chef obtains interesting and different results with this dish by ------- the ingredients he uses in the recipe.

(A) vary　　　　　　(B) varying
(C) varied　　　　　(D) varies

正確答案　P44

02 可以接動名詞做受詞的動作

❶ 只能接動名詞作受詞的動詞

享受	enjoy Ving 享受		
提議、考慮	suggest Ving 提議	recommend Ving 推薦	consider Ving 考慮
中止、延期	finish Ving 終止	quit Ving 放棄	discontinue Ving 結束
	give up Ving 放棄	postpone Ving 延期	
反面意義	dislike Ving 討厭	deny Ving 否認	mind Ving 介意
	avoid Ving 避免		

Russ will consider ~~to work~~ for a new company. Russ將會考慮去新的公司工作。
             working
→ consider 的受詞不是 to 不定詞（to work），而是動名詞（working）。

❷ to 不定詞和動名詞都可以作受詞。

• 動名詞作受詞時和 to 不定詞作受詞時，句意不變的情況。

Jane has just begun ~~learned~~ to drive. Jane 剛開始學開車。
                learning / to learn
→ 動詞 begin 後面既可以接動名詞（learning）也可以接 to 不定詞（to learn），而且句意不會有改變。類似於 begin 這種情況的動詞還有 like，love，prefer，hate，start，intend，attempt，continue 等。

• 動名詞作受詞時和 to 不定詞作受詞時，句意有變化的情況。

I remembered canceling that order. 我記得我取消了那個訂單。
I remembered to cancel that order. 我記得我要去取消那個訂單。

I stopped running. 我停止跑步了。
I stopped to rest. 我停止正在做的事情去休息。
→ forget，remember，stop 等動詞接動名詞或 to 不定詞作受詞時，句意會改變。動名詞作受詞時表示「過去」，to 不定詞作受詞時表示「未來、目的」。

注意！ advise，allow，permit，forbid 等動詞有「動詞 + 動名詞」或「動詞 + 受詞 + to 不定詞」的形式。

The hospital does not permit smoking in the building. 醫院不准在室內吸煙。
The hospital does not permit people to smoke in the building. 醫院不准人們在室內吸煙。

多益實戰考題　　　　　　多 益 會 出 這 樣 的 問 題

⊙ 區分動名詞和 to 不定詞並填空。

1. The small appliance manufacturer has recently begun ------- into the consumer electronics industry.

(A) expand　　　　　(B) expanded
(C) expanding　　　　(D) has expanded

2. It would be wise of you to consider ------- with your firm, as the job market is tough right now.

(A) renegotiate　　　　(B) renegotiated
(C) to renegotiate　　　(D) renegotiating

3. Do not forget ------- the application form before submitting it to Ms. Radowick at the front desk.

(A) signing　　　(B) sign
(C) to sign　　　(D) signed

正確答案　P44

03 動名詞 VS.名詞

❶ 動名詞可以接受詞，但名詞不能。

The chain was successful in ~~establishment~~ a new store. 那個連鎖店成功開了新店鋪。
establishing

→ 名詞（establishment）不能接受詞，所以要改成動名詞（establishing）。

注意！ 1. 動名詞和名詞後面沒有受詞時，應該用名詞。

We have just been informed about his arriving(→ arrival). 我們剛得知他到達的消息。

2. 不要把以下 Ving 形式的名詞誤認為是動名詞。

beginning 起源，開端	belongings 攜帶品	broadcasting 廣播	findings 發現（物），研究結果	gathering 聚會
lodging 寄宿，借宿	meeting 會議	opening 開始，空缺	shipping 船舶	training 訓練

❷ 動名詞前只能接定冠詞，但名詞（可數名詞）前可以接不定冠詞。

The bank has experienced a marked ~~increasing~~ in deposits in recent weeks. 這幾週銀行的存款有了明顯增加。
increase

→ 動名詞（increasing）前不能接不定冠詞 a，所以把動名詞（increasing）改為名詞（increase）。

❸ 與名詞有不同涵義的被名詞化的動名詞時，選擇涵義正確的一個。

advertising 廣告業 - advertisement 廣告	covering 蓋子 - coverage（保險）賠償範圍	funding 資金支援 / 資金調節 - fund 資金
marketing 營銷 - market 市場	meaning 涵義 - means 方法	processing 處理 / 步驟/加工 - process 過程 / 工程
seating 座位安排 - seat 座位	staffing 職員分配 - staff 職員	ticketing 售票 - ticket 票

For proper ~~process~~, submit all documents completely and accurately. 為了恰當的處理，要完整、精確地提交文件。
processing

→ 因為要表示「恰當的處理」的意義，只能用 processing（處理），不能用 process（過程 / 程序）。

After the phone lines went down, the company decided to seek out other ~~meaning~~ of communication with clients.
means

電話線斷掉後，公司打算找別的可以與顧客取得聯繫的方法。

→ 因為要表現「取得聯繫的方法」的涵義，所以只能用 means（方法），不能用 meaning（涵義）。

多益實戰考題　　　　　多益會出這樣的問題

⊙ 區分動名詞和 to 不定詞並填空。

1. By ------- paperwork, the Stamford Company is able to more efficiently accomplish routine tasks.

(A) reduce   (B) reduced
(C) reducing   (D) reduction

2. The frozen dinner company is utilizing consumer ------- on nutrition to formulate wholesome menus for its products.

(A) research   (B) to research
(C) researching (D) researched

3. The team met for three hours to discuss strategies for ------- the midmarket needs of small to medium-sized businesses.

(A) address   (B) to address
(C) addressing (D) addressed

正確答案　P44

❶ 動名詞句慣用表現

go Ving 去做…	be busy (in) Ving 忙於…
on Vng 做完…接著…	be worth Ving 值得做…
It's no use Ving 做…無用	keep (on) Ving 繼續做…
spend + Ving 時間 / 錢花在…	feel like Ving 想要做…
have difficulty(trouble, a problem) (in) Ving 做…有困難	cannot help Ving 不得不做…

We will be busy editing **this article.**
我們會忙於編輯這篇文章。

The company will have trouble carrying **out its plans.**
公司在實行計畫時遭遇困難。

❷ 介系詞 to + 動名詞

contribute to Ving 貢獻…	be committed to Ving 盡力於…
look forward to Ving 期待…	be dedicated to Ving 奉獻於…
object to Ving 反對…，對…提出疑義	be devoted to Ving 奉獻於…
lead to Ving …原因	be used to Ving 習慣於…

I look forward to **your** joining **the company.**
我期待你能加入公司。

The company is committed to providing **the best possible service.**
公司會盡力提供最好的服務。

注意！ 要注意 to 被連接詞連接時的情況。
We are looking forward to touring the area and <u>to see</u>(→ to seeing) the sights.
我們期待去那裡旅遊並看看名勝古蹟。
⇨ 「介系詞 to + 動名詞」（to touring，to seeing）被連接詞 and 所連接，所以要注意不能用 to see。

多益實戰考題　　　　　多 益 會 出 這 樣 的 問 題

⊙ 填動名詞。

1. Mr. Gray looks forward to ------- out more about investment opportunities with your growing company.

   (A) find　　　　　(B) finding
   (C) have found　　(D) be found

2. The overseas branches have had many difficulties in ------- the main branch's system to their local operations.

   (A) adapt　　　　(B) adapts
   (C) adapted　　　(D) adapting

3. Although the employees are satisfied with the training program, they object to ------- to travel an hour each way to get to the training center and back.

   (A) have　　　　(B) has
   (C) had　　　　　(D) having

正確答案 P44

Practice 1 選擇正確的答案。

01 Daniel is used to (work / working) under deadlines and in high pressure situations.

02 Ian forgot (to give / giving) sufficient notice about his resignation to his employers.

03 Be careful to use appropriate (word / wording) when writing up the contract.

04 Sheila decided to keep (working / to work) through most of her pregnancy.

05 Studies have shown that a positive environment can significantly improve worker (effectiveness / effecting).

06 The project contributed to (raise / raising) environmental awareness.

07 Shoppers cannot help (to wonder / wondering) why the prices at the department store are so high.

Practice 2 改正錯誤的地方。

08 Paul's job is take care of a request from his supervisor.

09 I would like you to prepare for your first day by reviewing company policies.

10 Many people cannot afford the cost of obtain medical care without health insurance.

11 It would be best to avoid to talk on the phone during work hours.

12 While he's an expert in buying stocks, he's not good at know when to sell.

13 I would prefer to have my salary wired to my account directly each month.

14 Her impressive volunteering record proves that Jessica is dedicated to help others in need.

Part V

01 Age-related changes can contribute to one's having problems ------- soundly.

(A) sleep   (B) sleeps
(C) slept   (D) sleeping

02 The government's report found that CIZMO Group had failed to take the necessary steps in ------- the building's cash vault.

(A) secured   (B) was secured
(C) securing   (D) has secured

03 Despite ------- to reach an agreement, negotiations between the company and the union remain at a standstill.

(A) attempted   (B) attempt
(C) attempts   (D) attempting

04 Because demand for sharp-toed boots has been decreasing, Martinique Shoemakers has decided to discontinue ------- this particular style.

(A) made   (B) making
(C) make   (D) to make

05 Especially in Western countries such as America and Canada, companies prefer not to ------- aside too much time for the professional development of their employees.

(A) set   (B) sets
(C) have set   (D) setting

06 The department is committed to ------- customers with a satisfactory resolution to their complaints.

(A) provision   (B) providing
(C) provides   (D) provided

07 Please indicate your desire to renew your membership with our club within ten days of ------- this notice.

(A) received   (B) receipt
(C) receive   (D) receiving

08 Mr. Fields helped his friend ------- a bank from which to take out a loan to start his own construction business with.

(A) find   (B) findable
(C) finding   (D) be found

09 The factory supervisor ------- equipment and machinery through a second-hand dealer who sells slightly used items at bargain prices.

(A) to purchase   (B) purchase
(C) purchasing   (D) purchases

10 The cosmetics division is considering ------- a product line for men, which will probably include facial creams and concealers.

(A) introduce   (B) introducing
(C) to introduce   (D) introduced

11 Investors should look closely at financial reports ------- the risks associated with a company.

(A) to analyze   (B) analyst
(C) analysis   (D) analyze

12 The managers involved with the negotiations are pleased with the progress of the talks and believe that they will reach a mutually beneficial -------.

(A) to conclude   (B) concluded
(C) concluding   (D) conclusion

13 The recent cuts in budget appropriations were aimed at ------- the company's year-end deficit.

(A) reduce   (B) reduced
(C) reducing   (D) reduction

14 Shopping websites can continue to ------- shoppers by ensuring product quality, offering low prices, and being user-friendly.

(A) attractive   (B) attract
(C) attracting   (D) attraction

15 Rather than go ------- at the local supermarkets, residents of the town are urged to buy produce straight from the farms.

(A) to shop   (B) shopping
(C) for shopping   (D) to shopping

16 ------- your business card to individuals you meet will allow you to advertise your business in an inexpensive and effective way.

(A) Hand   (B) Hands
(C) Handed   (D) Handing

17 I am calling to get some information on ------- the 15th International Symposium on Mobile Radio Communications in September.

(A) to attend   (B) attending
(C) attended   (D) attendance

18 A demonstration of the most recent PDA model will ------- place in the conference room on the third floor before it goes on sale.

(A) take   (B) be taken
(C) be taking   (D) have taken

19 The purpose of ------- our computer systems is to help us maintain a competitive edge in the market.

(A) upgrade   (B) upgrades
(C) upgrading   (D) upgraded

20 By May, the weather should become warm enough to permit ------ in the cellar or basement for longer periods of time.

(A) stay   (B) to stay
(C) staying   (D) stayed

21 ------- the difficult bar exam, he spent most of his waking moments reading reference materials at the library.

(A) For passing   (B) To pass
(C) By passing   (D) On passing

22 Sleek Inc. has begun ------- of a new line of stockings made from insulated polar fleece for the winter months.

(A) produces   (B) produced
(C) producing   (D) production

23 The promotion advisor, Mr. Dorsey, enjoys ------- with potential clients during the open house days held once a month.

(A) talk   (B) talked
(C) talking   (D) to talk

24 ------- the list of terms of agreement regarding your account before contacting one of our branch offices with account inquiries.

(A) See   (B) Saw
(C) To see   (D) Seeing

25 As there are no clear guidelines for ------- fairness in grievance procedures, management will hold a special meeting to address this problem.

(A) ensure   (B) ensured
(C) ensuring   (D) be ensured

26 Special discounts and incentives are being offered to residents to encourage them ------- energy at all times of the day.

(A) conserve   (B) conservative
(C) for conserving   (D) to conserve

27 City developers will begin ------- the parking lot into a luxury shopping center after the summer ends.

(A) convert   (B) converting
(C) to converting   (D) converted

28 In ------- an atmosphere conducive to studying, the library has painted the walls a color that is easy on the eyes of the students.

(A) establish   (B) establishing
(C) established   (D) establishment

Chapter 11

分詞

啊哈!! 愉快地打基礎

1 分詞（動詞 + ing，動詞 + ed）是基於動詞形成的，在句子中可以充當形容詞角色，而不是動詞角色。

I broken heart.（×）
The man was dying of a broken heart.（○）那個人遭受失戀的痛苦。
They removed all the marble blocks broken into several pieces.（○）
他們清理了很多碎成好幾塊的大理石。

根據上文分詞broken不當動詞，而是在名詞heart前修飾它或在名詞句the marble blocks後面修飾它，並當做形容詞。

2 分詞仍然有動詞的性質，所以可以接受詞或補語，還可以被副詞修飾。

There were a lot of people enjoying the nice weather. 很多人正享受著晴朗的天氣。
The car repaired yesterday is working well. 昨天修的汽車現在正常運轉著。

根據上文知道enjoying可以有受詞the nice weather，repaired也可以被副詞yesterday修飾。

但分詞在前面修飾名詞時，分詞與名詞間不能有受詞、副詞或補語。

The repaired yesterday car is working well.（×）

01 分詞的作用

❶ 分詞當形容詞。

• 就像形容詞一樣在名詞前或後修飾名詞。

名詞前修飾 　As a result of <u>increasing</u> demand, we are in a position to raise prices.
由於需求的增長，我們能夠提高我們產品的價格。

名詞後修飾 　The staff members (who were) <u>expected</u> to attend didn't turn up.
本該出席的職員沒有出現。
→ 底下畫線的部分是分詞的核心部分，多益考試中會常考這部分。

• 像形容詞一樣當做主詞補語或受詞補語。

主詞補語 　The task seems challenging. 這個任務似乎很難。

受詞補語 　Mr. Dover keeps his partners motivated. Dover 先生使他的合作夥伴們一直保持積極。

注意！ 分詞不與受詞或介系詞子句一起出現而是單獨出現時，通常會出現在名詞前作修飾角色，唯獨有 people questioned，people interviewed，people concerned 等表現時，分詞會在後面單獨修飾名詞。
The <u>people questioned</u> gave very different opinions. 被詢問的人提出了完全不同的意見。

❷ 動詞不能出現在分詞的位置。

She could have been a ~~lead~~ actress. 她有可能會成為優秀的女演員。
　　　　　　　　　　leading
→ 動詞（lead）不能修飾名詞（actress），所以要用可以當形容詞的分詞（leading）。

The candidate ~~hire~~ last week turned down the position. 上週被雇用的職員拒絕接受那個職位。
　　　　　　　hired
→ 動詞（hire）不能修飾名詞（candidate），所以要用可以當形容詞的分詞（hired）。

多益實戰考題　　　　　　多益會出這樣的問題

⊙ 填分詞。

1. Because flu is a ------- public concern, pharmaceutical companies have been marketing a variety of medications.

(A) grow　　　　　(B) grew
(C) growth　　　　(D) growing

2. Photo-Ops is a bimonthly publication ------- by an organization of amateur photographers devoted to their avocation.

(A) distributes　　(B) distributed
(C) are distributed　(D) will distribute

3. The resort keeps its patrons ------- by offering numerous services that ensure their comfort and well-being.

(A) satisfy　　　　(B) satisfies
(C) satisfied　　　(D) satisfaction

正確答案　P47

02 分詞片語

❶ 分詞片語在句子中作副詞，可以表示時間、原因、條件、伴隨等。

時間　<u>Having failed</u> the interview process, I returned to university. 在採訪過程失敗後，我回到了大學。
= After I had failed the interview process

原因　<u>Feeling</u> confident, Susan asked for a raise. 由於感到自信，Susan 要求提高薪資。
= Because she felt confident

條件　<u>Marketed</u> cleverly, the game will be very popular. 要是促銷手段夠聰明，這個遊戲將會廣受歡迎。
= If it is marketed cleverly

伴隨　The supermarket added a foreign foods section, <u>including</u> items from Southeast Asia.
= and it included items from Southeast Asia

那個超市新增了外國食品專櫃，包括了來自東南亞的食品。

→ 底下畫線的部分是分詞片語的核心部分，多益考試中會常考這部分。

注意！ 為了明確分詞片語的涵義，可以把子句中的連接詞放到分詞片語前。

<u>Before</u> signing the contract, make sure that you understand it fully. 簽合約之前，一定要充分了解合約內容。
You may enter the bank vault <u>when</u> accompanied by security personnel. 你可以在保全人員的陪同下進入銀行金庫。

❷ 動詞或名詞不能出現在分詞片語的位置。

~~Surprise~~ by the sudden drop in the value of the stock, the investor immediately sold his shares.
Surprised
被股票突然下跌驚嚇到，這位投資者立刻賣掉了他的股份。
→ 在分詞片語的位置上不能用 Surprise，要改為 Surprised。

When ~~application~~ for a transfer, explain your situation fully. 申請調職時，請充分說明你的情況。
　　　　applying
→ 子句中的連接詞（when）後分詞片語的位置上不能用名詞 application，要用 applying。

❸ 表示同時發生的狀況時，用「with + 受詞 + 分詞片語」。

Mrs. Sedrick walked by with papers falling out of her briefcase. Sedrick 夫人邊走她的公事包裡一邊掉出文件。
There was a problem with shipments (being) sent to the wrong address. 出了一個貨物被送到錯誤的地址的問題。

多益實戰考題　　　　　多 益 會 出 這 樣 的 問 題

⊙ 填（副詞子句連接詞 +）分詞片語。
常出現的子句連接詞有 unless，when，while，whenever，once（只要…就）等。

1. ------- completed the initial write-up of the study, the researcher submitted the draft to her supervisor for feedback.

(A) Had　　　　　　(B) Having
(C) Have　　　　　 (D) Has

2. Once -------, both corporations will examine what alternatives are available for the affiliates they separately own.

(A) merged　　　　(B) merge
(C) are merged　　 (D) have merged

3. After carefully ------- the holes in security, experts agreed that passwords should be changed once a month.

(A) review　　　　 (B) reviews
(C) reviewing　　　(D) are reviewed

正確答案　P48

03 現在分詞 VS.過去分詞

❶ 分詞修飾名詞時，被修飾的名詞與分詞是主動關係時用現在分詞，被動關係時用過去分詞。

We have seen a proposal recommending us to change company regulations.
我們已經看過一個提案建議我們改變公司的規定。
→ 被修飾的名詞（a proposal）與分詞「建議…」是主動關係，所以用現在分詞（recommending）。

The discount offer is not valid on tickets purchased on the internet.
在網上購買的票不能打折。
→ 被修飾的名詞（tickets）與分詞「購買」是被動關係，所以用過去分詞（purchased）。

❷ 分詞作主詞補語或受詞補語時，主詞和補語或受詞和補語是主動關係時用現在分詞，被動關係時用過去分詞。

The game became exciting. 那個遊戲變得很有趣。
→ 主詞（the game）和補語是「遊戲有趣」的主動關係，所以用現在分詞（exciting）。

The writer made the executive summary polished. 那個作家修改了執行大綱。
→ 受詞（the executive summary）和補語是「執行大綱被修改」的被動關係，所以用過去分詞（polished）。

❸ 對分詞片語來說，主句的主詞和分詞片語是主動關係時用現在分詞，被動關係時用過去分詞。

You must read the terms of the contract carefully before signing the agreement.
在同意書上簽字之前，你必須仔細閱讀合約中的條款。
→ 主句中的主詞（You）和分詞片語是「你簽字」的主動關係，所以用現在分詞（signing）。

Enclosed within the office compound, the restaurant is frequented by employees.
這間餐廳周圍都是辦公區，所以職員們經常去這間餐廳。
→ 主句中的主詞（the restaurant）和分詞片語是「餐廳被…圍住」的被動關係，所以用過去分詞（Enclosed）。

多益實戰考題　　　　　　　　　多　益　會　出　這　樣　的　問　題

⊙ 區分現在分詞和過去分詞並填空。
大體會出現區分主動或被動的現在分詞和過去分詞的題型。

1. The receipts attached to the travel report indicate the total amount ------- for the trip to the overseas branch.
   (A) pay　　　　　　　　(B) pays
   (C) paid　　　　　　　　(D) paying

2. Mr. Sanders has decided to take on the position at Barker Technologies because the work seems -------.
   (A) interest　　　　　　(B) interests
   (C) interesting　　　　(D) interested

3. ------- in the downtown area, the information center for expatriates provides various types of assistance and serves as a meeting place for young adults.
   (A) Locating　　　　　(B) Located
   (C) Locate　　　　　　(D) Location

正確答案　P48

❶ 現在分詞 + 名詞

during his opening remarks	當他講開場白時
maintenance of existing equipment	現有設備的保養
my missing luggage	我遺失的行李
leave a lasting impression on the school system	為學校系統留下長久的影響
leading commercial company	一流的廣告公司
The presiding officer will emcee the seminar.	主席會擔任研討會的主持
the most promising member of the team	團隊裡面最有前途的成員
improving techniques	改善中的技術
cf) improved techniques	被改善的技術

The interviewer met with the ~~promised~~ candidate to ask him about his long-term goals.
　　　　　　　　　　　　　promising

面試官為了問他的長期計畫，而面試了那個有前途的應徵者。

→ 表示「有前途的」涵義時，分詞要用現在分詞promising，而不是過去分詞promised。

❷ 過去分詞 + 名詞

提倡、資格	the preferred means of transportation	被提倡的交通手段
	the proposed plan of rebuilding	被提出的重建設計圖
	a qualified (skilled, experienced) programmer	熟練的程式設計師
標示、器材	designated parking area	被指定的停車場
	request a reserved parking space	要求一個預約的停車位
	view the detailed product information	閱讀詳細的產品資訊
	without written consent	沒有書面同意
	in limited warranty	在有限的保固期內
	limited items	限定項目
購入、製造	newly purchased computer hardware	新購買的電腦硬體
	heavy demand for customized products	對訂做產品的大量需求
	increase of the price of finished products	成品的加價
	the superior quality of the handcrafted pieces	手工製品的精湛品質
其他	repeated dismissal from the firm	來自公司的反覆拒絕
	explain in the attached document	在附加檔案中說明
	responsible for the damaged items	對損壞的物品負責

The trainer asked his ~~experiencing~~ assistant to help the participants.
　　　　　　　　　　experienced

教練員要求有經驗的助理來幫助那些參與者們。

→ 表示「熟練的」的分詞要用過去分詞experienced，而不是現在分詞experiencing。

多益實戰考題　　　　　　　多　益　會　出　這　樣　的　問　題

⊙ 區分現在分詞和過去分詞並填空。

1. For over three hundred years, cork has been the ------- means to cap wine bottles, but manufacturers are now looking into metal screw caps.

(A) preferred　　　　(B) preferring
(C) preference　　　 (D) preferably

2. The new company regulation states that ------- tardiness will be grounds for suspension from work without pay.

(A) repeating　　　　(B) repeats
(C) repeated　　　　 (D) repeatedly

3. The small shop recently won an award for the originality and outstanding quality of its ------- pieces.

(A) handcraft　　　　(B) handcrafts
(C) handcrafted　　　(D) handcrafting

正確答案　P48

Practice 1 區分並選擇現在分詞和過去分詞。

01 A deposit is required when (reserved / reserving) banquet space at this hotel.

02 We must make a (lasting / lasted) impression on our clients to maintain long-term relations with them.

03 Please have this signed and stamped by the date (writing / written) on this form.

04 Mr. Donaldson received an invitation (welcoming / welcomed) him to the wedding reception.

05 Rain poured relentlessly, (dampened / dampening) the company picnic.

06 Applicants (interesting / interested) in the early decision program should apply by September 1st.

07 This is just a reminder to keep your doors (locked / locking) at night for safety.

Practice 2 改正錯誤的地方。

08 We decided to try a restaurant served raw seafood and other dishes.

09 The proposed plan was acceptable to all members of the committee.

10 Felt lucky, Charles decided to ask his boss for a raise.

11 The bank will send the depositor an update statement of transactions.

12 Every day after eating lunch, Kate takes a short walk around the block.

13 Please include payment in the reply envelope providing in your catalogue.

14 We have searched everywhere for the missed reports, but they are yet to be found.

正確答案 P50

Part V

01 The hotel provides personal service and careful attention to detail, ------- that you have a relaxing and comfortable stay.

(A) be ensured   (B) ensure
(C) ensures   (D) ensuring

02 An invoice will be generated and included with the order being ------- to the address you indicated on the form.

(A) send   (B) sent
(C) sending   (D) sends

03 The head office is looking forward to meeting with branch representatives and to ------- any issues that have risen in the past quarter.

(A) discuss   (B) discussing
(C) have discussed   (D) be discussing

04 Although the latest PDA (personal digital assistant) has a number of exciting new features, it has a ------- warranty.

(A) limited   (B) limit
(C) limitation   (D) limiting

05 The editor spoke to his assistant about how to keep the writers ------- to write lively and interesting articles.

(A) have inspiration   (B) be inspired
(C) inspired   (D) inspiring

06 Net Connect furnishes its clients with ------- networking solutions, ranging from file and printer sharing to group calendar and scheduling.

(A) customize   (B) customizes
(C) customized   (D) customizing

07 The task force ironed out a plan to launch a more ------- promotional campaign for their new quick-education services.

(A) excited   (B) exciting
(C) excitingly   (D) excitable

08 The staff wishes ------- for the inadvertent deletion of the items you saved for future purchase on our website.

(A) apologizing   (B) apologized
(C) apologizes   (D) to apologize

09 In his ten years at Nortel Networks, Mr. Gutierrez has shown that he performs admirably when ------- with tight deadlines.

(A) face   (B) facing
(C) faces   (D) faced

10 Readers find the young writer's first novel ------- despite the fact that the initial reviews of the book were so dismal.

(A) fascinate   (B) fascination
(C) fascinating   (D) fascinated

11 From the moment he comes up with a concept, it usually takes Mr. Barnes a week to produce the ------- product.

(A) finished   (B) finishing
(C) finish   (D) finishes

12 The corporation head, who ------- a large city orphanage, will establish a non-profit computer learning center for the underprivileged.

(A) foundation   (B) founded
(C) found   (D) founding

13 The number of employees ------- to work at foreign branches in Asia and Europe will probably continue to increase.

(A) agree   (B) agreeing
(C) agreed   (D) agreement

14 The manager makes certain his employees keep themselves up-to-date on the latest high-tech news by giving them ------- reading every week.

(A) requiring   (B) requirement
(C) requires   (D) required

15 Even though the business trip was -------, a lot of headway was made with our future Swiss partner.

(A) tire (B) tired
(C) tiring (D) tiredness

16 If the front door is locked, punch in your access code, while ------- down the green button on the door handle.

(A) hold (B) holds
(C) held (D) holding

17 Facilities have been established to facilitate pick-ups and drop-offs for passengers ------- the train and subway stations.

(A) used (B) using
(C) use (D) will use

18 The symposium's ------- event is the Peace Ball, where delegates can meet members of the community.

(A) culminate (B) culmination
(C) culminating (D) culminated

19 Misuse or neglect can result in the equipment ------- damaged, requiring parts replacement or extensive repair.

(A) was (B) been
(C) having (D) being

20 Professor Watson just received an official letter ------- him to serve as a judge at the International Poem Reading Competition to be held in Cedar, Ohio in March.

(A) invited (B) is inviting
(C) inviting (D) has invited

21 Due to a significant change in the nation's tax laws, we are likely to see ------- investments by foreign individuals.

(A) decrease (B) to decrease
(C) decreases (D) decreased

22 We have adopted a new accounting system ------- us to monitor expenditures more closely than ever before.

(A) help (B) helps
(C) helping (D) helped

23 When ------- for a bank account, you must present an identification card with a recent picture.

(A) apply (B) applying
(C) application (D) applied

24 Mr. Morris and I ------- the section written by Ms. Wood because her conclusion was based on outdated information.

(A) excluding (B) am excluding
(C) was excluded (D) are excluding

25 Employees are expected to use the newly ------- reference materials to expand their knowledge of computer software and their applications.

(A) purchased (B) purchasing
(C) purchases (D) purchase

26 The willingness of the parties ------- on this new project to put forth extra effort is the main reason for the company's success.

(A) work (B) working
(C) are working (D) worked

27 The stadium was packed with thousands of people waiting to see the two soccer teams -------.

(A) playing (B) played
(C) to play (D) are playing

28 The state government has decided to introduce a program targeting unemployed men and women ------- to reenter a highly competitive job market.

(A) are trying (B) try
(C) trying (D) will try

正確答案 P50

Section 4 詞類

名詞

啊哈!! 愉快地打基礎

1 名詞是表示人、事物、地點或抽象概念的名稱。

teacher　cat　coffee　rain　match　dream　China

2 名詞可分為可數名詞和不可數名詞。

可數名詞
- 表示人 / 事物的普通名詞　　　　　manager, typist, ticket, letter ...
- 表示集體的名詞　　　　　　　　　family, people, police, team, committee ...

不可數名詞
- 特定的人 / 事物的專有名詞　　　　Seoul, Hong Kong, Tom, Christmas ...
- 表示概念 / 狀態 / 動作的抽象名詞　history, information, news, equipment ...
- 表示物質的名詞　　　　　　　　　paper, water, wood, glass, oil ...

3 名詞通常與限定詞一起使用。限定詞有冠詞、數量形容詞、所有格和指示詞等。

① 冠詞
We need a car for several weeks. 我們這幾週需要一輛車。
I decided to sell the car. 我決定賣掉這輛車。
「不定冠詞 + 名詞」形式的 "a + car" 表示沒有特別指定的一輛車，「定冠詞 + 名詞」形式的 "the + car" 表示是大家都知道的那一輛車。像這樣不定冠詞（a, an）用在沒有特定的名詞前，定冠詞（the）用在特定的名詞前。

② 數量形容詞
Some cars on the list are not available in Korea. 訂單上的幾種車在韓國是找不到的。

③ 所有格 / 指示詞
Mike parked his car two blocks from the bank. Mike 把車停在離銀行兩條街遠的地方。
I bought this car in 1998. 我 1998 年買了這台車。

01 名詞位置

❶ 名詞出現在句子中主詞、受詞、補語的位置。

主詞的位置	Customer satisfaction must be considered. 要考慮到顧客的滿意度。
及物動詞的受詞位置	The library will be accepting donations of used textbooks. 圖書館會接受舊教科書的捐贈。
介系詞受詞的位置	Suncorp moved to its new office last year. Suncorp（公司）去年搬到了新辦公室。
補語的位置	Having a strong corporate culture is an advantage for the company. 具備優秀的企業文化對公司有利。
	It was a great disappointment that an agreement was not reached. 沒有達成協議是令人很失望的事。

注意！ 名詞可以出現在非動詞的受詞位置。

They are trying to increase employee <u>productivity</u>. 他們致力於提升員工的生產力。

❷ 名詞常出現在以下詞類的前後

冠詞 + 名詞 + 介系詞	<u>the</u> features <u>of</u> the dishwasher 那個洗碗機的特性
形容詞、副詞 + 名詞	offers a lot of <u>practical</u> information 提供很多實用的資訊
所有格 + (形容詞) + 名詞	would like to express <u>his</u> disappointment 想表達他的失望
	<u>Latzer's</u> <u>second</u> edition is more useful than the old one. Latzer 第二版比以前的有用多了。
名詞 + 名詞〔複合名詞〕	meet the production schedule 趕上生產排程表

❸ 名詞的位置中不能出現動詞、形容詞等詞。

Tax incentives can be used to encourage ~~invest~~ in small businesses.
　　　　　　　　　　　　　　　　　investment

稅款補償政策可以用於獎勵小規模公司。

→ 因為是 to 不定詞 to encourage 的受詞位置，所以動詞（invest）要改成名詞（investment）。

They generally have lots of information regarding their ~~industrial~~.
　　　　　　　　　　　　　　　　　　　　　　　　industry

他們通常掌握許多跟自身產業相關的情報。

→ 因為是介系詞 regarding 的受詞位置，所以形容詞（industrial）要改成名詞（industry）。

多益實戰考題　　　　　多 益 會 出 這 樣 的 問 題

⊙ 填名詞。

2. The feasibility study which was postponed a few months ago is expected to resume in time for the New Projects Committee's -------.

(A) evaluated　　　　　(B) evaluation
(C) evaluator　　　　　(D) evaluates

1. I'd like to delay the ------- of the copy machine until we can move the old one into the basement.

(A) delivered　　　　　(B) deliver
(C) deliverable　　　　(D) delivery

3. Prescription service and the purchase of medication over the Internet are provided at great ------- to sickly and aging patients.

(A) convened　　　　　(B) convenient
(C) conveniently　　　(D) convenience

正確答案　P52

02 可數名詞與不可數名詞

❶ 可數名詞前面必須有冠詞或用複數形式，不可數名詞前不能有不定冠詞 a(n)，也沒有複數形式。

I need ~~chair~~ without arms. 我需要沒有把手的椅子。
       a chair / chairs

→ chair 是可數名詞，所以前面沒有冠詞或不用複數形式是錯誤的。必須是帶冠詞的（a chair）或複數形式（chairs）。

We need ~~a furniture / furnitures~~ to fill the room. 我們的房間裡還需要放一些傢俱。
       furniture

→ furniture 是不可數名詞，所以不能有不定冠詞，也不能用複數形式。

注意！ 1. 可數名詞分為表示一個可數名詞的單數名詞和表示兩個及兩個以上可數名詞的複數名詞。
單數名詞前帶不定冠詞，複數名詞字尾加-(e)s。
You can print <u>a coupon</u> from the web site. 你可以在網上列印優惠券。
<u>Boxes</u> are piled up in the office. 箱子堆積在辦公室裡。

2. 有些名詞看似不可以數，但包括在可數名詞裏。

a discount 打折	a price 價格	a purpose 目的	a refund 退款	a relation 關係
an approach 接近	a statement 報告書	a workplace 工作場所	a source 根源，來源	a result 結果
belongings 財產	measures 手段，方法	savings 儲蓄	standards 標準，基準	funds 基金

3. 有些名詞看似可數，但包括在不可數名詞裏。

access 門路	advice 忠告	baggage 行李	equipment 配備	information 資訊
luggage 行李	machinery 機械	news 新聞	stationery 文具	weaponry 武器

❷ 因意思相似，而容易混淆的可數名詞和不可數名詞。

可數名詞 － 不可數名詞	可數名詞 － 不可數名詞
an account 帳戶 － acounting 會計（學）	a lender 出借人 － lending 出借
an advertisement 廣告 － advertising 廣告（業）	a letter 信 － mail 郵件（物）
clothes 衣服 － clothing 衣類	a permit 許可書 － permission 許可
a fund 基金，資金 － funding 資金支援	a process 過程 procedures 順序，步驟 － processing 處理，步驟，加工
furnishings 傢俱，窗簾，地毯類 － furniture 傢俱	a seat 坐席 － seating 坐席（排列）
goods 商品 － merchandise 商品	a ticket 票 － ticketing 售票

多益實戰考題   多 益 會 出 這 樣 的 問 題

⊙ 區分可數名詞和不可數名詞後填入。
⊙ 區分單數名詞和複數名詞後填入。

1. With so many products to choose from, consumers demand a high ------- of customer service when choosing which company to support.

  (A) level   (B) leveling
  (C) levels   (D) leveled

2. Many of the policy holders of National Insurance receive ten percent ------- for cars or houses covered in their contracts.

  (A) discount   (B) discounts
  (C) discounting   (D) discounted

3. We became one of the most recognized digital camera manufacturers through an ------- that both young adults and parents could relate to.

  (A) advertise   (B) advertisable
  (C) advertising   (D) advertisement

正確答案 P52

03 限定詞與名詞

❶ 不定冠詞 a 只能在單數可數名詞前，不能在複數名詞和不可數名詞前。

She works for a foreign <u>company</u>. 她在外商公司工作。
Another factor contributed to ✗ higher fuel <u>prices</u>. 另一個要素使油價變貴的原因。
I've got ✗ interesting <u>information</u> about the event. 我得到了關於那個事件的有趣情報。
→ 不定冠詞 a / an 不可以出現在可數名詞複數的 prices 前和不可數名詞 information 前。

> 注意！ 在使用不定冠詞時，不管單字的拼寫，若緊跟其後的單字以子音開頭時用 a，以母音開頭時則用 an。
> a discount   a university   an effort   an hour

❷ 定冠詞 the 可以用在可數名詞單、複數和不可數名詞前。

I just bought the <u>book</u> that you recommended. 我剛買了你推薦的那本書。
I bought the <u>works</u> of Shakespeare. 我買了莎士比亞的書。
There is no charge to borrow the <u>equipment</u>. 借那個裝備不需要租金。

❸ 用在可數名詞、不可數名詞前的數量形容詞。

可數名詞前			不可數名詞	可數、不可數名詞前	
單數名詞	複數名詞				
one 一個　　each 每個	(a) few 幾個　fewer 更少的		(a) little 少	no 不是…	all 所有
every 每個	many 很多　several 數個的		less 更少的	more 更多	most 大部分的
	both 兩個都		much 很多	some 一些，某個	any 一些

~~Much~~ financial advisors will charge an hourly rate. 很多財政顧問是按小時計算費用的。
Many

→ advisors 是可數名詞，所以不能使用用在不可數名詞前的（much），而要使用用在可數名詞前的（many）。

The newest MP3 model boasted <u>several</u> new ~~feature~~. 最新款的 MP3 型號有數種新功能。
                                                    features

→ 與複數名詞一起使用的數量形容詞（serveral）後面不能接單數名詞（feature），而要用複數形式（features）。

> 注意！ all, more, most, other 與可數名詞一起使用時，用在複數名詞前。
> Most <u>tree</u> (→ trees) lose their leaves each fall, but some keep them over winter.
> 秋天的時候大部分的樹都會落葉，但有些樹到冬天也不落葉。

多益實戰考題　　　　　　多 益 會 出 這 樣 的 問 題

⊙ 填與名詞相對應的限定詞。
⊙ 填與限定詞相對應的名詞。

2. After spending a full year on redesign, our programmers have developed a program that offers customers several convenient new -------.

(A) to feature　　　　(B) feature
(C) featuring　　　　(D) features

1. ------- merchandise returned to the store after purchase must be checked for flaws or alterations before being put back on the shelf.

(A) An　　　　　　(B) There is
(C) Any　　　　　　(D) In that

3. ------- probationary accounting trainee must undergo six months' instruction before he is allowed to work in financial systems.

(A) All　　　　　　(B) Much
(C) Each　　　　　(D) A few

正確答案 P52

❶ 人物 / 事物 / 抽象名詞都可以用在名詞位置。但要用使句意自然、流暢的名詞。

accountant 會計師 — account 計算 — accounting 會計 applicant 申請者 — application 申請 — appliance 器具，裝置 occupant — 佔有者 occupancy 佔有 — occupation 職業 producer 生產者 — production 生產 — product 產品 receptionist 接待員 — reception 接見 — receptacle 容器 analyst 分析者 — analysis 分析 consultant 顧問 — consultation 諮詢 — consultancy 諮詢公司 arbitrator 仲裁者，主宰 — arbitration 仲裁 architect 建築師 — architecture 建築學 assembler 裝配工 — assembly 裝配 attendant 出席者 — attendance 出席 author 作家 — authorship 作者身份 authority 權力 — authorization 授權 beneficiary 受益者 — benefit 利益 committee 委員（會）— commitment 委託，獻身 consumer 消費者 — consumption 消費 contributor 貢獻者 — contribution 貢獻 donor 捐贈者 — donation 捐贈 editor 編輯者 — edition 版本 employee 員工 — employment 雇用 engineer 工程師 — engineering 工程學	expectant 期待者 — expectation=expectancy 預期 founder 創立者 — foundation 創立 illustrator 插畫家 — illustration 插畫 interpreter 翻譯員 — interpretation 翻譯 journalist 記者 — journal 報導，期刊 lender 出借人 — lending 出借 manager 經理 — management 經營，（集合）管理階層 manufacturer 製造業者 — manufacture 製造業 operator 司機，操作者 — operation 經營 owner 擁有者 — ownership 所有權 photographer 攝影師 — photograph 照片 president 總統 — presidency 總統職位 relative 親戚 — relation 關係 reminder 提醒者 / 物 — remembrance 記憶，紀念 representative 代表 — representation 代表 resident 居住者 — residence 居住 rival 競爭者 — rivalry 競爭 subscriber 期刊、雜誌訂戶 — subscription 訂閱款 supervisor 監督者 — supervision 監督 translator 翻譯者 — translation 翻譯 writer 作者 — writings 作品

An ~~architecture~~ carefully studies a site before making a perspective.
　　architect

建築師在畫透視圖之前會仔細研究現場。

→ 要表達的是「建築師」的涵義，所以不能用表示「建築」這個涵義的抽象名詞（architecture），而是要用表示「建築師」這個涵義的人物名詞（architect）。

The ~~founder~~ of the local art center reflects the city's commitment to artists and culture.
　　foundation

當地藝術中心的成立反應了該城市對藝術家和文化發展的支持。

→ 要表達的是「藝術中心成立」的涵義，所以不能用「創立者」涵義的人物名詞（founder），而是要用「成立」涵義的抽象名詞（foundation）。

多益實戰考題　　　　　　　　　　　　多 益 會 出 這 樣 的 問 題

⊙ 區分人物名詞和事物 / 抽象名詞並填空。

1. If long-term ------- is a possibility at this company, I would be interested and willing to relocate myself to this site.

   (A) employs　　　　(B) employee
   (C) employed　　　(D) employment

2. The chemical company gave local government officials a report detailing the ------- of its plant in Westbury.

   (A) operative　　　(B) operator
   (C) operation　　　(D) operate

3. It is common practice today for psychologists to serve as ------- to toy companies in the design of toys for children of different ages.

   (A) consult　　　　(B) consultants
   (C) consultancy　　(D) consultations

正確答案 P52

05 複合名詞

❶ 複合名詞由「名詞 + 名詞」組成。這時前面名詞的位置上不能用形容詞、分詞或動詞。

account number 帳號	enrollment form 登記表格	performance appraisals / evaluations 效益評價
application fee 申請費	exchange rate 匯率	product information 產品情報
application form 申請書	exercise equipment 運動器材	production schedule 生產排程
arrival date 到達日	expansion project 擴張計畫	reception desk 接待處
assembly line 裝配線	expiration date 截止日	reference letter 推薦信
attendance record 出勤（上班）記錄	feasibility study 可行性研究	registration form 登記書
communication skill 表達能力	growth rate 成長率	repair facility 修理設施
conference room 會議室	growth potential 成長潛力	research program 調查程序
confidentiality policy 保密政策	identification card 身份證	response rate 回應率
confirmation number 確認號碼	installment payment 分期付款	retirement luncheon 退休午宴
construction delay 工程延遲	interest rate 利息	return policy 退貨政策
convenience store 便利商店	investment advice 投資建議	safety inspection 安全檢查
currency market 貨幣市場	marital status 婚姻狀況	security card 社會安全卡
delivery company 快遞公司	occupancy rate 佔有率	service desk 服務台

Good ~~communicated~~ skills are essential to the project. 優秀的表達能力是此企畫不可或缺的。
communication

❷ 把複合名詞改為複數名詞時在後面名詞加-(e)s。

research program → research programs

注意！ 在複合名詞「名詞 + 名詞」中，前面的名詞不能加-(e)s。但有例外的「名詞 s + 名詞」形式複合名詞。

customs office 海關，public relations department 宣傳部，electronics company 電子公司，earnings growth 收入成長率，savings account / bank 儲蓄帳戶／銀行，sales division / promotion 銷售部門／促銷，human resources department 人力資源部

❸ 「數字 + 單位名詞 + 名詞」中的單位名詞不能加-s。

two thousands tickets（×）→ two thousand tickets（○）兩千張票
a four-years-old girl（×）→ a four-year-old girl（○）一個四歲的女孩

注意！ thousand, hundred, year 等名詞不修飾其他名詞而單獨使用時，要加 -s。
thousand(→ thousands) of tickets
She is four year(→ years) old.
⇨ 在這裡 year 沒有修飾 old。old 是在後面修飾 four years 的形容詞。

多益實戰考題　　　　多　益　會　出　這　樣　的　問　題

⊙ 填修飾其他名詞的名詞。

2. The ------- equipment at the new fitness club is guaranteed to help men and women achieve greater muscle tone in just a few weeks.

(A) exercise　　　　(B) exercisable
(C) exercising　　　(D) exercised

1. The anthropological ------- program is being financed privately, although the government is looking into the possibility of supporting the program.

(A) researching　　(B) researched
(C) research　　　 (D) researches

3. With nearly two ------- orders placed within the first twenty-four hours, the manager has decided to add another work shift to meet product demand.

(A) thousands　　　(B) a thousand
(C) thousand　　　 (D) thousands of

正確答案　P53

❶ 同形異義的單字

coverage（報導，保險，適用）範圍	cover 封面 covering 蓋子	the amount of media coverage 媒體報導數量
delivery 投遞	deliverance 解放，構造	the largest global delivery company 規模最大的全球快遞公司
entry 登記	entrance 入場，入口	do not accept any late entries 不接受遲到的登記
identification 身份證明	identity 身份	present a form of identification 出示一種身份證明
interests 利益	interest 興趣	the company's best interests 公司的最大利益 show great interest in alternative energy resources 對替代能源表示了很大的興趣
likelihood 可能性	likeness 類似	reduce the likelihood of system failure 減少系統錯誤的可能性
objective 目標 object 目標，物體	objectivity 客觀性 objection 反對	the objective of this program is to help ~ 這個專案的目的是幫…
percent 百分比	percentage 比例	ten percent on all items 所有項目有 10% 的… high percentage of the budget 高預算比率 ＊ percent 與數字一起使用，percentage 用於除此以外的情況。
permit 許可證	permission 許可	purchase a parking permit 購買停車許可證
procedure 步驟	proceedings 會議記錄	building security procedures 建立保全步驟
production 生產	product 生產品 produce 農產品 productivity 生產力	production remains steady 保持穩定的狀態生產 demonstrate the highest productivity 顯示出最高生產力
remainder 剩餘物	remains 遺物	throughout the remainder of the week 這週剩下的時間內
responsibility 責任	responsiveness 反映	accept responsibility for belongings left 對遺失物品的事件負責
segment 部分	segmentation 分割	the fastest growing segment of the automobile industry 在汽車產業裡成長最快的部分
sense 感覺	sensation 感動，興奮	have the business sense 擁有商業觀念
utilization 利用，活用	utility 效用，實利	the effective utilization of personnel at all levels 在所有階層內人事管理的有效利用

→寫在最左邊的單字通常是正確答案。

Pamela Hayes was given the ~~responsiveness~~ of preparing the equipment needed for the presentation.
responsibility

Pamela Hayes 負責準備發言時所需要的設備。

→ 要表達「負責」的涵義，所以不能用 responsiveness（反映），而要用 responsibility（責任）。

多益實戰考題　　　　　　　　多 益 會 出 這 樣 的 問 題

⊙ 區分涵義後填入名詞。

1. Any ------- submitted without the requirements listed in the contest rules will automatically be disqualified.

(A) enter　　　　　　(B) entries
(C) entering　　　　 (D) entrance

2. Visitors are not allowed to use the back of the building to park their cars without obtaining a parking ------- from the attendant.

(A) permit　　　　　　(B) permission
(C) permitting　　　　(D) to permit

3. Having a good business ------- can help one to plan a career that involves long-term goals and strategies.

(A) to sense　　　　　(B) sensing
(C) sensation　　　　 (D) sense

正確答案　P53

Practice 1 選擇正確的答案。

01 Laffless Law Firm is highly recommended for its (commit / commitment) to meeting its clients' needs.

02 The manufacturer accepts no (responsibility / responsiveness) for replacement if the product is broken due to misuse.

03 In an effort to meet the encroaching deadline, management has sped up its (producing / production) schedule.

04 In order to prevent the (likeness / likelihood) of malfunction, computer systems are now equipped to monitor themselves.

05 The financial (health / healthy) of the company was revived when the new marketing director devised a clever sales pitch.

06 All products must be removed from the shelves in accordance with the marked (expiring / expiration) date on each package.

07 Evaluations will be based not only on personal performance, but also employee (attendance / attending) records.

Practice 2 改正錯誤的地方。

08 The franchise is debating the locate of its new store.

09 Every application was given an official receipt for fees paid.

10 A workshop on the developer of economic relations between the EU and Japan took place in Tokyo.

11 The general manager handles the supervisor of all employees.

12 The frequent business traveling is allowed to enter to the airport's exclusive lounge.

13 Although his occupancy was teaching, he dabbled in stock trading.

14 The Power Health Club urges people to discover the beneficiaries of supervised exercise and treatments.

正確答案 P53

Part V

01 Mr. Cook of the accounting division is under enormous ------- to submit the financial statements by this afternoon.

(A) pressing   (B) pressed
(C) press   (D) pressure

02 The administrative supervisor will consider the ------- of his assistant's contract in light of suspicion regarding his loyalty to the company.

(A) cancel   (B) canceling
(C) cancelled   (D) cancellation

03 The report indicated that the company's average annual earnings ------- was much higher than analysts had estimated.

(A) grow   (B) growing
(C) growth   (D) grown

04 During Henry Ford's time, the ------- of the Model-T was divided into eighty-four distinct steps, with each step assigned to a single worker.

(A) assemble   (B) assembly
(C) assembler   (D) assembled

05 The manager would like to thank the factory workers for the highest ------- the company has had in the past twenty years.

(A) product   (B) productivity
(C) productive   (D) produce

06 The project implementation committee is staffed by a ------- group with years of experience in the formation of financial cooperatives.

(A) dedicated   (B) dedication
(C) dedicating   (D) dedicate

07 Unlike fossil fuels, which are expensive and limited in supply, renewable energy sources tend to emit fewer -------.

(A) pollutes   (B) polluted
(C) pollution   (D) pollutants

08 The factory supervisor said that there was no ------- but to shut down production until the technicians could repair the defective machine.

(A) alternate   (B) alternative
(C) alternation   (D) alternatively

09 It is vital to clearly state and define the ------- of the project before planning the first stage.

(A) objective   (B) objection
(C) objectivity   (D) objectionable

10 The ------- for the book cover went through several revisions before it was finally approved by the publisher.

(A) designed   (B) designing
(C) design   (D) designer

11 ------- numbers of former customers were maintained in the database for six months as part of the company's standard procedure.

(A) Account   (B) Accounts
(C) Accounting   (D) Accountable

12 For the ------- of today's seminar, we will focus on the growing need for interpreters in the global market.

(A) remain   (B) remained
(C) remaining   (D) remainder

13 To the surprise of the visitors, the elevator door in the old building opened suddenly while the lift was still in -------.

(A) moving   (B) moved
(C) move   (D) motion

14 In an effort to improve -------, we are installing laser-activated alarms at the front of every major entrance.

(A) secure   (B) securely
(C) secured   (D) security

15 Sales of the book, The Hours, ------- down following the last few days of the movie's run.

(A) was slowed   (B) has slowed
(C) slowed   (D) slowing

16 It is in the best ------- of the company to comply with environmental regulations although this may cut into its profits.

(A) interests   (B) interesting
(C) interestingly   (D) interested

17 If the ------- submitted do not meet federal requirements, the Embassy will be unable to issue a passport.

(A) photographs   (B) photography
(C) photographers   (D) photographic

18 Each customer is regrettably limited to one discount coupon per ------- during the sales promotion.

(A) purchase   (B) to purchase
(C) purchasing   (D) purchased

19 A personal finance report includes the credit status of an individual, and is used by the ------- to determine whether or not to grant a loan.

(A) lend   (B) lent
(C) lender   (D) lending

20 For inquiries on estimated arrival time for your order, please contact the --------company by clicking on the following link.

(A) deliver   (B) delivery
(C) deliverance   (D) deliverable

Part VI

Ms. Winona McBride
BioTech Inc.
Planning Department
67 Valley Road
Chicago, Ill. 98798

Dear Ms. McBride,
As we discussed in our meeting last week, I'm writing to detail our bid for ------- in erecting

21 (A) select   (B) selecting
(C) selective   (D) selection

BioTech's new state of the art research compound. Although we are not a state owned contractor, we receive ------- praise and recommendation from various renowned institutes such as The

22 (A) inclusive   (B) unanimous
(C) elevated   (D) declaratory

International Architects Guild and The Goethe Institute of Urban Design, and we have the utmost ------- that we are the ideal choice in cost-effectively building the most secure edifice. We

23 (A) optimism   (B) optimistic
(C) optimist   (D) optimistically

use up-to-code material and have a range of skilled structural engineers on our team, thus ensuring complete client satisfaction. Enclosed you will find a ------- account of the estimated cost and

24 (A) durable   (B) nutritious
(C) comprehensive   (D) presumptive

completion time frame for this endeavor. We hope to collaborate with you on this exciting project.

Sincerely,
Steven Shield
Mountain View Construction

正確答案 P54

Chapter 12 名詞 | 145

Chapter 13

代名詞

啊哈!! 愉快地打基礎

1

為了防止同一個名詞反覆使用多次，就用代名詞來代替名詞。因此代名詞也可以像名詞一樣在句中充當主詞、受詞或補語的角色。

I shut my cat in the room, and <u>my cat</u> scratched the door.
→ I shut my cat in the room, and it scratched the door.
我把貓關在房間裡，然後牠就抓門了。

it 是代替名詞 my cat 在後半句中充當主詞。

2

代名詞按用法的不同可分為人稱代名詞，反身代名詞，指示代名詞，否定代名詞等。

① 人稱代名詞（I, you, she, he, they 等）用來代替人或事物。
Helen quit her job because she didn't get along with her co-workers.
Helen 辭去她的工作，因爲她和同事處不來。

上文中的 she 用來代替 Helen，以避免重複使用。

② 反身代名詞（himself, herself, themselves 等）是人稱代名詞加 -self (-selves), 有（…自身）的涵義，即表示人稱代名詞自身。

單數	myself	yourself	himself, herself, itself
複數	ourselves	yourselves	themselves

James talks to himself when he works. James 工作時經常會自言自語。

在這裡 himself 是有「James 自身」涵義的反身代名詞。若在這裡把 himself 改為 him，那就不是「對 James 自身」的涵義，而是變為對「別的男生」說的涵義。

③ 指示代名詞（this / these, that / those 等）有「這個（些）」，「那個（些）」的意思，是指特定的人或事物。他們還可以以「這…」，「那…」意思的指示形容詞角色用在名詞前。
I have never seen scenery like this. 我從沒看過這樣的風景。
This book will be interesting. 這書會很有趣的。

上文中的 this 是「這個」意思的指示代名詞，下文中的 this 是「這個…」意思的指示形容詞。

④ 不定代名詞（some, any 等）用來表示未知事物，人或數量。他們又可以以「任一」、「某些」意思的不定形容詞角色用在名詞前。
Some of the visitors are single. 訪客中有幾位是單身。
Some visitors are single. 某些訪客是單身。

上文中的 some 是訪客中的「幾個」意思的不定代名詞，下文中的 some 是「某些…」意思的不定形容詞。

01 人稱代名詞的格

❶ 人稱代名詞的種類

人稱	數 / 性		主格	所有格	受格	所有格代名詞
第一人稱	單數		I	my	me	mine
	複數		we	our	us	ours
第二人稱	單 / 複數		you	your	you	yours
第三人稱	單數	男性	he	his	him	his
		女性	she	her	her	hers
		事物	it	its	it	-
	複數		they	their	them	theirs

❷ 主格用在主詞的位置。

They were given free tickets to the show. 他們被贈予了那場公演的免費門票。

He will go with us to the park as long as we take our bikes. 只要我們騎自行車,他就會和我們一起去公園。

❸ 所有格像形容詞一樣用在名詞前,表示「⋯的」涵義。

Many people make decisions based on their emotions. 很多人根據他們的感情做出決定。

注意! 所有格前不能接 a / an 一樣的不定冠詞,所以不能用 a my client,而要用所有格代名詞寫成 a client of mine。

❹ 受格用在及物動詞的受格和介系詞受格的位置。

The advisor helped them to understand the legal situation. 那個顧問幫他們瞭解法律上的情況。

Mr. Wilson works with me. Wilson 先生和我一起工作。

注意! 要注意不要看到介系詞就直接用受格。

I am satisfied with me(→ my) job. 我很滿意我的工作。

⇨ 後面有名詞 job,所以要用所有格 my。

❺ 所有格代名詞是代替「所有格 ＋名詞」,解釋成「⋯的」意思,用在主詞、受詞、補語的位置。

My book is about plants, but hers is about herbs. 我的書是關於盆栽,但是她的是關於草藥。

多益實戰考題　　　　　　　多 益 會 出 這 樣 的 問 題

⊙ 填正確的代名詞。

1. When the trade negotiators arrived at the airport, ------- were picked up and brought to their hotel.

   (A) them　　　　　(B) theirs
   (C) their　　　　　(D) they

2. After delivering ------- proposal, Mr. Douglas sat with committee advisors to listen to their comments.

   (A) he　　　　　(B) his
   (C) him　　　　(D) himself

3. If you experience any problem using the website, you may contact ------- at any of the following telephone numbers or send an e-mail to websiteop@unicom.net.

   (A) we　　　　　(B) us
   (C) our　　　　(D) ours

正確答案　P56

Hackers Skill　　所有格後面必須接名詞,但所有格代名詞後絕對不能接名詞。

Many people make decisions based on theirs(→ their) emotions.

My book is about plants, but her(→ hers) is about herbs.

02 反身代名詞

❶ 受詞主詞是一致的人事物時，在受詞的位置上用反身代名詞。這時不能省略反身代名詞。

Sometimes, Jessica talks to herself. (Jessica = herself) Jessica 有時會自言自語。
→ 受詞的位置上用了反身名詞 herself，說明 Jessica 跟自己說話。這時不能省略 herself。

cf) Sometimes, Jessica talks to her. (Jessica ≠ her) Jessica 有時會跟她說話。
→ 在受詞位置上用了受格 her，這說明 Jessica 不是跟自己，而是跟別的女人說話。

❷ 為了表示強調主詞或受詞，就在要強調的語句後面或在句子的最後加上反身代名詞。

The manager himself guided the group to the factory. 管理者親自迎接該團隊到公司。
I didn't have time to read the report myself. 我沒有時間親自看那個報告。
She liked the house itself, but not the location. 她喜歡那個房子的本身，但不喜歡那個地理位置。

注意！ 在命令句中省略了主詞 you，但即使沒有主詞也要用 yourself。
Don't try to do repairs oneself(→ yourself). 不要試圖親自去修。

❸ 有關反身代名詞的慣用表現。

> by oneself (= alone = on one's own) 獨自，靠自己的力量
> for oneself 為自己　of itself 自動　in itself 本質上

She prefers to travel by herself rather than with a tour group.
她更喜歡獨自旅行，而不想跟團隊一起。
You should judge by yourself. 你要靠自己去判斷。

多益實戰考題　多 益 會 出 這 樣 的 問 題

⊙ 填反身代名詞。

2. Chad Reyes's total sales for this year topped everyone else's in the entire company, so the manager gave ------ the top employee award.

(A) him　　　　　(B) he
(C) his　　　　　(D) himself

1. I have not been able to examine the statement ------- although it has been on my desk for the past two days.

(A) me　　　　　(B) myself
(C) mine　　　　(D) my

3. Karen got the job by ------- despite rumors that she has friends in high places.

(A) her　　　　　(B) she
(C) herself　　　(D) hers

正確答案 P56

Hackers Skill　充當受詞的代名詞與主詞不一致時，不能用反身代名詞，而要用受格。

Members of the Fulbright Council have granted themselves(→ them) scholarships.
Fulbright 委員會的會員們發給他們獎學金。
→ 主詞 Members 發獎學金的對象不是 Members 自己，而是其他人，所以用受格 them 是正確的。

148

03 指示代名詞 / 指示形容詞

❶ 指示代名詞 that / those 用來代替前面提過的名詞。

Mr. Schmidt's <u>performance</u> is far superior to that [of his associates]. Schmidt 先生的執行能力與他的同事相比很出色。

I think London's <u>restaurants</u> are better than those [of New York]. 我認為倫敦的餐廳比紐約的更好。

The only <u>warranties</u> applying to the vehicle are those [offered by the manufacturer].
那台車的唯一保證是就製造商提供的保證。

→ 這時 that 和 those 後面必須接修飾語。

注意! 1. that 不能代替人物名詞。

The blonde girl I saw was older than <u>that</u>(→ the one) you were dancing with.
我看到的那個金髮少女比跟你跳過舞的那位年紀要大些。

cf)The blonde girls I saw were older than <u>those</u> you were dancing with.

2. that / those 的位置上不能用 this / these。

Mr. Schmidt's performance is far superior to <u>this</u>(→ that) of his associates.
One company's products can be distinguished from <u>these</u>(→ those) of another company.
公司之間的商品應該是可以區分開來的。

❷ those 也可以用作「…的人們」的意思。

Those [who are responsible for this crime] will be severely punished.
對這次犯罪有責任的人會受到嚴懲。

Those [interested in joining the discussion] need to register in advance.
有意參加討論的人需要預先登記。

→ 這時 those 不代替前面的名詞，而是用作「…的人們」的意思。這時 those 後面也必須接修飾語。

注意! those 的位置上不能用 they 或 them。（因為 they 或 them 後面不能接修飾語。）

<u>They</u>(→ Those) interested in joining the discussion need to register in advance.

❸ this / that 和 these / those 以「這…」「那…」意思的指示形容詞角色用在名詞前。

<u>This</u> <u>meeting</u> will be difficult. 這次會議會很不容易。

<u>Those</u> <u>buildings</u> were built several decades ago. 那些建築是數十年以前建的。

注意! 指示形容詞有時不代表「這…」的意思，而像 "the" 一樣用是特別指定的意思。

<u>Those trainers</u>(= The trainers) who wish to attend the conference should register this month.
有意參加會議的講師們應在這個月登記。

<u>Those memories</u>(= The memories) which we acquire in early childhood rarely lose their vividness.
在幼年早期獲得的記憶很不容易遺忘。

多益實戰考題

多 益 會 出 這 樣 的 問 題

⊙ 填 that / those。

一般在 that / those 後面出現 of 子句，但也常出現 who 形容詞子句，分詞等。

1. This factory's shoes can be distinguished from ------- of another factory because of the spiral imprint on the bottom.

(A) this
(B) them
(C) that
(D) those

2. For ------- hoping to participate in this year's marathon, an application form has been made available online to facilitate quick and easy registration.

(A) those
(B) who
(C) ones
(D) them

3. Food prices in general rose nearly 14 percent, with the price of meat going up by 20 percent and ------- of vegetables by 5.8 percent.

(A) this
(B) that
(C) these
(D) those

正確答案 P57

04 不定代名詞 / 不定形容詞 1 one / another / other

❶ one 代替不定單數可數名詞。

I sold my old <u>car</u> and bought a new one. 我賣掉舊車後買了輛新車。
→ one 前必須有 one 所代替的名詞。

注意！ one 的複數形式為 ones，並代替數量不確定的複數可數名詞。
I sold my old books and bought new <u>ones</u>. 我賣掉舊書後買了些新書。

❷ another 是「已經提到之外的另一個」的意思。

One of the students is from Mexico. Another student is from Japan. (Another is from Japan.)
學生其中一名來自墨西哥，另一名來自日本。
→ another 用作形容詞使用時，後面必須接單數可數名詞，而且 another 前不能接 the 。

❸ other / others 是「已經提到之外的其他幾個」的意思。

One of the students is from Mexico. Other students are from Brazil. (Others are from Brazil.)
這些學生中有一名是來自墨西哥，其他都來自巴西。
→ other 用作形容詞時以代名詞的角色出現，後面接複數可數名詞。

注意！ other 後面也可以接不可數名詞。
We can get <u>other</u> information from the website. 我們可以在網路上獲得其他的資訊。

❹ the other(s) 是「除去特定之外，剩下的全部」的意思。

I have three books. Two are mine. The other book is yours. (The other is yours.)
我有三本書。兩本是我的，那一本是你的。

I have three books. One is mine. The other books are yours. (The others are yours.)
我有三本書。一本是我的，剩下的兩本是你的。
→ 剩下一個時用 the other + 單數名詞，或只用 the other。剩下兩個及以上時用 the other + 複數名詞，或只用 the others。

注意！ 表示「互相」的意思時常用 each other，one another 等。
Both parties should show respect for <u>each other</u>'s opinion. 兩個政黨應該尊重互相的意見。
They sat for two hours without talking to <u>one another</u>. 他們坐了兩個小時，完全沒有互相說話。

多益實戰考題　　　　　多 益 會 出 這 樣 的 問 題

⊙ 填不定代名詞 / 形容詞。

2. The company purchased most of its necessities from a single supplier, but ------- were ordered from special sources.

(A) other　　　　　(B) others
(C) the other　　　(D) both

1. The company has grown so quickly that its owners are planning to set up one branch in China and ------- in Japan.

(A) each other　　(B) one another
(C) other　　　　　(D) another

3. During the orientation for new employees, it was discovered that two of the workers already knew each -------.

(A) ones　　　　　(B) other
(C) another　　　(D) others

正確答案　P57

Hackers Skill　　another 後面接單數可數名詞，other 後面接複數可數名詞。

Other(→ Another) <u>candidate</u> has jumped into the presidential race. 另一個候選人投身總統大選。
We are willing to explore another(→ other) <u>options</u>. 我們願意來調查其他的選項。

05 不定代名詞 / 不定形容詞 2 some / any, no / none, most / almost

❶ some 常以「一些，若干個」的意思作代名詞和形容詞的角色，此時只用在肯定句中。 any 常以「一些，任何」的意思作代名詞和形容詞的角色，這時只用在否定句、疑問句、條件句中。

Some of the members didn't show up. 一些會員沒有出現。
I'm going to buy some clothes. 我買了一些衣服。
There's some ice in the freezer. 冰箱裡有一些冰塊。

We don't have any of the equipment. 我們沒有任何裝備。
Have you got any luggage? 你有任何行李嗎？
If there are any letters for me, can you send them to this address? 如果有任何要給我的信，能不能送到這個位址？

注意！ 1. 表示建議或請求意義的疑問句時使用 some 。
　　　　Would you like some coffee? （建議）要喝咖啡嗎？
　　　　Can I have some soup? （請求）我可以喝湯嗎？
　　　 2. any 用在肯定句時有「任何…」的意思。
　　　　Any equipment removed from the lab must be signed for. [=If there is any equipment]
　　　　要從研究室搬走任何裝備都要得到批准。
　　　　Anyone involved in the project can see the reports. 任何參加專案的人都可以看報告書。
　　　 3. something, somebody, someone 像 some 一樣在肯定句中，同理， anything, anybody, anyone 也像 any 一樣用在否定句、疑問句、條件句。
　　　　I don't want anything to eat. 我什麼也不想吃。 There's somebody at the door. 門旁邊有人。

❷ no 作為形容詞後面必須接名詞， none 作為代名詞單獨用在名詞位置。

We had to walk home because there was no bus. 因為沒有公車，所以我們只好走路回家。
All the tickets have been sold. There are none left. 所有的票都賣完了，一張也不剩。
None of the shops were open. 沒有一家商店營業。

注意！ 1. no one 不能被「of + 人」修飾， not 可以用在 a / an 前，表示強調的意味。
　　　　No(→ Not) one of them knew how to handle it. 他們之中沒人知道怎樣去掌控它。
　　　 2. Nothing 與 not anything 同義，也不能用在 anything 的位置上。
　　　　There is anything(→ nothing) to add to the list. 那個清單沒有任何需要補充的。

❸ most 以「大部分（的）」的意思作代名詞和形容詞， almost 以「幾乎」的意思作副詞。

Most of the people didn't enjoy the party. 大部分的人都不怎麼享受這次聚會。
Most people didn't enjoy the party. 大部分人都不怎麼享受這個聚會。
Almost all the people didn't enjoy the party. 幾乎所有的人都不怎麼享受這個聚會。

多益實戰考題　　　　　　　　　　多 益 會 出 這 樣 的 問 題

⊙ 填入不定代名詞 / 形容詞。

1. ------- of the clerks in the supply room faulted themselves for not accurately recording the inventory of supplies.

(A) No　　　　　　(B) One
(C) Some　　　　　(D) Any

2. We received the sales figures for last year, but there appears to be ------- of a discrepancy in third quarter.

(A) something　　　(B) everything
(C) anything　　　　(D) nothing

3. The project approval committee received 40 proposals, ------- of which were related to the transmission of electricity to rural areas.

(A) most　　　　　(B) the most
(C) any　　　　　　(D) almost

正確答案　P57

06 名詞、代名詞一致

❶ 代名詞和名詞的數要一致。即單數名詞對單數代名詞，複數名詞對複數代名詞。

	單數	複數
人稱代名詞	he / his / him, she / her / her, it / its / it	they / their / them
反身代名詞	himself, herself, itself	themselves
指示代名詞	this, that	these, those

Businesses should consider the social implications of ~~its~~ activities. 企業要考慮到它們的活動所帶來的社會意義。

their

Mr. Pak and the other employees tried to finish it by ~~himself.~~ Pak 先生和其他職員正努力去獨自完成這個任務。

themselves

A grandparent's job is easier than ~~those~~ of a parent. 祖父母的工作比父母的工作容易。

that

注意！ 像形容詞一樣用在名詞前面時，代名詞也要與名詞的數保持一致，所以用 this / that + 單數名詞、these / those + 複數名詞。

these(→ this) travel-expense report 這個旅行經費明細報告　　this(→ these) areas 這些地區

❷ 代名詞要與名詞保持性 / 人稱一致。

Mr. Jones enjoyed the work so much that ~~it~~ changed his career. Jones 先生非常喜歡那個工作，所以換了他的職業。

he

Mrs. Pringle and ~~his~~ husband attended an investment club. Prings 夫人和她丈夫都參加了一個投資俱樂部。

her

The firm wishes to announce the addition of Mr. Hopkins to ~~his~~ board of directors.

its

公司想要公佈 Hopkins 先生已加入董事會的訊息。

The country has become one of the largest natural gas producers by increasing ~~your~~ production.

its

那個國家透過增加生產而成爲天然氣的最大生產國之一。

多益實戰考題　　多益會出這樣的問題

⊙ 填與名詞的數 / 性一致的代名詞。

1. The library has its own collection of rare books, but ------- also sponsors local exhibits with books loaned by other libraries.

(A) they　　　　(B) he
(C) it　　　　　(D) we

2. Representatives of the fishing industry said that the decline in fish stocks was slowing down, but ------- progress was not expected to last.

(A) that　　　　(B) which
(C) those　　　 (D) whose

3. The executive committee decided that a task force would not have ------- own decision-making capability but would defer to management for resolutions.

(A) its　　　　　(B) his
(C) her　　　　 (D) theirs　　正確答案 P58

Hackers Skill　　為了解決名詞與代名詞一致的問題，要清楚地知道代名詞所代表的是前面名詞中的哪一個。

The firm wishes to announce the addition of Mr. Hopkins to his(→ its) board of directors.
在前面的名詞中代名詞指的是 the firm，所以不能用 his，而要用 its。

Practice 1 選擇正確的答案。

01 Cashiers are asked to report to (them / their) division heads if there is any discrepancy in the tills.

02 Tycon is a successful corporation because its employees are more skilled than (that / those) of other companies.

03 In order to process the request, we must have (your / yours) account number and permanent address.

04 If you need (another / other) application form, go to the reception desk and they will assist you.

05 Mrs. Gray was expected to arrive by (her / herself), but she couldn't find the conference center.

06 We consider (him / his) not only the best analyst in the industry, but also the top manager.

07 We will teach (that / those) individuals who want their own business how to manage daily operations.

Practice 2 改正錯誤的地方。

08 Labor unions are opposed to the bills, saying he would worsen conditions for temporary workers.

09 The problem is that construction companies saw all its 2004 profits disappear into steel costs.

10 By boosting our production, the company hopes to climb out of bankruptcy.

11 Although the marketing strategy failed, the CEO has decided to give them another try.

12 Absent employees must send in a letter explaining the reason for its absence.

13 We extend its sincerest appreciation to the National Consumer Committee for a job well done.

14 Compaq has decided to recall its laptops and upgrade themselves at no additional cost to the consumer.

正確答案 P58

Part V

01 The finance department would like to announce the addition of Jake Pasternak to ------- team of accountants.

    (A) its   (B) it
    (C) his   (D) him

02 One employee at the company prefers working during fixed hours, while ------- appreciates the flex-hour system recently installed by the manager.

    (A) any   (B) other
    (C) either   (D) another

03 Mr. Evans, head of advertising, had to miss the morning briefing in order to make ------- monthly medical checkup.

    (A) he   (B) him
    (C) his   (D) himself

04 We are waiting for Enron to turn in its annual fiscal report before we calculate -------.

    (A) us   (B) our
    (C) ourselves   (D) ours

05 Mr. Eisenhower was offered a number of positions in the company, ------- of which was exactly what he was looking for.

    (A) few   (B) none
    (C) both   (D) all

06 The company cannot let its present problem with organizational restructuring ------- its plans to merge with Macro Technologies.

    (A) affect   (B) affected
    (C) to affect   (D) affecting

07 Famous people sometimes make good use of ------- celebrity status by launching their own product lines.

    (A) they   (B) their
    (C) them   (D) themselves

08 The assistant accounting manager doesn't have ------- authority to release the documents the client is requesting.

    (A) another   (B) one
    (C) no   (D) any

09 Brenda Chastain asked the person sitting next to ------- whether there would be any more talks featuring the eminent cardiologist, Dr. Bernard.

    (A) she   (B) hers
    (C) her   (D) herself

10 It is the company's policy that the director ------- must abstain from any political involvement in carrying out his responsibilities.

    (A) him   (B) himself
    (C) he   (D) his

11 Employees working on an incentive-based contract are more efficient than ------- who are salaried and locked into a one-year term.

    (A) such   (B) that
    (C) those   (D) someone

12 ------- a single missing file has been retrieved from the main computer yet, causing widespread panic in the office.

    (A) No   (B) Any
    (C) None   (D) Not

13 Staff evaluators place heavy emphasis on employee ------- records, as punctuality is a sign of responsibility and stability.

    (A) attendance   (B) attending
    (C) attend   (D) attended

14 At the Svelte Health Club, all patrons should have ------- body fat percentage measured before they embark on an exercise regimen.

    (A) they   (B) them
    (C) their   (D) theirs

15 One associate remained in the main office with the visiting executives while ------- ran out to gather the prepared reports and documents.

(A) other   (B) the other
(C) each other   (D) one another

16 ------- them have had two or three years of experience in graphic design before coming to our company.

(A) Most   (B) Most of
(C) Almost   (D) Any of

17 A formal dinner will be held in honor of Bill Ward, who has been a client of ------- ever since the company established itself nearly thirty years ago.

(A) us   (B) our
(C) ours   (D) ourselves

18 Larger businesses are expected by the government to donate a certain percentage of ------- earnings to charities each year.

(A) its   (B) their
(C) it   (D) them

19 The wearing of proper headgear at all construction sites ------- by the company as an important safety procedure.

(A) are required   (B) require
(C) is required   (D) has required

20 The salesmen asked the president to reimburse ------- for expenses incurred while they were away on business.

(A) them   (B) themselves
(C) their   (D) they

21 Sally was so grateful for her promotion that ------- sent a dozen flowers to the supervisor who recommended her.

(A) it   (B) she
(C) its   (D) her

22 The bureau is hesitant to cut public sector health costs, but ------- proposal may be applied to the private sector by the end of the week.

(A) that   (B) those
(C) them   (D) theirs

23 You have illegally passed on confidential financial information to another corporation, so the police will have to be -------.

(A) notify   (B) notification
(C) notifying   (D) notified

24 The court ordered that both parties present their copies of the original contract to -------.

(A) another   (B) other
(C) other ones   (D) each other

25 ------- determined to earn their holiday bonus must not miss any days between now and the Christmas break.

(A) They   (B) That
(C) Those   (D) Someone

26 The finance expert received the proposals and will now sift through ------- before determining which one will best suit the company's interests.

(A) it   (B) them
(C) theirs   (D) ours

27 As soon as we ------- your payment, the packaging and shipping department will send your order.

(A) will receive   (B) receive
(C) are receiving   (D) having received

28 Many small businesses are consolidating ------- debt by refinancing with a government-sponsored low-interest loan.

(A) they   (B) them
(C) their   (D) theirs

Chapter 14

形容詞

啊哈!! 愉快地打基礎

1 形容詞限定或說明名詞的性質或狀態。

I like long hair. 我喜歡長頭髮。
The bridge is pretty long. 那座橋很長。

第一個句子是表示很多種類的髮型中喜歡長頭髮的意思，同時形容詞 long 限定了名詞 hair 的種類。第二個句子中的 long 則說明的是 bridge 的形態，與上面的有所不同。

2 形容詞通常以 -able, -al, -ible, -ic, -tive, -ous, -ful, -y 結尾。

advisable	formal	responsible	specific
effective	previous	successful	heavy

也有些形容詞以 -ly 結尾，所以不要與副詞混淆。

likely 有可能的 lively 有活力的 costly 昂貴的 deadly 致命的 friendly 親切的

01 形容詞的位置

① 形容詞用在修飾名詞的位置。

- （冠詞）+（副詞）+ 形容詞 + 名詞

  You will get <u>the</u> specific <u>information</u> about the meeting. 你將會得到這個會議的確切資訊。

  The <u>highly</u> successful <u>book launch</u> was attended by thousands of people.

  有數千人參加了這個非常成功的書本發表會。

- 形容詞 + 複合名詞（名詞 + 名詞）

  John was awarded for his exceptional <u>job performance</u> with a promotion.

  John 因為他出眾的工作表現得到了升職的獎勵。

- 名詞 + 形容詞

  The bank will take every <u>measure</u> possible to ensure the safety of the cashiers.

  銀行將採取一切措施來保證出納員的安全。

  注意！ 1. 形容詞在「形容詞 + 名詞」的構成中修飾名詞時，注意不要在形容詞的位置上錯用副詞。

    Please report the <u>totally</u>(→ total) financial expenses. 請回報所有財務上的花費。

  2. 以 -abl / -ible 結尾的形容詞在修飾名詞時放後面。

    The tickets <u>available</u> are for the day performance only. 公演的票只能在白天使用。

② 形容詞用在補語的位置。

主詞補語的位置   It is important to be creative in the field of advertising. 在廣告業界，創意很重要。

受詞補語的位置   Light-colored walls make a room bright. 亮色的牆會使房間看起來明亮。

③ 形容詞的位置上不能用副詞和名詞。

People can become overweight because of an ~~improperly~~ diet. 不當的日常飲食會使人們變得超重。

improper

→ 為了修飾名詞（diet），要用形容詞（improper），而不是副詞（improperly）。

There is an opening for an ~~experience~~ assistant professor. 有個職位需要有經驗的助理教授。

experienced

→ 為了修飾複合名詞 assistant professor，要用形容詞（experienced），而不是名詞（experience）。

多益實戰考題   多 益 會 出 這 樣 的 問 題

⊙ 填形容詞。

2. If we continue with the ------- production rate, inventory in all stores should be stocked by next week.

(A) present   (B) presented

(C) presently   (D) presenting

1. Commercial banks are advised to take ------- action to amend the serious currency shortfall.

(A) quickness   (B) quicken

(C) quickly   (D) quick

3. Workers in general are much less ------- to detail during the day if they haven't had sufficient rest.

(A) attentive   (B) attention

(C) attentively   (D) attentiveness

正確答案 P61

02 數量表示

❶ 可數名詞、不可數名詞前的數量表現

可數名詞前			不可數名詞前	可數、不可數名詞前	
單數名詞	複數名詞				
a / an 一個	one of …中一個	each of ～中每一個	(a) little 一點	no …都沒有	all 所有
each 每一個	(a) few 一些	fewer 更少的	less 更少的	more 更多	most 大部分的
one 一個	both 都	many 許多	much 許多	some 幾個，某些	any 任何
every 所有	several 幾個	numerous 大量的	a great deal of 許多	lots of 許多	a lot of 許多
another 另一個	various 多樣的	a variety of 多樣的	a large amount of 許多	plenty of 許多	other 其他的
a single 一個	a couple of 幾個	a number of 許多			

~~Much~~ customers benefited from the service. 很多顧客都從那項服務中受益。
Many
→ customers 是可數名詞，所以不能用不可數名詞前的數量表現（much）來修飾，而要用可數名詞前的數量表現（many）。

I was given ~~few~~ information at the help desk. 我在詢問處幾乎沒得到任何資訊。
little
→ information 是不可數名詞，所以其前面不能用可數名詞前的數量表現（few），而要用不可數名詞前的數量表現（little）。

注意！ all, more, most, lots of, a lot of, plenty of, other 等可以用在複數可數名詞前，修飾名詞。
All letter(→ letters) should be signed. 所有的信都要簽名。

❷ 當數量表現和名詞間有 of the 來限定名詞的部分或全部時，of 和 the 一個也不能省略。

one / two	each	all	both	none	
many	much	most	several		+ of the + 名詞
some	any	(a) few	(a) little		

Some ~~of / the~~ progress in sales was due to the unique ads. 業績成長的一部分原因是基於這些獨特的廣告。
of the
→ 數量表現（some）和名詞（progress）間不能只有 of 和 the 其中的一個，而是 of 和 the 一起使用。

注意！ 1. 特例：all 和 both 存在時可以不接 of。
All (of) the staff asking for time off must submit a request form. 所有申請休假的職員都要提交申請書。
2. 名詞前面的所有格可以替代 the 的出現。
All of our staff have full time jobs. 我們所有的職員都是全職。

多益實戰考題 多益會出這樣的問題

⊙ 填與名詞對應的數量表示。

1. ------- order that comes to our department is processed with the utmost care and attention.

(A) Many　　　　(B) All
(C) Every　　　　(D) Most

2. The unconventional manner of leadership by the company's new marketing manager was the cause of ------- debate in the office.

(A) much　　　　(B) many
(C) mostly　　　　(D) almost

3. Pharmacists have publicly refused to condone any cream which claims to provide ------- impossible cosmetic results and skin altering benefits.

(A) every　　　　(B) a lot
(C) many　　　　(D) some of

03 容易混淆的形容詞

❶ 注意容易混淆的同形異義的形容詞。

appreciable 相當可觀的 — appreciative 感激的 argumentative 好爭論的，爭論的 — arguable 可辯論的 beneficial 有益的 — beneficent 慈善的 careful 謹慎的 — caring 有愛心的 considerable 相當的，重要的 — considerate 考慮周到的 comparable 可比較的 — comparative 比較的 comprehensible 可理解的 — comprehensive 包括，綜合的 economic 經濟的 — economical 經濟的，節約的 exciting 興奮的 — excitable （人）易興奮的 impressive 印象深刻的 — impressed 感動的 informed 精通的，瞭解的 — informative 有益的	persuasive 有說服力的 — persuaded 確信的 probable 可能發生的 — probabilistic 可能性的 profitable 有利的，多益的 — proficient 熟練的 prospective 未來的 — prosperous 繁盛的 reliable 可信的 — reliant 依賴的 respectable 可敬佩的 — respective 各自的 responsible 有責任的，可信的 — responsive 反應的 satisfactory 符合（要求，目標）的 — satisfying 滿意的 seasonal 季節的 — seasoned 有經驗的 successful 成功的 — successive 連續的，相繼的 understanding 通情達理的 — understandable 可理解的

Background music has an ~~appreciative~~ effect on employee productivity.
appreciable

背景音樂對勞動生產力的提高可以產生相當可觀的效果。

→ 要表示的涵義是「相當可觀的效果」，所以不能用 appreciative（感激的），而要用 appreciable。

It is important to keep your supervisor ~~informative~~ about any problems.
informed

讓你的主管隨時瞭解所有的問題是很重要的。

→ 要表示的涵義是「瞭解的」，所以不能用 informative（有益的），而要用 informed。

Telephone representatives are trained not to be ~~arguable~~ with customers.
argumentative

電話訪問員們被訓練不能與顧客爭論。

→ 要表示的涵義是「爭論的」，所以不能用 arguable（可辯論的），而要用 argumentative。

~~Caring~~ use of the machine will prevent it from malfunctioning.
Careful

謹慎的使用機器可以減少故障的產生。

→ 要表示的涵義是「謹慎的」，所以不能用 caring（有愛心的），而要用 careful。

多益實戰考題   多 益 會 出 這 樣 的 問 題

⊙ 填恰當的形容詞。

1. Despite consumer opposition, Nokia will spend ------- time researching the potential benefits of adding GPS to its cell phones.

(A) consider
(B) considerate
(C) considerable
(D) consideration

2. Because his response to the questions was less than -------, the school officials decided to deny him acceptance into their graduate program.

(A) satisfaction
(B) satisfied
(C) satisfactory
(D) satisfying

3. Stunned by the ------- performance of the violinist, the magazine critic was at a loss for words when he sat down to write a review of the show.

(A) impress
(B) impressed
(C) impressively
(D) impressive

正確答案 P61

04 「be + 形容詞」片語

❶ 以下是形容詞用在 be 動詞後面時的慣用表現。

表現	例句
be apt to V = be likely to V = be liable to V 很有可能會…	Sales are likely to increase this season due to high consumer confidence. 因顧客信心增長，本季的銷售量很有可能會增加。
be available to V 可以做… be available for 有可能做…	The applicant indicated that she was available to start working immediately. 那個申請者表示她可以馬上開始工作。 Patricia Wells is usually available for private consultation on weekends only. Patricia Wells 一般只有週末才能做私人顧問。
be aware of = be conscious of = be cognizant of 注意到…	Everyone should be aware of the dangers of second-hand smoke. 每個人都應該注意到二手煙的危險性。
be capable of Ving 有能力…	The department is capable of providing specialized rescue service. 這個部門有能力提供專業的救助活動。
be comparable to 與…差不多	Export figures from this year are comparable to statistics from the past two years. 今年的出口額與前兩年的調查相差不多。
be consistent with 與…一致	Product quality and design must be consistent with customer demand. 商品的品質和設計要與顧客的要求一致。
be eligible for / to V 對…有資格	Freelance workers are not eligible for the company pension plan. 接案的工作人員沒有資格參加公司的退休金計畫。
be responsible for 對…有責任	The city police were responsible for the accident. 市區員警對這起意外是有責任的。
be skilled in / at 熟練於…	People who are skilled in website design are in high demand these days. 近來對技巧熟練的網頁設計人員有很高的需求。
be subject to 受到…，易受到… cf) be subjective to 以…不同，主觀的	Part of this presentation may be subject to revision. 這個報告中的一部分可能會受到修改的影響。 cf) Truth is subjective to the individual. 見仁見智。
be willing to V 願意做…	He is willing to do whatever it takes to succeed. 為了成功他願意做任何事情。

多益實戰考題

⊙ 填入恰當的形容詞。
⊙ 填形容詞。

2. Unless the company's proof of age requirement is satisfied, application for membership in the online shopping club may be ------- to rejection.

(A) subject   (B) subjects
(C) subjective   (D) subjecting

1. Given the recent trends in stocks and bonds, the market is ------- to drop by 2% in the next couple of quarters.

(A) like   (B) alike
(C) likely   (D) likelihood

3. Persons with disabilities are not ------- to apply for labor positions because of the extensive physical demands.

(A) eligibility   (B) eligibleness
(C) eligible   (D) eligibly

HACKERS PRACTICE ● ● ● ● ● ● ● ● ● ● ● ● ● ● ● ●

Practice 1 選擇正確的答案。

01 After a heated debate, the director and assistant manager both returned to their (respective / respectable) offices.

02 Once his father dies, Ben Gershwin will be the (successful / successive) heir to the family's textile business.

03 The weekly staff meeting is held (every / all) Wednesday morning in the presentation room.

04 In general, this year's gross output is (comparative / comparable) to that of the previous three years.

05 The government called for the (continued / continuation) intervention of inspectors in factories mass-producing corporate goods.

06 There is so (many / much) competition that prices are likely to stay low.

07 It was incredibly (considerable / considerate) of the director to give the workers extra vacation time this Christmas.

Practice 2 改正錯誤的地方。

08 The economical outlook portends steep rises in interest rates for business loans.

09 In preparation for the Olympics, many contractors are bidding for the construction of a permanently sports complex.

10 Once the new security system was put in, the store had fewer trouble with prowlers.

11 Rumor has it that Bank of America is like to merge with Fargo Wells next year.

12 A variety of difference factors have contributed to the company's failure, the main one being sales.

13 Todd is an understandable leader who makes all of the workers feel comfortable.

14 The government has announced that businesses contributing to locally charities will be given tax deductions.

正確答案 P62

Part V

01 Mr. Jefferson is a good leader because he is able to provide ------- criticism in a way that people are receptive to.

(A) constructs   (B) constructor
(C) constructive   (D) construction

02 Erickson & Co. has called in a number of professional ------- advisors to give their opinions about the company's potential merger.

(A) finance   (B) financial
(C) financed   (D) financing

03 To avoid giving clients misleading advice on investments, brokers must have access to information that is completely -------.

(A) reliance   (B) reliable
(C) reliant   (D) relying

04 When the analyst provides me with ------- details, I will write up the final report and send it to your office.

(A) almost   (B) a lot
(C) quite   (D) more

05 If there are any changes in the schedule and activities for next week's open house, your ------- will fill you in.

(A) supervision   (B) supervise
(C) supervising   (D) supervisor

06 Visitors to the United States often see signs in public places that state, "Management is not ------- for any loss or damage of personal belongings left unattended."

(A) responsibly   (B) responsible
(C) responsibility   (D) responsive

07 Many injuries at the construction site can be prevented or minimized with the use of ------- equipment.

(A) protect   (B) protects
(C) protective   (D) protecting

08 We think that the community center is the ------- venue for our annual company barbeque.

(A) ideal   (B) idealize
(C) ideally   (D) idealistically

09 All of the employees have been quite ------- with the police during the rigorous investigation of the company.

(A) cooperate   (B) cooperative
(C) cooperating   (D) cooperation

10 The report indicated that ------- independent broker agents in the European continent were being put out of business by larger corporations.

(A) the most   (B) almost
(C) most of   (D) most

11 The company now requires all newly-hired accountants to undergo two months of intensive ------- training before taking on any work responsibilities.

(A) formal   (B) formed
(C) forming   (D) formally

12 The sponsoring company has prepared a ------- online exhibit of the artist's paintings for individuals who do not have time to visit the art center.

(A) special   (B) specially
(C) specialist   (D) specialize

13 Larger discount stores that sell products in bulk are ------- to middle class families that lead busy lives.

(A) attracted   (B) attractive
(C) attraction   (D) attractively

14 The bank is offering a new service that will allow patrons to examine personal transactions listed in a ------- weekly statement.

(A) consolidate   (B) consolidator
(C) consolidated   (D) consolidation

15 The ------- interests of the corporation make it difficult for management to form definite decisions.

(A) diverse   (B) diversification
(C) diversifying   (D) diversity

16 Every means ------- will be used to ensure that your valuables are delivered quickly and safely.

(A) possibility   (B) possible
(C) possibilities   (D) possibly

17 The ------- size of the memory card in mobile phones which feature a built-in camera will allow users to save hundreds of images.

(A) reduce   (B) reducing
(C) reduced   (D) reduction

18 If inventory is well-planned and done in an orderly fashion, it will be ------- trouble than it was last year.

(A) fewer   (B) least
(C) a few   (D) less

19 ------- folder contains important and confidential documents and should be placed inside Mr. Berr's safe when he doesn't need it.

(A) This   (B) Which
(C) These   (D) Whose

20 At his retirement party, a number of Jack's colleagues congratulated him on a highly ------- career in the journalism field.

(A) succeed   (B) successive
(C) succeeded   (D) successful

Part VI

Emma Goldman
45 Green Valley Boulevard
Fargo, North Dakota 79706

Dear Mrs. Goldman,

I am writing to ------- the receipt of your application for our First Time Home Owner Variable

     21 (A) remark   (B) understand
          (C) suggest   (D) acknowledge

Interest Prime Mortgage Plan. I am pleased to inform you that your loan has been approved and we will be able to ------- you the amount requested. As indicated in your chosen plan,

     22 (A) lend   (B) lease
          (C) rent   (D) borrow

once the ------- monetary transaction is performed, you will be required to deposit monthly

     23 (A) initial   (B) initiate
          (C) initially   (D) initiated

installments covering the principal payment and interest into the bank account which will be opened for this purpose. The option to transfer into a closed interest rate package will remain ------- for a period of three years, after which time it will be mandatory for you to continue

     24 (A) effect   (B) effected
          (C) effective   (D) effectively

with the current plan. Please contact the bank to set up an appointment to begin the mortgage process.

Sincerely,
Thomas Mann
Mortgage Representative
M&T Bank

正確答案 P62

Chapter 15

副詞

啊哈!! 愉快地打基礎

1

副詞修飾除名詞之外的詞類，即形容詞、副詞、動詞或修飾片語、子句、句子整體等。

修飾形容詞	The sandwiches were really delicious. 那個三明治真地好吃。
修飾其他副詞	She likes this novel very much. 她非常喜歡這本小說。
修飾動詞	He carefully dug under the tree. 他在樹下小心地挖。
修飾片語	Ally left shortly before 9:00 p.m. Ally 在快 9 點的時候離開了。
修飾子句	I arrived long after the party began. 聚會開始很久後我才到達。
修飾句子整體	Usually, he works Monday to Friday. 他通常從星期一工作到星期五。

2

副詞一般是「形容詞 + ly」的形態。

通常與 calmly, completely, entirely, heavily, temporarily 相似的副詞都以 -ly 結尾。

但也有像 ahead, just, only, still, well 這樣不以 -ly 結尾的副詞。

She smiled in a friendly way. 她親切的微笑著。

這裡 friendly 雖然是以 -ly 結尾，但它卻是形容詞，故在此是以整個片語 "in a friendly way"（以友善的方式）當成是副詞來修飾 smile （微笑），而 friendly 則是以形容詞的形式修飾名詞 way（方式）。

01 副詞的位置

❶ 副詞修飾動詞時副詞的位置。

- 副詞出現在「動詞 + 受詞」的前後，但不能出現在動詞和受詞之間。

   Mr. Fields promptly <u>informed</u> his supervisor of the accident. Fields 先生迅速地把事件報告給他的主管。

   It is necessary <u>to filter</u> ~~individually~~ <u>each customer complaint</u> individually. 個別過濾顧客的抱怨是必須的。

- 修飾的是進行式、被動語態、完成式動詞時，副詞出現在「助動詞 + Ving / p.p.」之間或後面。

   They <u>are</u> still <u>arranging</u> the office to accommodate the new workers.
   為了安置新的職員，他們仍然在整理辦公室。

   Mr. Walker's retirement <u>has been</u> indefinitely <u>postponed</u>. Walker 先生的退休被無限延期。

   The new assistant <u>is adjusting</u> nicely to the corporate life. 新來的助理很適應公司的生活。

❷ 副詞修飾除動詞之外的詞性時，用在被修飾詞的前面。

He gave an exceptionally <u>profound</u> speech at the gathering. 他在聚會中做了意義特別深遠的演講。

The following is the list of the most frequently <u>asked</u> questions. 以下是常見問題列表。

She likes this novel very <u>much</u>. 她非常喜歡這本小說。

The service operates only <u>on the dates</u> listed below. 這個服務只在以下所列的日子裡才提供。

> **注意！** 修飾起形容詞作用的「數量表現」的也是副詞，而不是形容詞。
>
>   <u>Approximate</u>(→ Approximately) <u>10,000</u> workers will be laid off next term. 下一期大約一萬名的職員會被臨時解雇。

❸ 在副詞的位置上不能出現形容詞。

Expense accounts for traveling salesmen have been cut ~~substantial~~. 支付給出差人員工的出差費大大減少了。
                                                    substantially

→ 為了修飾動詞（have been cut），不能用形容詞（substantial），而要用副詞（substantially）。

Whether or not you quit is ~~entire~~ up to you. 你是否放棄完全取決於你。
                          entirely

→ 為了修飾片語（up to you），不能用形容詞（entire），而要用副詞（entirely）。

> **注意！** 在比較句中區分 as ~ as 之間的形容詞 / 副詞的位置時，先去掉 as ~ as，然後再區分會比較容易。
>
>   My computer was as <u>slowly</u> as a snail.(×) → My computer was <u>slowly</u>(→ slow). 我的電腦慢的像蝸牛。
>
>   You'd better eat as <u>slow</u> as possible.(×) → You'd better eat <u>slow</u>(→ slowly). 你最好盡可能地慢慢吃。

多益實戰考題　　　多 益 會 出 這 樣 的 問 題

⊙ 填副詞。

2. Recent advances in telephony have made it possible for mobile phone owners to ------- transmit clear and sharp images to other users.

(A) easy　　　　　(B) easier
(C) easiest　　　　(D) easily

1. A surveyor's inspection shows that it may be ------- impossible to lay the foundation for the memorial on the suggested site.

(A) technically　　　(B) technician
(C) technicality　　　(D) technical

3. He was fired ------- after getting into a heated debate with the manager about appropriate office etiquette.

(A) short　　　　　(B) shorter
(C) shortly　　　　(D) shorten

正確答案　P64

❶ 要注意同形異義的副詞

副詞	例句
hard 艱難的，努力的 hardly 幾乎沒有	Employees that work hard will be rewarded with bonuses. 努力工作的職員可以得到獎勵。 That was hardly enough time for lunch. 用來吃午餐的時間幾乎是不夠的。
high （高度、目標）高 highly （地位，評價，金額）高，非常	Her work has piled up high on her desk. 她的工作高高地堆在她的桌上。 Admittedly, I think highly of our company's founder. 正如所公認的，我對我們公司的創立者的評價也很高。 Private schooling is a highly lucrative industry in South Korea. 在南韓私立教育是一個收益很高的產業。
great 好 greatly 非常	You really have done great this year in terms of sales. 你今年在銷量方面的業績很好。 In spite of a lack of practice, her writing has greatly improved. 儘管缺乏練習，但她的寫作還是進步了很多。
late 遲的，晚的 lately 最近	The company president is scheduled to arrive late Friday evening. 星期五晚上董事長會晚點回來。 Mark has been missing the feedback sessions lately. 最近 Mark 都沒有參加報告會。
most 很，最多 mostly 大體，主要	The lack of coordination at the office annoys me most. 辦公室成員間缺乏配合使我很生氣。 My co-workers are mostly energetic and bright college graduates. 我的同事大部分都是活潑開朗的大學畢業生。
near 接近 nearly 幾乎	They placed the antique table near to the director's desk. 他們把那個古董桌子放在經理的書桌旁邊。 I was nearly finished when the phone rang. 電話響時，我的工作幾乎已經做完了。

注意！ 有時一個單字會同時擁有形容詞和副詞的涵義。

early 早的 / 很早地　late 遲的 / 來不及　hard 困難的 / 努力地　high 高的 / 高度地　long 長久的 / 長久地　fast 快的 / 迅速地
far 遠 / 遠遠地　near 近 / 近的　daily 每日的 / 每日地　weekly 每週的 / 每週　monthly 每月的 / 每月　yearly 每年的 / 每年

形容詞　Early submission of income tax returns is encouraged by IRS. IRS 鼓勵他們早點提交所得稅申報書。
副詞　　Eva always gets up early. Eva 總是早起。

多益實戰考題　　　　　　多 益 會 出 這 樣 的 問 題

⊙ 填入可以構成正確語意的副詞。

1. The manager sent a memo complaining about the timeliness of report submissions and mentioned that monthly reports are being submitted one or two days -------.

(A) lately　　　　　(B) later
(C) lateness　　　　(D) late

2. Sales of compact disc players have gone down ------- fifteen percent this fiscal year.

(A) nearly　　　　　(B) near
(C) quite　　　　　(D) very

3. Kurt Drew works -------, his communication skills are exemplary, and I have no doubt he will be an asset to your company.

(A) hardly　　　　　(B) harden
(C) hard　　　　　(D) hardened

正確答案 P65

03 選擇副詞 1：時間副詞 already / still / yet, ever / ago / once

❶ already / still / yet

- already 有「已經，早已」（用於肯定句）的涵義。

  She has already typed the report you left on her desk. 她已經把你放在她桌子上的報告書打好了。

- still 有「還，仍」（用於肯定句、否定句、疑問句）的涵義。

  The house is still up for sale. 那個房子仍在出售中。

- yet 有「還」（用於否定句），「已經，早已」（用於疑問句）的涵義，並用於詢問預想的事情發生與否。

  Have the reports been filed yet? 已經提出那個報告書了嗎？

注意！
1. 在否定句中 still 和 yet 都表示「還」的意思，但 still 用在 not 前，yet 用在 not 後。

   The funds for the event are <u>still</u> <u>not</u> sufficient. 這次活動的基金還不充足。
   They hadn<u>'t</u> even started the project <u>yet</u>. 他們甚至還沒開始進行那個專案。

2. have yet to + 原形動詞　還沒做…

   They <u>have yet to</u> turn in their last project. 他們還沒提交他們的最後專案。

3. finally（最終，終於）用於期待很久的事情終於發生時。

   After hours of discussion, the group <u>finally</u> agreed to scrap the project.
   經過幾個小時的討論，該團隊最後決定放棄那個計畫。

4. soon（立刻）用於某個事情不久會發生或預想某個事情即將要發生時。

   We expect the changes to come into effect <u>soon</u>. 我們期待立刻實行這些改革。

❷ ever / ago / once（之前）

- ever 表示未知的過去時間點，用在否定句或疑問句中。

  They hardly ever received encouragement from their parents.
  他們不曾沒有得到過他們父母的鼓勵。

- ago 用在時間後面，並表示以現在時間為基準之前發生的事件。

  Mrs. Baker joined our team here at ESCO <u>three years</u> ago.
  三年前，Baker 夫人在這裡加入了我們的 ESCO 團隊。

- once 用來表示未知的過去時間點，有時也修飾形容詞。

  He once managed this store. 他曾經營過這間店。
  Formerly a main source of fish, the area had many once <u>thriving</u> fish markets.
  那個曾經是主要漁場的地區，擁有很多繁榮一時的海鮮市場。

多益實戰考題　　　多益會出這樣的問題

⊙ 填時間副詞。

1. The traffic was so heavy that by the time we arrived at the theater, the award-winning play had ------- started.

   (A) yet　　　　　　(B) already
   (C) once　　　　　(D) still

2. Although infrastructure contracts should be awarded through open bids, the administration has not ------- devised a policy that would allow for it.

   (A) yet　　　　　　(B) still
   (C) never　　　　　(D) already

3. Union leaders have been negotiating with management representatives ever since most of the company's workers went on strike about two weeks -------.

   (A) already　　　　(B) once
   (C) ago　　　　　(D) yet

正確答案　P65

04 選擇副詞 2：頻率副詞 always, usually, often, hardly

❶ 表示頻率的副詞表現事情「發生得有多頻繁」，一般用在一般動詞前，或用在 be 動詞或助動詞的後面。

always 經常	almost 幾乎	often 常常	frequently 頻繁地	usually 通常
sometimes 有時	hardly / rarely / seldom / scarcely / barely 幾乎沒有		never 絕不	

She often tries to help me. 她常常試圖幫助我。

She is so tired that she can hardly keep awake. 她太累了，幾乎難以保持清醒。

He is usually very cheerful. 他通常很開心。

注意！　1. hardly ever 表示「幾乎不，很少」

　　　　　She <u>hardly ever</u> lies. 她幾乎不說謊。

　　　　2. usually 或 often 可以用在句子的最前面，但 always 不能。

　　　　　<u>Always</u>(→ Usually), the pizza delivery boy arrives within 15 minutes of receiving our order.
　　　　　通常，送披薩的少年在我們點完後 15 分鐘內到達。

　　　　　I go there <u>always</u>(→ often). 我經常去那個地方。

　　　　3. 注意不要在頻率副詞的位置上用時間副詞。

　　　　　Passengers with small children are <u>ever</u>(→ usually) given priority seating on planes.
　　　　　帶孩子們的乘客在飛機上通常可以享受到提前入座的待遇。

　　　　4. barely 有「好不容易」的意思。

　　　　　The rain had <u>barely</u> stopped before it came down in a torrential downpour.
　　　　　雨在還沒變成暴雨之前好不容易停了下來。

❷ hardly / rarely / seldom / scarcely / barely（幾乎不⋯）含有否定的涵義，所以不能與 not 等否定詞連用。

I had hardly ~~never~~ taken lunch outside of the office. 我幾乎沒有在辦公室外面吃過午餐。
　　　　　　ever

→ hardly 已經含有否定的涵義，所以不能與 never 一起使用。應該把 never 去掉或用 ever 代替。

注意！　像這樣的否定副詞在句子最前面有強調作用時，就會發生主詞-謂語的倒裝。

　　　　<u>Never</u> was the work at the plant harder than when demand peaked.
　　　　工廠裡絕對沒有比需求最高時更累的時候。

多益實戰考題　　　　　　多 益 會 出 這 樣 的 問 題

⊙ 填頻率副詞。

　會有透過文章的來龍去脈來區分頻率副詞，然後填空的題。

1. At Calvin's Outlet Store, evaluations of team leaders are ------- done at the end of every three month quarter.

(A) yet 　　　　　　　　(B) ever
(C) once 　　　　　　　(D) usually

2. We have the production laborers change schedules ------- to prevent laziness from too much routine.

(A) soon 　　　　　　　(B) often
(C) shortly 　　　　　　(D) hardly

3. ------- have I seen such an eager and enthusiastic recruit with so much experience in the work force.

(A) Ever 　　　　　　　(B) Although
(C) Seldom 　　　　　　(D) Even

正確答案　P65

05 選擇副詞 3：連接副詞 besides, therefore, however, otherwise

❶ 連接副詞是連接前後句涵義的副詞。

besides 而且	moreover 而且	furthermore 而且
therefore 所以	hence 因此	consequently 結果，必然地
however 然而	nevertheless 雖然如此	nonetheless 雖然如此
otherwise 否則，不同地	then 然後，那時	meantime / meanwhile 期間

Knowing he was going to be fired, he consequently didn't put effort into his work.
他知道了將會被解雇的事實，因此他就沒有努力工作。

Draw up a budget and then put it on my desk for review.
制訂好預算報告之後，請把它放在我的桌子上。

❷ 連接副詞也是副詞，所以不能單獨連接兩個句子，要與分號（；）一起使用。

It is too late besides you are tired. (×)
It is too late; besides you are tired. (○) 已經太遲了，而且你也很累了。
→ 連接副詞不同於連接詞，不能連接兩個句子。若要用連接副詞連接兩個句子，要在連接副詞前加分號（；）。

❸ 連接副詞不能與副詞子句中的連接詞重複使用。

Although we were tired and sleepy, ~~nevertheless~~ we kept on walking. 儘管我們又累又睏，但還是繼續走著。
→ 連接副詞（nevertheless）不能與連接詞（although）重複使用，所以要去掉 nevertheless。

注意！ 只有 then 可以用在 if 子句後面。

If you had known this all along, <u>then</u> you could have told me. 如果你一開始就知道，那時你就可以跟我說了。

多益實戰考題　　多益會出這樣的問題

⊙ 填連接副詞。

2. Unless ------- indicated, all the information in this set of records is up-to-date as of June 30, 2001.

(A) instead　　　(B) otherwise
(C) also　　　　(D) else

1. Employee suggestions are always accepted by management; -------, most suggestions are usually not acted upon until after the board meetings are held.

(A) therefore　　(B) otherwise
(C) instead　　　(D) however

3. Make out the check for the correct amount and ------- mail the payment to the address indicated on the invoice.

(A) moreover　　(B) then
(C) although　　(D) whereas

正確答案　P66

❶ just, right（剛剛）在前面強調 before 或 after。

Get in touch with the secretary just(=right) <u>before</u> coming to the office. 剛來辦公室的時候，請跟秘書聯繫。

注意！ 1. just enough 表示「剛剛好，勉強」

I have <u>just enough</u> time to eat lunch before my next class. 下節課開始之前，我有剛好吃午餐的時間。

2. just 修飾動詞時有「剛剛」的涵義。（兩個詞的意思一樣）

Sage Entertainment <u>just</u> announced the leading male actor for its upcoming epic film.
Sage Enterainment 剛剛宣布了這部史詩電影的男主角人選。

❷ only, just（僅）強調介系詞片語或名詞片語。

They hold barbecue parties only <u>during the summer.</u> 他們只在夏天舉辦烤肉會。

It's just <u>a simple manager-employee misunderstanding.</u> 那只是管理者和員工之間的單純誤會。

❸ well（遠遠）強調介系詞片語。

Stock prices are well <u>over market value</u> this week. 股價本週遠遠超過了市場價格。

注意！ well 是 good 的副詞形式，表示「很好地，優秀地」意思。

Tomas does his job <u>well</u>. Tomas 的工作表現很出色。

❹ even（甚至）用在單字或片語前，有強調作用。

Even <u>the anthropology professor</u> thought the speech was boring. 就連人類學教授也覺得那個演講很無聊。

We <u>will</u> even <u>provide</u> you with complimentary mints on your pillow. 我們甚至會免費在你的枕頭上加薄荷。

→ even 強調「助動詞 + 一般動詞」時用在助動詞和一般動詞之間。

❺ quite（相當）用在「a/ an+ 名詞」前，有強調作用

The new archiving system was quite <u>a success.</u> 新的資料庫系統相當成功

注意！ 1. not quite: 還沒完全地

I'm <u>not quite</u> ready to take the next step. 我還沒完全地準備好去執行下一步。

2. quite 跟動詞、形容詞、副詞合用時有「非常，相當，很」的意思。

The performance was <u>quite surprising</u>. 這個表演相當令人驚訝。

❻ nearly（幾乎），almost（幾乎），just（正好）強調原級；much, even, still, far, a lot, by far（遠遠）強調比較級；by far, quite（顯然）強調最高級。

She's just <u>as</u> intelligent and good-looking <u>as</u> her brothers and sisters. 她就像她的兄弟姐妹一樣聰明又好看。

There is a much <u>better</u> store around the corner. 轉角處附近有更好的店。

Joel Rivera is by far <u>the most forceful</u> of all the speakers at the convention.
顯然 Joel Rivera 是會議中最有說服力的演講者。

多益實戰考題   多 益 會 出 這 樣 的 問 題

⊙ 填程度副詞。

1. This business visa allows you to travel to your destination ------- on the days listed at the bottom of the paper.

(A) also   (B) only
(C) even   (D) however

2. Parmalat sold its ImClone stocks at a price that was ------- below the market value at that time.

(A) very   (B) so
(C) well   (D) such

3. The company decided that a ------- more aggressive approach to advertising was needed to pull ahead of the competition.

(A) so   (B) very
(C) much   (D) really

正確答案 P66

07 選擇副詞 5：so, such, very, too

❶ 雖然 so 和 such 都表示「非常」的意思。但 so 是副詞，所以用來修飾形容詞 / 副詞； such 是形容詞，用來修飾名詞。

The store was ~~such~~ busy that it had to hire additional part-time workers.
　　　　　　　so
那家店非常忙，所以額外雇用了兼職人員。

Sales items sold out ~~such~~ quickly that the shop had to close early.
　　　　　　　　　　so
因為商品賣的非常快，所以那家店只好早點關門。

→ such 不能修飾形容詞（busy）、副詞（quickly），所以要用 so 來修飾。

It's amazing that one company can have ~~so~~ dedicated employees.
　　　　　　　　　　　　　　　　　　　　　such
一個公司能擁有那麼賣力的職員是很令人吃驚的。

→ so 不能修飾名詞（employees），所以要用 such。

注意！ such 修飾單數可數名詞時後面要接 a / an。
　　　　He had never dealt with such an experienced negotiator before. 從來沒有和這麼有經驗的談判者交涉過。

❷ very（非常）和 so 是一樣的意思，但與 so 不同的是 very 不能與 that 子句一起使用。

The explanation in the book is very clear. 那本書的解釋非常清楚。

The staff was ~~very~~ argumentative that it took time before decisions were made.
　　　　　　　so
那個職員很喜歡爭論，所以下決定之前花了些時間。

❸ too（太）不同於 so / such / very，有「太…」的否定涵義。

The report was too long to read all at once. 那個報告書太長，以至於不能一口氣讀完。
→ 表達了「報告書太長，以至於沒有一口氣讀完」的否定涵義。

cf) The walk was very long, but the fresh air felt good. 雖然走了很遠，但新鮮空氣的感覺很好。
→ 表達的是「雖然走了很遠，但感覺不錯」的意思，這裡沒有否定涵義。

注意！ 1. too + 形容詞 / 副詞 + to 不定詞（太…，以至於不能…）
　　　　This is too complicated for the students to understand. 這個太複雜了，以至於學生們不能理解。
　　　　→ 在 too 和 to 不定詞之間，可以添加「for + 受詞」來充當 to 不定詞的形式主語。

　　　 2. too much / many + 名詞（太多的）（= far too much / many）
　　　　They had eaten too much food to go jogging in the park. 他們吃的太多，以至於不能去公園慢跑。

　　　 3. much too + 形容詞 / 副詞（太… / 太…的）（= far too）
　　　　This study is much too comprehensive for Carlos Sanchez to handle.
　　　　這個研究太廣泛了，使 Carios Sanchez 很難掌握。

多益實戰考題　　　　　　　　　　　多 益 會 出 這 樣 的 問 題

⊙ 區分 so, such, very, too 並填空。

1. The chess championships at the school are ------- popular events that the auditorium is always packed on tournament days.

(A) so　　　　　　　(B) huge
(C) such　　　　　　(D) too

2. Considering that the job was done in a rush, the director was ------- satisfied with the results.

(A) too　　　　　　　(B) such
(C) far　　　　　　　(D) very

3. Relative to the average gross revenue, taxes in the area are ------- heavy for the smaller businesses to handle.

(A) much too　　　　(B) such
(C) so　　　　　　　(D) much

正確答案　P66

❶ also / too / as well / either（而且）

- also 只能出現在句子前面或中間部分，不能出現在句子後面。

  I have shares in Samsung, Eurotunnel, and also Alba. 我不僅擁有 Samsung 和 Eurotunnel 的股份，還有 Alba 的。

  Each character represents a syllable of spoken Chinese and also has a meaning.
  每個中文字都表示中文口語中的一個音節，以及涵義。

- too 和 as well 放在句尾。

  There will be workshops offered next month too. 下個月還會舉行研討會。

  Mary wants to apply for the position as well. Mary 也想申請那個職位。

- 否定句表示「也」要用 either。

  Luis won't be going to the dinner party; Pedro won't be going either.
  Luis 不參加晚上的聚會，Pedro 也不會去。

❷ later（以後）/ thereafter（其後）/ since（自從）

- later 用在時間表現之後，是「那個時間以後」的意思。

  He was questioned about the scandal five months later. 過了 5 個月後，他才被問及關於那個醜聞的事情。

  Why don't we talk this over later? 我們何不晚點來討論這件事情？

  → later 若出現在沒有時間表現的情況下，就表示「現在之後（after now）」。

- thereafter 表示「之後（after that）」的意思。

  Sally left and her package was delivered shortly ~~later~~. Sally 離開了，隨後她的包裹很快被送走了。
  thereafter

  → later 在沒有時間表現時表示「現在之後」的意思，因此與該句想表達的涵義「之後」不符。

- since 表示「自從」的意思。

  Anne Keating was promoted and has since worked as head accountant.
  Anne Keating 自從升職後，就做了首席會計師。

❸ forward（向前）/ ahead（前面），backward（向後）/ behind（後面）

- 表示「方向」時用 forward / backward，表示「狀態」時用 ahead / behind。

  The director is working hard to push the company ~~ahead~~. 那個主任努力工作將公司的發展往前推進。
  forward

  → 表示向前推動的「方向」，所以要用 forward。

  They all knew that the days ~~forward~~ would be tiresome. 他們都認為等在前面的日子會很煩人。
  ahead

  → 表示到未來的時間還剩一些日子的「狀態」，所以要用 ahead。

多益實戰考題　　　　　　　　多 益 會 出 這 樣 的 問 題

⊙ 填副詞。

1. Ms. Peters thought the designs were marvelous, but she ------- needs to see what they would look like in a display window.

(A) not only　　　　(B) either
(C) also　　　　　　(D) as well

2. The plane will take off at about 3:15 P.M., and a light snack will be served to the passengers shortly -------.

(A) later　　　　　(B) thereafter
(C) already　　　　(D) suddenly

3. When Bernal became the CEO, we considered it a great step ------- because a woman was finally guaranteed formal say in company policy.

(A) ahead　　　　(B) forward
(C) towards　　　(D) backward

正確答案　P66

Practice 1 選擇正確的答案。

01 The design department has not (still / yet) finished constructing the model for the client's proposed building project.

02 Acting as the vice president of such a large company was (so / such) stressful that she retired early.

03 They prepared (much too / too much) food, believing that many people would be participating.

04 Fax the billing information to headquarters by 5 p.m.; (otherwise / however), we won't receive the payment on time.

05 Mrs. Jensen was (such / very) pleased with her new high rise office on 5ᵗʰ Avenue.

06 Evans Construction is a leading contracting company that provides bidding, contracting, and (also / as well) architectural support.

07 She was called away for an emergency meeting (ever / right) before the performance was about to start.

Practice 2 改正錯誤的地方。

08 Cocoa is exported wide to nearly every part of the world.

09 The actual annual report figures came closely to this year's production estimates.

10 Investors want the company to be sufficiently strong before they consider putting money into it.

11 The Christmas bonus, based on the company's yearly net profit, was divided impartiality between laborers and supervisors.

12 Mr. Jenkins final agreed to holding the meeting in the Grand Hotel.

13 The three-stage interview process helps administrators decide exactly which applicant is right for which position.

14 Morale among the staff has been raised substantial by the new espresso machine in the lounge.

HACKERS TEST

Part V

01 Mrs. Dorsey is ------- being considered for a promotion to the position of head manager for the company's technology division.

(A) present
(B) presently
(C) presenter
(D) presentation

02 The new Power Point software is the most ------- advanced presentation program on the market today.

(A) high
(B) higher
(C) highly
(D) highest

03 The drafting programs available at our firm are ------- too advanced for the trainees to use.

(A) well
(B) quite
(C) far
(D) pretty

04 Anonymous Writers is less expensive than the Writers' Consortium, and its work is ------- as dependable.

(A) as well
(B) very
(C) just
(D) while

05 Electric service will be restored as ------- as possible after the power outage problem on the second floor has been resolved.

(A) quick
(B) quickly
(C) quicken
(D) quickness

06 Two multi-million dollar corporations are ------- attempting to reach an agreement over the sale of one of the country's biggest banks.

(A) still
(B) once
(C) besides
(D) any more

07 Mr. Richards is such a dedicated supervisor that he works night and day and ------- ever takes time to relax.

(A) quite
(B) just
(C) nearly
(D) hardly

08 Although the restaurant is new, it has already been praised by Food Review and most of ------- restaurant rating services.

(A) other
(B) the other
(C) each other
(D) another

09 Consumer views are becoming an ------- important factor in determining the way a product is presented and packaged.

(A) increase
(B) increased
(C) increasing
(D) increasingly

10 We cannot always guarantee that everything in our catalog is in stock at our outlets, so please call ------- to make sure.

(A) ahead
(B) before
(C) if
(D) advance

11 A number of large investment projects have ------- sprung up in rural areas where agriculture is the main industry.

(A) lateness
(B) late
(C) later
(D) lately

12 To register for your online account, ------- proceed to the website's homepage and click on the 'sign-up' button.

(A) simply
(B) simple
(C) simplify
(D) simplicity

13 Sales of the new vacuum cleaner have gone beyond our initial estimate and we have ------- decided to increase production.

(A) therefore
(B) however
(C) although
(D) in contrast

14 All purchases made on the company credit card should be listed ------- on the monthly statement.

(A) direct
(B) directly
(C) directed
(D) directing

15 Drivers are constantly reminded by the head office to pull over as ------- as necessary to rest during long shifts.

(A) almost   (B) often
(C) well   (D) always

16 Copies of the popular children's book had been placed on bookstore shelves for not ------- several hours when they sold out.

(A) quite   (B) many
(C) still   (D) only

17 The task force spent an entire day selecting applications that most ------- matched the requirements of the positions being offered.

(A) closer   (B) closest
(C) closely   (D) close

18 Had the profits been shared ------- among the leading salesmen, there wouldn't be the fuss that there is now.

(A) equal   (B) equally
(C) equality   (D) equalize

19 ------- serving as president of the Board of the Giltmore Corporation, Mr. Bennett also works as a consultant to a few medium-size companies.

(A) Else   (B) Because
(C) As long as   (D) Besides

20 The fat content of food products sold in supermarkets should be labeled much more ------- to allow people to make informed decisions.

(A) clear   (B) clearly
(C) clearing   (D) clearness

Part VI

Marsha Berger
Medical Supplies Division
Tyrrell Manufacturing
89 Oak Drive
Portland, Oregon 78798

Dear Ms. Berger,

I'm writing to inform you that I will be unable to attend the conference in New Jersey as our company is currently undergoing restructuring, making it impossible for me to leave Portland. I am eager to ------- your proposals concerning incorporation of your products into our wide spectrum of distributed

21 (A) detract   (B) solicit
     (C) instigate   (D) resonate

goods. -------, you will be attending the next conference in July in Austin, allowing us the prime

22 (A) Almost   (B) Already
     (C) Mostly   (D) Presumably

chance to get together and discuss our prospects -------. I believe our companies are headed in

23 (A) soon   (B) almost
     (C) nearly   (D) usually

the same direction and a joint venture would be highly beneficial. Therefore I greatly look forward to the opportunity to converse with you at the next conference, unless ------- informed.

24 (A) besides   (B) customarily
     (C) afterward   (D) otherwise

Sincerely,
Justin White
Garnet Distribution

正確答案 P67

Chapter 16

介系詞

啊哈!! 愉快地打基礎

1

介系詞用在名詞前並表示地點、時間、原因等要素。

We had dinner at <u>a Korean restaurant</u>. 我們在韓式餐廳吃了晚餐。
The city hosts a jazz festival in <u>the summer</u>. 那個城市在夏天舉行爵士音樂節。
It is usually colder on the beach because of <u>the breeze</u>.
因為海邊吹來的微風,所以通常比較冷。

在這裡 at 是表示場所、in 是表示時間、because of 是表示原因的介系詞。這時把介系詞後面的 a Korean restaurant, summer, the breeze 叫做「介系詞的受詞」,並把「介系詞 + 介系詞的受詞(名詞片語 / 動名詞 / 代名詞)」的組合叫做「介系詞片語」。

2

介系詞片語在句子中充當修飾名詞的形容詞或修飾動詞的副詞等角色。

<u>The box</u> on the table is empty. 桌子上的箱子是空的。

I <u>exercise</u> in the evening. 我在晚上做運動。

介系詞片語 on the table 有修飾名詞 The box 的作用,in the evening 則是修飾動詞 exercise 的副詞。

01 選擇介系詞 1：時間和場所 in / at / on

❶ 時間介系詞 in / at / on

介系詞	用法	範例	
in	月，年度 季節，世紀 …時間之後，早上/下午/晚上	in August 在八月 in winter 在冬天 in three days 在三天之後	in 2005 在 2005 年 in the 21st century 在 21 世紀 in the morning / afternoon / evening 在早上/下午/晚上
at	時刻，時間點	at 7 o'clock 在 7 點 at the beginning / end of the month 在月初/月末	at noon / night / midnight 在中午/傍晚/午夜
on	日期，星期，特定日	on August 15 在八月 15 日	on Friday 在星期五　　　on Christmas Day 在耶誕節那天

❷ 場所介系詞 in / at / on

介系詞	用法	範例	
in	大空間內的場所	in the world / country 在世界/國家	in the city / room / town 在都市/房間/城鎮
at	地點，門牌號	at the intersection 在十字路口 at the station 在車站	at the bus stop 在公車站牌處 at 10 Franklin street 在 Franklin 十街
on	表面上，垂直的上方	on the table 在桌子上 on the 1st floor / level 在 1 樓	on the Han River 在漢江上 on the wall 在牆上

注意！ 同樣的場所與人物也要看意義來使用介系詞，當人物在場所內時使用 in，人物與場所為各自獨立關係時使用 at。

I was <u>in</u> the shop when he came in. 當他來時我正在店裡。

I stopped <u>at</u> the shop on the way home. 回家途中我順便逛一下商店。

❸ in / at / on 的常用表現

介系詞	表現		
in	in time 時間內 in place 在原地、在適當的位置 in a campaign 在活動中	in a sales event 在打折活動中 in the sales department 在業務部門 experience in relevant field 在相關領域的經驗	in the coming year 在明年 in the foreseeable future 在可見的未來
at	at once 馬上，在同時 at times 隨時 at least 至少 at the latest 最晚 at regular intervals 每隔一定時間	at a good pace 以良好的步調 at high speed 以高速度 at a low price 以低廉的價格 at 60 miles an hour 以每小時 60 碼 at your earliest convenience 在你方便時儘早	at the rate of 以…的比率、以…的速度 at the age of 以…的年齡 at a charge of 以…的費用 at one's expense 以…的費用
on	on time 及時 on a regular basis 有規律地	on the waiting list 在等候名單裡 on the recommendation of 以…的推薦	

多益實戰考題　　多益會出這樣的問題

⊙ 區別填 in / at / on。

1. The interchange with the real estate consultant is expected to take place tomorrow afternoon ------- 4:00.

(A) on　　　　　　(B) at
(C) to　　　　　　(D) for

2. If our new low-fat potato chip becomes a hot seller in Springfield, we are going to test-market it ------- 25 major cities across the US.

(A) on　　　　　　(B) in
(C) against　　　　(D) to

3. All of the drilling machines are ------- place and ready to begin oil production at the command of the chief executive.

(A) at　　　　　　(B) on
(C) in　　　　　　(D) for

正確答案 P69

02 選擇介系詞 2：時間點和期間

❶ 表示時間點的介系詞

> since 自從　　from 從…
> until / by 直到…　before / prior to …之前　+ 時間表現 (three o'clock, July, Friday morning 等)

The project team leader would like to see us before **5:00 p.m.** 這個企畫團隊的領導人想在下午 5 點之前跟我們見個面。

注意！ 1. until 表示「狀況、狀態持續到…為止」，by 表示「動作發生在…之前」。

The library will be open until 7. 圖書館開館時間到 7 點。
→ 圖書館開門的狀態會持續到 7 點。

You should submit the report by 7. 你要在 7 點前提交報告書。
→ 到 7 點之前，提交報告書的動作會結束。

2. 表示時間點的介系詞的常用表現

three weeks from now 從現在開始三週以後　three weeks prior to the date 這個日期的前三週　from 3 o'clock onward(s) 從 3 點以後

❷ 表示期間的介系詞

> for / during 在…期間
> over / through(out) 在…期間，從頭到尾 + 期間表現（three years, a decade, holiday 等）
> within …之內

Digital technology has become increasingly important over **the past few decades.**
電子技術在過去數十年的期間變得更重要。

注意！ 1. for 後面接時間表現，表示「持續了多長時間」；during 後面接名詞，表示「什麼時候發生」。

The mechanic has been working on the project <u>for</u> **two years.** 這位機械工做這個工程有兩年了。
Countless foreigners travel to Italy <u>during</u> **the Christmas season.** 有數不清的外國人在耶誕節期間去義大利旅遊。

2. in 後面可以接期間表現，這時的 in 表示「…之後、過…後、在…期間」的意思。

Your application for membership will be processed <u>in</u> **two days.** 你的會員資格申請在兩天以後會得到處理。

❸ 表示時間的介系詞和表示期間的介系詞的區別。

I will have this done ~~within~~ **the end of the month.** 我會在這月底之前完成這件事。
　　　　　　　　　　by
→ 介系詞 within 後面不能接表示時間點的片語（the end of month），所以要用 by。

We have been married ~~since~~ **2 years.** 我們已經結婚兩年了。
　　　　　　　　　　　for
→ 介系詞 since 後面不能接表示期間的片語（2 years），所以要用 for。

多益實戰考題　　　多 益 會 出 這 樣 的 問 題

⊙ 區別時間點 / 期間介系詞。

2. The rental deposit must be transferred to the landlord's bank account at least 15 days ------- the moving in date.

(A) by　　　　　　(B) until
(C) prior to　　　 (D) due to

1. Because fewer than five people have registered for the Computer Graphics Workshop to be held two weeks ------- now, the Training Department manager has decided to cancel the event.

(A) until　　　　　(B) before
(C) from　　　　　(D) for

3. To have any broken parts replaced without charge, the registration form must be mailed to the company ------- one month of product purchase.

(A) from　　　　　(B) within
(C) until　　　　　(D) by

正確答案　P69

03 選擇介系詞 3：位置

① 表示位置的介系詞

介系詞	例句
above / over …上	He lifted his hands above / over his head. 他把手抬到頭上。
below / under …下	Look in the cupboard below / under the sink. 請看水槽下的櫥櫃。
beside / next to …旁邊	I sat down beside / next to my wife. 我坐在妻子旁邊。
between/among …之間	There's a table between the two chairs. 兩個椅子之間有張桌子。 There's a table between a chair and a bookshelf. 椅子和書架之間有張桌子。 The midday meal was served between 2 and 4 o'clock. 午餐在 2 點到 4 點之間提供。 They walked among the crowds. 他們在人群中走著。
near …附近	I'd like to sit near a window. 我想坐在窗戶附近。
within …內	All staff should be aware of activities within the company. 所有職員都要注意到公司內的各項活動。
around …周圍	Some of the travelers wanted to walk around the night market. 幾個遊客想在夜市的周圍走走。

注意！ 1. between 用在「兩個之間」，而且可以表示時間和位置的「之間」。 among 用在「三個及以上的人、事、物之間」。

2. above / over 和 below / under 各自表示「…以上」和「…以下」的意思。
   You have to be <u>over</u> 18 to see this film. 你需要滿 18 歲才能看這部電影。
   You can't see this film if you're <u>under</u> 18. 如果你不滿 18 歲就不能看這個電影。

❸ 位置介系詞常用表現

介系詞	表現	
over	have the edge over 比…有利	
under	under new management 在新的管理下 under close supervision 在嚴格的監督下 under current contract 在現有合約下 under control 在控制下 under pressure 在壓力下	under investigation 在調查中 under review 在檢討中 under consideration 在考慮中 under discussion 在討論中 under development 在開發中
between	a difference / gap between A and B A 和 B 的區別	
within	within a radius of 在半徑…內	within the organization 在組織內
around	around the world 在全世界	around the corner 在附近

多益實戰考題　　　多益會出這樣的問題

⊙ 填介系詞。

1. A recent study mentions that prescription drug use has steadily increased ------- people aged 45 years and above over the past two decades.

(A) among　　　(B) within
(C) between　　(D) around

2. The annex to the office building on Lester Avenue will be ------- construction until the first week of April.

(A) in　　　(B) by
(C) on　　　(D) under

3. Last summer's heavy precipitation levels caused sales of beachwear to fall 20 percent ------- normal.

(A) after　　　(B) below
(C) behind　　(D) around

正確答案　P70

04 選擇介系詞 4：方向

❶ 表示方向的介系詞

介系詞	例句
from 在…，從…	The copy can be obtained from the office. 可以在辦公室拿到那份拷貝文件。
to 往…	They will send the package to your client. 他們會將包裹寄給你的顧客。
across 穿過… through 通過… along 沿著…	We walked across the ice. 我們徒步穿過了冰層。 I walked through the woods. 我徒步通過了森林。 Newman walked along the street. Newman 沿著街道走著。
for 往… toward(s) 向…（未知的方向）	I'm leaving for Busan. 我要前往釜山。 She walked toward me. 她向我走來。
into 到…裡 out of 從…裡（往外）	We moved all the luggage into the room. 我們把所有的行李搬到房間裡了。 I took the key out of my pocket. 我從口袋裡掏出鑰匙。

❷ 方向介係詞的表現

介係詞	表現		
from	from one's view points 從…的觀點來看		
to	to the relief of 使…安心 to be sure 的確，當然	to a great extent 到很大的程度 to one's satisfaction 使…滿意	to my knowledge 據我所知 to your heart's content 使你得到滿足
along across	along the shore 沿著海岸 across the street 路對面	along the side of 沿著…的邊 across from the post office 郵局對面	
out of	out of date 過時的 out of room 沒有空間 out of season 過時的 out of paper 缺紙	out of reach 搆不著的 out of print 絕版的 out of control 無法控制的	out of order 壞的 out of stock 無庫存的 out of town 在外地，在鄉下

多益實戰考題　　多益會出這樣的問題

⊙ 填介系詞。

2. The new highway, which will run ------ the mountains, is expected to cause irreversible damage to wildlife and the ecosystem.

(A) through　　(B) during
(C) out　　　　(D) against

1. Subscribers to the online newsletter were informed that their names would be removed ------- the list if they did not reply to the e-mail asking if they wished to be retained.

(A) to　　(B) from
(C) for　　(D) of

3. This product should be kept ----- reach of children as it contains many toxic agents.

(A) away with　　(B) out of
(C) up until　　　(D) without

正確答案　P70

05 選擇介系詞 5：理由，讓步，目的，除外，附加

❶ 表示理由，讓步，目的的介系詞

介系詞	涵義	例句
because of due to owing to on account of	因為…	We were late because of the rain. 我們因為下雨而遲到了。 * 介系詞 thanks to 表示「幸虧…」，as a result of 表示「…的結果」
despite in spite of with all	儘管…	Despite a poor economy, the shop has been doing well. 儘管經濟蕭條，但那家商店仍然經營得很好。
for	為了…	The club is hosting a party for all its members. 俱樂部正為所有的會員舉行聚會。

注意！ 包含介系詞 for 的表現

for your convenience 為了您的便利　　for future uses 供往後使用　　articles for sale 銷售物品
for safety reasons 為了安全上的考慮　for future reference 供往後參考　money for supplies 供應費

❷ 表現除外，附加的介系詞

介系詞	涵義	例句
except (for) excepting aside from apart from	除…之外	I cleaned all the rooms except (for) the bathroom. 我打掃了除浴室之外的所有房間。
barring without but for	若沒有（過）…	We should arrive at ten o'clock, barring any unexpected delays. 若沒有意想不到的耽擱，我們會在 10 點到達。 I would have been in real trouble but for your help. 若沒有你的幫助，我一定會有麻煩的。
instead of	代替	Use graphics instead of words. 用圖代替文字。
in addition to besides apart from	除…之外	In addition to the new offices, the building has a coffee house on the first floor. 除了新辦公室之外，這棟大樓還有一個咖啡館在 1 樓。 Besides writing summaries, she proofreads all of the professor's work. 除寫論文概要之外，她還檢查了那位教授的所有文章。

注意！ except 後面接「介系詞 + 子句（主語 + 動詞）」時，不能用 for。
I don't know anything about wine, except for that(→ except that) I like it.
除了我喜歡的那種之外，我對葡萄酒一竅不通。
→ except 後面最常接的是 that，但有時也會接 when, where, what, while 等。

多益實戰考題 多益會出這樣的問題

⊙ 填介系詞。

2. The manager said that ------- any changes, the proposal would be presented at a special meeting of sustainable development organizations.

(A) except　　(B) barring
(C) unless　　(D) because

1. The staff is planning to hold a farewell gathering ------- an employee who served the company for over twenty years.

(A) by　　(B) for
(C) to　　(D) from

3. Interest rates are falling ------- a governmental push to raise all mortgage rates for middle class homeowners.

(A) in spite of　　(B) according
(C) even though　　(D) in addition to

正確答案 P70

❶ A of B

用法	例句
涵義上 A 為動詞，B 為主詞時	the development of the company 公司的發展（←公司在發展） consent of the parent 父母的許可（←父母許可） the retirement of our colleague 我們同事的退休（←我們同事退休）
涵義上 A 為動詞，B 為受詞時	showing of his new movie 他新片的上映（←他的新片上映） the marketing of luxury brands 高級品牌的銷售（←銷售高級品牌） the shipment of wine 酒的運送（←運送酒） the utilization of health care services 健康管理服務的活用（←活用健康管理服務）
A 和 B 同一級別時	a chance of meeting someone new 認識新人的機會（←機會＝認識新人） the idea of producing handbooks 出版手冊的建議（←建議＝出版手冊） a balance of 100 dollars 100 美元的餘額（←餘額＝ 100 美元）
A 為 B 的部分，所屬時	this area of the city 那個城市的這個地區（←屬於那個城市的這個地區） the end of the month 月底（←屬於這個月的最後幾天） the employees of the branch 那個分店的職員（←屬於那個分店的職員）

❷ 「用作…」、「關於…」的介系詞

about	on	over
as to	as for	
concerning	regarding	
with / in regard to	with respect to	with / in reference to

The following is frequently asked questions concerning the internship program.
以下是在實習課程中常遇到的問題。

We take pride in complying with all regulations with regard to food safety.
我們為遵守所有關於食品安全的規定而自豪。

多益實戰考題　　　　　　　多 益 會 出 這 樣 的 問 題

⊙ 填介系詞。

1. The independent audit of the company is expected to be concluded by the end ------- this month.

   (A) in　　　　　(B) by
   (C) of　　　　　(D) on

2. Dr. Wilson will attend the workshop to moderate a panel discussion ------- ethics of new medical technology.

   (A) by　　　　　(B) to
   (C) on　　　　　(D) with

3. A dispute ------- workers' rights has caused union members employed at the factory to walk out in a week long strike.

   (A) over　　　　(B) above
   (C) of　　　　　(D) along

正確答案　P70

GRAMMAR | 語法

❶ 其他介系詞

介系詞	涵義	例句
by through	被… 由… 透過…	Authenticated access is obtained by providing a valid name and password. 透過提供有效姓名和密碼，就可以得到使用認證。 Competence is achieved through training. 能力是透過訓練而得到的。
with without	與…一起 沒有	The children will discuss it with their teacher. 孩子們將會與老師一起討論。 Headphones will enable you to listen to the music without disturbing anyone. 耳機可以讓你在不干擾任何人的情況下聽音樂。
as	作為…	He had served as a section director at the Ministry of Education. 他在教育部任職部門主管。
like unlike	像… 與…不同	Like jogging, walking should have a steady and continuous motion. 走路也像慢跑一樣需要穩定且不斷的移動。 Swimming, unlike jogging, is ideal for any age or physical ability. 與跑步不同，游泳適合於任何年齡或任何身體狀況的人。
amid	在…之間 / 在…之中	Stockholders sold their shares amid signs that the company was going bankrupt. 在公司出現破產的徵兆時，股東們賣掉了他們的股票。
against	反對… 依靠…	Some consumers have campaigned against the use of furs in luxury clothing. 一些消費者們舉辦活動來反對使用動物毛皮製作高級服飾。
beyond	超越… 比…優越	Its functions go beyond what is necessary for an mp3 player. 它的功能超越了 mp3 播放器所需要的。

❷ 其他介系詞的表現

介系詞	表現	
by through	by telephone / fax / mail 透過電話 / 傳真 / 郵件 by land 經陸地 through the use of 透過使用 through arbitration 經過仲裁	by cash / check / credit card 用現金 / 支票 / 信用卡 by law 依法 through (the) customs 通過海關 through cooperation 透過合作
with without	with no doubt 無可置疑 with the aim of 以…為目標	with no exception 無例外 without paying 無償地
against	against the laws 非法地	act against one's will 違反…的意願
beyond	beyond repair 不可修復 beyond description(expression) 無法解釋 beyond question(doubt) 無可置疑，確切	beyond one's capacity 超出…的能力範圍 beyond one's control 超過…的控制能力 beyond one's expectation 超出…的期待

多益實戰考題　　　多 益 會 出 這 樣 的 問 題

⊙ 填介系詞。

2. Companies can save hundreds on airfares ------ computer linkups which allow for international meetings without leaving the office.

(A) above　　　　(B) through
(C) into　　　　　(D) down

1. Prospects for higher interest rates are increasing this quarter ------- news of upcoming governmental intervention.

(A) amid　　　　(B) regarding
(C) about　　　　(D) near

3. Employees expressed content with their salaries and working hours ------- the exception of those in packing, who requested a pay increase.

(A) like　　　　(B) by
(C) for　　　　　(D) with

正確答案　P71

08 與動詞、名詞、形容詞一起使用的介系詞的表現

❶ 與動詞一起使用的介系詞表現

account for 說明	depend on(=rely on =count on) 依賴於	associate A with B 把A和B聯想在一起
add to 加	sympathize with 同情	congratulate A on B 向A祝賀B
comply with 服從	wait for 等待	direct A to B 把A送到B / 告訴A往B的路
consist of 由…構成	keep track of 記錄	return A to B 把A送回B
contribute to 貢獻於…	employ A as B 把A錄用為B（職位）	transfer A to B 把A轉移到B

They have only a few days left to comply with new regulations on factory safety.
再過幾天他們就要執行工廠安全的新規定。

The public associates the company name with trust and reliability. 大眾將這個公司的名稱和誠實可靠聯想在一起。

❷ 與形容詞一起使用的介系詞表現

absent from 缺席	equivalent to 與…相等	identical to 與…相同	consistent with 與…一致
responsible for 對…有責任	comparable to 與…媲美	similar to 與…相似	comparable with 可與…比較

Projects conducted by like organizations are similar to each other. 那些由類似機關管理的專案都很相近。

❸ 與名詞一起使用的介系詞表現

access to 接近，出入	exposure to 暴露於	advocate for (of) …的擁護者
cause / reason for 原因 / 理由	concern over 對…關心	lack of 缺乏
permission from 被…許可	problem with …的問題	dispute over 關於…的論爭
effect / impact / influence on 對…的影響	question about / concerning / regarding 關於…的問題	
respect for 對…的尊敬	decrease / increase / rise / drop in 減少 / 增加 / 上升 / 落下	

The client has a question regarding the arrangements for the trip.
那個顧客有旅遊行程安排的相關問題。

❹ 由2個以上的詞構成的介系詞

as of + 時間 從…	by means of 以…手段	in place of 代替…
contrary to 與…相反	in charge of 負…責任的	in respect of 關於…
instead of 代替…	in honor of 對……表示敬意	in violation of 違反…
regardless of 與…無關	in observance of 遵守…	on behalf of 代替…

Fred Sumner will be giving the speech in place of Mr. Trent, who is down with the flu.
Fred Sumner 會代替感冒的 Trent 先生演講。

多益實戰考題　　　　　　　多 益 會 出 這 樣 的 問 題

⊙ 填介系詞。

2. Education for Children, Inc. has always been an advocate ------- effective early education through home and school-based programs.

(A) to　　　　　　　(B) by
(C) for　　　　　　　(D) over

1. Management has decided to transfer certain responsibilities formerly held by the administrative division ------- the accounting department.

(A) at　　　　　　　(B) by
(C) to　　　　　　　(D) of

3. Ms. Turner asked us to use the original design for the product display ------- the one submitted by the team.

(A) because　　　　(B) instead of
(C) despite　　　　(D) when

正確答案　P71

Practice 1 選擇正確的答案。

01 The country has suffered from little investment (over / until) the past year as a result of political instability.

02 (Due to / Except for) rising oil prices, import prices went up by 16% in August.

03 In recent years, private investors have become increasingly attracted to this area (on / of) the city.

04 Requests for assistance via email or live Internet support are only monitored (since / during) regular hours of operation.

05 (At / Despite) a looming fiscal crisis, the country's economy has bounced back from a slump.

06 Workshops are offered (before / throughout) the year on a variety of job search tools and skills including résumé writing.

07 (Aside from / Long since) the acquisition costs, the manager anticipated additional costs for operational and restructuring expenses.

Practice 2 改正錯誤的地方。

08 A recent report said consumer prices could exceed 4 percent on the end of the year.

09 Professionals on the academic community frequently immigrate to places where their skills earn a better reward.

10 Guests can put their valuables in the hotel's safety deposit boxes for safekeeping.

11 Until approximately twenty years, the national debt is forecast to jump to four trillion dollars.

12 In observance for Labor Day, all US exchanges will be closed on Monday, September 6, 2004.

13 All documentation on local cost payments, including tender documents, must be retained to the future.

14 The expansion project will be completed since December 15 and will be eligible for sales tax exemption.

Part V

01 The company anniversary party will take place ------- August 26, so please mark the date on your calendars.

(A) in   (B) at
(C) on   (D) for

02 The innovative website allows a traveler to search and find locations of interest that lie ------- a fifty-mile radius of the city.

(A) among   (B) within
(C) into   (D) through

03 We need not remind everyone here today that mobile phones and pagers should be turned off ------- the symposium is in progress.

(A) due to   (B) meantime
(C) ever   (D) while

04 The BCN Company will not accept applications for transfers to overseas branches ------- the first of the month.

(A) by   (B) when
(C) until   (D) through

05 The Travel Holiday Group offers some of the best horseback tours ------- the coast of the Eastern Mediterranean basin.

(A) into   (B) along
(C) under   (D) among

06 The workshop teaches managers and employees how to dispute someone else's ideas ------- being disagreeable.

(A) except   (B) without
(C) whereas   (D) otherwise

07 The director wants all of the items shipped by the end of the week, ------- of the cost.

(A) regardless   (B) regard
(C) regarding   (D) regarded

08 The data will be posted on a secure password-protected server that is accessible ------- to authorized staff members.

(A) exclusive   (B) exclusivity
(C) exclusively   (D) exclusiveness

09 Country Air offered free tickets to every passenger that missed their holiday flight -------a malfunction in the plane's engine.

(A) owed to   (B) thanks for
(C) resulting in   (D) because of

10 Employees who are planning to extend holiday vacations with unused leave days must inform their supervisors ------- 31 October.

(A) at   (B) for
(C) by   (D) until

11 Human resources personnel are trained to tell the differences ------- a resolvable conflict and an irresolvable confrontation.

(A) upon   (B) about
(C) during   (D) between

12 We are holding a dinner this evening to congratulate Mr. Brian Banks ------- his twenty years with the Meyers Cold Cuts Company.

(A) to   (B) of
(C) on   (D) from

13 ------- the last ten years, professional and business services comprised 38 percent of the total job growth in the Washington region.

(A) In   (B) On
(C) Since   (D) While

14 As always, we here at Gray Consulting look ------- to assisting you with your future legal needs.

(A) up   (B) in
(C) forward   (D) around

15 The company's payroll office is located ------- the corner of Faribault and 23rd street, across from the Trade Center.

(A) at   (B) in
(C) of   (D) to

16 Wageworks Corporation is planning to lay off as many as 1,000 employees ------- the next two years.

(A) at   (B) by
(C) until   (D) over

17 Whatever your security needs, Armed Guard provides 24 hours ------- constant protection and service to our clients.

(A) around   (B) of
(C) over   (D) through

18 It would be better for business if we were associated ------- some of the trade officers at the embassy.

(A) to   (B) on
(C) with   (D) for

19 Teen magazine is offering a special promotion, which entitles ------- to gift certificates at top clothing boutiques.

(A) subscribe   (B) subscribing
(C) subscribers   (D) subscription

20 The manager hopes to increase production ------- introducing bonuses for all employees who improve their production quota.

(A) by   (B) from
(C) since   (D) about

Part VI

> **PACIFIC Reaching for the Clouds**
>
> As long distance travel becomes more commonplace ------- globalization, airlines take action to
>
>   **21** (A) as to   (B) due to
>   (C) in spite of   (D) in place of
>
> attract customers who have a wide range of options to choose from. PACIFIC Air with their spectacular ------- project, are focusing on speed, safety and innovation to increase revenue.
>
>   **22** (A) expansion   (B) existence
>   (C) exception   (D) experience
>
> They have purchased 5 more supersonic jets, and have refurbished their existing carriers with special paint resistant to -------, sofas instead of uncomfortable chairs, and personal
>
>   **23** (A) derision   (B) redemption
>   (C) conclusion   (D) corrosion
>
> computers with DVD and game playing functions. Extra security measures include buttons under armrests which report directly to security officers in the cockpit, and bomb detectors in the baggage compartments. PACIFIC Air aims to attract families and groups of 4 or more ------- these added features.
>
>   **24** (A) for   (B) through
>   (C) owing to   (D) because of
>
> 正確答案 P71

Section 5 連接詞與子句

Chapter 17

對等連接詞與成對的對等連接詞

啊哈!! 愉快地打基礎

對等連接詞有連接詞和詞、片語和片語、句子和句子的作用。

Use <u>fruits</u> and <u>vegetables</u> that are ripe.
請食用煮熟的水果和蔬菜。

The editor is responsible for <u>collecting articles</u> and <u>publishing newsletters</u>.
編輯負責收集文章和發行本會會報。

<u>It was raining</u>, so <u>I put on my rain coat</u>.
那時正在下雨,所以我穿了雨衣。

對等連接詞所連接的句子或子句中重複的單字可以省略。

The only way <u>to get (customers)</u> and <u>(to) keep customers</u> is through service.
獲取並維繫顧客的唯一方法是優良的服務。

They painted the wall and (they) fixed the window.
他們粉刷牆壁並修理窗戶。

2 **成對的對等連接詞是兩個單字組成一對一起使用的連接詞,有連接詞和詞、片語和片語、句子和句子的作用。**

Tuna is sold as both <u>steaks</u> and <u>fillets</u>.
的鮪魚可以以魚排和魚片兩種方式販賣。

You can make your payment either <u>in person</u> or <u>by mail</u>.
你可以本人直接支付或透過郵件。

It depends on neither <u>who you are</u> nor <u>what you know</u>.
這並非取決於你是什麼樣的人或你知道些什麼。

01 對等連接詞

❶ 對等連接詞的種類

and 和	or 或	but 但是	yet 然而	so 所以	for 因為

Eating should be healthful and enjoyable. 吃飯應該是有益健康且愉悅的。

I will go camping or canoeing this weekend. 我這週末會去爬山或划獨木舟。

There will be a party tonight, for he is retiring this week. 今晚會有個宴會，因為他這禮拜就要退休了。

注意！ 1. so 和 for 只能連接句子，不能連接「詞和詞」或「片語和片語」的格式。

　　　　I had to stay home, <u>for</u> it was too cold.（O）因為太冷了，所以我只好待在家。

　　　　His designs are bold <u>so</u> original.（X）他的設計既大膽又有獨創性。

　　　2. 對等連接詞的位置上不能是連接副詞（however, therefore, instead）或一般副詞（also）。

　　　　I wanted to clear my thoughts, <u>therefore</u>(→so) I went for a walk. 我想整理一下思路，所以就去散步了。

　　　3. and so（所以），and yet（可是），and then（然後）是搭配使用的對等連接詞和副詞，能更明確的表達涵義。

　　　　She hates horror films <u>and yet</u> she went to see one anyway. 她討厭看恐怖電影，但她還是去看了。

❷ 要選擇與句意相符的對等連接詞。

I will have a sandwich ~~but~~ a Diet Coke. 我吃三明治配健怡可樂。
　　　　　　　　　　　　and

→「三明治和可樂一起」是句子的主要意思，所以要用 and 而不是 but。

She wants to see the play, ~~so~~ he prefers to watch soccer on television.
　　　　　　　　　　　but / yet

她想看話劇，但他喜歡看足球轉播。
→ 她喜歡的和他喜歡的東西不一樣，所以要用 but 或 yet，而不是 and。

❸ 主詞用 and 連接時，be 動詞要用複數；用 or 連接時，be 動詞要視 or 後面的主詞而定。

My boyfriend and I <u>are</u> going to the concert. 我要和我的男朋友去看演唱會。
→ 主詞（My boyfriend, I）用 and 連接，所以用複數 be 動詞（are）。

I doubt that we or our teacher <u>is</u> going to solve the problem. 我懷疑我們或老師能不能解決這個問題呢。
→ 因為用 or 連接，後面的主詞（our teacher）是單數，所以用單數 be 動詞（is）。

多益實戰考題　　　　　　　　多 益 會 出 這 樣 的 問 題

⊙ 填對等連接詞。

1. The corporation's portfolio of clients consisted of representatives from 13 of the American states ------- 25 countries worldwide.

(A) in　　　　　　　(B) and
(C) by　　　　　　　(D) both

2. Your promotion offer is very appealing, ------- I'm afraid that I can't sacrifice my family life for my career.

(A) so　　　　　　　(B) but
(C) besides　　　　　(D) therefore

3. Mark Melendy ------- Scott Drake is going to represent Balmar Associates at the branch meeting on Friday.

(A) but　　　　　　　(B) and
(C) either　　　　　　(D) or

正確答案　P74

❶ 成對的對等連接詞的種類

both A and B A和B都	either A or B A或B中一個
neither A nor B 既不是A也不是B	not A but B = B but not A = (only) B, not A 不是A，而是B
not only A but (also) B = B as well as A 不僅A，B也	

Payroll is located not on the first floor, but near the elevator in the basement.
員工薪資名單不在1樓，而在地下室電梯附近。

The gift shop not only offered discounts but also gave away small souvenirs.
禮品店不僅有打折，還送小紀念品。

❷ 成對的對等連接詞的搭配要正確。

The papers are either in my briefcase and under the books on my desk.
                              or
那個報告不是在我的公事包裡，就是在我桌子上的書下面。
→ 能與成對的對等連接詞 either 正確的搭配是 or，不是 and。

Jack either knows her nor wants to get to know her.
     neither

Jack 不認識她，也不想認識她。
→ 能與成對的對等連接詞 nor 正確搭配的是 neither，不是 either。

❸ 要注意與成對的對等連接詞連接的主詞和動詞其單複數要一致。

與B一致的情況	not A but B either A or B neither A nor B not only A but also B
總是用複數動詞的情況	both A and B

Either bus or taxi is available from the airport. 從機場坐巴士或計程車都可以。
→ 在 Either A or B 中動詞單複數與B保持一致，所以與B單數名詞 taxi 保持一致，應該用單數動詞 is。

Both coffee and tea have long and historic pasts. 咖啡和茶都有悠久的歷史。
→ 在 Both A and B 後面總是用複數動詞，所以此處用複數動詞 have。

多益實戰考題　　　　　多　益　會　出　這　樣　的　問　題

⊙ 填成對的等連接詞。

2. Information will be presented on the means of global communication, but ------- on presentation technology or sales marketing.

(A) for　　　　　　(B) nor
(C) so　　　　　　(D) not

1. You can purchase a copy of his latest adventure novel either at a book store ------- through popular bookstore websites.

(A) or　　　　　　(B) nor
(C) and　　　　　(D) also

3. The director complained that the report submitted by the supervisor was ------- too lengthy but also too detailed.

(A) only　　　　　(B) not
(C) not only　　　(D) either

正確答案 P74

HACKERS PRACTICE ● ● ● ● ● ● ● ● ● ● ● ● ● ● ● ●

Practice 1 選擇正確的答案。

01 Brent tossed (but / and) turned all night over whether or not to quit his job.

02 She tried to reserve the hotel's conference room, (but / however) someone had already booked it.

03 Online customers can now use the website's order form (or / nor) fax in their order.

04 As coworkers, we see each other every day (and yet / therefore) we still find something to talk about.

05 John left for work early, (instead / for) he didn't want to risk being late again.

06 There are two receptionists, one by the elevator (so / and) the other next to the entrance.

07 Andrea received an excellent evaluation this year (and so / also) she is going to be given a raise.

Practice 2 改正畫線部分。

08 The company lounge is open to <u>not only</u> administrative staff and workers.

09 I'd advise you <u>neither</u> to approach these clients too eagerly, but rather cautiously.

10 The goal is not only to triumph, <u>and</u> also to demoralize the competing corporations.

11 It is <u>both</u> you or me that has to fly to Tokyo to negotiate the contract.

12 The manager is neither receiving <u>or</u> returning calls this afternoon, as it's his day off.

13 If it were up to me, the office's entrance sign would be both red <u>yet</u> brown.

14 Your salary can be either directly deposited <u>also</u> picked up at the payroll office.

Part V

01 The Maxwell Byrd Company prides itself on having established modern ------- efficient procedures unmatched in the industry.

(A) either
(B) so
(C) and
(D) too

02 All examinees should bring ------- a driver's license or passport and a pencil to the testing center.

(A) or
(B) and
(C) both
(D) either

03 To prevent electricity outages in areas where service is not readily available, use major appliances before noon ------- after 7 pm.

(A) neither
(B) nor
(C) either
(D) or

04 If you placed an order, ------- have not received your package, please wait two months from the day it was shipped before making an inquiry.

(A) but
(B) also
(C) then
(D) even

05 The training staff was instructed neither to give handouts before the sessions ------- to distribute the manuals until after the seminar had ended.

(A) yet
(B) nor
(C) or
(D) and

06 All of the workers were warned about wearing masks in the laboratory, ------- half of them ignored the advisory and got sick.

(A) yet
(B) by
(C) so
(D) both

07 The new interior design of the office has both increased employee productivity ------- drawn many positive remarks from the clientele.

(A) or
(B) yet
(C) like
(D) and

08 The chief executive is trying to decide whether to assign an individual ------- an entire team to evaluate last week's event.

(A) so
(B) but
(C) or
(D) nor

09 Better product advertising is needed that not only grabs the viewer's attention ------- stimulates consumer desire to spend money.

(A) or
(B) but
(C) and
(D) therefore

10 Candidates will be considered on the basis of their prior experience ------- on their level of dedication and loyalty.

(A) although
(B) based on
(C) as well as
(D) in addition

11 Your participation in ------- support of our charity benefit will help feed the thousands of starving children our company sponsors.

(A) and   (B) so
(C) because   (D) however

12 The severance request has been processed by the head office, ------- not by the accounting department as of yet.

(A) also   (B) or
(C) but   (D) unless

13 At the end of Sarah's first month of employment, the company evaluated ------- her daily performance and her total month's production.

(A) either   (B) both
(C) plus   (D) so

14 The objective of the session is to ------- managers to the new system that headquarters is planning to install next year.

(A) orientation   (B) orientated
(C) orientate   (D) orientating

15 Our store will be refinanced, ------- to save on long-term interest rates and to ensure a solid credit rating.

(A) either   (B) both
(C) neither   (D) not only

16 To create a ------- effect on the public, the firm utilizes hidden advertising in all of its print and television ads.

(A) last   (B) lasted
(C) lasts   (D) lasting

17 The restaurant critic advised patronizing ------- the newly-opened Greek restaurant nor the 20-year-old grilled food eatery.

(A) and   (B) either
(C) with   (D) neither

18 Make sure that copies of the agenda and the annual report ------- into the envelopes for each of the directors.

(A) put   (B) have put
(C) have been put   (D) are putting

19 You can either submit your application by e-mail ------- send the needed information by post.

(A) or   (B) and
(C) nor   (D) also

20 All new computer technicians should receive ------- and up-to-date training in the use and maintenance of state-of-the-art equipment.

(A) adequacy   (B) adequate
(C) adequateness   (D) adequately

正確答案 P74

Chapter 18

名詞子句

啊哈!! 愉快地打基礎

1 名詞子句是在句子中充當主詞、受詞、補語的必要角色。

What she read **was a story by** E.B. White. 她讀的是 E.B.White 寫的故事。
I know that he is innocent. 我知道他是無辜的。
My question is whether he is telling the truth. 我的問題是他是否在說真話。

名詞子句what she read充當句子的主詞、that he is innocent 充當know的受詞、whether he is telling the truth 充當補語的角色。

2 名詞子句由「引導名詞性子句的連接詞 +（主詞）+ 動詞」構成。

I can't tell whether you are bored or entertained. 我不知道你是無聊還是開心。
What makes him happy **is the desire for art.** 能讓他感到幸福的是對藝術的渴求。

第一個句子的受詞是由「連接詞（whether）+主詞（you）+動詞（are）」構成的名詞子句。
第二個句子的主詞是由「連接詞（what）+ 動詞（makes）」構成的名詞子句。

引導名詞性子句的連接詞有that, if / whether，疑問詞（who, what, which, when, where, how, why），複合關係代名詞（whoever, whatever, whichever）等。

01 名詞子句的位置與用法

❶ 名詞性子句像名詞一樣用在主詞、受詞、補語的位置。

主詞	Whether we have to work or not **is unclear.** 我們是否要工作還不清楚。
動詞的受詞	**Daniel said** that you had the file. Daniel 說你有那個檔案。
介系詞的受詞	**The group talked about** how the accident occurred. 那個團隊談論事故如何發生。
補語	**The problem is** who will bring a car for tomorrow's trip. 問題是誰會為明天的旅行準備車。

注意！ that 名詞子句也可以用來做動詞直接受詞的角色。

The landlord informed the tenant <u>that the rent would have to be paid immediately</u>.

那個房東通知房客要立即交房租。

→ 類型 4 動詞 informed 的間接受詞是 the tenant，直接受詞是 that。

❷ 引導名詞子句的連接詞的位置上不能用介系詞或代名詞。

The committee agreed ~~on~~ <u>the next meeting would take place in Geneva</u>.
　　　　　　　　　　　that

委員會同意下次會議在日內瓦舉行。

→ 因為介系詞（on）不能引導子句（the next meeting would take place ~），所以要用連接詞。而且還必須是可以作動詞（agreed）的受詞，所以用引導名詞子句的連接詞（that）。

He explained ~~it~~ <u>the contract must be approved at this meeting</u>.
　　　　　　　that

他解釋說這個合約必須在這次會議上通過。

→ 因為代名詞（it）不能引導子句（the contract must be approved ~），所以要用名詞子句的連接詞。而且還必須是可以做動詞（explained）受詞的名詞子句，所以用引導名詞性子句的連接詞（that）。

多益實戰考題　　　　　　多 益 會 出 這 樣 的 問 題

⊙ 填名詞子句連接詞。

1. The company's press relations officer confirmed ------- Selectric, Inc. would no longer be manufacturing pagers.

(A) about　　　　　(B) of
(C) that　　　　　(D) it

2. The banking industry reported ------- the past year saw a ten percent increase in international wire transfers.

(A) about　　　　　(B) this
(C) on　　　　　(D) that

3. Please submit your picks for employee of the month so that our manager can decide ------ will be given the award.

(A) those　　　　　(B) them
(C) who　　　　　(D) while

正確答案　P76

❶ that引導的名詞子句在句子中充當主詞，動詞的受詞，補語，同位語子句等。

主詞	That he won the first prize is hardly surprising. 他得第一並不是什麼奇怪的事。
動詞的受詞	I know that you didn't lie. 我知道你沒有說謊。
補語	The best thing about this guitar is that it stays in tune. 這個吉他最大的優點是它的音調得很準。
同位語子句	The claim that he stole the car is true. [the claim=he stole the car] 他說他偷了那輛車是事實。

注意！ 1. that子句不能用作介系詞的受詞。

I knew about that(→that) he had problems. 我知道他有問題。

2. that子句表示「說，報告，想，知道」涵義做動詞受詞時，可以省略that。
但用作主詞或同位語子句的that子句中的that則不可以省略。
I know (that) you didn't lie. 我知道你沒有說謊。
He won the first prize(→That he won the first prize) is hardly surprising. 他得第一並不是什麼奇怪的事。

❷ 可用於that子句的形容詞

be aware that 知道…	be glad / happy that 以…而高興	be sure that 確信…
be sorry that 對…感到抱歉	be convinced that 相信…	be afraid that 恐怕是…

The applicant is aware that the director is not in today. 那個申請人知道到今天主管不在。

The librarian is sure that the book was stolen. 那個圖書管理員確定那書被偷了。

❸ 可用於同位語子句的名詞

fact that …的事實	statement that 聲明…	opinion that …的意見	truth that …的事實
news that …的新聞	report that …的傳聞，報導	idea that …的建議	(re)assurance that 確信…
rumor that …的謠言	claim that …的主張	confirmation that 確定…	

The radio commentator announced the news that oil prices would increase.
這位廣播員報導了石油價格會提高的新聞。

The entire company was surprised by the report that their factory would have to shut down.
全公司的人都被工廠要倒閉的傳聞嚇壞了。

多益實戰考題　　　　　　　　多　益　會　出　這　樣　的　問　題

⊙ 填that。

2. Mr. Forster was convinced ------- his decision to sell his shares had been the right one when the value of the stock plunged the next day.

(A) which　　　　　(B) that
(C) about　　　　　(D) of

1. ------- Alice Diaz was willing to work over the weekends to ensure the success of the ceremony is evidence of her devotion to her work.

(A) That　　　　　(B) But
(C) Since　　　　　(D) After

3. During the meeting, the manager referred to the rumor ------- the business was losing money.

(A) then　　　　　(B) that
(C) which　　　　　(D) how

正確答案 P76

03 引導名詞子句的連接詞2：if, whether

❶ if或whether (or not) 引導的名詞子句表示「是否」的涵義，在句子中充當主詞、補語、受詞的角色。

主詞	**Whether we succeed** is not important. 我們能否成功並不重要。
補語	**The question is** whether this is true. 問題是這個是不是事實。
動詞的受詞	**I will check** if the movie is playing. 我會確認那個電影是否在上映中。
介系詞的受詞	**I can't answer the question of** whether or not computers can think. 我無法回答電腦是否能思考這個問題。

注意！ 1. whether子句也可以用作表示「不管…」涵義的副詞子句。
<u>Whether you like it or not</u>, I'm coming to see you. 不管你喜不喜歡，我都會去看你。

2. 表示「（如果）怎樣」涵義的if子句是副詞子句，並不是名詞子句，所以不能用whether代替if。
They will send you a catalog <u>whether</u>(→ if) you ask. 如果你提出要求，他們就會寄給你目錄。
→ 這是表示「如果你提出要求」的條件涵義的副詞子句，所以要用if，而不是whether。

❷ 可以用 "whether A or B"、"whether or not"，但不可以用 "if A or B"、"if or not"。

I don't know ~~if~~ she likes me or hates me. 我不知道她是否喜歡我還是討厭我。
      whether

→ 因為不可以用if A or B，所以此時要把if改為whether。

I can't tell ~~if~~ or not an email message is spam. 我不知道怎麼判斷一封電子郵件是不是垃圾郵件。
    whether

→ 因為不可以用if or not，所以在這裡要把if改為whether。

❸ if子句不能用在主詞的位置或介系詞的後面。

~~If~~ we succeed is not important. 我們的成功與否不重要。
Whether

→ 因為if子句（if we secceed）不能用在主詞的位置，所以把if改為whether。

I'm confused about ~~if~~ we should invite everyone in the class. 我對是否要邀請班上的所有人感到困惑。
        whether

→ 因為if子句（if we should invit everyone in the class）不能用在介系詞的後面，所以把if改為whether。

多益實戰考題　　　多益會出這樣的問題

⊙ 區別填if和whether。

1. The telecommunications industry should do even better this year ------- the government passes legislation that deregulates the industry.

(A) if   (B) though
(C) whether   (D) while

2. She is still thinking about whether ------- to boost the office's computer systems with the latest software programs.

(A) or   (B) or not
(C) and   (D) and not

3. The committee is still deciding about ------- to allocate funds for monthly training sessions for employees.

(A) if   (B) that
(C) whether   (D) which

正確答案　P76

❶ who, where, what, which 是疑問代名詞，引導名詞子句。因為它本身在名詞子句中充當主詞或受詞角色，所以疑問代名詞後面會接沒有主詞或受詞的不完整子句。

I don't know <u>who typed the letter</u>. 我不知道誰打了這封信。
<u>What he said</u> was unclear. 他所說的話並不明確。
I don't know <u>which is better</u>. 我不知道哪個比較好。

❷ whose, what, which 等疑問代名詞修飾後面的名詞並引導名詞子句。因為「疑問代名詞 + 名詞」充當名詞子句的主詞或受詞角色，所以後面會接沒有主詞或受詞的不完整子句。

I don't know <u>whose car it is</u>. 我不知道這是誰的車。
<u>What clubs you are in</u> is not important. 你屬於哪個俱樂部並不重要。
The discussion should be about <u>which plan is better</u>. 這個討論應該是關於哪個計畫比較好？

❸ when, where, how, why 是疑問副詞引導名詞子句，所以疑問副詞後面會接完整的子句。

The child will ask when <u>she can start piano lessons</u>. 孩子會問她什麼時後可以什麼時候開始上鋼琴課。
Where <u>I found the book</u> is a secret. 我在哪裡找到這本書是個秘密。
You need to practice how <u>you should handle client complaints</u>. 你有必要練習如何去處理顧客的不滿。
The shoppers wondered why <u>the book was so expensive</u>. 消費者很好奇為什麼這本書那麼貴。

注意！how 有時修飾形容詞或副詞，表示「多少」的意思。
　　　The clerk will tell me <u>how much</u> money I have to pay. 那位店員會告訴我該付多少錢。
　　　Can you tell me <u>how often</u> you eat vegetables? 能告訴我你通常多久吃一次蔬菜嗎？

❹ 「疑問詞 + to 不定詞」可以做名詞子句的角色，並可以換作「疑問詞 + 主詞 + should + 動詞」。

I have to decide when to do (=what I should do) first. 我必須決定先做什麼。
They don't know when to stop (=when they should stop). 他們不知道什麼時候該停下來。

注意！to 不定詞前疑問詞的位置上可以用 whether。
　　　The director hasn't decided <u>whether to release</u> the report. 主管還沒有決定是否公佈那個消息。

多益實戰考題　　　　　　　　　　　　多 益 會 出 這 樣 的 問 題

⊙ 填疑問詞。

2. To make preparations for the event, the caterer asked ------- many people would be present at the sit-down dinner.

(A) about　　　　　　(B) concerning
(C) how　　　　　　(D) what

1. The manager wants to know ------- prepared the employee profiles for the company website, as he finds them unprofessional and inappropriate.

(A) how　　　　　　(B) that
(C) which　　　　　(D) who

3. The company's lawyer will know ------- to do in this situation, so let's make an appointment to see him.

(A) what　　　　　(B) that
(C) which　　　　　(D) where

正確答案　P77

05 引導名詞子句的連接詞 4：複合關係代名詞 who(m)ever, whatever, whichever

❶ 複合關係代名詞引導的名詞子句在句子中有「代名詞 + 關係代名詞」的作用，並充當主詞和受詞。

whoever(= anyone who) 無論是誰	whomever(= anyone whom) 無論是誰（whoever的受格）
whatever(= anything that) 無論是什麼	whichever(= anything that, anyone who) 無論是哪個，無論是哪個人

主詞　　Whoever(= Anyone who) answered the phone **was very polite**. 無論是誰接電話（那個人）都很客氣。

受詞　　**You can select** whatever(= anything that) you want. 你可以選擇你所想要的一切。

注意！　1. 複合關係代名詞也可以引導副詞子句。
　　　　<u>Whatever you do</u>, you need courage. 無論做什麼，你都需要有勇氣。

　　　　2. 代名詞不可以代替複合關係代名詞（代名詞＋關係代名詞）。
　　　　<u>Anyone</u>(→Whoever) answered the phone was very polite. 無論是誰接電話都很客氣。

　　　　3. whoever 可以代替 whomever，但介系詞後面只能用 whomever。
　　　　You can give the box <u>to whoever</u>(→ to whomever) you want. 你可以把箱子給任何你想給的人。

　　　　4. whatever 和 whichever 可以修飾後面的名詞並做為複合關係形容詞。
　　　　<u>Whichever road</u> you take is a risk. 你選擇的每條路都充斥著危險。

❷ 複合關係代名詞本身做為名詞子句的主詞或受詞，所以後面接沒有主詞或受詞的不完整子句。

<u>Whoever</u> **visits my website** is asked for a username. 任何瀏覽我網頁的人都會被問帳號名稱。
Please choose <u>whichever</u> **theme you like**. 請選擇你喜歡的任何主題。

❸ 根據句意決定用複合關係代名詞還是疑問詞。

~~Who~~ did it was not an amateur. 不管是誰做的，這都不是外行人所為。
Whoever
→ 因為要表現的是「無論是誰做了那個」的意思，所以要用複合關係代名詞（whoever），而不是疑問詞（who）。

~~Whoever~~ did it was not important. 誰做了那個不重要。
Who
→ 因為要表現的是「誰做了那個」的意思，所以用疑問詞（who），而不是複合關係代名詞（whoever）。

I'll take ~~which~~ side you're not using. 我會選擇你不用的那邊。
　　　　whichever
→ 因為要表現的是「任何一邊」的意思，所以要用複合關係代名詞（whichever），而不是疑問詞（which）。

I have finally decided on ~~whichever~~ side I should choose. 我終於決定要選擇哪邊了。
　　　　　　　　　　which
→ 因為要表現的是「哪邊」的意思，所以用疑問詞（which），而不是複合關係代名詞（whichever）。

多益實戰考題　　　　　　　　　　多 益 會 出 這 樣 的 問 題

⊙ 填複合關係代名詞 / 複合關係形容詞。
⊙ 區別填複合關係代名詞 / 複合關係形容詞和疑問詞。
　　也會出一些區分複合關係代名詞的主格和受格的題目。

1. ------- is said at this very private meeting is confidential and should not leave the room for any reason.

(A) Whichever　　　　(B) Whatever
(C) Whenever　　　　 (D) However

2. The supervisor reminded us that ------- needed a certificate of employment for personal reasons should ask for Ms. Simon's assistance.

(A) who　　　　　　(B) whenever
(C) whoever　　　　(D) whomever

3. ------- team of sales representatives has sold the highest number of units will receive the Team of the Month award.

(A) Which　　　　　(B) Some
(C) Whichever　　　(D) These

正確答案　P77

06 what 和 that 的區別

❶ what子句在句子中只能充當名詞角色，但 that子句可以充當名詞、形容詞、副詞角色。

It's hard to decide <u>what</u> is right to do. 很難決定做什麼才是對的。
→ 出現在動詞（decide）後受詞位置的 what子句是有名詞作用的名詞子句。

I knew <u>that</u> there was a shortage of ink cartridges. 我知道墨水匣用完了。
→ 出現在動詞（knew）後受詞位置的 that子句是有名詞作用的名詞子句。

I have a plan <u>that</u> will help you stop smoking. 我有個幫你戒煙的計畫。
→ 在後面修飾名詞（plan）的 that子句是有形容詞作用的形容詞子句。

The movie was so funny <u>that</u> I watched it twice. 電影太好看了，所以我看了兩遍。
→ 出現在 so / such 後面的 that子句是在句子中有副詞作用的副詞子句。

❶ 當 what子句和 that子句用作名詞子句時，what子句後接不完整的子句，但 that子句後要接完整的子句。

I want to know what <u>＿＿＿ makes you happy</u>. 我想知道是什麼讓你如此開心。
→ what本身就是句子 "makes you happy" 的主詞，所以 what後面接不完整的子句。

That <u>you need more money</u> is obvious. 很明顯地，你需要更多的錢。
→ that後面接的是具備主詞和受詞的完整子句。

多益實戰考題

多 益 會 出 這 樣 的 問 題

⊙ 區別填 what 和 that。

2. Implementers understand ------- they cannot use company funds earmarked for project expenses on rest and recreation.

(A) about   (B) it
(C) what   (D) that

1. As an advertiser, it is absolutely vital to understand ------- most customers expect and want from manufacturers.

(A) how   (B) that
(C) what   (D) whether

3. New computer programs have made it so much easier to store information in databases ------- even a novice can compile one from a given set of data.

(A) that   (B) there
(C) what   (D) when

正確答案 P77

Hackers Skill

1. what不能引導形容詞子句或副詞子句。

I'm listening to <u>a CD</u> what(→ that) came out last week. 我正在聽上週發行的CD。
It was <u>such</u> a lovely day what(→ that) it was a pity to get up. 今天的天氣太好了以至於都不想起床。

2. 在名詞子句中，that後面接不完整子句或 what子句後面接完整子句都是錯誤的。

That(→ What) <u>he said ＿＿</u> was true. 他說的是事實。
→ that後面不能接缺受詞的不完整子句（he said），所以要用 what。

You will realize what(→ that) <u>the world is a global community</u>. 你會發現整個世界就是個地球村。
→ what後面不能接完整的子句（the world is a global community），所以要用 that。

202 |

HACKERS PRACTICE ● ● ● ● ● ● ● ● ● ● ● ● ● ● ●

Practice 1 選擇正確的答案。

01 It is definite (that / what) she will commence with the presentation tomorrow.

02 It is not certain (whose / which) of the representatives will be sent to one of our important clients.

03 Investors are afraid (that / what) the war on terror will cause stock shares to plummet.

04 They questioned her regarding her skills instead of (if / whether) she had the appropriate experience.

05 (Who / Whoever) has an interest in the position of field manager should send a résumé to the main office.

06 It is difficult to know (that / what) to expect on the first day of a job.

07 He was of the opinion (that / which) the marketing team needed a new leader.

Practice 2 找出名詞子句並區分它的作用。

08 Suppliers will have to decide when the time is right to make a change.

09 How the company manages to stay afloat with all its debt is a mystery.

10 The motorists were concerned about what roads had been blocked due to the accident.

11 New office chairs are what the receptionists have requested numerous times.

12 The company was founded on the idea that quality service should be provided to everyone.

13 The accountant doesn't understand why ten percent of profit must go to pension funds.

14 The fact is that some exports will have to be cut back because of inventory shortages.

正確答案 P78

Part V

01 ------- the holiday is only going to last three days is a disappointment to the entire staff.

(A) What   (B) That
(C) Although   (D) So

02 Our supervisor wants to know ------- we anticipate the final revisions will be made to the contract.

(A) what   (B) which
(C) that   (D) when

03 All responsibilities ------- the workers are accountable for are outlined in the training manual handed out on the first day.

(A) this   (B) that
(C) what   (D) why

04 At 6:00, ------- club members joining the special clambake at the beach should be at the entrance of the Lakeside Center.

(A) all   (B) somewhat
(C) when   (D) whichever

05 The major issue we face is ------- within the next month our spending will exceed the budget.

(A) the fact that   (B) coming from
(C) rather than   (D) the point at which

06 As the manager of the hotel, I can assure you that ------- room you choose will be of the highest standards.

(A) these   (B) some
(C) whose   (D) whichever

07 The tailor shop is requesting the customer to return the expensive suits ------- it mistakenly packed with his purchase.

(A) what   (B) whoever
(C) this   (D) that

08 Parking fees are calculated by the hour ------- are generally the same from city to city.

(A) or   (B) by
(C) and   (D) to

09 When questioned as to ------- he was planning to work for the competition, Mr. Graham said he would always be loyal to Sanford and Sons.

(A) whenever   (B) while
(C) whether   (D) whereas

10 We want all staff to be aware ------- security codes will be changed on the following Monday.

(A) concerning   (B) about
(C) that   (D) which

11 The company has provided customers who need to retrieve account information regardless of the time or place with multiple methods for -------.

(A) access   (B) accessing
(C) accessory   (D) accessed

12 Next week's workshop will focus on ------- to be an effective and trustworthy leader in the corporate world.

(A) which   (B) how
(C) what   (D) that

13 The candy shop maintains a certain temperature throughout the store so that the quality of its chocolates does not -------.

(A) be deteriorated   (B) deterioration
(C) deteriorate   (D) to deteriorate

14 A key to closing a deal is to realize ------- knowing how to negotiate means having a sense of how people think and feel.

(A) so that   (B) in that
(C) and that   (D) that

15 Employees are reminded ------- they should limit their use of office supplies, as budget cuts will be taking effect immediately.

(A) if　　　　　　(B) that
(C) still　　　　　(D) yet

16 Although staff members have some leeway when it comes to daily activities, the supervisor determines what tasks get done by -------.

(A) who　　　　　(B) whoever
(C) whom　　　　(D) whomever

17 ------- active participant should be provided with a headset to listen to real time translations as the conference takes places.

(A) Few　　　　　(B) Every
(C) Whole　　　　(D) Many

18 Martin's job is so demanding ------- he takes occasional three-day leave to get away from the pressures of office work.

(A) that　　　　　(B) there
(C) what　　　　　(D) where

19 ------- leaves the office last will be required to make sure all the lights are off and lock all doors behind them.

(A) Who　　　　　(B) Whom
(C) Whose　　　　(D) Whoever

20 You are welcome to stroll around the hotel grounds and use the swimming pool at night ------- you so desire.

(A) or　　　　　　(B) if
(C) except　　　　(D) whether

21 ------- interested in helping plan this year's Christmas party should contact Ms. Holly in Accounting who will be coordinating the event.

(A) Them　　　　(B) Some
(C) Whoever　　　(D) Anyone

22 We will be holding a meeting this afternoon to decide ------- needs to be revised before the report goes to print.

(A) what　　　　　(B) those
(C) whether　　　(D) there

23 For those who have made an investment, ------- happens during the first year is an important indicator of how successful the company will be.

(A) that　　　　　(B) as
(C) what　　　　　(D) how

24 The monthly financial reports will ------- to Mr. Hall's office, at which point he will review them to make a decision about future investments.

(A) be bringing　　(B) bring
(C) be brought　　(D) have brought

25 The new regulations state ------- if an employee contract does not meet legal requirements, the employer is obliged to adjust it immediately.

(A) about　　　　(B) what
(C) that　　　　　(D) it

26 Maintenance personnel cannot properly install the new security system in the office ------- employees are working at their desks.

(A) with　　　　　(B) while
(C) how　　　　　(D) whether

27 ------- wishes to participate in the company's annual charity run should begin collecting donations from sponsors before the end of the month.

(A) Some　　　　(B) Who
(C) Whenever　　(D) Whoever

28 Sales agents should be aware that most people do not understand the fine print ------- makes up much of an insurance policy.

(A) that　　　　　(B) when
(C) this　　　　　(D) what

Chapter 19

形容詞子句

啊哈!! 愉快地打基礎

1

形容詞子句是在句子中做形容詞角色,並修飾子句前面的名詞的修飾成分。

The woman who lives next door is kind.
I found a shop where I can get a discount.

Who lives next door 和 where I can get a discount 都有修飾子句前名詞 The woman 和 a shop 的形容詞作用,去除這些修飾成分也可以形成句子。把這樣的子句叫做形容詞子句,被形容詞子句修飾的名詞叫做「先行詞」。

2

形容詞子句可以分為限定前面名詞意義的限定性形容詞子句,和對前面名詞進一步補充說明的非限定性形容詞子句。

限定性 I have two sisters who are teachers. 我有兩個當老師的姊姊。
非限定性 I have two sisters, who are teachers. 我有兩個姊姊,她們都是老師。

在第一個句子中,形容詞子句(who are teachers)限定名詞(two sisters)的職業。在第二個句子中,形容詞子句對名詞進行補充說明。兩個句子似乎是相同的涵義,但第一句中不管說話者有多少姊姊,主要限定討論當老師的那兩位(即說話者有可能有第三位非老師的姊姊),而第二句中的說話者只有兩個姊姊,所以不需限定,而是給予「她們是老師」的額外訊息。

非限定性形容詞子句可以對子句前的整個句子進行補充說明。

Charlie became a lawyer, which surprised his friends.
Charlie 當上了律師,這個消息讓他的朋友們感到驚訝。

3

形容詞子句由「關係代名詞 +(主詞)+ 動詞」/「關係副詞 + 主詞 + 動詞」構成。

The reporter met the designer, who is now the company's president.
那個記者和身為公司現任董事長的設計師碰面。

The bookstore has a cafe where you can enjoy classical music.
那間書店裡有一家可以聽古典音樂的咖啡廳。

第一個句子中的先行詞 designer 得到由「關係代名詞(who)+ 動詞(is)」組成的形容詞子句的修飾,第二個句子中的先行詞 cafe 得到由「關係副詞(where)+ 動詞(can enjoy)」組成的形容詞子句的修飾。這時關係代名詞 who 有「連接詞 + 代名詞(and he / she)」的作用,關係副詞 where 有「連接詞 + 副詞(and there)」的作用。

關係代名詞有 who, whom, whose, which, that 等,關係副詞有 when, where, why, how 等。

01 形容詞子句的位置與用法

形容詞子句出現在具備修飾成分的位置，即主詞和動詞之間或句子的最後。

The tourists whom Eric guided **were from Germany.** Eric 所帶領的觀光客來自德國。
I can't find the book which was on the desk. 我找不到原來放在桌子上的那本書。

注意！形容詞子句不同於副詞子句，它不可以用在必要成分（主詞和動詞）前的修飾語的位置。

<u>Which is open 24 hours a day</u>, the library is comfortable for reading. 那個24小時開放的圖書館方便我們閱讀。

❷ 引導形容詞子句的關係代名詞或關係副詞的位置上不能用代名詞和副詞。

Fill out the application forms, ~~those~~ **are available online.** 請填好申請表，表格在網路上可得到。
                                    which

→ 因為是引導修飾 the application forms 的形容詞子句，所以用關係代名詞（which），而不是代名詞（those）。

We often go to a restaurant ~~there~~ **we can eat hearty meals.** 我們經常去那家我們可以吃到豐盛飯菜的餐廳。
                                  where

→ 因為是引導修飾 a rastaurant 的形容詞子句，所以用關係副詞（where），而不是副詞（there）。

❸ 要區分引導形容詞子句的關係詞和引導名詞子句的連接詞。

I know the boy ~~what~~ **broke this fence.** 我認識那個弄壞圍欄的少年。
                    who

→ 先行詞 the boy 不能用 what 來引導，而應該用關係詞 who 來引導。

I know ~~who~~ **the boy did to the fence.** 我想知道那個少年把圍欄怎麼了。
            what

→ 動詞 know 後面的受詞所使用的名詞子句，不能用 who 來引導，應該用名詞子句連接詞 what 來引導。

❹ 不能在形容詞子句的動詞位置上用不是動詞的形態（動名詞、不定詞、名詞、副詞）。

The company will reply only to those <u>who</u> ~~meeting~~ **our requirements.**
                                                    meet
公司只聯繫那些符合條件的人。
→ 不能在形容詞子句（who ~ requirements）的動詞位置上使用動名詞（meeting），而應該用動詞（meet）。

注意！形容詞子句的動詞要和形容詞子句的主詞保持單複數、時態、語態的一致。

I'm sitting in a room whose walls <u>is</u>(→ are) **dirty.** 我現在坐在牆壁骯髒的房間裡。
→ 因為形容詞子句的主詞（whose walls）是複數，所以也要用複數動詞（are）。

The tour group visited the museum, which <u>built</u>(→ was built) **in 1839.** 觀光團參觀了博物館，那個博物館始建於1839年。
→ 形容詞子句的先行詞 (museum) 和動詞 (build) 之間是被動關係，所以要用被動語態（was buil）。

多益實戰考題

⊙ 填關係代名詞。
⊙ 填形容詞子句內動詞。

1. Most of the products and goods ------- are traded on-line are sold directly by the owner.

(A) they   (B) those
(C) that   (D) these

2. Recently the director released the list of engineers who ------- to lead the bridge project.

(A) have nominated
(B) nominated
(C) have been nominated
(D) will be nominating

3. Dietary supplements ------- come from plants are generally known to be safe, but some may interfere with a wound's capacity to heal.

(A) whatever   (B) what
(C) whichever   (D) which

正確答案　P80

❶ 先行詞為人時用 who(m)，為事物時用 which。

We are looking for <u>someone</u> <s>which</s> is intelligent and dedicated. 我們在尋找一個既聰明又有奉獻精神的人。
　　　　　　　　　　 who
→ 先行詞為人（someone），所以要用 who，而不是 which。

<u>The files</u> <s>who</s> are stacked on his desk are due next week. 放在他桌子上的那些檔案下個禮拜就到期了。
　　　　 which
→ 先行詞為事物（the files），所以要用 which，不是 who。

注意！that 與先行詞的種類無關，用作主格或受格關係代名詞，但不能在逗號或介系詞後用 that。
　　　 The baker, <u>that</u> (→ who) is French, opened a new store in the area. 在那個地區開新店的是一位法國的麵包師傅。
　　　 The person <u>with that</u> (→ with whom) I talked last week is my lawyer. 我上週提到的那個人是我的律師。

❷ 關係代名詞有主格、受格、所有格。

格　　　　先行詞	主格	受格	所有格
人	who	whom, who	whose
事物・動物	which	which	whose, of which
人・事物・動物	that	that	-

I know the person <u>who is standing in line</u>. 我認識那個排隊的人。
The car <u>which is in the garage</u> is Steve's. 車庫裡的那台車是 Steve 的。
→ 主格關係代名詞（who / which）在形容詞子句中作主詞，緊接著主格關係代名詞（who, which）的是動詞（is）。

The girl (<u>whom/who</u>) <u>I met yesterday</u> is my best friend. 我昨天見的那個女孩是我最要好的朋友。
He took the medicine (<u>which</u>) <u>the doctor prescribed</u>. 他吃了醫生開的藥。
→ 因為受格關係代名詞（whom / which）在形容詞子句中作受詞，所以受格關係代名詞（whom, which）後面要緊接「主詞 + 動詞」結構。

I had to meet with my neighbor, <u>whose dog I have been watching</u>. 我必須跟我的鄰居見面，因為我在看著他的狗。
The students are writing a report, <u>the topic of which is Korean history</u>.
學生們正在寫的報告，而該報告的主題是韓國歷史。
→ 所有格關係代名詞（whose）在形容詞子句中以「…的」意思修飾名詞（dog）。人、事、物都可以用先行詞 whose，當先行詞為（a report）時可以用 of which 代替 whose。

多益實戰考題　　　　　　　　　多 益 會 出 這 樣 的 問 題

⊙ 填關係代名詞。
　有些題需要分清先行詞是人還是物，或分清關係代名詞的格才能解答。
　多益中主要會出現這類題型。

2. Gecko is an organization ------- mission is to provide financial relief to families left homeless by natural disasters.

　(A) which　　　　　　(B) that
　(C) whom　　　　　　(D) whose

1. Any contract ------- is not signed by the members of the Board of Directors would have no legal power even though its terms may have already been executed.

　(A) who　　　　　　(B) which
　(C) whom　　　　　(D) of which

3. Job candidates ------- are presently unemployed or are studying to obtain a degree must furnish this information on their application forms.

　(A) who　　　　　　(B) which
　(C) whom　　　　　(D) whose

正確答案　P81

03 介系詞+關係代名詞 / 數量表現+關係代名詞 / 省略關係代名詞+be 動詞

❶ 介系詞 + 關係代名詞

- 前句的名詞在後句中作介系詞的受詞時用「介系詞 + 關係代名詞」形式。

  I ran into a woman. + I had worked <u>with</u> her. 我偶然見到了一個女人。+ 我曾經跟那女人一起工作過。
  →I ran into a woman whom I had worked <u>with</u> ___. 我偶然見到了那位曾經共事過的女人。
  →I ran into a woman <u>with</u> whom I had worked ___.

- 「介系詞 + 關係代名詞」中的介系詞取決於與其構成片語的形容詞子句中的動詞。

  I had <u>a holiday</u> during which I was able to see my family. (↩during the holiday)
  我過了一個可以在休假期間跟我家人見面的假期。

  This is the book about which we <u>talked</u> yesterday. (↩talk about)
  這就是我們昨天談論過的那本書。

- 「介系詞 + 關係代名詞」後面接完整的子句。

  You have a sponsor to whom <u>you must submit a report</u>. 你有個贊助者，你得提交報告給他。

❷ 數量表現 + 關係代名詞

one / each	some / any	many / much / most	
all / both	several	half / the rest	+ of + 關係代名詞 (whom / which / whose + 名詞)

The program enrolls 20 students. + <u>All</u> of the students are women.
那個節目招收了 20 名學生。+ 所有的學生都是女性。
→The program enrolls 20 students, and <u>all</u> of them are women. 那個節目招收了 20 名學生，而且她們全都是女性。
→The program enrolls 20 students, <u>all</u> of whom are women. 那個節目招收了 20 名女性學生。

❸ 省略「關係代名詞 + be 動詞」

The place (which was) chosen for the reception is beautiful. 為歡迎會選定的那個場地很漂亮。
I want to know the person (who is) responsible for this mess. 我想知道應該對這起混亂事故負責的人。
The park (which is) around my house is open for day-use only. 我家附近的那個公園只在白天開放。
→ 因為可以省略「主格關係代名詞 + be 動詞」（which was / who is / which is），所以後面就會剩下分詞（chosen）、形容詞（responsible）、介系詞（around my house）等。

多益實戰考題　　多 益 會 出 這 樣 的 問 題

⊙ 填關係代名詞。
⊙ 填介系詞。
⊙ 填用在「省略關係代名詞 + be 動詞」部分後面的形式。

1. Electronic delivery methods such as e-mail and fax are the most common ways ------- which international communications are made these days.

(A) to　　　　(B) for
(C) by　　　　(D) of

2. There were more than 100 graduate students in attendance at our internship fair, many of ------- had prior work experience.

(A) who　　　(B) whom
(C) them　　　(D) that

3. Of the three applicants ------- for appointment to a managerial position, two have worked in an international setting.

(A) eligibility　　(B) eligible
(C) eligibly　　　(D) eligibleness

正確答案 P81

04 關係副詞

❶ 以先行詞的種類來決定關係副詞。

先行詞	關係副詞
時間（day, year, time）	when
原因（the reason）	why
場所（place, building）	where
方法（the way）	how（the way 和 how 不能一起使用，只能選擇其中一個）

Thursday is the last day when classes meet. 星期四是一週中有課的最後一天。

The place where I had lunch has a great salad bar. 我吃午飯的那個地方有不錯的沙拉吧。

The article explains the reason why customers are so indecisive. 那篇文章說明了顧客們猶豫不決的原因。

I tried to figure out the way/how the machine works. 我努力去理解那個機器是如何運作的。

❷ 關係副詞可以被「介系詞＋關係代名詞」結構替換。

The conditions where(= in which) the laborers work are unacceptable.
這些勞工工作的環境狀況是不被允許的。

The day when(= on which) he proposed to me was the best day of my life.
他向我求婚的那天是我人生中最美好的一天。

❸ 關係副詞後面接完整的子句，關係代名詞後面接缺少主詞或受詞的不完整子句。

Tomorrow is the last time when we will be able to see each other before you go.
明天是你離開之前，我們可以見面的最後一天。
→ 關係副詞（when）後面要接有主詞和受詞的完整子句。

That is the boy who broke my window. 那就是打破我的窗戶的男孩。
→ 關係代名詞（who）後面要接缺主詞或受詞的不完整子句。

多益實戰考題　　　　多 益 會 出 這 樣 的 問 題

⊙ 區別填關係代名詞與關係副詞。
　主要會出現與關係副詞比較後填關係代名詞的題目。

1. Any person ------- would like to visit the exhibition must have a written statement of permission from administration.

(A) who　　　　　　(B) when
(C) which　　　　　(D) whose

2. The new shuttle service, ------- has been operating since last year, serves all of the city's main stopping points.

(A) who　　　　　　(B) which
(C) what　　　　　(D) where

3. She applied to the company ------- she had previously worked when just out of university.

(A) which　　　　　(B) when
(C) of which　　　　(D) where

正確答案　P81

HACKERS PRACTICE ● ● ● ● ● ● ● ● ● ● ● ● ● ● ●

Practice 1 選擇正確的答案。

01 Mr. Gomez is familiar with Asian culture, (which / they) will help him as the liaison for Hong Kong.

02 All applicants (which / who) are waiting in line must have their documents ready.

03 Any staff writer (whose / that) proposal is selected for funding will receive an all-paid vacation.

04 The company purchased mobile communication devices (those / that) serve both as phones and e-mail portals.

05 Customers (who / they) wish to sign up for a store membership may stop by the information desk.

06 Working for the firm allows you to purchase stock options (which / who) are offered as incentives.

07 Persons (whom / whose) names are on the waiting list must call again tomorrow.

Practice 2 改正錯誤的地方。

08 On your desk is the receipt for the airline tickets where must be picked up tomorrow.

09 The number of entertainment programs that is directed at young adults is steadily increasing.

10 The upcoming workshop is the first one that the company having organized.

11 Miscommunication between coworkers is a problem when has caused a lot of tension in the office.

12 The main building, that houses the superior officers, has an electronically monitored gate.

13 The company manufactures diet pills and sleeping tablets, both of them are top sellers.

14 The surroundings where the employees work are pleasant.

正確答案 P82

Part V

01 The director developed a list of criteria for development, ------- he feels will boost the company's prestige.

(A) which   (B) that
(C) what   (D) who

02 A conference to discuss the terms of the settlement will be held at a time and place ------- to both parties involved.

(A) acceptance   (B) acceptingly
(C) accept   (D) acceptable

03 A1 Travel employed eight certified agents, all of ------- were trained at the same institute in Manhattan.

(A) what   (B) whom
(C) this   (D) their

04 ------- the government nor the private sector can provide a solution to the growing recession in the United States.

(A) When   (B) Both
(C) Neither   (D) Where

05 At a meeting yesterday, we studied the most recent budget proposal, ------- the board thinks will help pull the corporation out of debt.

(A) whether   (B) where
(C) which   (D) that

06 Changes in our organizational structure have created ways for employees to explore opportunities ------- were previously not available.

(A) what   (B) those
(C) that   (D) there

07 Lawless and Son is looking for a general accountant ------- duties will include balancing the books and preparing budget outlooks for each financial quarter.

(A) what   (B) whom
(C) when   (D) whose

08 People entering business administration need a broad knowledge of the culture in ------- they will eventually put their professional training to work.

(A) which   (B) that
(C) whom   (D) whose

09 The manager commented that the facts in the report were so incredible that she had to question ------- they could possibly be accurate.

(A) whether   (B) that
(C) whichever   (D) what

10 In an attempt to improve relations with his employees and be aware of their abilities, the boss decided to talk with ------- himself.

(A) anyone   (B) everyone
(C) ourselves   (D) themselves

11 Enclosed with this letter is a pre-addressed, stamped envelope ------- to mail your application for membership to our club.

(A) which   (B) in which
(C) what   (D) whenever

12 The units in the new apartment building have large kitchen and living room areas that ------- the growing demand for open space.

(A) reflects   (B) reflect
(C) reflecting   (D) is reflected

13 There have been some problems with the printer, ------- it is taking us longer to produce the advertising posters than expected.

(A) that   (B) furthermore
(C) so   (D) therefore

14 The package that ------- to Mr. Jones was returned to us when the mail carrier could not locate the address on the shipping label.

(A) sends   (B) have been sent
(C) sent   (D) was sent

15 Most heaters have a temperature dial ------- is best placed at the lowest setting for purposes of safety.

(A) what
(B) who
(C) in which
(D) which

16 GasCo sells more than 8 million gallons of oil a year, half of ------- is consumed in the United Sates alone.

(A) many
(B) which
(C) each
(D) whose

17 Please tell the person in charge to let us know ------- the assessment forms have been completed by the participants.

(A) when
(B) that
(C) what
(D) whatever

18 A dinner will take place next Friday to honor Richard Perkins, ------- has been a great asset to this bank for over thirty years.

(A) who
(B) which
(C) whose
(D) of which

19 After ------- informed of the planned federal increase of minimum wage, PennyPincher Inc. dismissed 30% of their entire workforce without notice or compensation.

(A) been
(B) was
(C) being
(D) were

20 George Rand's book, ------- examines the effects of culture on a society's economic sustainability, has already sold hundreds of copies in its first week.

(A) who
(B) this
(C) which
(D) what

21 Mr. McKenzie has been working on the campaign longer than anyone else ------- with the undertaking.

(A) associates
(B) association
(C) associating
(D) associated

22 Only Speedy Shipping offers a variety of delivery options that ------- both air and sea transportation.

(A) are utilized
(B) utilize
(C) utilization
(D) utilizing

23 The Mother Nature Garden Show, ------- annually demonstrates the newest technology in horticulture, draws over 5000 attendees during its week-long run.

(A) when
(B) which
(C) where
(D) whose

24 The conference was held in a banquet hall, ------- was remodeled just seven months ago.

(A) where
(B) which
(C) of which
(D) when

25 ------- during market slumps, the company refuses to lay off employees in order to reduce costs and increase profits.

(A) About
(B) Quite
(C) Although
(D) Even

26 We are currently seeking a partner firm whose marketing principles ------- to our own.

(A) similar
(B) similarity
(C) are similar
(D) has similarity

27 The renovations will usher in a new era for the historic Mandarin Oriental hotel, ------- one of Macau's most luxurious resorts.

(A) when
(B) once
(C) former
(D) past

28 An employee ------- performance during a specified period is satisfactory is entitled to a wage increase based on current pay standards.

(A) who
(B) whom
(C) whose
(D) in which

正確答案 P82

Chapter 20

副詞子句

啊哈!! 愉快地打基礎

1 副詞子句是在句子中有時間或條件等修飾成分的副詞。

Please call me before you leave. 請你在離開前給我打電話。
If he falls, he will get hurt. 如果他跌倒了，他會受傷的。

副詞子句before you leave 和 if he falls 在句中有時間和條件副詞的作用，是句子的修飾成分，句子沒有它們也能夠成立。

2 副詞子句由「引導副詞子句的連接詞 + 主詞 + 動詞」構成。

Once you have time, pay a visit to your grandmother. 你有時間就去探望奶奶吧。

第一個句子中的副詞子句由「引導副詞子句的連接詞（once）＋ 主詞（you）＋ 動詞（have）」構成。

引導副詞子句的連接詞有when, if, although, because, whatever 等。

副詞子句中的動詞為be動詞時可以省略（主詞 + be動詞）。
I would like to get it done today if (it is) possible. 如果可能的話我想今天就把這個做完。

01 副詞子句的位置與用法

❶ 副詞子句用在修飾成分的位置，主要是主詞和動詞這些必要成分的前後。

In case we don't get in touch next week, <u>I'll see you after the holidays</u>.
如果下週我們沒有聯繫的話，我會在假日之後去見你。

<u>I like to have a cup of coffee</u> while I'm getting ready in the morning.
我喜歡在早上一邊喝咖啡一邊作好準備。

❷ 副詞子句在句中起副詞的作用，與名詞子句不同。

副詞子句　I will lend you money if you pay me back tomorrow. 如果你明天還錢，我就會再借錢給你。

名詞子句　I demand that you pay me back. 我要求你必須還錢。

→ 在這裡副詞子句有表示條件的副詞作用，而名詞子句用在動詞（demand）的受詞位置，有名詞的作用。

❸ 副詞子句不同於那些有形容詞作用並在名詞後面修飾它們的形容詞子句。

副詞子句　She began cleaning when she learned that visitors were coming.
　　　　　當她知道訪客要來時，就開始打掃屋子了。

形容詞子句　Our home is <u>a warm place</u> where we can enjoy each other's company in safety.
　　　　　我們家是一個溫馨的地方，在那裡我們可以放心地享受互相的陪伴。

→ 與形容詞子句有修飾前面名詞的作用不同，副詞子句不修飾前面的名詞。

❹ 一般原則是引導副詞子句的連接詞用在子句的前面，但有些連接詞用在分詞片語（Ving, p.p.）前。

After <u>buying food at the market</u>, he prepared himself a delicious meal. 從市場裡買完食物後，他親自準備了美味的一餐。

The oil will burn quickly unless <u>placed on a low flame</u>. 不轉小火的話油很快就會燒過頭的。

→ 在這裡引導副詞子句的連接詞（After / unless）用在分詞片語（buying~ / unless~）前。

注意！　1. 不要用介系詞代替用在分詞片語前引導副詞子句的連接詞。

The oil will burn quickly <u>without</u>(→ unless) placed on a low flame.

2. 常用在分詞片語前引導副詞子句的連接詞。

when 當	before 之前	after 之後	since 自從	while 期間
whenever 無論什麼時候	once 一旦	until 直到	unless 除非	

多益實戰考題　　多益會出這樣的問題

⊙ 填副詞子句連接詞。

2. ------- the minimum wage has increased in some countries over the past few years, it is still below poverty level in many places.

(A) However　　　　(B) That
(C) Whereas　　　　(D) Despite

1. ------- the marketing head transfers to Singapore, there will be an open position at the main office.

(A) So　　　　　　(B) Wherever
(C) If　　　　　　(D) Whom

3. Customers who hear music on an open telephone line ------- placed on hold are less likely to hang up.

(A) to　　　　　　(B) as
(C) nearby　　　　(D) while

正確答案　P85

❶ 表示時間並引導副詞子句的連接詞。

連接詞	例句
until 直到… before …之前	He was not allowed to play until he had done his homework. 他不准去玩，直到他做完他的回家作業為止。 They lit the candles before they turned out the lights. 他們在關燈之前點了蠟燭。
when 當…時 as 當…時、依照 while 當…的時候 even as 恰好…時	When the doctor made the diagnosis, the patient was shocked. 當醫生下診斷時，患者大吃一驚。 While waiting for her son, Mrs. Cosby read a magazine. 在等她的兒子時，Cosby 夫人就看雜誌。 →表示在特定的時間點上發生事件時用 when，兩個動作或狀態持續較長時間時用 while。
since 自從… after …之後	I haven't eaten anything since I got home last night. 自從昨晚回家後我什麼也沒吃。 They left the theater after the singer gave an encore. 歌手唱完安可曲以後，他們就離開了劇場。
once 一旦… as soon as 一…就… (= immediately after)	They boarded the bus once everyone had arrived. 大家一到他們就坐上了巴士。 They stopped working as soon as dusk settled in. 天一黑他們就停止了工作。

注意! 　1. as 和 since 表示「因為」，while 表示「反而」的意思引導副詞子句。

　　　　　Her doctor ordered her to go on a diet since she had gained 30 pounds in two months.
　　　　　因為她在兩個月內多了 30 磅，她的醫生叮囑她要減肥。

　　　　　Some people like to take one long vacation, while others prefer many shorter trips.
　　　　　有些人喜歡享受一次長假，反而其他的人較傾向於有許多的短期旅行。

　　　2. 一個修飾成分的子句前不能有兩個連接詞，until after 是例外。

　　　　　Please stay here and wait until after I'm done with my meeting. 請在這裡等我直到我開完會。

❶ 為了表示未來時態，在表示時間的副詞子句連接詞後要用現在式。

They hope to finish the report before the library ~~will close~~. 他們希望能在圖書館關門之前完成報告書。
　　　　　　　　　　　　　　　　　　　　　　closes

→ 在表示時間的副詞子句連接詞（before）後，為了表示未來時態，要用現在式 closed 代替 will close。

注意! since 後面常用過去時態，這時主句要用現在完成式。
　　　The postman has delivered mail to community residents since he was in his twenties.
　　　這郵差從 20 歲起就開始給當地居民送信。

多益實戰考題　　　　　　　　　多　益　會　出　這　樣　的　問　題

⊙ 填副詞子句連接詞。

2. Staff members have reported hundreds of phone calls ------- the promotion was aired on television and radio a few hours ago.

(A) by　　　　　　　(B) before
(C) past　　　　　　(D) since

1. ------- all of the appropriate paperwork has been filed, you will be officially registered as an accountant at this firm.

(A) Whether　　　　(B) Once
(C) As if　　　　　　(D) Yet

3. Patrons who arrive more than twenty minutes ------- the opera begins should wait in the lobby until the doors to the main hall are opened.

(A) before　　　　　(B) when
(C) during　　　　　(D) while

正確答案 P85

03 引導副詞子句的連接詞 2：條件、讓步

❶ 表示條件並引導副詞子句的連接詞。

連接詞	例句
if 假如	Contact me if there is a problem. 如果有問題，就請聯繫我。
unless 除非（=if…not）	Let's go to the movie tomorrow, unless you have other plans. 我們明天去看電影吧，除非你有其他的計畫。
as long as, providing (that) provided (that), on condition that 只要（=only if）、倘若	You can use my car as long as you take good care of it. 只要你好好照料我的車，你就可以使用它。 You will get a discount providing you purchase two sets. 買兩套的話，就可以打折。
in case (that), in the event (that) 以防（在…情況下）	We have a back-up speaker in case Mr. Sanchez arrives late. 我們有候補的主講人，以防 Sanchez 先生遲到。 Call a customer representative immediately in the event that your credit card is stolen. 如果信用卡被盜，請立即與客戶代表聯繫。 →in case (that) 和 in the event (that) 用以表現「為可能發生事件準備對策的情況」。

注意！ 1. as long as 也可以以「跟…一樣久，在…的時候」的意思來引導副詞子句。

I won't smoke another cigarette <u>as long as</u> I live. 在我有生之年再也不抽煙了。

2. 在表示條件的副詞子句連接詞後，要用現在式來表示未來時態。

They will use the generator if the power <u>will</u>(→ does) not return. 假如不來電，他們就要使用發電機。

3. if 和 whether 都可以引導副詞子句和名詞子句。要注意引導名詞子句時兩個詞意思相同，但引導副詞子句時意思不同。

名詞子句 if=whether 是否　I don't know if (= whether) you like it. 我不知道你是否喜歡它。
副詞子句 if 如果…就　If you would like to use it, please ask. 如果你想用它就說吧。
　　　　 whether 不管　Whether you like it or not, you must admit it now.
　　　　　　　　　　 不管你喜不喜歡它，現在你必須認同它。

❷ 表示讓步並引導副詞子句的連接詞。

連接詞	例句
although, though, even if even though 雖然	Although he promised to come early, he was late again. 雖然他說好要早點來，但他還是遲到了。
whereas, while 相反地	The manager is aggressive, whereas his assistant is soft-spoken. 這位經理很強勢，相反地他的助理卻很溫和。

多益實戰考題　　多 益 會 出 這 樣 的 問 題

⊙ 填副詞子句連接詞。

2. The CEO has decided to bring Perry James along on his business trip ------- he is inexperienced and underqualified.

(A) if (B) so
(C) although (D) because

1. The value of the dollar will continue to drop ------- the American economy undergoes a dramatic revival.

(A) unless (B) whether
(C) even (D) or

3. Please refer to the enclosed manual or call one of our technicians ------- you are unable to fine-tune your device.

(A) unless (B) while
(C) whether (D) if

正確答案 P85

❶ 表示原因、目的、結果並引導副詞子句的連接詞。

連接詞	例句
because, as, since 因為 now that 既然 in that 在…點上	You should ask Mr. Carter since he is the expert. 因為 Carter 先生是專家，所以要問他一下。 Now that we are all here, let's begin the meeting. 既然大家都在這了，那就開始開會吧。 We are different in that you prefer to keep your opinions to yourself. 你通常不跟別人交流你的意見，在這一點上你跟我們不同。
so that ~ can, in order that 為了	He made changes in the presentation so that it could be more easily understood. 為了使陳述更容易理解，他做了修改。
so / such ~ that ~ 太…以至於…	Miguel was so tired from studying that he fell asleep in the library. Miguel 唸書唸得太累了，以至於在圖書館睡著了。 It was such a clear day that we could see the far-off mountains. 天氣很好，因此我們可以看到遠處的山。

❷ except that, but that（除…之外）

I have no problem with Daniel except that he never shows up on time.
除了他從不守時這一點，我對他這個人沒有任何意見。

❸ as if, as though, 這 (just) as（好像…似的）

It seemed as though there was something wrong with Jeff today. 今天 Jeff 好像遇到了什麼不高興的事情。

❹ given that, considering (that)（考慮到…，顧及…）

It is surprising how well Michael is doing, considering that he only got out of the hospital last week.
我們顧及 Michael 上週才剛剛出院，可能身體沒有恢復好，但令人吃驚的是他已經恢復得很好了。

多益實戰考題　　　　多 益 會 出 這 樣 的 問 題

⊙ 填副詞子句連接詞。

2. A number of our staff were late coming to the office today ------- the East bound A-train got stuck on the tracks.

(A) if   (B) because
(C) that   (D) unless

1. A gathering of all the company's senior managers has been arranged ------- we can discuss problems involving customer dissatisfaction.

(A) in order   (B) so that
(C) because   (D) such

3. ------- that exports have failed to recover the economy, the government is appealing to corporate entities for help.

(A) Considering   (B) Even so
(C) In case   (D) Unless

正確答案　P85

05 引導副詞子句的連接詞 4：複合關係副詞 whenever, wherever, whoever, whatever

❶ 複合關係副詞引導子句並在句中充當副詞作用。

whenever 無論何時	however 無論如何	whatever 無論什麼 / 無論怎麼樣
wherever 無論哪裡	who(m)ever 無論誰	whichever 無論哪一個

We were greeted with smiles ~~however~~ we went in that small town.
　　　　　　　　　　　wherever
在那個小村子裡，我們無論走到哪裡他們總是笑臉相迎。
→ 不是「無論如何」，而是「無論哪裡」的意思，所以用 wherever。

~~Whichever~~ calls on the phone, tell them I'm coming back from my trip tomorrow.
　Whoever
無論誰來電話，都跟他說我明天就會回來。
→ 因為是人打電話，所以要用指人的 whoever 來代替指物的 whichever。

注意！　1. who(m)ever, whatever, whichever 是用來引導名詞子句的複合關係代名詞。
　　　　Whatever we have to do is alright with me. 無論我們要做什麼，我都有時間。
　　　　→ 在這裡 whatever 引導的不是副詞子句，而是充當句子中主詞的名詞子句。像這樣引導名詞子句的 whatever 叫複合關係代名詞。關於複合關係代名詞的詳細內容在 Chapter 18 的名詞子句中。

　　　　2. however 常用作連接副詞。
　　　　The package arrived on time; however, some of the items inside were damaged.
　　　　包裹是按時到達了，可是裡面的一些東西受損了。

❷ however 常用的形式有「however + 形容詞 / 副詞 + 主詞 + 動詞」。

However often they visit the resort in Napa Valley, they never get bored.
無論他們去多少次 Napa Valley 的渡假名勝，都不會感到乏味。

However much that house is, I'm willing to pay the price.
無論那個房子多貴，我都願意支付。

注意！關於 however 的用法
　　　Visit however often you can. 儘量多參觀
　　　however much it costs 無論它有多貴
　　　however hard I try 無論我有多努力
　　　however well I perform 無論我做得多好

多益實戰考題　　　　　　　多益會出這樣的問題

⊙ 填複合關係副詞。
　　常出現選擇與句意相符的複合關係副詞的題目。

1. We at Grayson Automotive would appreciate it if you would fill out this service evaluation ------- it is convenient for you.

(A) whichever　　　　(B) whoever
(C) whenever　　　　(D) whatever

2. ------- much your company is paying you, I can guarantee twice that salary if you work for us.

(A) Whatever　　　　(B) However
(C) Whichever　　　(D) Whenever

3. Electronic communications make it possible to do business ------- you are in the world, whether in or out of the country.

(A) whenever　　　　(B) whomever
(C) wherever　　　　(D) whatever

正確答案　P86

06 引導副詞子句的連接詞 VS.介系詞

❶ 容易混淆的引導副詞子句的連接詞和介系詞。

涵義	引導副詞子句的連接詞	介系詞
時間	when …的時候 while 當…的時候 by the time, until 直到…才 after 在…之後 before 在…之前 once 一旦… as soon as 一…就… since 自從…	in, at 在 during 在…期間 by, until 到…為止 following, after 在…之後 before 在…之前 on(upon) Ving 一…就… since 自從…
條件	unless 除非 in case (that), in the event (that) 萬一，以防	without 在沒有…的情況，沒有… in case of, in the event of 假設，萬一
讓步	although, even though 雖然…while 反之	despite, in spite of 不顧…
原因	because, as, since 因為	because of, due to 因為
目的	so that ~ can~, in order that ~ can~ 為了	so as to, in order to 為了
例外	except that, but that 除了…之外	except (for), but (for) 除…以外
其他	given that, considering 考慮到… whether 不管… as if, as though 好像…似的 as 像…	given, considering 考慮到… regardless of 不管… like 像… as 做為…

❷ 引導副詞子句的連接詞用在「子句」前，介系詞用在「片語」前。

The meeting was postponed because <u>Mr. Stanley had urgent business to attend to</u>.
因為 Stanley 先生有急事要處理，所以會議延期了。

The meeting was postponed because of <u>urgent matters</u>. 因為有急事，會議延期了。
→ 「子句（主詞＋動詞）」前面要用引導副詞子句的連接詞（because）才對，而「片語」前面要用介系詞 because of。

注意！連接副詞不能引導子句，只能用引導副詞子句的連接詞來引導。

We will lose this client <u>otherwise</u>(→ unless) we can get the shipment in on time.
我們會失去這個顧客，除非我們能讓貨運準時到達。

多益實戰考題
多 益 會 出 這 樣 的 問 題

⊙ 填副詞子句連接詞。

2. Housing prices stabilized ------- interest rates on mortgages rose sharply due to the overall economic fluctuation.

(A) during   (B) in addition
(C) while   (D) meantime

1. Our office can begin filling out the order ------- the completed request form and instructions are sent via fax.

(A) once   (B) just
(C) upon   (D) still

3. ------- the company has been selling the same product for thirty years, it is still popular with consumers all over the country.

(A) In light of   (B) Nevertheless
(C) Therefore   (D) Even though

正確答案 P86

HACKERS PRACTICE ● ● ● ● ● ● ● ● ● ● ● ● ● ● ●

Practice 1 選擇正確的答案。

01 (As / For) my car broke down, I missed the meeting.

02 (Also / Although) his opportunities are wide open, he'd like to stay with the small company.

03 We can't confirm your order (until / while) you provide a transaction receipt.

04 (Even though / In spite of) the restaurant is always crowded, people still wait in line to be able to get a table.

05 Please provide an e-mail address with unlimited storage (therefore / in case) we have to send large files.

06 The library will be open to the public by February (so / if) the remodeling is completed before the second week of January.

07 Mr. Anderson has been given his own office (so that / hence) he can work in peace.

Practice 2 改正錯誤的地方。

08 They moved into the office even the electricity had not been turned on yet.

09 Despite the director retired last week, nobody has taken his place as of yet.

10 Total profit rose by twenty percent during Mr. Jameson acted as president of the company.

11 The company assured on delivery of the goods would be on time.

12 The hostess will mail out the invitations as soon they arrive from the printing shop.

13 We have to postpone the picnic while the weather forecaster said it would rain.

14 Nobody will be permitted inside this building unless when accompanied by a security guard.

正確答案 P86

Part V

01 The telephone information service is available round the clock ------- it is a special holiday.

(A) regardless   (B) whether
(C) despite   (D) even if

02 The new work schedule cuts back on extra hours ------- improving employee efficiency with longer lunch breaks.

(A) while   (B) but
(C) after   (D) since

03 At this company, quarterly bonuses are awarded, ------- all of the sales goals are met.

(A) so as   (B) depending on
(C) rather than   (D) provided that

04 The loan agency has been closed for investigation ------- claims were made that the owner dipped into overhead funds.

(A) when   (B) due to
(C) in spite of   (D) since

05 The company is currently looking for a certified senior business analyst ------- has strong problem-solving skills.

(A) her   (B) if
(C) who   (D) because

06 The club is so exclusive that visitors are not permitted to use its services ------- accompanied by a member.

(A) without   (B) otherwise
(C) but   (D) unless

07 Some of the suggestions proposed by the assistant manager had to be declined ------- they did not reflect the company's approach to employee relations.

(A) unless   (B) rather than
(C) because   (D) anyway

08 The company decided to change its policy regarding holiday breaks ------- the labor union initiated a strike.

(A) while   (B) where
(C) when   (D) whether

09 ------- Frank prefers having a quick meal at his desk, Carl would rather have a leisurely lunch at a good restaurant.

(A) As soon as   (B) While
(C) Because of   (D) However

10 ------- interested in taking extra classes in communications development should talk to Jessica at the main desk for information.

(A) One   (B) Anyone
(C) Whoever   (D) Them

11 ------- deciding whether or not to purchase an investment property, it is important to consider the terms of investment and the ongoing costs.

(A) Whatever   (B) However
(C) Whichever   (D) Whenever

12 Harold Grist became the company's top senior manager ------- successfully leading the firm through a period of near bankruptcy.

(A) with   (B) in
(C) after   (D) like

13 Employees are being asked to pull overtime ------- the current project has been completed.

(A) while   (B) until
(C) during   (D) upon

14 Visitors to the museum may approach the displays only to view the artifacts, but ------- to take any pictures.

(A) just   (B) but
(C) not   (D) yet

15 This color copier will last beyond its warranty ------- the machine is periodically maintained and worn-out parts are replaced.

(A) whereas   (B) in case
(C) unless   (D) as long as

16 ------- accompanied by an adult, children under the age of twelve are admitted free into the museum.

(A) With   (B) When
(C) Only   (D) By

17 An additional 78,000 job openings are available for entry-level workers ------- increasing foreign investments have spurred companies to establish new factories.

(A) that   (B) if
(C) as   (D) which

18 ------- the bank approves his application for a small business loan, Gary intends to open his shop by the end of the year.

(A) Providing   (B) Nevertheless
(C) The fact what   (D) Until

19 Included in this month's subscription is a coupon for a discounted year membership ------- you can introduce our magazine to your friends.

(A) in order   (B) so that
(C) in addition to   (D) such as

20 ------- the raw material needs of the company, we have had to explore other means to obtain the supplies we require.

(A) Consider   (B) Considered
(C) Considering   (D) Consideration

Part VI

> **Notice to all employees:**
>
> ------- it's the season when sleigh bells are ringing and snow is glistening, it's time to start the
>
> **21** (A) For   (B) As
>   (C) While   (D) Although
>
> preparations for our annual winter holiday party, this year entitled, "Another Notch on the Belt of Life." This event allows us the opportunity to unwind after an impressive 12 months of work and improve company -------. I have chosen December 21st at the tentative date and ------- I have
>
> **22** (A) duty   (B) morale   **23** (A) once   (B) afterward
>   (C) skill   (D) behavior   (C) yet   (D) while
>
> received ------- from you on whether this is convenient, your opinions on holiday food you would
>
> **24** (A) relevance   (B) dimensions
>   (C) objection   (D) feedback
>
> like served at the gathering, or any other suggestions, I will post the official date. I also require that you RSVP as to how many guest will accompany you so everyone will be accommodated. Please contact me in Human Resources Ext. 8768.
>
> Thank you,
> Brenda Lee

正確答案 P87

Section 6 特殊句型

Chapter 21

比較句型

啊哈!! 愉快地打基礎

1 比較句是把兩個以上的物件在數量或性質方面做比較的句子，並按比較物件的數量和比較方法分為三種。

表示兩個物件同等的比較句是「原級」句子。
Peter is as old as **John.** Peter跟John一樣老。（Peter和John的年齡一樣大。）

表示兩個物件中一個更優越的比較句是「比較級」句子。
Peter is older than **John.** Peter比John更老。

表示三個或三個以上物件中有一個是最優越的比較句是「最高級」句子。
Peter is the oldest **man in the band.** Peter是樂隊中最老的。

在這裡有很多對象以 **old** 來比較。比較句中經常出現比較多個物件的性質的情況，所以比較句中常出現形容性質的形容詞或副詞。

2 在原級、比較級、最高級中形容詞和副詞各有不同的形態。

當形容詞或副詞為單音節單字或以-er, -y, -ow, -some 結尾的雙音節單字時，有下列形態：原級、比較級、最高級的基本形態。

原級（形容詞或副詞的一般形態）	比較級（原級 + er）	最高級（原級 + est）
old	older	the oldest
clever	cleverer	the cleverest

當形容詞或副詞是以-able, -ful, -ous, -ive 結尾的雙音節單字或是 3 個以上音節的單字時，有以下形態。

原級（形容詞或副詞的一般形態）	比較級（more + 原級）	最高級（the most + 原級）
useful	more useful	the most useful
important	more important	the most important

有些形容詞和副詞不用-er / -est，而是用特定的比較級 / 最高級的形態。

原級	比較級	最高級
good / well	better	best
bad / badly	worse	worst
many / much	more	most
little	less	least
late	later / latter	latest / last

01 原級

❶ 原級以「像…一樣」的意思來表示兩個物件是同等的，原級的表現有「as + 形容詞 / 副詞 + as」形式。

Her hair was as black as coal. 她的頭髮像煤炭一樣黑。

The order was shipped as quickly as possible to the customer. 那個訂購品盡可能快速地被運送到客戶那裡。

注意！ 1. 表示「不像…一樣」的涵義時，用 "not as ~ as" 或 "not so ~ so" 來表示。

My report is not as / so comprehensive as yours. 我的報告書不像你的那樣充分。

2. 判斷 as ~ as 之間的形容詞 / 副詞的位置時，要先去掉 as ~ as 後再來區分。

Be as carefully as possible when going down wet stairs.(✕) → Be carefully(→ careful).
從潮濕的樓梯走下來時請盡可能小心點。

He drove on the icy roads as careful as he could.(✕) → He drove on the icy roads careful(→ carefully).
在有冰的路面，他盡可能小心地開車。

❷ 表示「像…一樣多 / 少」的涵義的原級表現時用「as + many / much / few / little 名詞 + as」。

I ate as many potato chips as you did. 我吃的洋芋片跟你吃的一樣多。

Please complete as much information as possible. 請盡可能地多完成資料。

→ 不能用原級表現「as + 名詞 + as」，所以必須在名詞前加形容詞（many / much）。

❸ 表示「與…一樣」涵義的原級表現為「the same（+ 名詞）+ as」。

Nelly has the same dress as I do. Nelly 有和我一樣的衣服。

Nelly's dress is the same as mine. Nelly 的衣服和我的一樣。

❹ 修飾形容詞或副詞原級的表現有 nearly（幾乎）、almost（幾乎）、just（一定）等。

The book, the second in a series, is nearly as exciting as the first.

這個系列的第二本書幾乎跟第一本一樣有趣。

多益實戰考題   多 益 會 出 這 樣 的 問 題

⊙填原級表現。

1. Management has decided to rotate workers to keep the assembly line running as ------- as possible.

(A) efficiency   (B) efficiently
(C) more efficient   (D) efficient

2. Studies have proven that laborers work twice ------- hours on average as skilled professionals in any field.

(A) much   (B) more
(C) as many   (D) more than

3. In order to serve you best, we ask that you take the time to fill out our questionnaire in ------- detail as possible.

(A) as   (B) more
(C) as much   (D) many

正確答案 P89

Hackers Skill   在「as + 形容詞 / 副詞 + as」中，後面的 as 不可以用 than 替換。

The wallpaper in the bedrooms is as simple than(→ as) the one in the living room. 臥室的壁紙和客廳的壁紙一樣簡單。

02 比較級

❶ 比較級以「比…更」的意思來表示兩個物件中更優越的一個，比較級的表現有「形容詞 / 副詞比較級 + than」形式。

Last month's test was harder than this one is. 上個月的考試比這次的更難。
She acted more cleverly than usual. 她比平時更機靈。

cf) The lesson we took up in class today was ~~harder~~. 今天我們學的課程很難。
                                             hard

→ 沒有比較物件時不能用比較級，所以要用原級（hard）。

注意！ 表示「比…不（少）」涵義時 用「less + 形容詞 / 副詞 + than」。
This report is <u>less important than</u> the first one you showed me. 這份報告沒有你第一次給我看的重要。

❷ 表示「比…更多 / 少」涵義的比較級表現是「more / fewer / less + 名詞 + than」。

More participants than last year came to the convention. 今年參加會議的人數比去年更多。

❸ 在比較級中不用the，但在下列情況下的比較級必須用the。

· the比較級…the 比較級（越…越…）

The more you eat, ∧fatter you will become. 你吃得越多，就會越胖。
                 the

→ 在上面比較句中如果沒有the就是錯誤的，而且即使有the卻沒用比較級，而只用原級the fat 也是錯誤的。

Daniel is ∧more intelligent of the two. Daniel是兩個人中較聰明的。
         the

→ 兩個人之間的比較句要使用the來表示出最高級

❹ 強調形容詞或副詞的比較級的表現有much、even、still、far、a lot、by far（更）等。

The effort you spent on achieving your dreams is much <u>more valuable than</u> the dream itself.

爲實現你的夢所做的努力，比你的夢想本身更有價值。

多益實戰考題　　　　　　　　多 益 會 出 這 樣 的 問 題

⊙填比較級表現。

1. Unfortunately the shipment will be delayed, as our factory is experiencing more technical problems ------- we anticipated.

   (A) or　　　　　　(B) while
   (C) whether　　　(D) than

2. ------- we put off finishing these cases, the more work there will be to do over the weekend.

   (A) Longer　　　　(B) Longest
   (C) The long　　　(D) The longer

3. Sending the memos by fax is far ------- than attempting to deliver them by express mail.

   (A) quickest　　　(B) quickly
   (C) quicker　　　(D) quick

正確答案 P89

Hackers Skill   出現比較級時後面必須有than，出現than時前面必須有比較級。

This apple is sweet(→ sweeter) <u>than</u> the one I ate yesterday 這顆蘋果比我昨天吃的那個還要甜。
We spent <u>more</u> money when/as(→ than) expected on travel. 我們在旅行的花費比預期的還要多。

03 最高級

❶ 最高級以「在…中最…」的意思表示在三個及三個以上的物件中最優越的一個，最高級的表現有「最高級 + of～ / in～ / that」的形式。

He is the funniest boy **of all the children**. 他是所有孩子中最有趣的一個。
It is the thickest book **in the world**. 這是世界上最厚的書。
It is the most informative documentary **(that) I've ever seen**. 這是我看過的最能增廣見聞的一部紀錄片。

cf) The ~~quickest~~ responses of the interviewee made the manager skeptical.
　　　 quick
面試者的匆忙回答會讓經理產生疑慮。
→ of不能表示「…中」的意思，也沒有比較物件時不能用最高級（quickest），而要用原級（quick）。

注意！ 1. 不管最高級後面的名詞是什麼，只要意思已經表現得很明顯時就可以省略。
　　　　He is <u>the funniest</u> of all the children.
　　　 2. 有關最高級的表現有one of the 最高級 + 名詞（…中最…的一個），at least（至少），at most（至多），at best（最多）等。
　　　　She is <u>one of the largest girls</u> in the group. 她是團體中個子最大的女孩之一。
　　　　I can drink <u>at least</u> six glasses of water a day. 我一天至少能喝六杯水。

❷ 「最高級 + 名詞」前必須加the，但the可以被所有格代替。

Snoopy was ⌒ most favorite cartoon character **when I was a kid**. 史努比是我小時候最喜歡的卡通人物。
　　　　　　the/my
→「最高級 + 名詞」的結構前沒有the是錯誤的，所以要在most前加the或所有格my。

注意！ 為了表示「第幾個最…的」意思，要在最高級前加序數。
　　　United Airlines is the <u>second</u> largest airline in the Unites States. United Airlines是美國第二大航空公司。

❹ 強調形容詞或副詞的最高級表現有by far，quite（絕對）等。

He was by far <u>the worst</u> roommate. 他絕對是最壞的室友。

多益實戰考題　　　　　　　　　　多　益　會　出　這　樣　的　問　題

⊙填最高級表現。

1. Of the many laborers at this plant, the ------- highly skilled will be transferred to a newly opened facility.

(A) so 　　　　　　(B) most
(C) such 　　　　　(D) much

2. Although less popular than the phonograph, the projection box was the ------- of the home viewing devices available in the early 1900s.

(A) success 　　　　(B) successful
(C) most success 　　(D) most successful

3. Erickson Brands offers customers the ------- variety of cellular phone accessories in the marketplace.

(A) wider 　　　　　(B) more widely
(C) most widely 　　 (D) widest

正確答案　P90

Hackers Skill　　有表示 "…中" 意思的of～、in～、that子句時要用最高級。

Bill is the slower(→ slowest) <u>of all the typists</u>. Bill是所有打字員中速度最慢的一個。
This building is the tall(→ tallest) <u>that I have ever seen</u>. 這是我見過最高的一棟建築物。

04 其他原級、比較級、最高級表現方式

❶ 比較級表現方式

表現	例句
more than + 名詞 …之上 less than + 名詞 …之下	There are more than <u>10,000 books</u> in the library. 圖書館有上萬卷的藏書。 Less than <u>five percent of the subscribers</u> chose not to renew. 訂閱者中5%以下的人決定不續訂。 *more than 或 less than 用在形容詞前起強調作用。 The meal he had at the cafeteria left him more than <u>satisfied</u>. 他在自助餐廳吃了非常滿意的一餐。
no later than 最晚…	The supervisor expects us to come in to work no later than 7:00. 監督者希望我們最晚7點來工作。
no longer 不再…	Mary no longer uses make-up. Mary 不再用化妝品了。
no sooner ~ than ~ 一…就…	No sooner did Pete put the phone down than it rang again. Pete 剛一掛電話，它就又響了起來。
other than 除…之外	Other than cornflakes, crispy bacon is her favorite breakfast food. 除玉米片之外，香脆的培根也是她最喜歡的早餐。
rather than 寧可…也不	The demonstrator stood his ground rather than run away like the others. 那個示威者寧可堅持站在那裡，也不願像那些人一樣逃跑。
would rather ~ than ~ 與其…不如…	I would rather read a book at home than watch a movie at the theater. 我與其在影院看電影，還不如在家看書。

❷ 用原級、比較級形態來表現最高級。

· 比較級 + than any other ~ （比別的…更）

This show is ~~the funniest~~ than any other sitcom on TV. 這個節目比別的電視連續劇更有趣。
                     funnier
→ 用最高級（the funiest）代替 than any other ～前的比較級是錯誤的。

· have never / hardly / rarely been + 比較級（從來沒有過…比）

Herbs have never been more popular than they are now. 草本植物以前從來沒有像現在這樣更受歡迎。

· no other ~ nothing + as 原級 as （沒有任何…像…一樣…）
  no other ~ nothing + 比較級 than（沒有任何…比…更…）

No other sitcom is as funny as this show. 沒有任何電視劇比這個節目更有趣。
When it comes to investing, nothing is more important than experience.
對於投資來說沒有任何比經驗更重要的東西了。

多益實戰考題　　　　　　　　多　益　會　出　這　樣　的　問　題

⊙ 填原級 / 比較級 / 最高級表現。

1. Customers wanting refunds must bring in the product and its receipt ------- one week after the date of purchase.

(A) no more than   (B) no later than
(C) no later as   (D) no more as

2. I would rather make the reservation now ------- risk not getting a ticket down the road.

(A) than   (B) else
(C) whereas   (D) rather

3. Garson's Manufacturing boasts in its advertisement that it can produce steel rods ------- than any other producer in the business.

(A) fast   (B) faster
(C) fastest   (D) the fastest

正確答案　P90

HACKERS PRACTICE ● ● ● ● ● ● ● ● ● ● ● ● ● ● ● ●

Practice 1 選擇正確的答案。

01 Due to flight cancellations, the convention will be held tomorrow rather (as / than) today.

02 Second-hand car parts were obtained (easiest / more easily) in the past than they are now.

03 Club members are allowed to join the raffle contest as (often / more often) as they wish.

04 (Hardly / No sooner) had the package arrived than we received a call from the sender.

05 Mr. Hanson's proposals are (by far / far) the most farsighted and well-balanced of all the propositions submitted.

06 Purchasing the entire program is less costly (than / rather) if components are bought and installed separately.

07 I believe Mr. Smith would be (much / just) as competent as the other candidate.

Practice 2 改正錯誤的地方。

08 The nearer you live to a major transportation facility, more costly your home will be.

09 Although the building had been remodeled, the windows were the same style to the previous ones.

10 Martha is the more talented designer that I have ever encountered.

11 Buying commodities in bulk is more economically than making several trips to get the same item.

12 The turnout for the grand opening was even greater when anticipated.

13 Please bring as much samples as you can to the interview.

14 The number of people interested in world affairs is much high than it was three years ago.

正確答案 P90

Part V

01 Improving our customer outreach program is ------- important than reorganizing our office system right now.

(A) better   (B) more
(C) well   (D) greater

02 The courses which have the ------- attendance records of the training department's offerings will be dropped from the program.

(A) poor   (B) poorest
(C) poorer   (D) poorly

03 Recent changes in the regulations and procedures at the American embassy have made it more difficult to get a visa ------- a timely manner.

(A) at   (B) on
(C) with   (D) in

04 A meeting sometime after the project deadline fits ------- for my schedule than trying to have one this week.

(A) better   (B) good
(C) any better   (D) any good

05 At this firm, young, motivated candidates who show enthusiasm have ------- value as experienced professionals.

(A) a lot   (B) also
(C) as much   (D) so many

06 It is the company's position that moving into a market with ------- competition will result in greater gains.

(A) a few   (B) least
(C) often   (D) less

07 ------- did the manager leave on vacation than the most important client walked in seeking an urgent consultation.

(A) Sooner   (B) No sooner
(C) The sooner   (D) Any sooner

08 It was fortunate that the company sold its shares ------- the price was high before the stock market crash.

(A) when   (B) why
(C) what   (D) which

09 Due to the alleged scandal, the corporation was receiving more attention ------- that which was good for business.

(A) so   (B) such
(C) too   (D) than

10 In the field of industrial arts and applied sciences, there are ------- positions open for entry-level candidates.

(A) lesser   (B) fewer
(C) sort of   (D) much

11 Piles of old newspapers must be stacked and tied as ------- as possible before being loaded into the truck and brought to the plant.

(A) tight   (B) tighter
(C) tightly   (D) tightest

12 Bringing all of the brochure and website information up to date is the ------- task the office team has ever faced.

(A) challenged   (B) challenging
(C) more challenged   (D) most challenging

13 Many financial organizations are finding that it is much ------- to survive through the national deficit than originally expected.

(A) hardness   (B) harder
(C) hardest   (D) hard

14 The senior officers have decided that the current computers are ------- adequate for what the staff must accomplish daily.

(A) enough poorly   (B) too much
(C) more than   (D) such

15 Of the two machine operators, the ------- qualified will be the one to run the new equipment in the factory.

(A) much   (B) lot
(C) better   (D) so

16 The more cutbacks we make in production expenses, the ------- the net profit ratio becomes.

(A) steep   (B) steeper
(C) more steeply   (D) steeply

17 Investors are nervously watching their stock shares ------- are being devalued by the recent presidential elections.

(A) where   (B) and
(C) but   (D) which

18 Installing a new blower for an air ventilation system may seem expensive but actually costs ------- in the long run than repairing an existing one.

(A) less   (B) lesser
(C) lessen   (D) least

19 Of all brain surgeons I have employed over the last 15 years, Mr. Mammoth is the -------.

(A) more intelligent   (B) more intelligently
(C) most intelligent   (D) most intelligently

20 The more ------- a camera is, the more the customers are willing to spend on the features that it provides.

(A) sophisticate   (B) sophisticated
(C) sophisticating   (D) sophistication

21 Commercial businesses are pleased that with the current state government, taxes have ------- been lower than they are now.

(A) quite   (B) none
(C) anything (D) never

22 It is well known that the storage capabilities of even the ------- powerful hard drive can't hold enough information to run an entire office system.

(A) so   (B) best
(C) most   (D) very

23 In determining whether to close a bank branch, the impact on the majority of community members is the ------- important factor.

(A) very   (B) most
(C) much   (D) mostly

24 Orders are filtered to separate departments when they arrive ------- given to the shipping personnel right away.

(A) than   (B) rather
(C) rather as   (D) rather than

25 Diet Trends, Inc. makes the ------- fat burning energizer of all those available in drugstores, but the product's safety is being questioned by the FDA.

(A) strong   (B) stronger
(C) strongest (D) strongly

26 Either the company increases its investment for the current year ------- it spends the same amount, risking a takeover by its competitors.

(A) but   (B) and
(C) or   (D) for

27 This is to remind you that employees are required to submit personal information changes to the administrative department ------- than December 20.

(A) no more   (B) no less
(C) no later   (D) no longer

28 All persons who wish to register for the Skills in Marketing Workshop must sign up at the main office ------- possible.

(A) as soon as   (B) as long as
(C) as much as   (D) as many as

正確答案 P90

Chapter 22

對等、倒裝句型

啊哈!! 愉快地打基礎

1 連接詞所連接的幾個項目有相同的詞性或構造並保持均衡時，叫做對等。

The interview was brief <u>and</u> informal. 那個面試既簡短又不正規。
Lectures will be held <u>either</u> in English <u>or</u> in French. 講演將會以英語或法語進行。

在第一個句子中被對等連接詞（and）連接的 brief 和 informal 都是形容詞，所以保持了均衡。
在第二個句子中被相關的對等連接詞（either ~ or）連接的 in English 和 in French 都是介詞片語，所以也保持了均衡。

2 把主詞和動詞的位置倒過來的現象叫倒裝，這樣做主要是為了強調特定的詞，而把謂語放到句子的最前。

Paula was <u>never</u> angrier than when she lost her ring. Paula 最生氣的時候就是她遺失戒指的時候。

<u>Never</u> was Paula angrier than when she lost her ring.

有助動詞（包含 have / be 動詞）時，助動詞要放到主詞前；但沒有助動詞，而只有一般動詞時，do 助動詞要放到主詞前，把原來位置上的動詞改為原形。

You can get a newspaper <u>only in the morning</u>. （主詞 + 助動詞）
→ <u>Only in the morning</u> can you get a newspaper. 只有在早晨才能收到報紙。

She has been thinking <u>only lately</u> about her future career. （主詞 + have 動詞）
→ <u>Only lately</u> has she been thinking about her future career. 她最近才考慮自己未來的職業。

The students were <u>never</u> so scared of the teacher. （主詞 + be 動詞）
→ <u>Never</u> were the students so scared of the teacher.
學生們從來沒有那麼害怕過老師。

Richard <u>rarely</u> steps out of the house on weekends. （主詞 + 一般動詞）
→ <u>Rarely</u> does Richard step out of the house on weekends.
Richard 週末幾乎不出家門。

01 對等句

❶ 在對等句中，連接詞連接的必須是相同的詞性。即名詞和名詞、動詞和動詞、形容詞和形容詞、副詞和副詞。

名詞　　His patience **and** intelligence made him a great leader. 他的耐心和智慧使他成為一名優秀的領導者。

動詞　　The researcher will collect **and** analyze the data. 研究員會收集並分析資料。

形容詞　The hostess at the party served hot **and** hearty food. 聚會的女主人提供了熱騰騰用心料理的食物。

副詞　　The motorist in the left lane was driving recklessly **and** desperately.
在左車道的駕駛員開得魯莽又危險。

注意！連接的是動詞時，要確認他們的單複數、時態是否一致。

If she finishes the project and clean(→cleans) up her work area, she may leave early today.
如果她完成這個企畫並且把周圍整理完後，今天她可以早點下班。

Jimmy Atkins sent out a dozen resumes and wait(→waited) for a company to call him.
Jimmy Atkins 寄出了許多履歷，現在等著公司來電話。

❷ 對等句要連接相同的構造。即動名詞片語和動名詞片語、不定詞片語和不定詞片語、介系詞片語和介系詞片語、名詞子句和名詞子句。

動名詞片語　Filling out applications **and** interviewing for jobs can be tiresome.
填寫求職申請書和做求職面試可能是令人覺得很疲勞的。

不定詞片語　I need to fix the ceiling **and** (to) paint it.
我需要修一下天花板並重新粉刷。

介系詞片語　Decorations hanging on the wall **and** from the ceiling were taken down.
牆壁和天花板上的裝飾物被卸了下來。

He wanted to tell me what he did **and** how he felt.
他想告訴我他做了什麼和他感覺如何。

注意！連接兩個to不定詞片語的對等句中，可以省略第二個to。

多益實戰考題　　　　　　　　多 益 會 出 這 樣 的 問 題

⊙填對等句。

1. For many companies, liaison offices have proven effective and ------- when establishing international connections in numerous countries.

(A) profits　　　　　(B) profitably
(C) profiting　　　　(D) profitable

2. Mr. Muir has been working on the assignment for the past three months and ------- to complete it by next week.

(A) plan　　　　　(B) plans
(C) to plan　　　　(D) planned

3. The responsibilities of a representative include ------- the company's sales goals and managing the special requests of customers.

(A) to achieve　　　(B) achieving
(C) achieved　　　　(D) achievement

正確答案　P93

Hackers Skill　　有對等、相關的對等連接詞時要確認並列的是不是對等關係。

For a middle-aged man, he is **witty** and energy(→ energetic). 以中年男子而言，他算是充滿智慧與活力。
The program includes both to cook(→ cooking) a meal with a group and **preparing** a dish individually.
這個節目包括與團體一起料理餐點以及單獨準備菜餚。

02 倒裝句

① 在假設語氣句子中省略 if 就會發生倒裝。

將來式	Should 主詞 動詞原形	, 主詞 will 動詞原形
過去式	Were 主詞	, would 主詞 would 動詞原形
過去完成式	Had p.p.	, 主詞 would have p.p.

Should you wish to visit, Mrs. Cameron will schedule a tour. (⇨ If you should wish ~)
如果您希望參訪，Cameron 夫人會預定參訪日程。

Were it not for my wife, I would be completely disorganized. (⇨ If it were ~)
若不是我妻子，我會搞得一團糟的。

Had he started cooking earlier, we would have eaten our meal on time. (⇨ If he had started ~)
如果他早點煮飯，我們就會準時開飯了。

注意! 關於假設語氣句子的倒裝在 Chapter 8-02，沒有 if 的假設語法中做了詳細說明。

② 不定詞（never, neither, nor, hardly, seldom, rarely, little）用於句子開頭時，句子會發生倒裝。

<u>Never</u> had he seen such an efficiently run business. (⇨ He had never seen ~)
他從來沒看過如此有效率地營業。

<u>Hardly</u> had he fallen asleep when the alarm went off. (⇨ He had hardly fallen ~)
當鬧鐘響起時，他幾乎不能再睡。

③ 「only + 副詞（子句 / 片語）」用於句子開頭時，句子會發生倒裝。

<u>Only recently</u> has Sharon begun to make her home look tidy. (⇨ Sharon has only recently begun ~)
最近 Sharon 才開始把房子收拾得看起來整潔些。

注意! 1.要注意倒裝句中主詞後面的動詞形態。

Only since the expensive vase broke has Maria <u>was</u>(⇨been) keeping the breakables upstairs.
自從那個昂貴的花瓶被打碎以後，Maria 才開始把易碎的東西放到高處。
Only in the evenings does Charlotte <u>takes</u>(⇨take) a walk. Charlotte 只有在傍晚才會去散步。
Seldom did Laura <u>used</u>(⇨use) the elevator, even when she was going to the tenth floor.
Laura 很少使用電梯，即使當她要去 10 樓的時候。

2.在 as（像⋯）或 than（比⋯）後面，有時發生倒裝，有時不發生倒裝。

I like to see movies, <u>as</u> do most of my friends.(= as most of my friends do)
和我大部分朋友一樣，我也喜歡看電影。
I spend more time working on reports <u>than</u> does my co-worker.(= than my co-worker does)
我比我的同事花了更長時間來做那個報告。

多益實戰考題 　　　　　　　　　多 益 會 出 這 樣 的 問 題

⊙填倒裝句。
　會出現填入引導倒裝句的詞或動詞的正確形式等
　問題。

1. Had we ------- that the event would not be a popular one with our customers, we would have dropped the plan in its early stages.

(A) realize　　　　　(B) realized
(C) been realized　　(D) realizes

2. Never did Mr. Lerner's penchant for details ------- with his capacity to see the whole picture when making management decisions.

(A) interfered　　　(B) to interfere
(C) interfering　　 (D) interfere

3. Only after a consensus was taken did the general manager ------- to forego having his employees do mandatory overtime work.

(A) decide　　　　 (B) decides
(C) decided　　　　(D) deciding

正確答案 P93

HACKERS PRACTICE ● ● ● ● ● ● ● ● ● ● ● ● ● ● ● ●

Practice 1 選擇正確的答案。

01 Tungsten Company's razor-sharp knives are designed to be (durable / duration) and slip-free.

02 (Ever / Seldom) does the team get into arguments about tasks.

03 Walking and (stretching / stretch) are two of the top suggested methods of daily stress relief.

04 The printing department will create and (distributing / distribute) company business cards to all staff.

05 (Should / Whether) you want more information on the subject, please call Ms. Terrell.

06 Only now does Kelly (understand / understood) the importance of organization.

07 Buston usually manufactures safe and (reliably / reliable) kitchen products.

Practice 2 改正錯誤的地方。

08 Mr. Richardson is giving hope and encourage to our staff.

09 Motorists must stay on the right side of the road and in single file.

10 Have Annie prepared better, she could have given an excellent presentation.

11 Both technical train and on-site experience are required for this position.

12 Henry often stops outside his door and turn around to get his briefcase.

13 The company promises incomparable customer support and satisfactory for all its products.

14 Mr. Lang's team works more diligently than Mr. Ford's team does.

正確答案 P93

01 Companies looking for ------- and competent staff may find it difficult to do so, especially when economic expansion leaves only the less qualified job seekers.

(A) experience   (B) experienced
(C) experiences   (D) experiencing

02 Patricia Wells applied for a transfer as soon as the branch in Honolulu opened, ------- did some of her co-workers.

(A) as   (B) too
(C) also   (D) thus

03 ------- accepting a job that is offered to you, carefully examine all possible alternatives.

(A) Whereas   (B) Finally
(C) Before   (D) Next

04 Applications that do not have the required documents will not be considered, and ------- will those that lack a clear career objective.

(A) also   (B) however
(C) neither   (D) only

05 We are seeking applicants whose ideas regarding design and layout are both creative and -------.

(A) originally   (B) originality
(C) origin   (D) original

06 Tokyo is a place ------- is frequented by businessmen who claim that navigating the circuitous city can be difficult.

(A) what   (B) why
(C) there   (D) that

07 The resume workshop teaches young professionals how to display their ------- and skills using sophisticated language and attractive formatting.

(A) educate   (B) educated
(C) education   (D) educational

08 Had the synopsis ------- earlier, we might have been able to include Mr. Roberson's proposal in our evaluation.

(A) deliver   (B) delivered
(C) be delivered   (D) been delivered

09 The department store has put out an advertisement announcing that it will hold a one-week sale on ------- and formal clothing.

(A) leisure   (B) leisurely
(C) leisured   (D) at leisure

10 Last week's issue of Fashion and Style featured Carrie Plimpton, an interior decorator with a special ability ------- a client's personality in her designs.

(A) of capture   (B) to capture
(C) capture   (D) capturing

11 It is best to keep a record of all checks you have written out, ------- it becomes necessary to substantiate a cancelled check.

(A) therefore   (B) even if
(C) in spite of   (D) in case

16 If you want to register to become one of our subscribers, fill in this ------- and simple information form.

(A) quick   (B) quickly
(C) quicker   (D) quickest

12 ------- have department stores seen such a decrease in sales of swimwear during the long hot months of July and August.

(A) Ever   (B) Even
(C) Although   (D) Seldom

17 Only lately ------- sales figures begun to show some growth in comparison to last month's total revenue.

(A) has   (B) been
(C) have   (D) are

13 Make sure to call the office immediately should ------- have any problems accessing your bank account.

(A) you   (B) your
(C) yours   (D) yourself

18 The Entrepreneur's Dream internet cafe has the ------- collection of information available on how to start your own business.

(A) wide   (B) widely
(C) more widely   (D) widest

14 The manufacturer is not responsible for injuries or harm caused by wrongful use of the product, ------- will they replace products broken by misuse.

(A) or   (B) nor
(C) and   (D) but

19 More and more individuals are turning to alternative therapies to treat a host of ailments and ------- pain.

(A) relieve   (B) relieves
(C) relieved   (D) relieving

15 Without sufficient contacts, finding an ideal location and ------- a good apartment can be a time consuming effort.

(A) to rent   (B) rent
(C) renting   (D) rented

20 With the marketing manager's impending resignation, an opening for a highly ------- and financially driven individual is now being advertised.

(A) motivate   (B) motivation
(C) motivating   (D) motivated

正確答案 P94

NEW TOEIC新多益必考單字

☑ 最核心！2212個必考單字，用最短的時間背最重要的單字

☑ 對症下藥！分第1順位、第2順位、第3順位單字，可清楚針對較弱單元加強

☑ 貼心規畫！針對「第一次準備參加TOEIC」、「曾經參加過TOEIC測驗」及「沒有時間準備考試」三種狀況提供不同的準備方式。

☑ 用聽的也能背單字！超過7小時的mp3，配合美式、英式腔調及中文翻譯，用聽的也能背單字。

VOCABULARY

VOCABULARY

1 多益單字的特點

- 多益中的單字都來自與實際商務交流相關的文章。

多益中的單字主要考察日常生活或公司業務中的英語活用能力。因此，如果不把重點放在學習實際商務交流中使用的單字，就會帶來很大損失。比如說function這個詞，在商業文章中不是指平時所說的「技能」這個意思，而是表示「儀式，宴會」的意思。所以對缺乏職場經驗的人，不能只侷限於日常學校或生活中的簡單會話，還要熟悉一些與商業有關的主題和單字。

- 多益單字問題不能光靠理解字彙的涵義，還需要熟悉它的用法（usage）。

多益考試旨在考察考試者對日常生活中單字運用的準確度。因此，大部分的多益單字問題不能光看單字的表面意義來解答。所以，需要時刻注意各個單字在日常生活中以什麼涵義使用的用法（usage）。不能停留在簡單的背單字階段，最重要的是熟悉在多益中可能出現的商業文章裡面的單字和用法。

2 多益考題的特點

- 片語、慣用語填空

這種題目是以常用慣用語和片語為空格，在四個選項中選出一個正確的答案來填空。不用理解句子全意，只要單字量多就能直接選出答案，所以這種題目是可以節省時間的獎勵題。最近有些題目中的片語有一個以上的可能選項，所以需要理解句子的全意才能選出最正確的答案。

[例題]

The Internet service provider is promoting broadband subscriptions by giving software programs ------- free.

(A) of　(B) from　(C) for　(D) at

解釋：該網路服務商以贈送免費軟體的方式來吸引顧客訂購寬頻上網。
解析：不需要理解句子全意也能看出空白後的free和（C）中的for是片語，所以選擇有「以免費」意思的片語for free來完成句子。

- 一般單字問題

這種題目要先理解句意並在四個選項中選擇一個正確的答案來填空。會出現與句意無關的選項或與正確答案相似的選項來迷惑考生，所以需要準確理解句意後選擇適合句子的單字。

[例題]

Although Bank-Tech, Inc. is as interested as any other company in making profits, it also adheres to a policy of social -------.

(A) assurance　(B) statement　(C) responsibility　(D) strategy

解釋：雖然Bank-Tech像別的公司一樣關心利益創造，但它也堅持遵守負起社會責任的政策。
解析：四個選項：保證（assurance），聲明（statement），責任（responsibility），戰略（strategy）中，最適合句意的是「責任」，所以選（C）responsibility來完成句子。

- 近義詞問題

這種題目是在意思近似的四個選項中選擇一個正確的答案來填空。四個選項的意思相近，所以很容易混淆。因此需要特別整理這些近義詞，同時與例句一起，記住各個單字的用法（usage）和它們之間的不同點。

[例題]

The entire plot of Mr. Scott's new book can be ------- into a few sentences.

(A) condensed　(B) minimized　(C) decreased　(D) contracted

解釋：Scott 先生的新書可以用幾句話來概括。

解析：四個選項都有「減少，收縮」的意思，但最適合句意的只有（A）condensed（condense 概括表示，摘要）。（B）minimize 是「最小化」（minimize risk 危險最小化），（C）decrease 是「減少」（decrease interest rates 減少利率），（D）contract 是「收縮」的意思，（metal contracts 金屬收縮），所以都不準確。

3 按類型／詞性出題比率

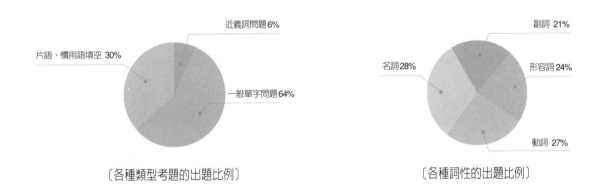

片語、慣用語填空 30%
近義詞問題 6%
一般單字問題 64%

〔各種類型考題的出題比例〕

副詞 21%
名詞 28%
形容詞 24%
動詞 27%

〔各種詞性的出題比例〕

4 NEW TOEIC 的趨勢與戰略

- 單字問題的比重大大增加。

NEW TOEIC Part 6 中取消了「改錯」但增設了「短文填空」。在「短文填空」中出現了很多單字問題，這使單字問題的比重增加。以已經出現的單字為中心努力學習多益範圍內的單字，並透過做題目來保持實戰的感覺是很有益處的。

- 做題時需要單字能力。

「短文填空」中的單字問題是在文章中的空白處選擇適合的單字，所以做題時需要單字能力。學習時徹底理解題目中出現的單字和表現有助於將來的快速解題。

Section 1 片語

Chapter 1

介系詞關聯的片語

「那座橋正在修建中」這句話該怎麼表達呢？

表達某事正在進行中我們一般用介系詞 on，那麼是用 "The bridge is on construction?" 嗎？寫出來後感覺又不太對。該怎麼知道這句話到底對不對呢？「在修建中」我們用 "under construction" 來表示。在網路上有時會看到某些冷清的網站主頁上荒唐的寫著兩個字 "under construction"，所以我們就能清楚知道這種用法是對的。在多益考試中會問到像這樣的介系詞關聯片語，但只要經常接觸片語就能飛快地答題，所以這種題目是可以節省時間的，讓我們把它當作遊戲來享受吧。

百發百中 出題類型與戰略

⊙ 會出現選擇適合片語的介系詞或名詞的問題。

⊙ 先看一下空白處前後的名詞或介系詞，然後再來選擇適合片語的選項。

⊙ 最後把選擇的選項代入句子中，並迅速判斷是否符合句意後確定答案。

例題 1

Requests for vacation time must be submitted ------- writing at least two weeks in advance.

(A) at　(B) of　(C) in　(D) on

解說　不用理解全句，只要看空白處前後的詞就能做答。能與 writing 搭配的只有 in，所以正確答案是（C）。

翻譯　休假申請必須要至少提前兩週以書面形式提交。

request [ɪ´kwɛ] 請求 / submit [səb´mɪt] 呈交 / in advance 提前

答案　(C)

例題 2

Morris Marina, the head of the small business software division, will be traveling to New Mexico tomorrow to attend a conference. As he will be gone for the whole of next week, he has designated his next in command, Hillman Avenger, to ------- of the division's business during

(A) be replaced　(B) be in charge
(C) be attuned　(D) be at odds

his absence.

解說　能與空白處後面的 of 組成片語的只有（B）be in charge，「be in charge 擔當…」帶入空白處就是「他不在時擔當公司的業務」的意思，句意自然順暢，所以正確答案是（B）。（A）replace 是「交替」的意思，（C）attune 是「（為樂器）調音」的意思。（D）at odds 用於「be at odds with 與…關係不好」，所以都不正確。

翻譯　小型企業的軟體部部長 Morris Marina 明天將會去新墨西哥州出席一個會議。因為下週他會去一整個禮拜，所以 Marina 指定部門副指揮 Hillman Avenger 在他不在時負責部門的業務。

division [ə´vɪʒə] 部門 / in command 指揮、受指揮 / absence [´æbsṇs] 缺席

答案　(B)

❶ subsequent to …之後

與「following …之後」同義。

Subsequent to the introduction of cost-cutting measures, expense accounts are being monitored.
在採用了減少支出的對策之後，經常費的支出正被觀察著。

❷ in exchange for 代替…，以…為代價

The company offered workers higher salaries **in exchange for** reduced health benefits.
公司以減少的健康保險金為代價，來給職員們增加薪水。

❸ to capacity 負載量，最大限度量

「be filled to capacity 滿員，裝滿」

The theater was filled **to capacity** every night of the week long performance.
在一週的演出期間，劇院每晚都是爆滿。

❹ in search of 尋找…

Mr. Smith is **in search of** talented and innovative personnel.
Smith先生在尋找既有才能又能創新的職員。

❺ to an absolute minimum 最小化

The new microphone system keeps background noise **to an absolute minimum**.
新麥克風系統可以使背景的噪音最小化。

❻ with the exception of 除…之外

No one is allowed beyond this point, **with the exception of** authorized security personnel.
除了得到許可的保全人員，誰也不能越過這個地方。

❼ as a result of 因…的結果

Many factories had to close **as a result of** new licensing regulations.
因新的認證規定的結果，有很多工廠不得不關門。

❽ out of one's reach 搆不著的

物品等在手搆不到的地方。

Ensure that blades for this razor are stored **out of the reach** of children.
確認這個刮鬍刀的刀片存放在孩子們搆不著的地方。

❾ at the latest　最遲

Send in your inquiry by next week **at the latest**.
最遲下週前必須把你的調查申請書送進來。

❿ at your earliest convenience　在您方便時儘快…

常用於商業文件中，與顧客書信中的表述，誠懇地請求對方盡可能地趕快處理某事。

Send some samples of your writing **at your earliest convenience.**
在您方便時請儘快將一些您寫的樣稿寄來。

⓫ until further notice　直到另行通知為止

notice 是「通知，通報」的意思。有時以「without notice 不預先通知」的意思出現。

The prices listed in the catalog are effective **until further notice**.
目錄裡的價格直到我們另行通知前都是有效的。

⓬ in one's absence　當…不在（缺席）時

The staff will hold a meeting **in the director's absence.**
當部長不在時職員們還是會開會。

⓭ in a timely manner　時機恰當的

The company processes job applications **in a timely manner.**
公司會在時機恰當的時候處理求職申請書。

⓮ in combination with　與…結合

This tablet, when taken **in combination with** vitamin C, helps strengthen immunity.
這個藥與維生素C同時服用可以幫助增強免疫力。

⓯ out of print　絕版

The first edition of the book is **out of print.**
這本書的最初版本已經絕版了。

⓰ above one's expectations　超出預期

Product sales last month were **above our expectations.**
上個月的商品銷售額超出了我們的預期。

HACKERS PRACTICE ● ● ● ● ● ● ● ● ● ● ● ● ● ● ●

◉ 在正確的前打 √ 標記。

01 be made ◇ **by** / ◇ **with** **hand**   用手製作的

02 **in conjunction** ◇ **with** / ◇ **from** the Lyons Community Center   與 Lyons Community Center 聯合

03 new procedures will be **in** ◇ **case** / ◇ **effect**   新的流程將會開始實施

04 **in** ◇ **commitment** / ◇ **comparison** **with** last year's performance   與去年的成績比較

05 write checks **in excess** ◇ **over** / ◇ **of** $5,000   超過 5000 美元時請開支票

06 Be reliable, and, ◇ **above all** / ◇ **foremost** , honest.   要令人信任，而且最重要的是要誠實

07 **in** ◇ **observance** / ◇ **observatory** of Independence Day   慶祝獨立紀念日

08 The economy is ◇ **on** / ◇ **in** the wane.   經濟正在衰退

09 a banquet **in** ◇ **honor** / ◇ **respect** of the mayor   為向市長表示敬意的宴會

10 Wear safety goggles ◇ **by** / ◇ **at** all times.   要時刻戴上護目鏡

11 give an estimate ◇ **of** / ◇ **for** free   免費估價

12 Visitors ◇ **in particular** / ◇ **on special** prefer outdoor cafes.   旅客們特別喜歡戶外咖啡館

13 Check the website **for** ◇ **quite** / ◇ **more** details.   更多的詳情請查看網站

14 **payment** ◇ **within** / ◇ **upon** delivery   貨到付款

15 Mr. Leeds is ◇ **during** / ◇ **out of** the office.   Leeds 先生外出中

16 be available **upon** ◇ **request** / ◇ **respect**   可於提出請求後提供

17 **work** ◇ **from** / ◇ **into** home   在家辦公

18 ◇ **with** / ◇ **at** **the aim** of increasing sales   以增加銷售額為目的

19 ◇ **in** / ◇ **on** **the recommendation of** the Board   按照董事會的推薦

20 Open 24 hours **for your** ◇ **convenience** / ◇ **promptness**   24 小時營業為您提供便利的服務

正確答案　P96

Part V

01 Staff members are requested to send in reports on equipment malfunctions at their earliest -------.

(A) requirement
(B) option
(C) choice
(D) convenience

02 All prices listed on the company website are effective until further -------.

(A) notice
(B) mark
(C) bulletin
(D) statement

03 The manufacturing contract awarded to Centrum was valued in excess ------- ten million dollars.

(A) to
(B) than
(C) of
(D) over

04 All household chemicals, such as cleaners or polishes, should be kept ------- reach of small children.

(A) out of
(B) away with
(C) up until
(D) without

05 High school students were paid on an hourly basis to distribute the company's promotional flyers ------- hand.

(A) through
(B) with
(C) by
(D) in

06 The department store offers the latest fashion apparel in a ------- of colors, ranging from light tints to dark shades.

(A) crowd
(B) type
(C) pack
(D) variety

07 Sales figures for agricultural products went up by 5% as a result ------- growth in the domestic and export markets.

(A) as
(B) about
(C) beyond
(D) of

正確答案　P96

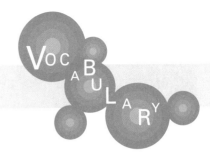

Questions 08-11 refer to the following notice.

Notice to Employees

Due to recent changes in occupational safety laws, Chubb Industries Inc. employees must agree to comply with the safety regulations described herein. It has been noticed that certain employees are reporting to work without their safety gear. Protection goggles and proper headwear must be worn ------- all times while working on the assembly line. When substituting at another

08 (A) of
(B) at
(C) by
(D) on

workstation for another employee during their absence, operate the machinery ------- in order to

09 (A) cautiously
(B) happily
(C) preventatively
(D) pessimistically

avoid injury, or seek assistance from a coordinator before using.

------- safety issues, occasional equipment malfunctioning has forced us to adopt biweekly

10 (A) In spite of
(B) Prior to
(C) Rather than
(D) Aside from

inspections and maintenance procedures to ensure that machinery is running at optimum efficiency. Be sure to allow the technicians full access to your workstation so that they can complete their work. In the event of any other ------- issues that may delay productivity, report

11 (A) unqualified
(B) unexpected
(C) unattached
(D) unstable

them immediately to the workstation supervisor.

Chapter 2

形容詞關聯的片語

「吃過沒有酸菜的牛肉麵嗎？」

呼～沒有酸菜至少多放點蔥吧？無緣無故提起牛肉麵話題是為了說明英語裡也有像牛肉麵和酸菜一樣形影不離的「形容詞和介系詞」片語。例如「be absent from 缺席」這種，在多益中需要知道 absent 與什麼樣的介系詞一起使用，知道了這些片語才能解題。多益委員們督促我們配菜時不要把牛肉麵和法國麵包合在一起吃，他們在試圖教我們正確的配菜方法，我對此感到很欣慰。今天已經上了「形容詞和介系詞」這道菜，那就我們來一起好好探討一下它的配菜方法。

百發百中 出題類型與戰略

- ◉ 主要會出現選擇適合的形容詞或介系詞的題目。
- ◉ 先看空白處前後的名詞、介系詞或形容詞，然後再來選擇適合片語的選項。
- ◉ 最後把選項內容代入句子，並迅速判斷是否符合句意後，確定答案是否正確。

例題 1

The company is looking for someone who is -------- of making important decisions in a fast paced environment and under time constraints.

(A) liable　(B) capable　(C) eligible　(D) subject

解說　先看看空白處的前後，我們知道能與空白處後面的介系詞 "of" 搭配的是形容詞（B）capable（be capable of Ving 有能力做…）。（A）liable 是「be liable to do 容易做…，有義務做…」，（C）eligible 是「be eligible to do 有資格做…」，（D）subject 是「be subject to 容易受到…的影響，容易成為…」的意思，所以都不正確。

翻譯　公司在尋找可以在瞬息萬變的環境和有限時間內迅速做出重要決定的人。

look for 尋找 / under time constraints 有限時間內 / pace [pes] 踱步，步調

答案　(B)

例題 2

Please extend a warm welcome to Thomas Little, the new vice president and general manager of our product development unit. He comes to us from Believe Inc., a Canadian computer graphics technology company, where he was -------- for all aspects of product design,

(A) knowledgeable　(B) independent
(C) responsible　　(D) subject

operations, and software processes.

解說　可以與空白處後面的 "for" 搭配的是形容詞（C）responsible（be responsible for 對…負責任）。（A）knowledgeable 是「be knowledgeable about 精通於…」，（B）independent 是「be independent of 獨立於…」，（D）subject 是「be subject to 容易受到…的影響，容易成為…」的意思，所以都不正確。

翻譯　請熱烈歡迎新任副社長兼開發部總經理 Thomas Little，他從加拿大電腦圖像技術公司 Believe 來加入我們，在那裡他全面負責產品設計、執行、軟體處理等業務。

extend [ɪkˋstɛ] 給予（恩惠）/ vice president 副社長 / operation [ˌapəˋreʃən] 執行 / process [ˋprasɛs] 處理，過程

答案　(C)

❶ be reflective of 反映⋯

Market conditions **are** often **reflective of** the current political state.
市場狀況常常會反映政治現況。

❷ be subject to 容易受到⋯的影響，需要得到（認可等），以⋯為條件

像「be subject to damage 容易受到傷害」或「be subject to colds 容易得感冒」這樣，有「容易受到⋯的影響」的意思。
也有特定情況「需要得到某人的（認可）」的意思。

Building foundations **are subject to** damage from water and wind.
建築物根基部分容易受到水和風的損害。

Employee leave applications **are subject to** management approval.
職員的休假申請書需要得到管理階層的批准。

❸ be compatible with 與⋯有相容性，與⋯相容

用來表示兩個事物互相相容的意思，例如軟體可以在不同系統中順暢的運作。與 "work well together" 同義。

Our software programs **are compatible with** the computer's hardware system.
我們這個程式軟體可以與這個電腦的硬體系統相容。

❹ be uncertain about 對⋯不確信

The committee said it **is uncertain about** the results of the study.
委員會表示對研究結果並不是很確信。

❺ be critical of 挑剔⋯

Human Resources managers should not **be critical of** employee suggestions.
人事部經理不能對職員的提議太苛刻。

❻ be accustomed to 熟悉⋯

Our regular customers **are accustomed to** consistently outstanding levels of service.
常客們都熟悉我們一向出眾的服務水準。

❼ be comparable to 可以與⋯媲美，可以與⋯比較

The size of the city **is comparable to** that of Philadelphia.
那個市的大小可以與費城相比了。

❽ Make your checks payable to + 支票受領者 給（支票受領者）開支票

美國常用個人支票（personal check），所以可以在貸款申請書上看到這些句子。
注意：在「payable to 應付給⋯」中要用介系詞 to。

Make your checks payable to Squibb, Inc.
請給 Squibb 公司開支票。

VOCABULARY I 片語

❾ be noted for 因…而出名

The company **is noted for** the quality of its furniture.
那個公司因其傢俱的優良品質而出名。

❿ be concerned about / over 擔心…

be concerned about / over 是「擔心… (be worried about)」的意思。

The organizers **are concerned about** the seating capacity of the room.
主辦者們擔心那個房間裡的座位夠不夠用。

cf) be concerned with 是「(書等的主題) 有關於…」的意思。

The article **is concerned with** the effects of a consumer boycott.
那個報導是關於消費者聯合抵制運動所帶來的影響的。

⓫ be known for 因 (…內容) 而眾所周知

be known for 是「因 (…內容) 而眾所周知」的意思，被眾所周知的內容出現在 for 後面。

The Ace Motors dealership **is known for** its excellent after-sales service.
Ace 汽車代理店因出色的售後服務而眾所周知。

cf) be known as 是「被認為是…」的意思，as 後面接身份、職位等詞。be known to 是「被…所知」的意思，to 後面接知道的主詞。

Mr. Carlson **is known to** the staff **as** a highly motivated CEO.
Carlson 先生被職員們認為是行動力極強的 CEO。

⓬ be responsive to 對…做出反應，回應

The health club staff **is responsive to** its members' requests.
健身俱樂部的職員要對會員們的要求做出反應。

⓭ be contingent on 以…為條件，依賴於…

「A is contingent on B： A 以 B 為條件，A 依賴於 B」

Funding for the project **is contingent on** the Board of Directors' decision.
專案資金的來源依賴於董事會的決定。

⓮ be cognizant of 意識到…，知道

與「be aware of 知道…」同義。

Physicians must **be cognizant of** medical regulations in the state where they practice.
醫生們要知道他們工作所在的州的醫療規定。

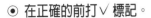

◉ 在正確的前打 ✓ 標記。

01 **be aware** ◊ **to** / ◊ **of** the circumstances　　　　意識到狀況

02 **be** ◊ **detached** / ◊ **dedicated** **to** pursuing a banking career　　　　專心追求銀行業務的工作

03 The effect **was opposite** ◊ **of** / ◊ **to** what we intended.　　　　效果與我們希望的相反

04 remarks that **are** ◊ **irretrievable** / ◊ **irrelevant** **to** the subject　　　　與主題無關的言論

05 prices **comparable** ◊ **of** / ◊ **to** those of competitors　　　　與競爭者的價格差不多

06 The new model **is** ◊ **exceptional** / ◊ **superior** **to** the previous one.　　　　新款的產品比前款的出色

07 **be consistent** ◊ **of** / ◊ **with** the company's code of ethics　　　　與公司的綱領一致

08 pillows ◊ **made** / ◊ **selected** **of** 100 percent cotton　　　　用100%純棉做的枕頭

09 **be absent** ◊ **from** / ◊ **to** the company gathering　　　　缺席公司聚會

10 **be full** ◊ **of** / ◊ **by** expectations　　　　充滿期待

11 **be ideal** ◊ **with** / ◊ **for** young teens　　　　對青少年來說是非常適合的

12 **be interested** ◊ **in** / ◊ **at** product quality　　　　對產品品質的關心

VOCABULARY | 字語

Part V

01 Before downloading and installing any program, staff members should check with the company technician whether it is ------- with the existing system.

(A) undeniable
(B) amenable
(C) favorable
(D) compatible

02 The company is committed to developing an excellent customer service department that is responsive ------- patrons' needs and wishes.

(A) on
(B) of
(C) to
(D) with

03 Individuals interested in establishing a business should be ------- of the regulations on company filing set down by the Securities and Exchange Commission.

(A) cognizant
(B) ambitious
(C) oblivious
(D) reticent

04 The formation of a new team of representatives remains ------- on how well the existing teams do by the end of the quarter.

(A) speculative
(B) contingent
(C) hopeful
(D) eventual

05 The new bank rules state that approval of a client's loan application is ------- to income verification and credit approval.

(A) necessary
(B) subject
(C) exposed
(D) internal

06 When ordering products from our mail-order catalogue, please ensure that all checks are made payable ------- Gillian Sanders.

(A) from
(B) in
(C) of
(D) to

07 The staff at Blue Ribbon Corporation is ------- to providing consistent, timely and quality service to company customers.

(A) pledged
(B) concentrated
(C) offered
(D) dedicated

正確答案 P97

Questions 08-11 refer to the following memo.

From: Richard Garfield, Vice President
To: All Employees, Marketing Department

According to the latest statistics, sales figures for the past quarter were subject to a negative trend, stemming from the ongoing national economic slump. The growth that we had become ------- to over the past two years has come to an abrupt end, with the public already

08 (A) familiar
(B) accustomed
(C) friendly
(D) acquainted

reacting by curbing their spending on high-end goods and services. The recent decline in our sales figures is ------- of this conservative consumer behavior.

09 (A) manageable
(B) thoughtful
(C) possible
(D) reflective

Senior Management staff have therefore decided to ------- reduce targets for our company's

10 (A) significantly
(B) exactly
(C) vaguely
(D) unnecessarily

Three Year Development Plan. We'll be making a presentation giving ------- information about

11 (A) maximum
(B) partial
(C) detailed
(D) constant

the new plan, which all marketing department employees will be required to attend, as the revisions will affect our advertising strategy. Check the website notice board for the date, time, and venue of the presentation.

Chapter 3

動詞關聯的片語 1

You jump, I jump, right? (鐵達尼號經典台詞)

緊跟著形容詞和介系詞這對情侶的影子之後，動詞和介系詞這對情侶也出來啦。仔細一看，原來動詞就是英文中的超級明星。你得給這小子想要的才能高枕無憂。動詞中有像「concentrate on 集中於…」一樣的動詞和介系詞情侶，多益考試中會出題目考察你們是否能正確地運用「動詞和介系詞」片語。當問到「concentrate 的另一半情侶介系詞是誰？」的時候，回答成「是in」，那你就是給「羅密歐和祝英台」作媒。聽說做錯媒可要挨三個耳光，那我可得好好記住「動詞和介系詞」這對情侶唷！

百發百中 出題類型與戰略

◉ 會出現選擇適合的動詞或介系詞的問題。

◉ 先看空白處前後的名詞或介系詞，然後選擇適合片語的選項。

◉ 最後把選項內容代入句子，並迅速判斷是否符合句意後確定答案是否正確。

例題 1

Although the director wants his staff to minimize mistakes, he also knows his employees can benefit ------- such experiences.

(A) from　(B) with　(C) to　(D) of

解說　不用理解全句我們就知道，能與空白處前面的benefit搭配的介系詞只有（A）from。把「benefit from 從…中獲益」代入整句之後句意也正確，所以最終確定正確答案是（A）from。

翻譯　雖然經理希望職員們能將他們的失誤最小化，但他也知道職員們可以從這些失誤中獲益。

答案　(A)

例題 2

There are a number of commonly-used psychological management techniques that can help achieve a successful outcome when dealing with difficult employees. For example, while they are speaking, you should ------- carefully to their arguments to let them know you value their

(A) pay　　　　(B) consider
(C) assist　　　(D) listen

opinions before firmly raising the issues which need to be addressed.

解說　仔細看空白處後面和選項我們發現listen和介系詞to可以構成片語。把listen代入空白處，構成「要仔細聆聽他們的意見」的通順意思，所以（D）是正確答案。（A）pay（支付），（B）consider（考慮），（C）assist（支援）都與句意不符，而且它們都是及物動詞，不能與介系詞to一起使用，所以不正確。注意：listen和to之間有carefully，即不及物動詞和介系詞之間可以有副詞修飾。

翻譯　很多心理管理方面的技術用在難以管理的職員身上有很不錯的成果。例如，果斷提出要改善的問題之前，你應該要仔細的聽取他們的反對的理由，讓他們知道你很看重他們的觀點。

psychological [ˌsaɪkəˈlɑdʒɪkl] 心理的 / outcome [ˈaʊtˌkʌm] 結果 / value [ˈvælju] 重視 / address [əˈdrɛs] 改善，改正（問題）

答案　(D)

❶ attribute A to B 把A歸因於B，A的原因是B

常用被動式的「A is attributed to B：把A歸因於B」。

Analysts **attribute** the current market boom **to** an increase in individual investors.
分析人士把最近市場興盛的原因歸因於個人投資者的增加。

❷ charge 購入品 **to** 支付來源 （把採購物品的花費）算在（支付來源）

Please **charge** the repairs **to** my credit card.
請把修理費算在我的信用卡上。

❸ result from 由…產生，由…引起

用來表示某事的起因。事件的原因放到from之後。

The manufacturer will not be accountable for damages **resulting from** misuse.
因錯誤使用而造成的損壞，製造商概不負責。

❹ dispose of 處理

When **disposing of** expired credit cards, it is wise to cut them in half.
當處理過期的信用卡時把它剪成兩半是很聰明的作法。

❺ contribute to 捐助，貢獻

Factors **contributing to** globalization include technological innovation and world economic integration.
貢獻全球化的要素有科學技術的革新與世界經濟的統合。

❻ congratulate 某人 **on** 祝賀內容 因（祝賀內容）而祝賀（某人）

We want to **congratulate** Mr. Grant **on** his recent promotion.
因Grant先生最近升職了，所以我們想向他表示祝賀。

❼ contend with 與…爭鬥，應付

Bakery companies have to **contend with** a decreasing demand for baked products.
麵包公司要應付烘焙產品需求量減少的情況。

❽ restrict 事物 **to** 特定集體 （事物）僅限於（特定人員、地點）

用來表示入場限制或僅限於特定人員，或物品只能在特定場所使用，「A is restricted to B：A限於B」。

Access **is restricted to** authorized personnel only.
得到許可的職員們才能進入。

⑨ be faced with 面對（問題）

face 作動詞時表示「面對…」的意思。注意：被動式時要與 with 一起使用。

Faced with a large debt, the company declared bankruptcy.
面對巨額的負債，公司宣佈倒閉了。

⑩ be associated with 與…有關。

associate 是不及物動詞，表示「把…聯繫在一起」的意思。常用於 be associated with 的形態。

The company's consultant **was** closely **associated with** a competing firm.
那個公司的顧問與一家競爭的公司之間有密切的關係。

⑪ check A for B 為確認 B，而檢查 A

It is recommended that consumers **check** their credit report **for** errors at least once a year.
消費者們最好一年檢查一次信用卡記錄來確保無誤。

⑫ comply with 規則 **遵守（規則、要求）**

Tenants are asked to **comply with** the building's rules and regulations.
承租人必須遵守本大樓規則和規定。

⑬ collaborate on 事物 **合作（事物）**

同時記住「collaborate with 某人」是「與…合作」的意思。

The two firms want to **collaborate on** a landmark research project on DNA sequencing.
兩個公司希望在劃時代的 DNA 排列研究項目上合作。

⑭ A is aimed at B A瞄準 B

表示產品瞄準特定消費群時，使用的是 aim（瞄準）的被動式。

The new F-series sports car **is aimed at** young business executives.
新 F-series 跑車瞄準了年輕企業家的消費群。

⑮ compensate A for B 因 B 補償 A

用於給某人提供補償損失時。

The broadcaster **compensated** Dr. Bland **for** the damage caused by the report.
廣播員補償 Bland 博士因這個報導所造成的傷害。

⑯ interfere with 妨礙，傷害

Chronic stress can **interfere with** the function of the immune system.
慢性壓抑會妨礙免疫系統的正常功能。

◉ 在正確的前打 ✓ 標記。

01 be accompanied ◊ **of** a cover letter　　　　　附上一封信
◊ **by**

02 prohibit customers ◊ **under** smoking　　　　禁止顧客吸煙
◊ **from**

03 experiment ◊ **with** feasible alternatives　　　試驗可行的對策
◊ **over**

04 Fill this out and ◊ **retrieve** it **to** the front desk.　填好這個後交回給接待處
◊ **return**

05 Price increases **depend** ◊ **of** the cost of gasoline.　價格膨脹與否取決於汽油價格
◊ **on**

06 The complex **consists** ◊ **by** two-bedroom houses.　這個綜合建築是由有兩個臥室的房子們所構成
◊ **of**

07 engage ◊ **in** a discussion　　　　參與討論
◊ **to**

08 The merger could **lead** ◊ **at** layoffs.　　這個合併案可能導致裁員
◊ **to**

09 compete ◊ **along** a promotion　　為升職而進行競爭
◊ **for**

10 Lockers will **be** ◊ **assigned** to all staff.　可上鎖的置物櫃將會分配給所有員工
◊ **assumed**

11 Employees **are** ◊ **entailed** to overtime pay.　職員們有權拿到加班費
◊ **entitled**

12 regard the decision ◊ **as** a mistake　把這個決定認為是一種失誤
◊ **to**

13 be subjected ◊ **to** high temperatures　容易受到高溫的影響
◊ **with**

14 Bonuses **are related** ◊ **for** performance.　獎勵是跟表現有關的
◊ **to**

15 cars **equipped** ◊ **by** an anti-theft device　配備防盜器的車輛
◊ **with**

16 ◊ **throw** the table **with** a cloth　用布裝飾桌子
◊ **drape**

17 be involved ◊ **at** designing the program　從事軟體設計工作
◊ **in**

正確答案　P98

VOCABULARY | 片語

Part V

01 Semiconductor companies around the world have had to ------- with increasingly lower demand and plummeting values on the stock exchange.

(A) replace
(B) contend
(C) group
(D) reward

02 Software Mode and a top Japanese electronics manufacturer will collaborate ------- the design and production of a new hand-held device.

(A) for
(B) by
(C) with
(D) on

03 ------- to the call for more proposals, our feasibility study writers worked overtime to produce one before the deadline.

(A) According
(B) Abiding
(C) Responding
(D) Awakening

04 After returning from his trip to Asia, the president ------- the branch heads on the agreement entered into by the firm.

(A) communicated
(B) told
(C) briefed
(D) explained

05 Admittance to the special showing is ------- to members of the club and their guests.

(A) conscripted
(B) restricted
(C) denied
(D) released

06 All visitors to the San Diego Zoo are kindly requested to refrain ------- feeding the animals.

(A) from
(B) with
(C) to
(D) of

07 The sudden increase in sales of Superslim mobile phones is ------- to their appearance in a popular television drama series which is currently showing on NATV.

(A) prohibited
(B) attributed
(C) contributed
(D) distributed

正確答案 P98

Questions 08-11 refer to the following letter.

Hi-Net Cable Internet
867 East Valley Trail NW
Great Falls, Montana 68750

To Whom It May Concern,

This letter is to notify you of an ------- amount which appears on the billing statement for my

        08 (A) ultimate
            (B) effective
            (C) incorrect
            (D) unclaimed

new account.
I applied for internet access last month on the understanding that the cost of the service was
$35 per month. However, to my surprise, I've discovered that an amount of $50 has been
charged ------- my first bill. It seems that when I applied, the clerk mistakenly registered me for a

  09 (A) to
       (B) of
       (C) at
       (D) by

high speed connection, despite the fact that I clearly asked for standard. I called my bank this
morning to alter the automatic payment on this account, but the first transaction had already gone
through and ------- cannot be reversed, hence this letter.

    10 (A) accurately
         (B) apparently
         (C) arguably
         (D) aggressively

Please reply as soon as possible, not only to confirm that future bills will be correct, but also to let
me know whether I am ------- to a refund for this month's erroneous charges.

       11 (A) entailed
           (B) entertained
           (C) entitled
           (D) entered

Sincerely,
Eleanor Briggs

動詞關聯的片語 2

讓飯菜更豐盛的動詞片語。

The flight touched down.做多益問題時看到了這個句子，很多人不懂是什麼意思。飛機到底怎麼樣啦？好像也不是墜落的意思？touch down是「(飛機)著陸」的意思，可以與land替換使用。那為什麼放著好端端的land不用，而非擠出這麼一句話？其實就像人會厭倦天天吃米飯，偶爾也會吃點麵一樣，語言這傢伙也不可能在一種用法中得到滿足。再說多益中也常問起這些動詞片語，因此大家就不得不吃這道菜啦！今天就好好吃吃「動詞片語」這道菜吧。

百發百中 出題類型與戰略

◉ 會出現要求選擇可以與空白處周圍的單字搭配的選項的問題。

◉ 先看空白處前後，然後再選擇適合片語的選項。

◉ 最後把選項內容代入句子，並迅速判斷是否符合句意後確定答案是否正確。

例題 1

Allan Parsons got ------- the required interviews and then waited a month before the company finally got in touch with him.

(A) about　(B) despite　(C) above　(D) through

解說　不需要理解全句，看了空白處前後和四個選項後，就可以發現只有 (D) through 能與空白處前面的get搭配使用，(get through 完成…)。把through代入句子中，句意正確，所以 (D) through 就是正確答案。別的介系詞不能搭配成get…形式，所以不正確。

翻譯　Allan Parsons完成了所要求的面試後等了一個月，那個公司才聯繫他。

require[rɪˊkwaɪr] 要求 / get in touch with 與…聯繫

答案　(D)

例題 2

Every time you begin and end a shift, you'll need to have your card swiped by the attendant at the staff entrance. If you lose your card during your shift, report it to security, where you will be able to apply for a new one and ------- out manually before leaving the building.

(A) block　　(B) fill
(C) sign　　(D) phase

解說　(C) sign 可以與空白處後面的 "out" 搭配，用於「走出建築之前用手＿＿」中，(sign out：用簽名記錄離開的時間，用簽名記錄外出) 句意通順，所以是正確答案。(A) block (阻止) 有「block out 阻止…進入」的片語，(B) fill (填) 有「fill out 填寫…」的片語，(D) phase (按階段調整) 有「phase out 分階段撤退」的片語，但都與題意不符，所以不正確。

翻譯　開始或結束輪班時，大家都要透過職員出口的接待員來刷職員卡。上班期間遺失職員卡者，請向保全部門報告，您可以在那裡申請新的卡片並在離開大樓前以手寫的方式記錄下班時間。

shift[ʃɪft] (輪班制的)一班 / swipe[swaɪp] 刷卡 / apply for 申請 / manually[ˊmænjuəlɪ] 手動，用手

答案　(C)

❶ draw on + 技術 / 經驗　以（技術、經驗）為參考

以自己的技術或經驗為參考來執行某事。

When starting your own business, **draw on** your experience as a customer.
開始自己創業時要參考自己身為顧客時的經驗。

❷ hold back　不透露…，隱瞞

對於意見與想法「隱藏不說出來」的意思。

Please don't **hold back** your opinions on the new product design.
請不要隱瞞地說出對新產品的意見。

❸ account for　佔（…的比例）

Benefits **account for** only 20 percent of payroll costs.
利潤只佔了薪水支出的20%。

❹ have A in common　有共同點A

The assembly line errors made this morning **have** nothing **in common**.
早上發生在組裝線上的幾個錯誤之間沒有共同點。

❺ have every intention of Ving　有強烈的意圖做…

The landlord **has every intention of** making improvements to the building.
地主非常想要改善這棟建築。

❻ place A on standby　讓A處在等待狀態

The passenger was **placed on standby** for the next possible flight.
乘客被安置等待下一班可能的飛機。

❼ defy description　無法描述

The subtle flavor of the soup of the day **defies description**.
今天這湯的微妙的味道是無法用語言來描述的。

❽ bring A to a halt　中斷，停止A

Without a generator, the loss of power will **bring** operations **to a halt**.
如果沒有發電機，會因電力損失而停止運轉。

❾ make sense　做（某事）妥當，合情合理

Hiring a full time technician **made** more **sense** than calling in a freelancer.
雇用一名全職技術人員比找外包更妥當。

VOCABULARY | 片語

⑩ go through 度過（困難等），堅持

The company **went through** a hard time financially, but is doing much better now.
公司度過了財政方面的困難，現在經營情況好了很多。

⑪ check in 辦理住宿手續或搭乘手續。

用在旅館或機場手續的辦理上。

Guests are required to **check in** before 10 am.
顧客需要在早上10點之前辦理住宿手續。

⑫ take ~ into account 參酌⋯，考慮

John **took** the past year's market conditions **into account** when writing the annual report.
寫年度報告時 John 參考了去年的市場狀況。

⑬ stand in for 代替（某人）

像代替同事工作一樣，表示當某人的代替角色時使用。

As Patrick Chuah is sick, Tallulah Morgan will be **standing in for** him today.
因為 Patrick Chuah 病了，所以 Tallulah Morgan 今天將代替他。

⑭ keep track of 持續追蹤⋯，持續獲得關於⋯的資訊

This software allows users to easily **keep track of** inventory.
這個軟體可以讓使用者輕鬆追蹤到存貨清單。

⑮ look over 檢查（檔案），查閱

The manager **looked over** the documents before making a decision.
經理在下決定之前查閱了公文。

⑯ look into 調查

The Finance Division has **looked into** the errors and corrected them.
財務部調查了錯誤並對其進行相關修正。

Cf 1) look for 尋找

The article gives advice on what to **look for** when buying a camera.
那個報導對於買相機時該挑選什麼提出了建議。

Cf 2) look upon A as B 把A看作B

The company **looks upon** Asia **as** a potential market for its products.
那個公司把亞洲看作公司自身產品的潛在市場。

⊙ 在正確的前打 √ 標記。

01 Office supplies are **running** ◊ **fast**
◊ **short**   辦公用品快要用完了

02 take ◊ **advantage**
◊ **benefit** **of** the lower prices   可利用較低價格的好處

03 The bill **comes into** ◊ **result**
◊ **effect** in July.   那個法案七月份施行

04 put ◊ **in for**
◊ **back in** a two week vacation   申請兩週休假

05 take ◊ **the care**
◊ **care** **of** the customer's complaint   處理顧客的不滿

06 check ◊ **in**
◊ **off** at the airport   辦理機場登機手續

07 The debate **came** ◊ **to**
◊ **in** an end.   爭論結束

08 ◊ **approach**
◊ **look** **for** full-time work   尋找全職工作

09 Spring sales helped **make** ◊ **out**
◊ **up** **for** a slow winter.   春季銷售彌補了冬天銷售的不振

10 care ◊ **with**
◊ **for** a family   負擔家計

11 follow ◊ **up on**
◊ **through to** the promise to raise salaries   對提高薪水的承諾做出後續的措施

12 do one's ◊ **innermost**
◊ **utmost**   全力以赴

Part V

01 The factory manager brings the assembly line to a ------- if a defective auto part is found.

(A) block
(B) quit
(C) stay
(D) halt

02 With the loss of 10 percent of their customer base over the past six months, the company is now ------- some major changes.

(A) pulling in
(B) going through
(C) looking over
(D) laying off

03 Following ------- his pledge to improve the company's working environment, Mr. Lawson has had the entire office renovated and equipped with up-to-date machines.

(A) out in
(B) throughout
(C) up on
(D) across with

04 The supplies at the photo developing shop were running -------, prompting Mr. Lark to send his assistant out to buy what was needed.

(A) deep
(B) long
(C) fast
(D) short

05 The factory owner ------- production on standby when it became impossible to meet product demand due to insufficient raw materials.

(A) placed
(B) viewed
(C) emitted
(D) occupied

06 Upon arrival at the airport, passengers must check ------- at any one of the designated counters.

(A) on
(B) off
(C) in
(D) up

07 Meeting attendees are requested not to hold ------- opinions which may contribute to the fulfillment of project goals.

(A) away
(B) from
(C) back
(D) at

正確答案 P100

Questions 08-11 refer to the following article.

With bank interest rates for savings continually on the decline, building a nest egg today isn't as easy as it used to be 30 years ago. Extensive financial knowledge is a highly beneficial ------- when

08 (A) draft
(B) evaluation
(C) asset
(D) margin

dealing with today's multitudes of ways in which to build personal investments. Due to the complicated nature of the field, most people choose to enlist the services of an experienced broker. However, personal investors are ------- relying on their own resources when handling their finances.

09 (A) optimistically
(B) increasingly
(C) extraneously
(D) idealistically

They ------- on media such as online forums, business journals, and periodicals, where they read

10 (A) seek
(B) select
(C) refer
(D) draw

up on companies' stability and profitability to upgrade their own expertise, rather than depending on a third party to do it for them. After having ------- over the vast amount of online and published

11 (A) seen
(B) looked
(C) viewed
(D) watched

information available, investors then use their newly-gained understanding of the market to safely decide where to invest their capital.

正確答案 P100

Chapter 5

名詞關聯的片語

看懂 "job description" 才能知道找的是什麼工作！

解答多益問題時始終會有一些傢伙像伏兵一樣突然出現，混亂考生的思緒，job description 就是其中一個。按字面來翻譯，它應該是職業描述的意思，但這樣的翻譯還是讓人搞不清楚這個詞的真正用意。

徵人時，應該會對職缺進行職務說明。比如會計要負責帳簿管理，像這樣的內容就是 job description（業務內容說明）。多益中有很多像這樣將名詞加上其他成分後組成片語的情況，學習時要是不留意，它們就會變得很難應付。學好名詞片語會使以後的多益之路順暢許多，那今天就一起來面對它們吧。

百發百中 出題類型與戰略

◉ 會出現選擇名詞片語、適合名詞的介系詞、適合介系詞的名詞等問題。

◉ 先看空白處前後名詞或介系詞，然後再選擇適合片語的選項。

◉ 最後把選項內容代入句子，並迅速判斷是否符合句意後，確定答案是否正確。

例題 1

Because of accumulated stress at work, many of our staff members choose to have more vacation time rather than a pay -------.

(A) growth　(B) lift　(C) increase　(D) climb

解說　看完空白處的前後，可以發現能與 pay 搭配的單字只有（C）increase（pay increase 提高薪水），所以（C）是正確答案。（A）growh 是「成長」，（B）lift 是「舉起」，（D）climb 是「爬」的意思，與句意不符，而且三個都不能與 pay 搭配，所以不正確。

翻譯　由於工作上累積的巨大壓力，我們很多職員寧可選擇有更多的休假時間，而非提高自己的薪水。

答案　(C)

例題 2

Today's Business Line column focuses on how to calculate your tax properly under the newly-introduced corporate tax system. It is written by Jan Delpratt, a senior executive of Merchant Associates, the nation's largest accounting firm, and a regular ------- to The National

(A) winner　(B) contributor
(C) participant　(D) contestant

Business Review.

解說　可以與空白處後面的介系詞 "to" 搭配使用的是（B）contributor（投稿者），構成 contributor to 的「關於…的投稿者」之意，代入句中就是 "The National Business Review 社的正式撰稿人"，句意通順，所以正確答案是（B）。（A）winner 是「贏家，獲勝者」，（C）participant 是「參與者」，（D）contestant 是「競爭者，爭論者」的意思，句意不符，而且都是與介系詞 "of" 一起使用，而不是 "to"，所以不正確。

翻譯　今天的 Business Line 專欄中，詳細說明了在新實施的公司稅體系下如何正確計算稅金的方法。這個專欄由 Jan Delpratt 撰寫，他既是全國最大會計公司 Merchant Associates 的高層管理者，也是 The National Business Review 的正式撰稿人。

focus on 重點說明 / corporate tax 公司稅 / accounting [əˋkaʊntɪŋ] 會計

答案　(B)

❶ mastermind behind （計畫等）的幕後主導者，策畫者

mastermind 是制定並主導重要計畫的「幕後主導者，策畫者」的意思。因為有表示在幕後主導計畫的語氣，所以與介系詞「behind …的後面，背後」一起使用。

Mr. Grieves is the **mastermind behind** the candidate's new campaign strategy.
Grieves 先生是那個候選人新競選活動戰略的幕後策畫者。

❷ safety precautions 安全防護措施

precaution 是預防措施的意思，它是可數名詞，所以前面要加冠詞 a 或用複數。也可以用作「fire precautions 火災預防措施」的意思。

Construction workers were reminded to follow **safety precautions** at all times.
建築工人被提醒要時刻遵守安全防護措施。

❸ performance appraisals 工作成果考核

雖然 performance 有「公演」的意思，但在這裡表示「成果，執行」的意思。apprasal 是「評價」的意思，因為是可數名詞，所以要加冠詞 an 或用複數。

The manager has to carry out monthly **performance appraisals**.
經理每月都要執行工作成果考核。

❹ a form of identification 身份證明文件

要求提出什麼證明文件時用 "a form of identification"。identification 是身份證明，form 是文件的意思。

A form of identification is necessary to collect the package at the post office.
到郵局取包裹時需要出示一種身份證明文件。

❺ system failures 系統故障

注意：failure 有「故障」的意思。

Due to repeated **system failures**, the current computer operating system will be changed.
由於反覆的系統故障，現有的電腦運作系統將會被更換。

❻ commitment to 致力於…，獻身

We have an abiding **commitment to** providing individualized service to customers.
我們一直致力於提供滿足顧客個人特性的服務。

❼ problem with …的問題，障礙

The staff is having a **problem with** their computers' operating system.
職員們遇到了電腦運作系統的問題。

⑧ baggage allowance 行李允許量

The standard **baggage allowance** is 20 kilos.
標準行李允許量為20公斤。

⑨ time constraints 時間限制

Due to **time constraints**, the staff will continue the discussion tomorrow.
因為時間限制，職員們明天會繼續討論這個問題。

⑩ taxes on …的稅

The Revenue Department decided not to impose extra **taxes on** rice imports.
國稅局決定不徵收額外的稻米進口稅。

⑪ confidence in 對…有信心。

I have every **confidence in** Mrs. Foster's ability to manage the project successfully.
我對Foster夫人成功地管理這個專案的能力很有信心。

⑫ staff productivity 職員生產力

The bestselling book talks about innovative ways to improve **staff productivity**.
那本暢銷書講述了提高職員生產力的創新方法。

⑬ office efficiency 辦公效率

Providing a comfortable environment will improve **office efficiency**.
提供舒適的環境會使辦公效率提高。

⑭ compliance with + 規則 遵守（規則）

The company operates in full **compliance with** current export laws.
那個公司的營運完全遵守現行的外銷法律。

⑮ media coverage 媒體報導

Media coverage of the new product launch helped raise the brand's profile.
新產品發表的媒體報導幫助品牌知名度的提升。

⑯ attendance records 上班記錄，出勤記錄

Employees' **attendance records** are confirmed each month before paychecks are issued.
在每月發薪水之前，會確認職員的出勤記錄。

HACKERS PRACTICE ● ● ● ● ● ● ● ● ● ● ● ● ●

◉ 在正確的前打 √ 標記。

01 ◇ **exposure**
◇ **enclosure** **to** moisture 　　　　　　　暴露在濕氣中

02 Check the ◇ **overhead**
◇ **overlaid** **compartments**. 　　　　確認頭上的儲物間

03 **guarantee** ◇ **of**
◇ **with** satisfaction 　　　　　　保證滿意

04 ◇ **Confidential**
◇ **Maximum** **security** will be enforced. 　　會採取最大限度的安全措施

05 the written **consent** ◇ **by**
◇ **of** the patient 　　患者的書面同意書

06 a keen **interest** ◇ **for**
◇ **in** suburban development 　　對郊區的發展有很高的興趣

07 **conference** ◇ **participants**
◇ **tenants** 　　　　　　會議參與者

08 **taxes** ◇ **on**
◇ **by** luxury goods 　　　　奢侈品的稅款

09 have little **regard** ◇ **for**
◇ **of** the safety of employees 　　幾乎不考慮職員們的安全

10 an **advocate** ◇ **of**
◇ **by** human rights 　　　人權擁護者

11 a **dispute** ◇ **above**
◇ **over** wheat prices 　　關於麵粉價格的紛爭

12 **questions** ◇ **concerning**
◇ **by** shipping charges 　　有關運送費用的問題

正確答案　P101

VOCABULARY | 片語

Part V

01 Because of time -------, Mr. Pelham scheduled a second meeting to discuss items that were not taken up on the agenda.

(A) inhibitions
(B) necessities
(C) obstacles
(D) constraints

02 The store's website charges local sales tax ------- all items purchased by individuals living in the state of Indiana.

(A) on
(B) by
(C) at
(D) in

03 Beginning next week, the bank will require two ------- of identification when cashing checks and making withdrawals.

(A) terms
(B) marks
(C) forms
(D) prints

04 Even for domestic flights, baggage ------- is three pieces of checked luggage as long as the largest bag does not exceed 62 inches in length.

(A) permission
(B) allowance
(C) estimation
(D) weight

05 The job ------- for accounting clerk includes assisting with accounts receivable, accounts payable, inventory and invoicing.

(A) topic
(B) interpretation
(C) description
(D) comment

06 Before your flight takes off, make sure the ------- compartments have been securely closed.

(A) overlaid
(B) overhead
(C) overdue
(D) overpowered

07 The museum director has full confidence ------- the new curator's ability to organize and revamp the exhibits.

(A) by
(B) with
(C) on
(D) in

正確答案 P101

Part VI

Questions 08-11 refer to the following article.

Security Chip Set to Reduce Fraud

In our rapidly modernizing world, more and more shoppers rely on plastic rather than paper to purchase every-day items, yet credit card consumers have become increasingly vulnerable to fraudulent transactions. But with the efforts and cutting-edge vision of Monica Hynde, the mastermind ------- a new, remarkably secure identification chip, shoppers will soon be able to make easier and

08 (A) below
    (B) among
    (C) behind
    (D) about

safer purchases. Her team of top researchers took two years to develop the technology, based on a small chip which contains the cardholder's personal information. Meticulous standards were followed in developing this unit, to ensure ------- with federal privacy regulations. The mechanism identifies

    09 (A) tolerance
        (B) compliance
        (C) application
        (D) reliance

purchasers and confirms their identity using ------- privacy software, minimizing potential consumer

    10 (A) continuing
        (B) random
        (C) ordered
        (D) progressive

risks when making transactions. Manufacturers anticipate that the new security chip system should be ------- by most major credit card companies by the end of next year.

11 (A) implemented
    (B) interpreted
    (C) notified
    (D) fulfilled

片語的用法

「問題」是question我們都知道，但「提出」這詞太難了。我們的語言中也有也有「給問題」這種說法，但是在英文裡面 "give a question" 是錯誤的表達方式。正確表達「提出問題」的應該是 "raise a question"。

百發百中 出題類型與戰略

◉ 會出現「形容詞＋名詞」、「動詞＋名詞」、「副詞＋形容詞」等片語。
  （例。broad knowledge，raise a question，readily available）
◉ 先選擇可以與空白處前後的詞搭配的選項。
◉ 最後把選項內容代入句子，並迅速判斷是否符合句意後確定答案是否正確。

例題 1

Applicants unable to ------- their appointment with the interviewer must call one day ahead of time.

(A) meet　(B) come　(C) carry　(D) keep

解說　可以與空白處後面的名詞「appointment（約會）」搭配的名詞是（D）keep（keep an appointment遵守約會（時間））。把 "keep" 代入空白處時句意通順，所以（D）是答案。其他選項都不能與 "appointment" 搭配，所以不正確。

翻譯　不能遵守時間與面試官見面的求職者，請提前一天電話通知。

　　　ahead of 在…前面 / keep an appointment 遵守約定

答案　(D)

例題 2

The city branch of Warehouse Office Products Ltd. is open for business between the hours of 9 a.m. and 5 p.m. Monday through Saturday. Parking is available in the lot on the corner of 7th and East Jefferson Streets in ------- spots only, so take care to ensure that you do not

(A) designated　(B) located
(C) replaced　　(D) received

park in a tow-away area.

解說　可以與空白處後面的「spots（場所）」恰當搭配的是（A）designated（指定的），在句中是指定的場所。把designated代入空白處，構成「只能在指定的場所停車」的意思，句意通順，所以（A）是正確答案。（B）located 是「位於」，（C）replaced 是「代替」，（D）received 是「收到」的意思，都與句意不符，不是正確答案。

翻譯　Warehouse Office Products市區分部的營業時間是從星期一到星期六期間每天上午9點到下午5點。只能在7號街和East Jefferson街拐角處的指定場所停車，所以請小心確認不要把您的車停在拖吊區。

　　　lot[lɑt]（土地的）一塊 / spot[spɑt] 區域，場所 / tow-away 強制拖吊（違規停車的車輛）

答案　(A)

❶ return to normal　回復正常

After unusually cold weather, the temperature should **return to normal** by Friday.
罕有的寒冷天氣過去後，星期五的氣溫將會回復正常

❷ strictly limited　嚴格限制的

The number of rebates is **strictly limited** to one per customer.
折扣的數量嚴格限制每個顧客只有一次。

❸ make a call　打電話

make有「make progress 進步」，「make requests 邀請」等用法。

When **making an** out-of-office **call**, remember to dial 9 first.
打外線電話時，請記住先按9。

❹ readily available　容易得到

readily是「容易（=easily）」的意思。available是「可得到」的意思

Applications are **readily available** at the administrative office.
申請書在行政辦公室很容易拿到。

❺ work extended hours　加班

To meet demand, factory employees will **work extended hours**.
為了滿足需求工廠職員們將會加班。

❻ heavily discounted　大幅度打折

heavily用作「大幅，嚴重」的意思。還可以有「rain heavily 下大雨」的用法。

High-performance computers have been **heavily discounted** after a slump in sales.
高性能電腦在度過銷售冷淡期後價格大幅度下降。

❼ surrounding cities　周邊都市

surrounding是「周邊的」的意思。

Tourism officials hope visitors from **surrounding cities** will attend the centennial celebration.
觀光考察官員們希望周邊都市的遊客們都來參加一百周年紀念儀式。

❽ economic forecast　經濟預測，經濟展望

forecast是「預測」的意思。

The newly released **economic forecast** predicts a rise in interest rates.
新發表的經濟展望做出了利率會上升的預測。

⑨ prospective employee　可能被錄取的人，求職者

prospective 是「想成為…的（=would-be）」的意思，用在某人希望得到特定的職位並有可能得到的情況。有時也用作「prospective buyer 預期的買家」

Prospective employees are required to make a five-minute presentation.
求職者被要求要發表5分鐘的演說。

⑩ highly qualified　有充分資格的

highly 是「非常，充分」的意思，並且有「highly successful 非常成功」和「highly unlikely 幾乎沒有可能」等用法。

The company is seeking a **highly qualified** candidate to fill the position.
公司為了補那個空缺正在尋找有充分資格的候補人員。

⑪ in the foreseeable future　在可預見的未來

foreseeable 是「可預見的」的意思。

The company does not expect a lag in demand **in the foreseeable future**.
那個公司並不認為在可預見的未來會產生需求停滯的狀況。

⑫ combined experience　結合經驗，多種經驗

意味著把幾種經驗結合在一起。combine 是「聯合（人、力量）」的意思的動詞，在這裡要用它的過去式。

The team's **combined experience** is a plus for the company.
團隊的整體經驗結合有利於公司。

⑬ do business with　與…做生意

The company is going to **do business with** a supplier in Southeast Asia.
這個公司會與東南亞的某供應商合作做生意。

⑭ established company　穩定的公司

意味著建設時間長、基礎穩定的公司。established 是「穩定」的意思。

UK Tools is an **established company** with a reputation for providing quality products.
UK Tools 社是一家以提供高品質的產品而負盛名的穩定公司。

⑮ fiscal year　會計年度

以一個年度期間來做編制、執行、核算預算報告叫會計年度。fiscal 是「會計的，財政的」的意思。

The financial outlook for the next **fiscal year** is promising.
我們對下一個會計年度的財政展望充滿希望。

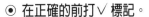

⊙ 在正確的前打 √ 標記。

01 an ◊ **hastily** ◊ **instantly** **recognizable** brand　　　　一個可立即辨識的商標

02 **take** customer privacy ◊ **soundly** ◊ **seriously**　　　　重視顧客的隱私

03 ◊ **generate** ◊ **elevate** funds　　　　籌備資金

04 The car lease agreement includes ◊ **uncontrolled** ◊ **unlimited** **miles.**　　　　租車合約包括無限制的哩數

05 **promotional** ◊ **offers** ◊ **judgements**　　　　促銷提案

06 ◊ **extremely** ◊ **exactly** **successful**　　　　非常成功的

07 an ◊ **invoked** ◊ **informed** **decision**　　　　根據情報的決定

08 a **gigantic step** ◊ **forward** ◊ **advance**　　　　長足的進步

09 Handle the crystal **with** ◊ **extreme** ◊ **steep** **care.**　　　　非常細心地處理水晶

10 be ◊ **pessimistically** ◊ **cautiously** **optimistic**　　　　謹慎樂觀的

11 a **vested** ◊ **ability** ◊ **interest**　　　　既得利益

12 the ◊ **famished** ◊ **finished** **product**　　　　成品

13 ◊ **visual** ◊ **observed** **aids**　　　　視覺教具

14 an ◊ **inherently** ◊ **insincerely** **risky** business　　　　本來就具有危險性的事業

15 **meet one's** ◊ **accountability** ◊ **needs**　　　　滿足…的需求

16 **reach one's** ◊ **high** ◊ **full** **potential**　　　　發揮…的最大潛力

17 ◊ **live** ◊ **alive** **broadcast**　　　　現場直播

18 ◊ **inquire** ◊ **raise** public **awareness**　　　　增進群眾的意識

正確答案　P102

VOCABULARY | 片語

Part V

01 The director has every confidence that the ------- qualified trainers will design a program that will meet the needs of the new accountants.

(A) highly
(B) acutely
(C) severely
(D) blandly

02 Many low-income full-time workers must take up a second job to ------- a decent wage.

(A) catch
(B) win
(C) gain
(D) earn

03 ------- employees must have a valid driver's license and two years experience in transporting dangerous chemicals.

(A) Probable
(B) Disgruntled
(C) Prospective
(D) Eventual

04 The packaging of a product is the first thing shoppers see, so it must be attractive enough to ------- their attention.

(A) decide
(B) bring
(C) catch
(D) notice

05 With market demand at an all-time low, the manager does not think he will be hiring any new workers in the ------- future.

(A) ongoing
(B) foreseeable
(C) surfacing
(D) prevalent

06 Unions and factory employees have actively involved themselves in the ------- mayoral election.

(A) forward
(B) prepared
(C) upcoming
(D) prospective

07 About half of the employees have volunteered to work ------- hours to meet consumer demand for the busy holiday season.

(A) potential
(B) fortified
(C) extended
(D) previous

正確答案 **P102**

Questions 08-11 refer to the following advertisement.

Bargain Book Bazaar!

Everyone loves reading, and reading has never been cheaper! Novel Ideas Bookstore will be holding its ------- overstock clearance between 9am and 4pm this Saturday, offering enormous discounts

08 (A) inherent
    (B) annual
    (C) happening
    (D) appearing

on all novels, periodicals, textbooks, travel guides, encyclopedias and catalogues. Just some of the bestseller titles available on sale include Janet Pratty's *Olga's Story*, Demetrios Petalas' *Autumn in Athens*, and the latest AMCLT translation award winner, *Snow Falling on Mountains*, by Tetsu Fujiwara. But why stop there when you can ------- your horizons by upgrading your business

                         09 (A) multiply
                                 (B) broaden
                                 (C) dilate
                                 (D) impress

etiquette, learning gourmet cooking, becoming a wine connoisseur, trekking around the world, or refreshing your knowledge of world history? All excess stock will be ------- discounted, with prices

                                      10 (A) busily
                                            (B) safely
                                            (C) solely
                                            (D) heavily

reduced by between 50 and 80%! As we only hold this closeout once a year, purchases will be ------- limited to eight books per person to enable everyone to get a fair share of the bargains.

11 (A) strictly
    (B) tensely
    (C) densely
    (D) compactly

Section 2 單字

Chapter 7

動詞

怎麼把「謝謝你的來信」翻譯成英語？

多益喜歡的 acknowledge 的意思是「答謝（來信等）」的意思。收到商業信件後的一般慣例是回覆「我對您的來信致謝」。這句話用英語說就是 "I am writing to acknowledge the receipt of your letter."。看了幾百遍不如記住「acknowledge 是與 the receipt of your letter 一起使用」，這就是多益片語的特徵。最好多記與多益動詞一起使用的名詞和介系詞。

百發百中 出題類型與戰略

◉ 會出選擇符合句意的動詞這樣的題目。

◉ 仔細分析句子的關鍵字和連接詞就很容易理解句意。

◉ 要注意及物動詞與受詞的搭配，以及及物動詞被動語態與主詞的搭配。

例題 1

The popularity of low-carbohydrate diets has been declining, so food companies have decided to ------- their production of low-carb products.

(A) discontinue　(B) disallow　(C) disband　(D) disengage

解說　「低碳水化合物減肥食品的人氣下降，所以食品公司決定___。」與這個句子的句意相符的動詞是（A）discontinue （中止）。（B）disallow 是「不允許」，（C）disband 是「解散（組織）」，（D）disengage 是「斷開（機器的連接）」的意思，都與句意不符，所以不正確。

翻譯　因為低碳水化合物減肥食品的人氣下降，所以食品公司決定中斷生產。

popularity[.pɑpjə´lærətɪ] 人氣 / carbohydrate[´kɑrbə´haɪdret] 碳水化合物 / diet[´daɪət] 特定的食物 / product[´prɑdʌkt] 產品

答案　(A)

例題 2

Workers are reminded to ensure that each workstation is clean and each machine is running up to code before signing out this evening. The annual inspection, which is scheduled for tomorrow afternoon, will be ------- by government-designated inspectors to ensure that factories are

(A) alerted　　(B) conducted
(C) protected　(D) engaged

operating according to safety standards.

解說　能與主語 "The annual inspection" 運用的動詞是（B）conducted，（conduct 執行（任務等），conduct an inspection 實施檢查）。（A）alert 是「警告」，（C）protect 是「保護」，（D）engage 是「使…參與…」的意思，不符合題意，所以都不正確。

翻譯　職員們切記在今晚下班之前要確認工作站是否清理乾淨並檢查機器運作是否符合規定。為了檢查工廠是否按安全標準營運，明天下午會有政府指派的檢查人員來進行年度檢查。

workstation[.wɝk.steən] （電腦）工作站 / up to code 按規定 / annual inspection 年度檢查 / safety standards 安全標準

答案　(B)

① distract 使精神散漫，使分散注意力

Conference participants were continuously **distracted** by noise from the construction site.
參加會議的人們不斷地被工地傳來的噪音分散注意力。

② retain 保留，保存

The new residents hope to **retain** the historical beauty of the area.
新居民們希望保留那個地區所呈現的古典之美。

③ veify 認證，確認

與confirm（確認）同義。

Please include the original receipt in order to **verify** the date of purchase.
請把原始收據一起附上以便確認購買日期。

④ violate 違反（規定）

Restaurateurs must be careful not to **violate** any health regulations.
餐廳經營者要注意別違反任何有關健康的規定。

⑤ convene （會員們等）會合，集合

The Board of Directors will **convene** next Monday to discuss the proposed expansion.
下週一將集合各董事開董事會討論提議的擴張計畫。

⑥ relocate 重新部署（公司、居民等）

Volentia announced plans to **relocate** its manufacturing plant to China.
Volentia 發佈了把製造工廠重新在中國部署的計畫。

⑦ represent 表明，意味著…

The figures **represent** a significant increase in sales.
那些數據資料表明在銷售上有了巨幅的增長。

⑧ hesitate 猶豫

「Do not hesitate to + 動詞原形　不要猶豫做…」

Do not **hesitate** to contact one of our representatives if you need any further information.
如果您需要其他額外情報時，請不要猶豫，立即聯繫我們其中任何一個代表。

⑨ rush 忙碌

The product development team **rushed** to complete the new design before the deadline.
產品開發組正忙著在最後期限之前完成新設計。

⑩ alter 變更，變換

與change同義。

The editor requested that the title of the article be **altered**.
編輯要求更改這篇文章的題目。

⑪ coordinate 調和，協調

He was assigned to **coordinate** the activities of the buyers and sellers.
他被指派去協調商家和消費者之間的活動。

⑫ curb 抑制

與restrain同義。

Higher energy costs will likely **curb** fuel and electricity usage.
能源價格的上漲會抑制燃料和電的使用量。

⑬ delegate 委任（責任、許可權等）

「delegate responsibility 委任責任」

Supervisors are expected to **delegate** responsibilities in a timely and efficient manner.
上司們應當在恰當時機有效地委派責任。

⑭ exceed 超過⋯

The firm's debts **exceeded** three million dollars this year.
今年公司的負債超過了300萬美元。

⑮ indicate 表示

常用用法是「Studies indicate that子句：研究結果表示⋯」。

Studies **indicate** that employee performance is linked to job satisfaction.
研究結果表示職員的表現與對工作的滿意度有關。

⑯ obstruct 遮擋，妨礙（視線、光等）

Before driving, adjust the rear view mirror so that nothing **obstructs** your view.
駕駛前要調整好後視鏡以免視線被阻擋。

⑰ supplement 補充（⋯的不足之處）

To **supplement** his income, he works a second job in the evening.
他晚上兼職來補充收入的不足。

⑱ emerge 浮現，嶄露頭角

「emerge as 以…嶄露頭角」

PharmaMed has **emerged** as a new force in the pharmaceutical market.
以製藥市場上新勢力的姿態，PharmaMed公司嶄露了頭角。

⑲ accommodate （建築、車輛）容納…

The luxurious beachfront rooms can easily **accommodate** up to seven guests.
豪華的海邊客房可以輕鬆容納七位客人。

⑳ implement 施行，執行（計畫等）

與carry out（施行…）同義。

Sun Telecom has **implemented** a new policy on long-distant rates
Sun Telecom在長途電話費上實行了的新政策。

㉑ patronize 經常光臨（商店等）

Younger people are more likely to **patronize** modern health facilities than the elderly.
年輕人比老年人更願意經常光臨現代健康機構。

㉒ alleviate 緩和，減輕

In an effort to **alleviate** traffic congestion, the city introduced new bus lanes.
為了緩和交通堵塞的情況，這城市引進了新的公車車道。

㉓ acquire 獲得（財產、權力等）

The developers wish to **acquire** land for a new industrial park.
開發者希望獲得土地來建設新工業園區。

㉔ deposit 存（款）

deposit money 存入金錢，deposit checks 存入支票

Payment must be **deposited** into our bank account by the last day of each month.
支付款要在每個月最後一天前存進我們的銀行帳戶。

㉕ inaugurate 正式開放…，舉行…的就職典禮

A new direct air route between Geneva and Bangkok was officially **inaugurated** yesterday.
昨天日內瓦和曼谷之間的新航線正式開通了。

Iona Yang was **inaugurated** Wednesday as the 5th president of the Board of Directors.
Iona Yang在星期三被任命為董事會的第五任董事長。

VOCABULARY｜單字

⊙ 在正確的前打 √ 標記。

01 anticipate a decrease in sales   Ⓐ預測到 Ⓑ體驗到 銷售額減少

02 justify the time spent   Ⓐ分析 Ⓑ合理化 消耗的時間

03 gauge the applicants' abilities   Ⓐ懷疑 Ⓑ評價 申請人的能力

04 solicit bids   Ⓐ拒絕 Ⓑ邀請 投標

05 release funds   Ⓐ釋放 Ⓑ收集 資金

06 The merger will help the company **diversify**.   合併會幫助公司的Ⓐ多元化 Ⓑ重新部署

07 curb the economic recovery   Ⓐ抑制 Ⓑ減輕 經濟恢復

08 inspect product quality   Ⓐ提升 Ⓑ檢查 產品品質

09 authorize a second printing   Ⓐ許可 Ⓑ開始 第二次印刷

10 terminate the agreement   Ⓐ簽訂 Ⓑ中止 協議

11 automate computer tasks   Ⓐ概括 Ⓑ自動化 電腦業務

12 utilize a new method   Ⓐ利用 Ⓑ提議 新方法

13 taste some local dishes   Ⓐ製作 Ⓑ品嘗 一些當地的料理

14 supply training handouts   Ⓐ提供 Ⓑ收集 訓練資料

15 prevent construction accidents   Ⓐ導致 Ⓑ預防 建設事故

16 His skills **match** the job responsibilities   他的技術能Ⓐ配合 Ⓑ分擔 那項工作的職責

17 a bus **bearing** a large advertisement   Ⓐ支持 Ⓑ附帶 大型廣告的公車

18 The name is **engraved** in gold.   名字Ⓐ刻 Ⓑ寫 在金子上

19 redesign the display window   Ⓐ重新設計 Ⓑ置入 展示窗的展示

20 devise a new plan   Ⓐ設計 Ⓑ變更 新的計畫

21 reveal the company's plan   Ⓐ制定 Ⓑ公開 公司的計畫

22 allocate funds for improvements   Ⓐ借給 Ⓑ分配 資金去做改善

23 audits are regularly **scheduled**   定期地Ⓐ安排 Ⓑ延期 審查

24 prohibit smoking indoors   Ⓐ允許 Ⓑ禁止 在室內吸煙

25 The work was **proceeding** as planned.   按計畫Ⓐ執行 Ⓑ縮小 業務

26 attract bargain hunters   Ⓐ吸引 Ⓑ嘲笑 尋找特價品的消費者

27 Your expertise **benefits** the company.   您的專業技術能Ⓐ幫助 Ⓑ告知 公司

28 be reprimanded for **procrastinating**　　　　因Ⓐ隱藏 Ⓑ耽擱 遭受譴責

29 **renew** the contract　　　　Ⓐ廢除 Ⓑ更新 合約

30 **affix** the stamp to the envelope　　　　郵票Ⓐ貼在 Ⓑ放進 信封上

31 need to **obtain** a license　　　　Ⓐ歸還 Ⓑ獲得 執照

32 **prescribe** diabetes medication　　　　Ⓐ研發 Ⓑ指定 糖尿病藥物

33 **handle** the packages with care　　　　仔細Ⓐ處理 Ⓑ包裝 包裹

34 **detach** the last section of the form　　　　將表格最後一欄Ⓐ撕下 Ⓑ填滿

35 **order** a new edition　　　　Ⓐ紀念 Ⓑ訂購 最新版

36 **adopt** a new strategy　　　　Ⓐ開發 Ⓑ制定 新戰略

37 **review** the year-end report　　　　Ⓐ再次檢查 Ⓑ發行 年末報告書

38 **reward** one's efforts　　　　Ⓐ報答 Ⓑ無視 某人的努力

39 Growth is not expected to **abate**.　　　　沒有預期成長會Ⓐ繼續 Ⓑ減少

40 **dilute** the concentrate with water　　　　把濃縮液用水Ⓐ提煉 Ⓑ稀釋

41 **bill** guests for room service　　　　對顧客Ⓐ要求支付 Ⓑ提供 客房服務

42 in order for the rebate to **apply**　　　　為了 Ⓐ適用於 Ⓑ進行 退款條件

43 **oversee** operations in Asia　　　　Ⓐ預測 Ⓑ監督 亞洲地區的營業

44 **refuse** damaged goods　　　　Ⓐ拒絕 Ⓑ退還 損壞的商品

45 **confirm** the reservation　　　　Ⓐ確認 Ⓑ接受 預約

46 **present** an official ID card　　　　Ⓐ發放 Ⓑ出示 正式的身份證

47 **submit** photocopies　　　　Ⓐ借 Ⓑ提交 影印本

48 The bar graph **illustrates** the dip in sales.　　　　柱狀圖表Ⓐ表示 Ⓑ說明 銷售額的下滑

49 **follow** the directions　　　　Ⓐ發表 Ⓑ跟隨 指示事項

50 The report **asserts** that reorganization is needed.　　　　這份報告書Ⓐ斷言 Ⓑ贊成 組織改造是必要的

51 **forfeit** one's driver's license　　　　Ⓐ偽造 Ⓑ沒收 某人的駕駛執照

52 **consolidate** their market standing　　　　Ⓐ強化 Ⓑ擴大 市場基礎

53 The message should be **conveyed** to new staff.　　　　這個訊息要Ⓐ發放 Ⓑ傳遞 給新職員

54 **require** more information　　　　Ⓐ需要 Ⓑ檢討 更多的情報

◉ 在正確的前打 √ 標記。

55 revenue estimates ◊ **gravitate** / ◊ **tend** to be optimistic　　　　收入評估似乎頗為樂觀

56 ◊ **accumulate** / ◊ **organize** one's thoughts　　　　整理思緒

57 ◊ **release** / ◊ **cause** a decline in sales　　　　導致銷售額的減少

58 ◊ **visit** / ◊ **travel** the head office　　　　訪問本部

59 It is ◊ **asked** / ◊ **expected** that the CEO will resign.　　　　預料 CEO 會辭職

60 ◊ **consider** / ◊ **think** the current market value　　　　考慮現在的市場價值

61 ◊ **send** / ◊ **use** a reliable delivery company　　　　利用可信賴的物流公司

62 the package ◊ **includes** / ◊ **surrounds** airfare　　　　該包套旅行方案包含機票費用

63 The analyst ◊ **predicts** / ◊ **prepares** that stock prices will rise.　　　　分析家預測股價會上升

64 ◊ **weaken** / ◊ **decline** the invitation　　　　拒絕邀請

65 ◊ **complete** / ◊ **notify** the paperwork　　　　完成文書作業

66 a new product will be ◊ **declared** / ◊ **introduced**　　　　將會介紹新產品

67 ◊ **examine** / ◊ **look** the files　　　　檢查檔案

68 ◊ **incline** / ◊ **expand** market share　　　　擴大市場佔有率

69 ◊ **labor** / ◊ **employ** outdoors　　　　在戶外工作

70 ◊ **renew** / ◊ **avoid** a production slowdown　　　　避免生產減緩

71 Employees are ◊ **reminded** / ◊ **remembered** that S + V　　　　希望職員們記住…

72 the shirt does not ◊ **wear** / ◊ **fit** the customer　　　　襯衫不適合顧客

73 ◊ **offer** / ◊ **control** patrons a better deal　　　　給顧客提供更好的交易

74 ◊ **induce** / ◊ **insert** the disk into the computer　　　　把光碟放入電腦光碟機

正確答案　P104

Part V

01 Some supervisors are reluctant to ------- responsibilities because they know they will be held accountable if something goes wrong.

(A) address
(B) delegate
(C) encourage
(D) share

02 The building owner generally does not ------- tenants to make renovations in their units.

(A) permit
(B) commit
(C) transmit
(D) submit

03 In order to ------- traffic on the roads, the Ministry of Transportation has begun a campaign to encourage individuals to use public transportation.

(A) alleviate
(B) assist
(C) deteriorate
(D) remove

04 Diners are more likely to ------- restaurants that serve excellent food and provide friendly service.

(A) encourage
(B) promote
(C) patronize
(D) nurture

05 A number of studies ------- that allowing employees greater leeway to make decisions gives them a greater sense of responsibility at the workplace.

(A) interpret
(B) indulge
(C) indicate
(D) induce

06 Residents can ------- the permit by downloading the form from the website and submitting the completed form to City Hall.

(A) tear
(B) enhance
(C) restore
(D) obtain

07 Your subscription to any of our online newsletters can be ------- at any time simply by submitting a request for cancellation by e-mail.

(A) terminated
(B) exterminated
(C) eliminated
(D) finished

08 The shareholders will ------- this afternoon to finalize resolutions on the use of the company's net income and the payment of year end dividends.

(A) accompany
(B) confide
(C) convene
(D) facilitate

09 In order to ------- a larger percent of the market share in cellular phones, OneWorld is attempting to appeal to a wider audience.

(A) produce
(B) inflate
(C) spread
(D) acquire

10 I am writing to ------- my attendance at the Symposium on Medical Technologies to be held next weekend.

(A) contact
(B) confront
(C) confirm
(D) contend

11 The client was satisfied with the new curtains, but she requested that the length be ------- so that they would not touch the floor.

(A) qualified
(B) diversified
(C) widened
(D) altered

12 Our financial adviser ------- that investments in new projects will increase as a result of lower bank interest rates.

(A) predicts
(B) ponders
(C) questions
(D) releases

13 Please do not ------- the first part of the form from the second, or it will be invalid.

(A) correspond
(B) write
(C) detach
(D) withdraw

14 In order to pay your bills through your account, you first need to ------- enough money to cover the balance of the bills.

(A) amount
(B) deposit
(C) coin
(D) lend

正確答案 P104

Questions 15-18 refer to the following notice.

Chicago Classical Music Hall
Additional Information Regarding Ticketing

This year we have added ten additional shows to the classical concert series and hope that many of you who missed last year's performances will have the opportunity to attend. There has been an unexpected and overwhelming demand for tickets, and with ------- seat capacity available for

15 (A) few
    (B) limited
    (C) little
    (D) partial

each performance, all buyers may purchase a maximum of 5 tickets only. This will ensure that a greater number of buyers are given the opportunity to attend performances.
Tickets may be picked up at the box office prior to each show. Proper identification, such as a driver's license, must be presented ------- with your credit card when obtaining tickets. This

16 (A) simultaneously
    (B) extraneously
    (C) stringently
    (D) concisely

procedure is necessary in order to ------- your identity so that others cannot take your tickets. Also,

17 (A) rearrange
    (B) complicate
    (C) discount
    (D) verify

if the original receipt has been -------, buyers can receive a free concert t-shirt at the box office. For

18 (A) contracted
    (B) collected
    (C) gauged
    (D) retained

any enquiries, please call 1500-1588-275 to speak with one of our customer representatives.

Chapter 8

名詞

理解 level 的真正涵義才能提升你的多益 level

如果你事先只背單字最普遍使用的涵義，進入考場後再確認句子語意的正確與否的話，那你已經輸掉了這場遊戲。Level 除了有「水準」的意思，還有「地位」的意思，要知道它可以用於「rise to the level of branch manager 升到分店經理的地位」這樣的句子中。這樣才能在時間緊迫的多益考試中穩操勝券。單字需要知道多種用法才能靈活使用，所以要記住那些與多益名詞搭配使用的動詞、修飾補語等。

百發百中 出題類型與戰略

◉ 會出現選擇符合句意的名詞這樣的問題。

◉ 仔細分析句子的關鍵字和連接詞、介系詞就很容易理解句意。

例題 1

Having a large directory of business ------- can be a plus for anyone in the travel industry.

(A) tactics   (B) combinations   (C) contacts   (D) indications

解說 「擁有很多企業上 ___ 的工商名錄是」能使這部分的句意順暢的選項是（C）contact（（為商業目的）聯繫的人），所以在句中就是 business contact，事業上的聯繫人。通常視為「接觸」意思的 contact 又出現了第三、四個涵義，增加了問題的難度。（A）tactic 是「傳授」，（B）combination 是「結合，聯合」，（D）indication 是「指出，暗示」的意思，都不符合題意，所以不正確。

翻譯 擁有很多企業聯絡人的工商名錄對從事旅遊業的人來說是很有利的。
directory [də´rɛktərɪ] 工商名錄 / plus [plʌs] 利益

答案 (C)

例題 2

At only a fraction of the normal registration price, joining has never been easier or more advantageous. Not only will you have access to all of our online services, but as an added ------- of membership, Info-Mate now provides full networking opportunities with other members

(A) petition   (B) course
(C) possibility   (D) benefit

in all its chapters.

解說 「基於會員權利的增加 ___，Info-Mate 提供了可以與其他分部的會員們見面聯誼的機會」符合這個句意的選項是（D）benefit（好處）。（A）petition 是「請願」，（B）course 是「課程，進程」，（C）possibility 是「可能性」的意思，都與句意不符，所以不正確。

翻譯 只用一般入會費的一小部分就能加入，所以加入比以往任何時期都容易，而且有更多優惠待遇。不僅可以讓您使用我們所有的線上服務，我們還為 Info-Mate 的會員提供了額外的好處，那就是可以與分部的其他會員們見面聯誼的機會。
at a fraction of 一小部分 / registration [ˌrɛdʒɪ´steʃən] 登記 / membership [´mɛmbə˞ˌʃɪp] 會員權，會員的地位
chapter [´tʃæptə˞] （組織、協會）的分部

答案 (D)

❶ stance 立場，態度

與position（立場）同義。

The spokesperson announced the company's **stance** on outsourcing.
代言人發表了公司在海外採購的立場。

❷ speculation 推測

Despite widespread **speculation**, the company offered no price cut on their products.
不管外界的廣泛推測，公司仍然沒有降低產品的價格。

❸ alternative 對策

「alternative to 對…的對策」

Taking two or more part-time jobs is a valid **alternative** to full-time employment.
做兩個以上的兼職工作是代替全職工作的有效對策。

❹ duration 持續期間

Vitamin C is known to reduce the **duration** of colds and flus.
維生素C被認為可以減少一般感冒和病毒性感冒的持續時間。

❺ effort 努力

「in an effort to + 原形動詞：在努力做…的環節上」

In an **effort** to increase output, management introduced production bonuses.
在努力提高生產力的環節上，管理階層引入了生產獎勵金制度。

❻ perception 認知，建議

Ms. Flick challenged the **perception** that a CEO needs to be over the age of 40.
Flick女士挑戰了大家CEO需要有超過40歲以上的認知。

❼ method 方法，方式

「method of payment 支付方法」

Customers may choose from several convenient **methods** of payment.
顧客可以在幾個便利的支付方法中進行選擇。

❽ assurance 保障，保證

與guarantee（保證）同義。

Completion of a university degree carries no **assurance** of earning a high salary.
大學畢業的學位不能保證帶來高薪水。

❾ cultivation 栽種，培養（關係）

表示穀物或植物的「栽種」，另外還表示人與人之間「培養（關係），增進（友誼）」的意思。

Experts recommend the **cultivation** of plants as a good means of relieving stress.
專家建議植物的栽種是緩解壓力的好方法。

Our business depends largely on the **cultivation** of a diverse network of clients.
我們的事業在相當程度上依賴於不同的顧客人脈的培養。

⑩ atmosphere　氛圍，氣氛

The restaurant is renowned for its comfortable **atmosphere**.
那個飯店以其舒適的氛圍而聞名。

⑪ advantage　有利點，好處

Having a broad knowledge of the computer industry is an **advantage** in this firm.
在這公司裡對電腦產業有廣泛知識是種利基。

⑫ chance　可能性

「a chance of rain 下雨的可能性」

The forecaster said there's a 20 percent **chance** of rain in the late afternoon.
天氣預報說傍晚下雨的可能性有20%。

⑬ force　勢力，力量

表示具有影響力的人或團體時用。

Although the company is relatively new, it has become a **force** to contend with.
雖然這個公司比較新，可是它已經變成一股競爭的力量。

⑭ function　儀式，宴會

表示儀式或大規模聚會，是 large formal dinner or party 的意思。

The hotel provides various facilities for social and business **functions**.
那個旅館為社交和事業上的宴會提供多種設施。

⑮ momentum　促進力，（運動物體的）動力

表示事情等受到促進而加速的情況，「gain momentum 得到促進力」。

The shift toward the use of environmental technologies is gaining **momentum**.
朝著使用環境技術方面的轉變正得到促進的力量。

⑯ morale　（職員等的）士氣，欲望

Morale is bound to dip when employees are laid off during a crisis.
在危機時期裁員會使員工的士氣大跌。

⑰ reimbursement　（費用等的）報銷，償還

在公司事務上花費個人的錢時，公司會把相應的金額還給當事者。這在英語中叫做 reimbursement（報銷）。

Traveling salesmen receive **reimbursement** for expenses incurred while on the road.
頻繁出差的業務員會收到在路程中所花費的報銷金額。

⑱ revenue　收入

「earn revenue 獲得利潤」、「large / high revenue 高利潤」，注意：money不能跟large 、 high 、 small 一起使用。

Portable mp3 players earn the largest **revenue** in the music player market.
攜帶型mp3 在音樂播放器市場上創造最大的利潤。

⑲ notification　通知（書）

Employees need to provide written **notification** of their intention to take leave.
職員們需要提出書面通知書說明休假的意圖。

⑳ expertise　專業知識，專業技術

Our consulting team is ready to provide **expertise** in internet broadcasting technology.
我們諮詢團隊已經準備好提供網路播放技術的專業知識。

㉑ profit　利益，利潤

The conference aims to help farmers gain **profits** from alternative crops.
那個會議目地在幫助農民們從替代的穀物中獲得利潤。

㉒ negotiation　協商，交涉

Planning for the next stage of **negotiations** is currently underway in New York.
下一階段的協商計畫現在正在紐約進行。

㉓ asset　資產，財產

Our staff here at EB Creative Services is our most valuable **asset**.
EB Creative Service公司的職員是我們最珍貴的資產。

㉔ monopoly　獨佔（權），專賣（權）

「monopoly on 獨佔…」

Clearnet lost its **monopoly** on internet services with the privatization of the telecommunications market.
隨著電子通訊產業的私有化，Clearnet失去了在網路服務的壟斷權。

㉕ hospitality　款待

「extend hospitality to 盛情款待…」

I'd like to thank you for the **hospitality** extended to me during my visit.
我想感謝您在訪問期間對我的盛情款待。

HACKERS PRACTICE ● ● ● ● ● ● ● ● ● ● ● ● ● ● ●

⊙ 選擇A和B中正確的一個。

01 The CD player is under **warranty**.　　　　　　　那個CD Payer在Ⓐ保固期內　Ⓑ修理中

02 in the closing **stage** of negotiations　　　　　在協商的最終Ⓐ發表　Ⓑ階段

03 his **unwillingness** to invest a large sum　　　Ⓐ決心　Ⓑ不情願　進行巨額投資

04 a **characteristic** of a good manager　　　　　優秀的管理者的Ⓐ特徵　Ⓑ條件

05 Speak to the manager for **clarification**.　　　需要Ⓐ許可　Ⓑ說明　的話請跟經理說

06 make **revisions** to the hard copy　　　　　　在列印原稿上做Ⓐ修正　Ⓑ複製

07 oversee the **coordination** of all projects　　監督所有計畫的Ⓐ協調　Ⓑ施行

08 **feedback** from a survey　　　　　　　　　　調查所呈現的Ⓐ意見　Ⓑ結果

09 a **budget** of one million dollars　　　　　　百萬美元的Ⓐ捐贈　Ⓑ預算

10 a **paper** on refinancing loans　　　　　　　關於籌集資金貸款的Ⓐ報導　Ⓑ論文

11 pay **dividends** on its preferred stock　　　　支付特別股的Ⓐ紅利　Ⓑ投資金

12 The CEO is calling for **proposals**.　　　　　董事長需要Ⓐ統計資料　Ⓑ提案

13 The bank statement showed **inconsistencies**.　銀行的交易明細表顯示出Ⓐ損失　Ⓑ不一致的地方

14 The contractor's main **concern** was the timetable.　訂約人主要Ⓐ關心的事　Ⓑ話題　是時間表

15 excellent **examples** of modern architecture　現代建築中優秀的Ⓐ外形　Ⓑ例子

16 Success depends on the **participation** of members.　成功取決於職員們的Ⓐ參與　Ⓑ意志

17 ensure the long-term **stability** of the program　確保方案長期的Ⓐ成功　Ⓑ穩定性

18 attach a letter of **reference**　　　　　　　附上一封Ⓐ表示感謝　Ⓑ參考　的信

19 the general **consensus**　　　　　　　　　一般的Ⓐ言論　Ⓑ評價

20 select some **candidates** for the award　　　挑選獲獎Ⓐ作品　Ⓑ候選人

21 after the **close** of bidding　　　　　　　　投標Ⓐ終結　Ⓑ公開後

22 **Competition** increased overnight.　　　　　Ⓐ競爭　Ⓑ訂購　連夜增加

23 reliable **analysis** of the balance sheet　　　資產負債表可信任的Ⓐ資料　Ⓑ分析

24 receive an **award**　　　　　　　　　　　獲得Ⓐ獎賞　Ⓑ學位

25	expand the **capacity** of the communication network	擴大通信網的 Ⓐ範圍 Ⓑ容量
26	The second floor will be closed for **renovation**.	二樓會因Ⓐ改裝 Ⓑ大清掃 而封閉
27	meet with company **representatives**	與公司Ⓐ顧問 Ⓑ代表 相見
28	fill out a **complaint** form	填寫Ⓐ客訴 Ⓑ申請 單
29	a large **gap** between supply and demand	需求和供應的巨大Ⓐ變動 Ⓑ差異
30	An education serves as the **foundation** for a career.	教育對職業做到Ⓐ訓練 Ⓑ打基礎 的作用
31	**agreement** with the proposal	對提案的Ⓐ滿足 Ⓑ同意
32	Some **studies** suggest that S + V	一些Ⓐ研究性論文 Ⓑ研究者 建議…
33	the **demand** for medical personnel	對醫療人員的Ⓐ需求 Ⓑ援助
34	**progress** toward a safer workplace	向更安全的工作場所的目標Ⓐ努力 Ⓑ進步
35	**requests** for grant proposals	對輔助金方案的Ⓐ申請 Ⓑ疑問
36	an important **step** in gaining equality	爭取平等的一個重要Ⓐ事項 Ⓑ階段
37	offer financial **incentives** to qualified patients	給資格的患者提供金錢上的Ⓐ基礎 Ⓑ鼓勵
38	**delays** in shipping	運輸的Ⓐ延遲 Ⓑ取消
39	They all belong to the **union**.	他們都屬於這個 Ⓐ公司 Ⓑ組織
40	use extreme **caution**	使用極度的Ⓐ注意力 Ⓑ集中力
41	**Attendees** must register today.	Ⓐ志願者 Ⓑ參與者 要在今天登記
42	an airtight **container** to store food	保管食品的密封Ⓐ倉庫 Ⓑ容器
43	**violation** of office rules	Ⓐ違反 Ⓑ遵守 公司規定
44	Plastic is resistant to **corrosion**.	塑膠能抵抗Ⓐ侵蝕 Ⓑ腐蝕
45	begin another **expansion** project	開始另一個Ⓐ擴張 Ⓑ支出 計畫
46	The menu includes a **selection** of wines.	菜單包括葡萄酒的Ⓐ目錄 Ⓑ選擇
47	the **purpose** of the meeting	會議的Ⓐ提案 Ⓑ目的

在正確的前打 √ 標記。

48 ◊ digits
◊ **developments** in technology   技術上的發展

49 seek ◊ **device**
◊ **advice** from a stockbroker   尋求股票經紀人的意見

50 express one's ◊ **applause**
◊ **appreciation**   表示某人的感謝

51 Professional ◊ **attire**
◊ **ambivalence** is necessary   需要專業的服裝

52 International ◊ **command**
◊ **commerce** has increased   國際貿易有所增加

53 The fire caused widespread ◊ **hurt**
◊ **damage**   火災造成了廣大的損失

54 the first stage of ◊ **environment**
◊ **development**   開發的第一階段

55 an ◊ **exception**
◊ **instance** might be made   可能會產生例外的情況

56 attend a public ◊ **lecture**
◊ **speaker**   參加一場公開的演講

57 manufacture ladies' ◊ **apparel**
◊ **applicants**   工廠製作女性服裝

58 Meals are your ◊ **responsibility**
◊ **requirement**   準備餐點是你的責任

59 put the form in the ◊ **envelope**
◊ **postage**   把這表格放進信封裡

60 There is room for ◊ **establishment**
◊ **improvement**   有改善的空間

61 We apologize for the ◊ **inclination**
◊ **inconvenience**   對於造成不便我們深感抱歉

62 a species in danger of ◊ **decadence**
◊ **extinction**   一個瀕臨絕種的物種

63 a large ◊ **collection**
◊ **connection** of artwork   一個豐富的藝術收藏

64 expect a gradual ◊ **slowdown**
◊ **rundown** in March   預計在三月逐漸的趨緩

65 a ◊ **bit**
◊ **minimum** of two years' experience   最少兩年的經驗

66 His ◊ **neutrality**
◊ **neutron** was in dispute.   他的中立性被質疑

正確答案　P106

Part V

01 One of the great ------- of working for Seal Corporation is its excellent treatment of employees.

(A) courtesies
(B) advantages
(C) profits
(D) favors

02 The new executive officer brings with him ------- in the areas of policy making, strategy formulation and business acquisitions.

(A) inquiry
(B) conversion
(C) jurisdiction
(D) expertise

03 Clarkson and Sons is in the last ------- of the study and will soon submit a report on its findings.

(A) paths
(B) drafts
(C) ways
(D) stages

04 The weather forecaster has announced that there is a ------- of showers later in the evening.

(A) speculation
(B) fate
(C) chance
(D) prospect

05 The local government has a total ------- of ten million dollars for job skills training for unemployed people.

(A) book
(B) budget
(C) money
(D) wallet

06 The risks in investing in Data-Tech are high, but it could bring substantial ------- in the future.

(A) rewards
(B) cash
(C) payments
(D) money

07 During the economic crisis, the company generated the smallest ------- in the history of its operation.

(A) finances
(B) charges
(C) money
(D) revenue

08 The PR Department of the Merrill Power Corporation issued a press release making clear the firm's ------- on current environmental issues.

(A) circumstance
(B) stance
(C) composition
(D) substitution

09 The most successful general managers assert that human resources are the most important ------- in any establishment.

(A) worth
(B) benefit
(C) asset
(D) personal

10 The firm has a total ------- on the apparatus because it is the only company authorized to produce it.

(A) monologue
(B) monograph
(C) monotone
(D) monopoly

11 A spokesperson from FutureNet Ltd. reported that there had recently been a number of innovative ------- in the networking industry.

(A) digits
(B) developments
(C) repetitions
(D) decisions

12 The financial ------- of the shipping industry is dependent on the continued growth and improvement of the country's fleet of cargo liners.

(A) stability
(B) allocation
(C) donation
(D) statement

13 The deadline for submission of ------- for the river cleaning project has been extended to the end of the month.

(A) intentions
(B) advice
(C) indications
(D) proposals

14 The restaurant is undergoing ------- in hopes of attracting more business-class clientele.

(A) formation
(B) magnification
(C) renovation
(D) boost

正確答案 P106

Questions 15-18 refer to the following memo.

From: Warren Reynolds, PR Department
To: All Staff

All employees at Burrows and Burrows Design Ltd. are hereby informed that a new
quality ------- program will be implemented as of next month. Stringent quality regulation

15 (A) acceptance
(B) assurance
(C) location
(D) confidence

procedures have been introduced to guarantee that our international reputation for excellence in
design services is maintained. While working on new design projects, staff will be ------- to keep

16 (A) interested
(B) compared
(C) compensated
(D) required

a detailed online record of all steps taken throughout the project to ensure that the new quality
specifications are met. On completion, the record will then be submitted to the management office
for -------, after which feedback will be provided. A special full-day induction seminar has been

17 (A) evaluation
(B) reservation
(C) expectation
(D) implication

scheduled for Saturday February 19th in the large conference room, at which the new quality
assurance specifications will be explained in detail. It is ------- for all staff to attend, and overtime

18 (A) decisive
(B) willing
(C) resourceful
(D) imperative

will be paid accordingly.

VOCABULARY | 單字

Chapter 9

形容詞

瞭解 Valid 的含義，在美國的生活就會輕鬆啦

消費大國美國是退換文化發達的國家。買完東西後覺得不滿意就可以憑收據去退換，這時商家會要求 valid receipt（有效的收據）。抽象化的 valid（有效的）在看到 valid receipt 這樣的用法就開始有實感啦。要記住與多益形容詞一起使用的名詞。

百發百中 出題類型與戰略

◉ 會出現選擇符合句意的形容詞這樣的問題。

◉ 用來修飾名詞時，要選擇符合「形容詞＋名詞」這個部分的句意。

◉ 仔細看句子的關鍵字、連接詞和介系詞就很容易理解句意。

例題 1

Information technology and computer networks have provided offices and homes with ------- gains in efficiency and productivity.

(A) overpowering　(B) noble　(C) affected　(D) impressive

解說　句意是「資訊技術和電腦網路在效率和生產方面為辦公室跟家庭帶來了___的利益」，能與其相符的選項是（D）impressive（令人印象深刻的），（impressive gains 令人印象深刻的利益、impressive special effects 令人印象深刻的特別影響）。（A）overpowering 是「壓制性的，強烈的（感情等）」，（B）noble 是「出色的，高尚的」，（C）affected 是「受到影響的」的意思，都與句意不符，不是正確答案。

翻譯　資訊技術和電腦網路在效率和生產方面為辦公室跟家庭帶來了令人印象深刻的利益。

gains [genz] 獲利 / efficiency [ɪˈfɪʃənsɪ] 效率 / productivity [ˌprodʌkˈtɪvətɪ] 生產力

答案　(D)

例題 2

We have carefully considered each of our valuable and talented employees for this award, but only one could be selected. It took much deliberation, but we have reached consensus that out of the hundreds of ideas to emerge over the past year, Brian Lee's have been the most -------.

(A) respective　(B) interested
(C) innovative　(D) attracted

解說　句意是「Brian Lee 的想法最___的」，能與其相符的選項是（C）innovative（創新的）。（A）respective 是「個別的」，（B）interested 是「（人）覺得有興趣的」，（D）attracted 是「（人）被吸引的」的意思，與句意不符，所以不正確。

翻譯　為了這個獎項，我們考慮過每個我們看重而且具有才能的職員，但只有一位能夠選上。這花了很多時間討論，但我們已經達成共識，在去年提出近百個想法中，Brian Lee 的想法是最創新的。

talented [ˈtæləntɪd] 有才能的 / deliberation [dɪˌlɪbəˈreʃən] 商討 / reach consensus 達成共識 / emerge [ɪˈmɝdʒ] 浮現

答案　(C)

❶ unprecedented 史無前例的

Record sales by such a small firm are **unprecedented**.
以這麼小的公司來做唱片銷售是史無前例的。

❷ tentative 暫時的，臨時的，可變更的

用來表示臨時制訂的計畫或日程。與provisional（暫時的）的意思相同。

The release date for the new product is still considered **tentative**.
新產品的出售日期仍暫定為先前考慮的日期。

❸ defective 有缺陷的

Store owners are offering refunds on all **defective** merchandise.
店主對所有缺陷的商品提供退費服務。

❹ illegible （文字）難辨認的，字跡模糊的

Because of a printing mistake, the documents are **illegible**.
由於印刷上的失誤，那個文件很難辨認。

❺ alert 細心的，謹慎的

Our team supervisor was **alert** enough to spot the errors in the report.
我們這組的管理者細心到足以避免報告裡的錯誤。

❻ annual 每年的，一年一度的

Those interested should register for the **annual** conference by next week.
有興趣參加年度會議的人請於下週前完成登記。

❼ promising 有希望的，有前途的

Job opportunities for new graduates will be more **promising** than before.
剛畢業的學生的就業機會比以前的人更有希望。

❽ respective 分別的，各自的

要與類似形態的respectful（恭敬的）區分。

All images on this web page are the property of their **respective** illustrators.
網頁上的所有圖片都歸那些各自的插畫家所有。

❾ insecure　不安的，不確信的

「insecure about 對…不安的」

Department store sales have decreased, as shoppers feel **insecure** about the current economy.
消費者對現有經濟狀況的不安導致百貨公司的銷售額減少。

❿ enviable　令人羨慕的，可羨慕的

Mr. Brown in telemarketing has an **enviable** sales record.
電話行銷部的 Brown 先生有很令人羨慕的銷售記錄。

⓫ affordable　價格合理的

Today's personal computers are **affordable** and accessible to most people.
現在的個人電腦對大部分的人來說是價格合理而且可接受的。

⓬ available　可利用的（事物），有空的（人）

表示設施、服務等可供人利用，「A（事物）is available to + B（利用的人）：A對B有用」。

Savings options are **available** to all customers of the American First Bank.
儲蓄選項可供所有 American First Bank 的顧客利用。

⓭ diverse　多樣的

Recent hires reflected the company's goal to have a **diverse** workforce.
最近的招聘反應了公司要擁有多樣人才資源的目標。

⓮ eligible　有資格的（人），合格的

有資格享受待遇或做某事的意思，「be eligible to + 動詞原形 / be eligible for + 名詞：有資格做…」。

Donors are **eligible** to become members of the Gold Star Club.
捐贈者有資格成為 Gold Star Club 的會員。

Workers are eligible for compensation.
職員們有資格得到補償。

⓯ liable　很有可能的，易…的

「be liable to + 動詞原形：很有可能的」（=be likely to + 動詞原形）

During an economic crisis, many small businesses are **liable** to fail.
經濟危機期間很多小型企業都有可能倒閉。

⑯ overdue　過期的，到期末付的

表示還書或支付貸款過期，「期間 + overdue：遲了⋯長期間」。

The books he had borrowed were two days **overdue**.
他借的書過期兩天啦。

⑰ unclaimed　無人要求的，所有者不明的

表示沒有主人的事物時使用。

The airport introduced new security procedures for **unclaimed** baggage.
機場為所有者不明的行李引進了新的保安措施。

⑱ consecutive　連續的，持續的

「for the + 序數 + consecutive year：⋯年間持續的」

ATLP announced that its stock value had risen for the fifth **consecutive** year.
ATLP公司宣佈自身股價在過去的五年裡持續上升。

⑲ unwavering　堅定的，不動搖的

Ecolife stated its **unwavering** commitment to preserving the local environment.
Ecoife公司表明了保護當地環境的堅定信念。

⑳ substantial　（量、大小）相當的

The company has invested a **substantial** amount of capital into its new projects.
公司在新計畫上投入了相當大的資本。

㉑ chronological　按年代順序排列的

「in chronological order　按年代順序的」

The newspaper listed the events in **chronological** order.
那個報紙把這些事件按年代順序的整理方式列出來。

㉒ unanimous　無異議的

The proposal to cut costs obtained **unanimous** shareholder approval.
減少費用的提案得到了股東們的一致贊同。

㉓ durable　（材料、物件）結實，耐久的

Playtoy products are **durable** enough to be used inside and outside the home.
Playtoy公司的產品結實耐用，無論用於室內或戶外都很合適。

⊙ 選擇A和B中正確的一個。

01 the **overall** effectiveness of the program 計畫方案Ⓐ整體的 Ⓑ向上的 效率性

02 The supervisor is extremely **demanding** on the staff. 那個主管對職員非常地Ⓐ關心 Ⓑ要求

03 The office is in a **desirable** location. 辦公室在Ⓐ讓人想要的 Ⓑ有名的 地方

04 **mounting** pressure Ⓐ起作用的 Ⓑ漸增的 壓力

05 **technical** problems Ⓐ本質上的 Ⓑ技術上的 問題

06 **reliable** employees Ⓐ可靠的 Ⓑ剩下的 職員

07 an **authorized** car repair center Ⓐ公認的 Ⓑ權威的 汽車修理廠

08 a **diversified** line of products Ⓐ類似的 Ⓑ各種的 商品系列

09 an **unbiased** opinion Ⓐ無偏見的 Ⓑ活潑的 意見

10 an **active** program to support small companies 對支援小型企業Ⓐ積極的 Ⓑ必要的 方案

11 **accurate** data Ⓐ公開的 Ⓑ準確的 資料

12 **detailed** information Ⓐ詳細的 Ⓑ有益的 情報

13 **required** application documents Ⓐ必要的 Ⓑ已提出的 申請公文

14 a totally **independent** agency 一個完全Ⓐ可利用的 Ⓑ獨立的 代理商

15 a **strategic** location Ⓐ戰略性的 Ⓑ正確的 位置

16 ensure the **efficient** processing of complaints 確保客訴Ⓐ迅速的 Ⓑ高效率的 處理

17 The slide projector was **unavailable**. 幻燈片投影機Ⓐ不能使用 Ⓑ不能交換

18 get **regular** check-ups 接受Ⓐ嚴格的 Ⓑ定期的 檢查

19 **delicate** issues involving civil rights   包含市民權力的Ⓐ深刻 Ⓑ敏感 問題

20 at a **rapid** pace   Ⓐ快速的 Ⓑ多樣的 步調

21 a **comprehensive** physical examination   Ⓐ恰當的 Ⓑ綜合的 身體檢查

22 **differing** opinion   Ⓐ正當的 Ⓑ有差異的 意見

23 on a **clear** day   Ⓐ晴朗的 Ⓑ打掃的 日子

24 the **reserved** room   Ⓐ改造後的 Ⓑ預約的 房間

25 It is **imperative** that you go to the meeting.   您Ⓐ沒有必要 Ⓑ有必要 參加會議

26 security has been **lax**   保全系統Ⓐ被採用了 Ⓑ鬆懈了

27 **powerful** engine   Ⓐ強力的 Ⓑ改良的 引擎

28 might be especially **beneficial**   將會特別地Ⓐ安全 Ⓑ有益

29 make the manual **accessible** to users   使說明書對使用者來說Ⓐ好理解 Ⓑ有需要

30 The company is not **progressive**.   那家公司是不Ⓐ進步的 Ⓑ保守的

31 be compensated for **unused** leave days   對Ⓐ不足的 Ⓑ沒有使用的 選休假日補償

32 the **medicinal** uses of aloe vera   蘆薈在Ⓐ醫學上的 Ⓑ無節制的 使用

33 **past** findings   Ⓐ過去的 Ⓑ重要的 發現

34 **incompetent** employees   Ⓐ新雇傭的 Ⓑ無能力的 職員

35 feel **apprehensive** during the interview   在面試期間覺得Ⓐ擔心 Ⓑ後悔

⊙ 在正確的前打 √ 標記。

36 manage an ◇ **increasing** / ◇ **cultivating** amount of work   管理增加的業務量

37 eat at a ◇ **popular** / ◇ **solicited** restaurant   在受歡迎的餐廳吃飯

38 The food was ◇ **worthy** / ◇ **worth** the long wait.   那道菜值得等

39 at ◇ **condensed** / ◇ **reasonable** rates   並不太高的價格

40 with a ◇ **damp** / ◇ **confident** manner   以自信的態度

41 an ◇ **unexpected** / ◇ **unqualified** result   想不到的結果

42 in the ◇ **consequent** / ◇ **coming** year   在明年

43 Milk is a ◇ **perishable** / ◇ **perceptible** food.   牛奶是容易變質的食品

44 revamp the company's ◇ **existing** / ◇ **occuring** systems   改造公司現存的體制

45 The sponsors were ◇ **pleased** / ◇ **accustomed** that the event was successful.   贊助商對活動的成功感到高興

46 have a ◇ **contradictory** / ◇ **complimentary** breakfast   有免費的早餐

47 a ◇ **relievable** / ◇ **rich** source of petroleum   豐富的石油資源

正確答案 P108

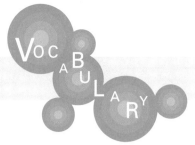

HACKERS TEST

Part V

01 Although stock options were previously offered only to management, the rank-and-file are now ------- to purchase options.

(A) appropriate
(B) eligible
(C) available
(D) befitting

02 If you have any problems using the handset, take it to any ------- service center for repairs.

(A) limited
(B) authorized
(C) permissive
(D) sufficient

03 When delivering ------- food, delivery companies use special refrigerated trucks and insulating materials to prevent the food from spoiling.

(A) perishable
(B) spoiled
(C) fragile
(D) durable

04 Although all members of the discount club may order items from the website, rebates are ------- only to those members who have kept their accounts active.

(A) creditable
(B) considerable
(C) approachable
(D) available

05 Media Creators, producer of family-oriented fast food restaurant advertisements, has won the coveted Advertising Award for the third ------- year.

(A) connected
(B) associated
(C) consecutive
(D) continuous

06 The shop specializes in furniture and table accessories that are ------- to low and medium-income households.

(A) curable
(B) believed
(C) excessive
(D) affordable

07 The manual was written in such a manner as to be readily ------- to laymen and nonprofessionals.

(A) acknowledgeable
(B) expressible
(C) familiar
(D) accessible

VOCABULARY | 單字

08 Plans for the consul's visit to the company are still considered -------, but our representative will call you once the arrangements are fixed.

(A) vigilant
(B) tentative
(C) contemporary
(D) infinite

09 For those who want to work as a business analyst, experience in market research is a highly ------- attribute.

(A) beneficial
(B) repetitive
(C) superficial
(D) expensive

10 Consumer Institute representative, Debbie Dorday, gave an ------- speech on digital cameras, and what to look for when purchasing one.

(A) indicative
(B) excited
(C) informative
(D) interested

11 Camping gear such as tents, sleeping bags, and backpacks are made from exceptionally ------- materials such as nylon or canvas.

(A) justifiable
(B) durable
(C) legible
(D) reversible

12 Despite the growing popularity of the internet, television advertising remains one of the most ------- ways to promote products.

(A) satisfied
(B) reluctant
(C) dependent
(D) effective

13 The job requirements are much too -------, even for staff who have the necessary skills and experience.

(A) demanding
(B) exciting
(C) revolting
(D) compelling

14 Few people would be ------- to relocate to areas that do not provide sufficient transportation facilities.

(A) convincing
(B) wishing
(C) willing
(D) starting

正確答案 P108

Part VI

Questions 15-18 refer to the following letter.

Infinicorp Ltd.
1246 Peartree Ave.
Denver, CO 80203

Norman Lord
246 Kandahar Crescent
Boulder, CO 80301

Dear Mr. Lord,

As I am sure you will be aware, Infinicorp Ltd. has posted a record profit for the past business year. Earnings came in at a staggering 837 million dollars, representing an ------- turnaround

15 (A) impenetrable
(B) immovable
(C) unprecedented
(D) insubordinate

since the company's huge loss two years ago. At that time, the corporation made a considerable loss of ------- 342 million dollars. The company's ------- rise back to power has been largely

16 (A) justly
(B) nearly
(C) mostly
(D) fluently

17 (A) unlimited
(B) impressed
(C) forbidden
(D) enviable

attributed to the formidable talents of CEO, Mr. Richard Baker, who was inaugurated only two years ago. This enormous profit translates into benefits for all shareholders. I am therefore delighted to announce that Infinicorp is turning this profit into a special dividend of 40 cents per share, an amount ------- over expected returns for this year. Based upon current earnings, we

18 (A) very
(B) so
(C) such
(D) well

anticipate further share price increases in the near future. Finally, I would like to thank you for remaining one of our most loyal and valued shareholders.

Sincerely,

Artimus Bertwhistle
Executive Director, Infinicorp Ltd.

Chapter 10

副詞

解答多益問題時，要 "Watch closely！"

多益中也會出現不少熟悉的副詞，但選起來並不容易。有時候需要把莫名其妙的字 "strictly" 填入「watch the proceedings___：細心地觀察步驟」的空白處中才能知道，closely 這個單字是否有「縝密地，細心地」的意思（strictly 有「嚴密地」的意思，但把 closely 跟 strictly 分別代入前面的片語，會發現 closely 是更合適的答案），這是很常見的情況。多益副詞要邊看例句邊掌握多益喜歡的用法，還需要同時看一下副詞修飾的形容詞和動詞片語。

百發百中 出題類型與戰略

⊙ 會出現選擇符合句意的副詞這樣的問題。

⊙ 仔細看句子的關鍵字和連接詞、介系詞就很容易理解句意。

⊙ 有時只看「副詞 + 副詞修飾的片語」部分就能選出答案。

例題 1

All individuals who use their credit card frequently should ------- check their transaction history to verify that no errors have been made.

(A) periodically　(B) precisely　(C) incidentally　(D) indefinitely

解說　根據句意「經常使用信用卡的人應該___檢查交易記錄」，適合的選項應該是（A）periodically（定期地）。（B）precisely 是「正確地」意思，不能與 check（檢查）一起使用，（know precisely 正確的知道），（C）incidentally 是「偶然地」，（D）indefinitely 是「不確定地」的意思，都不符合題意。

翻譯　經常使用信用卡的人應該定期地檢查交易記錄中是否有誤。

check[tʃɛk]（為了確認）檢查 / transaction history 交易記錄 / verify[ˈvɛrəˌfaɪ] 確認

答案　(A)

例題 2

In the past year, Threestar Automotive's automobile exports increased by 12.6%, bringing in gross profits of around \$500 million. The relatively new company has grown ------- in the five

(A) eagerly　　(B) immediately
(C) recently　　(D) rapidly

years since its inauguration, and considering the company's planned diversification into the pharmaceutical sector, the future looks bright indeed.

解說　想要表達「這個相當年輕的公司在過去五年內___成長」的句意，符合的選項應該是（D）rapidly（迅速地）。（A）eagerly 是「急切地」，（B）immediately 是「立即」，（C）recently 是「最近」的意思，都不符合題意。

翻譯　Threestar Automotive 公司去年的汽車出口額增長了 12.6%，並帶來約五億美元的總收入。這個相當年輕的公司從開始營運後在五年間迅速地成長，考慮到公司在藥品製造方面的經營多元化計畫，公司的未來看起來非常光明。

bring in 帶來（收入、利益）/ gross profit 總收入 / inauguration[ɪnˌɔgjəˈreʃən]（事業）開啟，就任
diversification[daɪˌvɝsəfəˈkeʃən] 經營多元化

答案　(D)

❶ enthusiastically　熱烈地

The staff **enthusiastically** applauded the boss' decision to increase wages.
職員們對社長要提高薪水的決定表示熱烈地歡迎。

❷ radically　根本地，徹底地

與 fundamentally（根本地）同義。

In an attempt to attract younger consumers, the ad campaign was **radically** changed.
為了吸引年輕一代的消費者這個廣告活動被徹底地改變了。

❸ solely　僅，只

The firm relied **solely** on word-of-mouth advertising.
那個公司只有靠直銷的方式行銷。

❹ directly　直接，立即

用來表示不經過中間人而直接與負責人聯繫的情況。

If you have any questions or comments, please contact me **directly**.
如果您有疑問或意見，請直接與我聯繫。

❺ immediately　立刻，馬上

單獨使用或以「immediately upon-ing / immediately after + 子句：一…就」形式使用。

Employees are instructed to punch in **immediately** upon arriving at work.
職員們被要求一上班就要馬上去打卡。

❻ minimally　最低限度地

Traffic will be only **minimally** affected during the construction work.
這工程的施工期間交通只會受到最低限度地影響。

❼ otherwise　另外，否則

用來表示與主要內容無關，而另外發生的情況。此外還常用作介系詞並表示「否則」的意思。

You will continue to receive these weekly newsletters unless **otherwise** requested.
您會每週繼續收到這些通訊，除非您提出另外的要求。

We must leave at once, **otherwise** we'll miss the beginning of the performance.
我們必須立即出發，否則就會錯過公演的開頭部分。

❽ consistently　一如既往，不斷地

要與類似形態的 respectful（恭敬的）區分。

Lewis' Law Firm has **consistently** provided quality services at affordable prices.
Lewis' Law 公司一如往常以合理的價格提供高品質的服務。

VOCABULARY | 單字

⑨ significantly　相當程度地

New drilling technologies are expected to **significantly** boost oil production capacity.
新鑽井技術預料會大幅地提高石油生產能力。

⑩ currently　現在

The fifth floor of this building is **currently** open for public tours.
這個建築的第五樓現在已經開放給大眾觀光客了。

⑪ simultaneously　同時

Training sessions given by the company are **simultaneously** funny and informative.
公司提供的教育課程很有趣,同時也很實用。

⑫ promptly　及時,準時地

The broken equipment at the plant must be repaired **promptly**.
工廠裡有故障的設備要及時維修。

The staff knows that Mr. Rich wants meetings to begin **promptly** at 8:00 am.
職員們知道 Rich 先生想在上午8點準時開始會議。

⑬ relatively　比較,相對

The increased crop yield was attributed to the past winter's **relatively** warm weather.
由於上次的冬天天氣比較溫暖,所以穀物的收穫量增加了。

⑭ densely　濃密地,濃厚地

「densely populated 人口密集的」

Heavy industry has been steadily moving out of **densely** populated areas.
重工業不斷地撤出人口密集的地區。

⑮ ahead　(時間上)提前,前

Be sure to call **ahead** for a reservation to avoid excessive delays.
為了避免嚴重耽擱,請提前打電話預約吧。

⑯ exclusively　獨佔地,全面地

A new department was created to concentrate **exclusively** on the emerging Asian market.
新部門的設立是為了把全部精力集中於新興的亞洲市場。

⑰ fully　充分地,完全地

The business community did not **fully** appreciate the marketing potential of the Internet.
這個業界沒有充分認識到網路市場的巨大潛力。

◉ 選擇A和B中正確的一個。

01 a **fairly** simple method Ⓐ過分 Ⓑ相當 簡單的方法

02 **accidentally** discover a confidential document Ⓐ偶然地 Ⓑ終於 發現了機密文件

03 record expenses **accurately** Ⓐ誇張地 Ⓑ準確地 記錄了費用

04 **carelessly** broke the rules Ⓐ有意地 Ⓑ輕率地 違反規則

05 On May 1, the store will **officially** open. 五月1日本商店會Ⓐ正式地 Ⓑ公然地 開放

06 choose **randomly** Ⓐ正確地 Ⓑ隨機地 選擇

07 has **consistently** arrived on time Ⓐ按預定 Ⓑ一貫地 準時到達

08 Customers **repeatedly** use the service. 顧客們Ⓐ免費地 Ⓑ重複地 使用那項服務

09 Prices increased **markedly**. 價格Ⓐ不合理地 Ⓑ顯著地 上升

10 Lateness will be **severely** penalized. 遲到會被Ⓐ嚴格地 Ⓑ持續地 處分

11 Visitors are **routinely** asked to show their IDs. 訪客會被Ⓐ依常規地 Ⓑ優先地 要求身份證件檢查

12 an **unusually** high profit return Ⓐ不尋常地 Ⓑ略高地 高利潤回收

13 **voluntarily** work overtime Ⓐ繼續 Ⓑ自發地 進行加班

14 His experience was **exclusively** in sales. 他的經歷Ⓐ只有 Ⓑ有些 在營業方面

15 Doctors were **previously** unable to cure the disease. 醫生們Ⓐ完全 Ⓑ以前 不能治療那種疾病

16 Regrettably, we have to close our doors.　　　Ⓐ的確　Ⓑ很遺憾地　我們只能結束營業

17 He will **undoubtedly** take the position.　　　他將Ⓐ無疑地　Ⓑ很感激地　接受那份工作

18 The equipment operates **properly**.　　　裝備Ⓐ正常地　Ⓑ快速地　運作

19 The partners worked **cooperatively**.　　　搭檔們Ⓐ協力地　Ⓑ獨立地　工作

20 be **adequately** wrapped to avoid damage　　　為防止損失Ⓐ壓縮後　Ⓑ適當地　進行了包裝

21 talk to patrons **politely**　　　Ⓐ安靜地　Ⓑ委婉地　告訴顧客

22 Our office has **recently** moved　　　我們的辦公室Ⓐ最近　Ⓑ全部　遷移了

23 deal with problems **appropriately**　　　Ⓐ適當地　Ⓑ急忙地　處理問題

24 expand **substantially**　　　Ⓐ階段性地　Ⓑ大規模地　擴張

25 cost **significantly** less　　　花費Ⓐ相當地　Ⓑ持續地　減少

26 follow the directions **carefully**　　　Ⓐ謹慎地　Ⓑ按原樣　遵照指示

27 The plant operates **efficiently**.　　　工廠Ⓐ正式地　Ⓑ有效地　運營

28 be **temporarily** out of stock　　　Ⓐ臨時　Ⓑ同時　售完

29 The hotel is **conveniently** located near the shopping district.　　旅館Ⓐ便利地　Ⓑ戰略性地　座落在購物區附近

30 The network system will **eventually** need upgrading.　　網路系統Ⓐ額外　Ⓑ最終　將需要升級

31 The restaurant stays open ◇ **late** / ◇ **far**　　　　餐廳營業到很晚

32 The bridge is ◇ **extremely** / ◇ **presently** under construction.　　　　那座橋現在還在建設中

33 cut spending, ◇ **scarcely** / ◇ **especially** on recreation　　　　減少費用，特別在娛樂的方面

34 pay ◇ **closely** / ◇ **separately**　　　　分開支付

35 He ◇ **distantly** / ◇ **initially** resisted the change.　　　　他最初反抗這項改變

36 ◇ **frequently** / ◇ **shortly** depend on donations　　　　頻繁地依賴捐款

37 ◇ **Presumably** / ◇ **Almost** , he left the building.　　　　可能他已經離開了大廈

38 fasten the strap ◇ **thickly** / ◇ **securely**　　　　牢牢地繫上帶子

39 the ◇ **before** / ◇ **once** famous celebrity　　　　曾經有名的名人

40 The product line will ◇ **once** / ◇ **finally** be launched.　　　　系列產品終於要上市了

41 Tourists visit ◇ **entirely** / ◇ **regularly** throughout the year.　　　　遊客們整年都有規律地來訪

42 ◇ **Nearly** / ◇ **Apparently** , she lost the original copy.　　　　顯然地，她把原始的版本給弄丟了

43 The book is read ◇ **equally** / ◇ **brightly** by both boys and girls.　　　　不管是少男還是少女都同樣地閱讀這本書

44 do one's job ◇ **even** / ◇ **well**　　　　很出色地工作

45 be ◇ **spaciously** / ◇ **widely** admired　　　　受到廣泛尊重的

Part V

01 Effective -------, the company will no longer accept applications for medical or sick leave without a certificate from a physician.

(A) financially
(B) immediately
(C) concurrently
(D) repeatedly

02 The use of alternative medicine among professionals in the city and suburbs is ------- widespread.

(A) directly
(B) quickly
(C) likely
(D) fairly

03 The company misled investors by not ------- reporting the losses it incurred in the first quarter.

(A) assuredly
(B) remarkably
(C) accurately
(D) deductively

04 The gift shop on Baker Street is popular with customers because it is conveniently located, and its products are ------- inexpensive.

(A) nearly
(B) hardly
(C) relatively
(D) scarcely

05 Cell phone users who -------send text messages should take advantage of the new plan being offered by the wireless carrier.

(A) totally
(B) greatly
(C) hugely
(D) frequently

06 Because the first speaker has another appointment, the convention must begin ------- at 9:00 AM.

(A) assertively
(B) cordially
(C) promptly
(D) especially

07 The company has ------- hired some new staff, so we will be holding a gathering at the cafeteria to introduce them.

(A) recently
(B) usually
(C) commonly
(D) freshly

正確答案 P110

Questions 08-11 refer to the following article.

Downtown Finance Center Facelift

The Downtown Finance Center is about to undergo an extensive modernization project, including a revamped facade and lobby. The aim of the work is to give the Finance Center a competitive edge in attracting high-end corporate lessees for its office space. After completion, the building will appear ------- different from now due to the addition of a mirrored glass exterior that changes colors based

08 (A) formerly
(B) radically
(C) allegedly
(D) primarily

on the time of day. Also, upgraded seating areas will ------- more people than before, with special

09 (A) appreciate
(B) articulate
(C) alienate
(D) accommodate

attention being given to comfort and space. In an unusual move, developers decided not to employ an entire design team to work on the new project, opting instead to allow freelance architect Janice Pana, designer of the New York Arts Center, to ------- create the new-look Finance Center.

10 (A) recently
(B) nearly
(C) solely
(D) surely

Because the Finance Center building will have to undergo extensive remodeling, ------- costs are

11 (A) concurrent
(B) characteristic
(C) minimum
(D) legible

expected to be around $150,000.

Section 3 近義詞

Chapter 11

意義相近的動詞

Stir the sauce 請攪拌調味料

想教外國朋友煮中國料理，可是發現不太懂「攪拌調味料」這句話怎麼說。想用 turn，好像也不對，一查才知道「攪拌（調味料）」是 stir，而 turn 是「（輪胎等的）轉動」的意思。這個章節主要收錄了一些表面上意義相似，但用於不同狀況和模式的動詞。請注意閱讀例句並好好記住它們的區別。

百發百中 出題類型與戰略

◉ 會出一些看起來意義相近的動詞，只有知道他們的正確用法才能選出正確答案的問題。

例題 1

A few bank cash machines can ------- as much as 30,000 dollars, but most carry less than half that amount.

(A) possess   (B) hold   (C) occupy   (D) grasp

解說　選項中的四個動詞看起來意思都一樣，但用法卻各有不同。符合句意的是（B）hold（（機器等）裝（物品））。（A）possess 是「（人）擁有…」（possess a membership card 擁有會員卡），（C）occupy 是「（人或事物）佔著（場所）」（Offices occupied the building 這棟大樓的佔用空間皆為辦公室），（D）grasp 是「（人）抓緊…」（grasp hands 抓緊手）的意思，都不符合題意，所以不正確。

翻譯　少數的銀行提款機能裝三萬美元，但大部分連一半都裝不下。
　　　bank cash machine 銀行提款機 / carry[ˌkærɪ] 攜帶，帶有

答案　(B)

例題 2

Steel Works Inc. has just announced plans to move their operations from the Michigan Steel Mill to a new location near Los Angeles. The company has officially ------- staff that the current plant

(A) explained   (B) informed
(C) expressed   (D) inquired

will be closing at the end of year, but jobs will be available for employees prepared to relocate.

解說　選項中的四個動詞看起來意思都一樣，但形式不同。空白處後面有人（staff），所以空白處要填以人為受語的動詞。因此 inform（通知（給人））的過去式，即選項（B）informed 是正確答案。（A）explain（說明…）的受詞只能是要說的內容，聽的人的前面必須加 to。（C）express（表示…）的受詞是感情、想法等，（D）inquire 是「inquire about 問及…」的意思，都不符合題意，所以不正確。

翻譯　Steel Works 公司剛剛宣佈公司的營運會從密西根州的煉鋼工廠移動到洛杉磯附近的新計畫。公司已正式通知員工現有工廠會在年底關閉，但準備參與重新部署的職員們可以繼續上班。
　　　announce[əˈnaʊns] 公佈 / operation[ˌɑpəˈreʃən] 營運 / officially[əˈfɪʃəlɪ] 正式地 / current[ˈkɝənt] 現在的
　　　plant[plænt] 工廠 / relocate[riˈloket] 重新部署

答案　(B)

❶ advise : recommend

advise　勸告

「advise 人 that 子句：給…勸告…」，that 子句前面要接人物受詞。

The lawyer **advised** the owner that filing for bankruptcy was his only option.
律師勸告業主宣告破產是他唯一的解決方法。

recommend　推薦

「recommend that 子句：推薦…」，that 子句前不能接人物受詞。

The stockbroker **recommended** that shares of the offering be purchased immediately.
股票經紀人推薦立即購買公開招募的股票。

❷ affect : effect

affect　影響（人物、事物）

The new security rules will **affect** all employees at the main headquarters.
新的安全規定會影響到總公司的所有職員。

effect　使（變化等）產生

The company cannot **effect** a change without closely examining its systems.
那個公司在沒有很仔細的檢測它的系統後是不會容許任何變化。

❸ attend : participate in

attend　參加（課程、行事等）

attend 後面直接接受詞。

The director is requiring all new employees to **attend** the session on insurance.
理事要求所有的新職員都參加關於保險的會議。

participate in　參加（課程、行事等）

用於「participate in + 受詞」的格式，而不能直接接受詞。

Our employer has asked us to **participate in** the company's open house event.
雇主要求我們參加這個公司的開放參觀日。

❹ broaden : multiply

broaden　擴大，加寬

用來表示擴大道路等物質或領域等的抽象物體。

The grant allows us to **broaden** our research into several different areas.
這筆補助金使我們能把研究擴大到一些不同的領域。

multiply　使增加，增加

He **multiplied** his fortune by choosing his investments carefully.
他謹慎選擇投資方式使得他的財產增加。

❺ condense : contract : minimize : decrease

condense 概要（表現等）

「condense A into B：把A概括成」

The CEO has asked us to **condense** an hour-long presentation into 20 minutes.
CEO要求我們把為時1個小時的發表演說概括成20分鐘。

contract 收縮

When exposed to cold temperatures, metal **contracts**.
金屬在低溫下會收縮。

minimize 極小化

Having a diversified portfolio can help investors **minimize** risk.
擁有多種的有價証券可以幫助投資者把風險降到最小。

decrease 減少（數量），減輕（強度）

The company has decided to **decrease** production of electric appliances.
公司決定減少電子產品的生產。

❻ contact : connect

contact 聯繫

表示通過電話、信件、訪問取得聯繫。

Please **contact** Ms. Brooks for any questions regarding your application.
關於申請方面有問題時，請與Brooks女士聯繫。

connect 連接

「connect A with / to B：把A連接到 / 於B」

Can you **connect** me to the Bookman Publishing Company, please?
你能幫我（把電話）接到Bookman出版社嗎？

❼ demonstrate : display

demonstrate （透過示範、舉例）說明…

透過示範、舉例來說明使用方法等。

The talk show guest **demonstrated** how to dress for success.
脫口秀來賓為大家示範講解該如何為了成功來穿著打扮。

display 展示

「展示」物品以便讓人們容易看到。

The latest styles of shoes are **displayed** in the shopwindows.
在展示窗展示了最新款的皮鞋。

❽ evaluate : estimate

evaluate 評價，評估

The feasibility of the projects has not been **evaluated**.
那些專案的可行性還未接受評估。

estimate 預測

Mr. Turner **estimates** that the non-stop flight to Switzerland will take 14 hours.
Turner先生預測此直飛瑞典的航班要花14個小時。

❾ expire : invalidate

expire （合約、有效日期）到期

它是不及物動詞，所以在「合約到期」中要用主動語態。

The contract **expired** a few days ago and will not be renewed.
那個合約幾天前就到期了，而且不會再更新了。

invalidate 使（合約、法）無效

它是及物動詞，所以表示「合約失效」的意思時用被動語態。

The contract **was invalidated** because the company failed to comply with the terms of the agreement.
那個公司沒有遵守合約，導致了合約失效。

❿ foster : enlarge

foster 促進，培養

「促進」事件或使思想得到發展的涵義。

The new agreement **fostered** exports between the two nations.
新協定促進了兩國間的出口貿易往來。

enlarge 擴大

表示「擴大」設施或實物的大小時使用。

The board plans to **enlarge** the sports complex by the end of the year.
董事會計畫年底前增加體育設施。

⑪ lend : borrow : rent

lend　借給

表示把東西借給某人。

The library does not **lend** books to individuals who have no borrower's card.
圖書館不會把書借給沒有借書證的人。

borrow　借

表示借的動詞。

A small businessman cannot **borrow** money from a bank without collateral.
沒有擔保的情況下，小型企業家不能獲得銀行的貸款。

rent　租（車、房子），租給

The company **rented** several cars for the overseas representatives to use.
公司租了幾輛車給海外業務代表使用。

⑫ note : notify : announce

note　注意，留意

The clerk told the customers to **note** that the store would be closed for two days.
店員告訴顧客要留意商店將要關閉兩天。

notify　通知給⋯

notify後面接受詞，即收到通知的人，「notify人of內容：給⋯通知⋯」。

The company **notified** its shareholders of the proposed merger.
公司向股東們通知了被提議的合併案。

announce　公佈

announce後面接受詞，即發佈的內容，收聽的人前必須加to，「announce（to人）that子句：（給⋯）公佈⋯。」

The chairman **announced** to the Board that the CEO had tendered his resignation.
會長向董事會公佈了CEO提出辭呈的消息。

⑬ raise : lift

raise　提出（問題等）

表示為慈善事業「籌措資金」或「提出」問題。

The concert was held to **raise** money for a charity.
演唱會是為籌備慈善基金而舉辦的。

The journalist **raised** a question about government spending policy.
記者提出了關於政府消費政策的問題。

lift　舉起⋯

「舉起」重物的意思。

Always bend your knees when **lifting** a heavy package.
當你要舉起重物時一定要彎下膝蓋。

⓮ shrink : reduce

shrink （布）縮水

Tightly woven fabrics are more likely to **shrink** when soaked in water.
編織緊密的紡織物被水浸濕後，更有可能縮水。

reduce 減少，使減少

To clear out old inventory, the owner decided to **reduce** prices by 50 percent.
為了清理舊的庫存，老闆把價格調降了50%。

⓯ speak : tell : say : express

speak 講述

要在聽的人和說的人前加介系詞，「speak to 人 about 內容：給…講…」。

Mr. Tokuyama will **speak** to management about production cuts.
Tokuyama先生將跟管理層級講述關於生產縮減的事。

tell 告訴…

tell 後面接受詞即收聽的人。注意：不能在收聽人前加介系詞，「tell 人 that 子句 / tell 人 about 內容：給…說…」。

We had to **tell** the client we would be unable to meet the deadline.
我們應該告訴顧客我們將不能在期限內做出來。

say 說

say 後面接受詞即收聽的人，而且收聽人前必須加to，「say（to 人）that 子句：（跟…）說…」。

The secretary **said** to Mr. Wills that the meeting had been postponed.
秘書跟Wills先生說會議延期了。

express 表達（感情、思想）

express 後面接表示感情或思想的名詞做受詞，「Express + 名詞：表達…」。

The buyer has **expressed** interest in purchasing the unused lot.
買家表示對購買這塊未被使用的地感興趣。

Part V

01 The contract stipulates that tenants must ------- the landlord of any major structural changes they wish to make to their apartment.

(A) forward
(B) announce
(C) notify
(D) arrange

02 In line with company policy, all new employees must first ------- a safety briefing before attempting to operate factory machinery.

(A) participate
(B) register
(C) attend
(D) go

03 Any agreements that have ------- are, without exception, placed in the company archives.

(A) invalidated
(B) expired
(C) violated
(D) submitted

04 A supervisor is expected to ------- a close relationship between his subordinates and himself.

(A) enlarge
(B) gain
(C) foster
(D) arise

05 I will leave a number with my assistant in case anyone needs to ------- me while I'm away on business.

(A) convey
(B) conform
(C) connect
(D) contact

06 In accordance with manufacturing policy, it must be printed on the label that this fabric will ------- if put into a drying machine.

(A) reduce
(B) shrink
(C) dwindle
(D) diminish

07 The Bank of Rhode Island has established a special program to ------- funds at low interest to those who develop local business initiatives.

(A) lease
(B) lend
(C) borrow
(D) rent

正確答案 **P111**

Questions 08-11 refer to the following information

Top Researcher to Speak on Solar Power

At the National Conference on Renewable Energy in Atlanta next month, Sunbeam Resources' top researcher, Dr. Robert Flack, will ------- about recent technological developments in solar power.

08 (A) say
     (B) speak
     (C) tell
     (D) discuss

To provide the most up-to-date information to consumers, he has ------- his essential research data

09 (A) minimized
     (B) condensed
     (C) contracted
     (D) decreased

into a two-hour presentation, explaining how solar energy can help preserve the global environment, and why people should convert to it. Dr. Flack will convey these ------- findings through charts and

10 (A) enveloping
     (B) disturbing
     (C) encouraging
     (D) approving

diagrams, illustrating solar power's efficiency and competitiveness. He will also explain how it has evolved into the most viable ------- to hydroelectric or nuclear energy, and how it can create a self-

11 (A) alternative
     (B) difference
     (C) equivalent
     (D) distinction

sustaining source of power. The conference will take place at the Sunseeker Hotel on Saturday November 17th. Online registrations are being accepted at www.ncre.org until the 15th.

Chapter 12

意義相近的名詞

不能區分 Scent 和 Odor

艾爾·帕西諾主演的影片《Scent of a Woman（女人香）》中，題目中的 Scent 是指「香氣」，表示帶有香氣的味道。相反，表示「氣味」的 odor 則包含各種味道的氣味，因此如果片名是《Odor of a Woman（女人的氣味）》，就會減少很多浪漫的氣氛。在此章節中，比較很多意義相近的名詞，請仔細體閱讀例題並努力記憶。

百發百中 出題類型與戰略

◉ 選項中名詞的意義非常相近，因此只有瞭解它們在用法上的差異，才能選擇正確的答案。

例題 1

One of the ------- of the campaign is to let the elderly know of various services available to them at community centers.

(A) aims　(B) beliefs　(C) reasons　(D) foundations

解釋　表面上看，選項中的四個單字都能做答案，但與句意相符且用法正確的單字只能有一個。要構成「活動的目的」之意，因此（A）aim（目的）是正確答案，（aim of …的目的）。（C）中的 reason 是「原因」的意思，選擇 reason 就要把空白處之後的 of 改成 for，（reason for …的原因）。（D）中的 foundation 是「基礎」的意思，（foundation of economic growth 經濟成長的基礎），以上三者都不符合題意，所以不正確。

翻譯　活動的目的之一是讓老人們知道社區中心有很多服務可供他們利用。

the elderly 年長者

答案　(A)

例題 2

Now into her second year as Mayor of Detroit, Francine Menendez outlined pending improvements to the city's infrastructure. First on her list is the urban ------- of the Lakeside

(A) refreshment　　(B) progress
(C) renewal　　　　(D) structure

Precinct, which includes the conversion of an abandoned dock area into recreational parklands, and a two-mile long pedestrian boardwalk with cafes and restaurants.

解釋　（A）、（C）都有「使變新」之意，因此很難做出選擇。但通過句意可知，正確答案應該是表示（更新，再開發）的（C）renewal，（urban renewal：城市再開發）。（A）refreshment 表示「恢復精神」之意，（B）progress 表示「進步」之意，（D）structure 表示「構造」之意，都不符合題意，所以不正確。

翻譯　Francine Menendez 在擔任底特律市長的第二年裡，對即將進行的公共建設改善做了概略的敘述。在她表定的第一項就是：對 Lakeside 區域進行再開發，此項計畫包括將廢棄的碼頭改建成含有休閒公園，和有咖啡廳和飯店的兩英里長散步道。

outline[ˋaʊtˏlaɪn] 概述 / pending[ˋpɛndɪŋ] 即將發生的，未決定的 / infrastructure[ˋɪnfrəˏstrʌktʃɚ] 公共建設（交通、管道、電等方面的設施）
precinct[ˋprisɪŋkt] 區域 / conversion[kənˋvɝʃən] 改變，轉變 / abandoned[əˋbændənd] 廢棄的 / dock[dɑk] 碼頭
parkland[ˋpɑrkˏlænd] 公園用地，公園休閒用地 / pedestrian[pəˋdɛstrɪən] 徒步的，步行的

答案　(C)

❶ access : approach

access　進入權，通路

有「進入權，通路」兩個意思，是不可數名詞，「have access to 對⋯有進入權，通往⋯的路」。

Members have unlimited **access** to the magazine's online archives.
會員們對雜誌的線上資料擁有毫無限制的登入瀏覽權。

The path behind the house has direct **access** to a hidden garden.
房屋後面的小路可以直接通往隱蔽的花園。

approach　（學問等方面的）接近法，出入口

表示「（學問等方面的）步驟方法」，也含有和access一樣的「出入口」之意，但approach是可數名詞，要與冠詞an一起使用。

The software developer has a new **approach** to business software.
軟體開發者對於商務軟體有新的處理方法。

The narrow alley is a little-used **approach** to the office building.
那條窄路是一條不常使用通往大廈的路。

❷ area : site

area　區域

There is only one caterer in the **area** that offers kosher food.
在那個地區，能夠提供猶太式食物的活動食品供應商只有一名。

site　（建築用）地址

The **site** for the memorial was changed several times due to a lack of support.
建造紀念館的位址由於資金不足而數度變更。

❸ brochure : catalog

brochure　小冊子

表示用照片等用於介紹商品或服務的「小冊子」，「travel brochure 旅行指導小冊」。

Refer to the enclosed **brochure** when selecting a suite for the duration of your stay.
在停留期間如果想選擇一個房間休息，可以參考隨信附上的小冊子。

catalog　（商品的）目錄，（圖書館）的圖書目錄

表示購買物品時可供參考的商品「目錄」，博物館或圖書館的物品目錄。

The admission ticket included a **catalog** of all the works shown in the exhibition.
入場門票裡包含了將在展示會展示的物品目錄。

❹ choice : option : preference

choice 選擇

「物主代名詞+choice of +名詞：…選擇的…」

The restaurant gives you a **choice** of appetizers when you order a main.
你點了主菜後，這家餐廳會讓你選擇開胃菜。

option 選擇權

Subscribers have the **option** of canceling their subscriptions at any time.
訂閱者有隨時取消訂閱的選擇權。

preference 偏愛

「preference for 對…的偏愛」

The new restaurant caters to diners with a **preference** for Italian food.
新的餐廳可以滿足偏愛義大利食品的用餐者的要求。

❺ copy : count

copy 一部，一冊（書等）

表示書、檔等的單位，「a copy of the report 一份報告」。

The secretary neglected to give the manager a **copy** of the supervisor's report.
秘書忘了把上司的報告交給經理。

count （數數時的）次數

用於通過數數來記時間，「for a count of ten 數10個數的時間」。

The exercise routine requires you to hold the position for a **count** of ten.
那個練習普通方式要求你一直保持那個姿勢從一數到十。

❻ description : information

description （產品等的）說明書，解釋

表示局部的說明或解釋，此時為可數名詞，「a description of 對…的說明」。

For a more detailed **description** of the courses, please see our website.
關於這些課程更詳細的說明，請參考我們的網站。

information 情報，訊息

是不可數名詞，因此不能與不定冠詞a一起使用，「information about / on 對…的情報」。

For more **information** about this promotion, please call this number.
想知道關於這次促銷活動的更多情報，請打這支電話。

❼ division : category : faction

division （公司的）部門

The corporation has considered closing the unprofitable automobile **division**.
公司考慮關閉利潤不佳的汽車部門。

category 主題，有共通性的單元

The poetry in the book was divided into several **categories**.
書中的詩集分別收錄在幾個主題內。

faction 小集團，組織內部持有不同意見的團體

The presidential candidate's goal was to unite the **factions** within his political party.
這位總統候選人的目標是整合他的政黨內的所有派別。

❽ fare : fee

fare 交通費用

「taxi fare 計程車費」

Can you estimate the cab **fare** from 5th Avenue to 42nd Street?
你能估計一下從第5路到42街需要多少計程車費嗎？

fee 各種手續費，小費

「an admission fee 入場費」

The admission **fee** for children under eight years of age is half price.
八歲以下兒童的票價為半價。

❾ fine : tariff : expense

fine 罰款

Drivers who park in no-parking areas are subject to a steep **fine**.
在禁止停車區域停車的司機，將必須支付非常高昂的罰鍰。

tariff 關稅

The government charges a **tariff** for luxury goods imported into the country.
政府對進口的奢侈品收取關稅。

expense 費用，支出

表示在任何事物或事情上支出的「費用」。

It's well worth the **expense** to invest in top-of-the-range equipment.
把費用投資在高級裝備上是非常值得的。

⑩ habit : convention

habit　個人習慣

The staff should make it a **habit** to submit reports on time.
職員要養成按時提交報告的習慣。

convention　社會習俗

It is still the **convention** in this country for men to pay for dinner on a date.
在約會時，男士付款仍舊是這個國家的習俗。

⑪ indication : show

indication　（暗示…的）標誌，徵兆

當有暗示性的想法或出現暗示性的狀況時使用，與that引導的子句或of一起使用。

There are clear **indications** that the economy is beginning to turn around.
有經濟復甦的明顯徵兆。

show　（感情、性能等）的表現

在主詞有意地表達感情時使用，「a show of affection　有好感的表現」。

The striking workers gathered at the company headquarters in a **show** of solidarity.
罷工的工人們為表示團結而聚集在了公司總部前。

⑫ majority : most

majority　大多數

用於「the majority of …的大多數」形式，注意：在majority前面要有定冠詞the。

The **majority** of credit card holders manage to keep up with payments.
大多數信用卡使用者都在設法還款。

most　（沒有冠詞）大多數

用於「most of the~ …的大多數」形式，注意：在most前面沒有冠詞。

Government bonds make up **most** of the national debt.
公債占了國家債務的大部分。

⑬ material : ingredient

material　物質，材料

A commonly used **material** in power transmission lines is aluminum.
一般在電力傳輸上採用的物質是鋁。

ingredient　（混合物的）成分，材料

表示混合物中的成分、食品的材料等，「the ingredients of a cake 蛋糕的材料」。

There are only five **ingredients** in this simple recipe for soup.
這道湯的配方簡單，只有五種食材而已。

⑭ **residence : venue**

┌─ residence　住處

Delegates are invited to visit the official **residence** of the Prime Minister.
代表們被邀請去參觀總理的官方住處。

└─ venue　（活動、會議等）召開的地點

表示活動或特定活動的開辦地點。

Event coordinators selected the Greyson Exhibition Hall as the official **venue**.
活動負責人把 Greyson 展示大廳定為官方會議地點。

⑮ **survey : research**

┌─ survey　抽樣調查

主要表示通過人們的問卷來獲得情報的「抽樣調查」，「conduct the survey　實施書面調查」。

The magazine conducted a **survey** to obtain reader feedback.
這個雜誌實施了一個抽樣調查以得到讀者的回應。

└─ research　研究，學術調查

努力地將特定的事實調查出來，具有「研究」的意義

The latest advertising strategy took into account the most recent market **research** findings.
最新的廣告戰略是將最近的市場調查結果考慮進去的。

⑯ **tour : trip**

┌─ tour　觀摩，（短途）旅行

表示「觀摩」工廠、設施或表示「短程旅行」，「give A a tour of B：使 A 觀摩 B」。

New employees will be given a **tour** of the company offices this afternoon.
新進的員工會在今天下午參觀公司辦公室。

└─ trip　出差，郊遊，（比較短的）旅行

The meeting was called to discuss the results of Ms. Black's business **trip**.
為討論 Black 女士的出差結果而召開了會議。

⑰ **value : worth**

┌─ value　（物品的）價格

表示與物品價值相當的價格

Store credit will be issued on returned items for the **value** of the purchase.
商店的信譽會因可以同等價格收回所賣的物品而為人所知。

└─ worth　值（多少），（物品的）價格

除了表示物品的價格之外，還有「值多少…」的意思，要注意用於「價格＋ worth of ＋物品：價值…的物品」形式。

A thousand dollars **worth** of merchandise was stolen from the gift shop.
那家禮品店被偷了價值一千美元的貨物。

Part V

01 A survey conducted by a research center revealed that the ------- of online shoppers are educated and have an annual household income of $50,000.

(A) majority
(B) summary
(C) addition
(D) most

02 Mr. Powell, the new researcher, has requested ------- to the company's archives to retrieve the information he needs for a feasibility study.

(A) entrance
(B) pass
(C) access
(D) approach

03 To prevent loss of information, staff members make it a ------- to make copies of all important documents.

(A) tradition
(B) hobby
(C) habit
(D) convention

04 A more detailed ------- of our new office machines is available in our product catalog.

(A) confirmation
(B) description
(C) inquiries
(D) information

05 The driver of the blue sedan received a hefty ------- for deliberately driving through a red light.

(A) fee
(B) fine
(C) damage
(D) dismissal

06 The owner purchased ten thousand dollars' ------- of party favors for the grand opening of his posh new restaurant.

(A) much
(B) value
(C) cost
(D) worth

07 Recent market trends are a good ------- that this will be an ideal year for investments in all sectors of the market.

(A) record
(B) show
(C) indication
(D) specification

正確答案 P113

Part VI

Questions 08-11 refer to the following letter.

Al Tapp
52 Southern Avenue
Great Falls, Montana 86503

Dear Mr. Tapp,

I am writing to inform you that I have been having problems with ------- plumbing in my apartment.

08 (A) underlying
(B) untrue
(C) deliberate
(D) defective

On Wednesday night I had a burst pipe in my kitchen and had to call in a plumber, according to whom the original system was not ------- installed. As a result, poor drainage over a long period led

09 (A) properly
(B) urgently
(C) exclusively
(D) valuably

to the pipes gradually clogging up until the increasing pressure caused them to burst.
Luckily there was no serious damage from the floodwater, although extensive repairs had to be made to the plumbing under the sink, replacing the old plastic pipes with new ones. Due to the urgent nature of the work, I had to pay for it out of my own pocket at considerable -------. The total came to

10 (A) fare
(B) tariff
(C) expense
(D) quantity

$785, with $365 for ------- and $420 for labor, as per the enclosed invoices. I'd appreciate it if I

11 (A) ingredients
(B) materials
(C) patterns
(D) stationery

could be reimbursed as soon as possible for the full repair amount.

Sincerely,

Polly Fawcet

Chapter 13

意義相近的形容詞、副詞

tightly 和 solidly 有什麼不同？

「把瓶子蓋緊」用英語表示為 Keep the bottle tightly clsed。熟記例句就會很容易理解「在緊緊蓋住某種東西的時候用 tightly」，但如果只知道中文的意思，在看到選項中的「solidly（堅固地）」時就會分不清該選哪個。事實上 solidly 是在表示建築物建造得很堅固時使用，因此，只有牢記例句才能成為最後的贏家！

百發百中 出題類型與戰略

◉ 選項中的形容詞、副詞意義非常相近，因此只有瞭解它們在用法上的差異，才能選擇正確的答案。

例題 1

It is clearly stated in the airline's policy that ------ luggage is in no way the responsibility of the company.

(A) wounded　(B) damaged　(C) impaired　(D) injured

解釋　表面上看，四個選項意思都很接近，但實際用法是不同的。像 luggage（行李）這樣的事物受到損壞時要用（B）damaged（（事物）受損）。而（A）wounded 表示「（人被武器等擊中而）受傷」(the wounded soldier　負傷的士兵)，（C）impaired 表示「（人、事物的機能）受損的」(the hearing impaired　聽力有障礙者)，（D）injured 表示「（人因事故等）受傷」(the injured man　受傷的人)。所以要選擇意義和用法相符的（B）。

翻譯　航空公司的規定裡明確表示，行李受損不是航空公司的責任。

答案　(B)

例題 2

Washington D.C. tourist transit buses regularly depart from the East Side Bus Depot for major monuments, museums, and art galleries. The bus for the Jefferson Memorial leaves hourly from 8:00 A.M., and the one for the Smithsonian Institution shortly -------, from 8:10 A.M.

(A) later　　　　(B) already
(C) suddenly　　(D) thereafter

解釋　此題選項中出現了像 later（過後）、thereafter（隨後）這樣的只記住中文意思就很容易混淆的副詞。要構成「Jefferson 紀念館方向的公車從 8 點開始，每隔 1 小時發一次車，而 Smithsonian 博物館方向的公車在隨後的 8:10 分開始發車」之意，因此空白處應填（D）thereafter（隨後）(shortly thereafter　在那之後馬上)。（A）later 強調的是「之後」(five months later　5 個月之後)，語意不恰當。

翻譯　華盛頓的觀光車從 East Side 公車站出發，向主要的紀念館、博物館還有美術館定時發車。Jefferson 紀念館方向的公車從 8 點開始，每隔 1 小時發一班車，而 Smithsonian 博物館方向的公車會在隨後的 8:10 分開始發車。

transit [ˋtrænsɪt] 運送，旅客 / regularly [ˋrɛgjələˑlɪ] 定期的 / depart [dɪˋpɑrt] 出發 / depot [ˋdipo] 停車場

答案　(D)

▶ 形容詞

❶ attached : connected

┌ attached　附加的

用於文書或檔案帶有附加的情況下使用，「attached file　附加檔」。

The **attached** schedule may be subject to last-minute changes.
附加的日程表可能會受到最後變更的影響。

└ connected　連接的

相互對等的兩個東西在意義關係上或在物理上有了聯繫時使用。

The technician said that all the computers in the room are **connected**.
技術員說辦公室的所有電腦都已連接上了。

❷ early : previous

┌ early　在時間上表示「早的」

意思是在時間上比普通的時候要早，「early retirement　提早退休」。

The company offers **early** retirement incentives.
公司提供提早退休的獎勵。

└ previous　在時間上表示「以前的」

表示在以前發生的事情或以前的時間。

Information from the **previous** events is available on the following pages.
過去的活動資料可以在以下的頁面看到。

❸ extensive : spacious

┌ extensive　（建築、知識、品目之類）較廣範圍的，概括性的

表示建築等座落在較寬廣的範圍裡。也用於知識或物品清單概括性地包含了很多種類的情況。

We guarantee the most **extensive** selection of quality wines in the city.
我們保證提供這座城市裡最多品項的優質葡萄酒。

└ spacious　（場地）寬廣的

與roomy（寬廣的）意思相同。

The company provides each executive with a **spacious** office that overlooks the harbor.
那家公司給各總經理提供了可以看到港口的寬敞辦公室。

❹ likely : possible

likely 像要做⋯，有可能⋯的

表示某種事情發生的可能性較高，「be likely to+動詞原形：像要做⋯」。

The report is **likely** to be released within the next week.
那份報告似乎會在下週之內發表。

possible 可能的，可實行的

在表示有實現可能的事時使用，「it is possible to+動詞原形：做⋯是有可能的」。

It is **possible** to protect sensitive information by installing the latest security software.
安裝最新的防護軟體，可以保護那些機密情報。

❺ marginal : petty

marginal （量）少的

表示在數量上少，與small有相同的意思，「marginal interest 關心較少」。

The client has shown **marginal** interest in investing in the new product line.
顧客對於新產品系列的投資表現出很小的興趣。

petty （金額）少的，（人）器量小的

表示少的意思時，主要是用於錢少，「petty cash 小錢，零用金」、「a petty person 一個器量小的人」。

The secretary takes money out of the **petty** cash box for deliveries.
秘書從零用金箱裡拿出錢來支付運送費用。

❻ outstanding : evident

outstanding 優秀的，顯著的，（負債等的）未付的

表示事物或人顯著、優秀。此外也表示負債等未付，「outstanding account 未付清的帳目」。

The marketing plan was so **outstanding** that it was immediately approved.
這個市場計畫非常優秀，因此立即被採用了。

evident 明顯的

表示事實等很明顯。

The participants reacted to the news with **evident** disappointment.
參加者對那個消息表示了明顯的不滿情緒。

❼ prevalent : leading

prevalent 普遍的，流行的，廣為傳播的

表示現象等廣為傳播、流行，與common意思相同。

Lawsuits have become more **prevalent** in today's society.
法律訴訟在現今社會普遍增多。

leading 傑出的，優秀的

表示人或事物在一定領域裡很傑出。

a **leading** figure in economic circles
在經濟領域非常傑出的人物。

❽ recent : modern : new

— recent 最近的

用來表示最近的事件或時間，也表示事物是最新的，「recent event 最近的事件」、「recent address 最新的住址」。

The **recent** promotion of Mr. Cummings was completely unexpected.
Cummings先生最近的升職完全出乎預料之外。

— modern 近代的，現代的

表示現在存在的，有別於過去的。

The staff was more than happy to move into the **modern** headquarters.
搬到現代化的本部使職員們都感到非常高興。

— new 新的

表示新做出來的或新形成的。

The CEO urged his copywriters to come up with **new** advertising ideas.
CEO催促他的廣告文案作家做出新的廣告創意。

❾ reserved : preserved

— reserved 預約的

常用於預約座位等情況。

Call the travel agent to confirm or change a **reserved** seat.
請打電話給旅行社確認或改變預約的位子。

— preserved 被保存的

表示狀態等沒有變化地被保存。

The area contains some excellently **preserved** examples of Gothic architecture.
那個地區有幾座保存非常良好的哥德式建築。

❿ unoccupied : discarded

— unoccupied （建築物裡）沒有人居住的

表示沒人居住的建築物，與empty有相同之意。

Although the building has been renovated, it continues to remain **unoccupied**.
雖然建築被重新整修過了，但還是一直沒有人住。

— discarded （事物）被丟棄的

表示被丟棄而不被使用。

The **discarded** programs littered the floor of the main hall after the event.
在活動結束後被丟棄的節目表散落在中央大廳的地板上。

▶ 副詞

⑪ away : far

── away 遠，在距離很遠的地方

在 away 前可以用距離單位，「100 miles away from 距離…100 英里遠」。

The City Hall is located one kilometer **away** from the Metro Station.
市政大廳在離地下鐵車站一公里遠的地方。

── far （距離、空間）遠

在 far 之前不能使用距離單位，因此 be located 10 miles far from the airport 是錯誤的用法。

The company's factory is located **far** from the headquarters.
那家公司的工廠離本部很遠。

⑫ continually : lastingly

── continually 繼續地，一再地

用來表現一件事情從發生到停止、重新發生、停止…如此反覆。

The new manager is **continually** giving orders to the staff.
新的總經理一再地給職員們下達指令。

── lastingly 持續地

表示效果等長時間不斷地持續。

Research is being conducted to find a **lastingly** effective treatment for the disease.
尋找治療此疾病有效方法的研究正持續進行著。

⑬ dramatically : numerously

── dramatically 急劇地，戲劇性地

表示量的變化。常與 increase, climb, grow 這樣表示減少、增加的動詞一起使用。

Sales are expected to increase **dramatically** once prices go down.
據預測，一旦價格下降，銷售量就會急劇地上升。

── numerously 多數地，無數地

表示數量眾多。

The jazz concert is expected to be **numerously** attended.
這場爵士音樂會預計將有許多人參加。

⑭ primarily : firstly

primarily 主要地，根本上地

表示根本、主要的目的和内容，與 chiefly 意義相近。

The new laptop computers are **primarily** marketed for business users.
新型的筆記型電腦主要市場對象為商業用戶。

firstly 首先，第一

在列舉多個事件時使用，與 in the first place 意義相同。

Firstly, Mr. Moore will give a few remarks before we proceed with the agenda.
首先，在我們進行議程之前，Moore 先生會給我們講幾句話。

⑮ prominently : markedly

prominently （事物）顯著地，引人注目地

用於某些事情引人注目。

Exit signs must be **prominently** placed on all floors.
出口標誌必須要顯著地設置在所有的樓層。

markedly （變化或差異）顯著地，突出地

在表示發生顯著變化或差異時使用，「change prominently 顯著地變化」、「be markedly different 有顯著地差距」。

Recent consumer trends are **markedly** different from those of the previous generation.
當今消費者的消費傾向與以前的年代有顯著的差別。

⑯ strongly : stringently

strongly 強烈地

表示程度強烈。

The foreman **strongly** recommends that the structure's flooring be removed.
領班強烈地建議建築物的底板要搬走。

stringently 嚴格地

用於表示法律或規則被嚴格執行。

Because of the accident, safety rules will likely be enforced more **stringently**.
因為這場意外，安全規定將有可能被更嚴格地執行。

HACKERS TEST

Part V

01 Because the students seemed to show only a ------- interest in the new course that was offered this semester, university officials decided to drop the course.

(A) rational
(B) petty
(C) intentional
(D) marginal

02 The tenth floor office was vacated some two years ago and has remained ------- ever since.

(A) unoccupied
(B) concealed
(C) suppressed
(D) discarded

03 Trendy coffee shops are replacing many of the fast-food spots that were once so ------- in this town.

(A) leading
(B) prevalent
(C) habitual
(D) foremost

04 The security system allows almost every part of the building to be ------- monitored by personnel at a surveillance center.

(A) timelessly
(B) lastingly
(C) continually
(D) movingly

05 Due to an unexpected illness, the executive officer was forced to submit a letter announcing his ------- retirement.

(A) mature
(B) early
(C) ready
(D) previous

06 To prevent the cream from becoming discolored, keep the jar ------- closed and store it away from sunlight.

(A) tightly
(B) hardly
(C) solidly
(D) cleanly

07 A ------- downturn in the company's financial situation forced management to contemplate carrying out mass employee layoffs.

(A) stable
(B) modern
(C) recent
(D) casual

正確答案 P114

Part VI

Questions 08-11 refer to the following memo.

FROM: Human Resources
TO: All Staff
SUBJECT: Revisions to Health Care Scheme

The Human Resources Department is pleased to advise that in an ------- to better accommodate all

08 (A) objection
(B) effort
(C) opinion
(D) influence

employees' medical welfare needs, a new health care scheme has been devised, taking effect from August 1st.

After ------- and thorough research, we have put together our most comprehensive package yet,

09 (A) spacious
(B) distracted
(C) extensive
(D) occasional

which includes optical and dental care benefits, as well as additional regular health services. For more information, please consult the ------- analysis of the old and new systems. It shows that by

10 (A) attached
(B) joined
(C) connected
(D) matched

means of a combination of decreased prescription fees, more affordable premiums, and increased mental health benefits, employees will be significantly better off under the new plan.

Any suggestions or objections should be sent to Zoe Peabody in HR within the next two weeks, who will then pass them on to senior management for consideration. If there are any questions regarding this matter, do not ------- to contact the Human Resources Department .

11 (A) separate
(B) hesitate
(C) necessitate
(D) alternate

NEW TOEIC新多益題庫大全

☑ 首創1！新多益考試深度分析特別版

☑ 首創2！「英、澳、美、加」四國口音，完全比照新多益考題錄製方式

☑ 親身體驗！韓國新多益大師金大均參加考試經驗談

☑ 完全命中！韓國讀者公認最精確的模擬考題

☑ 高分保證！分析題目陷阱，短時間內掌握新多益解題法

☑ 一看就懂詳解！制伏多益快又有效

☑ 含閱讀4小時mp3！相當於4片CD，全書可用聽的隨時隨地準備

☑ 特殊雙書設計！讀者使用更靈活

R^EA D I_NG

1 多益閱讀測驗的特徵

- 多益閱讀測驗中的題目來自與日常生活或商業活動密切相關的短文

多益閱讀測驗所要測試的是考生在日常生活或商業活動中,正確使用英語的能力。閱讀短文也是由商業活動中實際使用的文章所組成的。因此,對職場生活不太瞭解的人,也要掌握基本商業活動中用到的信件、公告、介紹等。

- 多益閱讀測驗所要測試的是基本閱讀能力

多益閱讀測驗不僅測試考生在實務中對英語的實際運用能力,也像其他英語考試一樣,測驗正確理解短文並解答問題的基本閱讀測驗能力。因此,平時透過廣泛地閱讀英語,提高閱讀理解能力是非常重要的。

2 短文類型比例

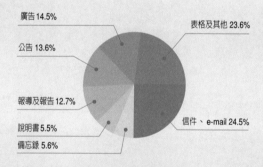

廣告 14.5%
公告 13.6%
報導及報告 12.7%
說明書 5.5%
備忘錄 5.6%
表格及其他 23.6%
信件、e-mail 24.5%

〔各類型短文出題比例〕

3 多益閱讀測驗核心技巧

- 必須先閱讀在短文之前出現介紹短文的句子

各閱讀短文,在開始之前都有「Questions 題號 refer to the following 短文種類」這種形式的句子,用來介紹短文的類型。如果事先知道短文的類型,閱讀短文就會更有效率。在本書中,對經常出現的問題類型進行了分類系統的分析,使讀者能夠自然地熟悉問題的類型。

- 初級或中等程度的學習者要先看問題選項再看短文，而高等程度的學習者要先閱讀短文再解題。

對於初級或中等程度的學習者來說，在短時間內快速閱讀短文並理解短文的意思並不容易。因此先閱讀題目，再於閱讀短文時尋找與題目相關的內容，就能節省時間，並且能夠較容易地選出正確答案。相反，如果是單字量很大的學習者，就應該先快速地閱讀短文，了解大致的內容，然後閱讀題目，回到短文中的相關段落重新重點閱讀，找出答案。

- 學會區分有相同意義，但用不同形式表現的語句（Paraphrasing）。

不使用原本的敘述，而用同義詞或可代替詞來表示相同意思的表現形式叫做Paraphrasing。在多益閱讀測驗中，短文中出現的句子不會直接呈現在選項中，而是換成與它意思相近的其他表現形式，以此來測試應試者的理解能力。因此要透過練習熟記表示同一種意思的多種表現形式。

[例題] **Share prices increased.** 股價上升了。
　　　➡ **The value of the stocks went up.** 股票價格上升了。

---

4 NEW TOEIC 趨勢及戰略

- 題目數量增加

閱讀測驗的題目由以前的40題增加到了48題。和以前相較之下，閱讀量增加了，因此答題時間更容易不夠用。平時要閱讀多種類型的文章，通過不斷的練習加快閱讀速度。

- 新增雙篇文章（Double Passage）類型的題型。

「雙篇文章」類型的題型是閱讀完兩篇相關的短文後，解答5道題目的題型。由於短文的長度並不太短，會帶來一定的負擔，但各短文和問題的類型和「單短文（Single Passage）」相同，因此運用以前的解題策略就可以解決。但是偶爾也會出現需貫通兩篇短文來解答的問題，要注意加強練習這種類型的題型。

- 新增找同義字的問題

新增加了找同義字的題目，這種題目要求理解單字在短文中用於何種意義，然後找出「同義字」。建議在學習單字時，參考英英辭典或同義字辭典，並在例句中學習同義字。

Section 1
各類型問題攻略

Chapter 1

找主題的問題

找主題的問題，是指詢問主題或目的的問題。多益考試裡出現的短文，是以信件、公告等傳遞消息為主的應用文。文章的主旨會在文章開頭出現，而詳細內容則在後面。因此，找主題的問題在短文的前面就可以找到答案。找主題的問題主要出現在信件、公告、報導、備忘錄等體裁的文章中。

百發百中 出題類型與戰略

⊙ 頻繁出現的問題類型

文章的目的	What is the purpose of this notice?
文章的主題	What is the main topic of this article?
	What is the main idea of this report?
	What is this letter about?
寫文章的理由	Why was this memo written?

⊙ 核心戰略

要找出文章中的主題句。

主題句一般在短文的前面。

偶爾也會有主題句在短文的中間部分或後半部分，或者隱藏在整篇文章中的短文。這種情況，則要從頭開始閱讀短文，然後概括短文的主題。

例題 1

> In a press conference, Armor Wear announced that it had selected Benjamin Harper as its new spokesperson. Armor Wear's chief executive officer said that Harper was chosen mainly because of his excellent reputation as a go-between for businesses and the general population. He is well-known for his superior communication skills, as well as for being fluent in Japanese, Russian, and French. Both Armor Wear and Mr. Harper are excited about the deal.

主題

詳細內容

Q : What is the purpose of this article?　　**A : To announce a hiring decision**

→在短文的前面提到了文章的主題。此句是 "In a press conference, Armor Wear announced that it had selected Benjamin Harper as its new spokesperson."

例題 2

> I am the personal assistant to Mr. Gregory Murphy who will be staying at your establishment next week. According to the itinerary, Mr. Murphy will be arriving at Boston International on February 2nd, at 5 p.m. Your shuttle van is to pick him up and bring him back to the airport on February 7th. He will be staying at your hotel from the 2nd to the 7th, which is a total of six nights, at the rate of $329.99 per night. If there are any discrepancies between the information contained in this letter and your records, please contact me immediately by either phone or e-mail.

Q : Why was this letter written?　　**A : To confirm hotel arrangements**

→短文中沒有主旨句，因此要透過閱讀整篇短文來概括文章的主題。從前面開始閱讀，就可以從確定住宿日期和價格看出，這篇短文是為預定旅館的各種事項而寫的信件。

短文解釋 P116

HACKERS PRACTICE ● ● ● ● ● ● ● ● ● ● ● ● ●

⊙「找主題的問題」練習
閱讀短文並回答問題

01

Yesterday our office received the package of book covers you sent on November 3ʳᵈ. The order came to us complete and earlier than expected. After reviewing the designs, one of our staff will contact your office to let you know of our choice.

Q. What is the main purpose of this letter?

(A) To select the appropriate cover design
(B) To confirm the receipt of a shipment
(C) To place an order for book covers

02

Anyone who has ever been to Greece knows that if there is one thing you can always find there, it is sun. And now the country's Department of Natural Resources is suggesting the nation turn almost entirely to solar power to avoid the economic pitfalls of high oil prices. Recent rises in costs of barrels of crude oil have left many less developed nations in a state of energy crisis. While some countries lack the natural energy sources to make up for the loss, Greece is fortunate to be able to utilize its almost year-round solar power.

Q. What is the purpose of this article?

(A) To explain Greece's response to the energy crisis
(B) To explore energy options for poor nations
(C) To inform about the benefits of solar energy

03

Recently I saw your advertisement in the paper for a receptionist at your main office. I would like some more information regarding the opportunity to work for your company. Please send any pertinent information to the address at the top of this letter.

Q. Why was this letter written?

(A) To advertise a job opening
(B) To inquire about employment
(C) To apply for the position

04

Please be aware that the clean-up we announced last week will take place on the evening of May 1st for Building A. All interior and exterior glass as well as floors, walls and carpets will be cleaned with toxic chemical agents. Individuals should prepare by putting all their materials into the drawers of their desks and bringing home any important documents or valuable personal items. Cleaning personnel are only allowed to move office furniture and appliances. Rest assured that the office will be de-fumigated before anyone is permitted back into the building.

Q. What is the purpose of this memo?

(A) To announce the replacement of old carpets
(B) To remind occupants of moving in procedures
(C) To ask for cooperation regarding the cleaning

⊙ Paraphrasing 練習

請選擇與短文內容一致的句子。

05

> Melrose Bank recently discovered that some clients who signed up for our special banking service have been paying an additional ATM fee. The second ATM fee will be reimbursed to our clients' accounts next week.

(A) Customers of the bank will no longer pay any ATM fees.

(B) The bank will pay clients through their bank accounts.

06

> Protect-It zipper-lock plastic bags are effective at protecting anything from the elements. Ordinary plastic bags cannot keep water out, but Protect-It bags have a patented closure and material design that prevents moisture from entering the bag.

(A) Protect-It bags can hold large amounts of water.

(B) Protect-It bags are made of weather resistant material.

07

> Capital Alliance, Inc. is looking for a degreed accountant or a CPA. The ideal candidate should have three to five years auditing and accounting experience.

(A) Knowledge of the newest accounting principles is required.

(B) A university diploma is a requirement for the job.

08

> The top two car companies are planning to trim production as the increasing cost of gasoline has caused a prolonged slump in sales of trucks and cars. Faced with an inventory pile-up, Ace Motors and Townsend Cars will be cutting production by fifteen percent over the next two quarters.

(A) Poor sales are causing top automobile manufacturers to cut production.

(B) Reduced production can offset increasing gas prices.

09

> To make your stay at the Paradise Beach Resort a pleasant one, please pay strict attention to our rules on cleanliness. Because it is costly and difficult to remove debris and spilled liquids, guests who leave their huts dirty will forfeit the $100 key deposit for use of a hut.

(A) Customers will have to put down a deposit in case of damage to the room.

(B) The deposit will not be refunded if the hut is not left clean.

10

> The Wells Community Center is seeking monetary donations to cover the cost of buying computers for children of low-income families in the Wells Community.

(A) Private money will be used to finance the purchase of computers.

(B) Donations of old computers are being requested.

11

> Cabot Systems in Hong Kong is in the process of acquiring US-based Flexpoint, a multimedia technology company for mobile phones. Cabot Systems wants to be the dominant supplier for the mobile industry by using Flexpoint's technologies.

(A) Two companies have signed an agreement to produce mobile phones.

(B) Cabot Systems is buying out Flexpoint to gain control of the market.

12

> After having a guest editor supervise *The Journal of Commerce* for November, soon-to-retire JOC editor Bill Conley is now accepting applications for the editorship of JOC. Mr. Conley said that he is having an active hand in selecting his own replacement.

(A) JOC's editor is seeking his successor.

(B) The guest editor will take over permanently.

正確答案 P116

Question 1 refers to the following notice.

To:	All Staff
From:	Chad Ballmer, Head Technician
Re:	Network Upgrade

We regret to inform that as of next week we will be performing network repairs at one of our facilities, which will consequently result in frequent interruptions to the online system. The network is experiencing difficulties after a system-wide breakdown that occurred yesterday around 2:34 PM. Unfortunately there is no other option but to service the entire network, which will inevitably cause temporary inconveniences. The servers themselves will remain up, but will experience loss of connectivity. This disconnection will occur at the beginning of the servicing and will last a little more than 2 hours total. The process will consist of two separate sessions, with each session lasting from 11pm to 1am. During repair, you may experience a slowdown in speed and up to 3 network outages varying in duration from 10 to 30 minutes. The first session is scheduled for Friday, January 14. Further notification for the second window will be sent at least 48 hours in advance. We would like to assure you that the problem will be completely resolved by the first week of February. We apologize for any inconveniences this may cause.

1. What is the purpose of this notice?

(A) To remind staff to turn off their computers
(B) To inform staff of a change in management
(C) To warn of upcoming system disruptions
(D) To respond to complaints of slow connectivity

Question 2 refers to the following schedule and e-mail.

Alternative Energy Conference Proceedings
18 August

9:00 - 10:30	Opening Ceremony and Keynote Speech George J. Soap, St. Lukes Business Association
10:30 - 1:00	Energy Generation for the Future: Our Needs and Options Kees Vanderhout, State Electric Company
1:00 - 2:00	Lunch
2:00 - 4:00	Environmental and Social Impact Assessment Assoc. Prof. Jonathan Lee, Queensland University
4:00 - 4:30	Afternoon Break
4:30 - 6:00	Decision-Making Session Rachel Wilde-Prosser, St. Lukes River Development Board

---

TO: Norman Salisbury, Water Resource Management Consulting Ltd.

FROM: George J. Soap, St. Lukes Business Association

SUBJECT: Energy Conference

Dear Norman:

Sorry you were not able to make it yesterday. Here is a brief overview of what you missed, along with my own thoughts on the matter. We heard that by the end of the decade, our demand for electricity will be about 3000 MW, but that we have a present generating capacity of 2400 MW. This means that with our current limitations, we face at a 20% shortfall in seven years. The least expensive solution for this problem would be constructing a 500 MW hydroelectric dam on the St. Lukes River, at a projected cost of $250 million.

Jonathan Lee, however, raised an interesting issue, noting that thousands of acres of forest habitat for wild animals and plants would be lost beneath the waters of the dam's reservoir. This convinced me that the environmental impact of a hydro dam does need to be taken into account. My recommendation therefore is that we consider other kinds of energy generation, especially wind power projects, before we make the decision to build a hydro dam.

Regards,
George J. Soap

---

2. What is the purpose of the e-mail?

(A) To report on plans to develop the forestry industry
(B) To ask a question about the environment
(C) To request technical details on a windfarm project
(D) To explain the contents of a conference

正確答案 P118

六個要素原則

此類型的題目是測驗學習者是否掌握了文章中有關何人、何時、何地、何事、為何、如何進行（5W1H）等方面細節的問題。解答這種類型題的重點是，在短文中迅速找出有關問題核心的線索。由於可以在只看一部分短文的情況下就作答，因此這些是可以快速解答的問題。此類型題的出題頻率占了 Part 7 的 60% 以上。

百發百中 出題類型與戰略

⊙ 頻繁出現的問題類型

什麼時候做？	When does the special discount apply?
誰在做？	Who should be contacted for registration?
在做什麼？	What accompanies the letter?
多久時間做一次？	How often will classes be held?

⊙ 核心戰略

1. 最好先大致閱讀一下短文，掌握文章內容之後再看題目。

2. 看完問題之後確定疑問詞和核心單字。

例）Who should be contacted for registration?

⇨ 疑問詞：who 核心單字：contact, registration

3. 藉由問題的核心單字或核心單字的變化形式在短文搜尋題目的解答。

大部分的表現狀況是會把短文中相當於題目解題線索的部分以變化過的核心單字形式呈現。

注意

Richensia has announced the closing of one of its largest apartment complexes. The building, which is currently located in the Bronx area of Manhattan, will be demolished next week. Spokespersons from Richensia say that the main contributing factor to the closedown has been low occupancy rates. Richensia is planning to replace the loss with a new complex closer to the downtown area, in a more economically stable environment. However, formal plans have yet to be discussed.

Q : Why did the apartments close down?
A : Inadequate number of tenants

問題所問的是 "why"，問題的核心單字是 "close down"。與問題內容相關的部分是短文中的 "contributing factor to the closedown has been low occupancy rates."（動詞中的 "close down" 在短文中以名詞 "the closedown" 表示），而 "low occupancy rates" 在答案中變成了 "Inadequate number of tenants"。

短文解釋 P119

HACKERS PRACTICE ● ● ● ● ● ● ● ● ● ● ● ● ● ● ● ●

⊙ 「六個要素原則」練習

閱讀短文並回答問題

01

> The Sun Times Daily gave its "Worst Corporation" award to Inrun Corporation for embezzling its employees of investments they made in the company's stock. Two other companies were runner-ups for the award. These were Auditing Systems, Inc. for concealing anomalies in audits it did for several firms and Country Talents for promoting no-talent singers.

Q. Which business defrauded its workers?

  (A) Auditing Systems, Inc.
  (B) Country Talents
  (C) Inrun Corporation

02

> We greatly regret the delay of product delivery. Our factory is currently experiencing labor shortages due to a number of recent strikes. Consequently, there are fewer employees to sort and send packages. Although I can't give an exact date, I can assure you that your package will arrive within two weeks. Please accept our sincere apology and thank you for your patience.

Q. What does the writer guarantee?

  (A) Product delivery within a specified time
  (B) High level of product quality
  (C) End of strikes by next week

03

> All rentals must be returned to the drop box by the due date on the top of this form. Even if the store is open, please use the deposit box for the convenience of the staff. Customers who return videos and DVDs after the deadline will have an additional fee charged to the credit card number listed below.

Q. For what would patrons be given an extra charge?

  (A) Bringing something back late
  (B) Returning a rental without the box
  (C) Damaging a DVD or video

Chapter 2 六個要素原則 | 361

請選擇與短文內容一致的句子。

04

> Staff evaluations are an important training tool that can help your staff stay on course and make adjustments for improvement. Regular one-on-one discussions should be conducted between the immediate supervisor and the staff being evaluated.

(A) Regular feedback improves the relationship between supervisor and subordinate.

(B) Assessment of employees' work encourages improvement in performance.

05

> To reduce the incidence of mold in your home, you need to keep moisture to the minimum. You can do this by keeping all rooms well-ventilated. Turn on your electric fan when you are cooking or when you notice the windows misting.

(A) To prevent mold, keep the air flowing in your home.

(B) To reduce moisture, keep an electric fan on at all times.

06

> The Watley Department Store is holding a sweepstakes for all brides-to-be. To be eligible, you must have made plans to get married between June 1, 2004 and May 31, 2005. Register at the Wedding Gown Section of the Women's Clothing Department.

(A) Entrants must have a definite wedding date to qualify for the sweepstakes.

(B) The Watley Department Store is having a sale on wedding gowns.

07

> Tree planting is being considered as an inexpensive means of reducing CO_2 in the atmosphere. Trees absorb CO_2, offsetting carbon emissions by fossil fuels. However, the degree to which trees can be used will depend on local policies and technology.

(A) Tree planting will reduce the amount of fossil fuels used.

(B) Cultivation of trees is a cost-effective way of lessening CO_2 emissions.

08

> Recommendation: Please supply a replacement unit for the customer mentioned at the top of this form, as the heater she purchased is clearly defective.

(A) The defective heater will be repaired at no cost.

(B) The customer should be sent a new product.

09

> To reduce the cost of delivering services, the Piedmont Corporation is changing its policy regarding outsourcing. The company has discovered that by accepting outsourcing proposals and hiring fewer staff, it can save on support services costs.

(A) Costs can be decreased by hiring an outside firm.

(B) Costs can be reduced by accepting recommendations.

10

> Tenants must report any problems with rodents and bugs. We have a contract with a pest control vendor who will examine your apartment unit and make recommendations. Tenants may book an appointment with our vendor at no charge.

(A) Tenants should hire the services of a pest control vendor.

(B) Tenants can schedule a time and date for inspection.

11

> Mark your calendars for Saturday, March 23rd, when a large benefit dinner will be held at the city's convention center. The event is sponsored by Branding Consultancy, a marketing company in Hollywood.

(A) A company based in Hollywood has supported Branding Consultancy.

(B) Branding Consultancy has funded and organized a gathering.

Questions 1-3 refer to the following list of events.

Greenhills Country Club

Our events for the month of April

Campfire Barbeque
Date and Time   2nd, 4th Wednesday of the month, 5:00 ~ 9:00 p.m
Open to   Members of the country club and their guests
Time Details   Refreshments: 5 p.m
                        Barbeque Dinner: 7 p.m

Special Lecture   "Think Like a Golf Pro" by John Turlington
Date and Time   April 8
Open to   Public

Exhibit   "History's Greatest Golfers" Exhibit and Lecture
                        - Dr. Ed Brubaker, Lecturer,
                        renowned sports history professor at Wesson University
Date and Time   April 10 ~ April 13, Whole day exhibit
Open to   Public
Time Details for Dinner Reservations on April 13
                        Cocktails: 5:30p.m
                        Dinner: 6:30p.m
                        Lecture by Dr. Ed Brubaker: 7:30p.m

Jazz Night   (Musicians to be determined)
Date and Time   Every Wednesday, 6:00 p.m ~ 1:00 a.m
Open to   Public

---

1. Which activity takes place every other week?

(A) Jazz Night
(B) "History's Greatest Golfers" Exhibit
(C) "Think Like a Golf Pro" Lecture
(D) Campfire Barbeque

2. What is the exhibition about?

(A) The origins of golf as a sport
(B) The premier golf players of all time
(C) How to be the best golfer
(D) Wesson University's sports program

3. Why isn't information given about the musicians for "Jazz Night"?

(A) There are no performers that night.
(B) It is a surprise event.
(C) The performers have yet to be decided.
(D) It is not public information.

Questions 4-5 refer to the following advertisement and e-mail.

ℋome Equipment

1035 Washburn Ave. South Denver, CO 55306-1035

To all our valued customers:

From now until Memorial Day we are offering a substantial discount on our easy-grip dirt vacuum cleaner. This cleaner is made of the highest quality recycled plastic and has been approved by the Federal Conservation Board. It boasts three different attachments for your domestic needs, including a three-foot tube for hard to reach areas of the household. In addition, this cleaner uses a reusable dirt holder to save on paper! This promotion is only valid until Memorial Day, so with only four weeks to go, act now! Recent studies have proven that our product is the leading cleaner in the market. It beats out the competition with a revolutionary easy-to-grip handle, making it a snap to tackle even the dirtiest of environments. For these reasons, we guarantee absolute satisfaction with your order. As a show of our confidence in the product, you can have a free two week trial period! Within that first month, you can send the product back if you're in any way not satisfied with your purchase. If the product malfunctions, we will replace your machine at no additional cost, with all related charges and expenses being billed to us. Don't waste another minute missing out on this fabulous offer!

TO: Customer Service Center, Home Equipment
FROM: Joseph Grumbler
SUBJECT: Faulty Vacuum Cleaner

I ordered a vacuum cleaner under the two-week trial period and have been using it for seven days. At first, the product seemed to work well, especially with specifications such as the reusable dirt holder, and user-friendly handle. Unfortunately, the plastic rim of the three-foot extension tube is defective, and seems to have been warped by the heat of the motor after only a few days. As a result, I've decided to return it. However, rather than exchanging it for a new vacuum cleaner, I would prefer to get my money back. Please let me know if this is possible, and I will make arrangements to send it in.

Regards,

Joseph Grumbler

4. How is this vacuum different from others?

   (A) It is comfortable to hold.
   (B) It has a long tube.
   (C) It uses recycled plastic.
   (D) It is refundable.

5. Which part of the product is faulty?

   (A) The vacuum cleaner's motor
   (B) The dirt holder
   (C) The easy-to-grip handle
   (D) The extension tube

正確答案 P120

Chapter 3

Not / True 問題

Not / True 問題是根據短文的內容在題目的 4 個選項中，哪一個選項是不符合 / 符合的。因此需要一一對照各選項和短文中的內容，需要較長的時間。解題時，首先要略讀短文，掌握文章的內容之後，找出與問題相關的部分，然後再一一對照來作答。

百發百中 出題類型與戰略

⊙ 頻繁出現的問題類型

[Not 問題]	不是…的是？	What is NOT a feature of the item?
	在文章中沒講到的是？	What is NOT stated in the article?
[True 問題]	對…正確的是？	What is true about the library cards?
	文章中提到的是？	What is stated in the article?

⊙ 核心戰略

在短文中找出與選項有關的部分，然後一一對照。

大部分的選項，在文章中會用另一種形式表現。

各選項中的線索分佈在整個短文的情況很多。

例題 1

Offering season tickets for this year's performances

If you are a theater lover thirsting for shows to keep you entertained throughout the year, then look no further than the Manchester Arts Center located in the Farthings suburb of London. Purchasing a season ticket ensures you admittance to any performance all year long, as well as guaranteeing priority seating in section B. As an added bonus, season ticket holders can bring one guest to every show for 50% off the normal ticket price.

Q : What is NOT mentioned as a benefit of season tickets?

(A) Favorable seating options　　**(B) Entry to all shows**
(C) First choice on all seats　　**(D) Reduced rates for friends**

→ 要先在文章中找出與 season ticket 相關的內容，然後與選項中的內容一一對照。（A）是短文中 "priority seating in section B" 的另一種表達方式，（B）是 admittance to any performance 的另一種表達方式，(D) 是 "bring one guest to every show for 50% off the normal ticket price" 的另一種表現形式。但是，（C）"priority seating in section B" 在文中並沒有與之對應的內容，因此答案為（C）。

例題 2

The Earphone Depot was founded in 1957 by James Clayton who was a disc jockey for Louisville, Kentucky's WPPI. He designed his first earphones in 1950 and has since been selling brand earphones as well as his own creations. The company is now being managed by his son Jeff, the designer of the C7e.

Q : What is true about the Earphone Depot?

(A) It was established in 1950.　　**(B) It is a subsidiary of WPPI.**
(C) It operates in Louisville.　　**(D) It is a family business.**

→ 要先在文中找出與 Earphone Depot 關聯的部分，然後與選項對照。（A）與文中的 The Earphone Depot was founded in 1957 矛盾，因此不正確。（B）中的 WPPI 和（C）Louisville 雖然在文章內有出現，但文中內容與選項中的內容不一致，也不正確。（D）與文中的 "The company is now being managed by his son Jeff" 內容上一致，因此正確答案為（D）。

短文解釋　P122

HACKERS PRACTICE ● ● ● ● ● ● ● ● ● ● ● ● ● ●

⊙ 「Not / True 問題」練習

閱讀短文並回答問題

01

> You are invited to attend this weekend's seminar on Aligning Project Management with Corporate Strategy. The aim of the seminar is to give you an in-depth analysis of the process of business strategy formation from a project management perspective. Today, a manager must take into account the expectations and interests of all parties that have a stake in the project outcome. Several keynote speakers will present on a variety of issues related to these corporate challenges.
>
> Topics of this seminar include:
>
> ⌐ The Changing Face of Business   ⌐ Implementation of Strategy   ⌐ Project Stakeholder Management
> ⌐ Project Prioritization   ⌐ Paradigm Shifts   ⌐ Effective Business Strategy

Q. What is NOT one of the topics to be discussed?

(A) How to balance investor needs
(B) How to actualize a plan
(C) How to market a project

02

> Ultra Perm Hair Dryer
>
> The brand new Ultra Perm Hair Dryer hit the stores yesterday for the first time. Its popularity is evident by record sales on only the first day. The dryer contains the following features:
>
> ⌐ Five settings according to hair length   ⌐ Soft-bristled brush option
> ⌐ Waterproof casing for bathroom use   ⌐ Flat plug for child safety
> ⌐ Temperature auto-control

Q. What is NOT one of the new dryer's features?

(A) Temperature setting options
(B) Protection from water damage
(C) A variety of modes depending on user

03

> Internationally acclaimed track star David Fliers will endorse Cascade's new running shoe, TRAX. Cascade, which specializes in athletic footwear and sports training gear, introduced its product two months ago in response to consumer demand. TRAX, which was an immediate success, has nonetheless failed to bring in the revenue the company's president expected. The CEO of Cascade, Mr. Avery White, is hopeful that the 2003 star's image will boost sales and reignite the interest of young fans wanting to imitate the running legend. The advertisements will target consumers in their teens and early 20s, as these are the groups most frequently influenced by endorsements by famous faces.

Q. What is stated about Cascade's TRAX?

(A) It was started by David Fliers.
(B) It is aimed at consumers in their 10s and 20s.
(C) Its sales have met the CEO's expectations.

請選擇與短文內容一致的句子。

04

> We are holding a job opportunities information session for university senior students and fresh graduates. This is a one day session scheduled for May 25ᵗʰ. Registration is not required, but attendees will be accepted on a first-come, first-served basis only.

(A) Only university students may attend the session.
(B) Limited seating is available for participants.

05

> The Bergerson Industries Corporation will be relocating its factory to the east side of the city. Roger Bergerson, sole proprietor, said the transfer will facilitate delivery of materials to the warehouse.

(A) Roger Bergerson is the owner of the company.

(B) Roger Bergerson is the company spokesman.

06

> Do you find dust balls under your dresser and bed even if you've already swept the floor? Our new Whoosh vacuum cleaners are so mighty that floors, carpets, and even curtains can become spotless in just a few minutes.

(A) The Whoosh vacuum cleaner can make draperies clean.

(B) There's no need to sweep the floor again after you've used Whoosh.

07

> The governor's travel schedule tomorrow includes a stopover at Lincoln, Nebraska, where he intends to deliver a speech on his plans to run for a second term. The talk will be delivered at the Lincoln Chamber of Commerce.

(A) The governor will talk about issues on commerce.

(B) The governor will discuss his plans for re-election.

08

> From 8:00 AM to 11:00 PM, the prices of children's bicycles at the Mega Bike Shop will be marked down by as much as 20 to 25 percent!

(A) The store is selling all bicycles at marked down prices.

(B) The store will hold a sale on select items.

09

> The Carmichael Group, Inc. said that plans for the construction of a 450 million dollar office building had been approved but that work on the building would not proceed until investors provide the initial outlay needed.

(A) Construction will begin when financial backing is given.

(B) The Carmichael Group will invest in the building when the plans are finalized.

10

> The owner of the building was informed that renovations are needed to meet the accessibility requirements of workers with disabilities. One important change mentioned is the installation of suitable door handles on all building entrances.

(A) Properly installed doors are needed at all building entrances.

(B) Renovations will enable disabled workers to reach door handles.

11

> Write to Home Remodeling Contractors for a home remodeling guide. Aside from home reconstruction ideas and plans, the guide includes a picture catalog for every room in your house. You can also get a free quote on any room you want to remodel.

(A) The company gives a free estimate.

(B) The guide is free for customers.

Question 1 refers to the following notice.

Taxi Service Guidelines
- A Reminder for all Travelers

The following are guidelines for passengers in taxi cabs:

Riders should be aware that cab drivers cannot refuse to provide taxi service based on the distance of the trip. Additionally, the meter must be turned on when the service begins. The taxi driver cannot charge you more than what is indicated on the meter. The only exception to this is a trip to or from the airport. There is a flat charge of $21 for airport service. You will not be charged extra for additional passengers, but having more than four passengers in the vehicle is considered illegal. Hence, do not expect a cab driver to accept the fifth passenger. Credit cards are accepted by most cab drivers. Cab drivers are not allowed to play their own music or smoke in their cabs. Passengers are also prohibited from smoking. Tipping is appreciated. An appropriate tip for satisfactory service is 10% of the total fee. However, the amount of tip is left to the discretion of the customer. If you experience any problems, report the taxi number, license plate, and driver's name to the National Taxi Association.

Thank you for cooperation and patronage.

1. What is NOT a taxi regulation?

   (A) People in the taxi can't smoke cigarettes.
   (B) Drivers are obligated to take riders regardless of distance.
   (C) All fees and charges must be paid in cash.
   (D) The maximum capacity is four people.

Questions 2-3 refer to the following advertisement and e-mail.

Office Space for Lease

A superior office space is available for lease on Hubbard Ave., centrally located in the downtown Denver area. The building is in the heart of the shopping and dining district of the city, as well as minutes away from the city's main expressway. For both residential and commercial purposes, this is an ideal location for a business.

∨ *24-hour manned security and elevator access*

∨ *Central heating and air already installed*

∨ *Coded security locks on all entrances*

∨ *1,932 sq. ft. of open space available immediately*

∨ *Built last year!*

The terms of the lease include a one-year renewable contract, utilities included in the rent, designated company parking, and a two-month cancellation notice agreement. Installation of dividing walls will be at the tenant's expense. All other interior work must be approved first by the building owner. The property is available for immediate rent, although a thorough background check will be performed by the landlord before a contract is signed. For more information, send an email to frank@dtre.com.

TO: Frank Wright, Downtown Real Estate
FROM: Harry Peabody, Maxx Finance

Dear Mr. Wright:
Thank you for showing us around the office space yesterday. I was impressed with the building and the facilities, especially the state-of-the-art security system. However, there are a few changes we would like to have made to the contract. To begin with, we would like to extend the term of the contract to two years, repaint the interior in our company's signature color of pale blue, and attach some signage to the wall in the reception area. Secondly, it's our understanding that the cost of installation of dividing walls is usually met by the building owner, so we would like this part of the contract to be changed too.
Sincerely,
Harry Peabody.

2. What does the advertisement say about the property?

(A) It will be ready to rent next month.
(B) It's pre-equipped with temperature control.
(C) It was renovated last year.
(D) It is separated into cubicles.

3. What is NOT mentioned in Mr. Peabody's list of amendments?

(A) The interior decoration
(B) The security system
(C) The terms for installing dividing walls
(D) The length of the agreement　　正確答案　P124

Chapter 4

推論問題

本類型題目要根據短文的內容做出推理然後作答。推論問題大致上可以分為「解題線索分散在整篇短文」和「解題線索在短文的某一部分內容當中」這兩種情況。在第一種情況中,一般有「這篇文章的對象是誰?」「這篇文章通常出現在什麼地方?」等問題。在第二種情況中,一般有「關於…這篇文章表示了什麼?」等問題。推論問題必須根據文章中的內容找出答案。

百發百中 出題類型與戰略

⊙ 頻繁出現的問題類型

這篇文章通常出現在什麼地方?	Where will this text most likely appear?
這篇文章的對象是誰?	Who is this announcement intended for?
這篇文章的語氣如何?	What is the tone of the letter?
這篇文章意味著什麼?	What does the article suggest?
關於…這篇文章表示了什麼?	What does this memo imply about the recipient?

⊙ 核心戰略

1. 分析文章的核心單字,找出答案的線索。

閱讀整篇短文才能做出判斷的情況,要根據短文中的核心單字來進行判斷。

2. 要找出文章中提供判斷根據的句子。

閱讀文章的某一部分內容做出判斷的情況,要在文章中找出問題的核心單字所在的部分,然後對照內容來解答。

例題 1

Ceramics Auction

On July 1, Macy's Antiques will be hosting a ceramics auction at the city hall. Examples of auction items include a variety of cups and plates from the Elizabethan Period, as well as bowls from Ancient Greece. Also represented will be medieval vases and Byzantine wine glasses. Persons wishing to attend the event must register at Macy's Antiques before June 29th. Buyer numbers will be handed out promptly at 4 p.m., one hour before the first item is to be auctioned.

Q:Who is the announcement for?   A:Collectors of old china

→ 可以根據短文中的單字,推斷出文章提到的對象。通過 Auction, bowls from Ancient Greece, medieval vases 等詞可以看出,這篇文章是寫給古董瓷器收藏家。

例題 2

A number of companies are now switching to rotating shift schedules in an attempt to allay the tediousness of repetitive tasks. However, some workers have reported experiencing additional stress with this type of schedule. Owners all admit that you cannot schedule in a single method that will satisfy the entire staff, but most agree that the day must be divided into multiple shifts.

Q:What does the article suggest about rotating shift scheduling?
A:It does not always appeal to employees.

→ 要先找出文章中與 rotating shift scheduling 相關的內容,然後與選項一一對照。 "you cannot schedule in a single method that will satisfy the entire staff" 是答案的根據,同時透過 "some workers have reported experiencing additional stress with this type of schedule",我們也可以得到一些線索。

HACKERS PRACTICE ● ● ● ● ● ● ● ● ● ● ● ● ● ● ● ● ●

⊙ 「推論問題」練習

閱讀短文並回答問題

01

Dear Edward,

Thank you for the outline of yesterday's presentation. I'll get right on the completion of the architectural models. My team will most likely have them finished before the weekend. Make sure to make any final modification requests by this afternoon, as we will be working off of the original drafts sent last week. I will have a delivery person bring the replicas to your office by Monday morning at the latest. Have a good day.

Q. What will Edward most likely do in response to this memo?

(A) Arrange for delivery service
(B) Make copies of the original plans
(C) Send off any last-minute changes to the plans

02

As always, it is a pleasure doing business with our friends at Lake Homes. It was a great surprise to receive the complimentary copy of your magazine in the mail last week. We have always displayed copies of your catalogs in our lounge for customers' viewing pleasure, which has produced a considerable number of orders for your company. We will continue to showcase and refer your company to our clients.

Q. What is the tone of this letter?

(A) Surprised
(B) Grateful
(C) Flattered

03

Your dream of owning a family vacation home in the sunny Mediterranean is not as far away as you think. Properties in the regions of western Greece, southern Spain, and northern Italy are rapidly developing without the typical prices of luxury properties in more trendy areas. Two, three and four bedroom villas, as well as renovated town homes, are available and displayed on our website. Let European Dreamscapes assist you in fulfilling your investment, retirement, and vacation needs.

Q. Who is this brochure targeting?

(A) Middle class families
(B) Corporate property investors
(C) Wealthy luxury travelers

請選擇與短文內容一致的句子。

04

For those interested in becoming a Light Goods Vehicle (LGV) driver, we recommend Veritas Training, the only training company that provides free retest training should the driver fail the first test.

(A) The training may be repeated once without charge.

(B) Veritas recommends that an LGV driver sign up for training.

05

Henson Speakers provides the finest quality speakers available in the market. With zero tolerance for defects, Henson has made an enormous investment in a high-tech measurement system.

(A) Henson invested a great deal of money to ensure a high quality standard.

(B) Henson has purchased a new system due to a lack of quality products.

06

Our cellular service plans are individually tailored to fit the financial situation of each of our customers. Aside from the basic plan, Cell-Com provides extra services to make your entire cellular package fit your wireless communication needs.

(A) The basic plan is suitable for all communication needs.

(B) Pricing options are available for all budgets.

07

Management has noted some opposition to the proposal for the company's reorganization. To address your concerns, we will be issuing a memorandum that will provide answers to your questions. We hope that this memo will lay your worries to rest.

(A) A conference is being scheduled for management and employees.

(B) There is an existing plan to restructure the company.

08

> Doctors have been looking into alternative medicine as one way of speeding up a patient's recovery from an operation. In particular, herbs look very promising.

(A) Herbs can promote faster healing from surgery.

(B) Doctors use herbs during surgical operations.

09

> We specialize in carpet, upholstery, drapery, walls, and floor cleaning. Our services feature exclusive patented cleaning methods. For those using our services for the first time, mention this ad and we will give you 10 percent off.

(A) Patented cleaning methods are used if requested by the homeowner.

(B) The caller can enjoy a discount if he refers to the advertisement

10

> The Kennedy Business Center is giving a free one-time seminar on business financing options on August 24. Pre-registration is required as there are not enough seats.

(A) You need to sign up in advance to attend the seminar.

(B) The seminar is limited to employees only.

11

> This Sunday, down at the beachfront by the pavilion, the City Council will be hosting a community breakfast. The goal is to gather residents of the neighborhood for a morning outdoors, in support of reconstructing the pavilion's floor. Coffee and pastries, courtesy of Henry's Bakery, will be available from 8 a.m. to noon.

(A) A bakery is hosting a fundraiser to build a pavilion in the morning.

(B) A bakery will give out free food before noon.

READING | 各類型問題攻略

Question 1 refers to the following article.

n recent airline industry news, two of the top companies have merged in an attempt to offer more direct services to popular international destinations. A representative from BlueSky was recently interviewed by members of the press, at which point he announced the company's decision to join forces with Atlantic Air. The decision comes after months of negotiation. The main cause of the merger is the increasing competition with some of the major U.S. airliners who are able to offer direct service flights for the most popular business routes.

In a world increasingly obsessed with convenience and where time is a commodity, industry leaders agree that less time-consuming travel is the wave of the market. Although both companies acknowledge the risk involved in joining the airlines, there is confidence that the new services will sway public opinion. Ashley Hampton, a member of BlueSky's executive board, reminded the press of the main reason for the switch. She stated, "If a customer calls one of our representatives needing a flight from Tokyo to Seattle, we can refer her/him to the Atlantic Air service line. It is a mutually beneficial relationship and we are excited about the possibilities."

1. What can be learned from this article?

(A) BlueSky doesn't offer direct service anywhere.
(B) Atlantic Air doesn't fly to Tokyo.
(C) BlueSky doesn't have a flight from Tokyo to Seattle.
(D) Atlantic Air has only direct flights.

Questions 2-3 refer to the following document and e-mail.

Comparison of Laptops

Brand	Display Quality	Provided Software	Battery Life	Weight/Size	Storage Space
Creativity	★★★	★★★★	★★★★	★★★★	★★★
Riverpoint 440	★★★★★	★★★★★	★★★★★	★★★★★	★★★★★
Liquid Nitro	★★	★★	★★★★	★★	★★★
Excel 910	★★★	★★★★★	★★★★★	★★★★★	★★★
Sensory	★★★★	★★★★★	★★★	★★★★	★★★★★

★★★★★ excellent   ★★★★ good   ★★★ fair   ★★ poor   ★ terrible

Overall, Creativity and Riverpoint 440 met shoppers' expectations where display quality, software, battery life, weight/size and storage space are concerned. Riverpoint edged out Creativity by 7 points. Excel 910 and Sensory did fairly well, but Excel's storage space was at issue with its largest capacity being only 20 gigabytes. Shoppers complained about Sensory's battery life, which appears to run out after only 2 hours of use.

To: John Dyson, PR Department
From: Michael Boss, Executive Director
Subject: 'Comparison of Laptops' Article

Dear John:
I saw this in article yesterday, and am quite concerned about it to say the least. At this point, I'm not sure whether we should really trust these findings since we can't be sure that the survey was conducted systematically. However, based on these results, we didn't compare favorably to most other main brands at all. I think this matter deserves closer investigation. Get in touch with Paul Minnow in Marketing and put together a presentation comparing this article with our own market research findings, and then arrange a time for a seminar. Since we might have to look at upgrading our product, have Jennifer Lackey from Technology Development attend too.
Michael Boss

2. Where would you most likely find the first passage?

(A) In a magazine of product reviews
(B) On the product's box
(C) In a product brochure
(D) In a newspaper advertisement

3. What does the e-mail suggest?

(A) The brand's popularity has fallen due to the article.
(B) The company needs a better marketing strategy.
(C) The data reported in the article might not be accurate.
(D) They have recently upgraded their laptops.

Chapter 5

找同義字的問題

此題型是新多益的新增題型，要求在選項中選出與文章中的特定單字意義相同的單字。先瞭解相關單字所在的句子，然後再選擇與句中單字意思相同的選項就可解答。有些題目的指定單字有許多意思，選項中的單字是它的同義字，這時就要根據句意來選擇答案。

百發百中 出題類型與戰略

⊙ 頻繁出現的問題類型

與第…段、第…行的…意思相同的單字是？ The word "run" in paragraph 1, line 5, is closest in meaning to

⊙ 核心戰略

1.先瞭解句子中單字的意思之後，在選項中選擇與該單字意思相同的單字。

題目出現含有許多意思的單字的時候，選項中會有雖然是相關單字的同義字，但與文章用法不符的選項，此時就要認真分析句意再做選擇。

2.將多益單字與它們的同義字一起記憶是很好的做法。

推薦使用英英字典和同義字字典來幫助學習。有多個意思的單字，最好是先瞭解它各自的意義，然後再利用例句牢牢記住單字。

例題1

> With frequent downsizing and budget cuts becoming commonplace in today's economy, many enterprises are uniting with others to prolong their life span and increase business opportunities. A merger combines both a competing organization and your own, producing a single company. This can comprise of two parties who offer similar products and services, or two dissimilar ones who have a complementary relationship. As a result of a merger, a corporation can possibly dominate the industry in which they compete, thereby streamlining the marketplace and decreasing competition.
>
> While attempts at these types of alliances are high in number, only a limited amount of organizations are actually able to manage the process successfully. While this option may sound enticing for the company at risk, it is impossible unless adequate funds are available. An amount at least as much as the other company's value must be offered in order for a merge to be considered.
>
> The final decision is made by shareholder vote, so if you possess a large percentage of stock, then your vote has a large degree of leverage. Therefore, if it is possible to buy more than half of the company's stock, your proposal for a merger will most likely be authorized.

Q:The word "manage" in paragraph 2, line 2, is closest in meaning to

(A) unite   (B) regulate   (C) withstand   (D) handle

→ 此題問的是：與第二段、第二行的 manage 意思最相近的單字是什麼？在 "only a limited amount of organizations are actually able to manage the process successfully" 一句中用到的 manage 表示的是「制定、處理」，因此答案應該是（D）handle（制定）。雖然（B）regulate（規定）是 manage 的同義字，但 manage 在此句中並沒有「規定」之意，因此（B）不正確。

短文解釋 P128

⊙動詞

❶ **accommodate** = lodge 容納
[əˋkɑməˏdet] This hotel can **accommodate(= lodge)** 150 guests. 這家飯店可以容納150名客人。

❷ **assess** = evaluate 評估
[əˋsɛs] **assess(= evaluate)** the value of the house 評估房子的價格

❸ **curtail** = reduce 減少
[kɝˋtel] **curtail(= reduce)** the expenses 減少費用

❹ **extend** = lengthen 延長
[ɪkˋstɛnd] **extend(= lengthen)** the term of a loan for three months 將借出的期限延長3個月

= offer 給予，提供（親切感等）
extend(= offer) our hospitality 盛情款待

❺ **gauge** = measure 稱
[gedʒ] **gauge(= measure)** the weight of the box 稱箱子的重量

❻ **generate** = produce 使發生
[ˋdʒɛnəˏret] **generate(= produce)** enough electricity 產生充足的電力

❼ **govern** = control 支配
[ˋgʌvɚn] **govern(= control)** the price of goods 支配物價

❽ **observe** = follow 遵守
[əbˋzɝv] **observe(= follow)** the rules 遵守規則

❾ **quote** = estimate 估計
[kwot] **quote(= estimate)** a price for building a new house 估計新房子的建造費用

❿ **raise** = elevate 提高
[rez] **raise(= elevate)** wholesale prices 提高批發價格

= bring up 養育
raise(= bring up) two kids 養育兩個孩子

⓫ **run** = manage 經營
[rʌn] **run(= manage)** a restaurant 經營飯店

⓬ **suggest** = recommend 推薦
[səˋdʒɛst] **suggest(= recommend)** the Italian restaurant 推薦那家義大利餐廳

= imply 意味著
suggest(= imply) a lack of interest 意味著沒有興趣

⓭ **violate** = infringe 違反
[ˋvaɪəˏlet] **violate(= infringe)** company regulations 違反公司規定

⓮ **work** = operate 運作
[wɝk] get the radio to **work(= operate)** 使收音機開始運作

⊙名詞

❶ bill
[bɪl]

= **invoice** 帳單
pay the **bill**(= **invoice**)

= **legislation** 法規
pass the **bill**(= **legislation**) unanimously 使法規無異議通過

❷ commission
[kə`mɪʃən]

= **fee** 手續費
a 15% **commission**(= **fee**) on every order 對所有訂單附加15%的手續費

= **committee** 委員會
the Securities and Exchange **Commission**(= **Committee**) 證券交易委員會

❸ commodity
[kə`mɑdətɪ]

= **goods, merchandise** 商品
household **commodities**(= **goods, merchandise**) 居家用品

❹ counterfeit
[`kaʊntɚ͵fɪt]

= **forgery** 偽造品
This watch may be a **counterfeit**(= **forgery**). 這個手錶有可能是偽造品。

❺ feasibility
[͵fizə`bɪlətɪ]

= **viability** 實施可能性
the **feasibility**(= **viability**) of building a shopping center 建造購物中心的可能性

❻ feature
[fitʃɚ]

= **characteristics** 特徵
the main **features**(= **characteristics**) of this program 這個節目的主要特徵

❼ occupation
[͵ɑkjə`peʃən]

= **job** 職業
choose accounting as one's **occupation**(= **job**) 選擇會計為職業

❽ operation
[͵ɑpə`reʃən]

= **surgery** 手術
recover rapidly after the **operation**(= **surgery**) 手術後快速恢復

❾ paycheck
[`pe͵tʃɛk]

= **salary, wage** 薪水
an increased **paycheck**(= **salary, wage**) 增加薪水

❿ proprietor
[prə`praɪtɚ]

= **owner** 所有者
a hotel **proprietor**(= **owner**) 飯店所有者

⓫ replacement
[rɪ`plesmənt]

= **successor** 繼任者
a **replacement**(= **successor**) for the secretary who resigned 離職祕書的繼任者

⓬ stock
[stɒk]

= **inventory** 庫存品
Our **stock**(= **inventory**) of office supplies is exhausted. 辦公室用品的庫存用完了。

= **shares** 股份
20% of the company's **stock**(= **shares**) 這家公司的20%股份

⓭ term
[tɜm]

= **conditions** 條件
according to the **terms**(= **conditions**) of the contract 依據合同上的條件

= **period** 期間
the **term**(= **period**) of validity 有效期限

⓮ voucher
[`vaʊtʃɚ]

= **coupon** 優惠券
a discount **voucher**(= **coupon**) for 15% off your next order
一張讓你在下次訂購時有15%折扣的優待券

⊙形容詞

❶ apprehensive
[ˌæprɪˈhɛnsɪv]
= **fearful** 擔心的
feel **apprehensive**(= **fearful**) about the result of the exams 擔心考試成績

❷ contagious
[kənˈtedʒəs]
= **infectious** 傳染病的
a highly **contagious**(= **infectious**) disease 傳染性高的疾病

❸ effective
[ɪˈfɛktɪv]
= **efficient** 有效率的
effective(= **efficient**) analytical methods 有效率的分析方法

= **valid** 有效的
The discount is **effective**(= **valid**) through January. 折扣優惠在一月份有效。

❹ liable
[ˈlaɪəbl̩]
= **likely** 似乎要⋯
The market is **liable**(= **likely**) to crash. 市場似乎快要崩潰。

= **responsible** 負責的
be **liable**(= **responsible**) for damages 對損失負責任

❺ profitable
[ˈprɑfɪtəbl̩]
= **lucrative** 收益好的
a very **profitable**(= **lucrative**) business 收益非常好的公司

❻ sophisticated
[səˈfɪstɪˌketɪd]
= **complex** 複雜的
a **sophisticated**(= **complex**) computer system 複雜的電腦系統

= **refined** 老於世故的
a **sophisticated**(= **refined**) sense of humor 老於世故的幽默感

❼ unbiased
[ʌnˈbaɪəst]
= **impartial** 公正的
unbiased(= **impartial**) information 客觀的資訊

❽ unwavering
[ˌʌnˈwerərɪŋ]
= **consistent** 堅定的，不動搖的
unwavering(= **consistent**) loyalty 忠心耿耿

⊙副詞

❶ approximately
[əˈprɑksəmɪtlɪ]
= **around, about** 大約
The plane will be landing in **approximately**(= **around, about**) 10 minutes.
飛機大約在10分鐘之後到達。

❷ consecutively
[kənˈsɛkjətɪvlɪ]
= **successively** 連續地
work for 10 days **consecutively**(= **successively**) 在10天內連續工作

❸ exceptionally
[ɪkˈsɛpʃənəlɪ]
= **especially** 尤其
exceptionally(= **especially**) fine jewellery 特別精美的寶石

❹ exclusively
[ɪkˈsklusɪvlɪ]
= **solely** 唯一，單獨
exclusively(= **solely**) for the use of members 只有會員可以使用的

❺ inherently
[ɪnˈhɪrəntlɪ]
= **fundamentally** 本質上
Venture businesses are **inherently**(= **fundamentally**) risky. 投機事業本質上是危險的。

❻ initially
[ɪˈnɪʃəlɪ]
= **originally** 最初
more sales than **initially**(= **originally**) expected 比最初預計的銷售量更多

❼ substantially
[səbˈstænʃəlt]
= **considerably** 相當
a **substantially**(= **considerably**) reduced workload 減少了相當多的工作量

IX

01 launch a new perfume   Ⓐ develop Ⓑ introduce

02 a **vacancy** for a mailroom assistant   Ⓐ opening Ⓑ career

03 curb company spending   Ⓐ analyze Ⓑ restrain

04 have a previous **engagement**   Ⓐ reservation Ⓑ appointment

05 maintain the company's reputation   Ⓐ preserve Ⓑ assert

06 complimentary copies of the new book   Ⓐ praiseworthy Ⓑ free

07 He **assumed** that prices would rise.   Ⓐ presumed Ⓑ asserted

08 assess the financial **damage**   Ⓐ risk Ⓑ loss

09 Gas prices are **falling**.   Ⓐ decreasing Ⓑ inflating

10 a **discrepancy** in accounts   Ⓐ inconsistency Ⓑ transaction

11 execute the task   Ⓐ delegate Ⓑ perform

12 Imports have **markedly** increased.   Ⓐ distinctly Ⓑ primarily

13 meet the board's requirements   Ⓐ satisfy Ⓑ encounter

14 heavy **precipitation**   Ⓐ rainfall Ⓑ involvement

15 operate a business   Ⓐ work Ⓑ run

16 his **impending** retirement   Ⓐ approaching Ⓑ voluntary

17 a **meager** salary   Ⓐ insufficient Ⓑ generous

18 Remuneration is **contingent** on success.   Ⓐ dependent Ⓑ essential

19 demonstrate how to use the fax machine   Ⓐ explain Ⓑ protest

20 Consumption of luxury goods dropped **abruptly**.   Ⓐ significantly Ⓑ suddenly

21 for the **remainder** of this month   Ⓐ rest Ⓑ end

22 The final meeting will **occur** next week.   Ⓐ conclude Ⓑ happen

23 pay the **tariff**   Ⓐ fine Ⓑ duty

24 The report **implicates** that a recession is coming. Ⓐ implies Ⓑ denies

25 a **steep** price   Ⓐ sharp Ⓑ high

26 Our license **expires** next month.   Ⓐ perishes Ⓑ finishes

27 No **gratuities** accepted.   Ⓐ tips Ⓑ discounts

28 raise wholesale prices   Ⓐ elevate Ⓑ gather

29 weave **fabric**   Ⓐ string Ⓑ cloth

30 honor Ms. Haught for what she has achieved   Ⓐ respect Ⓑ approve

31 **face** the competition   Ⓐ defeat   Ⓑ confront

32 a **thorough** search for missing luggage   Ⓐ complete   Ⓑ random

33 **suspend** his decision   Ⓐ postpone   Ⓑ defend

34 the expense of a lengthy **litigation**   Ⓐ journey   Ⓑ lawsuit

35 **accrue** interest at 12% per annum   Ⓐ pay   Ⓑ accumulate

36 women's **apparel** production   Ⓐ garment   Ⓑ jewelry

37 a **meticulously** planned schedule   Ⓐ considerably   Ⓑ carefully

38 **affect** the economic state   Ⓐ influence   Ⓑ pretend

39 be **anxious** to begin the new project   Ⓐ worried   Ⓑ eager

40 a drop in industrial **output**   Ⓐ profit   Ⓑ production

41 **relieve** his heavy workload   Ⓐ alleviate   Ⓑ endure

42 a supermarket **patron**   Ⓐ supporter   Ⓑ customer

43 the **balance** of power between producers and retailers   Ⓐ equilibrium   Ⓑ remainder

44 **star** in the film   Ⓐ direct   Ⓑ feature

45 be **cognizant** of the problem   Ⓐ conscious   Ⓑ confident

46 The task **entails** much stress.   Ⓐ involves   Ⓑ relieves

47 as a **consequence** of the decision   Ⓐ result   Ⓑ objective

48 **aggravate** the downturn in economic activity   Ⓐ intensify   Ⓑ extend

49 the country's economic **clout**   Ⓐ closedown   Ⓑ influence

50 **remove** old stains   Ⓐ dismiss   Ⓑ eliminate

51 the **provision** in the contract   Ⓐ clause   Ⓑ supply

52 **solicit** for donations   Ⓐ ask   Ⓑ support

53 **outstanding** natural beauty   Ⓐ exceptional   Ⓑ excessive

54 a nice **spot** for a picnic   Ⓐ destination   Ⓑ place

55 Demand for imported goods has **skyrocketed**.   Ⓐ increased   Ⓑ dropped

56 **volatile** oil markets   Ⓐ constant   Ⓑ changeable

57 **fix** a machine   Ⓐ organize   Ⓑ repair

58 There was a lot of **speculation** about the new design.   Ⓐ conjecture   Ⓑ configuration

59 **surpass** everyone's expectations   Ⓐ exceed   Ⓑ increase

60 keep a person in **custody**   Ⓐ detention   Ⓑ suspense

正確答案　P129

✍ *Bali Palm Hotel and Resort* ✍
Notice to All Guests

Arrival and Departure
Please check in before 8pm, and check out before 10am.

Security
The Bali Palm Hotel goes the extra mile to guarantee the safety of your possessions. Card-swipe door locks have recently been fitted to rooms, and safety-deposit boxes for valuables are provided at the front desk. This service is available for a maximum of three items per room.

Room Service
An extensive menu is placed in the information package on your desk, offering the highest-quality international cuisine, delivered to your door 24 hours a day. Dial 123 on the telephone in your room to order.

Restaurant
Our restaurant is conveniently located adjacent to reception on the first floor, serving a variety of delicious international meals between the hours of 6a.m. and 11p.m. daily. Special discounts are offered for guests who hold a National Hotel and Inn Association membership card.

Housekeeping Services
The Bali Palm Hotel make every effort to maximize your comfort while being environmentally conscious. Housekeeping services can change bed linen and towels freshly each morning. However, if you wish to help preserve the environment, please place the designated signs on the bed and in the bathroom in order to reuse towels and sheets.

---

1. The word "hold" in paragraph 4, line 3 is closest in meaning to

(A) restrain
(B) conduct
(C) possess
(D) accommodate

Question 2 refers to the following article and e-mail.

Web Development Tips
Written by Patricia Musetti, GreenLight Web Design

Before embarking on any web design project you should ask yourself the following question: what do you want a website for? Is it to simply showcase your products and services, or are you planning something more substantial that allows you to conduct business online? The more thoroughly you can answer these questions, the better of a position you'll be in to brief the web development company. They will then produce a proposal, which should show a clear understanding of your goals, and a tentative assessment of the cost.

Once you have reached a consensus on the preliminary design, the developers will prepare a site map. You should spend time carefully assessing whether the specifications meet your needs, as changing them later will be costly and frustrating. Remember the rule: form is less important than function. A great-looking site is useless if people can't get what they want within a few mouse clicks. Last but not least– make sure your launch date is realistic before announcing it to your customers. Don't forget to submit your site to search engines– and never launch a site half-built.

From : Russell Bowman, President, Friend Consulting
To : Rosemary Naidu, Marketing Department, Friend Consulting
Subject: Web development project

Rosemary:
I've forwarded this article to you as I feel it contains some very useful information that we could apply to our new website project. Had we had access to this information when we first launched our site, I think we could have avoided some of the costly pitfalls that we experienced. The part saying that function is more important than form particularly resonates. I suggest we try to get in touch with Ms. Musetti at GreenLight and see if she is available to discuss a proposal. Look over the text and then get back to me with your thoughts on the matter.

2. The word "consensus" in paragraph 2, line 1, of the article is closest in meaning to
(A) adoption
(B) additive
(C) adjustment
(D) agreement

Section 2
各類型短文攻略

Chapter 6

信件（Letter）

每次考試都會出現三次以上關於信件和電子郵件的短文類型，大體可分為商業信件和個人生活信件兩種。商業信件主要是表現公司之間交易情況的信件，而個人生活信件是諸如出租人和承租人之間、銀行和顧客之間的書信，主要表現生活上的內容。電子郵件比信件的格式更為簡單，主要用於表現公司內部員工之間的意見交換。

百發百中 出題類型與戰略

⊙ 頻繁出現的問題類型

信件的目的是？	What is the purpose of this letter?
要求事項是？	What is Robert Payne being asked to do?
隨信附帶的是什麼？	What is enclosed with this letter?
其他細節	When did Ms. Dwyer first contact Mr. Frazier?

⊙ 核心戰略

1. 要瞭解英文的書信格式

   要先寫寄信人的名字，再寫收信人的名字。寄信人的姓名也可以省略不寫。

2. 要瞭解信件的基本構成

   在信件的最開始先表明寫信的目的，說明有附件等內容時要在信的中間寫，信的最後通常會提出邀請。

3. 如果熟記一些相關的表現手法，就可以很容易地找到信件的目的、附件、要求等事項的相關問題。

例題

Mark Spencer
Johnson Wholesale
967 Crescent Road
New York, NY 20132
　
寄信人（letter head）

November 23　寫信日期

Patrick Jameson
Production Manager
Jameson Sewing
Panchita, Columbia
　
收信人

Dear Mr. Jameson:
I am writing to inform you that the fabric sample we received from your factory was not satisfactory. The color was off from the original and the threads were too far apart. There is no possibility of our store purchasing fabric of this quality. I have enclosed a sheet of instructions about how to alter the sample to our liking. Please correct the mistakes and send another piece of fabric back to me for reconsideration.

寫信的目的／有關細節與附件／邀請事項

Sincerely,
Mark Spencer
Mark Spencer
Purchasing manager

結語／署名／寄信人姓名／寄信人的職業或公司

Q：Who is Mark Spencer?　A：A customer of a textile factory

→ 此題需要知道 Mark Spencer 是寄信人，並且要知道收信人與他的關係。

⊙ 信件中經常出現的慣用句

❶與信件目的有關的起始句

I am writing to + 動詞原形　為…原因而寫信。

I am writing to inquire about a discrepancy between an order I made and the amount I was charged.
寫信是想詢問一下訂購物品的價格與所付費用不符的問題。

This letter is to + 動詞原形　此信是為…原因而發送的。

This letter is to confirm your registration for the upcoming conference on financial service providers.
寫這封信是要確認一下您是否報名了即將舉辦的金融服務企業會議。

❷附加的內容

We have enclosed ~　隨信附上…

We have enclosed a copy of the quarterly report and a synopsis of upcoming projects for the coming fiscal year. 隨信附上本季報告的影本和即將提交的財政年度方案概況。

Enclosed you will find ~　隨信附上的是…

Enclosed you will find information on the services you indicated interest in and contact numbers for each service. 隨信附上的是您所諮詢的服務資訊和各項服務的聯繫方式。

❸邀請事項

Please ~　請…

Please send any comments or questions you have to Ms. Stevens at the following e-mail address.
如果有意見或疑問，請聯絡 Stevens 女士，電子信箱地址如下。

I would be grateful if you could ~　若…，我將非常感謝

I would be grateful if you could give me some information about the position you advertised in *The Financial Herald*. 如果貴公司能提供在 The Financial Herald 上所刊登的徵才廣告的職位相關資訊，我將非常感激。

⊙ 信件中經常出現的單字

❶貿易往來

bargain over prices 議價	mutual funds 共同基金
cargo [ˋkɑrgo] 貨物	order [ˋɔrdɚ] 訂購
clause [klɔz]（合同）條款	overcharge [ˋovɚˋtʃɑrdʒ] 報價過高
commerce [ˋkɑmɝs] 商業	postage [ˋpostɪdʒ] 郵資
commission [kəˋmɪʃən] 傭金	quota [ˋkwotə] 定額
consignment [kənˋsaɪnmənt] 委託	quote [kwot] 使用（設施）
contract [ˋkɑntrækt] 合同	shipment [ˋʃɪpmənt] 船運，貨運
courier [ˋkʊrɪɚ] 運送機關	specifications [ˏspɛsəfəˋkeʃən] 詳細說明書
customs [ˋkʌstəmz] 海關	subcontractor [sʌbˏkənˋtræktɚ] 轉包商
delivery [dɪˋlɪvərɪ] 運送	tariff [ˋtærɪf] 關稅
embargo [ɪmˋbɑrgo] 禁運	trade [tred] 貿易
freight [fret] 貨物	transit [ˋtrænsɪt] 運送
invoice [ˋɪnvɔɪs] 發貨清單	transaction [trænˋzækʃən] 事務，交易
multilateral [ˋmʌltɪˋlætərəl] 多國間的	vendor [ˋvɛndɚ] 賣主

❷流通‧販賣

catalog [ˈkætəlɔg] 目錄

charge [tʃɑrdʒ] 索價

client [ˈklaɪənt] 客戶

commodity [kəˈmɑdətɪ] 商品

customer [ˈkʌstəmɚ] 顧客

discount [ˈdɪskaʊnt] 折扣

distribution [ˌdɪstrəˈbjuʃən] 銷售量

goods [gʊdz] 商品

inventory [ˈɪnvənˌtorɪ] 存貨清單

merchandise [ˈmɝtʃənˌdaɪz] 貨物

net price 淨價

outlet [ˈaʊtˌlɛt] 銷路

purchase order 訂單

retailer [ˈritelɚ] 零售商

stock [stɑk] 庫存商品

supplier [səˈplaɪɚ] 供應廠商

transport [ˈtrænsˌpɔrt] 運輸

warehouse [ˈwɛrˌhaʊs] 倉庫

❸個人經濟生活

account [əˈkaʊnt] 帳戶

bank statement 銀行交易記錄

bounced check 拒付收據

cardholder [ˈkɑrdˌholdɚ] 持卡人

cash a check 兌現支票

checking account 抵押存款

collection notice 募捐通知

credit [ˈkrɛdɪt] 信用貸款

creditor [ˈkrɛdɪtɚ] 貸方

debit card 信用卡

debt [dɛt] 債務

deduct [dɪˈdʌkt] 扣除

delinquent [dɪˈlɪŋkwənt] 拖欠的

deposit [dɪˈpɑzɪt] 存款

due date 支付期限

endorse [ɪnˈdɔrs] 簽署

insurance [ɪnˈʃʊrəns] 保險

insurance policy 保險單

interest [ˈɪntərɪst] 利息

loan [lon] 貸出

mortgage [ˈmɔrgɪdʒ] 抵押

outstanding balance 未支付餘額

overdraw [ˈovɚˈdrɔ] 透支

overdue [ˈovɚˈdju] 到期未付

premium [ˈprimɪəm] 額外費用

savings account 存款帳戶

transaction record 交易記錄

utility bill 公共支出

wire [waɪr] 匯款

❹居住生活

building [ˈbɪldɪŋ] 建築

cozy [ˈkozɪ] 舒適的

demolition [ˌdɛməˈlɪʃən] 破壞

dweller [ˈdwɛlɚ] 居住者，居民

estimate [ˈɛstəˌmet] 估計

evacuate [ɪˈvækjuˌet] 疏散

furnished [ˈfɝnɪʃ] 配置傢俱

garage [gəˈrɑʒ] 車庫

inhabitant [ɪnˈhæbətənt] 居住者，居民

landlord [ˈlændˌlɔrd] 房東

lease [lis] 租借

let [lɛt] 出租

occupant [ˈɑkjəpənt] 居住者，持有人

outskirt [ˈaʊtˌskɝt] 郊區，邊界

parlor [ˈpɑrlɚ] 起居室

premises [ˈprɛmɪsɪz] 土地，房地產

real estate 房地產

remote [rɪˈmot] 遙遠的

rent [rɛnt] 房租

residence [ˈrɛzədəns] 住宅

spacious [ˈspeʃəs] 寬敞的

storage room 倉庫

tenant [ˈtɛnənt] 租客，房客

tenure [ˈtɛnjʊr] 佔有權

vacant [ˈvekənt] 空的

valuation [ˌvæljuˈeʃən] 估計

⊙「信件」類型題練習

閱讀短文並回答問題。

01

July 7, 2004

Samantha Chan
220 Lake Road
Wilkes-Barre, PA

Dear Ms. Chan,
Based on our initial interview, we are proceeding with the prefabrication of the ceiling. However, our representative will need to sit down with you to discuss the details of your renovations, in particular, the kitchen, bedrooms and bathroom. We can begin renovations next month and expect them to take a total of three months.

Q. When is the construction expected to start?

    (A) In July
    (B) In August
    (C) In November

02

Thank you for your interest in our travel club. Per your request, I have enclosed a number of brochures, information sheets, and pamphlets about our services. There is a plethora of information in these materials regarding our travel services, packages, and guided tours. If you have any further questions, please don't hesitate to call or e-mail our office anytime. Our 24-hour telephone operators are readily available to assist you with any questions you may have.

Q. Why was the letter written?

    (A) To advertise a new club
    (B) To respond to an inquiry for information
    (C) To provide contact details for the agency

03

Your attendance at the 2004 Global Communications Conference is anticipated. Enclosed in this letter you will find a print-out schedule of the weekend's events. Changes to the itinerary will be posted on the bulletin board in the main hall on the first day of the conference. Please indicate on the form which events you plan to attend and send it back to our office by the end of the month.

Q. What accompanies this letter?

    (A) An itinerary of the conference activities
    (B) A statement of participation for the event
    (C) An invitation to the weekend's festivities

正確答案 P134

Questions 1-2 refer to the following letter.

Savory Cheeses
Suite 34, Glass Complex
Chicago, IL 73456

Dear Mr. Jones,

Let me begin by expressing our company's excitement at the upcoming opportunity to do business with your establishment. On behalf of Alpha Carriers, I extend a show of gratitude for entrusting us with your valuable goods. Considering that this is the first time we will do business together, we want to take special care to ensure a smooth and faultless transaction.

To begin, I'd like to review the details of the shipment. The dairy goods will be picked up on the morning of September 25th in a refrigerated cargo truck. The truck will drive the goods to Seattle, Washington by the afternoon of September 26th along the route agreed upon in the contract. Please refer to the copy of the contract attached to this letter. The trucker will sign the shipment over to the handlers at the Savory Cheeses branch store and their people will unload the goods. Once the goods are unloaded, our trucker will take down the mileage and time of transaction and the shipment will be complete.

If there are no problems with the above noted plans, we shall begin preparing for your shipment immediately. Any problems or questions regarding your goods can be directed to the customer service representatives on call 24 hours every day. They are authorized to track the status of any shipment as long as a confirmation number is provided.

Thank you again for using Alpha Carriers. We look forward to a future of great business with you!

Best regards,

James Walker
James Walker
Alpha Carriers

1. What does Alpha Carriers provide?

(A) Loading and unloading services
(B) Cooled trucks for delivery service
(C) Packaging of goods
(D) Security insurance for products

2. What is enclosed with this letter?

(A) Plans for the shipping of the goods
(B) An itemized billing for the upcoming job
(C) A duplicate of the agreement and route plans
(D) A certificate of guarantee with a confirmation PIN

Questions 3-4 refer to the following e-mail.

To:	Steve Corcoran
From:	Mary Henry
Re:	Architectural consideration

It has come to my attention lately that a number of potential clients have asked what we offer in terms of paneling. Up until recently, I never considered this method of construction as a viable option, but customer demand is making me think otherwise. Our researchers have found that many urban buildings are now constructed using panels that attach like jigsaw puzzles. The benefits are that it is cheap, easy to put together, and has a very modern look. Customers seem to like this clean and sharp image in their offices and homes in comparison to the cement or sheetrock walls available before. The bumps and grooves characteristic of the splattered paint style of old construction methods are taking a back seat to the smooth, glossy finish of factory-made panels. Given the surprisingly high consumer demand for this style of building, I would like to know whether it is a possibility for this firm to offer it as a construction option. I feel this is in the best interests of our company. Let me know what you think of this idea. I will be sending some research files for your review within the next 24 hours. When it is convenient for you, let's schedule a time to discuss this proposal.

3. What is the sender inquiring about?

(A) When paneling will be marketed
(B) How to put together a paneled building
(C) Why the new style is so popular
(D) Whether offering paneling is feasible

4. What does the passage suggest?

(A) The company is not currently using jigsaw-like panels.
(B) Modern consumers prefer the more traditional walls.
(C) Customers are hesitant about urban-style interiors.
(D) The company has thoroughly researched paneling options.

Chapter 7

廣告（Advertisement）

在每次考試中都會出現兩篇關於廣告的短文。廣告可以分為徵才廣告和產品廣告。徵才廣告在每次考試中都會出現，它有固定的文章結構，只不過每次考試都換一種職業。因此，如果熟練掌握徵才廣告的結構，就可以節省很多時間。產品廣告羅列出了有關產品的各種特點，經常會出關於產品特徵的 NOT / True 類型的題目。

百發百中 出題類型與戰略

⊙ 頻繁出現的問題類型

[徵才廣告]	職務要求的資格是？	What is a requirement for the position?
	工作職責是？	What is one of the responsibilities of the job?
	薪資及福利是？	What is the stated benefit?
[產品廣告]	廣告的商品是？	What is being advertised?
	何者不是產品特徵？	What is NOT a feature of the item?
	其他細節	When does the special discount apply?

⊙ 核心戰略

1. 表示職務的職責是 responsibilities。表示所需資格的是 qualifications 或 requirement。要找到相應的語句，仔細確認情況。

2. 產品廣告要先在題目上確認產品的大致情況，然後確認特徵、打折優惠、購買方法等。

   在題目或文章前半部分會出現所廣告的商品，因此可以快速地確認產品的種類。

   在說明產品的特徵之後，會出現有關打折情況和購買方法的說明。

例題

Linguistic Specialist

The Boston Herald is seeking a professional Japanese translator for a full-time, one year position. He or she must edit and translate articles from English to Japanese. Responsibilities also include researching newspapers based in Japan and conducting surveys on interests of Japanese readers. The ideal applicant must have at least two years experience in a similar position. The candidate should demonstrate leadership, self-motivation, and a keen sense of detail. Applicants must also possess the Certificate of Proficiency for the Japanese language. Salary will be determined by experience. If interested, please email your application, including all certificates and licensures, to hrd@bostonherald.com.

— 題目
— 招聘職業
— 職務說明
— 資格要求及待遇
— 申請方法

Q : According to the advertisement, what does the job require?

A : Official proof of fluency in the foreign language

→ 資格要求一般會出現在職務說明之後。根據文中的 Applicants must also posses the Certificate of Proficiency for the Japanese language，我們可以知道它對應徵者的要求是要有日語能力證書。因此答案應該是 "Official proof of fluency in the foreign language"。

短文解釋 P136

⊙ 出現在招聘廣告中的主要內容

❶ 招聘的職業類型

公司名 is seeking 職業名　在…公司招聘…職業的人員

Cell-Tech is seeking an innovative and dynamic individual to facilitate business development at our new branch in Chicago. Cell-Tech 正在招募有創意、有活力的人員來促進我們在芝加哥的新分公司的企業成長。

❷ 負責業務

Candidates will be responsible for ~　申請者會負責…工作

The successful candidate will be responsible for budget management, accounts reconciliation and inventory control. 合格的申請者將負責預算管理、對帳、管理庫存等工作。

❸ 資格事項

A candidate is required to have ~　申請者要具備的資格是…

The candidate is required to have five or more years experience in a similar role.
申請者需要有五年以上相關職務的工作經驗。

❹ 申請方法

Interested persons should send ~　有意願的人請發送…

Interested persons should send or fax a cover letter, resume, and references before the August 15 deadline. 有意願的人要在八月15日之前把附信、履歷表和推薦函等郵寄或傳真到公司。

⊙ 廣告中常出現的單字

❶ 錄用

application [ˌæpləˈkeʃən] 申請

apply for 申請…

be fluent in 對…熟練的

bilingual [baɪˈlɪŋgwəl] 雙語的

candidate [ˈkændədet] 求職者

certificate [səˈtɪfəkɪt] 證明書

communication skills 溝通技術

competent [ˈkɑmpətənt] 有能力的

cover letter 推薦函

diploma [dɪˈplomə] 畢業證書

employ [ɪmˈplɔɪ] 雇用

employment [ɪmˈplɔɪmənt] 聘僱

experienced [ɪkˈspɪrɪənst] 有經驗的

hire [haɪr] 雇用

in-house job posting 內部求職廣告

interview [ˈɪntəˌvju] 面談

job vacancy 職缺 =job opening

proficient [prəˈfɪʃənt] 熟練的

qualification [ˌkwɑləfəˈkeʃən] 申請資格

recruit [rɪˈkrut] 新進職員

reference letter 推薦書 =letter of recommendation

résumé [ˌrɛzjuˈme] 履歷表

skill [ˈskɪl] 技術

specialist [ˈspɛʃəlɪst] 專家

trustworthy [ˈtrʌstˌwɝðɪ] 可信賴的

dependable [dɪˈpɛndəbl̩] 可相信的

prerequisite [ˌpriˈrɛkwəzɪt] 必要條件

professional [prəˈfɛʃənl̩] 專門的

❷職業

accountant [əˋkauntənt] 會計師
analyst [ˋænˌlɪst] 分析員
attorney [əˋtɝnɪ] 代理人，律師
bookkeeper [ˋbukˌkipɚ] 簿記員
cashier [kæˋʃɪr] 出納員
chemist [ˋkɛmɪst] 化學家
counselor [ˋkaunslɚ] 商談者，顧問
engineer [ˌɛndʒəˋnɪr] 技術員

expert [ˋɛkspɚt] 專家
janitor [ˋdʒænɪtɚ] 看門人
operator [ˋɑpəˌretɚ] 接線生
physician [fɪˋzɪʃən] 內科醫生
researcher [riˋsɝtʃɚ] 研究員
salesman [ˋselzmən] 銷售員
secretary [ˋsɛkrəˌtɛrɪ] 秘書

❸工資

allotment [əˋlɑtmənt] 特別收入
allowance [əˋlauəns] 定期補助
benefit [ˋbɛnəfɪt] 津貼
bonus [ˋbonəs] 特別獎金
cut the number on payroll 裁員
incentive [ɪnˋsɛntɪv] 獎金

income [ˋɪnˌkʌm] 收入
payroll [ˋpeˌrol] 薪資單
pension [ˋpɛnʃən] 退休金
reward [rɪˋwɔrd] 獎勵
salary [ˋsælərɪ] 薪水
wage [wedʒ] 工資

❹工作狀態

be on duty 工作中的
be on leave 休假中的
day shift 每日工作
freelance [ˋfriˋlæns] 自由工作者
internship [ˋɪntɝnˌʃɪp] 實習醫師
maternity leave 產假
newcomer [ˋnjuˋkʌmɚ] 新人

night shift 夜間值班
orientation [ˌorɪɛnˋteʃən] 職業預備教育
part-time 兼職的
probationary period 實習期間
sick leave 病假
temporary [ˋtɛmpəˌrɛrɪ] 臨時工

❺購買

auctioned [ˋɔkʃən] 拍賣的
bid [bɪd] 投標
bill [bɪl] 帳單
due [dju] 到期的
expense [ɪkˋspɛns] 費用
payable [ˋpeəbl] 需支付的

payment [ˋpemənt] 支付，付款
purchase [ˋpɝtʃəs] 購買
raffle [ˋræfl] 抽獎
receipt [rɪˋsit] 收據
toll-free 不用付電話費的

⊙「廣告」類型題練習
　　閱讀短文並回答問題。

01

> Carson's Law Office is currently seeking a receptionist with the following qualifications:
>
> ✓ Typing speed of over 80 wpm
> ✓ Excellent communication skills
> ✓ Mastery of word processing programs
> ✓ Knowledge of Excel a plus
>
> If you feel that you meet these requirements, please stop by our office to set up an interview. Leave your resume and letters of reference with the front desk.

Q. What is mentioned as a requirement for employment?

(A) Master's degree in computer programming
(B) Ability to communicate in a foreign language
(C) Expertise with document processing software

02

> **Position:**
> - Market Analyzer
>
> **Specific duties and responsibilities:**
> - Research market competitors
> - Prepare portfolios and presentations with which to demonstrate your findings
> - Creatively design and plan suggestions for market share increase
>
> **Qualifications:**
> - Excellent research skills
> - Knowledge of cosmetic products
> - At least five years' experience
> - Specialized training at university or college

Q. What is NOT mentioned as a responsibility of the job?

(A) Instructing staff on market trends
(B) Giving presentations of research results
(C) Finding information about competing companies

03

> **Professional Tour Guides**
> Available for daily, weekly, or monthly excursions
>
> For your security and convenience:
> • All guides certified by the American National Tourist Association
> • Tours available all year round
> • Guides screened by National Security Department
> • Refunds given if not satisfied with the trip

Q. What is being advertised?

(A) An American travel agency
(B) A hostel for backpackers
(C) A travel escort service

正確答案　P136

Questions 1-2 refer to the following advertisement.

Management Position Available for a Qualified Professional

The Pacific Pacesetters Training Corporation is accepting applications for a Customized Training Director. This is a full-time position. The Director will be responsible for the overseeing and sales of customized training programs for companies, colleges, public offices and organizations on a city-wide scale. He or she will build relationships with local officials, company heads, colleges and professional organizations for the purpose of cultivating and growing new markets. Local travel is required. Candidate must have a Master's degree and two years experience in a similar position. Strong computer and instructional technology is required. Ability to speak and read in Spanish is a plus. The Pacific Pacesetters Training Corporation provides a competitive salary commensurate with the candidate's qualifications. Please send a letter of interest to Administrative Services, Pacific Pacesetters Training Corporation, Route 67 West, Boston, MA 02101 or: hrd@pptc.com.

1. What must a successful applicant possess?

(A) A vehicle
(B) City-wide contacts
(C) Computer expertise
(D) Second-language fluency

2. What does the advertisement suggest?

(A) The Director will conduct trainings.
(B) The pay is in accordance with the applicant's background.
(C) The candidate must be of Spanish descent.
(D) The applicant must be well-traveled.

Questions 3-4 refer to the following advertisement.

Spring Sale!!!

Stock up on spring savings!

From now until March 12, the prices on many food products have been slashed as a way of celebrating the end of winter. Great deals include:

- *10% off all canned fruits, vegetable, and legumes*
- *15% off dairy products*
- *20% off fresh, local produce*
- *20% off entire stock of frozen pizzas and microwave dinners*

In order to take advantage of these discounted prices, each customer must present a coupon, which can be found in the Gregory's Grocery bulletin, or in the local Sunday paper. Bring the coupon next time you visit our store and take advantage of reduced prices on all your favorite provisions! Remember, the sale only lasts until March 12, so hurry over! Don't waste another minute!

3. During the sale, which items will be reduced the least?

(A) Packaged meals
(B) Milk and eggs
(C) Tomatoes and plums
(D) Non-perishable produce

4. How can a person receive a reduced price?

(A) Applying for a membership card
(B) Subscribing to the newspaper
(C) Bringing in a discount ticket
(D) Checking the store's website

Chapter 8

公告（Notice & Anouncement）

公告是為告知新實行的方針或因現有規定變更而寫的文章。此類型的題目每次考試都會出現兩則，主要是關於公告的主題、場所、時間、要求事項等方面的問題。公司內部的公告會有人事或系統變化、設施維修或清掃預告、日程安排等內容。一般公告會有停車場或航空公司的規定、交通路線變更等多元化的內容。

百發百中 出題類型與戰略

⊙ 頻繁出現的問題類型

文章的目的是？	What is the purpose of this notice?
文章的要求事項是？	What are people being asked to do?
其他細節	When is compensation offered?
	What is NOT required when reporting problems?

⊙ 核心戰略

1. 瞭解公告的基本構造，就可以快速掌握文章重點。

   在文章的前半部分，會提出公告的目的。

   在文章的中間部分，會提到所談事項的時間、方法、要求事項等細節內容。

   在文章的結尾處，會提供聯繫方式。

2. 首先掌握公告的事項，然後一邊預測由此帶來的具體事項一邊進行閱讀。

   掌握了主題，就可以縮小場所、要求事項等方面的範圍，就可以做到邊預測邊閱讀。

例題

Notice
Approved by the Allegheny Police Department

The Allegheny Friendship Festival is expected to bring thousands of residents and visitors to the downtown area from January 23 to January 25. Please be informed that the following streets will be closed from 6 AM Friday, January 23 until 4 PM Sunday, January 25:

　　Main Street at 1st Street, 2nd Street, 3rd Street and Giss Parkway

　　Maiden Lane at 2nd Street, 3rd Street and Giss Parkway

Motorists are advised to take a detour through Penny Lane and to exercise caution when driving near the festival area. Please get in touch with John Shriver, festival administrator, if you have any questions.

主題

具體事項及要求事項

聯繫方式

Q : Who should motorists contact if they have any concerns?

A : John Shriver

　→ 此題問的是公告中談到的聯繫方法，所以確定解題線索在文章的結尾部分。從最後一句 Please get in touch with John Shriver, festival administrator, if you have any questions 可以看出，聯繫方式是找 John Shriver。

短文解釋 P138

⊙ 廣告中頻繁出現的主要內容

❶ 與公告的目的相關的表現

We are pleased to announce ~ 　很高興通知您…

We are pleased to announce the publication of the 2002 edition of The Journalist's Reference Book. 很高興通知您 The Journalist's Reference Book 的 2002 年修訂版已經出版。

Please be aware that ~ 　希望您能瞭解…

Please be aware that there is a service charge for bank patrons whose checks are returned due to insufficient funds. 如果出現支票因資金不足而被退回的情況,將會收取服務費用,希望您能瞭解。

❷ 要求事項

人 is requested to + 動詞原形 　要求…做…

Drivers are requested to collect a parking voucher from the dispensing machine before entering the garage. 進入車庫以前,司機被要求要從自動發票機拿停車證。

❸ 聯繫方式

If you have any concerns, please contact ~ 　如果有任何問題,請聯繫…

If you have any concerns, please contact us at the address indicated at the end of this policy. 如果有任何問題,請依照保險單最下方的地址聯繫我們。

⊙ 公告中常出現的單字

❶ 公司業務中的一般單字

accomplish [ə`kɑmplɪʃ] 執行	implement [`ɪmplə‚mɛnt] 執行
acquisition [‚ækwə`zɪʃən] 獲得,獲利	mediate [`midɪ‚et] 調解
agenda [ə`dʒɛndə] 應辦事項	negotiation [nɪ‚goʃɪ`eʃən] 協商
assign [ə`saɪn] 分配,指定	oversee [`ovə`si] 監督
assignment [ə`saɪnmənt] 分配,任務	performance [pə`fɔrməns] 執行,成果
circulate [`sɝkjə‚let] 傳閱	recipient [rɪ`sɪpɪənt] 接收者
compromise [`kɑmprə‚maɪz] 妥協	reimburse [‚riɪm`bɝs] 償還
consensus [kən`sɛnsəs] 合意	routine [ru`tin] 日常事務
coordinate [ko`ɔrdn̩et] 協調	set out to do 開始做…
correspondence [‚kɔrə`spɑndəns] 書信往來	submission [sʌb`mɪʃən] 提出
dispute [dɪ`spjut] 爭論	take on 承擔事情
dress code 服裝規定	undertake [‚ʌndə`tek] 承擔,開始
embark [ɪm`bɑrk] 投資	workload [`wɝk‚lod] 作業量
evaluate [ɪ`vælju‚et] 評價	

❷生產

apparatus [ˌæpəˈretəs] 儀器，設備

assembly line 生產線

component [kəmˈponənt] 構成要素

construct [kənˈstrʌkt] 建設

conveyor [kənˈveɚ] 運輸裝置

defect [dɪˈfɛkt] 缺陷

device [dɪˈvaɪs] 器具

equipment [ɪˈkwɪpmənt] 裝備，設備

facilitate [fəˈsɪləˌtet] 使容易

facilities [fəˈsɪlətɪ] 設施

fully-equipped 完備的

inspection [ɪnˈspɛkʃən] 精密檢查

instrument [ˈɪnstrəmənt] 器具，器械

machinery [məˈʃinərɪ] 機器類

malfunction [mælˈfʌŋʃən] 故障

maintenance [ˈmentənəns] 維修

manufacture [ˌmænjəˈfæktʃɚ] 製造

maximize [ˈmæksəˌmaɪz] 最大化

mechanical [məˈkænɪkl] 機械化的

minimize [ˈmɪnəˌmaɪz] 最小化

output [ˈaʊtˌpʊt] 生產

outsourcing [ˈaʊtˌsɔrsɪŋ] 外包

plant [plænt] 工廠

process [ˈprɑsɛs] 工程

produce [prəˈdjus] 生產

productivity [ˌprodʌkˈtɪvətɪ] 生產力

prototype [ˈprotəˌtaɪp] 原型，範例

quality [ˈkwɑlətɪ] 品質

quantity [ˈkwɑntətɪ] 數量

renovate [ˈrɛnəˌvet] 修復，革新

resources [rɪˈsors] 資源

shift [ʃɪft] 輪班

standardize [ˈstændɚˌdaɪz] 標準化

unit [ˈjunɪt] 構成單位

update [ʌpˈdet] 更新

upgrade [ˈʌpˈgred] 改良品質

yield [jild] 出產

❸機場

air fare 航空票價

aircraft [ˈɛrˌkræft] 飛機

airsickness [ˈɛrˌsɪknɪs] 暈機

aisle seat 靠走道的座位

aviation [ˌevɪˈeʃən] 飛行

baggage [ˈbægɪdʒ] 行李

boarding pass 登機證

departure [dɪˈpɑrtʃɚ] 出發

destination [ˌdɛstəˈneʃən] 目的地

duties [ˈdjutɪ] 稅金、關稅

duty-free shop 免稅店

emergency [ɪˈmɝdʒənsɪ] 緊急情況

flight attendant 空服員

go through customs 通過海關

immigration [ˌɪməˈgreʃən] 出入國管理、審查

jet lag 時差症候群

land [lænd] 著陸

local time 當地時間

luggage [ˈlʌgɪdʒ] 行李

renew [rɪˈnju] 更新

stand-by 等待者

take off 起飛

visa [ˈvizə] 簽證

window seat 靠窗的座位

⊙ 「公告」類型題練習

閱讀短文並回答問題。

01

For the next month, the local student council will be accepting submissions for the youth essay contest. The council is in need of qualified people to judge the entries after the deadline has passed. If interested, please contact principal Howard and send your resume to the council's e-mail address.

Q. What is the purpose of this notice?

(A) To recruit evaluators for a writing contest
(B) To bring in more participants for the contest
(C) To promote the student council

02

Due to an increase in customer demand, Johnson Tailor has had to reorganize its order completion process. From now on, all customers will receive an itemized receipt when picking up their mended or tailored clothing. A list of the made alterations will appear on the left hand side of the paper.

Q. How will the adjustments be indicated?

(A) They will be explained to the patron upon pick-up.
(B) They will be printed on the receipt.
(C) They will be listed on the clothes.

03

Electricians will be working with maintenance personnel to replace some of the wires on the first and second floors this morning at 10:00. The maintenance work will result in a loss of electric service for approximately one hour. A few minutes before the power outage is scheduled to begin, an announcement will flash on your screen, instructing you to save your data and turn off your computers.

Q. What should employees do when they are signaled?

(A) Turn out the lights
(B) Delete suspect files
(C) Shut down their computers

正確答案 P138

Questions 1-4 refer to the following notice.

The Belcan Corporation would like to announce that it has established a biennial award for enterprising employees who by action or idea have contributed to the growth of the corporation. The award is to be known as the John Belcan Award in honor of the man who founded the Belcan Corporation 50 years ago. His impeccable character and enormous energy for making the Belcan Corporation a well-known name in the electronics industry has positively influenced all who have known and worked with him.

The winner of the award should have the same outlook and determination that John Belcan had. He should also possess the devotion and high principles that Belcan had for family, work and society. The winner will receive a commemoration plaque, as well as a promotion complete with a 10% raise. Nominations should be submitted to the Employee Awards Selection Committee using the Employee Awards Form available at the administrative services office and on the company website. Supervisors can only nominate employees directly working under them and who have received a performance evaluation within the past three months. Although supervisors may be nominated by the manager they work under, managers are not eligible for this award. The Employee Awards Selection Committee shall make a selection based on the enterprising contributions made by each candidate. The full criteria for selections will be posted on the website by Monday of next week.

1. What is the purpose of this award?

(A) To celebrate the 50th anniversary of Belcan Corporation
(B) To recognize an employee who follows the spirit of the founder
(C) To commemorate the recently deceased founder
(D) To honor the founding of the Belcan Corporation

2. How often is this honor given?

(A) Twice a year
(B) Twice a month
(C) Once every other year
(D) Once per year

3. What does the winner get as an award?

(A) Free company products
(B) A paid vacation
(C) A trophy
(D) A salary increase

4. What is NOT correct about the announcement?

(A) The form must be given to the selection committee.
(B) The complete criteria is given in the announcement.
(C) The award was recently established.
(D) The award was named after the company's founder.

Questions 5-6 refer to the following notice.

FRIENDLY SKIES AIRLINES

We here at Friendly Skies Airlines would like to remind all passengers that security will be increased during the holiday season. It is customary for the level of alert to be higher during peak travel times. As you are already aware, tighter security means a few more restrictions for passengers flying on any of the days marked red by Homeland Security. For your own convenience and safety, please review the following restrictions:

- Each ticketed passenger is allowed only one piece of checked luggage and one piece of carry-on luggage, plus a purse, or brief case or laptop computer.

- When luggage is carried on-board the aircraft, it must be of a size and shape to allow for storage in aircraft overhead compartments, or underneath the seat in front of the passenger. This piece of luggage must not exceed 45 linear inches (9 inches by 14 inches by 22 inches) and also must not exceed 40 pounds.

- Passengers should arrive at the airport 75 minutes prior to departure for domestic flights. For international flights, you should arrive at least 2 hours in advance. Those travelers who arrive late will not be admitted into the main terminal area.

- Passengers who made reservations with e-tickets must claim them at one of the airline's automatic printers at least 90 minutes before their scheduled flight, whether domestic or international.

- Passengers traveling with disabled travelers who need any extra help are recommended to report to the airport at least 1 hour prior to the customarily recommended time, as listed above.

We appreciate your care and participation during the holiday times. As always, we hope you have safe travels and that we can serve you again soon in the future.

5. Who does the notice address?

(A) Flight attendants
(B) Pilots
(C) Airline passengers
(D) Travel agents

6. What time should regular passengers arrive for domestic flights?

(A) At least two hours prior to departure
(B) At least sixty minutes before departure
(C) At least ninety minutes prior to departure
(D) At least one and a quarter hour before departure

正確答案 P138

Chapter 9

報導（Article & Report）

報導和報告在每次考試中平均會出現兩次，它主要針對國際經濟或企業狀況，一般由環境保護、能源節約、公司業務、健康等方面的內容構成。大部分報導都先明確指出主題，然後再敘述詳細內容。題目類型是從找主題類型到推論題類型平均分配的。該類題目對單字量的要求較高，而且短文長度較長的情況也很多，因此屬於比較有難度的短文類型。

百發百中 出題類型與戰略

⊙ 頻繁出現的問題類型

文章的主題是？　　What is the main idea of this article?

詳細內容　　　　What is a worker's right according to the article?
　　　　　　　　What is NOT recommended when traveling in developing countries?

文章意味著什麼？　What does this article suggest?

⊙ 核心戰略

1. 報導一般都會在一開始點出主題，要先確認文章前面提到的內容。

　　在文章前面正確掌握文章的目的，就會在下面的閱讀中非常順暢。

2. 要盡量掌握多種領域的單字。

　　閱讀報導需要很大的單字量，因此最好掌握好本書中收錄的 Part 7 部分中的有關經濟、政治、社會、健康的單字。

例題

Gregory & Mills has announced that it is going to transfer its corporate headquarters to the southernmost provinces of the country. It has said that the fierce competition and high tariffs in New York are too much for the company to handle financially. Seasonal demands, which were expected to stimulate overall profits, weren't as high as anticipated. The decrease in consumption is closely linked to the sluggish economy shaking the nation's financial foundations, which is not forecasted to improve in the near future. The combined factors of the national recession and inflation in the Manhattan district have depleted Gregory & Mills' funds. Therefore, it has picked Texas as its new home and will host the office near the state's capital, Austin.

主題

具體事項

Q : What is the purpose of this article?
A : To declare an upcoming move

→ 從文章開頭部分的 Gregory & Mills has announced that it is going to transfer its corporate headquarters to the southernmost provinces of the country，可以看出文章的目的是要通知即將進行的搬遷事宜。

⊙ 報導中頻繁出現的核心表現

人物 / 機關 announced that ~　…宣佈了…

FB Network Associates announced today that it has signed an agreement with Data Technologies to develop network applications.

FB Network Associates 宣佈，今天與 Data Technoloies 公司簽署了協議書來發展網路的申請。

人物 / 機關 point out that ~　…指出…

Economists point out that the declining value of the dollar is helping exporters sell their goods in overseas markets.

經濟學家指出，美元的貶值將有助於出口商把他們的產品賣到國外市場去。

⊙ 報導中常出現的單字

❶一般經濟

adverse [æd`vɝs] 不利的，相反的	monetary [`mʌnəˌtɛrɪ] 貨幣的
bankrupt [`bæŋkrʌpt] 破產的	monopoly [mə`nɑplɪ] 獨佔，壟斷
boom [bum] 急速發展	prosperity [prɑs`pɛrətɪ] 繁榮
boost [bust] 促進	recession [rɪ`sɛʃən] 經濟衰退期
capital [`kæpət|] 資本	remit [rɪ`mɪt] 匯出
circulation [ˌsɝkjə`leʃən]（金融的）流通	sluggish [`slʌgɪʃ] 呆滯的
currency [`kɝənsɪ] 貨幣	soar [sor] 暴漲
downturn [`daʊntɝn] 低迷時期	speculation [ˌspɛkjə`leʃən] 投機
flourish [`flɝɪʃ] 繁榮	stagnation [stæg`neʃən] 停滯
fluctuate [`flʌktʃʊˌet] 變動	stimulate [`stɪmjəˌlet] 刺激
inflation [ɪn`fleʃən] 通貨膨脹	surge [sɝdʒ] 波動
market research 市場調查	tax exemption 免稅的
market share 市場佔有率	tax-deductible 減免稅後的
marketability [ˌmɑrkɪtə`bɪlətɪ] 市場性	thrifty [`θrɪftɪ] 節省的
merge [mɝdʒ] 合併	

❷企業經濟

accounting [ə`kaʊntɪŋ] 會計	finance [faɪ`næns] 財政
analysis [ə`næləsɪs] 分析	fiscal year 會計年度
analyst [`ænḷɪst] 分析師	liability [ˌlaɪə`bɪlətɪ] 責任
assets [`æsɛts] 財產	overhead [`ovɚˌhɛd] 一般支出
audit [`ɔdɪt] 檢查	portfolio [port`folɪˌo] 有價證券
budget [`bʌdʒɪt] 預算	profitability [ˌprɑfɪtə`bɪlətɪ] 收益性
dividend [`dɪvəˌdɛnd] 紅利	revenue [`rɛvəˌnju] 稅收
downsize [`daʊn`saɪz] 節儉	set up a business 創立事業
earnings [`ɝnɪŋz] 所得	strategy [`strætədʒɪ] 策略

❸損益

be in the black 獲利

be in the red 赤字

benefit [ˋbɛnəfɪt] 利益

cost [kɔst] 費用

damage [ˋdæmɪdʒ] 損失

deficit [ˋdɛfɪsɪt] 虧空，赤字

expenditure [ɪkˋspɛndɪtʃə] 支出

expense [ɪkˋspɛns] 支出

gross [gros] 總共的

gross income 總收入

income [ˋɪn͵fʌm] 收入

loss [lɔs] 損失

lucrative [ˋlukrətɪv] 賺錢的

margin [ˋmɑrdʒɪn] 利潤

net profit 淨利

profit [ˋprɑfɪt] 利潤，盈餘

profitable [ˋprɑfɪtəbl̩] 有利的

surcharge [ˋsɝ͵tʃɑrdʒ] 額外支出

surplus [ˋsɝpləs] 盈餘

❹環境

acid rain 酸雨

coal [kol] 煤，木炭

conserve [kənˋsɝv] 保存

contamination [kən͵tæməˋneʃən] 污染

crude [krud] 天然的

disposal [dɪˋspozl̩] 處理

ecology [ɪˋkɑlədʒɪ] 生態學

endangered [ɪnˋdendʒəd] 瀕臨絕種的

environment [ɪnˋvaɪrənmənt] 環境

habitat [ˋhæbə͵tæt] 棲息地

hazardous [ˋhæzədəs] 危險的

humidity [hjuˋmɪdətɪ] 濕度

mine [maɪn] 礦山

natural resources 天然資源

ozone layer 臭氧層

purify [ˋpjurə͵faɪ] 淨化

recycle [riˋsaɪkl̩] 再利用

timber [ˋtɪmbə] 木材

wildlife [ˋwaɪld͵laɪf] 野生生物

❺醫療‧健康

allergy [ˋælədʒɪ] 過敏

antibiotic [͵æntɪbaɪˋɑtɪk] 抗生素

diagnosis [͵daɪəgˋnosɪs] 診斷

fatigue [fəˋtig] 疲勞

medication [͵mɛdɪˋkeʃən] 藥物

nutrition [njuˋtrɪʃən] 營養

prescription [prɪˋskrɪpʃən] 處方

symptom [ˋsɪmptəm] 徵兆，症狀

vaccination [͵væksn̩ˋeʃən] 接種疫苗

❻國家政治

authorize [ˋɔθə͵raɪz] 授權

bureau [ˋbjuro] 局

consulate [ˋkɑnsl̩ɪt] 領事館

diplomat [ˋdɪpləmæt] 外交官

election [ɪˋlɛkʃən] 選舉

embassy [ˋɛmbəsɪ] 大使館

enactment [ɪnˋæktmənt] 法令

federal [ˋfɛdərəl] 聯邦的

legislation [͵lɛdʒɪsˋleʃən] 立法

mandatory [ˋmændə͵torɪ] 強制的，命令的

municipal [mjuˋnɪsəpl̩] 地方自治的

provisions [prəˋvɪʒən] 規定

summit [ˋsʌmɪt] 首長，高層

violation [͵vaɪəˋleʃən] 違反

HACKERS PRACTICE ● ● ● ● ● ● ● ● ● ● ● ● ● ● ●

01

> For many first-time home buyers, high interest rates or shaky market prices act as deterrents against property purchase. Most people find it discouraging to get rejected by bank after bank, even with perfect credit histories. In the meantime, home-seekers usually tire of the search and instead come to appreciate the simplicity of renting an apartment or condominium. Thus, in the end, the number of actual buyers is quite low.

Q. What obstacle do many first-time home owners face?

(A) Finding affordable housing
(B) Paying for rent and a mortgage at the same time
(C) Getting approved for a loan

02

> The so-called "Avian Flu" is wreaking havoc in some of Asia's easternmost provinces, most notably Thailand. The epidemic has had adverse effects on the country's already sluggish economy. Two of the largest industries in the nation are being hit the hardest, the chicken and tourist industries. Chicken farming, which makes up over 2% of the country's total GDP, is expected to continue its recession, while measures are being taken to stimulate tourism, which accounts for just under 6% of the nation's income.

Q. What is likely to happen to Thailand's chicken industry?

(A) It will derail Thailand's booming economy.
(B) It will suffer more losses.
(C) It will stay at a standstill.

03

> The Black and White Furniture Factory in Nogales, Arizona is closing down for good. It has had a glorious 80-year history, but Nogales is changing. Like many cities in Arizona, industries are no longer the main source of income for most residents. Service-oriented businesses are now flourishing in Nogales and provide the main source of employment for 90 percent of its working residents.

Q. Why is Black and White Furniture Company shutting down?

(A) It cannot compete with other furniture factories.
(B) It no longer provides a main work source for residents.
(C) The factory is old and broken down.

Questions 1-3 refer to the following article.

As cold approaches and temperatures drop below zero, protection against winter weather is foremost on everyone's minds. Not only the means of defense, but the expenditure needed to do so. Companies, which are inevitably burdened by large spaces, can trim their heating costs this winter by taking simple steps.

Initially, all corporations should assess their chosen means of fuel. It is recommended that any company using electricity for heat convert to another fuel, as electricity costs three times more than gas or oil. Some smaller companies, particularly those in less urban areas, might opt to go with propane. Some companies can harness byproducts, such as steam from a manufacturing process, to heat their facilities.

Companies in some urban areas and industrial districts might have access to district heating plants, where steam travels through tunnels and gets piped into buildings. There are serious restrictions, though. These districts are limited, and even companies that operate within districts might have to put up significant capital costs in order to take advantage of the energy.

For companies using oil or gas, experts say it pays to shop around. Even homeowners know that oil prices and services vary from company to company. Experts also recommend that companies, like homeowners, should make sure their heating equipment is as efficient as possible and their buildings are sufficiently insulated. The simple step of watching the thermostat is also recommended. Some people mistakenly believe that turning the temperature way down overnight conserves energy and lowers bills. In reality, though, it takes a lot of energy to bring a building's temperature back to comfortable levels in the morning. Multiple thermostats can help keep costs down; companies can shut off seldom-used areas so that these areas do not have to be heated.

1. What is the purpose of this article?

(A) To explain why companies use electricity
(B) To examine why companies spend so much on heating
(C) To provide information on conserving energy sources
(D) To discuss how a company can reduce heating expenses

2. What is the limitation of district heating plants?

(A) Government authorization is required.
(B) There aren't many that exist.
(C) Residential buildings are prioritized.
(D) Industrial districts compete for their use.

3. What does the article suggest?

(A) All oil and gas costs the same price.
(B) Raising heat costs less than sustaining it.
(C) Heating should be left on during the night.
(D) Electricity is an efficient source of energy.

Questions 4-5 refer to the following report.

Briggs Pharmaceuticals is almost ready to introduce its latest asthma medication into the market. For the past nine months, researchers have been developing ways to reduce the amount of chemical agents used in inhalers. This was propelled by a number of patient complaints regarding headaches, twitching and nausea after using the company's inhalation product.

A number of test studies and laboratory experiments have led to the discovery of a pill that attaches itself to the inner lining of the esophagus, releasing vapors that ease asthmatic symptoms. This method is less abrasive than other medications and is also more cost effective. The reduction in chemicals will potentially reduce the side effects normally considered a way of life for asthma sufferers.

4. What prompted Briggs to alter its asthma medication?

(A) There was significant competition.
(B) The price of the original product was too high.
(C) It had too many negative side effects.
(D) Inhalers are no longer popular.

5. What is NOT a benefit of the new drug?

(A) The price is much lower than that of the inhaler.
(B) It won't cause the patient as much suffering.
(C) It will make the lives of people with asthma easier.
(D) It will cure asthma patients at a much faster rate.

正確答案 P141

READING II 各類型短文攻略

Chapter 10

備忘錄（Memo）

備忘錄是公司內部傳達議事內容時用到的通告文。格式與電子郵件相似，但前後沒有問候語，以內容為重點。主要由公司內的公告和類似的公司設施、使用程式、業務次序變更通知等內容構成。每次考試平均出一篇。

百發百中 出題類型與戰略

⊙ 頻繁出現的問題類型

文章的目的是？　What is the purpose of this memo?

詳細內容　　　　When will the new procedures be initiated?

Why must the employees go to Room 3490?

Who will distribute the cards?

⊙ 核心戰略

1. 最好的備忘錄格式

左側上方寫制定日期、收信者和寄信者。在 "Subject:" 或 "Re:" 之後會表明主題，要以此為參考，邊猜測文章內容邊閱讀。

2. 掌握了備忘錄的基本架構，就可以邊猜測文章內容，邊進行流暢地閱讀。

表明備忘錄的主題之後，才會開始提到時間、方法、要求事項等細節。

例題

> Due to new attendance policies, every employee will have to remember to check-out everyday before leaving. The new system is managed online by OfficeSmart Corporation. Rather than filling out the old time cards, with the new policy you will have to type in your name and password onto the online attendance sheet by logging onto the company's website. Work performed outside of the office may be recorded by this system, but employees are cautioned that anyone attempting to take advantage of the new attendance record will be reprimanded. Conveniently, the program will automatically sign you in or out, unless you forget to report to the website. If you still do not yet have a password and sign-in ID, please report to the main office and request a change of identification. Thank you for your cooperation.

主題

具體事項

Q : Why was this memo written?
A : To inform employees of a change in procedure.

→ 此題問的是寫備忘錄的目的。從文章前半部分的 "Due to new attendance policies, every emplyee will have to remember to check-out everyday before leaving." 可以看出，這篇文章是在通知新的程式變更。因此答案是 "To inform employees of a change in procedure"。

短文解釋　P142

⊙ 備忘錄中頻繁出現的主要內容

❶與備忘錄的目的相關的表現

I am sending this memo out to + 動詞原形　為…而發送這篇備忘錄。

I am sending this memo out to all seminar participants to remind you of the change in schedule for tomorrow's presentations.
這篇備忘錄是為了提醒所有參加研討會的人，明天發演會的行程安排有變更。

We regret to inform you that ~　很遺憾地通知您…

We regret to inform you that your account has been suspended pending payment of all outstanding debts.
很遺憾地通知您，在您的債款未償還之前，您將無法使用您的帳戶。

⊙ 報導中常出現的單字

❶人事

allocate [`ælə͵ket] 分配

appoint [ə`pɔɪnt] 任命

appraisal [ə`prez!] 評價

aptitude [`æptə͵tjud] 素質、才能

curtail [kɜ`tel] 減少

cut back 削減

dismiss [dɪs`mɪs] 解雇

dispatch [dɪ`spætʃ] 急件

field [fild] 領域、現場

fire [faɪr] 解雇

get a promotion 獲得升遷

incumbent [ɪn`kʌmbənt] 在職人員

layoff [`le͵ɔf] 解雇

profile [`profaɪl] 人物概要

promote [prə`mot] 晉升

qualified [`kwɑlə͵faɪd] 有資格的

quit [kwɪt] 放棄

relocate [ri`loket] 重新部署

replacement [rɪ`plesmənt] 替換、後繼者

resign [rɪ`zaɪn] 辭職

resignation [͵rɛzɪg`neʃən] 辭職

retirement [rɪ`taɪrmənt] 退休

training session 訓練期間

transferred [træns`fɜ] 傳送

turnover [`tɜn͵ovə] 營業額

❷管理職位的業務

advise [əd`vaɪz] 忠告

alter [`ɔltə] 變更

appropriate [ə`proprɪ͵et] 適合的

assign [ə`saɪn] 分配

consult [kən`sʌlt]（與專家）商談

demanding [dɪ`mændɪŋ] 高要求的

head [hɛd] 領導

manage [`mænɪdʒ] 管理

proper [`prɑpə] 適合的

relevant [`rɛləvənt] 切題的

review [rɪ`vju] 檢查

streamline [`strim͵laɪn] 流線型

supervise [`supə͵vaɪz] 監督

time-consuming 費時間的

❸ 公司 日常

affiliate [ə`fɪlɪɪt] 使附屬
branch [bræntʃ] 分公司
colleague [`kɑlig] 同事
company [`kʌmpənɪ] 公司
competitor [kəm`pɛtətɚ] 競爭者
conglomerate [kən`glɑmərɪt] 企業集團
corporation [ˌkɔrpə`reʃən] 股份有限公司
division [də`vɪʒən] 部門
enterprise [`ɛntɚˌpraɪz] 企業
expansion [ɪk`spænʃən] 擴張

firm [fɝm] 公司
head office 總公司
headquarters [`hɛd`kwɔrtɚz] 總公司
Inc.(Incorporated) 股份有限公司
Ltd.(Limited) （公司）有限的
managerial [ˌmænə`dʒɪrɪəl] 經營上的
merge [mɝdʒ] 合併
parent company 總公司
subsidiary company 子公司

❹ 職位

administrative [əd`mɪnəˌstretɪv] 行政的
administrative assistant 行政助理
assistant [ə`sɪstənt] 輔助者，輔助的
associate [ə`soʃɪɪt] 副的，共事的
CEO(Chief Executive Officer) 執行總裁
chairman [`tʃɛrmən] 董事長
consultant [kən`sʌltənt] 顧問
coordinator [ko`ɔrdn̩ˌetɚ] 協調者
deputy [`dɛpjətɪ] 代理的
director [də`rɛktɚ] 主管
employee [ˌɛmplɔɪ`i] 受雇者
employer [ɪm`plɔɪɚ] 雇主
entrepreneur [ˌɑntrəprə`nɝ] 企業家

executive [ɪg`zɛkjutɪv] 主管，執行者
immediate supervisor 頂頭上司
manager [`mænɪdʒɚ] 部長，經理
managerial position 管理職
ownership [`onɚˌʃɪp] 所有權
position [pə`zɪʃən] 職位
representative [rɛprɪ`zɛntətɪv] 代表
senior [`sinjɚ] 上司
staff [stæf] 職員
supervisor [ˌsupɚ`vaɪzɚ] 管理人
trainee [tre`ni] 受訓者
vice-president 副董事長

❺ 部門

accounting department 會計部
board of directors 董事會
consumer affairs department 客服部門
engineering department 技術部門
head office 總公司
human resources department 人力資源部門
marketing department 行銷部門

overseas divisions 海外業務部
payroll department 薪資部門
personnel department 人事部門
public relations department 公關部門
sales department 營業部門
shipping department 船運部門

⊙「備忘錄」類型題練習

閱讀短文並回答問題。

01

> We regret to inform you that after ten years with Accutron Corporation, Stacy Burke will be stepping down as senior manager. Ms. Burke saw Accutron through some of its most exciting years, contributing to a 100 percent increase in product sales and devising a system that saved the corporation twenty million dollars in annual expenses.

Q. What is the purpose of this memo?

  (A) To congratulate a recently hired manager
  (B) To announce an increase in sales
  (C) To announce the resignation of a supervisor

02

> During the following two weeks, construction will be underway in the main lobby. There is a need to perform immediate repairs and maintenance before it can be used again. We ask that during this time you take the back door entrance and exit, or enter the building through the sliding doors adjacent to the river. Only construction crew members and high-ranking staff in management will be able to pass through the lobby while under construction.

Q. What is going to occur soon?

  (A) Staff will be using temporary offices.
  (B) The main entrance will be closed for repairs.
  (C) The company will be shut down temporarily.

03

> This year, we have accumulated 15 boxes of manuscripts that need treatment and rebinding in order to preserve them. These manuscripts are rare but still in demand; hence, the head librarian would like the salvaging work to take place as quickly as possible. While an expert technician has been hired to take the lead, staff members will be rotated to work with him on a two days per week basis.

Q. What is the purpose of this memo?

  (A) To ask for volunteers to work overtime
  (B) To inform staff of maintenance activities
  (C) To remind staff members of work load

Questions 1-2 refer to the following memo.

Date : 8 Nov 2004

To : Warehouse Personnel

From : Meredith Glover, Supervisor

Subject : Work Schedule for Winter Season

We are expecting orders for our products to peak this coming holiday season. Demand has already increased by 10 percent in the first week of November. We are not, at this time, planning to hire new packers and other warehouse personnel for the season, however. Therefore, we would like to announce that it will be necessary for all warehouse personnel to increase their work hour load beginning November 11 until the first week of January. An additional break will be provided during the shift. Each warehouse staff must increase his total weekly work load by 12 hours. Management is asking that employees who work the morning shift turn in their schedule requests to their supervisors. Those who work the afternoon shift must pick from the hours available on the sign up sheet located in the main office. Graveyard workers are expected to meet with their department heads individually to arrange their shifts. As usual, extra work will be remunerated with overtime wages, compensatory time off, or free products. Previously, we offered grocery coupon books, but that option has been discontinued.

---

1. Why was this memo written?

   (A) To inform staff of the hiring of temporary employees
   (B) To permanently change the work schedule
   (C) To inform staff of new work benefits
   (D) To announce a plan for meeting increased orders

2. What must people who work second shift do?

   (A) Make a list of desired hours
   (B) Choose from hours posted
   (C) Contact their supervisors
   (D) Arrange a time to talk

Questions 3-5 refer to the following memo.

TO :   Employees of Anderson Furniture
FROM :   Richard K. Norse, Director of Building Security
DATE :   15 April 2004
SUBJECT :   Security System

Please be aware that beginning next week Thursday the security system for this building is going to be replaced. Instead of the code accessible doors currently in place, there will be audio/visual monitors and armed personnel present at every entryway. This change is taking place due to the fact that a few employees have given their codes to persons not authorized to be in this building. We feel that using maximum security measures will benefit both the corporation and the staff.

According to our new policy, all employees must display their ID badges on their shirt pockets or around their necks at all times. Starting Thursday, anyone without proper identification will not be allowed into the premises. Guests will be ushered to the front information desk to fill out a visitor's application and will be issued a temporary ID before entering secure areas of the building. If you forget your pass, you will have to be screened by the front office before being allowed into your workplace.

In the case that you don't yet have your ID, stop down in the records department in the basement floor. Bring a passport size photograph and your social security card, as well as a signed copy of your contract. These documents will be retained for two days while your badge is being processed and the identification card will be valid for one year as of the issue date. You will also find a copy of this information in the weekly agenda in your mailboxes. Thank you for your cooperation.

3. Why is the security system being changed?

(A) Identification cards have been frequently lost.
(B) The code accessible doors have malfunctioned.
(C) Some people had unapproved access to the building.
(D) Employees have complained about theft.

4. What happens if employees don't wear the ID?

(A) They will be investigated before entering the building.
(B) They will have to be issued a temporary ID.
(C) They will have to fill out a visitor's application.
(D) They will be detained by security.

5. How long is the ID effective?

(A) For two days after the documents are processed
(B) For a year from the date of assignment
(C) For a year from the issue date of this notice
(D) For a year from next Thursday

Chapter 11

說明書（Information）

這種短文是產品說明書或登記書，以及與介紹公共設施的使用相關等在日常生活中可以接觸到的文章。由於經常問到文章提及的物件和提到的場所等，因此掌握文章的全盤狀況很重要。每次考試平均會出現一篇說明書。

百發百中 出題類型與戰略

⊙ 頻繁出現的問題類型

該類文章通常在哪裡可以看見？	Where would this information most likely be found?
此文以誰為對象？	Whom is this document intended for?
詳細內容	Why should customers send back the card?
	What is true about online orders?
	What is NOT available at the ticket office?

⊙ 核心戰略

1. 要掌握在哪裡、做什麼、對象是。

分析主要單字的表現，就可以得知是關於什麼的說明書，並且可得知說明的是什麼情況。文章的物件和看到此類文章的場所一般不會明白點出，偶爾會在推論題中問到。因此要理解文章的整體情況，推論出答案。

例題 1

Thank you for purchasing the Cellular Microphone. The Cellular Microphone is a state of the art communications device designed for people on the go. In order to assure the quality and performance of your new microphone, follow the guidelines below:

Instructions
1. Put two AAA batteries into the machine.
2. When the red light comes on, insert the microphone cord into the appropriate slot on the side of the box (indicated by a picture of headsets) and attach the other end of the cord to your cellular phone.
3. Turn both the cellular phone and the microphone box to 'on' and begin using your new microphone.

DO NOT
... place the microphone box in or around water (or other liquids).
... attempt to use another company's cord in this machine.

Q : Whom is this document intended for?
A : Purchasers of the Cellular Microphone

→ 此題問的是文章以誰為對象。觀察文章前半部分的 "Thank you for purchasing the Cellular Microphone."，可知是在為 Cellular Microphone 的購買表示感謝。因此答案應該是 "Purchasers of the Cellular Microphone。

⊙ 說明文中常出現的單字

❶交通

bypass [`baɪ͵pæs] 繞路

car maintenance 汽車維護

commute [kə`mjut] 通勤

fare [fɛr] 費用

fuel [`fjuəl] 燃料

highway [`haɪ͵we] 高速公路

intersection [͵ɪntə`sɛkʃən] 十字路口

launch [lɔntʃ] 出發

limousine [`lɪmə͵zin]（機場等接送旅客的）小型巴士

mechanic [mə`kænɪk] 機械的

passenger [`pæsṇdʒə] 乘客

pedestrian [pə`dɛstrɪən] 行人

public transportation 大眾交通

pull over 停車、停在路邊

route [rut] 通道、路

shortcut [`ʃɔrt͵kʌt] 捷徑

shuttle [`ʃʌtḷ] 接駁車

sidewalk [`saɪd͵wɔk] 人行道

toll [tol] 通行費

traffic congestion 交通擁擠

traffic jam 交通擁擠

transfer [træns`fɝ] 轉乘

vehicle [`viɪkḷ] 車輛

vessel [`vɛsḷ] 船

❷旅行

accommodation [ə͵kɑmə`deʃən] 住宿設施

book [bʊk] 預約

cancellation [͵kænsḷ`eʃən] 取消

car rental 汽車租用

check-in 登記

checkout [`tʃɛk͵aʊt] 退房

collect call 支付電話費

confirmation [͵kɑnfə`meʃən] 確認

courtesy [`kɝtəsɪ] 優惠

inn [ɪn] 小旅館

itinerary [aɪ`tɪnə͵rɛrɪ] 旅行日程

lodge [lɑdʒ] 住宿

long distance call 長途電話

make reservation 預約

reserve [rɪ`zɝv] 預約

scenery [`sinərɪ] 景色

telephone directory 電話號碼簿

valid [`vælɪd] 有效的

❸休閒活動

admission [əd`mɪʃən] 入場費

amusement park 娛樂公園

attendance [ə`tɛndəns] 出席人數

concert [`kɑnsɚt] 音樂會

display [dɪ`sple] 表演

exhibition [͵ɛksə`bɪʃən] 展覽

festival [`fɛstəvḷ] 慶祝

film [fɪlm] 電影

guided tour 有導遊的遊覽

membership [`mɛmbə͵ʃɪp] 會員

museum [mju`zɪəm] 博物館

performance [pɚ`fɔrməns] 表演

remains [rɪ`menz] 遺跡

souvenir [`suvə͵nɪr] 紀念品

READING II 多益閱讀文攻略

❹ 飯店

appetizer [ˈæpəˌtaɪzɚ] 開胃菜

bill [bɪl] 帳單

cafeteria [ˌkæfəˈtɪrɪə] 咖啡廳

chef [ʃɛf] 廚師

cuisine [kwɪˈzin] 料理

franchise [ˈfrænˌtʃaɪz] 特權

grocery store 雜貨店

recipe [ˈrɛsəpɪ] 食譜

refreshments [rɪˈfrɛʃmənt] 茶點

serving [ˈsɝvɪŋ] 招待

vegetarian [ˌvɛdʒəˈtɛrɪən] 素食者

voucher [ˈvaʊtʃɚ] 收據

❺ 產品

brand-new 最新的

built-in 安裝的

convenient [kənˈvinjənt] 便利的

cost-effective 划算的

durable [ˈdjʊrəbl] 耐用的

enduring [ɪnˈdjʊrɪŋ] 持久的

fragile [ˈfrædʒəl] 易碎的

fuel-efficient 省燃料的

lasting [ˈlæstɪŋ] 持續的

permanent [ˈpɝmənənt] 永久的

portable [ˈportəbl] 攜帶型的

reliable [rɪˈlaɪəbl] 可信賴的

state-of-the-art 最新的，流行尖端的

transparent [trænsˈpɛrənt] 透明的

user-friendly 容易使用的

waterproof [ˈwɔtɚˌpruf] 防水的

❻ 顧客服務

authorized [ˈɔθəˌraɪzd] 公認的

claim [klem] 要求、請求

compensation [ˌkɑmpənˈseʃən] 賠償

complaint [kəmˈplent] 控告

customer service 顧客服務

customized [ˈkʌstəmˌaɪz] 定做

description [dɪˈskrɪpʃən] 說明

expiration date 到期日

guarantee [ˌgærənˈti] 保證

inconvenience [ˌɪnkənˈvinjəns] 不便

instructions [ɪnˈstrʌkʃən] 使用說明書

label [ˈlebl] 商標

manual [ˈmænjʊəl] 說明書，手冊

patron [ˈpetrən] 顧客

questionnaire [ˌkwɛstʃənˈɛr] 調查問卷

recall [rɪˈkɔl] 收回

refund [ˈrɪˌfʌnd] 退款

repair [rɪˈpɛr] 修理

setup [ˈsɛtˌʌp] 裝配、構成

warranty [ˈwɔrəntɪ] 保證書

❼ 氣象預報

blizzard [ˈblɪzɚd] 暴風雪

climate [ˈklaɪmɪt] 氣候

drought [draʊt] 乾旱

flood [flʌd] 洪水

hail [hel] 冰雹

inclement [ɪnˈklɛmənt] 天氣惡劣的

overflow [ˌovɚˈflo] 氾濫

precipitation [prɪˌsɪpɪˈteʃən] 降水（量）

rainfall [ˈrenˌfɔl] 降雨量

shower [ˈʃaʊɚ] 陣雨

storm [stɔrm] 暴風雨

temperature [ˈtɛmprətʃɚ] 氣溫

torrential [tɔˈrɛnʃəl] 猛烈的

weather [ˈwɛðɚ] 天氣

weather forecast 氣象預報

⊙「說明書」類型題練習

閱讀短文並回答問題。

01

Anti-Cough is a non-prescription, over-the-counter medicine used to treat colds, cold symptoms, and related complications. Specifically, Anti-Cough attacks fluid trapped in the lung sacs. To use this medicine, patients should take the appropriate dosage as listed on the side of the bottle 2-3 times daily until symptoms have disappeared. It is best to take this medicine thirty minutes after eating food. If you experience nausea, severe headaches, a rash outbreak, or itching in your throat or on your face, discontinue use of this product immediately and seek medical assistance.

Q. When should you stop taking Anti-Cough?

(A) Two to three days after first taking it
(B) When you have side effects
(C) Thirty minutes after first taking it

02

FastLane Motors is calling in all of its 2003 Bentley models. The need to bring the cars back into the shop is due to a malfunction of the air bag on the passenger side of the car. When hit head-on, the car's airbag fails to deploy, leaving the passenger in great danger of head or facial injuries. There have been over twenty reported incidents of malfunction, enough to do a reassessment according to the National Car Association's guidelines.

Q. What is this information about?

(A) A recall notice for an automobile
(B) A user warning for a Bentley model
(C) A recent accident report

03

In order to apply for a Sense MasterCard, you must first fill out the application form available both online and at branches near you. You will need a driver's license, social security number, and checking account information in order to complete the application. Once you have sent that in, our processing department will respond with a letter of acceptance and your new MasterCard will arrive within ten days of acceptance.

Q. What is NOT needed to get a credit card?

(A) Personal identification
(B) Bank account number
(C) Proof of residence

Questions 1-2 refer to the following information.

FLAT PANEL SCREEN

Thank you for purchasing a Glaremaster Flat Panel Monitor! We're sure you'll be very satisfied with our products. Working on the computer all day can take its toll on your eyes. The Glaremaster screen filter helps relieve eyestrain by eliminating 99.9% of the glare coming from your computer monitor. And it does so without changing colors or brightness. The image is always true, never distorted.

Your flat panel monitor offers other advantages over older computer monitors. The Glaremaster takes 20% less power to run than other commercial brands and emits significantly less radiation and emissions than competing brands. It is also space efficient, as its small size requires less desk area to hold it. However, this doesn't mean it lacks in viewing area, as its LCD monitor is larger than all other monitors of its caliber.

On the back of the monitor are the connections with which to plug your new screen into the computer. Be sure to use the appropriate connector and to insert it into the portal marked with a circle. Adjust the color and contrast of the image with the buttons on the bottom front of the monitor. The button marked with a sun symbol controls brightness, while the wavy lines symbol indicates contrast. Additionally, you can reset the clock, day, or monitor volume by hitting the MENU button on the bottom left-hand corner of the screen. Remember to never touch the screen with water or any other fluid, as it may distort the picture. If you experience any difficulties, contact one of our technical support staff at the number listed below.

1. Where would you find this type of information?

(A) In a consumer magazine review
(B) In an electronics shop
(C) On a product package
(D) In a newspaper advertisement

2. What advantage does the flat panel monitor NOT have?

(A) It does not use as much electricity.
(B) It causes less eye fatigue.
(C) It includes a larger display.
(D) It has more connections than other monitors.

Questions 3-5 refer to the following information.

AVAILABLE PARKING

Due to an increase in the number of people needing vehicle parking during business hours, the building's private lot has been renovated for public use. The underground parking area now has four levels (A, B, C and D) open to both workers of this building and the general public. Each level can accommodate up to fifty cars, while level B is reserved for those who have monthly concession cards, which will cost $100 a month. Concessions are available only for employees working in this building.

Full-fare:
Up to an hour: $ 2.00
Each additional 30 minutes: $ 1.00
A day in business hours: $ 25
A week in business days: $ 120
A month: $ 450

Concession:
Up to an hour: $ 1.00
Each additional 30 minutes: $ 0.5
A day in business hours : $ 18
A week in business days : $ 80
A month: $ 300

Please note that all customers must take a ticket upon entering the facility. If the parking receipt is not visibly attached to the windshield of the vehicle, the vehicle will be charged double the rate of the fee. If you are a concession holder, you must attach the concession sticker on the window. If a vehicle parked in the reserved area does not show the certificate properly, it will be regarded as illegally parked and will be towed away at the owner's expense. For information or more details, contact your department supervisor.

3. How much do card holders pay for daily parking?

(A) $ 2.00
(B) $ 18.00
(C) $ 25.00
(D) $ 80.00

4. Which level is restricted for visitors?

(A) A
(B) B
(C) C
(D) D

5. What will happen to a car parked without a permit in the reserved area?

(A) The owner will be charged a fine.
(B) The car will be transferred to a different level.
(C) The owner will be charged twice the original rate.
(D) The vehicle will be removed from the parking spot.

正確答案 P145

Chapter 12

表格及其他（Forms）

此類型短文是生活中經常使用的表格和其他應用文，包括發票（invoice）、旅行指南（itinerary）、電話留言（telephone message）和履歷表（resume）。面對陌生的表格會對瞭解各項內容帶來困難，給應試者帶來心理負擔，因此要掌握各種表格的結構。表格類型的短文平均會在每次考試中出現三次，是頻繁出現的短文類型。

百發百中 出題類型與戰略

⊙ 頻繁出現的問題類型

這篇文章的類型是什麼？	What kind of document is this?
詳細內容	When was this invoice written?
	Who purchased the window?
	What is given to customers who return the form?

⊙ 核心戰略

1. 要掌握各種類型表格的構造結構

發票是購買物品時的支付證明書，包括購買品的詳細情況、支付總額、支付方式等內容。

履歷表以最近經歷的事項開始，按時間反向條列事件。

電話記錄中有打電話的人（From: ～）、接電話的人（Taken by: ～）、應接受電話記錄的人（To: ～），容易使人混淆，因此要熟悉各項的表現形式。

例題

Invoice
Maxwell Office Supply Inc.
521 Southern Avenue. Chicago, IL 60622

發票發送者

Bill to: The Madison Law Firm   Date: April 4th
        781 N. Tower Rd   Account Number: 39882
        Madison, WI
        53713-4483

支付日期

Product Description	Quantity	Price	Amount
20 piece Bic pens	5	$3.50	$17.50
A4 computer paper	20	$2.35	$47.00
		Sub-Total	$64.50
		Sales Tax	$6.50
		Total Balance Due	$71.00

物品細目及價格

支付總額

Make payable to: Maxwell Office Supply Inc.
        P.O. Box 77385
        Chicago, IL 60622

收款單位

Q：Who has to pay for the office supplies?
A：The Madison Law Firm

→ 問題是問誰是應支付費用的人。由上段中的 "Bill to"（給…開帳單）可知，隨後出現的公司是應該支付費用的一方。因此正確答案是 The Madison Law Firm

短文解釋 P146

⊙ 表格中常出現的單字

❶ 日程

agenda [ə`dʒɛndə] 日常工作事項

call off 取消

cancellation [,kænsḷ`eʃən] 取消

conference [`kɑnfərəns] 會議

convention [kən`vɛnʃən] 集會

enroll [ɪn`rol] 登記

make arrangements 準備

meeting [`mitɪŋ] 會議

notification [,notəfə`keʃən] 通知

registration [,rɛdʒɪ`streʃən] 登記

schedule [`skɛdʒʊl] 日程表

seminar [`sɛmə,nɑr] 研討會

speech [spitʃ] 演講

tentative schedule 臨時性的計畫

workshop [`wɝk,ʃɑp] 專題討論會

❷ 活動

annual [`ænjʊəl] 每年的

association [ə,sosɪ`eʃən] 協會，聯合

attendance [ə`tɛndəns] 參加

auditorium [,ɔdə`torɪəm] 觀眾席

banquet [`bæŋkwɪt] 宴會

charity [`tʃærətɪ] 慈善

committee [kə`mɪtɪ] 委員會

contribute [kən`trɪbjut] 貢獻

donate [`donet] 捐獻

exhibit [ɪg`zɪbɪt] 展示

foundation [faʊn`deʃən] 基金會

fundraising [`fʌnd,rezɪŋ] 籌款的

invitation [,ɪnvə`teʃən] 招待

keynote address 主題演講

nominate [`nɑmə,net] 提名

participant [pɑr`tɪsəpənt] 參與者

preside over a meeting 主持會議

representative [rɛprɪ`zɛntətɪv] 代表者

session [`sɛʃən] 會期

turnout [`tɝn,aʊt] 出席者

voluntary [`vɑlən,tɛrɪ] 自動自發的

❸ 社會

arbitration [,ɑrbə`treʃən] 仲裁

boycott [`bɔɪ,kɑt] 抵制

commit [kə`mɪt] 犯罪

controversial [,kɑntrə`vɝʃəl] 引起爭論的

copyright [`kɑpɪ,raɪt] 著作權

counterfeit [`kaʊntɚ,fɪt] 偽造

custody [`kʌstədɪ] 管理、監禁

detention [dɪ`tɛnʃən] 拘留

forfeit [`fɔr,fɪt] 罰款

forgery [`fɔrdʒərɪ] 偽造

fraud [frɔd] 欺騙

illegal [ɪ`ligḷ] 非法的

indict [ɪn`daɪt] 起訴

infringement [ɪn`frɪndʒmənt] 侵權

litigation [`lɪtə`geʃən] 訴訟

obliged [ə`blaɪdʒd] 有義務的

ordinance [`ɔrdɪnəns] 法令，規定

patent [`pætn̩t] 專利權

plaintiff [`plentɪf] 原告

press conference 記者會

prosecutor [`prɑsɪ,kjutɚ] 檢察官

provision [prə`vɪʒən] 法律條款

punishment [`pʌnɪʃmənt] 處罰

settlement [`sɛtḷmənt] 解決

strike [straɪk] 罷工

violation [,vaɪə`leʃən] 違反

❹ 意見交換

accommodate [əˋkɑməˌdet] 接受（要求）

approve [əˋpruv] 承認

argument [ˋɑrgjəmənt] 爭論

assert [əˋsɝt] 主張

brainstorming [ˋbrenˌstɔrmɪŋ] 腦力激盪

briefing [ˋbrifɪŋ] 簡報

clash [klæʃ] 衝突，對立

concede [kənˋsid] 讓步

consent [kənˋsɛnt] 同意

deadlock [ˋdɛdˌlɑk] 停滯狀態

debate [dɪˋbet] 辯論

disapprove [ˌdɪsəˋpruv] 反對，不承認

discuss [dɪˋskʌs] 討論

negotiate [nɪˋgoʃɪˌet] 協商

object to 反對

opposition [ˌɑpəˋzɪʃən] 反對

persuade [pɚˋswed] 說服

presentation [ˌprizɛnˋteʃən] 發表

proponent [prəˋponənt] 擁護者

proposal [prəˋpoz!] 提案

refuse [rɪˋfjuz] 拒絕

unanimous [juˋnænəməs] 一致的

withstand [wɪðˋstænd] 抵擋

❺ 電話

answer the phone 接電話

contact [ˋkɑntækt] 聯絡

disconnect [ˌdɪskəˋnɛkt] 切斷

extension [ɪkˋstɛnʃən] 分機

give a call 打電話

hang up 掛斷

leave a message 留言

pick up the phone 接電話

return one's call 回覆電話

take a message 收到電話留言

voice mail 語音留言

❻ 廣播 · 出版

archive [ˋɑrkaɪv] 資料庫

authorship [ˋɔθɚˌʃɪp] 原作者

biography [baɪˋɑgrəfɪ] 傳記

biweekly [baɪˋwiklɪ] 雙週的

broadcast [ˋbrɔdˌkæst] 廣播

censorship [ˋsɛnsɚˌʃɪp] 審查

commercial [kəˋmɝʃəl] 廣告

coverage [ˋkʌvərɪdʒ] 報導

edition [ɪˋdɪʃən] 版

exclusive [ɪkˋsklusɪv] 獨佔的

issue [ˋɪʃju] 發行，發佈

newsletter [ˋnjuzˌlɛtɚ] 時事通訊

periodical [ˌpɪrɪˋɑdɪk!] 期刊

press [prɛs] 言論

publication [ˌpʌblɪˋkeʃən] 出版

quarterly [ˋkwɔrtɚlɪ] 季度的

release [rɪˋlis] 發表，發行

satellite [ˋsætḷˌaɪt] 衛星

subscription [səbˋskrɪpʃən] 訂閱

❼ 日常生活

apologize [əˋpɑləˌdʒaɪz] 道歉

apparel [əˋpærəl] 衣服

appreciate [əˋpriʃɪˌet] 道謝

attire [əˋtaɪr] 服裝

complimentary [ˌkɑmpləˋmɛntərɪ] 免費的

dietary [ˋdaɪəˌtɛrɪ] 飲食的

disappointed [ˌdɪsəˋpɔɪntɪd] 失望的

favorable [ˋfevərəbḷ] 有利的

household [ˋhausˌhold] 家族

personal belongings 個人行李

preferable [ˋprɛfərəbḷ] 偏愛

reluctant [rɪˋlʌktənt] 不情願的

utility [juˋtɪlətɪ] 公共設施

⊙ 「表格及其他」類型題練習
閱讀短文並回答問題

01

Time	Event	Venue
09:15-10:15	Lecture on Types of Insurance Policies Session Handlers: James Gimbel and Ted Lee	Main Hall
10:15-10:30	"Labor Claims" Speaker: James Gimbel	Room 503
10:30-12:30	"How broad is Your Insurance Coverage?" Speaker: Michael Shapiro	Rooms 504 - 505

Q. Who will give a lecture on the extent of insurance protection?

(A) James Gimbel

(B) Michael Shapiro

(C) Ted Lee

02

In November, 1968 Buick Hall was completed and dedicated in honor of William Buick, one of the founders of the American Academy of Physical Education. Located at the corner of Rojas Boulevard and Union Avenue, the Hall houses the College of Health Professions, the Recreational Sports Department, and the Department of Dance. The building also contains three gymnasiums, exercise and weight training facilities, and a swimming pool. Originally 107,363 square feet in size, a 12,500 square foot annex was added in August, 2002 for a fitness center and a climbing wall.

Q. What does Buick Hall feature?

(A) A 12,500 square-foot swimming pool

(B) A rock-climbing facility

(C) A stadium for football games

03

What kind of water filter you choose will depend on the contaminations specific to your home and environment. Each filter is designed to address certain toxicity problems, but no one filter can perform all possible functions.

BRAND	PERFORMANCE	MONTHS	COST	RATING/COMMENT
Aquitania	80% chlorine removed	6 months	$69	AAAA (Product shipped fully plumbed)
Wellers	80% chlorine removed Dual, high flow system	4 months	$249	AAAA (Water pressure can be reduced)
Paradise	50% chlorine removed	3.5 months	$59	AAA (Customer preferred model for 2002,3)

Q. Which product is best if one wants to adjust the force of the water?

(A) Aquitania

(B) Wellers

(C) Paradise

正確答案 P147

Questions 1-3 refer to the following document.

Silicon Computer Supplies

750 Melrose Avenue, San Francisco, CA

Item	Price	Total Price
5 noise filters	$ 4.85	$ 24.25
3 mouse pads	15.96	47.88
3 wrist rests (gel-filled)	3.92	11.76
30 rewritable CDs 700 MB capacity	.85	25.50
10 boxes of 3.5' disks (a dozen in each box)	4.02	40.20
	TOTAL	$ 149.59
	DEPOSIT	–
	BALANCE DUE	$ 149.59

Any damage to goods in transit, or shortages, must be notified to the carriers immediately and to the company within 24 hours of receipt in writing by email or fax. Refunds and/or product replacements, as guaranteed in our warranty, will be sent within one week of notification. Questions or complaints may also be posted online at www.scs.org, or made by phone at 1-800-455-SILI.

1. Why was this document written?

(A) To apologize for sending damaged goods
(B) To explain the shipping options available
(C) To notify a customer of price changes
(D) To provide an invoice for products delivered

2. What is NOT mentioned as a way to report delivery problems?

(A) Send a memo by fax
(B) Visit the company's headquarters
(C) Speak to a customer representative
(D) Write an electronic letter

3. How much is one box of 3.5' disks?

(A) $3.92
(B) $4.02
(C) $4.85
(D) $40.20

Questions 4-5 refer to the following telephone message.

Message

To : Ms. Garner

Date : April 16, 2004

Time : 9:45 AM

☐ TELEPHONED   ■ PLEASE CALL

☐ RETURNED YOUR CALL   ☐ WILL CALL AGAIN

Message   James Dean from the Department of Tax and Revenue has been trying to get in touch with you for the past two weeks. He needs to speak with you regarding the business tax report filed last year. The matter is of some urgency, so he expects you to return his call promptly.

Taken By   Sherry Hill, Accounting

4. Who received the phone call?

   (A) Mr. James Dean
   (B) The Department of Tax and Revenue
   (C) Ms. Garner
   (D) Ms. Sherry Hill

5. What was the reason for the phone call?

   (A) Need for an urgent lunch meeting
   (B) Missing tax reports that need to be filed
   (C) Concerns over an old report
   (D) A mistake by the accounting department

Cheap Travel

554 Edmonton Drive, Madison, WI 53725
TEL: (612) 310-5788 / FAX: (612) 310-6473

Sales representative: Jenna Carlson
Customer: Christina Fielding

Issue Date: 28 May

15 JUNE MONDAY
TransGlobal Airlines	FLT: 669	ECONOMY	TWO MEALS
LV MSP	17:30	8HR 20MIN	
DEPART: Gate 55	VIA Paris		

16 JUNE TUESDAY
AR Paris	8:50
ARRIVE: Gate 23	

16 JUNE TUESDAY
TransGlobal Airlines	FLT: 832	ECONOMY	ONE MEAL
LV Paris	13:30	4HR 30MIN	
DEPART: Gate 16			

16 JUNE TUESDAY
AR Istanbul	19:00
ARRIVE: Gate 05	

23 JUNE TUESDAY
TransGlobal Airlines	FLT: 911	ECONOMY	THREE MEALS
LV Istanbul	13:30	12HR 45MIN	
DEPART: Gate 33			

23 JUNE TUESDAY
AR Minneapolis	18:15
ARRIVE: Gate 05	

TOTAL CHARGES (TX INC): $1255.68
If full payment is not made at least seven days prior to the departure date, your seat will be automatically canceled and no refund of any prior payments will be given. As always, we at Cheap Travel appreciate your business and hope to see you again soon.

6. When will the passenger leave from Istanbul?

(A) June 15th
(B) June 16th
(C) June 18th
(D) June 23rd

7. When is the airfare due?

(A) On the date of departure
(B) Upon receipt of the bill
(C) One week before travel
(D) On the date of issue

Questions 8-10 refer to the following resume.

Meghann Weiner

324 Sunshine Road, St. Croix Falls, WI 54024
(715) 483-9630; aphroathena@gmail.com

OBJECTIVE

To work in a position that affords me the opportunity to supervise and enhance my leadership abilities in an atmosphere that fosters respect, challenge and professionalism.

SKILLS / QUALIFICATIONS

- Three years experience in coffee sales and coffee shop management
- Excellent interpersonal communication skills
- Ability to delegate responsibilities

EDUCATIONAL BACKGROUND

MBA Marketing
Richfield School of Business; Richfield, MN, 2000-2002

BA Communications
University of Minnesota-Duluth; Duluth, MN, 1996-2000

WORK EXPERIENCE

Assistant Manager
Caribou Coffee; Duluth, MN, 2003-present
- Supervised a team of 23 café workers, organized their schedules, interviewed applicants, and dealt primarily in conflict resolution
- Organized and administered training of all new employees
- Participated in weekly evaluations of both staff and overall business
- Personally resolved any customer disputes

Sales Representative
Caribou; Seattle, WA, 2002-2003
- Delivered presentations to potential investors
- Sold the franchising concept to companies nationwide
- Increased overall corporation profits by 0.7%

8. What kind of position is Ms. Weiner seeking?

(A) Any kind of sales position
(B) A managerial position
(C) An entry level position
(D) A sales position in the coffee market

9. What is NOT one of Ms. Weiner's qualifications?

(A) A degree in economics
(B) Experience overseeing staff
(C) Ability to effectively interact with people
(D) Experience promoting company interests

10. What did Ms. Weiner do at her first job?

(A) Designed sales advertisements
(B) Provided training for new workers
(C) Gave investment opportunity speeches
(D) Dealt with customer concerns

Chapter 13

雙篇文章（Double Passage）

這種類型的短文由兩段相關的文章組成，並提出5個問題。由於有兩篇短文，所以閱讀量要比「單篇文章（Single Passage）」大，但問題類型和解題方法上沒有多大的區別，因此只要認真閱讀短文並對照問題就可以正確解答。在「雙篇文章」中，會有聯繫兩段短文的題目，這類題目尋找答案的時間要更長，因此要多加練習，熟悉這種類型。

百發百中 出題類型與戰略

⊙ 頻繁出現的問題類型

表格 & 有關聯的短文	對會議記錄和會議內容進行推斷並討論的郵件
	活動邀請函和活動日程表
	產品評估和與此評估有關的公司內部郵件
廣告 & 有關聯的短文	履歷表和公司回覆信件
	產品廣告和消費者諮詢郵件
	產品廣告和使用者的郵件
	兩份不同的徵才廣告
公告 & 有關聯的短文	計畫方案公告和諮詢郵件
	公共服務價格的變更公告和支付申請書
報導 & 有關聯的短文	公司的訂貨單和相關作業時間的傳單
	新聞報導和要求修改報導的讀者來信
備忘錄 & 有關聯的短文	公佈公司規定的備忘錄和職員們的諮詢郵件
	表明職員疑問的備忘錄和職員的回覆郵件
信件 & 有關聯的短文	信件及其回覆
	信件及其附件

⊙ 核心戰略

1. 透過觀察前面部分的短文類型，來確認會出現什麼樣的相關短文。

    透過 "Questions ~ refer to the following agenda and e-mail" 可以看出，下面的短文應該是會議記錄和與之關聯的郵件。

2. 快速閱讀短文的內容，並掌握兩篇短文的關係。

    未掌握兩篇短文的關係會難以理解題目的意思，若能先掌握兩篇短文的關係，再理解短文的意思就會使答題很有效率。

3. 按順序思考問題，仔細閱讀短文中的相關內容並選擇答案。

    讀完題目之後，要在短文中找出能提供解題線索的部分。將相關部分的內容與選項對照後選出正確答案。

4. 只閱讀一篇短文不能作答時，要綜合考慮兩篇短文。

    「雙篇文章」裡會出現綜合兩篇短文的內容來作答的題型。只閱讀一篇短文無法作答時，要綜合兩篇短文選擇答案。

例題　Questions 1-5 refer to the following agenda and e-mail.

Blueprint Imaging Services, Ltd.
Agenda for Meeting with Advanced Machinery

9:00 a.m.　　Ordering Quantity & Timeframe
　　　　　　Helen Clark: Asset Management, Blueprint Imaging
9:15 a.m.　　Customized Manufacturing Specifications
　　　　　　Heather Hughes: Engineering and Design, Advanced Machinery
9:45 a.m.　　Advanced Machinery Procedural Review
　　　　　　Winston Peters: Logistics and Distribution, Advanced Machinery
10:15 a.m.　Post-purchase Maintenance and Servicing
　　　　　　Peter Dunne: Technology services, Advanced Machinery
10:40 a.m.　Q & A about Orders
　　　　　　Rodney Hide: Financial Services, Blueprint Imaging

TO: Winston Peters, Advanced Machinery
From: Helen Clark, Blueprint Imaging
Subject: Monday's Meeting

Dear Winston:

It was a pleasure meeting with you on Monday. We were especially impressed by the presentation on consumer-tailored production, as our current supplier's products have become somewhat outdated and inflexible. The information you provided helped bring us one step closer to making a purchase. Now that we have an idea of your product range and started to explore our final ordering requirements, I would like to discuss a topic which we briefly touched on at the meeting; namely the prospect of a reduction in the purchasing price for large-quantity orders.

Assuming that we do choose to purchase Advanced Machinery products now and in the future, each order is likely to be in the range of 50-60 units, and therefore we would expect a significant markdown in your quoted market price. The basic functions of your products seem for the most part to cater to our needs, and we should be able to get back to you with a contract on Friday as long as we can have the necessary adaptations made to the machinery, as well as receive the abovementioned discount.

Regards,
Helen

Q1 : Why was the meeting held?
A : To discuss details of a machinery order
→ 此題問的是召開會議的理由，可以在第一篇短文裡找到相關線索。從 Ordering Quantity, Q & A about Orders 等內容可以看出這是有關產品訂購的會議。從議程表的 7～8 行 "Post-purchase Maintenance and Servicing ～ Advanced Machinery" 可以看出銷售的產品為 machinery，因此會議的目的就是 To discuss details of a machinery order。

Q2 : What is the main purpose of Ms. Clark's email to Mr. Peters?
A : To follow up on a meeting with Advanced Machinery
→ 此題問的是寄信的目的，要從第二篇短文中找答案。從 4～6 行的 "I would like ～ large-quantity orders." 可以看出，信裡提出了對會議內容進一步討論的意見。因此答案應該是 To follow up on a meeting with Advanced Machinery。

Q3 : Whose presentation had the greatest impact on the decision to order?
A : Heather Hughes
→ 此題需要綜合兩篇短文的內容來作答。從第二篇短文的 1～3 行可以看出，對交易產生很大影響的是 "consumer-tailored production" 發表的文章。為找到發表者，需要參考第一篇短文。在第一篇短文的第 3 行裡，可以找到 "consumer-tailored production" 的另一種表現形式 "Customized Manufacturing"，因此發表這篇文章的就是 Heather Huges。

Q4 : What is suggested in the e-mail?
A : Blueprint is generally satisfied with Advanced Machinery's products.
→ 此題問的是從信件裡可以看出什麼，因此要從第二篇短文中找答案。從第 9 行的 "The basic functions of your products seem for the most part tocater to our needs" 可以看出，答案應該是 "Blueprint is generally satisfied with Advanced Machinery's products"。

Q5 : When does Blueprint expect to finalize the contract?
A : By Friday
→ 此題問的是 Blueprint 何時敲定合約，因此要看提到 contract 的第二篇短文。從第 10 行的 "we should be able to get back to you with a contract on Friday" 可以看出，答案應該是 By Friday。

短文解釋　P150

⊙「雙篇文章」類型題練習
　　閱讀短文並回答問題。

01

02

Downs Business Academy announces details of this semester's third-year marketing course, MRT 302. Content includes information systems, data analysis, and critical-thinking skills in solving marketing problems. Prerequisites are: ACCT 201, ECN 211, or the consent of the instructor. Please contact the department head, Dr. Higginbotham (higginbotham@downs.edu), with any enquiries.

Dear Dr. Higginbotham:
I have a problem with the prerequisites for MRT 302. Basically, because I received a language scholarship this year, I had to take CHIN 101 last semester, which meant that I didn't have space in my schedule for ECN 211, but I did complete the other course with excellent marks. In light of these circumstances, I would like special permission to enter this program.
Regards,
Shaggie Mopp

Q1. What is NOT mentioned as being taught in the Marketing course?

(A) How to analyze information
(B) How to think in a critical way
(C) How to offer quality service

Q2. What request does Mr. Mopp make in his letter?

(A) To be admitted into a marketing course
(B) To be considered for a language scholarship
(C) To have his grades reconsidered and marked up

03

04

Hickory, Dickory, Dock & Company has a rare opportunity for someone with a strong financial background and experience to join our team of investment banking professionals. The ideal candidate should have a postgraduate qualification in commerce and at least three years of experience in the investment banking sector.

To Whom It May Concern:
I have extensive practical experience as an investment banker and would love the opportunity to work for such an eminent firm as yours. My current job involves advising clients on acquisition opportunities, so I believe I would be perfect for the job. Please contact me should you require further information.
Benjamin Prudhomme

Q3. What is the purpose of the advertisement?

(A) To praise especially talented staff members
(B) To solicit applications for a vacant position
(C) To convey new criteria for staff promotions

Q4. What does Mr. Prudhomme do in his present job?

(A) Gives customers advice on buying other businesses
(B) Offers investment advice to potential shareholders
(C) Helps businesses devise advertising strategies

05
06

Australia Post has invented a fun, inexpensive way to add a special touch to your Christmas envelopes this year with a personalized postage stamp service. Your favorite photo will be electronically added to your choice of 10 different stamp designs. Customers must go in person to a post office with their chosen digital image, as mail orders for photographs are not accepted.

TO: All Staff
FROM: Violet Beauregarde, Promotions Manager
We have decided to order a special batch of personalized stamps to be used on all company Christmas mail. It will be a unique way to familiarize clients with our team while sending Festive Season greetings at the same time. Therefore, employees will be required to attend a group photography session in the conference room on the first floor at 3pm tomorrow afternoon.

Q5. What is stated in the article?

(A) Customers can send in their favorite digital image by e-mail
(B) Customers must bring their photograph to a post office
(C) Customers can use the personalization service free of charge

Q6. Why does Mr. Beauregarde want to use this service?

(A) To advertise a service to clients
(B) To increase profits over the festive season
(C) To introduce the staff to customers

07
08

SoundByte magazine announces its convenient new online advertising registration service, available at www.soundbyte.org. Advertisement submissions are accepted until 5pm on Fridays for Category A (Non-Profit Organizations and Individuals) and before 12 noon on Tuesdays for Category B (Businesses). Rates are $5 for Category A and $25 for Category B. The magazine is out on newsstands Wednesdays for the low price of $3.

Name: Natalie Beaglehole	
Billing Address: 283 Moa St, Pt. Chevalier, Auckland	
Advertising Category: A	
Write text below. Maximum 5 lines.	
TEXT: T4-A custom-built speakers for sale. Compact design, professional audio grade sound quality. Have a great room-shaking base sound due to high-performance loudspeakers. Only owned for 6 months, good as new. $1600 neg.	

Q7. How much will Natalie's advertisement cost?

(A) $3
(B) $5
(C) $25

Q8. What is NOT mentioned about the speakers?

(A) They have sound that is of a professional standard.
(B) They have a very loud volume capacity.
(C) They have a special insulated casing.

正確答案 P150

Questions 1-5 refer to the following advertisement and memo.

Buddha's Bungalow
45 Sunset Drive, NW

Located in the historic and quiet residential area of Sunnydale, Buddha's Bungalow has the comforts of home, close to home. Relax while experiencing the remarkable service, fine dining, and fresh tastes of Asia. We use only the highest quality organic ingredients, along with flavors and spices imported from the East, to ensure you a taste extravaganza you'll never forget. We're taking things a step further with our exciting New Daily Deals Lunch Specials!

Pop in for Monday Madness where we offer a delectable selection of appetizers for only $9.99. On Tasty Tuesday, our head chef whips up a culinary masterpiece of his own invention, and it's bound to be superb. Mouth Watering Wednesdays leaves you licking your lips because every dish comes with a fresh fruit shake! Order any entree off our menu on Terrific Thursday for 60% off the regular price! Drop by on Fantastic Friday, and finish your meal with a complimentary dessert. Don't miss out on a chance to awaken your taste buds. Hurry to Buddha's Bungalow today!

"Buddha's Bungalow offers the most abundant lunch specials in town. Choose from a selection of sizzling curries and tempting noodle dishes, all served with a generous bowl of rice, a variety of appetizers and your choice of authentic teas. You are guaranteed to leave full."
Amber Jasperson, Food Critic

"Filled with authentic smells, cushions, wall ornaments and trinkets from South East Asia, walking into Buddha's Bungalow is like being whisked away to Thailand."
Carrie Dwight, *Food Choice* Writer

From: Ted Wong, Manager

To: All employees

In a sign of solidarity with our sister company, Little China is now offering our employees special mileage cards for use at Buddha's Bungalow. Every time you dine at the Bungalow, simply have your card stamped by your server. Collect five stamps and get a complimentary appetizer. Redeem 10 stamps for a free t-shirt at Little China. Cash in 30 stamps and treat yourself and 3 of your closest friends or family to a 5 course dining dream, on the house, at Buddha's Bungalow. Please pick up your cards from Helen, the Head Server. Thank you.

1. What is emphasized about the food in the restaurant?

   (A) It is made hot and spicy.
   (B) It is made in Thailand and flown in.
   (C) It is made by Asians.
   (D) It is made from ingredients without chemicals.

2. When does the customer get a discount?

   (A) On Monday
   (B) On Wednesday
   (C) On Thursday
   (D) On Friday

3. What does the critic say about the restaurant?

   (A) The decor imitates the Thai environment.
   (B) They offer cuisine from all round Asia.
   (C) The food portions are comparatively large.
   (D) The downtown location is convenient.

4. Why is Little China providing mileage cards to its employees?

   (A) To attract more business
   (B) To support their affiliate
   (C) To promote sales of Asian foods
   (D) To promote family ties

5. What do both the advertisement and the e-mail have in common?

   (A) Both discuss the taste of their cuisine.
   (B) Both extend discounts to employees.
   (C) Both offer a benefits card.
   (D) Both tender free food.

Questions 6-10 refer to the following article and letter.

The Daily Rove
Unemployment and Economy Figures Diverge

Figures have just been released by the Department of Finance showing that the national economy has grown by 4% over the past 12 months, demonstrating a healthy recovery since the previous year. The projected economic growth figure for next year has been set at a conservative 5%, though the actual rate could be higher. The Department of Finance attributed the economic recovery to the government's recent lowering of interest rates.

However, the rosy economic outlook has been offset by gloomy predictions for unemployment over the same period. While the Department of Labor claims that it is not yet able to release its unemployment estimate for next year, last year's figures show that unemployment grew to as much as 6%, the highest in five years. Moreover, in an interview with The Daily Rove yesterday, Swan Recruiting's Executive Director, Karen McGredy, conjectured that there would be no relief in sight for the unemployed, forecasting a further 2% rise in unemployment next year.

To the Editor:

I am writing with regard to yesterday's article, Unemployment and Economy Figures Diverge. You claimed that I foresaw a 2% rise in unemployment over the next year, when what I actually said was that I predicted a 2% fall in unemployment on the strength of the recent economic upturn. I did, however, add that since the situation is quite volatile and unpredictable, that it wasn't inconceivable for there to be a short-term rise in unemployment first, before it levels off and drops. I believe that this comment was the source of the confusion.

Certainly, according to our placement figures for the last month, the employment market is far from gloomy, with many more new placements, and a marked rise in enquiry call volumes from potential employers. I therefore request that you publish a revision in tomorrow's paper correcting your projected unemployment figure.

Sincerely,
K. McGredy, Swan Recruiting

6. Why did the economy improve?

   (A) Exports grew by 4%.
   (B) The exchange rate was lowered.
   (C) Tax cuts were introduced.
   (D) Interest rates were reduced.

7. According to the newspaper, how much will unemployment rise next year?

   (A) 2%
   (B) 4%
   (C) 5%
   (D) 6%

8. What does the article suggest?

   (A) Government measures will be introduced to reduce unemployment.
   (B) The Labor Department has released unemployment figures.
   (C) The economy was in decline last year.
   (D) There are too many people on welfare benefits.

9. What is the purpose of the letter?

   (A) To comment on a rise in unemployment
   (B) To point out a misquotation
   (C) To analyze reasons for the economic recovery
   (D) To report on the employment market

10. What is NOT mentioned in the letter?

   (A) Job placements have risen.
   (B) Telephone enquiries have increased.
   (C) The employment market looks healthy.
   (D) Working conditions have improved.

Questions 11-15 refer to the following letters.

Mr. Ray Green
Harborside Community Center
134 Alberta Ave
Harbourside, ME 04046

30th July

Dear Mr. Green:

We are a large multinational corporation and proud contributor to the local community, and due to a recent large-scale systems upgrade, we are looking to discard some equipment. I'm happy to say that in response to your newspaper advertisement, your organization has been selected as the lucky recipient, and therefore we would like to donate $50,000 worth of our old IT hardware to be used for your Community Development Project.

As far as logistical matters go, at this stage it looks like there will be a short delay before the equipment is available to be picked up, as it needs to be processed before being delivered to our warehouse sometime after August 13th. Should you choose to accept this offer, please send us a formal written notification of acceptance. Also, I'd like to take this opportunity to invite you to participate in the official presentation ceremony, to take place during our Annual General Meeting on Friday January 14th at the Harbourside Hotel Convention Center. Once again, Brightside Computers is proud to contribute to the local community, and we hope to continue doing so well into the future.

Yours Sincerely,
Marcie Wilton

Ms. Marcie Wilton
Brightside Computer Corporation
266 Water St. Augusta, ME 04330

1 August

Dear Ms. Wilton:

We would like to accept your kind donation to our Community Development Project, and I would like to personally take this opportunity to express our heartfelt gratitude. As you will know, the Harborside area has experienced a considerable rise in population, in response to which we have undertaken extensive renovations to our center. We now offer a crime prevention center, a free medical clinic for underprivileged families and the disabled, and an extended main building, where we will place your computers to be used for public internet access terminals.

Unfortunately, we do have a slight problem with transportation. We don't have a vehicle big enough to transport such a large amount of equipment, and I was wondering if it would be possible for you to deliver them, since we are less than 30 minutes from your offices, right next to the public library. I'll look forward to hearing from you soon.

Sincerely,
Ray Green

11. What is Mr. Green being offered?

(A) A $50,000 cash donation
(B) A large-scale IT systems upgrade
(C) Used computer appliances
(D) A discount on newspaper advertising

12. What is stated in Ms. Wilton's letter?

(A) An official ceremony will take place at the Community Center.
(B) Notification of acceptance should be made by telephone.
(C) There are several recipients for the donations.
(D) It will take some time to prepare the equipment.

13. According to Mr. Green's letter, what has happened in the community recently?

(A) The population has grown
(B) Crime has decreased
(C) Transportation services have deteriorated
(D) Unemployment has increased

14. What was included in the renovations?

(A) An access ramp for the disabled
(B) An environment protection center
(C) A health center for the poor
(D) A new public library

15. What is Ms. Wilton asked to do?

(A) Supply a larger amount of equipment
(B) Provide advice on renovations
(C) Deliver the computers within one week
(D) Provide a means of transport for the goods

Questions 16-20 refer to the following report and letter.

Gerald Hummer, Chief Inspector
Building and Safety Department
City of Henderson
Annual Inspection Report

File No.: C876-88
Business Owner: Kevin Dunst
Address: 64 East Hastings
Inspection Result: Renovation Requirement

The mandatory annual building and safety review was conducted by the City's Building Inspector in accordance to the Municipal Building Code. We ask that the following improvements take place. The law allows a period of 3 months to accomplish repairs. If you do not do as required, you will be asked to appear before the licensing board to have your case re-evaluated. If you fail to appear within a month of being notified, your license will be suspended.

1. The stairwell leading from the second to the third floor must be repaired. We found a few of the stairs to have loose tiles, which is a safety hazard.
2. The swimming pool filtration system must be replaced. It is old and not up to sanitation standards (code 465).
3. According to new By-Law 1098, all rooms must be equipped with emergency rope ladders, along with clear and concise instructions for use.

When all the alterations have been made, contact the City Building Department and arrange an appointment with your Inspector. Be sure to compile all necessary documentation, such as receipts or invoices for work done, and bring them along as proof that the work has been done. If the Inspector finds your documents in order, he will then determine a date to hold an on-site re-evaluation and assess whether your building meets code requirements.

The Sleep Easy Hotel
64 East Hastings

To: The Department of Building and Safety
ATTN: Gerald Hummer, Chief Inspector

As requested by your department, I have made renovations to my hotel. I completed #1 and #3 but I could not perform #2 in the allotted period of time due to complications with the equipment. It will take another 2 months or so for the necessary parts to arrive and be installed. Thank you for your patience and I promise to take safety more seriously. I have also performed a few additional non-essential improvements, to avoid future complications in terms of the Municipal Building Code. I installed state-of-the-art Smart Fire Alarms and improved the marking of fire exits.

Sincerely,
Kevin Dunst

16. What will happen to Mr.Dunst if changes are not made within 3 months?

(A) His license will be suspended.
(B) He will be given 2 more months to make changes.
(C) The board will go over his case.
(D) He will be fined.

17. What is the final step in verifying the repairs?

(A) The owner shows the inspector the required documents.
(B) The inspector checks that they conform to the law.
(C) The owner schedules a meeting with the inspector.
(D) The inspector calls the owner.

18. What requirement did Mr. Dunst mention he has not met?

(A) Installing escape devices
(B) Reattaching stairwell flooring
(C) Refurbishing the pool
(D) Improving kitchen sanitation

19. Why wasn't one of the repairs performed?

(A) Mr.Dunst thought fire alarms were more important.
(B) Mr.Dunst decided it was too expensive to complete.
(C) Mr.Dunst completed different repairs instead.
(D) Mr.Dunst must wait for the necessary parts.

20. Why did Mr. Dunst install the new alarm system?

(A) To comply with the city's safety regulations
(B) To perform all the required repairs
(C) To protect his guests
(D) To improve how fire exits were marked

實戰模擬測驗
Actual Test
*Answer Sheet 附錄在教材最後一頁。

多益實戰模擬測驗1

101 The readers agreed that the section on plot formation was ------- the best part of the fiction-writing handbook.

(A) defined   (B) definitive
(C) definite   (D) definitely

102 He has applied for the positions of both sales representative ------- general manager in the same company.

(A) and   (B) either
(C) also   (D) moreover

103 The new apartment building is being constructed in the ------- central residential district of San Antonio.

(A) erectable   (B) desirable
(C) permissible   (D) seasonable

104 I am calling on behalf of Piltdown Corporation to remind you about a payment that has been long ------- .

(A) extensive   (B) comprehensive
(C) overdue   (D) unpunctual

105 Two of the interior designers had graduate degrees in design, ------- only one was acquainted with the rudiments of architecture.

(A) or   (B) but
(C) so   (D) as

106 Part-time employees will be compensated on a monthly basis, ------- is the norm for workers doing 16 hours per week.

(A) who   (B) which
(C) whose   (D) what

107 There are some doubts as to ------- interest
rates will drop down enough this quarter.

(A) however   (B) although
(C) whether   (D) yet

108 Internet access is still not available to
everyone, ------- in communities that are small
and isolated.

(A) scarcely   (B) especially
(C) habitually   (D) hardly

109 All of the firm's associates will be ------- at the
local French restaurant tonight to celebrate
the recently won case.

(A) dining   (B) dine
(C) diner   (D) to dine

110 Inter-office communications are improved
------- seminars and workshops run by the
human resources department.

(A) along   (B) about
(C) through   (D) from

111 The trainers are expecting a ------- group of
participants ranging from fresh college
graduates to high-salaried professionals.

(A) diverse   (B) diversity
(C) diversely   (D) diversify

112 The new water treatment plant is -------
automated and requires minimal supervision.

(A) finely   (B) intently
(C) loyally   (D) fully

113 The Beeker Street Journal has ranked
Eibert's Clearing House ------- among the list
of newly established publishing firms.

(A) high   (B) highly
(C) higher   (D) highest

114 You should always consult with the CEO
------- any final decisions are made regarding
the operations of this office.

(A) before   (B) despite
(C) for   (D) with

115 The supervisor will conduct an information
session ------- new safety policies and
practices this Wednesday.

(A) across   (B) about
(C) during   (D) in

116 The customer has every ------- of paying off
his outstanding debt to keep his account up-
to-date.

(A) objective   (B) motive
(C) intention   (D) purpose

117 Natalie was offered a position in ------- at one of the top advertising agencies in the city.

(A) manager (B) managing
(C) manages (D) management

118 Their reconstruction and revitalization plans were inconsiderately overshadowed by ------- of a competing corporation.

(A) that (B) them
(C) those (D) they

119 A battery recharger is provided free of ------- with every purchase of an emergency lamp at any of our retail outlets.

(A) charge (B) rate
(C) fare (D) price

120 ------- your address has changed, in which case you should report it to payroll, your paycheck will be mailed directly to your home.

(A) Otherwise (B) Unless
(C) Without (D) Except

121 Fred is the most ------- member of the team because of his unending curiosity and positive attitude.

(A) promising (B) promised
(C) promise (D) promises

122 The popular cosmetics company magnate wants ------- a perfume that epitomizes the freedom-loving woman of today's generation.

(A) creating (B) created
(C) create (D) to create

123 One ------- of a good manager is the capacity to admit mistakes and to allow those mistakes to be corrected.

(A) position (B) characteristic
(C) attempt (D) regard

124 The quieter the workers are, the ------- suspicious the overseer becomes of what they are planning.

(A) most (B) many
(C) more (D) much

125 Under the leadership of Charles Pankow, Digital Arts became a major ------- in the graphics industry.

(A) force (B) assembly
(C) competition (D) arena

126 The exhibit ------- attracted so many customers to the dealership was the display of next year's sports car models.

(A) there (B) who
(C) where (D) that

127 A notice warning you of legal action will be sent to you unless payment is ------- by the second week of February.

(A) remit (B) remitted
(C) remitting (D) remittance

128 Please fill out the survey form and ------- it to Ms. Turner at the counter.

(A) revisit (B) retrieve
(C) return (D) replace

129 Customers have complained nearly ------- about the long lines and disgruntled workers at the store.

(A) continuous
(B) continued
(C) continuing
(D) continuously

130 Only the managers and staff members involved in the project are required to ------- the meeting this evening.

(A) participate
(B) enroll
(C) attend
(D) go

131 The Speedway Motor Company will be ------- its BBA Classic motorcycle before putting it on the market because of a problem with its muffler.

(A) advertising
(B) redesigning
(C) introducing
(D) developing

132 All questions on your current account and bank statement are subject to address -------.

(A) verification
(B) verify
(C) verified
(D) verifies

133 Internet providers are trying to catch up with the ------- demand for faster broadband.

(A) investing
(B) increasing
(C) cultivating
(D) activating

134 Problems with the company's old database system, ------- replaced, caused some loss of customer data.

(A) ever
(B) well
(C) since
(D) yet

135 We here at Home Remodeling remain ------- to reliable service, quality product, and long-term trust and dedication.

(A) committing
(B) commits
(C) commit
(D) committed

136 Households headed by persons 45 years of age and older ------- for half of all disposable income in the United States.

(A) account
(B) take
(C) feature
(D) replace

137 While I'm away from the office, contact me only ------- there is an urgent and dire situation that needs attending to.

(A) though
(B) if
(C) by
(D) to

138 Mr. Evans left the corporate world and is now running a ------- business from his home in Minneapolis.

(A) personally
(B) personalize
(C) personal
(D) personalizing

139 All complaints will be dealt with and resolved by our customer service representatives ------- a timely manner.

(A) on
(B) at
(C) with
(D) in

140 Order forms should be submitted for ------- at the end of each business day to ensure timely shipment and delivery.

(A) processing
(B) process
(C) processes
(D) processed

Directions: In this part, you will be asked to read an English text. Some sentences are incomplete. Select the word or phrase that correctly completes each sentence and mark the corresponding letter (A), (B), (C), or (D) on the answer sheet.

Questions 141-143 refer to the following article.

Urban Planning and Real Estate

Urban planning greatly affects people's quality of life. For instance, a well planned city center can integrate businesses and living spaces so people do not have to travel far to work. This cuts down on the amount of time spent commuting, which saves on transportation costs. It also hinders the phenomenon of urban sprawl, which can be detrimental to the natural environment. Unfortunately, in a recent survey, many people indicated that they do not want to live in ------- areas. Homes are

141 (A) rural
(B) marginal
(C) downtown
(D) popular

usually smaller than in the suburbs and much more expensive. In purely ------- areas, building

142 (A) habitual
(B) residential
(C) financial
(D) recreational

construction is cheaper and not limited by space. The best compromise for real estate businesses is to offer condominium complexes with better ------- for family entertainment, or townhouses that

143 (A) examples
(B) organizations
(C) facilities
(D) services

provide individual yards. That way, home owners can have the best of both scenarios.

Questions 144-146 refer to the following information.

The 7ᵗʰ Annual Medical Practitioners Convention

Medical advancements and improved healthcare technology are ------- introduced into the field.

144 (A) slowly
(B) constantly
(C) assuredly
(D) suddenly

The dynamic nature of the business can be a significant challenge to medical practitioners, who must remain informed at all levels in order to provide their patients with medical treatment that is current and effective. Therefore, it is the purpose of the 7th Annual Medical Practitioners Convention to provide a forum for doctors to ------- ideas on how to access and utilize information

145 (A) elevate
(B) exaggerate
(C) generate
(D) renovate

about recent and critical changes. The opening address by Billington Hospital's renowned Chief of Surgery, Chad Meyers, ------- attendees an introduction to the overarching issues.

146 (A) will give
(B) is giving
(C) has given
(D) to give

This will be followed by a series of talks and workshops touching on a variety of ways to stay abreast of additions to medical knowledge. For more information, please contact Katherine Hicks at (345) 432-0011 or send an e-mail to khicks@medcon.org.

Questions 147-149 refer to the following notice.

Attn.: All Employees

As some of you were made aware at the last staff meeting, the company's fiscal budget has been -------. Therefore, I'm required to inform you that our company must now implement

147 (A) explained
(B) set
(C) enlarged
(D) exceeded

new provisions to curb wasteful spending. This is also an opportune time to remind everyone that personal transportation, meals or accommodation expenditure is not to be charged to the company without prior authorization. We will begin monitoring any purchases more ------. Employees will be held personally responsible for failing to observe company

148 (A) strictly
(B) generally
(C) rarely
(D) occasionally

purchasing procedures. Commencing -------, any purchases must first be approved by the head

149 (A) immediate
(B) immediately
(C) immediacy
(D) in immediacy

of each department. Please show your dedication to the business by demonstrating your commitment to our company's fiscal welfare.

Ivy Lee Goethe,
Human Resources

Questions 150-152 refer to the following letter.

Access Credit Company
9234 Furly Drive
Climax, Colorado
90352

I am writing to inform you that I wish to cancel my credit card with the Access Credit Company. I am very disappointed in the customer service I have recently received from your company. As I mentioned to you in my last letter, my credit card was stolen on September 10, and I immediately reported the theft. The customer service representative informed me that my account would be put on hold until I submitted a written statement. She also assured me that no new charges would be ------- to my account. I ------- the letter, as per your request, and a copy of my latest bill

150 (A) supplied
(B) complied
(C) replied
(D) applied

151 (A) will send
(B) sent
(C) sending
(D) send

for your records. However, this month, I received a bill for several items that were charged after my account was put on hold. These purchases were ------- and I do not intend to pay for them.

152 (A) superficial
(B) ineffective
(C) unauthorized
(D) imbalanced

Regards,
Sylvia Handlemaas

Directions: In this part, you will be asked to read several texts, such as advertisements, articles or examples of business correspondence. Each text is followed by several questions. Select the best answer and mark the corresponding letter (A), (B), (C), or (D) on your answer sheet.

Questions 153-154 refer to the following survey.

Dear customer,

We at Kramer's Windows would like to thank you for your continued patronage. Being a progressive company, we are always looking for ways to serve you better. Please help us by taking a few minutes to fill out this survey. You can send back this survey form through the postpaid envelope or you can take the survey online at www.kramers.com. Thank you so much for your time. We value you as a customer and we hope to continue serving you and providing you with top notch products!

Standard	Rating		
Product quality	☐ poor	☐ fair	■ good
Timeliness	☐ poor	☐ fair	■ good
Customer Service	☐ poor	☐ fair	■ good
Prices	☐ poor	■ fair	☐ good

The space below is for any comments you may have:

My order arrived on time, but I was disappointed when I opened the package and realized that one of the windows I had ordered was cracked. I called your service number and the customer care representative said that it was the company's fault. She said she would have a replacement shipped that very same day and that I wouldn't be charged for shipping. I received the package in just two days. I am pleased with the promptness with which my problem was resolved.

153 What is the purpose of the text?

(A) To inform customers of the company's new website
(B) To let the customers know how the company is doing
(C) To generate customer interest in a new product line
(D) To ask customers about what they think of the company

154 What did the customer say about an order he had received?

(A) A product he ordered was in the wrong color.
(B) It contained damaged goods.
(C) It was never delivered.
(D) Shipping costs were higher than expected.

Questions 155-156 refer to the following letter.

Jazz on the Park

653 Nickel Plaza, Minneapolis, MN 55403

Dear valued customer:

We here at Jazz on the Park would like to take this opportunity to thank you for being one of our most valued customers. Whether you realize it or not, your patronage has made a significant contribution to the development of our store. As a show of appreciation, we'd like to offer you a number of discounts to help fill the wardrobe now that the winter season is approaching. Here is what we have to offer you!

Discounted Item	Reg. Price	Discount Price
Men's leather bomber	$159.99	$99.99
Women's silk evening gown	$239.50	$159.50
Suede down jacket	$189.00	$149.00
Cotton t-shirts	$7.99	$5.00

These special prices are only offered for a limited time and discounts can only be received with this original letter and a valid form of identification. Bring in this letter and see the savings yourself!

If you have friends you'd like to introduce to us, have them fill out the membership application form attached to this letter and send it back to the address above. If for some reason there is no application form, go to our website where your companion can register online. Finally, you may also have your friend call one of our customer representatives at the toll free number located on the bottom of this sheet.

We hope to hear from you soon!

Sincerely,

Jeffrey Brown

Jeffrey Brown
Jazz on the Park Customer Relations Manager

---

155 What is the purpose of this letter?

(A) To inform customers of the new store
(B) To advertise the winter season inventory
(C) To offer price deductions on merchandise
(D) To have customers fill out a survey

156 What is NOT mentioned as a way to sign up for a membership?

(A) Mailing in an application form
(B) Completing an internet form
(C) Going to the store directly
(D) Contacting the company by phone

Questions 157-159 refer to the following invoice.

INVOICE

Trans-Continental Connections
3125 W Franklin Ave, Los Angeles, CA 55783

To: Dan Carlson, Director of Avis Consulting
Suite 44, 869 Oak Park, Phoenix, AZ, 88945

Date: April 4th
Invoice No: 673093

Item	Quantity	Unit Price	Amount
Installation of Video Teleconferencing Software	-	$156.00	$156.00
Web Camera	8	$26.00	$208.00
Super Deluxe Wall Screen	1	$1399.00	$1399.00
Audio Devices(Installation included)	6	$65.00	$390.00
		Sub total	$2153.00
	Outstanding Balance from March		$221.00
	Total Amount Due		$2374.00

Make payable to Trans-Continental Connections
Mail to: P.O. Box 73259
Los Angeles, CA 55783-73259

Thank you for choosing our company. We hope to continue to supply you with your communication equipment. We are continuously improving our quality and any suggestions from our customers are always welcome.

157 Who will receive payment for this invoice?

(A) Director of communications
(B) Dan Carlson
(C) Trans-Continental Connections
(D) Avis Consulting

158 What service does Trans-Continental Connections NOT offer?

(A) Communications consulting
(B) Software set-up
(C) Equipment sales
(D) Assistance arranging devices

159 How much is the previous account balance?

(A) $208.00
(B) $2153.00
(C) $2374.00
(D) $221.00

Questions 160-162 refer to the following article.

South Beach resident Jack Striden is setting an example for the rest of the world. He has introduced the idea of tree planting to his hometown and has been ardently persuading many others to do the same. Through speeches, flyers, discussion groups and personal example, Striden has exposed his conservation ideas to not only his community, but the entire nation.

Tree planting is a relatively inexpensive project said to hold many benefits. According to Jack, it is effective and environmentally beneficial, but the key to its success is education. He emphasizes the need to involve the youth in such projects. He additionally highlights the importance of environmental issues at the community level. For example, people informed about the effects trees have on oxygen levels are much more likely to put energy into planting trees and flowers. This would in turn improve the overall health of the community's environment, by eliminating some of the pollutants and toxic chemicals endangering our lives everyday. For these reasons, Striden feels that initiation of tree planting is necessary.

In fact, Jack is volunteering for a national environmental group whose goal is to educate the public. This team has requested the mayor to impose a new law regulating the cutting down or uprooting of plants without the government's permission. They have played an instrumental role in passing similar regulations in metropolitan areas such as San Francisco, Seattle, Boston and Madison. Of course, all of this must first be marketed and proposed to the citizens. However, there is not much convincing to be done. Most people know that planting trees will decrease air contamination and improve oxygen distribution.

160 What does Jack Striden think is needed for tree planting to be successful?

(A) An emphasis on the environmental benefits
(B) Awareness of environmental issues
(C) A reduction in air pollution
(D) The passing of a new law

161 What has the environmental campaign group accomplished thus far?

(A) Reduced car pollution
(B) Petitioned for legislative action
(C) Encouraged many residents to put in trees
(D) Nothing because they just got started

162 What does this article suggest?

(A) The group's efforts have already had success.
(B) More youth have become involved in community projects.
(C) Environmental problems will continue to grow.
(D) It isn't useful to make children environmentally aware.

Questions 163-165 refer to the following notice.

The WTE municipal plant will begin picking up recycling on October 29th. Although residents have participated in previous pick-ups, there have been problems due to large numbers of non-recyclable items placed into the recycling bins. To avoid this occurrence in the future, we have created and advertised the guidelines below. Any questions should be directed to the phone number listed on WTE's website.

Recyclable	Non-recyclable	Notes/Special Instructions
Unbroken glass containers (Beverage containers, jars, food containers)	Plate glass, window glass, light bulbs, mirrors, broken glass (hazardous to handlers)	Lids must be placed in metals. Containers should be washed thoroughly with the label peeled off completely.
Empty metal cans, caps, lids, bands and foil, ferrous metal	Full cans, spray cans (unless instructed), cans with paint or hazardous waste	Metals can be recycled repeatedly. Do not recycle metals used in scientific experiments, as they may contain hazardous substances.
Mixed paper: junk mail, magazines, photocopies, cereal boxes, shredded paper, newspaper.	Stickers, napkins, tissues, waxed paper, milk cartons, carbon paper, paper towels, wet or food-stained paper.	When in doubt, throw it out.
Plastic bottles stamped #1 or #2 on the bottom (all bottle colors are OK).	#3-#7 plastic types, plastic bags, plastic dishes or eating utensils.	Empty bottles and remove caps. Wrong types of plastic will be sent to the landfill.

163 What is the purpose of this table?

(A) To advertise the recycling collection schedule
(B) To promote the use of recyclable products
(C) To describe what is acceptable for recycling
(D) To explain the different types of recycling bins

164 Which of the following can be reused many times?

(A) glass
(B) metals
(C) paper
(D) plastics

165 What item is NOT reusable?

(A) Paper used to wrap hamburgers
(B) Lids of glass containers
(C) Used office paper
(D) Pickle jars

Questions 166-169 refer to the following document.

At this point we are in the midst of the planning phase for the franchising and public image enhancement of our restaurant. The projected locations are in two separate neighborhoods of the Edina area, which is a neighborhood well known for its taste in fine establishments. It also has an atmosphere that supports nightlife, with its many bars and theater venues. What's more, according to market research, the dining market has been showing an increase at the annual rate of 23%, making it the greatest market rise seen in the past three decades. Additionally, an average consumer in that sector eats out ten times a month and spends an average of $32 each time. These feasibility figures indicate great potential for the expansion of high-end venues. We will cater to upper-class residents between the ages of 23 to 55. Our estimated annual income will be mainly derived from dinner service, although, we anticipate a fair amount of patronage during lunchtime if we offer a buffet. Monthly expenditures are estimated at around 10,000 dollars per venue and initial investment would be around 500,000 dollars. After 30 months, initial expense will break even with the total revenue.

166 What is the planned project?

(A) Renovation of a local neighborhood
(B) Expansion of a food business
(C) Inclusion of a buffet style meal at midday
(D) Relocation of a restaurant into a more trendy area

167 Who does the business target?

(A) Senior citizens
(B) Business people
(C) Teenagers
(D) Wealthy locals

168 What is NOT included in the franchise plan?

(A) Opening in a new district
(B) Offering fine dining
(C) Catering services
(D) A convenient lunchtime meal

169 What do the market figures suggest?

(A) People are willing to pay for quality.
(B) Customers will not want pricey menus.
(C) Edina is an industrial area.
(D) There has been a decrease in consumer spending.

Questions 170-172 refer to the following e-mail.

To : Webpage designer, BFI
From : Eileen Bont
Date : 7/24/05

To Whom It May Concern:

Good afternoon. I'm writing to make your bureau aware that there are some mistakes on the Bureau of Financial Investigation's website. I'm a shop owner in Nebraska who recently attempted to contact your office regarding some discrepancies in my accounting records. The feasibility study I had done was not corresponding to actual figures. Therefore, I went to the website and found the Personnel Data page. I scrolled down to the appropriate department and attempted to telephone someone from that office for help. However, the number that appeared on the screen led me to an entirely different person from who I expected, and after several attempts, I finally gave up.

As a result of this mishap, I haven't been able to consult a federal official about my dilemma and this has in turn delayed my being able to send the bureau my financial assessment. I would highly recommend making the necessary updates and alterations to your webpage, as listings of personnel are of the utmost importance to the general public. Although I understand that the bureau recently underwent a number of changes and reorganization, I still feel that the website maintenance should be of the highest priority.

Thank you for your time and consideration in this matter.

---

170 What is the purpose of this e-mail?

(A) To complain about an official at the bureau
(B) To ask about the results of a financial assessment
(C) To request modifications to the website
(D) To inquire as to how to contact the bureau

171 What happened due to the mistake?

(A) The writer had discrepancies in accounting records.
(B) The writer failed to submit a financial assessment.
(C) The bureau underwent a recent reorganization.
(D) The writer could not conduct a proper feasibility study.

172 What explanation does the writer provide for the mistake?

(A) The website recently underwent changes.
(B) The website manager is gone.
(C) The bureau has been reordered.
(D) The priorities at the bureau are misplaced.

Questions 173-176 refer to the following brochure.

Full Check-Up!

When was the last time you had a check-up? The National Health Association recommends having your physical health checked at least twice a year. We here at the School of Physiology invite you to come to our clinic for your next routine physical. Our 150 well-trained students and post-graduates are offering discounted services in exchange for the opportunity to practice and enhance their medical skills. Quality care is assured by the Dean of the school.

However, potential patients should be aware that a physical assessment does not include prescriptions or treatment. A general check-up includes evaluation, but there will not be x-rays, medication suggestions, long-term health consultations, or treatment planning. It is recommended that you see a general physician for more specific needs. A list of authorized and recommended health care professionals in the area is posted on the bulletin board outside of the reception area.

In the case that you wish to partake of this offer, please contact our reception desk to make an appointment. Fees vary according to the patient's insurance status. Ask the reception desk for more detailed information about applicable charges. All new patients will first have to be screened by a medical assistant, so arrive at least thirty minutes prior to your scheduled visit. Assistants are on staff from 9-5, Monday to Friday. A professor of medicine is also on staff full time in case of difficulties or questions. In addition, comment cards are available at the front desk for patients to evaluate our staff and facilities. Take advantage of this great opportunity and let us help lead you to a more fit life!

173 What is included in a health check-up?

(A) A long-term medication plan
(B) X-ray pictures of patients' joints
(C) Surgical consultation
(D) A complete physical assessment

174 For whom is the offer NOT beneficial?

(A) Those who want to be healthier
(B) Patients who haven't checked on their health lately
(C) Patients with specific medical problems
(D) People who only want an educated evaluation

175 Why must people contact the reception desk?

(A) To find out about consultation costs
(B) To schedule an appointment with a medical practitioner
(C) To look into examination options available at the clinic
(D) To receive a discount on medical care

176 The word "screened" in paragraph 3, line 4, is closest in meaning to

(A) concealed
(B) evaluated
(C) obscured
(D) shown

Questions 177-180 refer to the following instructions.

How to use your Central Cooler

To program: It is highly recommended that you first program your cooling system. To do so, first enter your access code into the keypad on the left hand side of the apparatus. For larger spaces, each individual room or area may have its own settings. To assign temperatures, press the Settings button on the lower right side of the button pad. When prompted, type in the degree you want, followed by the name of the room or group using that setting. Once you press Save, the temperature is entered. There are a number of other programming functions detailed on the reverse side of this instruction manual.

To access your Central Cooler: To use the cooler, enter your room or group name using the letter buttons on the bottom-left of the machine face. Press Enter and wait for the prompt to enter the four-digit access code. Once entered onto the keypad, press Enter again and you should be logged into the machine and able to make changes as needed.

How to maintain your Central Cooler: In order to keep your cooler running smoothly and ensure its long lifespan, it is advised that the filter be changed every 3 months and the compartment cleaned. To do this, simply slide off the back panel, remove the existing filter, and proceed to cleanse the interior surface a soft soapy cloth. Be sure not to allow moisture into any other part of the machine. Insert the new filter.

For technical difficulties: If you have any difficulties, please contact us and one of our service representatives will handle your problems. However, before you call us, just turn off the apparatus and reboot the power after 5-10 minutes. In the case that there has been an electrical shortage or a power failure, the system may experience difficulties restarting. In such circumstances it would be best to immediately seek counsel with a qualified technician.

177 Whom is this information written for?

(A) Makers of the Central Cooler
(B) New employees to the company
(C) The general public
(D) Purchasers of cooling machines

178 What is necessary to program the machine?

(A) Administrative officials need to be called.
(B) The machine has to be turned on and off.
(C) An entry code is required.
(D) The back of the instruction manual must be read.

179 What is stated about the filter?

(A) It has a long lifespan.
(B) It should be washed with water.
(C) It is guaranteed for 3 months.
(D) It should be regularly replaced

180 What is the first action to take if problems arise?

(A) Contact the Central Cooler representative
(B) Restart the entire system
(C) Enter the access code again
(D) Change the password

Questions 181-185 refer to the following advertisement and e-mail.

ABC Outsourcing– You Don't Have to Face Today's IT Challenges Alone!

As your business grows, inefficient IT management can lead to inadaptability and budget blowouts, which no business can afford in today's tough corporate environment. Yet there is a solution! Let ABC Outsourcing manage all or part of your IT systems, yielding cost efficiencies and adaptability, and leaving you free to concentrate on core business operations.

We offer you an exclusive service to make the outsourcing transition as smooth as possible, by allowing you to retain command over your system even after you outsource it. Essentially, we work in close consultation with you through the entire process, so you remain informed the whole way, deciding what to keep and what to give away. And don't forget that our Technology Help Service is just a phone call away. Our team of friendly IT experts are on call 24 hours a day to deal with all your technical needs.

If you'd like to find out more, simply send your name, company name, and daytime work number to info@ABC.com and we'll send you a detailed 23-page brochure outlining all our services. Then, if you're still interested, we offer a free initial consultation session.

To: Whom it may concern
From: Martha Thwaite, PanState Insurance

I am the executive director of PanState, a medium-sized insurance company which has been successfully catering to clients in our area for the past ten years. As a result of growing business transactions we shifted from our old system to an updated IT environment five months ago, but management of this system has proven complex, and to cut a long story short, our company's IT budget has become untenably high. Thus, we're looking to simplify our system and increase our flexibility through outsourcing, but without completely losing command over it, which is why your advertisement appealed to me. As we are really not sure of the best way to go, we would appreciate your thoughts on this matter, and I would be keen to make time to meet with one of your consultants in the near future.

Sincerely,

Martha Thwaite

Questions 1-2 refer to the following letter.

181 What does ABC Outsourcing offer to do?

(A) Develop IT hardware
(B) Improve IT efficiency
(C) Organize IT seminars
(D) Monitor IT security

182 What is an advantage of ABC's service?

(A) Clients can maintain control.
(B) Clients can remotely access information.
(C) Clients can lease hardware.
(D) Clients can oversee IT costs.

183 What information is NOT required for a brochure?

(A) A contact name
(B) A company name
(C) An office telephone number
(D) A home telephone number

184 What does Ms. Thwaite say about her company?

(A) It has been in operation for five years.
(B) Business transactions have suddenly increased
(C) It still uses an old IT system
(D) Managing its IT system is too expensive

185 What does Ms. Thwaite want to do?

(A) Estimate next year's IT budget
(B) Protect her company's IT technology
(C) Make her IT system less complicated
(D) Update her IT system to a new version

It is a foregone conclusion that the key to a successful business is efficiency. Employers have been struggling for years trying to determine the best ways to ensure that their staff maintains maximum possible performance on the job. Numerous on-site tests have shown that the most successful companies are ones that offer incentive based wages.

The objective of incentive-based compensation is to provide a real incentive for constant improvement and overall excellence in line with an organization's goals. While money is not the only motivating force, it is the most powerful incentive and the one most easily understood by employees.

There are two major components in a general salary compensation system. The first major component of this type of system is salary. Salary provides satisfactory earnings in proportion to the experience, talent and energy an employee brings to the organization. The second component is fringe benefits, such as health care, retirement plans, child care, etc.

On the other hand, an incentive-based compensation system has an additional component, an incentive bonus plan, which is designed to motivate and acknowledge each employee's contribution in achieving the organization's goals. Analysts say persons who work on commission were found to be 23% more productive overall than salaried employees. The idea that employees are sharing profits generated from their achievements is believed to provide a strong driving force for better performance.

TO: Oscar Carter-Lynch, CEO, Viva Corporation
FROM: Fiona Shakespear, HR Manager

Dear Oscar:

This article from Wednesday's CEO Monthly captured my interest since we had just been discussing restructuring our salary system. I was impressed by the statistics regarding workers' productivity, and think we could profit from a similar scheme. The only problem is I don't think employees would be that happy about being paid purely by commission, rather than salary.

Nevertheless, I don't see why we shouldn't be able to blend the best parts of the two systems mentioned in the article. For example, we could continue to offer health care and retirement benefits, but reduce monthly salaries and bring in commission-based compensation with no upper limit. That way, employees would theoretically have unlimited earning potential. Let me know what you think.

Regards,
Fiona

186 What is the purpose of this article?

(A) To analyze how successful companies do business
(B) To determine how to boost morale at the workplace
(C) To explain the benefit of the incentive-based system
(D) To describe a new type of wage system

187 What could NOT be considered a fringe benefit?

(A) Paid leave
(B) Medical insurance
(C) Commission
(D) Educational reimbursement

188 What is NOT true about an incentive-based system?

(A) It was proven to be more efficient than a salary-based system.
(B) It encourages employees to perform better.
(C) Its wages are solely determined by employee performance.
(D) It has been adopted by many leading companies.

189 What does Ms. Shakespear recommend?

(A) Compiling statistics on productivity
(B) Abolishing health care benefits
(C) Offering higher salaries to workers
(D) Changing their current pay system

190 What does the email suggest?

(A) Businesses tend to avoid paying by commission.
(B) Viva Corporation restructured their financial system.
(C) Employees prefer salary-based compensation.
(D) This year's profit margin decreased.

Green Thumbs

Dear green gardener,

It has come to our attention that your subscription to Green Thumbs will be coming to an end within the next two months. We would like to continue to provide you with up to date information on new gardening products and tools, tips to save you time and help your garden grow, and our monthly features on different species of plants. If you renew now, we'd like to give you our special Valued Customer Offer! Sign up for a 2 year subscription and save up to 70% off the newsstand price. That means almost a $100 in savings! Simply complete the form below and drop it in the mailbox to have 24 full-color glossy issues of Green Thumbs delivered straight to your door!

Name: _____

Account number: _____

☐ yes, sign me up for 2 more years of Green Thumbs for the low price of $43.20

☐ yes, sign me up for 1 more year, with the regular subscription price $48.00

☐ Postal Payment (by certified check or money order only) Amount: _____	‹ Payment by credit card Card number: _____ Expiration date: _____

* You can still pick up a copy every month, where all magazines are sold, for the regular price of $5.95 per issue and $71.40 per year.

To Whom It May Concern:

Enclosed you will find a check for $43.20. I would like to renew my subscription to your magazine. There is only one problem, though. I am currently residing at 927 Small Oak Rd, Great Falls, MT 45820; however, at the beginning of November, I will be moving. Please make sure that all issues are sent to my new address: 87 Huntington Blvd, London, England, UK 156-890. I'd be grateful if you'd please inform me if there will be an additional amount to pay for international delivery.

In addition, I suspect that a couple of issues of the magazine have gone astray in the mail, as I did not receive August and September's issues. I was particularly desirous to read the latter, as I am undertaking some work to rejuvenate the garden before the house goes on the market, and that issue contains an article on how to create a miniature fountain. I'd appreciate it if you'd kindly forward me a copy as soon as possible. I will look forward to your reply.

Regards,
Anna Fiaz

191. For whom is the form intended?

    (A) For new gardeners
    (B) For interested advertisers in Green Thumbs
    (C) For current subscribers of Green Thumbs
    (D) For Green Thumbs magazine

192. What is NOT accepted as payment for subscriptions?

    (A) Credit card
    (B) Check
    (C) Cash
    (D) Money order

193. How many more issues does Anna subscribe for?

    (A) 1
    (B) 12
    (C) 18
    (D) 24

194. What does Ms. Fiaz want to know?

    (A) Whether the cover price has increased
    (B) Whether the magazine is sent by air or regular mail
    (C) Whether the publication is available in Arizona
    (D) Whether there is an extra charge

195. Why does Ms. Fiaz want the missing issue?

    (A) It contains advice on planting annual flower beds.
    (B) It offers advice on pruning techniques.
    (C) It includes instructions on making a water feature.
    (D) It explains where to buy quality garden plants.

Dear Mr. Blige,

In a recent phone conversation with a representative of your office, I was directed to contact the shipping department via the order processing department, which you presumably work for. My name is James Duffley of Brighton Street in Dolton County and I'm writing in regards to the contractual agreement we signed in June.

As we agreed in the terms and conditions of the contract I signed on June 15, the large screen television I ordered will be delivered to my home on July 3rd. My payment has already been made and the delivery charges set by the company have also been compensated for. According to our contract, the T.V. will be brought to my current address on the agreed upon date and time.

Unfortunately, I have just been informed that my lease has expired and that my landlord has already rented the apartment to another tenant. Therefore, I will be spending the next month trying to find a suitable residence in the Frisco area. This area is within the delivery range set by your company. As today is June 29th, there is no possibility of my having moved into a new place by the expected delivery date, although I do expect to be moved at the end of July.

I am requesting, therefore, that the delivery date and location clause of the contract be changed. I would like to postpone the date until I have found a more permanent place to live. Of course, I will provide your store with my new information as quickly as possible, as I am eager to enjoy my new purchase. Your patience and flexibility in this matter would be greatly appreciated. I look forward to receiving your response and apologize for any inconvenience this may cause.

Very sincerely yours,

James Duffley

James Duffley

Dear Mr. Duffley:

While we do not usually accept alterations to terms of delivery, yours has been deemed an exceptional case. I am therefore pleased to inform you that your request has been approved. However, as the delivery schedule is rapidly filling up, we must insist on a fixed date for delivery.

The shipping department has informed me that there are still spaces available in the week beginning July 25th, with the exception of the 28th, which is National Day. Kindly let me know as soon as possible which date you would prefer. Also, it is my duty to inform you that as delivery service is only offered within six weeks of purchase, after August 1 we would have to charge an extra fee for delivery.

Kind Regards,

Oliver Blige, Order Processing Department

196 Where does Mr. Duffley live?

(A) In Frisco
(B) On Brighton
(C) On Dolton Street
(D) In Wheaton

197 When will Mr. Duffley relocate?

(A) July 3rd
(B) Late July
(C) June 29th
(D) July 15th

198 What is Mr. Duffley's reason for the request?

(A) He doesn't want the item anymore.
(B) He is renovating his apartment.
(C) He is considering changing residences.
(D) He's being forced out of his home.

199 What is Mr. Duffley asked to do?

(A) Pick up the TV himself
(B) Pay an extra service fee
(C) Decide on a delivery date
(D) Call Mr. Blige in six weeks

200 What does the letter suggest?

(A) Delivery is not available on public holidays
(B) Delivery is not possible after August 1st
(C) Terms of delivery can usually be changed
(D) The delivery schedule is already full

多益實戰模擬測驗2

101 Next spring, Grace will ------- as assistant director at this company for 10 years.

(A) acting   (B) act
(C) have been acting   (D) has acted

102 Meredith Baxter has been a ------- associate of mine for the past fifteen years.

(A) close   (B) closeness
(C) closely   (D) closest

103 The ink used for the copier is of inferior quality and is ------- to fade after a few days.

(A) proper   (B) owing
(C) capable   (D) liable

104 Management has been discussing whether ------- advertising strategy will have a positive effect on generating product interest.

(A) them   (B) their
(C) they   (D) of them

105 Video rental shops require patrons to return extremely ------- videos within 24 hours of borrowing them.

(A) popular   (B) recommended
(C) solicited   (D) acquainted

106 The new technician is ------- more skilled than one would guess by looking at his résumé and work experience.

(A) so   (B) very
(C) far   (D) real

107 If the supervisor decides that overtime is necessary, ------- in the office should plan on staying after regular work hours.

(A) whoever
(B) whomever
(C) everywhere
(D) everyone

108 The enormous increase in the working population of this city is ------- due to the influx of individuals from the rural areas.

(A) quite
(B) largely
(C) liberally
(D) roundly

109 We are having difficulty deciding ------- the documents should be sent by FedEx or by international courier.

(A) both
(B) than
(C) whether
(D) after

110 Although there are a variety of sources from which companies can obtain consumer data, Hartley Company ------- relies on the Consumer Data Industry Association.

(A) quickly
(B) shortly
(C) frequently
(D) eventually

111 The advertising team has come up with a strategy that they believe will outshine the competition ------- consumer interest soars.

(A) even as
(B) even so
(C) as if
(D) so if

112 After he ------- his current contract, Gary will negotiate for a higher salary and more vacation time and resign with the company.

(A) is finishing
(B) finishes
(C) will be finishing
(D) finished

113 Oberlin Industries, Inc. yesterday launched a new advertising campaign that is expected to be dispersed rapidly ------- the country.

(A) following
(B) into
(C) toward
(D) throughout

114 It is difficult for professionals in the real estate industry to make decisions when they are ------- about property values.

(A) unsafe
(B) uncertain
(C) unknown
(D) unstable

115 Mr. Howard is enforcing a rule that bars employees from entering the building unless they are properly -------.

(A) dresses
(B) dress
(C) dressed
(D) to dress

116 ------- among staff members is low when there is little communication between management and the rank-and-file.

(A) Skill
(B) Behavior
(C) Duty
(D) Morale

117 ------- to her acceptance into the MBA program, Cathy was interning at a multi-national corporate headquarters.

(A) Ahead   (B) Prior
(C) Earlier   (D) Formerly

118 Employees who are eligible for vacation leave days are offered ------- for any leave days not taken.

(A) investment   (B) reimbursement
(C) foundation   (D) standard

119 The entire staff has been given a day off, as the deadline was met and office productivity has increased -------.

(A) consideration   (B) considerable
(C) considerably   (D) considered

120 The team leader was struck by the ------- of his members to make their views known whenever the manager sat in on their meetings.

(A) unwillingness   (B) discouragement
(C) indifference   (D) indecision

121 The people who entered this year's sales ------- prepared their marketing pitches months before they hit the floors.

(A) competitor   (B) competitive
(C) competing   (D) competition

122 Mr. Stevenson is tasked with ------- the activities of the teams involved in the product launch.

(A) pending   (B) intending
(C) coordinating   (D) collaborating

123 The company issued another profit warning, because, ------- its sales haven't slowed down, it hasn't been able to draw in enough new business.

(A) while   (B) still
(C) either   (D) instead

124 The company's storage room will soon be remodeled ------- an archive of documents and paper files.

(A) in including   (B) for inclusion
(C) to include   (D) with included

125 As equal partners in the business, the three contractors decided to divide the profit gains ------- themselves evenly.

(A) through   (B) within
(C) inside   (D) among

126 Health for Women provides its subscribers weekly email updates to ------- the magazine it releases every two months.

(A) pursue   (B) add
(C) supplement   (D) impose

127 To ensure that his employees' time is spent -------, the supervisor requires a weekly plan to be submitted every Monday.

(A) productively   (B) productive
(C) productivity   (D) productiveness

128 Long-time managers ------- to hire candidates who possess an outlook that reflects the principles on which the company was based.

(A) lead   (B) tend
(C) suppose   (D) force

129 What good project proposals have in ------- are a clear identification of project needs and a strategy to meet those needs.

(A) common   (B) habit
(C) usual   (D) normal

130 Having customers send payments by mail is not working, so we must develop an ------- method of compensation.

(A) alternated   (B) alternating
(C) alternative   (D) alternator

131 It is true that ------- the recruits is time consuming, but in the end it is worth the investment.

(A) train   (B) trained
(C) training   (D) trainer

132 She accepted our offer, ------- the fact that Mercer's Fashion offered her a better package.

(A) whereas   (B) despite
(C) unless   (D) apart

133 The hand-made lace handkerchiefs being sold at the resort's gift shop are the ------- of any available.

(A) finest   (B) fine
(C) finer   (D) fineness

134 Unnecessary expenditures have been reduced significantly, ------- monitoring employee write-offs and conserving on supply costs.

(A) between   (B) for
(C) with   (D) by

135 The magazine deals with the recent and pressing law ------- that have risen from the technological and economic concerns of the 21st century.

(A) issuing   (B) issues
(C) issuers   (D) issuable

136 This product, in ------- with a balanced diet and an exercise program, can help the individual with his weight loss goals.

(A) combination   (B) contribution
(C) coalition   (D) condition

137 The buyer has agreed to purchase the painting for 56 million dollars, making it the largest payment ever made for a single artwork ------- fifty years.

(A) by   (B) from
(C) in   (D) since

138 For some newly hired employees, working with a ------- group like ours can be both intimidating and challenging.

(A) profession   (B) professions
(C) professionally   (D) professional

139 The hiring committee's second interview is ------- interviewers are allowed to pose questions that would enable them to discern the candidates' special strengths.

(A) why   (B) when
(C) what   (D) how

140 Analysts ------- in their opinions of how quickly the stock market will recover from the latest crash.

(A) swap   (B) adjust
(C) alter   (D) differ

PART VI

Directions: In this part, you will be asked to read an English text. Some sentences are incomplete. Select the word or phrase that correctly completes each sentence and mark the corresponding letter (A), (B), (C), or (D) on the answer sheet.

Questions 141-143 refer to the following article.

Keeping the Work Force Healthy

A number of technological advances have allowed for the mechanization of many manual labor jobs, ------- the necessity for employees to move. This, along with an increase in poorly ventilated

141 (A) leaving
(B) reducing
(C) losing
(D) expanding

and overcrowded work environments, has resulted in an unhealthy work force. -------, a majority of

142 (A) However
(B) Furthermore
(C) For instance
(D) Consequently

employees have low levels of Vitamin D due to insufficient exposure to sunlight. One strategy suggests investing in quality organic multivitamins to supplement a healthy diet and provide the missing ingredients that protect against common illnesses. Since cardiovascular fitness is essential, employees are reminded to routinely exercise; activities ranging from simple stretches at your desk to full workouts at the gym or a brisk walk can help to ------- a longer lifespan and a

143 (A) ensure
(B) afford
(C) offer
(D) define

healthier life.

Questions 144-146 refer to the following letter.

Tracks Delivery
75 Bounty Drive
Newark, New Jersey 98695

To Whom It May Concern,

I am writing ------- the misplacement of a crucial document which I had arranged to be shipped

      144 (A) in respect for
           (B) respecting to
           (C) in regard to
           (D) regarding to

from my firm in Athens to a client in San Francisco. Not only did the package fail to reach its destination, but I was also met with hostility whenever I contacted a representative in your Athens branch to inquire of its whereabouts. I've been a ------- of your company for many years because

      145 (A) supporter
           (B) detractor
           (C) worker
           (D) competitor

for the service. Following this incident, however, I will no longer be holding Tracks Delivery in such high regard. You advertise your service to be -------. However, when there is an issue, there

      146 (A) fast
           (B) reliable
           (C) unlimited
           (D) operational

doesn't seem to be a contingency plan in place to deal with the problem at hand. Due to your company's poor conduct, I expect to be compensated for the damage done to both my client and me.

Marsha Glade

Questions 147-149 refer to the following e-mail.

From : Elliot Young, Director
To   : All Staff
Re   : Archive DB

Since *Food and Home* magazine was first published, back issues have been kept in our in-house library for staff use. Management has become increasingly aware of the ------- staff members face

      147 (A) simplicities
           (B) inconvenience
           (C) usefulness
           (D) speed

when conducting research using these paper copies. For this reason, we have developed a database called Archive DB, which contains all our old articles in text format. Archive DB ------- to equip staff

148 (A) was created
(B) will be created
(C) has created
(D) is creating

members with an efficient and convenient way to retrieve articles published in past issues for reference purposes. We are confident that the database will demonstrate its practicality to users with its advanced search functionality. To access Archive DB, a personal identification number will be ------- to staff members. Write this number down and do not lose it or lend it to anyone else

149 (A) shared
(B) assigned
(C) returned
(D) posted

because lost PIN numbers cannot be recovered.

Questions 150-152 refer to the following article.

The local government has conducted a poll on the implementation of additional trains on popular routes during peak hours in the morning and evening. According to the poll, the reaction of city residents to the service has been -------. One regular passenger said, "With the extra service, if

150 (A) uncertain
(B) accepted
(C) surprising
(D) positive

I miss my train, I can ------- catch the next train to my destination in three minutes' time. I don't

151 (A) affordably
(B) conveniently
(C) only
(D) usefully

have to wait around ten minutes or longer for my train to arrive." The new schedule ------- nearly

152 (A) was established
(B) might be established
(C) will be established
(D) has been established

two months ago when the city's local officials received numerous complaints about overcrowded trains and poor service.

Directions: In this part, you will be asked to read several texts, such as advertisements, articles or examples of business correspondence. Each text is followed by several questions. Select the best answer and mark the corresponding letter (A), (B), (C), or (D) on your answer sheet.

Questions 153-154 refer to the following information.

All copiers bought at our store have three year warranties guaranteeing your satisfaction and twenty-four hour technical support. As of this year, when customers turn in their completed registration cards, the copier's date of purchase is recorded in order to ensure the validity of the warranty. Any copier registered at any of our stores can be exchanged in the case that it doesn't meet the customer's satisfaction. All one must do to register is to fill out and bring back the card taped onto the top of the new machine.

Additionally, anyone who purchases a copier this month will automatically get the opportunity to participate in the prize giveaway event. An extra receipt with a name and phone number is printed out and put into the prize box for the drawing date. On the last day of the month, three names will be pulled out and the awards sent to their home addresses. The 1st prize winner will get a 1000 dollar gift certificate, while a scanner and company products worth 100 dollars will be given to 2nd and 3rd prize winners. Hurry and don't miss this great opportunity! We are eager to serve you!
(Please direct any questions to the information desk located at the back of the store.)

153 Why should customers return the card?

(A) To enter the contest
(B) To purchase a copier
(C) To secure their purchase
(D) To file complaints or questions

154 What will be given to the 1st prize winner?

(A) A large cash prize
(B) A brand-new image scanner
(C) Products from the business
(D) A redeemable voucher

Questions 155-156 refer to the following letter.

October 26, 2004
Tony Phan
Collection Department
Visa Express
Vanderbilt Building Rm. 501

Earl Ray
1219 North Avenue Apt. 202
Arlington, VA

Dear Mr. Ray,

We're sorry to inform you that your account is now seriously delinquent and, as a result, we've been forced to terminate your account. We value you as a customer and hope that you will help us continue to serve you by bringing your account up-to-date immediately. Payments can be made monthly by registering for the online banking services, or the entire sum may be paid in one check. When the total amount has been reimbursed, you may opt to reopen your account. In this case, you may contact any of our representatives by phone or send in an e-mail request. We would like to emphasize, however, that if the check is not received within seven days, we regret that your account will be turned over to a collection agency. This can be avoided by sending us money now or by calling to inform us when you will be sending due monetary requital.

Thank you.

Sincerely yours,

Tony Phan

Tony Phan
Manager

155 Why was the letter written?

(A) To update credit card payments
(B) To make the customer aware of a closed account
(C) To apologize for an accounting error
(D) To inform a customer that his application was approved

156 What is likely to happen if the check isn't received on time?

(A) Mr. Phan will meet the recipient in person.
(B) A bank representative will meet the recipient.
(C) Mr. Phan will close the recipient's bank account.
(D) A third party will handle the matter.

Notice for Changes in Flight Routes 4

Beginning on May 23rd, the airline will be rerouting all of its international flights due to heavy flight traffic. Passengers who have already purchased tickets for flights that will be changed will automatically be issued tickets based on the new schedule. Dates and times of original flights will be kept as close as possible to the new itineraries. Please refer to the table below for specific dates and instructions. If you have any questions or complaints, please pick up the phone and call a customer representative at 1-800-COME-FLY. We apologize for any inconvenience.

Flight	Rerouting Date	Instructions/Alternative Flights
NRT (Tokyo-Narita) - MSP (Minneapolis)	May 23rd	Service also available at Tokyo-Haneda International Airport
JFK (New York) - CDG (Paris)	June 15th	Service only to Charles De Gaulle
LAX (Los Angeles) - ATH (Athens)	July 4th	This route includes a stop-over in Frankfurt
LHR (London) - ICN (Seoul) (East bound)	October 11th	This route will be non-stop

157 Why will a number of flights be changing their path?

(A) Airports have put restrictions on flights.
(B) Too many passengers bought tickets.
(C) There are too many flights en route at once.
(D) They are expanding their destinations.

158 What should passengers unable to get the Narita - Minneapolis flight do?

(A) Use a different airline
(B) Change their destination
(C) Buy a ticket for a different date
(D) Go to another airport

159 What will happen to the London-Seoul flight in October?

(A) It will be used as an alternative route.
(B) The route across Asia will become a direct flight.
(C) There will be two stops along the way.
(D) A new airline will use that route.

Questions 160-162 refer to the following e-mail message.

> **To :** All Employees
> **From :** James Cole, Training Department
> **Date :** March 4
> **Re :** Apprenticeship Training Programs
>
> The Department of Labor and Industry has recently written us to encourage employable individuals to take advantage of apprenticeship training programs available in the state. Fields of specialty include construction, plant maintenance, graphic arts, manufacturing, services, and professional technical industries. I have attached a list of available occupations and courses; however, this list is not complete. Beside each course you will find the venue and the class days and hours.
>
> The training programs teach the employee higher-level skills than entry level positions require in order to make them more competitive in the job market. Depending on the level of learning difficulty of the occupation, a program may be as short as 2,000 hours, but will not exceed 10,000 hours. Because of the hour requirement, classes will be held daily except on Sundays.
>
> Employers need well-trained recruits, so we encourage you to take a look at what's available. Before enrolling in a course, it would be a good idea to get more information about the course, the requirements, and the trainers. You may call 284-5090 or 342-5434. Remember, it is essential that you are fully committed before you start a program.

160 Where will the classes be held?

(A) At the Department of Labor and Industry
(B) At the workplace
(C) The venue depends on the course
(D) At a university

161 How often will classes be held?

(A) Every day
(B) Three days a week
(C) Five Days a week
(D) Six days a week

162 What should be done before an employee begins a training program?

(A) Get a complete list of courses available
(B) Obtain needed information about a program
(C) Complete 2,000 hours in an entry-level position
(D) Secure permission from the employer

Questions 163-165 refer to the following form.

LEAVE OF ABSENCE FORM

Employee should fill all blanks and attach appropriate required documentation.
Please see the back of this form to check what documents you may need to attach.

Department : Research and Development

Name : Carol Yu

Commencement of Date of Leave : June 15, 2004

Expected Return Date from Leave : June 30, 2004

Description of Leave : ■ Paid Leave   ☐ Unpaid Leave

Type of Leave :   ☐ Sick Leave   ☐ Vacation Leave   ■ Maternity Leave
                         ☐ Educational Leave   ☐ Military Leave   ☐ Family Illness

Contact Number While on Leave : (415) 553-7581

Department of Pension Contributions (please indicate which contributions will be maintained by the department while you are on leave) :

Both employee and employer's contributions :   ■

Employer's contributions only :   ☐

Neither employee's nor employer's contributions :   ☐

For information regarding the financial implications for any of these options, please contact the Pensions Office.

....

Approval   Manager/Supervisor : _____   Date : _____

Original   Human Resources Department

Copies   Manager/Supervisor, Employee

Original to be held on file in the Department of Human Resources, 3rd Floor

---

163 Why is the time off from work required?

(A) To care for a newborn child
(B) To go on a trip
(C) To take care of a health problem
(D) To pursue a degree

164 Who will give final authorization for the request?

(A) Human resources
(B) A doctor
(C) The manager
(D) The employee

165 Where will the form be kept?

(A) In Carol Yu's desk
(B) With the head supervisor
(C) In the manager's files
(D) At the HR office

Questions 166-168 refer to the following notice.

NOTICE

This is a warning regarding upcoming construction in your district. The Washington County Licensing Bureau has approved the proposed highway project. The project involves the addition of one northbound lane and one southbound lane from Arbor Road to I-65 in Washington County, extensive improvements to the interchange at I-65, and pavement rehabilitation from Arbor Road south to Sharon Road in Washington County. The start date is March 2006. The project is expected to be completed in June 2007. Most of the work will be completed by the end of 2006. The final course of asphalt will be laid in April 2007.

The roads and construction dates:

> Arbor Road - March 17, 2006. To be reopened September 26, 2006.
> Sharon Road - April 7, 2006. To be reopened November 4, 2006.
> Crescent Road - August 11, 2006. To be reopened December 18, 2006.

The Department of Transportation strongly encourages all motorists to plan ahead and consider alternate routes in an effort to avoid the affected areas whenever possible. Please do your part to reduce congestion on local roads during the upgrade.

166 What is the purpose of the construction?

(A) To reduce the amount of traffic
(B) To make improvements on I-65 and area roads
(C) To lay asphalt on the existing I-65
(D) To make an alternate transport route

167 When will the pavement of the roads be finished?

(A) In March 2006
(B) In June 2007
(C) By December 2006
(D) In April 2007

168 What are drivers asked to do?

(A) Donate funds to the project
(B) Consider taking alternative means of transportation
(C) Avoid using their vehicles during rush hours
(D) Map out and take other possible routes

Questions 169-172 refer to the following article.

HG Motors has failed to achieve expected sales revenue due to an unexpected decrease in automotive sales in Asia. The abrupt change in transportation trends is largely attributed to the increasing use of public modes of transport in rural areas of South East Asia. Another contributing factor has been HG Motors' lack of high-end cars. Of course, Asia's recent merge into the international vehicle trade has also put stress on the auto industry to meet increasingly specific needs. Quite simply, the company hasn't been able to keep up with consumer demands.

In response, HG Motors is planning to produce a line of sport-utility and compact cars to reposition itself in the line of automobile sales. The first product will be a super-deluxe sports coupe aimed at the elite clientele. It will boast precision speed, full options, interactive GPS, and performance features. The initial expenditure of this plan is expected to pay off within three months of product release. Another measure taken by the company will be to downsize its assembly staff by 35% to cut labor costs. While unions have already voiced opposition to such a move, little active contestation is anticipated.

While some critics and analysts are skeptical about the company's ability to rebound from such a deficit, HG representatives insist that the financial outlook is positive. They argue that the proposed strategy takes into account all possible risks. Admittedly, this is the company's final chance to put itself back into the automotive market. If it can make a name for itself in the industry again, it is possible that consumer interest will rise. In the end, success will depend primarily on two factors. The first is the competition's reaction to HG's daring move, and the second being the company's ability to quickly create enough overhead to eat up the costs of initial losses.

169 For what reason is HG Motors struggling?

(A) Asia's economy is declining.
(B) Exports to other countries have decreased.
(C) It can't fulfill customer needs.
(D) Their automobiles are too expensive.

170 How does HG Motors plan to recover its sales?

(A) By increasing production of current models
(B) By introducing new models
(C) By imitating competitors
(D) By hiring a video technology expert

171 Why is HG Motors confident it can survive?

(A) It has a solid business plan.
(B) It has a relatively small deficit.
(C) It is favored by the public.
(D) It will focus on overseas sales.

172 What will eventually determine the outcome for HG Motors?

(A) Response from the consumers
(B) The quality of design for the new models
(C) The amount of beginning costs of production
(D) Rate of paying off business expenses

Questions 173-176 refer to the following announcement.

From : Human resources department
To : All staff

There is a position open for a currently employed staff member. The research department needs one more person to assist with the investigation of competing companies and products. The information gathered by the research department is then given to the strategists for consideration. Duties of this job include continuous product inquiry, performing feasibility studies, generating findings reports, and presenting information to marketing analysts and strategists. Research is mainly conducted on the internet, although some field work is required at times. Therefore, this employee will be provided with her/his own office and a computer equipped with all the necessary software.

The ideal candidate will have worked with our company for at least three years, have a background in marketing, and have a minimum of one year experience in the field of research (not necessarily with this company). Background and reference checks will be performed on all applicants.

If you are interested in this position and feel that you are qualified for the job, see Sally in the Human Resources Department for more details. Applicants should report their intentions to their department supervisor when the application is being considered.

173 Where will this document most likely be found?

(A) A company brochure
(B) A company notice board
(C) Attached to employees' pay stubs
(D) In an envelope in the mailboxes

174 Which of the following is true about the advertised job?

(A) It involves doing extensive field work.
(B) It is open to outside applicants.
(C) Researchers will sometimes work out of the office.
(D) Only trained professional researchers will be considered.

175 What is one of the requirements for the position?

(A) Working in a field at times
(B) Producing new marketing strategies
(C) Holding a marketing degree
(D) Having relevant experience

176 What should applicants do while the application is being processed?

(A) Get specific information from the personnel department
(B) Communicate their interest to a supervisor
(C) Schedule an interview with the research department
(D) Send a resume to Sally

Questions 177-180 refer to the following memo.

To : Company Employees

From : Board of Directors, Cathy Severson

This is a notice to all employees regarding some upcoming changes to our reception system. The board of directors recently held a meeting to discuss whether or not to implement a plan to overhaul the entire company's services system. A decision was reached after a nearly unanimous vote. The board feels that in order to increase customer and employee satisfaction, quality service must be the first priority.

Beginning tomorrow, a gentleman from Avris Communications will observe our method of call answering, in order to assess the company's special needs. We ask that you not change anything about how you go about your work. It is vital that the visitor get an accurate depiction. Additionally, he'll be recording and installing a new voice messaging system. It is possible that he will be asking people to record their voices, replacing phones, and handing out instruction sheets. Please participate with his requests and answer his questions honestly and to the best of your ability. We have received a guarantee from the consulting agency that as little disruption as possible will be made.

The upcoming procedures detailed in this memorandum will come into effect as of tomorrow, October 3rd, at nine o'clock. We expect this process to be completed by the beginning of November and will be rewarding bonuses to those employees we deem have contributed to the overall effort. Questions or concerns should be brought forth the director of personnel, Roger Kim. Your cooperation and understanding are greatly appreciated.

177 What is the purpose of this memo?

(A) To warn employees about an intruder
(B) To express concern regarding productivity
(C) To announce modifications soon to be made
(D) To introduce a new staff member

178 What was decided at the board of directors' meeting?

(A) Proposed changes were passed.
(B) More employees would be hired to improve service.
(C) Departments will be reorganized.
(D) A proposal was rejected unanimously.

179 What does the board ask of the employees?

(A) To ignore the questions of the consultant
(B) To give the consultant full cooperation
(C) To give a good impression to the consultant
(D) To approve the new plans for improvements

180 What is NOT stated in the memo?

(A) Employees should stick to their regular work routine.
(B) The office will be closed for a few days.
(C) Existing telephones may be exchanged for new ones.
(D) The work will be completed in November.

Fitness and Fun in Chelsea

Over the past few years, the staff here at New York's Freedom Fitness Center has re-defined the idea of exercise by introducing a revolutionary new approach to training. The success of our extremely popular health clubs is attributable to our unique philosophy, based on a holistic approach to exercise. Through a combination of the latest technology and health education, we offer excellence at a reasonable price. And now, in addition to its 10 great locations throughout the city, Freedom Fitness announces the opening of its new Chelsea Branch, so you can workout at the latest facility on the West Side!

Don't miss our Grand Opening Party on June 1. Run in and enjoy energy drinks and take a tour of the high tech equipment rooms! Also, come and greet the fittest and friendliest staff in town, and learn about our fitness classes. All of our trainers have over 10 years' experience, which competitors cannot match. If you like what you see, you can begin enjoying your new lifestyle as soon as our doors open on June 5th. As a special opening promotion, we're offering free trial classes to new members who join before June 30, so stop by quickly!

If you already have a membership at another branch, you can enjoy the freedom of working out at the Chelsea gym too! Please note, however, that only New York State memberships are valid.

To: Freedom Fitness, admin@freedomfitness.com
From: Penelope Crustacine, pcrustacine@hotmail.com

Dear Freedom Fitness:

I am so excited to hear that I will now be able to work out in close proximity to my apartment in Chelsea, and pleased to hear that you have the latest variety of exercise machines.

Even though my current gym is conveniently located near my office, it isn't up to standard. Not only is the equipment over ten years old, but to make matters worse, the management refuses to change them. In addition, only a few trainers seem to have any certification in their field, with the rest having received a few weeks of training at the center. A majority of them are only able to provide basic health and fitness consultations, such as measuring overall body fat and suggesting elementary tips on stretching.

As a result, I am planning on changing to Freedom, but before I do so, can you tell me if there is a reduced membership fee if both my friend and I join? I read in an advertisement for another Freedom Fitness branch that joint membership discounts were possible

Thank you,
Penelope

Questions 1-2 refer to the following letter.

181 Why is the Health Center successful?

(A) It's the largest fitness chain in New York.
(B) It specializes in group training classes.
(C) It has a unique marketing strategy.
(D) It adopted a new concept in fitness training.

182 When will the center open to the public for use?

(A) May 25
(B) June 1
(C) June 5
(D) June 30

183 What is NOT stated about Freedom Fitness Club?

(A) Their fees are inexpensive.
(B) You can inspect the club's facilities.
(C) Non-local membership users can attend the club.
(D) Energy drinks are available there.

184 Why did Ms. Crustacine write this e-mail?

(A) To inquire about fitness training
(B) To ask about group discounts
(C) To inquire about the location of the gym
(D) To ask about exercise machinery

185 What does Ms. Crustacine say about her current gym?

(A) The staff lacks interdisciplinary expertise.
(B) It is not far from her current place of residence.
(C) They insist on retaining old outdated equipment.
(D) They don't professionally measure client's body fat ratio.

Strathclyde Health Board

Rachel Adams
Bainer Pharmaceuticals
446 E. Audubon, Fresno, CA 93720

Dear Ms. Adams,

Thank you for applying to take part in the Strathclyde Health Board's trials of the latest influenza vaccine, which has been developed to combat a strain of the virus spreading from South America. I am pleased to inform you that your business has been selected for participation in the program, the projected time frame for which breaks down as follows: First, a representative from your organization will be required to come to a briefing with our staff on March 7th. Immediately following the briefing, we will be dispatching forms that all candidates must fill out with particulars concerning their general medical background before sending them back to us by March 20th. We will commence administration of the vaccines in the first week of April, and continue for three weeks. A post-trial survey about reactions to the vaccine will then be sent to each volunteer at the beginning of May, which they must fill out. The results will be analyzed, and a report about the vaccine's performance will be prepared and posted on our website at the end of June. Any inquiries should be directed to: avrilsoares@strathclydehealth.gov.

Sincerely,
Avril Soares

TO: Avril Soares
FROM: Rachel Adams, Bainer Pharmaceuticals
DATE : February 18th

Dear Ms. Soares:

I was pleased to meet you at the vaccine trial briefing on the 7th, and am glad that our company will be able to assist with the trials. Unfortunately, I have to inform you that we've encountered a few problems with the health information forms that you said would be mailed out. After waiting almost two weeks, I'm afraid to say that we only received them today, very tardy considering that we are supposed to fill them out and have them sent back by the 20th. I'm certain that we won't be able to get them completed and returned to your offices in time for that deadline. As well, we were quite disappointed to find that in some parts of the forms, the print was so minute as to be virtually illegible. To make matters worse, there were only 37 forms in the envelope, insufficient for our all of our 56 volunteers. Considering the extremely extenuating nature of the circumstances, I entreat you to forward us 19 more forms by express courier as soon as possible. Thank you for your understanding.

Sincerely,
Rachel Adams

Questions 1-2 refer to the following letter.

186. What is the purpose of Ms. Soares' letter?

    (A) To schedule a date for the initial gathering.
    (B) To inform an applicant of their inclusion in a study.
    (C) To request staff to take the influenza vaccine.
    (D) To advertise a vaccination for traveling to South America.

187. What is stated in Ms. Soares' letter?

    (A) Candidates will begin undergoing vaccination procedures in early April.
    (B) Data from the survey will be analyzed over a three-week period.
    (C) A representative from the Health Board will visit participating organizations.
    (D) They have more than enough volunteers for the process.

188. When will forms be sent out?

    (A) After candidates' medical information has been submitted.
    (B) After the participants have been screened.
    (C) After the initial briefing has been completed.
    (D) After the results have been thoroughly analyzed.

189. What is Ms. Soares asked to do?

    (A) Extend the deadline by a few days.
    (B) Collect the forms from Bainer Pharmaceuticals in person.
    (C) Dispatch the extra forms by fast delivery.
    (D) Change the scheduled dates of the program.

190. What problem is NOT mentioned in the email?

    (A) There aren't enough forms.
    (B) The incorrect forms were sent.
    (C) The forms arrived late.
    (D) It's difficult to read the forms.

Questions 191-195 refer to the following notice and form.

Notice to all Customers from Top Insurance Company
December 1st

Dear Valued Customers:

At Top Insurance, we appreciate that superior service and competitive pricing lead to customer satisfaction and loyalty. That's why we're introducing a new no-claims bonus scheme for our home, car, and health insurance policyholders. The system works in the following way: if you don't apply for any insurance payouts for one year, the next year's premium is discounted by 15% yearly over a maximum of five years. After that, the discount remains at 75%, as long as you don't make any insurance claims, bringing you significant savings!

If you've had a policy with us since December 31st last year and have not claimed against it in the past 12 months, we'll automatically start you off on the bonus from January 1st. Please note that the filing of counterfeit insurance claims will result in the discount being cancelled. Finally, we'd like to thank you for choosing Top Insurance, the nation's leading Personal Insurance Company since 1956, and hope to enjoy your continuing patronage.

Top Insurance Ltd.
Insurance Premium Invoice

Customer Name: Jeremiah Flaherty
Customer Number: 043-2202-523
Billing Period: Dec 31 - Jan 31
Installments: Yearly ☐ Monthly ■ Weekly ☐
Last Payment Received: Dec 15 Thank You!
Next Payment Due: Jan 15

Policy Number & Type	Claims Made Last Year	Base Premium	No-Claims Discount	Amount Payable
L21042 Car	0	$70.80	$10.62	$60.18
H67917 House	0	$50.00	$7.50	$42.50
N24518 Health	2	$97.25	$0.00	$97.25
TOTAL:	2	$218.05	$18.12	$199.93

All special promotions and premium rates for new and existing accounts are advertised on both the official website and on the new automatic answering system. If you have any questions regarding our products, feel free to call us at 0800 INSURANCE. Not only can you check your billing details and alter your insurance information, but it is also possible to apply for new policies.

191 In which case will the bonus be canceled?

(A) The client refuses to cash in on the payout.
(B) The company changes its insurance plans.
(C) The customer keeps the same policy for more than 3 years.
(D) The policyholder makes a fake insurance claim.

192 What is stated about the no-claims scheme?

(A) All customers will end up with a 75% discount.
(B) The discount increases by 15% per year for five years.
(C) It is different from other companies' schemes.
(D) After 5 years, the bonus will no longer apply.

193 Why is there no discount on Mr. Flaherty's health insurance?

(A) Health discounts are not offered until January 15.
(B) He made insurance claims in the past year.
(C) The policy is less than one year old.
(D) He didn't pay his last bill.

194 What is NOT mentioned as something people can do over the telephone?

(A) Change their policy details
(B) Settle insurance disputes
(C) Find out how much they owe
(D) Get information about products

195 How often does Mr. Flaherty make insurance payments?

(A) Once a year
(B) Once a month
(C) Once a week
(D) Once every three months

Questions 196-200 refer to the following memo and e-mail.

To :	All employees
From :	Records Department

We would like to remind all employees about bank policies regarding transaction reports, as recently there have been many missing files, causing financial data and statistics to be inaccurate. Please regard carefully the following information in order to help guarantee the success of our institution.

New employees may be used to filing reports once a month, but it is our bank's policy to do transaction accounts every Monday morning. There is no official system to monitor the completion of such work, so we put our trust into our employees' abilities to complete it once a week, in addition to keeping customer interaction logs once a day. It is common practice at this branch for staff to remind each other that it is "report day." This method of peer pressure seems to work quite well. We also recommend that you make a note in your computer calendar as a reminder. Some people set the alarm on their phone to signal when the report must be finished. However you choose to remind yourself, make sure to complete an accurate record of completed transactions on time. If you forget to perform this task, immediately contact your supervisor for further instructions.

TO: Helen Prendergast
FROM: Nadine Ford
DATE: Monday, June 6th

Dear Helen:

I've recently joined the team here and have some concerns I need to express regarding the memo that was circulated last Friday. I carefully read through the outline of transaction report filing procedures and now feel very lucid about the bank's policies. However, prior to receiving the memo, I was unaware of such guidelines and consequently didn't stick to protocol. Reports at my previous employer were filed monthly, and I erroneously assumed that this would be the case here too.

While I sincerely regret this mistake, I feel that the situation is redeemable. Since I haven't filed in the past two weeks, I can look back over my records, organize the transactions and file the missing reports by the end of the day. I guarantee that from now on I will follow the appropriate procedures without fail.

Sincerely,
Nadine Ford

Questions 1-2 refer to the following letter.

196 How often should transaction reports be made?

(A) Once a day
(B) Once in a while
(C) Once a week
(D) Once a month

197 How does the memo suggest keeping the task in mind?

(A) By setting your alarm clock for earlier than usual
(B) By purchasing a new calendar
(C) By calling your supervisor
(D) By bringing it to the attention of coworkers

198 What should you do when you don't remember to file the report?

(A) Talk to your administrative officer
(B) File a report with management
(C) Make a new one
(D) Contact a colleague

199 What is implied in the e-mail?

(A) Nadine Ford's previous employer's filing system was changed
(B) Helen Prendergast was recently employed by the bank
(C) Nadine Ford was not informed of the proper procedure
(D) The bank caters to high-end corporate investors.

200 The word "assumed" in Paragraph 1, Line 5, of the e-mail is closest in meaning to

(A) consented
(B) pretended
(C) believed
(D) acquired

必考單字

* 收錄Part V，VI 中已經出現的單字

星號（*）表示出題頻率。沒有星號的是出題時常以錯誤選項出現的單字。

第一天

abandon [ə`bændən]　v. 放棄，終止

ability [ə`bɪlətɪ]　n. 能力

accept [ək`sɛpt]　v. 接受，領受

acceptable [ək`sɛptəbl]*　a. 可以接受的

accidentally [.æksə`dɛntl̩ɪ]*　ad. 偶然地

accomplish [ə`kɑmplɪʃ]　v. 完成，實現

according to *　phr. 據⋯所載，據⋯所說

acknowledge [ək`nɑlɪdʒ]*　v. 告知收到信件等，承認

at all times * *　phr. 在任何時候

a variety of * *　phr. 種種

a vested interest *　phr. 既得利益

baggage allowance *　phr. 行李允許數量

balance [`bæləns]　n. 結存，均衡

be absent from * *　phr. 缺席

calculate [`kælkjə.let]　v. 計算

calculated [`kælkjə.letɪd]　a. 計算而得的

calculation [.kælkjə`leʃən]*　n. 計算

care for * *　phr. 照料

catch one's attention *　phr. 吸引（某人的）注意

comprehensive [.kɑmprɪ`hɛnsɪv]* *　a. 無所不包的

damage [`dæmɪdʒ]* *　n. 損害，損失　v. 損害，毀壞

damaged [`dæmɪdʒd]* *　a. 受損壞的

damaging [`dæmɪdʒɪŋ]　a. 有害的

damagingly [`dæmɪdʒɪŋlɪ]　ad. 有損害性地

deal with * *　phr. 應付，處理

decide [dɪ`saɪd]　v. 決定，解決

deciding [dɪ`saɪdɪŋ]　a. 決定性的

decision [dɪ`sɪʒən]* *　n. 決定，決心

decisive [dɪ`saɪsɪv]　a. 決定性的（=critical）

engage in *　phr. 從事

eager [`igɚ]　a. 渴望的

eagerly [`igɚlɪ]　ad. 熱切地

eagerness [`igɚnɪs]　n. 熱心，熱切

earn [ɝn]* *　v. 賺得，掙得

faint [fent]　a. 模糊的

fall in value *　phr. 價值跌落

fluently [`fluəntlɪ]　ad. 流利地，流暢地

found [faʊnd]*　v. 建立，建造

foundation [faʊn`deʃən]*　n. 建立，創辦

founder [`faʊndɚ]*　n. 創立者，締造者

gap [gæp]*　n. 裂口

gate [get]* *　n. 出入口，登機門

gauge [gedʒ]*　v. 估計，判斷（=measure）

get through *　phr. 通過，完成

good [gʊd]　a. 好的，有效的

goods [gʊdz]　n. 商品，貨物

habit [`hæbɪt]*　n. 習慣

habitual [hə`bɪtʃuəl]*　a. 習以為常的

idea [aɪ`diə]*　n. 概念，意見

ideal [aɪ`diəl]*　a. 理想的

idealistically [.aɪdiəl`ɪstɪklɪ]　ad. 理想上地

idealize [aɪ`diəl.aɪz]　v. 將⋯理想化

ideally [aɪ`diəlɪ]　ad. 理想地，完美地

international [.ɪntɚ`næʃənl]* *　a. 國際性的（=global）

internationally [.ɪntɚ`næʃənlɪ]　ad. 國際性地

lasting [`læstɪŋ]*　a. 持久的，持續的

latch [lætʃ]　n. 門閂

magnification [.mægnəfə`keʃən]　n. 放大，擴大

maintain [men`ten]* *　v. 維持（=preserve），主張（=assert）

name [nem]* *　v. 說出⋯的名字（=nominate），叫⋯

namely [`nemlɪ]　ad. 即，那就是

obey [ə`be]　v. 服從，聽從

paint [pent]* *　v. 油漆，畫

paper [`pepɚ]*　n. 紙，報紙，論文

per [`pɚ]*　prep. 每

rainfall [`ren.fɔl]*　n. 下雨，降雨量

raise [rez]* *　v. 舉起，籌款，提出問題

safekeeping [`sef`kipɪŋ]*　n. 安全保護，妥善保管

season [`sizn]*　n. 季，季節　v. 給⋯調味，加味於

seasonal [`siznəl]* *　a. 季節性的，週期性的

seasoning [`siznɪŋ]*　n. 調味料

suitable [`sutəbl]　a. 適當的，合適的

suitably [`sutəblɪ]　ad. 適當地，相配地

tactics [`tæktɪks]　n. 戰術，策略

talk [tɔk]* *　v. 講話，商談，商討

wage [wedʒ]*　n. 薪水

wrongly [`rɔŋlɪ]　ad. 錯誤地，不正確地

第二天

abate [ə`bet]*　v. 減少，減弱

abduct [æb`dʌkt]　v. 誘拐，綁架

accelerate [æk`sɛlə.ret]*　v. 使增速

access [`æksɛs]* *　n. 接近，進入的權利；使用

accessible [æk`sɛsəbl]*　a. 可（或易）接近的

accessory [æk`sɛsərɪ]　n. 配件，附加物件

accordingly [ə`kɔrdɪŋlɪ]　ad. 相應地，於是

at one's expense * *　phr. 由（某人）付錢

barely [`bɛrlɪ]　ad. 僅僅，勉強，幾乎沒有

barring [`bɑrɪŋ]* *　prep. 除⋯以外

belong [bə`lɔŋ]　v. 屬於

belongings [bə`lɔŋɪŋz]　n. 攜帶物品，財產

call [kɔl]　v. 叫喊，呼叫

campaign [kæm`pen] * n. 運動，活動

continual [kən`tɪnjuəl] a. 連續的

continually [kən`tɪnjuəlɪ] * * ad. 不停地

continuation [kən,tɪnju`eʃən] n. 延續，延長

continue [kən`tɪnju] * * v. 繼續

continuity [,kɑntə`njuətɪ] * n. 連續性

continuous [kən`tɪnjuəs] a. 連續的

decline [dɪ`klaɪn] * v. 衰退

decline in * phr. 在…的減少

easily [`izɪlɪ] * * ad. 容易地

easiness [`izɪnɪs] n. 容易

easy [`izɪ] * * a. 容易的

established company * phr. 已建立的公司

forever [fə`ɛvə] ad. 永遠

gear [gɪr] n. 裝置 v.與…協調地工作，準備好（活動）

handle [`hændl] * * v. 操作，對待

have an influence on * phr. 影響於…

health [hɛlθ] * * n. 健康，保健

healthful [`hɛlθfəl] a. 有益於健康的

in a timely manner * * phr. 及時

intricate [`ɪntrəkɪt] * * a. 錯綜複雜的

irregularly [ɪ`rɛgjələlɪ] ad. 不規則地

just enough to + 動詞原型 * * phr. 恰好足夠做…

keep track of * phr. 不斷追蹤…

lag behind * phr. 落後

lease [lis] * * v. 出租 n. 租賃（契約）

lecture [`lɛktʃə] * n. 授課，演講

mail [mel] n. 郵件 v. 郵寄

mailing [`melɪŋ] * n. 郵寄，郵件

make all checks payable to + 某人 * phr. 所有支票支付給（某人）

narrow [`næro] v. 使變窄 a. 狹窄的

narrow down A to B * * phr. 將 A 縮小成 B 的範圍

object [`ɑbdʒɪkt] * v. 反對

objection [əb`dʒɛkʃən] n. 反對，異議

objective [əb`dʒɛktɪv] * * n. 目的 a. 客觀的

objectively [əb`dʒɛktɪvlɪ] ad. 客觀地

oblivious [ə`blɪvɪəs] a. 不注意的，不以為意的

parallel [`pærə,lɛl] * a. 平行的

qualified [`kwɑlə,faɪd] * a. 勝任的，合格的

quality [`kwɑlətɪ] * * n. 品質，質量

randomize [`rændəm,aɪz] v. 作任意排列

randomly [`rændəmlɪ] * ad. 任意地

rapid [`ræpɪd] * * a. 快的，迅速的

rapidly [`ræpɪdlɪ] * * ad. 很快地，迅速地

rate [ret] * * n. 比例（=percentage），費用，速度

rating [`retɪŋ] n. 評價，評估值，信用度

sale [sel] * * n. 出售，(pl.) 銷售額 a. 出售的

spontaneously [spɑn`tenɪəslɪ] ad. 自發地

superio [sə`pɪrɪə] * a. 優秀的，傑出的（=top-of-the-line）

talented [`tæləntɪd] * a. 有天賦的，有才幹的

tariff [`tærɪf] n. 關稅

trouble [`trʌbl] * * v. 使煩惱，使憂慮 n. 憂慮

ultimate [`ʌltəmɪt] a. 最後的，最終的

understand [,ʌndə`stænd] * * v. 理解，懂

understandable [,ʌndə`stændəbl] a. 可理解的

understanding [,ʌndə`stændɪŋ] * * n. 理解，協議 a. 善解人意的

uniform [`junə`fɔrm] n. 制服

vacancy [`vekənsɪ] n. 空缺，空額，(pl.) 空辦公室，空房

vacant [`vekənt] * a. 空著的，空缺的

vacate [`veket] * * v. 空出，搬出

valor [`vælə] n. 勇氣，勇猛

weaken [`wikən] v. 削弱

weakness [`wiknɪs] n. 弱點，缺點

whole [hol] a. 全體的

第三天

accomplice [ə`kɑmplɪs] n. 共犯

accord [ə`kɔrd] n. 一致，調和，協議

account [ə`kaʊnt] * * n. 解釋，說明

accountable [ə`kaʊntəbl] a. 應負責任的，可說明的

accountably [ə`kaʊntəblɪ] ad. 可說明地

acquaint [ə`kwent] v. 使認識，使熟悉

at the latest * * phr. 最晚

beneath [bɪ`niθ] prep. 在…之下

beneficial [,bɛnə`fɪʃəl] * a. 有益的，有利的（=advantageous）

beneficiary [,bɛnə`fɪʃərɪ] n. 受益人，受惠者

benefit [,bɛnəfɪt] * * n. 利益，津貼

bid [bɪd] v. 拍賣 n. 出價

broad [brɔd] * a. 寬的

broaden [`brɔdn] * * v. 使寬，擴大

broadly [`brɔdlɪ] ad. 寬廣地，大體上

calm [kɑm] a. 安靜的，平靜的

calmly [`kɑmlɪ] * * ad. 平靜地，寧靜地

calmness [`kɑmnɪs] n. 平靜，沈著

candidate [`kændədet] * n. 候選人

common [`kɑmən] * a. 共同的

commonly [`kɑmənlɪ] ad. 一般地

decrease [dɪ`kris] v. 減少，減小

delegate [`dɛləgɪt] * v. 把…委託給 n. 代表

delegation [,dɛlə`geʃən] * * n. 代表團

early [`ɝlɪ] * * a. 早的 ad. 早

faction [`fækʃən] 黨派，派別

famished [`fæmɪʃt] a. 饑餓的

finished product * * phr. 完成品

generalization [,dʒɛnərəlaɪ`zeʃən] n. 一般化

必考單字 | 495

generalize [ˋdʒɛnərəlˏaɪz] v. 概括，綜合

generally [ˋdʒɛnərəlɪ] * * ad. 一般地

generate [ˋdʒɛnəˏret] * * v. 發生（=produce），引起

generate funds phr. 籌措資金

graceful [ˋgresfəl] a. 雅致的，典雅的

gracefully [ˋgresfəlɪ] * ad. 雅致地，溫文地

handcrafted [ˋhændˏkræftɪd] * a. 手工製作的

higher salary * phr. 較高的薪水

identical [aɪˋdɛntɪkl] a. 同一的

identifiable [aɪˋdɛntəˏfaɪəbl] a. 可識別的

identification [aɪˏdɛntəfəˋkeʃən] * * n. 身份證

identify [aɪˋdɛntəˏfaɪ] v. 確認，使合作

identity [aɪˋdɛntətɪ] n. 身份

illustrate [ˋɪləstret] * v. 說明，闡明

illustrator [ˋɪləsˏtretə] * n. 插圖畫家

impact [ˋɪmpækt] * n. 影響，作用 v. 產生影響

intuitive [ɪnˋtjuɪtɪv] a. 憑直覺獲知的

late [let] * * a. 遲的 ad. 遲到

lately [ˋletlɪ] * * ad. 最近

lateness [ˋletnɪs] n. 遲，晚

latest [ˋletɪst] * a. 最近的

lessen [ˋlɛsn̩] v. 使變小，使變少

maneuver [məˋnuvə] v. 實施調動，用計謀

negotiation [nɪˏgoʃɪˋeʃən] * * n. 談判，協商

obligate [ˋɑbləˏget] v. 使負義務，強使

obtain A from B * * phr. 從 B 那裡得到 A

pass [pæs] * v. 通過，經過 n. 穿過，通行證

payment upon delivery * phr. 貨到付款

reach [ritʃ] * * v. 到達，取得聯繫

reaction [rɪˋækʃən] * n. 反應，感應

react to * phr. 對…作出反應

satisfaction [ˏsætɪsˋfækʃən] * * n. 滿足

satisfactorily [ˏsætɪsˋfæktərɪlɪ] ad. 令人滿意地

satisfactory [ˏsætɪsˋfæktərɪ] * * a. 符合要求的

satisfied [ˋsætɪsˏfaɪd] * a. 感到滿意的

satisfy [ˋsætɪsˏfaɪ] v. 使滿意

satisfying [ˋsætɪsˏfaɪɪŋ] a.（以成就感）滿意的，充分的

scrutinize [ˋskrutn̩ˏaɪz] v. 詳細檢查

send A to B * phr. 把 A 發送給 B

sure [ʃʊr] * a. 確信的

take care of * phr. 照顧，負責

tend [tɛnd] * v. 傾向

under construction * * phr. 架構中

union [ˋjunjən] n. 組織，團體

update [ʌpˋdet] * * v. 使…合乎時代，更新

verify [ˋvɛrəˏfaɪ] v. 證明，證實

what the future holds for +某人 * * phr. 某人的未來

第四天

above all * phr. 最重要的是

accommodate [əˋkɑməˏdet] * * v. 給…方便，收容（=lodge）

accurate [ˋækjərɪt] * a. 準確的

accurately [ˋækjərɪtlɪ] * * ad. 準確地

at the time * phr. 在那時

be accompanied by * * phr. 伴隨著

border [ˋbɔrdə] n. 邊界 v. 與…有共同邊界

capacity [kəˋpæsətɪ] * * n. 能力，容積

care [kɛr] v. 憂慮，照料

careful [ˋkɛrfəl] * * a. 仔細的

carefully [ˋkɛrfəlɪ] * ad. 仔細地

carelessly [ˋkɛrlɪslɪ] ad. 粗心大意地

check A for B * phr. 為確認 B 的存在檢驗 A

dedicate [ˋdɛdəˏket] * * v. 奉獻，把（時間、精力等）用於

dedicated [ˋdɛdəˏketɪd] * * a. 奉獻的

dedication [ˏdɛdəˋkeʃən] n. 奉獻

deem [dim] v. 認為，視作

defy description * phr. 無法全部闡述

degree [dɪˋgri] n. 程度，等級

elect [ɪˋlɛkt] * * v. 選舉

election [ɪˋlɛkʃən] n. 選舉，當選

eliminate [ɪˋlɪməˏnet] * v. 排除

fare [fɛr] n. 票價，車費

fill [fɪl] * v. 裝滿，填滿

find out phr. 找出…

give in to * phr. 遷就…

grant [grænt] * * v. 給予，授予

have A in common * phr. 共同擁有 A

honor [ˋɑnə] * * n. 榮譽 v. 尊敬（=respect）

impair [ɪmˋpɛr] v. 削弱，損傷

improvement in * phr. 對於…的改進

job description * phr. 工作說明

lend [lɛnd] * * v. 借給

lender [ˋlɛndə] * * n. 貸方，出借人

level [ˋlɛvl] * * n. 水平，程度

master [ˋmæstə] v. 精通，掌握

need [nid] * * v. 需要 n. (pl.) 需要，要求

neediness [ˋnidɪnɪs] n. 貧窮，困窘

needlessly [ˋnidlɪslɪ] ad. 不必要地

needy [ˋnidɪ] a. 貧窮的

neuter [ˋnjutə] n. 中性 a. 中性的

neutral [ˋnjutrəl] a. 中立的

neutrality [njuˋtrælətɪ] * * n. 中立（狀態），中立政策

neutralize [ˋnjutrəlˏaɪz] v. 使中立化

neutrally [ˋnjutrəlɪ] ad. 中立，保持中立

neutron [ˋnjutrɑn] n. 中子

partial [ˋpɑrʃəl] a. 部分的，偏袒的

partially [`pɑrʃəlɪ] *   ad. 部分地

partition [par`tɪʃən]   n. 分割，劃分

partner [`pɑrtnə]   n. 合夥人，同夥

patronize [`petrən‚aɪz] *   v. 贊助，庇護

permanent [`pɝmənənt] * *   a. 永久的，永恆的

quick [kwɪt] * *   a. 快的

quicken [`kwɪkən]   v. 加快

quickly [`kwɪklɪ]   ad. 立即

quickness [`kwɪknɪs]   n. 敏捷，敏銳

rare [rɛr]   a. 稀有的，罕見的

salvage [`sælvɪdʒ]   n. 海難救助，搶救

scent [sɛnt] *   n. 氣味，香味

search [sɝtʃ]   v. 搜查，搜尋

still [stɪl] * *   ad. 還，仍舊

technical [`tɛknɪkl] *   a. 專門的，技術性的

technicality [‚tɛknɪ`kælətɪ]   n. 專門性，專門語

technically [`tɛknɪklɪ] *   ad. 技術上

technician [tɛk`nɪʃən]   n. 技術人員，技師

technique [tɛk`nik]   n. 技術，技法

technology [tɛk`nɑlədʒɪ]   n. 技術

temporal [`tɛmpərəl]   a. 時間的，世俗的

temporarily [`tɛmpə‚rɛrəlɪ] * *   ad. 暫時地，臨時地

temporary [`tɛmpə‚rɛrɪ] *   a. 臨時的，暫時的

unanimous [ju`nænəməs] *   a. 全體一致的

valid [`vælɪd] *   a. 有效的

validation [‚vælə`deʃən]   n. 批准，確認

view [vju]   v. 觀看   n. 看法，觀點

weight [wet]   n. 重量，體重

willing [`wɪlɪŋ] *   a. 願意的，樂意的

willingness [`wɪlɪŋnɪs]   n. 自願，樂意

第五天

accompany [ə`kʌmpənɪ] *   v. 陪同

accountant [ə`kaʊntənt] * *   n. 會計師

accounting [ə`kaʊntɪŋ]   n. 會計（學）

acutely [ə`kjutlɪ]   ad. 尖銳地，劇烈地

at your earliest convenience *   phr. 在你最方便的時候

beside [bɪ`saɪd] * *   prep. 在…近旁

besides [bɪ`saɪdz] *   prep. 除…之外   ad. 而且

blend [blɛnd]   v. 混和

budget [`bʌdʒɪt] *   n. 預算   v. 編列預算

categorize [`kætəgə‚raɪz]   v. 將…分類

category [`kætə‚gorɪ]   n. 部屬，類別

claim [klem]   v. 要求   n. 要求，要求物

concisely [kən`saɪslɪ]   ad. 簡潔地

defend [dɪ`fɛnd]   v. 防禦，保衛

economic [‚ikə`nɑmɪk] *   a. 經濟上的，經濟學的

economical [‚ikə`nɑmɪkl] * *   a. 經濟的，節約的

economically [‚ikə`nɑmɪklɪ]   ad. 節約地

economics [‚ikə`nɑmɪks]   n. 經濟學

economist [i`kɑnəmɪst]   n. 經濟學者

economize [i`kɑnə‚maɪz]   v. 節約

economy [ɪ`kɑnəmɪ] * *   n. 經濟

favor [`fevə]   n. 偏愛，善意

favorable [`fevərəbl] *   a. 善意的，有希望的（=promising）

favorably [`fevərəblɪ] * *   ad. 善意地

favorite [`fevərɪt]   a. 特別喜愛的

growing [`groɪŋ]   a. 越來越多

growth [groθ]   n. 成長

impart [ɪm`pɑrt]   v. 告知，透露

in accordance with +（規定、規範）*   phr. 依照（規定、規範）

irrelevant [ɪ`rɛləvənt] *   a. 無關的

keep the appointment *   phr. 遵守約定

largely [`lɑrdʒlɪ] * *   ad. 主要，大部分

lead to +名詞 *   phr. 通到，導致

leverage [`lɛvə‚rɪdʒ]   n. 槓桿作用，影響力

license [`laɪsn̩s]   n. 許可，特許

lift [lɪft]   v. 舉起，抬起

limited capacity *   phr. 有限的容量、生產能力

make sure + that 子句 * *   phr. 確定…

manners [`mænəz]   n. 禮節，風俗

marginal [`mɑrdʒɪnl] *   a. 微小的，不重要的

marginally [`mɑrdʒɪnəlɪ]   ad. 少量地

match [mætʃ] *   v. 相配，相適合

neglect [nɪg`lɛkt]   v. 忽視，忽略

next to *   phr. 緊鄰著…

obstruct [əb`strʌkt]   v. 妨礙，阻擾

occasion [ə`keʒən]   n. 場合，機會

occasional [ə`keʒənl]   a. 偶爾的，非經常的

occasionally [ə`keʒənlɪ] *   ad. 偶爾，間或

on behalf of   phr. 代表

pattern [`pætən]   n. 花樣，形態，樣本

pay [pe] * *   v. 支付

payment [`pemənt]   n. 支付，付款

periodic [‚pɪrɪ`ɑdɪk]   a. 週期的，週期性的

periodically [‚pɪrɪ`ɑdɪklɪ]   ad. 週期性地，定期地

place A on standby *   phr. 將 A 設為待命狀態

play [ple]   v. 演奏，彈奏   n. 戲劇（=drama）

pronouncement [prə`naʊnsmənt]   n. 宣言，公告

recite [rɪ`saɪt]   v. 背誦

refrain from Ving *   phr. 克制住…

resign [rɪ`zaɪn]   v. 辭去

resignation [‚rɛzɪg`neʃən] * *   n. 辭職，放棄

resigned [rɪ`zaɪnd]   a. 已辭職的

resignedly [rɪ`zaɪnɪdlɪ]   ad. 順從地

seem [sim] * v. 看來好像，似乎

select [sə`lɛkt] v. 選擇

selection [sə`lɛkʃən] * n. 選擇，挑選

specific [spɪ`sɪfɪk] * * a. 具體的

specifically [spɪ`sɪfɪklɪ] ad. 具體地

specification [ˌspɛsəfə`keʃən] n. 說明書

specify [`spɛsəˌfaɪ] v. 詳細指明，明確說明（=state）

specification for * phr. 對…的詳細說明

straightly [`stretlɪ] ad. 直接地

surface [`sɝfɪs] n. 表面

sustained [sə`stend] a. 持久的，持續的

tenant [`tɛnənt] n. 居住者，承租人

tire [taɪr] * v. 使疲倦

wellness [`wɛlnɪs] n. 健康

第六天

above one's expectation * phr. 超過（某人的）期望

accost [ə`kɔst] v. 接近（不識者）與之攀談

accrue [ə`kru] * v.（利息等的自然）滋生（=accumulate）

accumulate [ə`kjumjəˌlet] v. 累積，積聚

accumulation [ə`kjumjəˌleʃən] n. 積累，積聚

achievement [ə`tʃivmənt] n. 成就，成績

adamantly [`ædəməntlɪ] ad. 堅決地

be aimed at * phr. 著眼於

block [blɑk] v. 妨礙 n. 阻塞（物），障礙（物）

build [bɪld] * * v. 建築

builder [`bɪldə] n. 建設者

built-in [`bɪlt`ɪn] * a. 嵌入的，固定的

bulk [bʌlt] * n. 體積，容積

cause [kɔz] n. 原因 v. 導致，引起

certifiable [`sɝtəˌfaɪəbl̩] a. 可保證的

certification [ˌsɝtɪfə`keʃən] * * n. 證明書

certified [`sɝtəˌfaɪd] a. 被證明的，公認的

certify [`sɝtəˌfaɪ] * v. 證明，保證

check in * phr.（旅館、空航）到達並登記

collaborate [kə`læbəˌret] * v. 共同工作，合作

command [kə`mænd] v. 命令

construe [kən`stru] v. 解釋

declaratory [dɪ`klærəˌtɔrɪ] a. 宣言的

declared [dɪ`klɛrd] a. 公開宣佈的，公然的

deflate [dɪ`flet] v. 緊縮

emerge [ɪ`mɝdʒ] v. 出現

employ [ɪm`plɔɪ] v. 雇用

employed [ɪm`plɔɪd] a. 受雇於

employee [ˌɛmplɔɪ`i] * * n. 雇員，從業員工

employer [ɪm`plɔɪə] n. 雇主

employment [ɪm`plɔɪmənt] * * n. 雇用，受雇

feature [`fitʃə] * * n. 特徵

featured [`fitʃəd] a. 作為特色的，作為號召的

find [faɪnd] * v. 找到，發現

findings [`faɪngɪŋz] * n. 調查結果

grip [grɪp] v. 緊握，理解

guided tour * phr. 有導遊的遊覽

implement [`ɪmpləmənt] v. 履行，實施

inability [ˌɪnə`bɪlətɪ] n. 無能，無力

likelihood [`laɪklɪˌhʊd] * * n. 可能，可能性

likely [`laɪklɪ] * * a. 很可能的

likeness [`laɪknɪs] n. 相像，相似

make requests * phr. 提出請求

mark [mɑrk] n. 痕跡，標記 v. 做記號於，留痕跡於

markedly [`mɑrkɪdlɪ] * ad. 顯著地

measure [`mɛʒə] v. 測量

obtain [əb`ten] * * v. 得到，獲得

occupancy [`ɑkjəpənsɪ] n. 居住，佔有

occupant [`ɑkjəpənt] n. 居住者

occupation [ˌɑkjə`peʃən] * * n. 職業

occupy [`ɑkjəˌpaɪ] v. 佔領，佔據

office efficiency * phr. 事務效率

penalty [`pɛnltɪ] n. 處罰，罰款

pending [`pɛndɪŋ] a. 懸而未決的，迫近的

pessimistically [pɛsə`mɪstɪklɪ] ad. 悲觀地

probabilistic [ˌprɑbəbɪ`lɪstɪk] a. 可能性的

possibility [ˌpɑsə`bɪlətɪ] * n. 可能性

probable [`prɑbəbl̩] * * a. 有充分根據（但未經證實）的，可信的

probably [`prɑbəblɪ] * ad. 或許

reason [`rizn̩] n. 理由，理性

reasonable [`riznəbl̩] * a.（價錢）公道的，合理的，通情達理的

remark [rɪ`mɑrk] v. 察覺，看到，說 n. 注意，評論

remarkably [rɪ`mɑrkəblɪ] a. 明顯的，顯著的

represent [ˌrɛprɪ`zɛnt] v. 出現

representative [ˌrɛprɪ`zɛntətɪv] * * n. 代表人，代理人

seat [sit] * * n. 坐席 v. 使就座，容納…人

sect [sɛkt] n. 派別，黨派

sentence [`sɛntəns] v. 宣判

sign out * phr. 登出

take A into account * phr. 考慮 A

unused [ʌn`juzd] * * a. 未使用的，未用過的

utility [ju`tɪlətɪ] n.（電、煤氣等）公用事業

utilization [ˌjutl̩ə`zeʃən] * * n. 利用

utilize [`jutl̩ˌaɪz] v. 利用

utilizer [`jutl̩ˌaɪzə] n. 利用者

under the new management * * phr. 根據新的管理

with the aim of * phr. 其目的是

第七天

adapt [ə`dæpt] *   v. 適應，改造

adaptation [ˌædæp`teʃən]   n. 適應，改造

caution [`kɔʃən] *   n. 小心，謹慎

cautious [`kɔʃəs]   a. 十分小心的，謹慎的

cautiously [`kɔʃəslɪ] * *   ad. 小心地

chance [tʃæns] * *   n. 可能性，機會

charge [tʃɑrdʒ] * *   v. 索價，收費

commute [kə`mjut] * *   v. 通勤

defy [dɪ`faɪ] *   v. 挑戰，對抗

demand [dɪ`mænd] * *   n. 需要 v. 要求

demanding [dɪ`mændɪŋ] * *   a. 使人吃力的，苛求的

demandingly [dɪ`mændɪŋlɪ]   ad. 苛求地

depend on *   phr. 依靠

desirable [dɪ`zaɪrəbl] *   a. 值得嚮往的

efficiency [ɪ`fɪʃənsɪ] * *   n. 效率

efficient [ɪ`fɪʃənt] * *   a. 效率高的，有能力的

efficiently [ɪ`fɪʃəntlɪ] * *   ad. 效率高地

encase [ɪn`kes]   v. 將…裝進容器

enormously [ɪ`nɔrməslɪ]   ad. 巨大地

every hour on the hour *   phr. 每一個小時整點

fast [fæst] * *   a. 快的，迅速的 ad.快

fee [fi]   n. 費，服務費

fill in / fill out *   phr. 填寫

finish [`fɪnɪʃ] *   v. 結束，完成

finished [`fɪnɪʃt] * *   a. 完成的，結束了的

give out   phr. 讓出

hard [hɑrd] * *   a. 困難的

harden [`hɑrdn̩]   v. 使變硬

hardened [`hɑrdn̩d]   a. 變硬的，堅定的

hardly [`hɑrdlɪ] * *   ad. 幾乎不

hardness [`hɑrdnɪs]   n. 硬，堅硬

have an impact on   phr. 對…產生影響

immune [ɪ`mjun]   a. 免疫的

impartial [ɪm`pɑrʃəl]   a. 公正的

impartiality [ˌɪmpɑrʃɪ`ælətɪ]   n. 公平

impartially [ɪm`pɑrʃəlɪ] *   ad. 公平地

imply [ɪm`plaɪ] * *   v. 暗示，包含

impose [ɪm`poz]   v. 徵稅，加（負擔等）於

in addition   phr. 此外

in addition to *   phr. 除了

incidence [`ɪnsədn̩s]   n. 發生率

incident [`ɪnsədn̩t]   n. 事件

incidental [ˌɪnsə`dɛnt!] * *   a. 偶然發生的

incidentally [ˌɪnsə`dɛnt!ɪ]   ad. 附帶地，偶然地

lax [læks]   a. 鬆弛的，放縱的

leave for *   phr. 動身去

make up for *   phr. 彌補

marriage [`mærɪdʒ] *   n. 結婚（典禮）

material [mə`tɪrɪəl] *   n. 物質，材料

materialistic [məˌtɪrɪəl`ɪstɪk]   a. 唯物主義的

meet one's needs   phr. 符合（某人的）需要

nominal [`nɑmən!] * *   a. 很少的，微不足道的

nominally [`nɑmən!ɪ]   ad. 表面地，在名義上

notice [`notɪs] * *   n. 公告，注意

noticeable [`notɪsəbl̩]   a. 顯著的，顯而易見的

occur [ə`kɝ]   v. 出現，發生

odor [`odɚ]   n. 氣味

pay increase *   phr. 加薪幅度

perform [pɚ`fɔrm] *   v. 履行

performance [pɚ`fɔrməns] * *   n. 成果，演出

perishable [`pɛrɪʃəbl̩] * *   a. 易腐爛的，易毀滅的

perish [`pɛrɪʃ]   v. 死去，枯萎，消滅

question concerning / about *   phr. 質詢

raise questioins *   phr. 提出問題

receptacle [rɪ`sɛptəkl̩] * *   n. 容器，貯藏所

reception [rɪ`sɛpʃən] *   n. 歡迎會，接待處

receptionist [rɪ`sɛpʃənɪst]   n. 接待員

receptiveness [rɪ`sɛptɪvnɪs]   n. 接受能力

recipient [rɪ`sɪpɪənt]   n. 受領者

recline [rɪ`klaɪn]   v. 靠，依賴

recognize [`rɛkəgˌnaɪz] * *   v. 識別，認出

recommend [ˌrɛkə`mɛnd] *   v. 推薦

set [sɛt] *   v. 校正，佈置

setting [`sɛtɪŋ]   n. 環境

shake [ʃek] *   v. 搖動

strictly [`strɪktlɪ]   ad. 嚴密地，嚴格地

terminate [`tɝməˌnet] *   v. 結束，終止

track [træk]   n. 行蹤，軌道

tradition [trə`dɪʃən]   n. 傳統

transcribe [træns`kraɪb] * *   v. 抄寫，翻譯

unwavering [ˌʌn`wevərɪŋ] *   a. 不動搖的，堅定的

第八天

acquire [ə`kwaɪr] *   v. 取得，獲得

addition [ə`dɪʃən]   n. 加，附加

additional [ə`dɪʃən!] *   a. 附加的，額外的

additionally [ə`dɪʃən!ɪ]   ad. 附加地，此外

address [ə`drɛs] * *   n. 住址 v. 寫地址

book [bʊk]   v. 預訂

characteristic [ˌkærəktə`rɪstɪk] *   n. 特徵

chart [tʃɑrt]   n. 圖表

climb [klaɪm]   v. 登上，上升

consciously [`kɑnʃəslɪ]   ad. 有意識地

credible [`krɛdəbl̩]   a. 可信的

credit [`krɛdɪt]　n. 信用　v. 存款

creditable [`krɛdɪtəbl]　a. 可信的

delay [dɪ`le] *　n. 延遲　v. 使延期

derivation [ˌdɛrə`veʃən]　n. 起源，衍生

derive [dɪ`raɪv]　v. 衍生，發生

electron [ɪ`lɛktrɑn]　n. 電子

electronic [ɪlɛk`trɑnɪk]　a. 電子的

electronically [ɪˌlɛk`trɑnɪkl̩ɪ] * *　ad. 透過電子的方法

electronics [ɪlɛk`trɑnɪks]　n. 電子學

encircle [ɪn`sɝkl̩]　v. 環繞，包圍

finance [fɑɪ`næns]　n. 財政，財務

financial [faɪ`nænʃəl] * *　a. 財政的

financially [faɪ`nænʃəlɪ]　ad. 財政上

financing [faɪ`nænsɪŋ]　n. 財經融資

fire [faɪr] * *　v. 解雇

guard [gɑrd]　v. 看守，守衛

improve [ɪm`pruv] * *　v. 改善

improvement [ɪm`pruvmənt] * *　n. 改善，增進

inaugurate [ɪn`ɔgjəˌret] *　v. 開始，舉行就職典禮

line [laɪn]　n. 線，（貨物等的）種類

mildly [`maɪldlɪ]　ad. 溫和地

no later than *　phr. 不會比…遲

notification [ˌnotəfə`keʃən] *　n. 通知，通告

notify [`notəˌfaɪ] * *　v. 告知，通知

novelty [`nɑvl̩tɪ]　n. 新穎，新奇

offer [`ɔfɚ] * *　v. 提供，提議

office [`ɔfɪs] * *　n. 辦公室，營業處

omission [o`mɪʃən]　n. 省略，遺漏

on one's own *　phr. 自己一個人

permission [pɚ`mɪʃən]　n. 許可，允許

permissive [pɚ`mɪsɪv]　a. 許可的

permit [pɚ`mɪt] * *　v. 允許

place an emphasis on *　phr. 視…為重點

promotional offers *　phr. 推廣優惠

quiet [`kwaɪət]　a. 安靜的

quietly [`kwaɪətlɪ] *　ad. 安靜地

quietness [`kwaɪətnɪs]　n. 平靜

real [`riəl]　a. 真的，真正的

realism [`riəlˌɪzəm]　n. 寫實主義

realist [`riəlɪst]　n. 現實主義者

realistic [riə`lɪstɪk] *　a. 現實主義的，寫實主義的

realistically [ˌriə`lɪstɪkl̩ɪ] * *　ad. 寫實地

reality [ri`ælətɪ]　n. 現實（性）

realize [`riəˌlaɪz]　v. 領悟，瞭解

record [`rɛkɚd] *　v. 記錄

regard A as B *　phr. 把 A 當成 B

safety precautions * *　phr. 安全措施

scarce [skɛrs]　a. 不足的

scarcely [`skɛrslɪ]　ad. 幾乎不，幾乎沒有

shield [ʃild]　v. 保護，掩蓋

spend 錢 on 事物 * *　phr. 把錢花在…

stringently [`strɪndʒəntlɪ]　ad. 嚴格地

take advantage of * *　phr. 利用

take steps *　phr. 採取步驟

unattached [ˌʌnə`tætʃt]　a. 不依附的

unavailable [ˌʌnə`veləbl̩]　a. 無法利用的

until further notice * *　phr. 直至另行通知為止

upcoming [`ʌpˌkʌmɪŋ] * *　a. 即將來臨的

valuable [`væljuəbl̩]　a. 值錢的，貴重的

valuation [ˌvælju`eʃən]　n. 估價

value [`vælju] * *　n. 價值　v. 尊重，評價

with reference to　phr. 參考

work [wɝk] * *　n. 事　v. 工作，操作

workplace [`wɝkˌples] *　n. 工作場所

第九天

act [ækt]　v. 行動

active [`æktɪv] *　a. 活潑的

actively [`æktɪvlɪ]　a. 積極地，主動地

activeness [`æktɪvnɛs]　n. 活躍

activity [æk`tɪvətɪ] * *　n. 活動，運動

advance [əd`væns] * *　n. 進步，晉升

advantage [əd`væntɪdʒ] * *　n. 優點，優勢

adversely [æd`vɝslɪ]　ad. 逆向地

be applied to *　phr. 適用

check [tʃɛk] * *　n. 支票　v. 檢查，檢驗

choice [tʃɔɪs] *　n. 選擇

clear 事物 through customs *　phr. （東西）通過海關

close [kloz]，[klos] * *　v. 關閉　a. 近的

closed [klozd] *　a. 關閉的

closedown [`klozˌdaʊn]　n. 關閉

closely [`kloslɪ] * *　ad. 接近地，親密地

closeness [`klosnɪs]　n. 密閉，親密

comply [kəm`plaɪ] * *　v. 依從，順從

consequently [`kɑnsəˌkwɛntlɪ]　ad. 因此，必然地

develop into　phr. 發展成

encourage [ɪn`kɝɪdʒ]　v. 促進，鼓勵

encouragement [ɪn`kɝɪdʒmənt] * *　n. 鼓勵，獎勵

encouraging [ɪn`kɝɪdʒɪŋ]　a. 鼓勵的，促進的

except [ɪk`sɛpt] * *　prep. 除…之外

excepting [ɪk`sɛptɪŋ]　prep. 除…之外

exception [ɪk`sɛpʃən] * *　n. 例外，除外

exceptional [ɪk`sɛpʃənl̩] * *　a. 例外的，異常的

exceptionally [ɪk`sɛpʃənəlɪ] *　ad. 例外地，異常地

except for * *　phr. 除…之外

fit [fɪt] *　　v. 適合，符合

focus on * *　　phr. 集中於…

go shopping *　　phr. 去購物

impatient [ɪm`peʃənt]　　a. 無耐心的，不耐煩的

include [ɪn`klud] * *　　v. 包含

inclusion [ɪn`kluʒən]　　n. 包括，包含

inconsistency [ˌɪnkən`sɪstənsɪ] * *　　n. 不一致，矛盾

list [lɪst] *　　n.目錄　v. 把…編列成表

means [minz] * *　　n. 手段，方法

mediation [midɪ`eʃən]　　n. 調解

operate [`apəˌret]　　v. 運轉，起作用（=work），營運（=run）

operation [ˌapə`reʃən] * *　　n. 作用，營運

operational [ˌapə`reʃənl] * *　　a. 操作上的，經營上的

operative [`apərətɪv]　　a. 操作的，運行著的

operator [`apəˌretə] *　　n. 接線員

place [ples] *　　v. 放置，安置

placement [`plesmənt]　　n. 佈置（=staffing）

potentially [pə`tɛnʃəlɪ] *　　ad. 潛在地，可能地

prospective employee *　　phr. 準雇員

recent [`risn̩t] * *　　a. 最近的

recently [`risn̩tlɪ] * *　　ad. 最近

redesign [ˌridɪ`zaɪn] *　　v. 重新設計

securable [sɪ`kjurəbl̩]　　a. 可獲得的

secure [sɪ`kjur]　　a. 安心的　v. 保證

securely [sɪ`kjurlɪ] *　　ad. 安全地

security [sɪ`kjurətɪ] *　　n. 保安

sensation [sɛn`seʃən]　　n. 感覺，激動

sense [sɛns] * *　　n. 感覺，意識

shock [ʃɑk] * *　　v. 使震驚　n. 震驚

shop [ʃɑp]　　v. 購物

strongly [`strɔŋlɪ] *　　ad. 強有力地，堅固地

thorough [`θɝo]　　a. 徹底的，完全的

thoroughly [`θɝolɪ] * *　　ad. 徹底地，完全地

thoroughness [`θɝonɪs]　　n. 徹底，完全

transfer [træns`fɝ] *　　v. 搬，轉換　n. 遷移，移交

transferable [træns`fɝəbl̩] * *　　a. 可轉移的

transference [træns`fɝəns]　　n. 轉移

unbiased [ʌn`baɪəst]　　a. 無偏見的，公正的

uncertain [ʌn`sɝtn̩]　　a. 不明確的，含糊的

unlimited miles * *　　phr. 無限距離

upgrade [`ʌp`gred] *　　v. 升級，提高品級

violation [ˌvaɪə`leʃən]　　n. 違反（法律），侵犯（權利）

widely admired *　　phr. 受敬佩

worth [wɝθ] * *　　a. 值得　n. 值一定金額的數量，價值

worthwhile [`wɝθ`hwaɪl]　　a. 值得做的

worthy [`wɝðɪ]　　a. 有價值的

第十天

account for *　　phr. 說明，對…負有責任

add [æd]　　v. 添加，增加

addict [ə`dɪkt]　　v. 使沉溺，使入迷

advance in * *　　phr. 對…的進步

advice [əd`vaɪs] * *　　n. 勸告，忠告

advisable [əd`vaɪzəbl̩] * *　　a. 適當的，明智的

advise [əd`vaɪz] * *　　v. 忠告

advisor [əd`vaɪzə] / adviser [əd`vaɪzə] * *　　n. 勸告者

advisory [əd`vaɪzərɪ]　　a. 勸告的，忠告的

afterwards [`æftəwədz]　　ad. 後來

announce [ə`naʊns] *　　v. 宣佈，發佈

announcement [ə`naʊnsmənt] *　　n. 通告，佈告

be associated with * *　　phr. 與…有關聯

boost [bust]　　v. 增加

broad knowledge *　　phr. 淵博的知識

clear A from B *　　phr. 把 A 從 B 中除去

collate [ka`let]　　v. 對比，對照

concentrate [`kɑnsɛnˌtret] *　　v. 集中

contributor to *　　phr. 對…的貢獻者

criticize [`krɪtɪˌsaɪz] *　　v. 批評，非難

current [`kɝənt] *　　a. 現時的，通用的

currently [`kɝəntlɪ] *　　ad. 現在

defective [dɪ`fɛktɪv] *　　a. 有缺陷的，不完美的

delicate [`dɛləkət]　　a. 纖弱的

deliver [dɪ`lɪvə]　　v. 傳送，運送

deliverable [dɪ`lɪvərəbl̩]　　a. 可以傳送的

deliverance [dɪ`lɪvərəns]　　n. 釋放，解救

delivery [dɪ`lɪvərɪ] *　　n. 投遞，傳送

dramatic [drə`mætɪk]　　a. 戲劇的

dramatically [drə`mætɪkl̩ɪ] * *　　ad. 戲劇性地

electric [ɪ`lɛktrɪk]　　a. 電的，導電的

electricity [ɪˌlɛk`trɪsətɪ] *　　n. 電流，電力

endurance [ɪn`djurəns]　　n. 持久（力），耐久（力）

engrave [ɪn`grev] *　　v. 雕刻，刻

flow [flo]　　v. 流動　n. 流

happily [`hæpɪlɪ] *　　ad. 幸福地，幸運地

imperative [ɪm`pɛrətɪv] *　　a. 命令式的，必須服從的（=essential）

inconvenience [ˌɪnkən`vjnjəns] *　　n. 不便

increase [ɪn`kris] * *　　v. 增加，增大（=grow）

increasing [ɪn`krisɪŋlɪ] * *　　a. 增加的，增大的

increasingly [ɪn`krisɪŋlɪ] *　　ad. 越來越多地

incur [ɪn`kɝ]　　v. 惹起，帶來（損失）

indecision [ˌɪndɪ`sɪʒən]　　n. 優柔寡斷

lend A to B *　　phr. 把 A 借給 B

locate [lo`ket] * *　　v. 使…座落於，找出

location [lo`kʃən] * *　　n. 位置，場所

medic [`mɛdɪk]　　n. 醫生

medical [`mɛdɪk]]* a. 醫學上的

medically [`mɛdɪklɪ] ad. 醫學上地

medicate [`mɛdɪ.ket] v. 加藥品於

medicinal [mə`dɪsɳ]]* a. 藥的，藥用的

meet [mit]** v. 滿足，符合（=satisfy），遇到（=encounter）

moreover [mor`ova] ad. 並且，加之

on the recommendation of* phr. 在…的推薦下

opponent [ə`ponənt] n. 敵手，反對者

opportunity [.apə`tjunətɪ] n. 機會

oppose [ə`poz] v. 反對

opposition [.apə`zɪʃən]** n. 反對

petition [pə`tɪʃən] n. 請願，請求

phase [fez] n. 相，面

pledge [plɛdʒ] v. 誓言

precisely [prɪ`saɪslɪ] ad. 精確地

redemption [rɪ`dɛmpʃən] n. 贖回，買回

refine [rɪ`faɪn] v. 提煉，精煉

reflect [rɪ`flɛkt]** v. 反映（=demonstrate）

relate [rɪ`let] v. 敘述，使有聯繫

relation [rɪ`leʃən]** n. 關係，關聯

relative [`rɛlətɪv] n. 親戚 a. 相對的

relatively [`rɛlətɪvlɪ]** ad. 相對地，比較而言

series [`siriz] n. 連續，系列

shrink [ʃrɪŋk]* v. 收縮，縮短

tend to +動詞原型* phr. 有…的傾向

translation [træns`leʃən]** n. 翻譯

undoubtedly [ʌn`daʊtɪdlɪ]* ad. 毫無疑問地

usual [`juʒʊəl] a. 通常的，平常的

usually [`juʒʊəlɪ]** ad. 通常地，慣常地

withdraw [wɪð`drɔ] v. 收回，提取（錢）（=take out）

withdrawal [wɪð`drɔəl] n. 收回，撤回

第十一天

acquaint 某人 with 某物* phr. 使某人瞭解某物

adequate [`ædəkwɪt] a. 適當的，足夠的

adhere [əd`hɪr] v. 粘附，緊粘

adjust [ə`dʒʌst] v. 調節，調整

agenda [ə`dʒɛndə]** n. 待議諸事項，議程

aggression [ə`grɛʃən] n. 侵略行動，侵犯行為

aggressive [ə`grɛsɪv] a. 侵略的，侵犯的

aggressively [ə`grɛsɪvlɪ]** ad. 侵略地，攻擊地

aggressiveness [ə`grɛsɪvnɪs] n. 侵犯

agree [ə`gri]** v. 同意

agreement [ə`grimənt]** n. 一致，協定，協議

ahead [ə`hɛd]** ad. 預先，在前

be aware of* phr. 意識到

be capable of** phr. 有能力做

busy [bɪzɪ]* a. 忙碌的，（尤指電話線）正被佔用的

chronological [.krɑnə`lɑdʒɪk]]* a. 依時間前後排列的

clarification [klærəfə`keʃən] n. 澄清，說明

clarify [`klærə.faɪ]** v. 澄清，闡明

clarity [`klærətɪ] n. 清楚，明晰

clear [klɪr]** a. 清楚的 v. 清除，收拾

clearance [`klɪrəns] n. 清除，整理

clearly [`klɪrlɪ]** ad. 明確地，清楚地

clearness [klɪrnɪs] n. 明晰，明確

collaborate on** phr. 共同工作

commitment to** phr. 信奉，獻身於…

consider [kən`sɪdə]** v. 考慮

considerable [kən`sɪdərəb]]** a. 相當大的

considerably [kən`sɪdərəblɪ]* ad. 相當

considerate [kən`sɪdərɪt] a. 考慮周到的

consideration [kənsɪdə`reʃən]* n. 考慮

considering [kən`sɪdərɪŋ]** prep. 就…而論，考慮到

constraint [kən`strent]* n. 強制，限制

dedication to** phr. 奉獻於

delighted [dɪ`laɪtɪd]* a. 高興的，快樂的

demolish [dɪ`mɑlɪʃ] v. 廢除

digit [`dɪdʒɪt] n. 數字

dimension [dɪ`mɛnʃən] n. 尺寸，大小

diminish [də`mɪnɪʃ] v. 減少，減小

disqualified [dɪs`kwɑlə.faɪ] a. 被取消資格

do one's utmost* phr. 竭力，盡全力

enroll [ɪn`rol] v. 記錄，登記

ensure [ɪn`ʃur]** v. 保證，擔保

entrance [`ɛntrəns] n. 入口

entry [`ɛntrɪ]** n. 參加，加入（=admission）

especially [ə`spɛʃəlɪ] ad. 尤其

fascinate [`fæsɳ.et] v. 迷住，使神魂顛倒

fascinating [`fæsɳ.etɪŋ]** a. 迷人的

fascination [`fæsɳ.eʃən] n. 魅力，有魅力的東西

follow up on* phr. 跟進

force [fors] n. 力量，勢力 v. 強迫

halt [hɔlt]* v. 停止，終止

have every intention of Ving* phr. 有意向

indicate [`ɪndə.ket]** v. 指示，指出

indication [`ɪndə.keʃən]** n. 指示，跡象

indicative [ɪn`dɪkətɪv] a. 表示的，象徵的

inherently risky** phr. 內在風險

least [list] a. 最小的，最少的

mention [`mɛnʃən]** v. 說起

message [`mɛsɪdʒ] n. 信息，口信

migration [maɪ`greʃən] n. 遷移，遷徙

mostly [`mostlɪ] ad. 大部分地，通常

nominate [`nɑmə.net]* v. 任命，指定

nomination [`nɑmə,neʃən]　n. 提名，任命

optimist [`ɑptəmɪst]　n. 樂觀者

optimistic [,ɑptə`mɪstɪk] * *　a. 樂觀的

optimistically [ɑptə`mɪstɪklɪ]　ad. 樂觀地

optimize [`ɑptə,maɪz] *　v. 持樂觀態度

phone [fon]　n. 電話 v. 打電話

photographer [fə`tɑgrəfə] *　n. 攝影師

piece [pis]　n. 部分

process [`prɑsɛs] * *　n. 過程，進程　v. 處理

procession [prə`sɛʃən]　n. 行列，行進

refresh [rɪ`frɛʃ]　v. 更新

refreshment [rɪ`frɛʃmənt]　n. 茶點，便餐

solicit [sə`lɪsɪt] *　v. 懇求（=ask）

transmit [træns`mɪt]　v. 傳送，傳達

visit [`vɪzɪt] * *　v. 參觀，拜訪

第十二天

adopt [ə`dɑpt]　v. 採取

agree on *　phr. 對…取得一致意見

agree with * *　phr. 和…意見一致

aim [em] * *　n. 目標，目的　v. 把…瞄準

alike [ə`laɪk]　ad. 一樣地，相似地

alliance [ə`laɪəns]　n. 結盟，聯盟

be cognizant of *　phr. 認識

borrow [`bɑro] *　v. 借

combination [,kɑmbə`neʃən] *　n. 結合，組合

combined [kɑm`baɪnd] *　a. 聯合的，相加的

compensate [`kɑmpən,set] * *　v. 補償

compete [kəm`pit]　v. 競爭

competition [,kɑmpə`tɪʃən] * *　n. 比賽，競爭（=rivalry）

competitive [kəm`pɛtətɪv] * *　a. 競爭性的

competitor [kəm`pɛtətə]　n. 競爭者

deprive [dɪ`praɪv]　v. 剝奪，使喪失

deride [dɪ`raɪd]　v. 嘲笑，嘲弄

derision [dɪ`rɪʒən]　n. 嘲笑，嘲弄

enclosed [ɪn`klozd] * *　a. 與世隔絕的

enclosure [ɪn`klozə]　n. 圍住，封入

enclose [ɪn`kloz]　v. 圍住，圈起

enhance [ɪn`hæns] * *　v. 提高，增加

enter [`ɛntə] * *　v. 進入

envelope [`ɛnvə,lop] * *　n. 信封

envelopment [ɪn`vɛləpmənt]　n. 包，裹，封，封皮

eventually [ɪ`vɛntʃuəlɪ] * *　ad. 最後，終於

exposure to * *　phr. 暴露於

fiscal year * *　phr. 會計年度

focus [`fokəs] *　v. 使聚焦　n. 焦點

forbidden [fə`bɪdn̩]　a. 被禁止的

forecast [`for,kæst]　n. 預測，預報　v. 預報，預測

give 某人 one's support *　phr. 支持某人

heavily [`hɛvɪlɪ] * *　ad. 沉重地，猛烈地

heaviness [`hɛvɪnɪs]　n. 重，沉重

heavy [`hɛvɪ] *　a. 重的，沉的

house [haus]　v. 給…房子住

in advance *　phr. 在前面，預先

inclination [,ɪnklə`neʃən]　n. 傾向，意向

incline [ɪn`klaɪn]　v. 使想要

indulge [ɪn`dʌldʒ]　v. 沉迷於，滿足

ineptitude [ɪn`ɛptə,tjud]　n. 不適當

inside [`ɪn`saɪd]　prep. 內部，裡面

listen to * *　phr. 聽，聽從

normal [`nɔrml̩]　a. 標準的

normalcy [`nɔrml̩sɪ]　n. 正常

normality [nɔr`mælətɪ]　n. 正常

normally [`nɔrml̩ɪ] *　ad. 正常地

option [`ɑpʃən]　n. 選擇，選擇權

perfect [`pɝfɪkt] *　a. 完美的

perfection [pə`fɛkʃən] * *　n. 完善，完成

perfectly [`pɝfɪktlɪ] *　ad. 完全地，絕對地

pioneer [,paɪə`nɪr] *　n. 拓荒者

plan [plæn] *　n. 計畫，方案　v. 計畫，打算

plate [plet]　n. 盤子，盆

precede [pri`sid]　v. 處在…之前

proficient [prə`fɪʃənt]　a. 精通的，熟練的

recover [rɪ`kʌvə]　v. 重新獲得，恢復

refuse [rɪ`fjuz]　v. 拒絕，拒受

regard [rɪ`gɑrd] *　v. 把…看作，把…認為

regarding [rɪ`gɑrdɪŋ] * *　prep. 關於，就…而論

regardless [rɪ`gɑrdlɪs] * *　ad. 不顧一切地

regardless of *　phr. 不管，不顧

regret [rɪ`grɛt]　n. 遺憾　v. 為…抱歉

regrettably [rɪ`grɛtəblɪ] * *　ad. 抱歉地，遺憾地

settlement [`sɛtl̩mənt]　n. 解決，定居

shape [ʃep]　n. 形狀，樣子

sheet [ʃit]　n. 床單，單張（紙）

solve [sɑlv]　v. 解決

sophisticate [sə`fɪstɪ,ket]　v. 使懂世故　n. 久經世故的人

sophisticated [sə`fɪstɪ,ketɪd] * *　a. 老於世故的

sophistication [sə`fɪstɪ,keʃən] *　n. 老於世故

tight [taɪt] *　a. 牢固的

tightly [taɪtlɪ] * *　ad. 緊緊地

tightness [taɪtnɪs]　n. 堅固

transpire [træn`spaɪr]　v. 發生，散發

unclaimed [ʌn`klemd] *　a. 無人領取的，物主不明的

without a doubt *　phr. 無疑地

第十三天

affix [ə`fɪks] * *　　v. 貼上，把…固定

almost [`ɔl.most] *　　ad. 幾乎，差不多

altruism [`æltru.ɪzəm]　　n. 利他主義

analysis [ə`næləsɪs] * *　　n. 分析

analyst [`ænḷɪst]　　n. 分析者

analyze [`ænḷ.aɪz] *　　v. 分析

around the world *　　phr. 世界各地

be comparable to * *　　phr. 與…比得上的

be compatible with * *　　phr. 與…可比較的

comment [`kamɛnt]　　n. 注釋，解釋

commerce [`kamɝs] *　　n. 商業，貿易

come from　　phr. 來自

compile [kəm`paɪl] *　　v. 彙編，編輯

complain [kəm`plen] * *　　v. 抱怨

complaint [kəm`plent] * *　　n. 抱怨，不滿

describe [dɪ`skraɪb] *　　v. 描寫，敘述

description [dɪ`skrɪpʃən] * *　　n. (物品) 說明書

entitle [ɪn`taɪtḷ] *　　v. 給…權力

equip [ɪ`kwɪp]　　v. 裝備，配備

equipment [ɪ`kwɪpmənt]　　n. 配備，設備 (=apparatus)

follow [`falo] * *　　v. 跟隨，領會

following [`faləwɪŋ]　　a. 接著的，其次的　prep. 在…以後

for free *　　phr. 免費的

form [fɔrm] * *　　n. 形狀，外形

formal [`fɔrmḷ] * *　　a. 正式的，形式上的

formality [fɔr`mælətɪ]　　n. 拘泥形式，(pl.) 正式手續

formalize [`fɔrmḷ.aɪz]　　v. 使形式化

formally [`fɔrmḷɪ]　　ad. 正式地，正規地

formalness [`fɔrmḷnɪs]　　n. 形式的

formation [fɔr`meʃən]　　n. 形態，結構

herein [.hɪr`ɪn]　　ad. 此中，於此

highly qualified *　　phr. 有充分資格的

infusion [ɪn`fjuʒən]　　n. 注入，灌入

ingredient [ɪn`gridɪənt]　　n. (混合物的) 組成部分，(烹調的) 原料

in the foreseeable future * *　　phr. 不久的未來

jeopardize [`dʒɛpə·d.aɪz]　　v. 使瀕於危險境地

logic [`ladʒɪk]　　n. 邏輯，邏輯學

luggage [`lʌgɪdʒ]　　n. 行李 (=baggage)

momentum [mo`mɛntəm] *　　n. 動力，衝力

necessarily [`nɛsəsɛrɪlɪ] * *　　ad. 必需地

necessary [`nɛsə.sɛrɪ]　　a. 必要的，必需的

necessitate [nɪ`sɛsə.tet]　　v. 使成為必需，需要

necessity [nə`sɛsətɪ]　　n. 必需品，必要性

note [not] *　　v. 注意，注目

on the waiting list * *　　phr. 在等候名單上的

order [`ɔrdə·] * *　　v. 定購，叫 (菜或飲料)

organize [`ɔrgə.naɪz] * *　　v. 組織，安排

---

outcome [`aut.kʌm]　　n. 結果

personal [`pɝsṇḷ] *　　a. 個人的

personality [.pɝsṇ`ælətɪ]　　n. 個性

personalize [.pɝsṇəl.aɪz]　　v. 使人格化，使個性化

personally [.pɝsṇḷɪ] * *　　ad. 就個人而言

plenty [`plɛntɪ]　　n. 豐富，大量

point [pɔɪnt]　　n. 要點，特徵

policy [`paləsɪ] *　　n. 政策，方針

predict [prɪ`dɪkt] * *　　v. 預料，預報

prediction [prɪ`dɪkʃən]　　n. 預言，預報

pretty [`prɪtɪ]　　ad. 相當，頗，很，非常

prior to * *　　phr. 在…以前

public [`pʌblɪk]　　a. 公共的，公用的

regular [`rɛgjələ·] * *　　a. 規則的，正規的

regularity [.rɛgjə`lærətɪ]　　n. 規則性

regularize [`rɛgjələ.raɪz]　　v. 使有規則，調整

regularly [`rɛgjələ·lɪ] *　　ad. 有規律地

reimbursement [.riɪm`bɝsmənt] * *　　n. 償還，賠償

reject [rɪ`dʒɛkt] * *　　v. 拒絕

sharp [ʃɑrp]　　a. 鋒利的，尖的

short [ʃɔrt] * *　　a. 短缺的，不足的

shorten [`ʃɔrtṇ]　　v. 使變短，縮短

shortly [`ʃɔrtlɪ] *　　ad. 立刻

show [ʃo]　　n. 展覽會，表示　v. 顯示

suddenly [`sʌdṇlɪ]　　ad. 忽然

total [`totḷ] * *　　a. 總括的，全體的

uncommon [ʌn`kamən]　　a. 罕見的，非凡的

use [juz] * *　　v. 用，使用　n. 用，使用

used [`just]　　a. 舊的

usefulness [`jusfəlnɪs]　　n. 有用，有益

user [`juzə·] *　　n. 使用者，用戶

第十四天

alert [ə`lɝt]　　v. 使警覺

apart [ə`pɑrt] * *　　ad. 分開地

apparatus [.æpə`retəs]　　n. 儀器，設備

apparel [ə`pærəl] *　　n. 服裝

appearance [ə`pɪrəns]　　n. 外貌，外觀

aside from　　phr. 除此之外

be concerned about *　　phr. 擔心…

be conscious of * *　　phr. 意識到

come in + 場所 *　　phr. 進到…

commission [kə`mɪʃən]　　n. 傭金，委員會

commit [kə`mɪt]　　v. 把…交托給，把…提交給

commitment [kə`mɪtmənt] * *　　n. 承諾，保證

committee [kə`mɪtɪ] *　　n. 委員會

complete [kəm`plit] * *　　v. 完成，結束　a. 完全的

completely [kəm`plitlɪ] * *　ad. 完整地

completeness [kəm`plitnɪs]　n. 完全，徹底

completion [kəm`pliʃən] *　n. 完成，結束

concede [kən`sid]　v. 承認，容許

design [dɪ`zaɪn] * *　v. 計畫，設計

designated [`dɛzɪɡ.net] * *　a. 已指定的

designed [dɪ`zaɪnd]　a. 設計好的，故意的

destroy [dɪ`strɔɪ]　v. 破壞

direct 某人 to 場所　phr. 為某人指路到…

discouragement [dɪs`kɝɪdʒmənt]　n. 沮喪，氣餒

eligible [`ɛlɪdʒəbl] *　a. 有資格當選的，合適的

embarrassing [ɪm`bærəsɪŋ]　a. 使人尷尬的

escalate [`ɛskə.let]　v. 使逐步上升（增強或擴大）

escalation [ɛskə.leʃən]　n. 逐步上升，逐步擴大

escalator [`ɛskə.letɚ] * *　n. 電扶梯

final [`faɪnl] *　a. 最後的，最終的

finalize [`faɪnl.aɪz]　v. 完成，結束

finally [`faɪnlɪ] * *　ad. 最後，終於

forfeit [`fɔr.fɪt] * *　v. 喪失 n. 喪失的東西，沒收物

forfeiture [`fɔrfɪtʃɚ]　n. （財產等的）沒收，（權利、名譽等的）喪失

hesitantly [`hɛzətəntlɪ] * *　ad. 遲疑地，躊躇地

hesitate [`hɛzə.teʃən]　v. 躊躇，猶豫

hesitation [.hɛzə`teʃən]　n. 躊躇，猶豫

improper [ɪm`prɑpɚ] * *　a. 不合適的

inaccurate [ɪn`ækjərɪt] *　a. 不正確的

inhalation [.ɪnhə`leʃən] *　n. 吸入（劑）

inhale [ɪn`hel]　v. 吸入（氣體）

inhibition [.ɪnhɪ`bɪʃən]　n. 禁止，抑制

join [dʒɔɪn] * *　v. 使結合，參加，加入

legible [`lɛdʒəbl]　a. 易讀的

liable [`laɪəbl] *　a. 易患…的，負有法律責任的

live broadcast *　phr. 直播

make telephone calls *　phr. 打電話

merge [mɝdʒ] * *　v. 合併

orientate [`orɪɛn.tet]　v. 使適應

pollutant [pə`lutənt] * *　n. 污染物，污染源

pollute [pə`lut]　v. 污染，弄髒

polluted [pə`lutɪd]　a. 受污染的

pollution [pə`luʃən]　n. 污染

post [post] * *　v. 揭示

regulate [`rɛgjə.let]　v. 約束，調整

regulation [.rɛgjə`leʃən] * *　n. 規定，約束

regulatory [`rɛgjələ.torɪ]　a. 管理的，控制的

relay [rɪ`le]　v. 給…換班

relevance [`rɛləvəns]　n. 關聯，適宜

reliability [rɪ.laɪə`bɪlətɪ]　n. 可靠，可信賴性

reliable [rɪ`laɪəbl] * *　a. 可信賴的

reliably [rɪ`laɪəblɪ]　ad. 可靠地

reliance [ru`laɪəns]　n. 信賴，信任

rely on *　phr. 依賴

routinely [ru`tinlɪ] *　ad. 常規地

sight [saɪt] *　n. 景色，景象

sign [saɪn] *　n. 徵兆，表示

signed [saɪnd]　a. 已寫入的

speculate [`spɛkjə.let]　v. 沉思，推測

speculation [.spɛkjə`leʃən]　n. 思索，投機

speculative [`spɛkjə.letɪv]　a. 思索的，推測的

stand in for *　phr. 承擔…任務（或職責）

thanks to *　phr. 幸虧，由於

transport [træns`port]　v. 運送，運輸

transportable [træns`portəbl]　a. 可運輸的，可運送的

transportation [.trænspɚ`teʃən] * *　n. 運輸，輸送

第十五天

afford [ə`ford]　v. 有足夠的…（去做…）

affordable [ə`fordəbl] *　a. 負擔得起的 (=inexpensive)

age [edʒ] * *　n. 年齡，時代

ageless [`edʒlɪs]　a. 不會老的，永遠的

alleviate [ə`livɪ.et] *　v. 減輕，緩和 (=relieve)

allocate [`ælə.ket] *　v. 分派，分配

apparently [ə`pærəntlɪ] *　ad. 表面上，似乎

appeasement [ə`pizmənt]　n. 平息，緩和

applause [ə`plɔz]　n. 鼓掌歡迎，喝彩

appliance [ə`plaɪəns]　n. 器具，用具，裝置

applicant [`æpləkənt] * *　n. 申請人

application [.æplə`keʃən] * *　n. 請求，申請書

applied [ə`plaɪd] * *　a. 應用的，實用的

apply [ə`plaɪ] * *　v. 申請，請求

assign A to B * *　phr. 把 A 歸於 B，分配

be consistent with *　phr. 與…一致的

be contingent on *　phr. 以…為條件的

cognizant [`kɑgnɪzənt] *　a. 已認知的

come into effect * *　phr. 生效，被實施

communicate [kə`mjunə.ket]　v. 通話，連接

communication [kə`mjunə.keʃən] *　n. 訊息，情報

communicator [kə`mjunə.ketɚ]　n. 傳播者

concern [kən`sɝn] * *　v. 使擔心 n. 關心的事

concerning [kən`sɝnɪŋ] * *　prep. 關於

cordially [`kɔrdʒəlɪ] * *　ad. 熱誠地，誠摯地

departed [dɪ`pɑrtɪd]　a. 過去的，死去的

detach [dɪ`tætʃ] * *　v. 分開，使分離

dish [dɪʃ]　n. 盤，菜餚

escort [`ɛskɔrt] * *　v. 護衛，護送

establish [ə`stæblɪʃ] *　v. 建立，設立

established [əs`tæblɪʃt] *　a. 已建立的，已確立的

establishment [ɪs`tæblɪʃmənt]　n. 建立，設立

evaluate [ɪ`vælju‚et]　**　v. 對…評價（=assess）

evaluation [ɪ‚vælju‚eʃən]　**　n. 估價，評價

fiscal [`fɪskḷ]　**　a. 財政的，會計的

for more details　*　phr. 需要更多細節的話

highly [`haɪlɪ]　**　ad. 非常，很

horizontal [‚harə`zɑntḷ]　a. 水平的

in combination with　**　phr. 與…結合

in conclusion　phr. 最後，總之

inquire [ɪn`kwaɪr]　*　v. 詢問

inquiry [ɪn`kwaɪrɪ]　n. 質詢，疑問

insert [ɪn`sɝt]　*　v. 插入，嵌入

insertion [ɪn`sɝʃən]　n. 插入

instantly recognizable　*　phr. 可立即辨識的

jurisdiction [‚dʒʊrɪs`dɪkʃən]　n. 司法權，審判權

monologue [`mɑnḷ‚ɔg]　n. 獨角戲

overhead compartment　*　phr.（船艙）頂板的貨艙

performance appraisals　*　phr. 業績

postage [`postɪdʒ]　n. 郵資，郵費

power [`paʊɚ]　n. 力量，權力

powerful [`paʊɚfəl]　**　a. 強有力的，效力大的

prescribe [prɪ`skraɪb]　*　v. 開（藥方）

prescription [prɪ`skrɪpʃən]　n. 處方，規定

present [`prɛzṇt]　*　v. 提供，提示　a. 現在的

presentable [prɪ`zɛntəbḷ]　a. 可見人的，可上演的

presentation [‚prizɛn`teʃən]　n. 提出

presenter [prɪ`zɛntɚ]　n. 提出者

presently [`prɛzṇtlɪ]　**　ad. 現在

prohibit [prə`hɪbɪt]　*　v. 禁止，阻止

prompt [prɑmpt]　a. 迅速的　v. 激起

prompter [`prɑmptɚ]　n. 激勵人

prompting [`prɑmptɪŋ]　n. 刺激，鼓勵

promptly [`prɑmptlɪ]　**　ad. 迅速地，立即地

promptness [`prɑmptnɪs]　n. 敏捷，迅速

release [rɪ`lis]　*　v. 釋放，發表

remain [rɪ`men]　**　v. 保持，仍是

remainder [rɪ`mendɚ]　**　n. 剩餘物，殘餘

remember [rɪ`mɛnbɚ]　v. 記得

remembrance [rɪ`mɛmbrəns]　n. 記憶，回憶

remind [rɪ`maɪnd]　**　v. 使想起

remittance [rɪ`mɪtṇs]　n. 匯款（額）

situation [‚sɪtʃʊ`eʃən]　n. 處境，情況

skill [`skɪl]　n. 技術，技能

spend [spɛnd]　**　v. 花（錢），花費

spending [`spɛndɪŋ]　*　n. 開銷，花費

spoil [spɔɪl]　v. 搞砸

第十六天

adequately [`ædəkwɪtlɪ]　**　ad. 適當地，足夠地

allow [ə`laʊ]　**　v. 允許，准許

allowance [ə`laʊəns]　n. 允許，認可

alter [`ɔltɚ]　v. 改變，修改

annual [`ænjʊəl]　*　a. 每年的，一年的

approach [ə`protʃ]　n. 接近，入口　v. 接近，靠近

appropriately [ə`proprɪ‚etlɪ]　*　ad. 適當地，合適地

be dedicated to　*　phr. 奉獻於

be divided into　*　phr. 被分割成

bring [brɪŋ]　**　v. 帶來，引起

come to an end　*　phr. 結束

conclude [kən`klud]　v. 作出（最後）決定

conclusion [kən`kluʒən]　**　n. 結論

conclusive [kən`klusɪv]　a. 決定性的

conclusively [kən`klusɪvlɪ]　ad. 決定性地，確定地

correctly [kə`rɛktlɪ]　**　ad. 正確地

deteriorate [dɪ`tɪrɪə‚ret]　v. 使惡化，使下降

detract [dɪ`trækt]　v. 轉移（注意等）

distraction [dɪ`strækʃən]　n. 分散注意的事物，注意力分散

evident [`ɛvədənt]　a. 明顯的，明白的

evidential [‚ɛvə`dɛnʃəl]　a. 作為證據的

evidently [`ɛvədəntlɪ]　*　ad. 明顯地，顯然

evidence [`ɛvədəns]　n. 證據，證明

examine [ɪg`zæmɪn]　*　v. 檢查，調查

example [ɪg`zæmpḷ]　*　n. 例子，樣本

forward [`fɔrwɚd]　**　ad. 向前，今後

forwarding [`fɔrwɚdɪŋ]　n. 轉交

in conjunction with　*　phr. 與…協力

in contrast　phr. 相反，大不相同

insist [ɪn`sɪst]　v. 堅持

inspect [ɪn`spɛkt]　**　v. 檢查，視察

interest in　*　phr. 對…有興趣

introduce [‚ɪntrə`djus]　**　v. 介紹，引進

introduction [‚ɪntrə`dʌkʃən]　n. 介紹，傳入

justify [`dʒʌstə‚faɪ]　v. 證明…是正當的

light [laɪt]　a. 輕的

likeable [`laɪkəbl]　a. 可愛的，令人喜愛的

look for　*　phr. 尋找，期待

look into　**　phr. 窺視，瀏覽

look over　**　phr. 從…上面看，察看

minimal [`mɪnəməl]　a. 最小限度的

minimally [`mɪnɪmlɪ]　*　ad. 最低限度地

minimize [`mɪnə‚maɪz]　v. 將…減到最少

minimum [`mɪnəməm]　**　n. 最小值，最小化

missing [`mɪsɪŋ]　a. 不見的，缺少的

modify [`mɑdə‚faɪ]　v. 更改，修改

morale [mə`ræl]　n. 士氣，民心

more than adequate ＊　phr. 太多，夠多

nevertheless [ˌnɛvɚðəˈlɛs]　ad. 仍然，不過

outdated [ˌaʊtˈdetɪd]　a. 過時的，不流行的

outstanding [ˈaʊdˈstændɪŋ] ＊　a. 突出的，顯著的

overbear [ˈovɚˌbɛr]　v. 壓倒，克服

overcome [ˌovɚˈkʌm]　v. 戰勝，克服

petty [ˈpɛtɪ]　a. 小的，不重要的

plain [plen]　a. 明白的，平常的

poor [pʊr] ＊ ＊　a. 可憐的，乏味的

poorly [ˈpʊrlɪ] ＊　ad. 貧窮地，貧乏地

practice [ˈpræktɪs]　n. 實行，實踐　v. 實施

preamble [ˈpriæmbl]　n. 導言

precept [ˈprisɛpt]　n. 規則

prefer [prɪˈfɝ] ＊　v. 更喜歡，寧願

preferably [ˈprɛfərəblɪ] ＊　ad. 更適宜

preference [ˈprɛfərəns]　n. 偏愛，優先選擇

profess [prəˈfɛs]　v. 表示

profession [prəˈfɛʃən]　n. 職業

professional [prəˈfɛʃənl]　a. 專業的

professionalism [prəˈfɛʃənlˌɪzəm]　n. 專家的地位，專業主義

professionally [prəˈfɛʃənəlɪ]　ad. 專業地

proper [ˈprɑpɚ]　a. 適當的，正確的

reach solutions ＊　phr. 達到目標

reluctant [rɪˈlʌktənt]　a. 勉強的

remote [rɪˈmot]　a. 遙遠的

report [rɪˈport] ＊　n. 報告　v. 彙報

secondary effect ＊ ＊　phr. 二次影響

slowdown [ˈsloˌdaʊn] ＊　n. 降低速度

state [stet]　v. 聲明，陳述　n. 狀態

travel [ˈtrævl] ＊　v. 旅行，行進　n. 旅行

第十七天

anxious [ˈæŋkʃəs]　a. 擔憂的，渴望的

approval [əˈpruvl] ＊ ＊　n. 贊成，承認

approve [əˈpruv] ＊ ＊　v. 贊成，批准

approved [əˈpruvd]　a. 經核准的，被認可的

approvingly [əpˈruvɪŋlɪ]　ad. 贊許地

be entitled to ＋ 權力／資格 ＊　phr. 有權力的／有資格的

be equipped with　phr. 裝備

be faced with ＊ ＊　phr. 面臨

compensate for ＊ ＊　phr. 賠償

complex [ˈkamplɛks] ＊ ＊　n. 聯合體

compliance [kəmˈplaɪəns]　n. 依從，順從

compliment [ˈkampləmənt]　n. 稱讚，恭維

complimentary [ˌkampləˈmɛntərɪ] ＊　a. 誇獎的，免費贈送的

component [kəmˈponənt]　n. 成分

conduct [kənˈdʌkt] ＊ ＊　v. 實施

confide [kənˈfaɪd]　v. 信賴

confidence [ˈkanfədəns]　n. 信心

confident [ˈkanfədənt] ＊ ＊　a. 確信的

confidential [ˌkanfəˈdɛnʃəl]　a. 機密的

develop [dɪˈvɛləp] ＊ ＊　v. 發展，開發

developer [dɪˈvɛləpɚ]　n. 開發者

developing [dɪˈvɛləpɪŋ] ＊ ＊　a. 發展中的

development [dɪˈvɛləpmənt] ＊ ＊　n. 發展

exceed [ɪkˈsid] ＊ ＊　v. 超越

exclude [ɪkˈsklud] ＊　v. 把…排除在外，排斥

exclusion [ɪkˈskluʒən]　n. 排除，除外

exclusively [ɪkˈsklusɪvlɪ] ＊ ＊　ad. 排外地，專有地

exclusiveness [ɪkˈsklusɪvnɪs]　n. 獨佔，排外

exclusivity [ɛkskluˈsɪvətɪ]　n. 獨佔

foster [ˈfɔstɚ] ＊　v. 養育，鼓勵

fragment [ˈfrægmənt]　n. 碎片，斷片

in comparison with ＊　phr. 與…比較

in compliance with ＋ 規定　phr. 順從（規定）

instigate [ˈɪnstəˌget]　v. 唆使，慫恿

instrument [ˈɪnstrəmənt]　n. 工具，手段（＝apparatus）

interest [ˈɪntərɪst] ＊ ＊　n. 興趣，利息

interested [ˈɪntərɪstɪd] ＊ ＊　a. 感興趣的

interesting [ˈɪntərɪstɪŋ] ＊ ＊　a. 有趣味的

kindly [ˈkaɪndlɪ] ＊　phr. 和善的，親切地，爽快的

look forward to ＋ ＊ ＊　phr. 期望…

motion [ˈmoʃən] ＊　n. 運動，動作

nicely [ˈnaɪslɪ] ＊　ad. 精細地，優秀地

overdrawn [ˈovɚˈdrɔ]　a. 已透支的

overexpose [ˈovərɪkˈspoz]　v. 使感光過度

pleasant [ˈplɛzənt] ＊　a. 令人愉快的

please [pliz] ＊ ＊　v. 使喜歡，使滿足

pleased [plizd] ＊　a. 高興的，滿足的

pleasurable [ˈplɛʒərəbl]　a. 愉快的

pleasure [ˈplɛʒɚ] ＊ ＊　n. 快樂

premium [ˈprimɪəm] ＊　n. 保險費

preside [prɪˈzaɪd] ＊　v. 主持

press [prɛs]　v. 壓，逼迫

pressure [ˈprɛʃɚ] ＊ ＊　n. 壓力

renew [rɪˈnju] ＊ ＊　v. 更新，重新開始

renewal [rɪˈnjuəl] ＊　n. 更新，恢復

repeated [rɪˈpitɪd]　a. 重複的

repeatedly [rɪˈpitɪdlɪ]　ad. 重複地

repetition [ˌrɛpɪˈtɪʃən]　n. 重複，迴圈

repetitiously [ˌrɛpɪˈtɪʃəslɪ]　ad. 重複地

revise [rɪˈvaɪz]　v. 修正，修改

revision [rɪˈvɪʒən] ＊　n. 修改，修正

seldom [ˈsɛldəm] ＊ ＊　ad. 很少，不常

simple [ˈsɪmpl]　a. 簡單的，天真的

simplicity [sɪm`plɪsətɪ]　n. 簡單，簡易

simplify [`sɪmplə‚faɪ]　v. 單一化，簡單化

simply [`sɪmplɪ] * *　ad. 簡單地，完全地

slight [slaɪt]　a. 輕微的，微小的

slightly [`slaɪtlɪ] *　ad. 些微地

slightness [`slaɪtnɪs]　n. 些微，少許

spectator [spɛk`tetə]　n. 觀眾

staff [stæf] *　n. 職員，社員

stage [stedʒ] *　n. 舞臺，發展的進程

stimulate [`stɪmjə‚let] * *　v. 刺激，激勵

stir [stɝ] * *　v. 搖動，攪和

tax on *　phr. 消費稅

undecided [‚ʌndɪ`saɪdɪd]　a. 未定的

upcoming mayoral election *　phr. 即將舉行的縣市長選舉

第十八天

advocate of *　phr. …的擁護者

annex [ə`nɛks]　v. 併吞，附加　n. 附件

aptitude [`æptə‚tjud]　n. 恰當，聰明

arbitration [ɑrbə`treʃən]　n. 仲裁，公斷

arbitrator [ɑrbə`tretə]　n. 仲裁人，公斷者

assist with * *　phr. 協助…

be full of *　phr. 充滿

be happy with *　phr. 因…感到幸福

be ideal for *　phr. …是理想的

compete for + 競爭目標 *　phr. 為…競爭

concur [kən`kɝ]　v. 觀點一致

concurrence [kən`kɝəns]　n. 同意，觀點一致

concurrent [kən`kɝənt]　a. 同時發生的

concurrently [kən`kɝəntlɪ] * *　ad. 同時發生的

confirm [kən`fɝm] * *　v. 確認

confirmation [‚kɑnfə`meʃən] * *　n. 確認

confirmed [kən`fɝmd] *　a. 證實的

conform [kən`fɔrm]　v. 依照，遵從

contact [`kɑntækt] * *　n. 接觸，聯繫人　v. 聯繫

diagnose [`daɪəgnoz]　v. 診斷

diagnosis [‚daɪəg`nosɪs]　n. 診斷

diagnostic [‚daɪəg`nɑstɪk]　a. 診斷的

diagnostically [‚daɪəg`nɑstɪkə`laɪ]　ad. 診斷上

enlightening [ɪn`laɪtɪŋ] *　a. 啟迪，教化

execute [`ɛksɪ‚kjut]　v. 實行（=perform），完成

exile [`ɛksaɪl]　n. 放逐，流放

expand into *　phr. 擴大為

fixed [fɪkst]　a. 固定的，確定的

frequency [`frikwənsɪ]　n. 頻率

frequent [`frikwənt]　a. 頻繁的

frequently [`frikwəntlɪ] * *　ad. 常常

huge [hjudʒ]　a. 巨大的，極大的

hugely [hjudʒlɪ]　ad. 巨大地，非常地

implicate [`ɪmplɪ‚ket]　v. 使牽連其中（=associate），含意

implication [‚ɪmplɪ`keʃən] * *　n. 牽連，含意

in detail * *　phr. 詳細地

incomparable [ɪn`kɑmpərəbl]　a. 無與倫比的

incompetent [ɪn`kɑmpətənt] *　a. 不勝任的

in effect * *　phr. 有效

institute [`ɪnstətjut]　v. 創立，設立　n. 協會

instruct [ɪn`strʌkt]　v. 教，教導

instruction [ɪn`strʌkʃən]　n. 指示，教育

knowledge [`nɑlɪdʒ] *　n. 知識

monitor [`mɑnətə]　v. 監控，監督（=check）

monotone [`mɑnə‚ton]　a. 單調的

mounting [`maʊntɪŋ]　a. 上升，增加　n. 架設，裝備

overall [`ovə‚ɔl] *　a. 全部的，全面的

overdue [`ovə`dju] * *　a. 到期未付的

overlap [`ovə`læp]　v. 重疊，重複

overlay [`ovə`le]　v. 覆蓋

premonition [‚prɪmə`nɪʃən]　n. 前兆

preparation [‚prɛpə`reʃən]　n. 準備

prepare [prɪ`pɛr]　v. 準備，預備

prevent [prɪ`vɛnt] * *　v. 防止，預防

preventable [prɪ`vɛntəbl]　a. 可阻止的

prevention [prɪ`vɛnʃən]　n. 預防，防止

preventively [prɪ`vɛntɪvlɪ]　ad. 預防性的

price [praɪs]　v. 給…定價　n. 價格

prosperity [prɑs`pɛrətɪ] * *　n. 繁榮

receipt [rɪ`sit]　n. 收據

receive [rɪ`siv] * *　v. 收到，受到

received [rɪ`sivd]　a. 被承認的，被認為標準的

renovate [`rɛnə‚vet] *　v. 刷新，修復（=refurbish）

renovation [‚rɛnə`veʃən] *　n. 革新

rent [rɛnt]　v. 租借　n. 租金

reservation [‚rɛzə`veʃən] *　n. 預約

reserve [rɪ`zɝv] *　v. 儲備（=retain），n.預約（=book）

reserved [rɪ`zɝvd] *　a. 預訂的

resolution [‚rɛzə`luʃən]　n. 決定，解決

separately [`sɛpərɪtlɪ] * *　ad. 個別地

separation [‚sɛpə`reʃən]　n. 分離，分開

stamp [stæmp]　n. 郵票

standard [`stændəd] *　n. 標準，規格

statement [`stetmənt]　n. 報告書，聲明書

streamline [`strim‚laɪn] * *　v. 使有效率

thereafter [ðɛr`æftə] * *　ad. 從那時以後

work extended hours *　phr. 加班

第十九天

allergic reaction * 　phr. 過敏反應

anticipate [æn`tɪsə.pet] * * 　v. 預期，期望

apologize [ə`pɑlə.dʒaɪz] * 　v. 道歉

appeal [ə`pil] * 　v. 求助，訴請　n. 請求，呼籲

architect [`ɑrkə.tɛkt] * 　n. 建築師

area [`ɛrɪə] * 　n. 範圍，區域

arena [ə`rinə] 　n. 競技場

be in charge of * 　phr. 管理

be interested in * * 　phr. 對…感興趣

be involved in * * 　phr. 涉及，與…有關

busy telephone lines 　phr. 通話中

coming [`kʌmɪŋ] * 　a. 就要來的

comply with + 規則 * * 　phr. 順從，遵守（規則）

confront [kən`frʌnt] 　v. 使面臨

confuse [kən`fjuz] 　v. 使糊塗

confusion [kən`fjuʒən] * 　n. 混淆

connection [kə`nɛkʃən] 　n. 連接，關係

conquest [`kɑnkwɛst] 　n. 征服

conserve [kən`sɝv] * * 　v. 保存，保護

differ [`dɪfə] * * 　v. 不一致，不同

difference [`dɪfərəns] 　n. 差異

different [`dɪfərənt] * * 　a. 不同的

differently [`dɪfərəntlɪ] * * 　ad. 不同地

dilute [daɪ`lut] * 　v. 淡的，稀釋的

entire [ɪn`taɪr] * 　a. 全部的，完整的

entirely [ɪn`taɪrlɪ] * * 　ad. 完全地

exhibit [ɪg`zɪbɪt] 　v. 展出，展示（=display）

existence [ɪg`zɪstəns] * 　n. 存在，實在

existing [ɪg`zɪstɪŋ] * 　a. 現有的

expand [ɪk`spænd] * * 　v. 張開，發展

expanse [ɪk`spæns] 　n. 寬闊的區域

expansion [ɪk`spænʃən] * * 　n. 擴充，開展

expansive [ɪk`spænsɪv] * * 　a. 易擴張的，廣闊的

go through 　phr. 經歷（困難等）

have no idea * 　phr. 完全不知道

hurt [hɝt] 　v. 傷害，（使）痛心

immediately [ɪ`midɪɪtlɪ] * * 　ad. 立即，馬上

in ending 　phr. 在結尾

intend [ɪn`tɛnd] 　v. 想要（=plan），打算

intensify [ɪn`tɛnsə.faɪ] 　v. 加強

intensive [ɪn`tɛnsɪv] 　a. 強烈的，透徹的

interviewer [`ɪntə.vjuə] 　n. 採訪者

international flight * 　phr. 國際航班

live [laɪv] * 　a. 實況轉播的

manage [`mænɪdʒ] * * 　v. 管理（=handle），控制

manageable [`mænɪdʒəbl] * * 　a. 易處理的，易管理的

management [`mænɪdʒmənt] * * 　n. 經營，管理

manager [`mænɪdʒə] * * 　n. 經理，管理人員（=supervisor）

managing [`mænədʒɪŋ] 　a. 管理的

monopolize [mə`nɑpl.aɪz] * 　v. 獨佔

monopoly [mə`nɑplɪ] * 　n. 壟斷

overhead [ovə`hɛd] * 　a. 在頭上的

overpower [ovə`pauə] 　v. 制服，壓倒

overprice [.ovə`praɪs] 　v. 將…定價過高

polite [pə`laɪt] 　a. 有禮貌的，客氣的

politely [pə`laɪtlɪ] * * 　ad. 客氣地，斯文地

politeness [pə`laɪtnɪs] 　n. 有禮，優雅

president [`prɛzədənt] 　n. 會長，行長

print [prɪnt] * 　v. 印刷，出版

proceed [prə`sid] * * 　v. 進行，繼續下去

proceeding [prə`sidɪŋ] * 　n. 行動，(pl.) 法律行動，訴訟

procrastinate [pro`kræstə.net] * 　v. 耽擱

repairable [rɪ`pɛrəbl] 　a. 可修理的

repair [rɪ`pɛr] * * 　v. 修理，修補

resource [rɪ`sors] 　n. 資源

resourceful [rɪ`sorsfəl] 　a. 資源豐富的

seriously [`sɪrɪəslɪ] * 　ad. 認真地

speak [spik] * * 　v. 說話，談話

step [stɛp] * * 　n. 腳步，臺階

stratagem [`strætədʒəm] 　n. 戰略，計謀

strategic [strə`tidʒɪk] * * 　a. 戰略的

strategical [strə`tidʒɪkl] 　a. 戰略的，戰略上的

strategically [strə`tidʒɪklɪ] * 　ad. 戰略上

strategist [`strætɪdʒɪst] 　n. 戰略家

strategize [`strætə.dʒaɪz] 　v. 制訂戰略

strategy [`strætədʒɪ] * * 　n. 策略，軍略

thickly [`θɪklɪ] 　ad. 厚地，濃地

第二十天

appear [ə`pɪr] * 　v. 出現，看來

appoint [ə`pɔɪnt] 　v. 任命，指派

arrival [ə`raɪvl] 　n. 到達

aspiration [.æspə`reʃən] 　n. 熱望，渴望

backward [`bækwəd] 　ad. 向後地，反向地

be irrelevant to * 　phr. 與…無關的

be known for 　phr. 因…而眾所周知

concentrate on * * 　phr. 全神貫注於

console [kən`sol] 　v. 安慰

consolidate [kən`sɑlə.det] * * 　v. 鞏固，合併

consolidation [kən.sɑlə`deʃən] 　n. 鞏固，合併

consolidator 　n.（海運業的）併櫃業者

complimentary light breakfast * 　phr.（旅館等）免費贈送的早餐

designated area * * 　phr. 指定區域

direct [də`rɛkt] 　v. 指引，指示　a. 直接的

direction [dəˈrɛkʃən] n. 方向，指示

directive [dəˈrɛktɪv] a. 指導的

directly [dəˈrɛktlɪ] ** ad. 直接地，立即

director [dəˈrɛktə] n. 主任，主管

disallow [ˌdɪsəˈlaʊ] v. 不接受

expect [ɪkˈspɛkt] ** v. 期待，預期

expectancy [ɪkˈspɛktənsɪ] n. 期待，期望

expectant [ɪkˈspɛktənt] a. 預期的，期待的

expectantly [ɪksˈpɛktəntlɪ] ad. 期待地，期望地

expectation [ˌɛkspɛkˈteʃən] ** n. 期待，預料

expected [ɪkˈspɛktɪd] ** a. 已預料的

expedite [ˈɛkspɪˌdaɪt] ** v. 加速，發送

fume [fjum] n. 煙，氣體

function [ˈfʌŋkʃən] * n. 功能，典禮，儀式

furniture [ˈfɝnɪtʃə] ** n. （工廠等的）設備，傢俱

give a speech * phr. 演說

incorrect [ˌɪnkəˈrɛkt] * a. 錯誤的，不正確的

in error ** phr. 錯誤地

in excess of phr. 超過

interpret [ɪnˈtɝprɪt] v. 解釋，口譯

interpretation [ɪnˌtɝprɪˈteʃən] ** n. 口譯

interpreter [ɪnˈtɝprɪtə] n. 口譯員

invention [ɪnˈvɛnʃən] n. 發明，創造

loath [loθ] a. 不情願的，勉強的

local [ˈlokl] ** a. 地方的

locale [loˈkæl] n. 現場，場所

locality [loˈkælətɪ] n. 位置，地點

localize [ˈloklˌaɪz] v. 使具有地方性，使局限於某一地區內

localization [ˌloklaɪˈzeʃən] * n. 局部化

locally [ˈloklɪ] ** ad. 在地方上

maturity [məˈtjʊrətɪ] ** n. 完備，成熟

on the wane * phr. 逐漸衰落

popular [ˈpapjələ] ** a. 通俗的，流行的，受歡迎的

produce [prəˈdjus] * v. 生產

producer [prəˈdjusə] n. 生產者，製作者

producible [prəˈdjusəbəl] a. 可生產的

product [ˈpradəkt] n. 產品，產物

production [prəˈdʌkʃən] ** n. 生產，產品

productive [prəˈdʌktɪv] a. 生產性的

productively [prəˈdʌktɪvlɪ] ad. 有結果地

productivity [ˌpradʌkˈtɪvətɪ] ** n. 生產力

prohibit A from Ving phr. 禁止 A 做…

prudent [ˈprudnt] a. 謹慎的

replace [rɪˈples] ** v. 取代，替換

replace A with B * phr. 把 A 換成 B

reply [rɪˈplaɪ] v. 回答

responsibility [rɪˌspansəˈbɪlətɪ] ** n. 責任，職責

responsible [rɪˈspansəbl] ** a. 有責任的

responsibly [rɪˈspansəblɪ] ad. 有責任地

result [rɪˈzʌlt] ** n. 結果 v. 以…為結果

severely [səˈvɪrlɪ] * ad. 嚴格地，激烈地

somewhat [ˈsʌmˌhwat] ad. 稍微，有點

strike [straɪk] v. 罷工

striking [ˈstraɪkɪŋ] * a. 顯著的，驚人的

struggle [ˈstrʌgl] v. 努力，奮鬥

study [ˈstʌdɪ] * n. 研究，學科 v. 學習，研究

subject [ˈsʌbdʒɪkt] ** n. 主題 v. 受制於

subjection [səbˈdʒɛkʃən] n. 征服

unexpected [ˌʌnɪkˈspɛktɪd] a. 想不到的，意外的

unfair [ʌnˈfɛr] a. 不公平的

unfairly [ʌnˈfɛrlɪ] * ad. 不公平地，不公正地

unfairness [ʌnˈfɛrnɪs] n. 不公平，不公正

visual [ˈvɪʒuəl] * a. 看的，視覺的

第二十一天

annotated [ˈænoˌtetɪd] a. 有註解的

appreciate [əˈpriʃɪˌet] * v. 鑑賞，欣賞（=enjoy）

appreciation [əˌpriʃɪˈeʃən] * n. 感謝，欣賞

approximate [əˈpraksəmɪt] v. 近似，接近

approximately [əˈpraksəmɪtlɪ] * ad. 近似地，大約

approximation [əˌpraksəˈmeʃən] n. 接近，走近

asset [ˈæsɛt] * n. 資產

assimilation [əˌsɪmlˈeʃən] n. 同化，同化作用

beforehand [bɪˈforˌhænd] * ad. 預先

be liable to * phr. 有…傾向的

be made of ** phr. 用…造成

be noted for * phr. 因…而著名

comparable [ˈkampərəbl] a. 可比較的

compare [kəmˈpɛr] v. 比較，相比

comparison [kəmˈpærəsn] ** n. 比較

compatible [kəmˈpætəbl] a. 諧調的，一致的

construct [kənˈstrʌkt] v. 建造

construction [kənˈstrʌkʃən] ** n. 建築

constructive [kənˈstrʌktɪv] * a. 建設性的

constructor [kənˈstrʌktə] n. 建造者

consult [kənˈsʌlt] v. 商量

consultant [kənˈsʌltənt] ** n. 顧問，商議者

container [kənˈtɛntmənt] * n. 容器，集裝箱

contentment [kənˈtɛstənt] n. 滿意，知足

contest [ˈkantɛst] n. 論爭，競賽

contestant [kənˈtɛstənt] n. 競爭者，爭論者

dependent [dɪˈpɛndənt] a. 依靠的

disappoint [ˌdɪsəˈpɔɪnt] ** v. 使失望

disappointed [ˌdɪsəˈpɔɪntɪd] * a. 失望的

disappointing [ˌdɪsəˈpɔɪntɪŋ] a. 使人失望的

disappointment [ˌdɪsəˈpɔɪntmənt]＊＊ 　 n. 失望

disband [dɪsˈbænd]　 v. 解散，遣散

discharge [dɪsˈtʃɑrdʒ]　 v. 釋放，解放（=release），履行

durability [ˌdjurəˈbɪlətɪ]　 n. 經久，耐久力

durable [ˈdjurəbl]＊＊　 a. 持久的，耐用的

duration [djuˈreʃən]　 n. 持續時間，為期

equal [ˈikwəl]＊　 a. 相等的，均等的

equally [ˈikwəlɪ]＊＊　 ad. 相等地，平等地

equivalent [ɪˈkwɪvələnt]　 a. 相等的　 a. 相當的（人）

expend [ɪkˈspɛnd]　 v. 花費

expenditure [ɪkˈspɛndɪtʃə]　 n. 支出，花費

experience [ɪkˈspɪrɪəns]＊＊　 n. 經驗，體驗

experienced [ɪkˈspɪrɪənst]＊　 a. 富有經驗的

for the sake of　 phr. 為了

incidental expenses＊　 phr. 雜費

invalidate [ɪnˈvælə‚det]　 v. 使無效

in good condition＊　 phr. 情況良好

marketing on＊　 phr. 行銷，買賣

motivate [ˈmotə‚vet]　 v. 激發

motivation [ˌmotəˈveʃən]　 n. 動機

near [nɪr]＊　 prep. 在…旁邊　 a. 近

nearly [ˈnɪrlɪ]＊＊　 ad. 幾乎

nearness [ˈnɪrnɪs]　 n. 靠近，接近

observably [əbˈzɝvəblɪ]　 ad. 顯著地

observance [əbˈzɝvəns]＊＊　 n. 遵守，嚴守

observant [əbˈzɝvənt]　 a. 深切注意的

observantly [əbˈzɝvəntlɪ]　 ad. 敏銳地

observation [ˌɑbzɝˈveʃən]＊＊　 n. 觀察，觀測

observatory [əbˈzɝvə‚torɪ]　 n. 天文臺，氣象臺

observe [əbˈzɝv]　 v. 觀察，遵守（=follow）

oversee [ˈovəˈsi]　 v. 監視（=supervise）

proliferate [prəˈlɪfə‚ret]　 v. 增生擴散

properly [ˈprɑpəlɪ]＊＊　 ad. 適當地，完全地

reproduce [ˌriprəˈdjus]　 v. 再生，複製

repulse [rɪˈpʌls]　 v. 擊退，使厭惡

repulsion [rɪˈpʌlʃən]　 n. 嚴拒，反駁

request [rɪˈkwɛst]＊＊　 v. 請求　 n. 邀請

respond to＊　 phr. 回答

retirement [rɪˈtaɪrmənt]　 n. 退休，引退

reunion [riˈjunjən]　 n. 重聚

subscriber [səbˈskraɪbə]＊　 n. 訂戶，捐獻者

subscription [səbˈskrɪpʃən]　 n. 捐獻，訂閱

succeed [səkˈsid]　 v. 成功，繼承

success [səkˈsɛs]＊　 n. 成功

successful [səkˈsɛsfəlɪ]＊　 a. 成功的

successfully [səkˈsɛsfəlɪ]　 ad. 成功地

successive [səkˈsɛsɪv]　 a. 繼承的，連續的

第二十二天

arise [əˈraɪz]　 v. 出現，形成

arrange [əˈrendʒ]　 v. 安排，排列，協商

atrium [ˈatrɪəm]＊　 n. 中庭，正廳

attempt [əˈtɛmpt]＊　 n. 嘗試　 v. 嘗試

belatedly [bɪˈletɪdlɪ]　 ad. 已經遲了的

be opposite to＊　 phr. 與…相反

be put out of gear　 phr. 齒輪脫落

be related to＊　 phr. 和…有關係

congratulate on＊　 phr. 為（某人）祝賀（某事）

consume [kənˈsjum]　 v. 消耗，消費

consumer [kənˈsjumə]＊　 n. 消費者

consumption [kənˈsʌmpʃən]　 n. 消費

contend [kənˈtɛnd]＊　 v. 主張

convenience [kənˈvinjəns]＊＊　 n. 便利，方便

convenient [kənˈvinjənt]＊＊　 a. 便利的，方便的

conveniently [kənˈvinjəntlɪ]＊＊　 ad. 便利地

convention [kənˈvɛnʃən]　 n. 大會，協定，習俗

convergence [kənˈvɝdʒəns]　 n. 集中，收斂

disclose [dɪsˈkloz]　 v. 揭露（=reveal），透露

discontinue [ˌdɪskənˈtɪnju]＊　 v. 停止，中斷

discount [ˈdɪskaʊnt]＊＊　 v. 打折　 n. 折扣

draft [dræft]　 n. 草稿，草案

experiment [ɪkˈspɛrəmənt]　 n. 實驗

expertise [ˌɛkspəˈtiz]　 n. 專門技術

expiration [ˌɛkspəˈreʃən]＊　 n. 期滿，終止

expire [ɪkˈspaɪr]　 v. 期滿，終止

expired [ɪkˈspaɪrd]　 a. 過期的

explain [ɪkˈsplen]＊　 v. 說明

extraneously [ɛkˈstrenɪəslɪ]　 ad. 無關係地，外來地

foreseeable [forˈsiəbl]＊＊　 a. 可預知的

impress [ɪmˈprɛs]　 v. 使感動（=touch），留下印象

impressed [ɪmˈprɛsd]　 a. 感動的

impressive [ɪmˈprɛsɪv]＊＊　 a. 給人深刻印象的

impressively [ɪmˈprɛsɪvlɪ]　 ad. 令人難忘地

incredible [ɪnˈkrɛdəbl]　 a. 難以置信的

incredibly [ɪnˈkrɛdəblɪ]　 ad. 不能相信地

in honor of＊＊　 phr. 向…表示敬意

initial [ɪˈnɪʃəl]　 a. 最初的　 v. 字首大寫字母

initially [ɪˈnɪʃəlɪ]＊　 ad. 最初，開頭

initiate [ɪˈnɪʃɪ‚et]　 v. 開始

issue [ˈɪʃju]　 n. 問題，爭論

once [wʌns]＊＊　 conj. 一旦

owe [o]　 v. 欠

personal belongings＊＊　 phr. 個人資產

premier [ˈprimɪə]　 a. 第一的，首要的　 n. 總理

profusion [prəˈfjuʒən]　 n. 豐富

progress [ˈprɑgrɛs]　 n. 進行

progression [prə`grɛʃən]　n. 前進

progressive [prə`grɛsɪv] *　a. 前進的，進行的

proof [pruf]　n. 證據

readily available *　phr.易利用的，容易得到的

require [rɪ`kwaɪr] * *　v. 需要，要求

required [rɪ`kwaɪrd] * *　a. 必需的

requirement [rɪ`kwaɪrmənt]　n. 請求（=prerequisite），要求

requisition [͵rɛkwə`zɪʃən]　n. 申請書，需要，要求

research [rɪ`sɝtʃ] * *　v. 研究，調查　n. 研究，調查

researcher [rɪ`sɝtʃə]　n. 研究員，調查員

resent [rɪ`zɛnt]　v. 憤恨，怨恨

revenue [`rɛvə͵nju] * *　n. 收入，稅收

reward [rɪ`wɔrd] *　n. 報酬，酬勞

rundown [`rʌn͵daʊn]　a. 衰弱的

special [`spɛʃəl] *　a. 特別的

specialist [`spɛʃəlɪst]　n. 專家　n. 專家

specialize [`spɛʃəl͵aɪz] * *　v. 專門研究

specially [`spɛʃəlɪ]　ad. 特別地

steep [stip] *　a. 陡峭的，險峻的

steeply [`stiplɪ]　ad. 險峻地

suffice [sə`faɪs]　v. 足夠，使滿足

sufficiency [sə`fɪʃənsɪ]　n. 充足，自滿

sufficient [sə`fɪʃənt]　a. 充分的

sufficiently [sə`fɪʃəntlɪ] * *　ad. 充分地

sum [sʌm]　n. 總數，和

summarize [`sʌmə͵raɪz]　v. 概述，總結，摘要

summary [`sʌmərɪ]　n. 摘要，概要

think about *　phr. 考慮…

think of *　phr. 想…

timelessly [`taɪmlɪslɪ]　ad. 永久地，無限地

第二十三天

assail [ə`sel]　v. 攻擊

assemble [ə`sɛmbl]　v. 集合，聚集

assembled [ə`sɛmbl]　a. 裝配，組合

assembly [ə`sɛmblɪ]　n. 裝配（機械），集會

attire [ə`taɪr] *　n. 服裝

average [`ævərɪdʒ]　n. 平均　a. 通常的，平均的

below [bə`lo] *　prep. 在…下面，在下

be responsible for * *　phr. 為…負責

be responsive to *　phr. 對…反映

contract [kən`trækt]，[`kɑntrækt]　v. 訂約，收縮　n. 契約

contraction [kən`trækʃən]　n. 收縮，緊縮

control [kən`trol] *　v. 支配，管理

convene [kən`vin]　v. 召集（會議）

copy [`kɑpɪ] * *　n. 副本，一冊

corporation [͵kɔrpə`reʃən] *　n. 法人，公司

corrosion [kə`roʒən] * *　n. 侵蝕，腐蝕狀態

cost [kɔst]　n. 成本　v. 花費

discover [dɪs`kʌvə]　v. 發現

discriminate [dɪ`skrɪmə͵net]　v. 區別，識別

discuss [dɪ`skʌs] * *　v. 討論

discussion [dɪ`skʌʃən] * *　n. 討論

disengage [͵dɪsɪn`gedʒ]　v. 解除，釋放

drape（某物）with（布料等）* *　phr. 用（布料等）蓋住（某物）

duty [`djutɪ]　n. 義務，職責

elevate [`ɛlə͵vet]　v. 舉起，提拔

elevation [͵ɛlə`veʃən]　n. 上升，高地

expose [ɪk`spoz]　v. 暴露，揭露

exposure [ɪk`spozə] * *　n. 暴露，揭露

extremely [ɪk`strimlɪ] * *　ad. 極端地，非常地

former [`fɔrmə]　a. 從前的，以前的

head for *　phr. 前往…

independent [͵ɪndɪ`pɛndənt] *　a. 獨立自主的，不受約束的

in light of　phr. 按照，根據

in observance of *　phr. 遵守…

invite [ɪn`vaɪt] * *　v. 邀請，招待

involve [ɪn`valv] *　v. 包括，使陷於

involved [ɪn`valvd] * *　a. 有關的

involvement [ɪn`valvmənt]　n. 連累

move [muv] *　v. 移動，遷居　n. 移動

outside [`aʊt`saɪd]　prep. 在…外

paid [ped] * *　a. 已支付的

proposal [prə`pozl] * *　n. 提議，建議

propose [prə`poz] *　v. 計畫，建議（=suggest）

proposition [͵prɑpə`zɪʃən]　n. 主張，建議

prospect [`prɑspɛkt] * *　n. 前景，期望

prospective [prə`spɛktɪv] *　a. 預期的

prosper [`prɑspə]　v. 繁榮

prosperity [prɑs`pɛrətɪ] * *　n. 繁榮

prosperous [`prɑspərəs]　a. 繁榮的

prosperously [`prɑspərəslɪ]　ad. 繁榮地

protect [prə`tɛkt]　v. 保護

protection [prə`tɛkʃən]　n. 保護

protective [prə`tɛkɪv] * *　a. 保護的

resist [rɪ`zɪst]　v. 抵抗，反抗

respectable [rɪ`spɛktəbl]　a. 值得尊敬的

respect [rɪ`spɛkt]　v. 尊敬，尊重

respectful [rɪ`spɛktfəl]　a. 尊敬的

respectfully [rɪ`spɛktfəlɪ] *　ad. 尊敬地，謙恭地

right [raɪt] * *　a. 正確的，對的　n. 權利

rightful [`raɪtfəl] *　a. 公正的

rightfully [`raɪtfəlɪ]　ad. 正直地，正當地

rightly [`raɪtlɪ]　ad. 正當地，正確地

risk [rɪsk]　n. 風險，危險

rival [`raɪvḷ] *   n. 競爭者

serve [sɝv] * *   v. 招待，侍候

service [`sɝvɪs] * *   n. 服務，招待（客人）

serviceable [`sɝvɪsəbḷ]   a. 有用的

suggest [sə`dʒɛst]   v. 建議（=recommend），暗示（=imply）

suggestion [sə`dʒɛstʃən]   n. 提議

supervision [ˌsupɚ`vɪʒən] * *   n. 監督，管理

supplement [`sʌpləmənt] *   v. 補充   n. 補充，附錄

supply [sə`plaɪ] *   v. 供給   n. (pl.) 供應品

time constraints *   phr. 時間限制

triple [`trɪpḷ]   a. 三倍的

unknown [ʌn`non]   a. 不知道的

unlimited [ʌn`lɪmɪtɪd] * *   a. 無限的，無約束的（=unrestricted）

upon request * *   phr. 一經要求

第二十四天

admission [əd`mɪʃən]   n. 允許進入，入場費

admit [əd`mɪt] *   v. 容許，承認

ambivalence [æm`bɪvələns]   n. 正反感情並存

apprehensive [ˌæprɪ`hɛnsɪv] *   a. 擔心的，憂慮的

assert [ə`sɝt] *   v. 斷言，聲稱

assign [ə`saɪn]   v. 分配（=allocate），指派

assignment [ə`saɪnmənt]   n. 分配，課題

assist [ə`sɪst]   v. 幫助

be restored to * *   phr. 恢復…

be subject to *   phr. 受制於，取決於

blandly [`blændlɪ]   ad. 溫和地

bowl [bol]   n. 碗

card [kard] * *   n. 紙牌，卡片

complacent [kəm`plesn̩t]   a. 自滿的

confidence in *   phr. 對…的信心

conscious of * *   phr. 意識…

conversion [kən`vɝʃən]   n. 變換，轉化

convert [kən`vɝt]   v. 使轉變

convey [kən`ve]   v. 搬運，傳達

cooperate [ko`apəˌret]   v. 合作

cooperation [ko͵apə`reʃən]   n. 合作

cooperative [ko`apəˌretɪv] * *   a. 協力的

cooperatively [ko`apəretɪvlɪ] * *   ad. 合作的，共同的

customer [`kʌstəmɚ]   n. 顧客

customization [`kʌstəm͵aɪzeɪʃən]   n. 專用化，定制，客制化

customize [`kʌstəm͵aɪz] * *   v. 訂製，用戶化，客制化

densely [`dɛnslɪ] *   ad. 濃密地

deposit [dɪ`pazɪt] * *   n. 押金   n.抵押

determined [dɪ`tɝmɪnd]   a. 堅決的，決定了的

dislocate [`dɪslə͵ket]   v. 使…脫位，脫離

dismiss [dɪs`mɪs] *   v. 開除

dispatch [dɪ`spætʃ] *   v. 派遣

displace [dɪs`ples]   v. 替代，撤換

enlarge [ɪn`lard3]   v. 擴大

exact [ɪg`zækt]   a. 精確的，準確的

exacting [ɪg`zæktɪŋ]   a. 嚴格的，吃力的

exactly [ɪg`zæktlɪ] * *   ad. 正確地，嚴密地

exactness [ɪg`zæktnɪs]   n. 正確

extra [`ɛkstrə]   a. 額外的，另外

faculty [`fækḷtɪ]   n. 才能，本領

fairly [`fɛrlɪ] *   ad. 公正地

frenetic [frɪ`nɛtɪk]   a. 發狂的，狂熱的

indifference [ɪn`dɪfərəns]   n. 不關心

in one's absence *   phr. 當…不在時

in particular *   phr. 特別

leave [liv] *   v. 離開   n. 許可

move away *   phr. 離開

obstacle [`abstəkḷ]   n. 障礙，妨害物

officially [ə`fɪʃəlɪ] *   ad. 職務上地

out of print *   phr. 絕版的

own [on] *   v. 擁有

owner [`onɚ] *   n. 所有者

ownership [`onɚˌʃɪp]   n. 所有權

participant [par`tɪsəpənt]   n. 參與者

participate [par`tɪsəˌpet]   v. 參與

participation [par͵tɪsə`peʃən] * *   n. 參與，分享

premeditate [pri`mɛdəˌtet]   v. 預先考慮

presumably [prɪ`zuməblɪ] * *   ad. 大概

presumptive [prɪ`zʌmptɪv]   a. 假定的

procedural [pro`sidʒərəl]   a. 程式上的

procedure [prə`sidʒɚ] * *   n. 程式，手續

protest [prə`tɛst]   v. 主張，抗議

prove [pruv]   v. 證明，證實

resonate [`rɛzəˌnet]   v. 迴響，反響

respond [rɪ`spand] * *   v. 回答，回應

respondent [rɪ`spandənt]   n. 回答者

response [rɪ`spans]   n. 回答，反應

simultaneously [saɪmḷ`tenɪəslɪ] *   ad. 同時地

stress [strɛs]   n. 逼迫，強調   v. 強調

structure [`strʌktʃɚ] * *   n. 結構，構造

tension [`tɛnʃən]   n. 緊張，壓力

term [tɝm]   n. 期間，條件

try [traɪ]   v. 試圖，努力   v. 試圖，努力

uniquely [ju`niklɪ]   ad. 獨特地，唯一地

upcoming school year *   phr. 下學年

upstart [`ʌp͵start]   n. 傲慢無禮的人

assume [ə`sjum] *　v. 假定，設想（=presume）

attach [ə`tætʃ] * *　v. 使依附，繫上

attached [ə`tætʃt] * *　a. 附屬的

behavior [bɪ`hevjə]　n. 舉止，行為

be superior to *　phr. 優越於

be uncertain about *　phr. 不能確定

brief [brif] *　a. 簡短的　v. 摘要

brief 某人 on 某事　phr. 向（某人）簡要介紹（某事）

briefly [`brifli]　ad. 簡要地

coordinate [ko`ɔrdn̩et] *　v. 調整，協調

coordination [ko`ɔrdn̩ˌeʃən] *　n. 同等，調和

correlate [`kɔrəˌlet]　v. 使相互關聯

counsel [`kaʊnsl]　n. 商議　v. 勸告（=advise）

detail [`ditel]　n. 細節，詳情

detailed [`diˈteld] * *　a. 詳細的，逐條的

dispute over *　phr. 爭論

disrupt [dɪs`rʌpt] *　v. 使中斷，使陷於混亂

dissatisfy [dɪs`sætɪsˌfaɪ] *　v. 使感覺不滿

distribute [dɪ`strɪbjut] * *　v. 分配，分佈

distributed [dɪ`strɪbjutɪd] * *　a. 分散式的

distribution [ˌdɪstrə`bjuʃən]　n. 分配，發行

distributor [dɪ`strɪbjətə] * *　n. 發行人，分配者

exportation [ˌɛkspor`teʃən]　n. 輸出，輸出品

express [ɪk`sprɛs] * *　v. 表達，表示

expression [ɪk`sprɛʃən]　n. 表達

expressive [ɪk`sprɛsɪv]　a. 表現的，富於表情的

fondness [`fɑndnɪs]　n. 愛好，溺愛

for your convenience * *　phr. 為了您的方便

glance [glæns]　n. 一瞥

growth rate　phr. 生長率

hospitality [ˌhɑspɪ`tæləti] * *　n. 好客，盛情

incentive [ɪn`sɛntɪv]　n. 動機，刺激

indefinitely [ɪn`dɛfənɪtli]　ad. 不確定地

individual [ˌɪndə`vɪdʒʊəl]　a. 個人的　n. 個人，個體

individualism [ˌɪndə`vɪdʒʊəlˌɪzəm]　n. 個人主義

individualist [ˌɪndə`vɪdʒʊəlɪst]　n. 個人主義者

individuality [ˌɪndəˌvɪdʒʊ`æləti]　n. 個性

individually [ˌɪndə`vɪdʒʊəli] * *　ad. 個別地

in place of　phr. 代替…

in spite of *　phr. 不管…

internment [ɪn`tɝmənt]　n. 扣留，收容

limitation [ˌlɪmə`teʃən]　n. 限制，局限性

limited [`lɪmɪtɪd] * *　a. 有限的

maximum [`mæksəməm]　n. 最大量

multiply [`mʌltəplaɪ]　v. 乘，增加

presumptuous [prɪ`zʌmptʃʊəs]　a. 太過分的，放肆的

prevalent [`prɛvələnt] *　a. 普遍的，流行的

previous [`priviəs] *　a. 之前的

previously [`priviəsli] * *　ad. 之前地，以前

provide [prə`vaɪd] * *　v. 供給，準備

provided [prə`vaɪdɪd] * *　conj. 倘若

providing [prə`vaɪdɪŋ] * *　conj. 倘若

provision [prə`vɪʒən]　n. (pl.) 供應品，預備

publish [`pʌblɪʃ] * *　v. 出版

responsive [rɪ`spɑnsɪv] *　a. 回應的，作出回應的

responsiveness [rɪ`spɑnsɪvnɪs]　n. 敏感度，回應率

restore [rɪ`stor] * *　v. 恢復，修復

restrained [rɪ`strend]　a. 受限制的，拘謹的

restructure [rɪ`strʌktʃə] *　v. 更改結構，重建構造

return A to B * *　phr. 把 A 歸還給 B，歸還

signifier [`sɪgnɪˌfaɪə]　n.（概念或意義的）象徵，意象

signify [`sɪgnəˌfaɪ]　v. 表示，意味

sincerely [sɪn`sɪrli]　ad. 真誠地

sticky [`stɪkɪ]　a. 黏的，黏性的

substantial [səb`stænʃəl] * *　a. 堅固的，實質的

substantiality [səbˌstænʃɪ`æləti]　n. 實在性，實質性

substantially [səb`stænʃəli] * *　ad. 充分地

substantiate [səb`stænʃɪˌet]　v. 證實

submit A to B *　phr. 把 A 遞交給 B

support [sə`port]　v. 支持，支援　n. 支持，支援

tour [tʊr]　n. 旅行　v. 旅行

turn [tɝn] *　v. 轉動　n. 變化，轉化

unoccupied [ʌn`ɑkjəˌpaɪd] * *　a. 沒有人住的（=vacant）

unrecoverable [ˈʌnrɪ`kʌvərəbl̩]　a. 無法收回的

unusually [ʌn`juʒʊəli] *　ad. 顯著地，異乎尋常地

unwillingness [ʌn`wɪlɪŋnɪs] *　n. 不情願

venture [`vɛntʃə] * *　n. 冒險，投機

venturesome [`vɛntʃəsəm]　a. 敢於冒險的

第二十六天

advertisement [ˌædvə`taɪzmənt] *　n. 廣告

attend [ə`tɛnd] *　v. 參加

attendee [əˈtɛndi] *　n. 參加者

because of *　phr. 因為

benefit from * *　phr. 受益於

brightly [`braɪtlɪ]　ad. 明亮地

circumstance [`sɝkəmˌstæns]　n. 環境，境況

collection [kə`lɛkʃən] * *　n. 收藏，搜集品

collective [kə`lɛktɪv]　a. 集體的

collector [kə`lɛktə]　n. 收藏家

condensed [kən`dɛnst]　a. 濃縮，簡潔的

consist of * *　phr. 由…組成

correspond [ˌkɔrɪ`spɑnd]　v. 相應

correspondence [ˌkɔrə`spɑndəns] * *　n. 相應，通信，信件

corresponding [ˌkɔrɪˈspandɪŋ]　a. 相應的

correspondingly [ˌkɔrəˈspandɪŋlɪ]　ad. 相對地

create [krɪˈet] * *　v. 創造，引起

creation [krɪˈeʃən]　n. 創造，創作

creative [krɪˈetɪv] * *　a. 創造性的

creatively [krɪˈetɪvlɪ]　ad. 創造性地

creativeness [krɪˈetɪvnɪs]　n. 創造力

creativity [ˌkrieˈtɪvətɪ]　n. 創造力，創造

dealing [ˈdilɪŋ] *　n. 交易

decadence [ˈdɛkədəns]　n. 頹廢

disturb [dɪsˈtɝb]　v. 打擾

disturbance [dɪsˈtɝbəns]　n. 騷動，動亂

disturbing [dɪsˈtɝbɪŋ] * *　a. 煩擾的

divest [dəˈvɛst]　v. 剝奪

excellent [ˈɛkslənt] *　a. 卓越的（=preeminent）

excessive [ɪkˈsɛsɪv]　a. 過分的

experiment with * *　phr. 對⋯進行實驗

extend [ɪkˈstɛnd]　v. 延長（=lengthen），擴充

extended [ɪkˈstɛndɪd]　a. 延長的

extension [ɪkˈstɛnʃən] * *　n. 延長，擴充，電話分機

extensive [ɪkˈstɛnsɪv] * *　a. 廣闊的，廣泛的

extensively [ɪkˈstɛnsɪvlɪ]　ad. 廣闊地

fine [faɪn] *　n. 罰款，罰金　a. 優良的

finely [ˈfaɪnlɪ]　ad. 細微地，美好地

firm [fɝm]　n. 公司　a. 結實的

firmly [ˈfɝmlɪ] *　ad. 堅定地，穩固地

fresh [frɛʃ] *　a. 新鮮的

freshen [ˈfrɛʃən]　v. 使顯得新鮮

freshly [ˈfrɛʃlɪ]　ad. 新鮮地

freshness [ˈfrɛʃnɪs] *　n. 新鮮，生氣勃勃

full [fʊl] *　a. 充滿的，完全的

fully [ˈfʊlɪ] * *　ad. 充分地，完全地

increasing market pressure *　phr. 日益增加的市場壓力

increment [ˈɪnkrəmənt]　n. 增加，增量

inspiration [ˌɪnspəˈreʃən] * *　n. 靈感

install [ɪnˈstɔl] * *　v. 安置

installation [ˌɪnstəˈleʃən]　n. 安裝

insubordinate [ˌɪnsəˈbɔrdnɪt]　a. 不順從的，不聽話的

in summary　phr. 摘要

intention [ɪnˈtɛnʃən] *　n. 意圖，目的

in the past　phr. 在過去

manufacturer [ˌmænjəˈfæktʃərə] *　n. 製造業者

maximum security *　phr. 最大的防護措施

origin [ˈɔrədʒɪn] *　n. 起源

original [əˈrɪdʒɪnl] *　a. 原始的，獨創的

originality [əˌrɪdʒəˈnælətɪ]　n. 創意

originally [əˈrɪdʒɪnlɪ] * *　ad. 最初，原先

originate [əˈrɪdʒəˌnet]　v. 引起，發起

possible [ˈpasəbl] *　a. 可能的，可能存在或發生的

purchase [ˈpɝtʃəs] * *　v. 買，購買　n. 買，購買

purchased [ˈpɝtʃəsd] * *　a. 已購買的

question [ˈkwɛstʃən] * *　n. 問題，疑問　v. 審問，懷疑

refund [rɪˈfʌnd]，[ˈrɪˌfʌnd] *　v. 退還，償還　n. 退還，償還

return [rɪˈtɝn] * *　v. 返回，回答

returned [rɪˈtɝnd] * *　a. 被送回的，歸來的

reveal [rɪˈvil] * *　v. 展現，暴露

revelation [rɛvlˈeʃən]　n. 揭露，揭示

review [rɪˈvju] * *　v. 回顧，複習

site [saɪt]　n. 地點，場所

stare [stɛr]　v. 凝視

struck [strʌk]　a. 受罷工影響的

suppress [səˈprɛs]　v. 鎮壓

第二十七天

arguable [ˈargjuəbl]　a. 可辯論的

argument [ˈargjəmənt] *　n. 爭論

argumentative [ˌargjəˈmɛntətɪv] * *　a. 好辯的，爭論的

automate [ˈɔtəˌmet] * *　v. 使自動化

automatically [ˌɔtəˈmætɪklɪ] * *　ad. 自動地

avert [əˈvɝt]　v. 防止（某件將要發生的事），轉移（視線）

avoid [əˈvɔɪd] *　v. 避免，消除

award [əˈwɔrd] *　v. 授予　n. 獎

be restricted to　phr. 限制於

beyond one's control *　phr. 難控制的

cancel [ˈkænsl]　v. 取消

cancellation [ˌkænslˈeʃən] * *　n. 取消

commencement [kəˈmɛnsmənt]　n. 開始，開端

condition [kənˈdɪʃən] * *　n. 條件，情形

conditional [kənˈdɪʃənl]　a. 有條件的

count [kaʊnt] *　v. 數，計算

countdown [ˈkaʊntˌdaʊn]　n. 倒數計秒

curb [kɝb] *　v. 抑制（=restrain）

difficulty [ˈdɪfəˌkʌltɪ] * *　n. 困難，難點

dissentingly [dɪˈsɛntɪŋlɪ]　ad. 好爭論的，爭吵的

divide [dəˈvaɪd]　v. 劃分，分開

divided [dəˈvaɪdɪd] *　a. 分開的

dividend [ˈdɪvəˌdɛnd] *　n. 分配物（=allotment）

division [dəˈvɪʒən] * *　n. 分割，區分

double [ˈdʌbl] * *　v. 使加倍　a. 兩倍的

drop [drap] *　v. 落下　n. 落下，下降

empathic [ɛmˈpæθɪk] * *　a. 移情作用的

environmental [ɪnˌvaɪrənˈmɛntl] *　a. 環境的

environmentalism [ɪnˌvaɪərənˈmɛntlɪzəm]　n. 環保主義

environmentalist [ɪnˌvaɪərənˈmɛntlɪst]　n. 環保者

environmentally [ɪnˌvaɪrənˈmɛntlɪ]　ad. 要求環境保護的

exertion [ɪgˋzɝʃən] * n. 努力，運用	amaze [əˋmez] * v. 使吃驚
feedback [ˋfid͵bæk] * n. 反饋，反應	amazed [əˋmezd] * a. 吃驚的
further [ˋfɝðɚ] * a. 更多的，深一層的	amazement [əˋmezmənt] * * n. 驚訝
furthermore [ˋfɝðɚ͵mor] ad. 此外，而且	amazing [əˋmezɪŋ] * a. 令人驚訝的
inherently [ɪnˋhɪrəntlɪ] * * ad. 天性地，固有地	apportionment [əˋporʃnmənt] n. 分配，分派
intact [ɪnˋtækt] a. 完整無缺的	ascertain [͵æsɚˋten] v. 查明，弄清
in theory phr. 理論上	bear [bɛr] * v. 負擔，忍受（=endure）
in writing * * phr. 書面上	bill [bɪl] * v. 給⋯開帳單 n. 帳單
majority [məˋdʒɔrətɪ] * * n. 多數，大半	bring（某事）to a halt * phr. 使（某事）停止
member [ˋmɛmbɚ] n. 成員，會員	by telephone * phr. 用電話
otherwise [ˋʌðɚ͵waɪz] * * ad. 否則，不同地	by hand * phr. 用手
out of the office * phr. 不在辦公室	capitalize [ˋkæpətḷ͵aɪz] v. 以大寫字母寫，供給資本
personal check * phr. 個人支票	capture [ˋkæptʃɚ] v. 捕獲，奪取
position [pəˋzɪʃən] n. 位置，職位	contend with * phr. 與⋯抗爭
precipitation [prɪ͵sɪpɪˋteʃən] * n. 降水量	courteous [ˋkɝtjəs] * a. 有禮貌的
provide 某人 with 某物 * phr.給（某人）供給（某物）	courteously [ˋkɝtɪəslɪ] ad. 有禮貌地
pursue [pɚˋsu] v. 追趕，追蹤	courteousness [ˋkɝtjəsnɛs] n. 有禮貌
pursuit [pɚˋsut] n. 追擊	courtesy [ˋkɝtəsɪ] n. 禮貌
quite [kwaɪt] ad. 相當	customs [ˋkʌstəmz] n. 進口稅，海關
rather [ˋræðɚ] ad. 寧願，有點	customarily [ˋkʌstəm͵ɛrɪlɪ] ad. 通常
relic [ˋrɛlɪk] n. 遺物，遺跡	customary [ˋkʌstəm͵ɛrɪ] a. 習慣的，慣例的
respect for * phr. 尊敬	demonstrate [ˋdɛmən͵stret] * v. 示範，證明（=prove）
revolve [rɪˋvɑlv] v. 旋轉，迴圈	detect [dɪˋtɛkt] v. 察覺，發覺
rise [raɪz] * * v. 上升，增長（=increase）	distantly [ˋdɪstəntlɪ] ad. 遙遠的
significance [sɪgˋnɪfəkəns] n. 意義，重要性	distinct [dɪˋstɪŋkt] a. 清楚的，明顯的
significant [sɪgˋnɪfəkənt] * a. 重大的，重要的	distinction [dɪˋstɪŋkʃən] n. 區別，差別
significantly [sɪgˋnɪfəkəntlɪ] * * ad. 意味深長地，值得注目地	distinctive [dɪˋstɪŋktɪv] a. 與衆不同的，有特色的
slowly [ˋslolɪ] * ad. 慢慢地，遲緩地	distinctively [dɪˋstɪŋktɪvlɪ] * ad. 特殊地
subjective [səbˋdʒɛktɪv] * a. 主觀的	donate [ˋdonet] * * v. 捐贈
subjectively [səbˋdʒɛktɪvlɪ] ad. 主觀地	donation [doˋneʃən] * * n. 捐贈品，捐款
succeed in Ving * phr. 在⋯方面成功	due to * phr. 由於
surround [səˋraʊnd] v. 圍繞	expense [ɪkˋspɛns] * * n. 費用，開支
surrounding [səˋraʊndɪŋ] a. 周圍的 n. (pl.) 環境	expensive [ɪkˋspɛnsɪv] * * a. 昂貴的
suspend [səˋspɛnd] * v. 保留，推遲（=postpone）	expensively [ɪkˋspɛnsɪvlɪ] ad. 昂貴地
swap [swɑp] v. 交換	expensiveness [ɪkˋspɛnsɪv] n. 昂貴
taste [test] * v. 品嘗 n. 味道	extinction [ɪkˋstɪŋkʃən] * * n. 消滅
type [taɪp] * n. 種類，樣式	flex [flɛks] v. 彎曲，伸縮
vaguely [ˋveglɪ] ad. 模糊地	flexibility [͵flɛksəˋbɪlətɪ] * * n. 彈性，適應性
vapor [ˋvepɚ] n. 水蒸氣 n. 水蒸氣	flexible [ˋflɛksəbḷ] a. 柔軟的
variation [͵vɛrɪˋeʃən] n. 變更，變化	in danger of extinction phr. 瀕臨絕種的
varied [ˋvɛrɪd] a. 各式各樣的	industry [ˋɪndəstrɪ] * n. 產業
variety [vəˋraɪətɪ] * * n. 變化，多樣（性）	influence [ˋɪnfluəns] * * n. 影響 v. 影響
variously [ˋvɛrɪəslɪ] ad. 各種各樣地	insert A into B phr. 把 A 插入 B
vary [ˋvɛrɪ] * * v. 變化，不同	invest [ɪnˋvɛst] v. 投資
	investment [ɪnˋvɛstmənt] n. 投資
	investor [ɪnˋvɛstɚ] * * n. 投資者
第二十八天	investigation [ɪn͵vɛstəˋgeʃən] * * n. 調查，研究
amalgamate [əˋmælgəmet] v. 合併	lead [lɪd] v. 導致（結果）

outweigh [aʊt`we] * *   v. 在重量（或價值等）上超過

overly [`ovə·lɪ]   ad. 過度地，極度地

override [ˌovə·`raɪd]   v. 高過於

primal [`praɪml]   a. 最初的，主要的

primarily [praɪ`mɛrəlɪ] * *   ad. 首先，主要地

primary [`praɪˌmɛrɪ]   a. 主要的，基本的

prime [praɪm]   a. 主要的

principal [`prɪnsəpl] *   a. 主要的

proximity [prɑk`sɪmətɪ]   n. 接近，親近

readily [`rɛdɪlɪ] *   ad. 容易地

ready [`rɛdɪ]   a. 有準備的

removal [rɪ`muvl]   n. 切除

remove [rɪ`muv]   v. 除去（=eliminate）

repeal [rɪ`pil]   v. 廢止，撤銷

restricted [rɪ`strɪktɪd] *   a. 受限制的，有限的

revolutionary [ˌrɛvə`luʃənˌɛrɪ]   a. 革命的

rich [rɪtʃ] *   a. 充足的，豐富的

share [ʃɛr]   v. 共用   n. (pl.) 股份（=stock）

softly [`sɔftlɪ]   ad. 柔軟地，溫柔地

staff productivity * *   phr. 員工勞動生產率

submit [səb`mɪt] * *   v. 提出

throughout the day * *   phr. 一整天

two forms of identification * *   phr. 兩種身份證明文件

unsafe [ʌn`sef]   a. 不安全的，危險的

unstable [ʌn`stebl]   a. 不牢固的，不穩定的

ventilation [ˌvɛntl`eʃən]   n. 通風，流通空氣

whereabouts [`hwɛrə`baʊts]   n. 下落，行蹤

第二十九天

appraisal [ə`prezl] *   n. 評價，鑑定

associated [ə`soʃɪˌetɪd] *   a. 關聯的

assorted [ə`sɔrtɪd]   a. 多樣混合的

assurance [ə`ʃurəns]   n. 確信，保證

assure [ə`ʃur]   v. 保證，擔保

by means of * *   phr. 依靠

by no means   phr. 絕不

catch [kætʃ] *   ad. 捕獲，抓住

consecutive [kən`sɛkjutɪv] *   a. 連續的

consensus [kən`sɛnsəs] *   n. 一致同意，輿論

consent [kən`sɛnt]   n. 同意，容許

consent of * *   phr. 同意

consistent [kən`sɪstənt] *   a. 一致的

consistently [kən`sɪstəntlɪ] * *   ad. 一貫地，始終如一地

contract out   phr. 退出合同

device [dɪ`vaɪs]   n. 裝置（=gadget），策略

devise [dɪ`vaɪz]   v. 想出

do business with *   phr. 與…做生意

effect [ɪ`fɛkt] * *   n. 結果，影響   v. 招致

effective [ɪ`fɛktɪv] * *   a. 有效的

effectively [ɪ`fɛktɪvlɪ]   ad. 有效地

effectiveness [ə`fɛktɪvnɪs]   n. 有效性，有效果的

excitable [ɪk`saɪtəbl]   a. 易興奮的

excite [ɪk`saɪt]   v. 使興奮，使激動

excited [ɪk`saɪtɪd] * *   a. 興奮的

excitedly [ɪk`saɪtɪdlɪ]   ad. 興奮地

excitement [ɪk`saɪtmənt]   n. 興奮，激動

exciting [ɪk`saɪtɪŋ] * *   a. 令人興奮的，使人激動的

face [fes] *   v. 面臨（=confront）

guarantee of *   phr. 對…擔保

induce [ɪn`djus]   v. 勸誘，促使

inflate [ɪn`flet]   v. 抬高，膨脹

inflated [ɪn`fletɪd]   a. 膨脹的，誇張的

inflation [ɪn`fleʃən] * *   n. 通貨膨脹，（物價）暴漲

injured [`ɪndʒə·d]   a. 受傷的，受損害的

insincerely [ˌɪnsɪn`sɪrlɪ]   ad. 無誠意地

instead of * *   phr. 代替

integrate [`ɪntə·gret] *   a. 合併

interfere [ˌɪntə·`fɪr]   v. 干涉，妨礙

open [`opən]   v. 打開，開放   a. 開著的，公開的

opening [`opənɪŋ] * *   n. 空缺，缺席

overload [`ovə·lod]   v. 使超載，超過負荷

owing to * *   phr. 由於，因…之緣故

persuadable [pə·`swedəbl]   a. 可以說服的

persuade [pə·`swed]   v. 說服

persuasion [pə·`sweʒən]   n. 說服

persuasive [pə·`swesɪv] * *   a. 善說服的

persuasively [pə·`swesɪvlɪ]   ad. 口才好地

precaution [prɪ`kɔʃən] * *   n. 預防

preserve [prɪ`zɝv] *   v. 保護，守護

prize [praɪz] * *   n. 獎賞

probability [ˌprɑbə`bɪlətɪ]   n. 可能性

purpose [`pɝpəs] * *   n. 目的，意志

reduce [rɪ`djus] * *   v. 減少，縮小

reduction [rɪ`dʌkʃən] * *   n. 減少，縮影

reductive [rɪ`dʌktɪv]   a. 減少的

register [`rɛdʒɪstə·] * *   v. 登記

renegotiate [ˌrini`goʃɪˌet]   v. 重新談判

run short * *   phr. 缺少

space [spes]   n. 空間   v. 隔開

spacious [`speʃəs]   a. 廣大的（=roomy）

spread [sprɛd]   v. 展開，傳播

stability [stə`bɪlətɪ] * *   n. 穩定性

stable [`stebl]   a. 穩定的

stay [ste] *   v. 停留   n. 止住

touch down * *   phr. （飛機）降落

treat [trit]　v. 視為，對待

undergo [ˌʌndɚ`go]＊　v. 經歷，遭受

voluntarily [`vɑlən͵tɛrəlɪ]＊＊　ad. 自動地

voluntary [`vɑlən͵tɛrɪ]　a. 自動的

volunteer [ˌvɑlən`tɪr]＊　n. 志願者　v. 自願

warranty [`wɔrəntɪ]＊　n. 保證

wash [wɑʃ]　v. 洗，洗滌

whereas [hwɛr`æz]　conj. 反之

第三十天

affect [ə`fɛkt]＊＊　v. 影響（=influence）

affection [ə`fɛkʃən]　n. 友愛，愛情

attract [ə`trækt]＊＊　v. 吸引

attraction [ə`trækʃən]　n. 吸引力，吸引人的事物

authorization [ˌɔθərə`reʃən]　n. 授權，認可

authorize [`ɔθə͵raɪz]＊＊　v. 批准

authorized [`ɔθə`raɪzd]＊＊　a. 經授權的

authorship [`ɔθɚ`ʃɪp]　n. 原創作者

available [ə`veləbl]＊＊　a. 可用到的，可利用的

by way of　phr. 經由，作為

challenge [`tʃælɪndʒ]　v. 向…挑戰　n. 挑戰

challenging [`tʃælɪndʒɪŋ]　a. 挑戰性的

configuration [kənˌfɪgjə`reʃən]　n. 配置，外形

contingent [kən͵tɪndʒənt]＊　a. 依條件而定的

contribute [kən͵trɪbjut]　v. 捐助

contribution [ˌkɑntrə`bjuʃən]　n. 捐獻

contributor [kən͵trɪbjutɚ]＊＊　n. 捐助者

cover [`kʌvɚ]　v. 確保，入保險加以保護，足以支付

coverage [`kʌvərɪdʒ]＊＊　n. 保險範圍，新聞報導，覆蓋度

cut back　phr. 修剪，削減

cultivate [`kʌltə͵vet]　v. 耕作

cultivation [ˌkʌltə`veʃən]　n. 耕作，培養

diverse [daɪ`vɝs]＊＊　a. 變化多的

diversification [daɪ͵vɝsəfə`keʃən]　n. 變化，多樣化

diversified [daɪ`vɝsə͵faɪd]＊　a. 多變化的，各種的

diversify [daɪ`vɝsə͵faɪ]＊＊　v. 使多樣化

diversity [daɪ`vɝsətɪ]　n. 多樣性

edit [`ɛdɪt]　v. 編輯

edition [ɪ`dɪʃən]＊＊　n. 版本，版

editor [`ɛdɪtɚ]　n. 編輯，編者

encounter [ɪn`kaʊntɚ]＊　v. 偶遇

engage [ɪn`gedʒ]　v. 從事，使參加

engineer [ˌɛndʒə`nɪr]＊　n. 工程師

escort 某人 to 某處＊＊　phr. 護送（某人）到（某處）

estimate [`ɛstə͵met]＊　n. 估計，估價　v. 估計，估價

estimated [`ɛstə͵metd]　a. 推測，估計

estimation [ˌɛstə`meʃən]　n. 估計，評價

exercise [`ɛksɚ͵saɪz]＊＊　n. 鍛鍊

facilitate [fə`sɪlə͵tet]＊　v. 使容易，促進

facilitation [fə͵sɪlə`teʃən]　n. 促進

facilitator [fə`sɪlə͵tetɚ]　n. 促進者，使容易的人

facility [fə`sɪlətɪ]＊＊　n. 設備，設施

fleetly [`flitlɪ]　ad. 迅速地，快速地

from now　phr. 從現在開始

grasp [græsp]　v. 抓住，抓緊

hold [hold]＊＊　v. 持有，擁有

implant [ɪm`plænt]　v. 灌輸，注入

inform [ɪn`fɔrm]　v. 通知（=notify）

informative [ɪn`fɔrmətɪv]＊＊　a. 情報的

informatively [ɪn`fɔrmətɪvlɪ]　ad. 情報地，有益地

informed [ɪn`fɔrmd]＊＊　a. 消息靈通的

informed decision＊　phr. 根據情報的決定

innovative [`ɪno͵vetɪv]＊＊　n. 革新的

inordinate [ɪn`ɔrdɪnɪt]　a. 超過適當限度的

instantly [`ɪnstəntlɪ]＊　ad. 立即地

interfere with＊＊　phr. 妨礙

offend [ə`fɛnd]　v. 違反

particularly [pɚ`tɪkjələ͵lɪ]＊　ad. 獨特地

possess [pə`zɛs]　v. 擁有，持有

problem with　phr. 關於…的問題

profile [`profaɪl]　n. 輪廓　v. 人物概評

profit [`prɑfɪt]＊　n. 利益，利潤

profitable [`prɑfɪtəbl]＊＊　a. 有利可圖的

profiteer [ˌprɑfə`tɪr]　n. 奸商

project [prə`dʒɛkt]＊　n. 事業，計畫

put in for＊＊　phr. 申請

refer [rɪ`fɝ]＊　v. 涉及，參照（=consult）

reference [`rɛfərəns]＊　n. 參考

rich source of information＊　phr. 豐富的情報

schedule [`skɛdʒul]＊　v. 確定時間　n. 時間表

segment [`sɛgmənt]＊＊　n. 部分，片

segmentation [ˌsɛgmən`teʃən]　n. 區分，分割

turn down＊　phr. 向下折轉，拒絕

widely [`waɪdlɪ]＊＊　ad. 廣泛地，普遍地

widen [`waɪdn]　v. 加寬

Actual Test 1 – Answer Sheet

准考證號						
姓名 中 文						
英 文						

READING (Part V~VII)									
NO.	ANSWER A B C D	NO.	ANSWER A B C D	NO.	ANSWER A B C D	NO.	ANSWER A B C D	NO.	ANSWER A B C D
101	Ⓐ Ⓑ Ⓒ Ⓓ	121	Ⓐ Ⓑ Ⓒ Ⓓ	141	Ⓐ Ⓑ Ⓒ Ⓓ	161	Ⓐ Ⓑ Ⓒ Ⓓ	181	Ⓐ Ⓑ Ⓒ Ⓓ
102	Ⓐ Ⓑ Ⓒ Ⓓ	122	Ⓐ Ⓑ Ⓒ Ⓓ	142	Ⓐ Ⓑ Ⓒ Ⓓ	162	Ⓐ Ⓑ Ⓒ Ⓓ	182	Ⓐ Ⓑ Ⓒ Ⓓ
103	Ⓐ Ⓑ Ⓒ Ⓓ	123	Ⓐ Ⓑ Ⓒ Ⓓ	143	Ⓐ Ⓑ Ⓒ Ⓓ	163	Ⓐ Ⓑ Ⓒ Ⓓ	183	Ⓐ Ⓑ Ⓒ Ⓓ
104	Ⓐ Ⓑ Ⓒ Ⓓ	124	Ⓐ Ⓑ Ⓒ Ⓓ	144	Ⓐ Ⓑ Ⓒ Ⓓ	164	Ⓐ Ⓑ Ⓒ Ⓓ	184	Ⓐ Ⓑ Ⓒ Ⓓ
105	Ⓐ Ⓑ Ⓒ Ⓓ	125	Ⓐ Ⓑ Ⓒ Ⓓ	145	Ⓐ Ⓑ Ⓒ Ⓓ	165	Ⓐ Ⓑ Ⓒ Ⓓ	185	Ⓐ Ⓑ Ⓒ Ⓓ
106	Ⓐ Ⓑ Ⓒ Ⓓ	126	Ⓐ Ⓑ Ⓒ Ⓓ	146	Ⓐ Ⓑ Ⓒ Ⓓ	166	Ⓐ Ⓑ Ⓒ Ⓓ	186	Ⓐ Ⓑ Ⓒ Ⓓ
107	Ⓐ Ⓑ Ⓒ Ⓓ	127	Ⓐ Ⓑ Ⓒ Ⓓ	147	Ⓐ Ⓑ Ⓒ Ⓓ	167	Ⓐ Ⓑ Ⓒ Ⓓ	187	Ⓐ Ⓑ Ⓒ Ⓓ
108	Ⓐ Ⓑ Ⓒ Ⓓ	128	Ⓐ Ⓑ Ⓒ Ⓓ	148	Ⓐ Ⓑ Ⓒ Ⓓ	168	Ⓐ Ⓑ Ⓒ Ⓓ	188	Ⓐ Ⓑ Ⓒ Ⓓ
109	Ⓐ Ⓑ Ⓒ Ⓓ	129	Ⓐ Ⓑ Ⓒ Ⓓ	149	Ⓐ Ⓑ Ⓒ Ⓓ	169	Ⓐ Ⓑ Ⓒ Ⓓ	189	Ⓐ Ⓑ Ⓒ Ⓓ
110	Ⓐ Ⓑ Ⓒ Ⓓ	130	Ⓐ Ⓑ Ⓒ Ⓓ	150	Ⓐ Ⓑ Ⓒ Ⓓ	170	Ⓐ Ⓑ Ⓒ Ⓓ	190	Ⓐ Ⓑ Ⓒ Ⓓ
111	Ⓐ Ⓑ Ⓒ Ⓓ	131	Ⓐ Ⓑ Ⓒ Ⓓ	151	Ⓐ Ⓑ Ⓒ Ⓓ	171	Ⓐ Ⓑ Ⓒ Ⓓ	191	Ⓐ Ⓑ Ⓒ Ⓓ
112	Ⓐ Ⓑ Ⓒ Ⓓ	132	Ⓐ Ⓑ Ⓒ Ⓓ	152	Ⓐ Ⓑ Ⓒ Ⓓ	172	Ⓐ Ⓑ Ⓒ Ⓓ	192	Ⓐ Ⓑ Ⓒ Ⓓ
113	Ⓐ Ⓑ Ⓒ Ⓓ	133	Ⓐ Ⓑ Ⓒ Ⓓ	153	Ⓐ Ⓑ Ⓒ Ⓓ	173	Ⓐ Ⓑ Ⓒ Ⓓ	193	Ⓐ Ⓑ Ⓒ Ⓓ
114	Ⓐ Ⓑ Ⓒ Ⓓ	134	Ⓐ Ⓑ Ⓒ Ⓓ	154	Ⓐ Ⓑ Ⓒ Ⓓ	174	Ⓐ Ⓑ Ⓒ Ⓓ	194	Ⓐ Ⓑ Ⓒ Ⓓ
115	Ⓐ Ⓑ Ⓒ Ⓓ	135	Ⓐ Ⓑ Ⓒ Ⓓ	155	Ⓐ Ⓑ Ⓒ Ⓓ	175	Ⓐ Ⓑ Ⓒ Ⓓ	195	Ⓐ Ⓑ Ⓒ Ⓓ
116	Ⓐ Ⓑ Ⓒ Ⓓ	136	Ⓐ Ⓑ Ⓒ Ⓓ	156	Ⓐ Ⓑ Ⓒ Ⓓ	176	Ⓐ Ⓑ Ⓒ Ⓓ	196	Ⓐ Ⓑ Ⓒ Ⓓ
117	Ⓐ Ⓑ Ⓒ Ⓓ	137	Ⓐ Ⓑ Ⓒ Ⓓ	157	Ⓐ Ⓑ Ⓒ Ⓓ	177	Ⓐ Ⓑ Ⓒ Ⓓ	197	Ⓐ Ⓑ Ⓒ Ⓓ
118	Ⓐ Ⓑ Ⓒ Ⓓ	138	Ⓐ Ⓑ Ⓒ Ⓓ	158	Ⓐ Ⓑ Ⓒ Ⓓ	178	Ⓐ Ⓑ Ⓒ Ⓓ	198	Ⓐ Ⓑ Ⓒ Ⓓ
119	Ⓐ Ⓑ Ⓒ Ⓓ	139	Ⓐ Ⓑ Ⓒ Ⓓ	159	Ⓐ Ⓑ Ⓒ Ⓓ	179	Ⓐ Ⓑ Ⓒ Ⓓ	199	Ⓐ Ⓑ Ⓒ Ⓓ
120	Ⓐ Ⓑ Ⓒ Ⓓ	140	Ⓐ Ⓑ Ⓒ Ⓓ	160	Ⓐ Ⓑ Ⓒ Ⓓ	180	Ⓐ Ⓑ Ⓒ Ⓓ	200	Ⓐ Ⓑ Ⓒ Ⓓ

Actual Test 2 – Answer Sheet

READING (Part V~VII)									
NO.	ANSWER A B C D	NO.	ANSWER A B C D	NO.	ANSWER A B C D	NO.	ANSWER A B C D	NO.	ANSWER A B C D
101	Ⓐ Ⓑ Ⓒ Ⓓ	121	Ⓐ Ⓑ Ⓒ Ⓓ	141	Ⓐ Ⓑ Ⓒ Ⓓ	161	Ⓐ Ⓑ Ⓒ Ⓓ	181	Ⓐ Ⓑ Ⓒ Ⓓ
102	Ⓐ Ⓑ Ⓒ Ⓓ	122	Ⓐ Ⓑ Ⓒ Ⓓ	142	Ⓐ Ⓑ Ⓒ Ⓓ	162	Ⓐ Ⓑ Ⓒ Ⓓ	182	Ⓐ Ⓑ Ⓒ Ⓓ
103	Ⓐ Ⓑ Ⓒ Ⓓ	123	Ⓐ Ⓑ Ⓒ Ⓓ	143	Ⓐ Ⓑ Ⓒ Ⓓ	163	Ⓐ Ⓑ Ⓒ Ⓓ	183	Ⓐ Ⓑ Ⓒ Ⓓ
104	Ⓐ Ⓑ Ⓒ Ⓓ	124	Ⓐ Ⓑ Ⓒ Ⓓ	144	Ⓐ Ⓑ Ⓒ Ⓓ	164	Ⓐ Ⓑ Ⓒ Ⓓ	184	Ⓐ Ⓑ Ⓒ Ⓓ
105	Ⓐ Ⓑ Ⓒ Ⓓ	125	Ⓐ Ⓑ Ⓒ Ⓓ	145	Ⓐ Ⓑ Ⓒ Ⓓ	165	Ⓐ Ⓑ Ⓒ Ⓓ	185	Ⓐ Ⓑ Ⓒ Ⓓ
106	Ⓐ Ⓑ Ⓒ Ⓓ	126	Ⓐ Ⓑ Ⓒ Ⓓ	146	Ⓐ Ⓑ Ⓒ Ⓓ	166	Ⓐ Ⓑ Ⓒ Ⓓ	186	Ⓐ Ⓑ Ⓒ Ⓓ
107	Ⓐ Ⓑ Ⓒ Ⓓ	127	Ⓐ Ⓑ Ⓒ Ⓓ	147	Ⓐ Ⓑ Ⓒ Ⓓ	167	Ⓐ Ⓑ Ⓒ Ⓓ	187	Ⓐ Ⓑ Ⓒ Ⓓ
108	Ⓐ Ⓑ Ⓒ Ⓓ	128	Ⓐ Ⓑ Ⓒ Ⓓ	148	Ⓐ Ⓑ Ⓒ Ⓓ	168	Ⓐ Ⓑ Ⓒ Ⓓ	188	Ⓐ Ⓑ Ⓒ Ⓓ
109	Ⓐ Ⓑ Ⓒ Ⓓ	129	Ⓐ Ⓑ Ⓒ Ⓓ	149	Ⓐ Ⓑ Ⓒ Ⓓ	169	Ⓐ Ⓑ Ⓒ Ⓓ	189	Ⓐ Ⓑ Ⓒ Ⓓ
110	Ⓐ Ⓑ Ⓒ Ⓓ	130	Ⓐ Ⓑ Ⓒ Ⓓ	150	Ⓐ Ⓑ Ⓒ Ⓓ	170	Ⓐ Ⓑ Ⓒ Ⓓ	190	Ⓐ Ⓑ Ⓒ Ⓓ
111	Ⓐ Ⓑ Ⓒ Ⓓ	131	Ⓐ Ⓑ Ⓒ Ⓓ	151	Ⓐ Ⓑ Ⓒ Ⓓ	171	Ⓐ Ⓑ Ⓒ Ⓓ	191	Ⓐ Ⓑ Ⓒ Ⓓ
112	Ⓐ Ⓑ Ⓒ Ⓓ	132	Ⓐ Ⓑ Ⓒ Ⓓ	152	Ⓐ Ⓑ Ⓒ Ⓓ	172	Ⓐ Ⓑ Ⓒ Ⓓ	192	Ⓐ Ⓑ Ⓒ Ⓓ
113	Ⓐ Ⓑ Ⓒ Ⓓ	133	Ⓐ Ⓑ Ⓒ Ⓓ	153	Ⓐ Ⓑ Ⓒ Ⓓ	173	Ⓐ Ⓑ Ⓒ Ⓓ	193	Ⓐ Ⓑ Ⓒ Ⓓ
114	Ⓐ Ⓑ Ⓒ Ⓓ	134	Ⓐ Ⓑ Ⓒ Ⓓ	154	Ⓐ Ⓑ Ⓒ Ⓓ	174	Ⓐ Ⓑ Ⓒ Ⓓ	194	Ⓐ Ⓑ Ⓒ Ⓓ
115	Ⓐ Ⓑ Ⓒ Ⓓ	135	Ⓐ Ⓑ Ⓒ Ⓓ	155	Ⓐ Ⓑ Ⓒ Ⓓ	175	Ⓐ Ⓑ Ⓒ Ⓓ	195	Ⓐ Ⓑ Ⓒ Ⓓ
116	Ⓐ Ⓑ Ⓒ Ⓓ	136	Ⓐ Ⓑ Ⓒ Ⓓ	156	Ⓐ Ⓑ Ⓒ Ⓓ	176	Ⓐ Ⓑ Ⓒ Ⓓ	196	Ⓐ Ⓑ Ⓒ Ⓓ
117	Ⓐ Ⓑ Ⓒ Ⓓ	137	Ⓐ Ⓑ Ⓒ Ⓓ	157	Ⓐ Ⓑ Ⓒ Ⓓ	177	Ⓐ Ⓑ Ⓒ Ⓓ	197	Ⓐ Ⓑ Ⓒ Ⓓ
118	Ⓐ Ⓑ Ⓒ Ⓓ	138	Ⓐ Ⓑ Ⓒ Ⓓ	158	Ⓐ Ⓑ Ⓒ Ⓓ	178	Ⓐ Ⓑ Ⓒ Ⓓ	198	Ⓐ Ⓑ Ⓒ Ⓓ
119	Ⓐ Ⓑ Ⓒ Ⓓ	139	Ⓐ Ⓑ Ⓒ Ⓓ	159	Ⓐ Ⓑ Ⓒ Ⓓ	179	Ⓐ Ⓑ Ⓒ Ⓓ	199	Ⓐ Ⓑ Ⓒ Ⓓ
120	Ⓐ Ⓑ Ⓒ Ⓓ	140	Ⓐ Ⓑ Ⓒ Ⓓ	160	Ⓐ Ⓑ Ⓒ Ⓓ	180	Ⓐ Ⓑ Ⓒ Ⓓ	200	Ⓐ Ⓑ Ⓒ Ⓓ

沿虛線剪下